David Singmaster
30 Jul 2009

PUBLISHED BY T.M.FOWLER & JAMES B. MOYER

MACUNGIE,
Lehigh County Pennsylvania,
1893.

Katy Gaumer
and other stories of
Millerstown

The village of Millerstown (derived from the two words Miller's Town), now the Borough of Macungie, was established in 1776 by Peter Miller when he purchased 150 acres of land along the Kings Highway in what was then a portion of Northampton County. The small village was formally incorporated as the Borough of Millerstown on November 13, 1857. In 1875, the inhabitants of the borough petitioned the Court of Quarter Sessions of Lehigh County to change the name of the borough from Millerstown to Macungie, taking the original Lenape Indian name for the region. The petition was granted on November 8, 1875, and the name of the village was officially changed to the present-day Borough of Macungie.

Katy Gaumer

and other stories of

Millerstown

Elsie Singmaster, circa 1895–96
Lindenmuth Studio, Allentown
Macungie Historical Society collection

"*In so many ways she resembles one of her own characters; even her physical appearance does much to bear out this impression.... And she possesses that same sturdy uprightness and honesty and kindly humor that one admires in the men and women of her creation.*"

Dayton Kohler,
The Bookman, February 1931

Katy Gaumer

and other stories of

Millerstown

by

Elsie Singmaster

A Publication of the
Macungie Historical Society
Macungie, Pennsylvania

2008

Copyright © 2008 by the Macungie Historical Society, Inc.
All rights reserved

No part of this book may be reproduced or utilized in any form or by any means, electronic or mechanical, including photocopying, scanning, recording, or by any information storage and retrieval system, without advance permission in writing from the Macungie Historical Society, Inc.

All inquiries should be addressed to
Macungie Historical Society
Post Office Box 355
Macungie, Pennsylvania 18062
www.macungie.org

Managing Editor
Dale Eck

Book Design and Editor
Ann Bartholomew

Original Pen and Ink Illustrations
Jane Ramsey

Library of Congress Control Number: 2007936670
ISBN 978-0-9789483-0-6

Publication of this book was made possible by a generous contribution from Fay Funk Ginther (1933–2006)

Printed in the Commonwealth of Pennsylvania on acid free paper

Published in 2008 by the
Macungie Historical Society, Inc.

DEDICATION

This book is dedicated to the memory of
Elsie Singmaster Lewars,
whose charming stories of Millerstown
and its Pennsylvania German inhabitants
captivated a nation nearly a century ago.

ACKNOWLEDGMENTS

The publication of this book would not have been possible without the encouragement and support of Mrs. Elizabeth Weaver Moatz, great granddaughter of Millerstown's first burgess, a founding member of the Macungie Historical Society, and the last surviving Singmaster descendant to live within the Borough of Macungie. Betty's wonderful memories of "Aunt Elsie" have been the prime inspiration for again publishing Elsie Singmaster's delightful series of Millerstown stories.

Ann Bartholomew spent many hours serving as editor, proofreading, and designing the book. Macungie artist Jane Ramsey designed the jacket and contributed the charming illustrations that evoke memories of the long-past Millerstown of the stories. Kathy Eck typed the novel and many of the stories, and proofread multiple drafts of the book. Judy Reppert and Lucille Schwartz diligently typed the remaining stories, and Ann Marie Ellis proof read the final copy. We also remember Mrs. Fay Funk Ginther, whose generosity and love of Macungie made publication of this book financially possible.

Sincere thanks to the Adams County Historical Society, Mr. Wayne E. Motts, Executive Director, and to Ms. Judith K. Sandt, Reference Librarian, Penn State Lehigh Valley, for their help in locating many of the stories and researching sources used for this publication.

Very special thanks to Ms. Susan Colestock Hill of Gettysburg, whose detailed research and academic writings on the life of Elsie Singmaster have provided much of the biographical and background information contained in this volume. A friend and dedicated research partner for more than ten years, Susan's help has been invaluable in the acquisition of Singmaster research materials, and she continues to provide us with her unique insight into the life and writings of Elsie Singmaster.

And finally, our most grateful appreciation to Mr. Alan L. Singmaster and the Estate of Elsie Singmaster Lewars for their encouragement and support of our efforts to reintroduce the writings of Elsie Singmaster to a new generation of readers.

Dale T. Eck, President
Macungie Historical Society

CONTENTS

Elsie Singmaster Lewars xv
Select Bibliography xxvi

KATY GAUMER

I.	The Great News	1
II.	The Belsnickel	10
III.	The Great Man	18
IV.	The Koehlers' Christmas Day	27
V.	Another Christmas Day	35
VI.	The Millerstown School	48
VII.	The Bee Cure	57
VIII.	William Koehler makes his Accusation for the Last Time	67
IX.	Change	77
X.	Katy makes a Promise	83
XI.	Katy finds a New Aim in Life	86
XII.	Katy borrows so that she may lend	92
XIII.	Emptiness	104
XIV.	Katy plans her Life Once More	110
XV.	An Old Way out of a New Trouble	118
XVI.	Bevy puts a Hex on Alvin	127
XVII.	Alvin does Penance and is shriven	137
XVIII.	A Silver Chalice	144
XIX.	The Squire and David take a Journey by Night	151
XX.	The Mystery deepens	161
XXI.	The Squire and David take a Journey by Day ..	165
XXII.	Katy is to be educated at Last	173

SHORT STORIES OF MILLERSTOWN

Big Thursday	185
In Defiance of the Occult	201
The Vacillation of Benjamin Gaumer	209
The Millerstown Yellow Journal	228
The Miracle	237
The Persistence of Coonie Schnable	243
Henry Koehler, Misogynist	257
The Restoration of Melie Ziegler	265
The Long Courting of Henry Kumerant	272
When Town and Country Meet	282
The Organ at Zion Church	290
Mrs. Weimer's Gift of Tongues	297
The County Seat	305
The Old Régime	313
The Ghost of Matthias Baum	322
Elmina's Living-Out	331
The Covered Basket	340
The Exiles	348

THE ETERNAL FEMININE	357
THE SQUIRE	364
THE MAN WHO WAS NICE AND COMMON	372
THE SUFFRAGE IN MILLERSTOWN	380
THEIR SENTIMENTAL JOURNEY	388
THE CURE THAT FAILED	394
THE SPITE FENCE	401
THE "ROSE-AND-LILY" QUILT	410
THE PICTURE-TAKER	417
THE DEVICE OF MISS BETSEY	425
A MILLERSTOWN PRODIGAL	430
THE SAVING GRACE	437
THE CHILD THAT WAS TAKEN TO RAISE	444
THE EIGHT-HOUR DAY	451
THE HIGH CONSTABLE	459
SARAH ANN'S DELIVERANCE	466
MOTHER'S GIRLS	474
THE MUSIC LESSON	481
GRANDMOTHER'S BREAD	488

Elsie Singmaster Lewars, circa 1944
Macungie Historical Society collection

ELSIE SINGMASTER LEWARS
1879–1958

ELSIE SINGMASTER LEWARS is perhaps Macungie's most famous citizen. She was a descendant of the Macungie Singmasters and the granddaughter of James Singmaster (1823–1896), who was elected as the town's first burgess when Millerstown was incorporated as a borough in November of 1857. She became one of the nation's most prolific writers during the early decades of the twentieth century. Her stories regularly appeared in nationally syndicated journals and magazines, including *Atlantic Monthly*, *Century*, *Collier's*, *Good Housekeeping*, *Harper's*, *Ladies' Home Journal*, *Lippincott's*, *McClure's*, *Outlook*, *Pictorial Review*, *Saturday Evening Post*, *Scribner's*, *Woman's Home Companion*, and *Youth's Companion*, as well as in numerous short-story anthologies compiled and printed by the major publishing houses of her day.

Born in the Saint Matthew's Lutheran Church parsonage in Schuylkill Haven, Pennsylvania, on August 29, 1879, Elsie was the daughter of the Rev. John Alden Singmaster (1852–1926), a fifth-generation Pennsylvania German, and Caroline Hoopes Singmaster (1852–1931), a descendant of English Quakers. The Singmaster family had a long history of service to the Lutheran Church. Elsie's great-great-great-grandfather, Rev. Jacob van Buskirk (1739–1800) of Millerstown, was the first Lutheran minister to be born, educated, and ordained in America. He was ordained on October 12, 1763, by Dr. Heinrich Melchior Mühlenberg, who is generally recognized as the patriarch of Lutheranism in America. In 1868, when part of the Millerstown congregation of Solomon's Evangelical Lutheran and Reformed Union Church separated to form the new Saint Matthew's Evangelical Lutheran parish, Elsie's grandfather donated the land and helped finance the construction of a new church building at 530 East Main Street. A published Singmaster family genealogy, *Ein Jahrhundert aus der Geschichte der Familie Zangemeister* (Dr. Ascan Westermann, Heidelberg: Heidelberger Berlagsanstalt und Druckerei, 1911), also indicates that a sixteenth-century Singmaster (Zangemeister) ancestor studied under Martin Luther at Wittenberg, Germany.

Elsie was the only daughter, and the second of five Singmaster children including brothers James Arthur (1878–1962), John Howard (1881–1957), Edmund Hoopes (1884–1969), and Paul (1887–1950). Her father grew up in Macungie, and her family resided in the borough from 1882 to 1885 while Rev. Singmaster was pastor of Saint Matthew's Lutheran Church. Although her mother always insisted that her children speak English at home, her father preached in both English and German, and Elsie quickly acquired a knowledge of the Pennsylvania German language from her playmates and neighbors. Elsie's earliest years of public school were spent in Macungie where her teacher spoke the local "Dutch" dialect; and it was in Macungie that she first absorbed the customs, traditions, folklore, superstitions, religions, and language of the Pennsylvania Germans.

During this early period in her life, the family lived in the former Wescoe Baptist Meeting House, located on the Singmaster family farm known today as Kalmbach Memorial Park. Elsie described her childhood memory of Macungie in a 1933 autobiography published in *Authors Today and Yesterday* (New York: The H. W. Wilson Company):

> When I was four years old, my father became pastor of a charge comprising six churches lying between Allentown and Reading, and we lived for several years in Macungie, the Pennsylvania German village where he was born and where many of his kinsfolk lived. It was quiet and tree-shaded, lying at the foot of a wooded hill we called 'the mountain.' … During a part of the time we lived in the oldest building in the neighborhood, an enlarged, weather-boarded loghouse, with darkened ceiling beams, a tremendous central chimney and many interesting traditions. Across the road, beside an ancient [saw] mill, steps were built into the race for the convenience of Baptists who had held services in the house and immersed in the race-box. A mile away there rose abruptly from the green fields one of the blast-furnaces then common in eastern Pennsylvania. It was a perfect period in our lives — the fields and streams were ours, affection and good will surrounded us.

Macungie and the Wescoe Meeting House held a special significance for the Singmaster family. According to O. P. Knauss, writing in the July 2, 1891, issue of the *Macungie Progress*: "Part of the building was used many years ago for holding religious meetings and Rev. Singmaster became converted to Christ therein. It has since been repaired and furnished mostly for the [Singmaster] family's occupancy, as Mr. Singmaster has a sacred regard for the old house." In 1887, the family left Macungie to accompany Rev. Singmaster at ministry sites in Brooklyn (1887–1890) and Allentown (1890–1900); but Elsie and her brothers delighted in their return to Macungie and the Wescoe home to spend weekends and summers with their parents and paternal relatives.

> Because of my father's affection for his home and because it was a safe place for children, we returned there for many summers, leaving first Brooklyn, New York, then Allentown, Pennsylvania, with rapture the instant that school closed on the last day of June and returning with drooping heads on the first of September.

Above is the Singmaster family farm in Macungie. From left to right: the farmhouse, the Wescoe Baptist Meeting House, and the barn. The Wescoe house was the home of Rev. John Alden Singmaster and his family during the years they lived in Macungie. It was razed circa 1959. The farmhouse and barn still exist and are now part of Kalmbach Memorial Park.

Below is the Wescoe Baptist Meeting House. This is the old weather-boarded log house described in Elsie Singmaster's autobiography. Pictured (left to right) are most likely Caroline Hoopes Singmaster, William Singmaster Weaver (in carriage), Elsie Singmaster, Edna Mae Weaver, Ella Singmaster Weaver, and Edmund Singmaster. Both photographs by William Mickley Weaver, circa 1887.   Macungie Historical Society collection

Elsie Singmaster (right) and her cousin Edna Mae Weaver (left) enjoying tea on the back porch of the home of William M. Weaver, 10 East Main Street, Macungie. Photograph by William Mickley Weaver, circa 1887.
Macungie Historical Society collection

In 1900, Dr. Singmaster accepted a position as Professor of Biblical Theology at the Lutheran Theological Seminary at Gettysburg, and in 1901 the family moved into a new home built for the Singmaster family on the Seminary campus. (The home was designed by noted York and Adams County architect John Dempwolf. Today it is known as the Singmaster House and currently serves as the Seminary conference center.) In 1903, Dr. Singmaster was chosen to succeed Dr. Milton Valentine as Professor of Systematic Theology and Chairman of the Faculty, a position that in 1906 was changed to President of the Seminary. In 1925, the family moved into a new home that Dr. Singmaster had built in anticipation of his retirement. Although Elsie and her family would periodically return to Macungie and the Lehigh Valley for numerous visits, her permanent residence remained on the campus of the Gettysburg Seminary for the majority of her adult lifetime. (Elsie's home, built by her father in 1925, was purchased by the Seminary from the Singmaster Estate in 1958. It currently serves as the residence of the Seminary president.)

~ ~ ~ ~ ~

Elsie Singmaster graduated from Allentown High School in 1894 at the age of fourteen. After attending West Chester Normal School (1894–1896) as a preparation for college, she entered Cornell University in September 1898 to study literature and "set out upon the long, arduous, and blissful path of the writer."

> It was eleven o'clock on a September morning when I entered the English classroom, my heart thumping. I wished to write stories, and here, I believed, was my chance to learn. Unless I could learn, life would not be worth living.

It was during this early time in her writing career that Elsie began to create fictional Pennsylvania German stories in order to fulfill a daily college writing requirement. Richard T. Sutcliffe, writing for the June 8, 1949, issue of *The Lutheran*, relates a conversation from Elsie's early days at Cornell. After submitting a composition about Pennsylvania Germans to one of her professors, she was questioned: "Who are these queer, unreal people?" She replied: "They're NOT queer! And they're very real. They are my people living in the traditional ways of their ancestors!" To which the professor heartily responded: "Then write more about them!"

Elsie left Cornell in 1900 after her sophomore year, "having taken most of the English courses under a far too elective system," and returned to Gettysburg to begin her literary career. She wrote while studying English, German, and history at home. In 1903, she sold her first story, "Big Thursday," to *The Century Magazine* (although it was not published until the January 1906 edition). In 1905, "The Lèse-Majesté of Hans Heckendorn" became the first story published in her long professional writing career, appearing in the November issue of *Scribner's Magazine*. Encouraged by the literary response to these early stories, Elsie enrolled at Radcliffe College in the fall of 1905 to reinforce her writing with a stronger academic background. While at Radcliffe, she published seventeen short stories, including some of the earliest stories of her Millerstown series. In 1907, she graduated Phi Beta Kappa with a Bachelor of Arts degree in English.

On April 17, 1912, Elsie married Harold Steck Lewars (1882–1915) at her parents' home on Gettysburg's Seminary Ridge. Harold was the son of Valeria M. (Steck) Lewars (1852–1943) and the Rev. William Henry Lewars (1849–1897), who had coincidently served as pastor of Saint Matthew's Lutheran Church in Macungie from 1881 to 1882, immediately preceding Rev. Singmaster's ministry there. Harold was a 1903 graduate of Gettysburg College, where he also received a Master of Arts degree in 1906. After three years of teaching English at Steelton High School (1903–1906), he returned to Gettysburg College as an assistant professor of English (1906–1910). In 1910, he resigned his position and left the academic world to study music at the newly organized Institute of Musical Art (now the Juilliard School of Music) in New York City. He eventually settled in Harrisburg, Pennsylvania, where he became a music teacher, hymn writer, and church organist. Harold authored Lutheran Sunday

School hymnals published in 1914 (*Hymns and Songs for the Sunday School*) and 1915 (*The Primary Hymnal*), and composed the music for six hymns included in the 1918 *Common Service Book of the Lutheran Church* (Philadelphia: The United Lutheran Church in America). After their wedding, the new couple took up residence at Harold's home in Harrisburg. Unfortunately, the marriage was short-lived, ending less than three years later when Harold, fighting rheumatic fever, became acutely ill while visiting Elsie's parents during the Christmas holidays. He died in Gettysburg on March 14, 1915, leaving Elsie pregnant with their only child. Tragically, their son, Harold Singmaster Lewars, died at birth just two months later on May 10, 1915. Both Harold and their infant son were buried in Fairview Cemetery, directly across from Saint Matthew's Evangelical Lutheran Church in Macungie. After Harold's death, Elsie moved back to her parents' home in Gettysburg. She never remarried.

In 1916, Elsie received an honorary Doctor of Literature degree from Gettysburg College, becoming the first woman to receive an honorary degree from that institution. In later years, she was honored with a Doctor of Literature degree by Muhlenberg College (1929), a Doctor of Letters degree from Wilson College (1934), and for more than forty years was listed in *Who's Who in America*. She also received numerous literary awards during her lifetime, including a Newberry Honor Award in 1934 for her Civil War novel, *Swords of Steel* (Houghton Mifflin Company, 1933). In 1950, based on her lifetime contribution to Pennsylvania literature, Elsie Singmaster was named a "Distinguished Daughter of Pennsylvania" by Pennsylvania Governor James H. Duff.

Dayton Kohler, writing in a biographical article published in *The Bookman* for February 1931, described Elsie as a diminutive woman with strong Victorian-era ideals who "never condescended to the literary mode of the moment."

> In a ministerial household Elsie Singmaster first learned to apply to her daily life those simple but wholly adequate standards of living which she has made so unerringly her own: the music of Johann Bach, novels by Jane Austen and those older writers who are somewhat out of fashion today, a high regard for scholarship, a delight in hospitality, a garden in which she can plant and dig. In so many ways she resembles one of her own characters; even her physical appearance does much to bear out this impression. She is small and squarely built, her eyes are dark, her cheek bones broad, and her jaw firm and resolute. Her features and manner combine to give one the impression of tireless energy. And she possesses that same sturdy uprightness and honesty and kindly humor that one admires in the men and women of her creation.

Elsie Singmaster Lewars, on the porch of the Singmaster house on Seminary Ridge, Gettysburg, circa 1924. Macungie Historical Society collection

Singmaster's greatest strength as an author was in the telling of the short story, and she would continue to write these stories under the Elsie Singmaster pen name throughout her lifetime. Often described as "local color" and numbering more than 350, her stories and other articles appear more than 500 times in American literary journals, short-story anthologies, and popular magazines of the day. Forty-two books were also published during her lifetime, primarily with the New York and Boston publishing house, Houghton Mifflin Company. But Elsie's appeal as an author extended far beyond the boundaries of her home state of Pennsylvania. Her talent in telling delightful stories of children and young adults dealing with the challenges and moral values of a simple Pennsylvania German community also found popularity with an international audience. *The Magic Mirror* (Houghton Mifflin Company), her 1934 novel centered around a Pennsylvania German family living in Allentown, was published in Germany by Verlag Ferdinand Schöningh. Other Singmaster works were published in Great Britain, France, Sweden, and Denmark.

The fictional setting for a large portion of Elsie's early stories about the Pennsylvania Germans and their culture was the Lehigh County village of Millerstown, renamed Macungie in 1875. Set in the late nineteenth and early twentieth centuries, Macungie's actual citizens most likely provided prototypes for the characters who appeared serially in these stories. Now known as the Millerstown series, these stories not only delighted and entertained the reader, but also celebrated Pennsylvania German and Lehigh County history, religious life, superstitions, dialect, and social customs. Republished in this volume, the Millerstown stories provide a rare, incisive glance for today's reader into the issues, culture, and ways of life that formed and affected Pennsylvania German immigrants and their descendants. Courting practices, home life, workplaces, gender roles, holiday celebrations, ethnic foods, village political structures, language differences, aging, and other topics each take center stage as Singmaster's Millerstown population slowly transitions into the American mainstream while attempting to preserve its cultural identity. Elsie Singmaster identified strongly with, and throughout her lifetime remained an outspoken advocate for, the capable yet misrepresented Pennsylvania Germans, and her Millerstown and other Pennsylvania German writings highlighted the positive virtues of these loyal, hardworking, productive, artistic people whose identifiable but different language and culture had separated them from the broader American scene.

The combination of Singmaster's excellent prose and the timely public fascination with the Pennsylvania German way of life provided informative, uplifting, and entertaining stories for curious American readers of the period. In a review of her first book, *When Sarah Saved the Day* (Houghton Mifflin Company, 1909), a juvenile story about a young, ambitious Pennsylvania German farm girl who dreamed of an education, *The Pennsylvania-German* (December 1909) wrote: "It is … the first time that the Pennsylvania German people have been presented in a decent way and in a manner that does them justice." And when one of her Millerstown stories, "Their Sentimental Journey," was first published in *The Youth's Companion* (September 5, 1912), the *Germantown Independent Gazette* noted: "Miss Singmaster comes nearer than any other writer to delineating the life of the Pennsylvania German with fidelity. … She presents quaint traits, their failings and their virtues, and she writes with a pen devoid of sting or ill will. … It is probably no exaggeration to say that this little tale is the best Pennsylvania German story ever written."

Singmaster's first full-length adult novel, *Katy Gaumer* (Houghton Mifflin Company, 1915), was also set in the village of Millerstown. Reflecting on her carefree days of childhood in Macungie, Elsie tells the story of a teenage girl, passionate with a desire for higher education, growing up amid the school, churches, iron furnace, and Sheep Stable of the late nineteenth-century Millerstown. Mary Rice Hess, in her 1929 master's thesis submitted to the English Department at Penn State University, concludes that "*Katy Gaumer* is natural and simple. It is vigorous in the expression of the healthful normal life portrayed and is a worthwhile contribution to the best type of fiction. In the clear, straightforward style of depicting her characters, [Singmaster] is unique." More than fifty years later, a biography written by Abigail Ann Hamblen for the publication *American Women Writers* (New York: Frederick Ungar Publishing Company, 1982) observed that "*Katy Gaumer* was [originally] praised for its picture of the Pennsylvania Germans, but as time went on critics pointed out the technical excellence of her fiction as seen in structure, characterization, and comprehension of life."

Elsie incorporated a large amount of Pennsylvania German dialect into her earliest Millerstown stories. At first, she tried to record dialect as it would have sounded in everyday farm and village life; and in order to capture that reality, she widely misspelled words to mimic their "Dutchified" pronunciation. She would also reverse the order of English words, and frequently inserted idioms and German words into the dialogue to imitate a typical ethnic conversation. By 1911, however, she began to limit her use of dialect. Her later stories contained only a few Pennsylvania German word clues to create an impression of dialect, but not to overcome the story line by trying the patience of her readers. Elsie would later criticize her heavy use of dialect in the early Millerstown stories: "If I should ever compile my earlier stories, I would eliminate almost all dialect. Much more can be effected by one word or expression here and there. ... dialect, like sex, is such a great strain that a little of it goes a long way." (Mary Spotten Groff, *Elsie Singmaster: Pennsylvanian*, master's thesis submitted to the University of Maine at Orono, 1945).

In a reprint of an academic paper entitled "Contemporary Fiction on the Pennsylvania-Germans" published in the July 3, 1943, Allentown *Morning Call* column, 'S Pennsylfawnisch Deitsch Eck, Donald Radcliffe Shenton called Singmaster a pioneer in proper dialect writing and recommended her work as a model for future novelists who wished to create credible Pennsylvania German fiction. He believed that her ability to demonstrate their dialect and culture without denigrating the Pennsylvania Germans "can be achieved not by mastery of their idiom alone, but only by the instinctive knowledge of one who has shared childhood with these people." Throughout her lifetime, Singmaster maintained a personal relationship with the Pennsylvania German people of Macungie and the greater Lehigh Valley. And with few exceptions, local reviews of Singmaster stories in Macungie and Allentown area newspapers expressed a warmth and gratitude over time toward the woman who succeeded in bringing informed public awareness to Pennsylvania German communities and their people.

When Singmaster was not writing or conducting research for her books and stories, her time was divided among personal interests and community affairs. Exemplifying what she asked of others, Elsie used her skills and knowledge professionally and publicly for the betterment of society. She was active in the American Red Cross, the Gettysburg Civic Nursing Association, the Adams County Historical Society, the Adams County Public Library System, The Women's Missionary Society, and

Elsie Singmaster Lewars in front of the first Adams County Public Library at 135 Carlisle Street, Gettysburg, 1948. Macungie Historical Society collection

her beloved Lutheran Church. She was also a strong advocate for women's education and continually encouraged her readers to seek self-improvement through education. She often took much delight in encouraging and sponsoring young men and women who showed talent and promise. Donald P. McPherson, Jr., best summarized her many charitable contributions in the August, 1959, memorial issue of the *Lutheran Theological Seminary Bulletin*: "her greatest contribution to the community was herself. ... Her calm personality, her incisive mind, her energy, her love of life, the sparkle in her eye at the prospect of another venture, and her Christian love left a deep impact. All who met her were fortunate. ..."

On September 30, 1958, at the age of seventy-nine, Elsie Singmaster Lewars died in her sleep at a Gettysburg convalescent home after an extended illness. Her funeral service was held at Christ Lutheran Church in Gettysburg on October 2nd. The next day, her remains were returned to her ancestral home town of Macungie for burial in Fairview Cemetery, where she now rests beside her parents, husband, and infant son. Shortly before her death, Preston A. Barba, noted Pennsylvania German writer, scholar, historian, and long-time editor of the Allentown *Morning Call* column, 'S Pennsylvaanisch (Pennsylfawnisch) Deitsch Eck, wrote:

> No other writer of fiction has portrayed the Pennsylvania Germans and depicted their lifeways with so much sympathetic understanding, and with so much integrity and art over so long a period of time as Elsie Singmaster.

In a July 11, 1965, Allentown *Sunday Call-Chronicle* article, arts and entertainment editor Albert G. Hofammann, Jr., posed the rhetorical question: "Who was Elsie Singmaster? Not too long ago almost any Lehigh Valley resident, particularly a school child, would have viewed the person who asked this question with amazement." Unfortunately today, very few people in the Lehigh Valley community have any knowledge of this remarkable woman, even though many of her stories continue to be published in contemporary collections. Her work is considered technically and historically sound and humorous, though somewhat idealistic. It is still valued for its preservation of the Pennsylvania German culture, for its skillful and realistic Pennsylvania regional representation, and for its insights into another time and place in the American human experience.

Dale T. Eck
with Susan Colestock Hill

Singmaster Family Portrait: (seated L to R) Caroline Hoopes Singmaster, Rev. John Alden Singmaster, Edmund Hoopes Singmaster; (standing L to R) Paul Singmaster, James Arthur Singmaster, John Howard Singmaster, and Elsie Singmaster, circa 1895-96.

Lindenmuth Studio, Allentown
Macungie Historical Society collection

SELECT BIBLIOGRAPHY

Barba, Preston A. "To Our Readers." 'S Pennsylvaanisch Deitsch Eck, *The Morning Call*, Allentown: Call-Chronicle Newspapers, Inc., June 16, 1956.

Groff, Mary Spotten. "Elsie Singmaster, Pennsylvanian." Master's thesis, The University of Maine, Orono, 1934.

Hamblen, Abigail Ann. "Elsie Singmaster," *American Women Writers*, New York: Frederick Ungar Publishing Company, Inc., 1982.

Hess, Mary Rice. "Elsie Singmaster." Master's thesis, The Pennsylvania State University, 1929.

Hill, Susan Colestock. "Seeking Fruitfulness: The Life of Elsie Singmaster, Victorian Woman in Ministry." Master's thesis, Lutheran Theological Seminary at Gettysburg, 1999.

_____. "Seeking Fruitfulness–Elsie Singmaster Lewars: Victorian Women in Ministry." Paper presented at Lutheran Historical Conference, Milwaukee, WI, October 19–21, 2000. Published in *Essays and Reports–Lutherans in America–A Twentieth Century Retrospective*, Vol 19.

_____. "Elsie Singmaster Lewars: Storyteller for the Region." *Witness at the Crossroads: Gettysburg Lutheran Seminary Servants in the Public Life*, ed. Frederick K. Wentz, Lutheran Theological Seminary at Gettysburg, 2001.

_____. *Heart Language: Elsie Singmaster and Her Pennsylvania German Writings*. University Park: The Pennsylvania State University Press, 2009.

Hofammann, Albert G. Jr. "Elsie Singmaster Wrote of Dutch." *Sunday Call-Chronicle*, Allentown: Call-Chronicle Newspapers, Inc., July 11, 1965.

Kohler, Dayton. "Elsie Singmaster." *The Bookman*, February 1931.

McPherson, Donald P. Jr. "Elsie Singmaster Memorial Issue." *Lutheran Theological Seminary Bulletin*, Lutheran Theological Seminary at Gettysburg, August 1959.

Moyer, Anna Jane. "Out of the Past, Reflections Downstream." *Gettysburg*, the alumni magazine of Gettysburg College, August 1985.

Shenton, Donald Radcliffe. "Contemporary Fiction on the Pennsylvania-Germans," in 'S Pennsylfawnisch Deitsch Eck, *The Morning Call*, Allentown: Call-Chronicle Newspapers, Inc., July 3, 1943.

Singmaster, Elsie. "Autobiographical Sketch." *Authors Today and Yesterday*, ed. Stanley J. Kunitz, New York: The H. W. Wilson Company, 1933.

Sutcliffe, Richard T. "Meet Elsie Singmaster!" *The Lutheran*, June 8, 1949.

Westermann, Dr. Ascan. *Ein Jahrhundert Aus Der Geschichte Der Familie Zangemeister*. Heidelberg: Heidelberger Berlagsanstalt und Druckerei, 1911.

Elsie Singmaster, circa 1920
Macungie Historical Society collection

"Elsie Singmaster has surmounted the insurmountable problem of dialect, though few critics — because they do not understand the magnitude of the problem — have observed her triumph. I believe that the future novelist, writing of the Dutch, will do well to study her example, and he will pay tribute to the pioneer."

Donald Radcliffe Shenton, 1943
Contemporary Fiction on the Pennsylvania-Germans

Katy Gaumer

Boston and New York: Houghton Mifflin Company
The Riverside Press, Cambridge

The first two chapters of *Katy Gaumer* were originally published as a Millerstown short story under the title of "The Belsnickel" in *The Century Magazine* for January 1911.

Copyright 1910 by The Century Company
Copyright 1915 by Elsie Singmaster Lewars

First published February 1915

KATY GAUMER

CHAPTER I
THE GREAT NEWS

Every Wednesday evening in winter Katy Gaumer went to the Millerstown post-office for her grandfather's "Welt Bote," the German paper which circulated among the Pennsylvania Germans of Millerstown. By six o'clock she and Grandfather Gaumer and Grandmother Gaumer had had supper; by half past six she had finished drying the dishes; by half past seven she had learned her lessons for the next day; and then, a scarlet shawl wrapped about her, a scarlet "nubia" on her head, scarlet mittens on her hands, Katy set forth into Millerstown's safe darkness.

Sometimes — oh, the thrill that closed her throat and ran up and down her spine and set her heart to throbbing and her eyes to dancing at sound of that closed door! — sometimes it rained and she pushed her way out into the storm as a viking might have pushed his boat from the shore into an unfriendly sea; sometimes it snowed and she lifted her hot face so that she might feel the light, cold flakes against her cheek; sometimes deep drifts lay already on the ground and she flung herself upon them or into them; sometimes she danced back to say a second good-bye that she might enjoy her freedom once more; sometimes she stole round under the tall pine trees and knocked ponderously at the door, knowing perfectly well that her grandmother and grandfather would only smile at each other and not stir.

Sometimes she crossed the yard in snow to her knees to rap against the kitchen window of Bevy Schnepp, who kept house for Great-Uncle Gaumer, the squire. Bevy's real name was Maria Snyder, but Katy had renamed her for one of the mythical characters of whom Millerstown held foolish discourse, and the village had adopted the title. Bevy was little and thin and a powerful worker. She was cross with almost every one in the world, even with Katy whom she adored and spoiled. There was a tradition in Millerstown that she was once about to be married, but that at the ceremony her spirit rebelled. When the preacher asked her whether she would obey, she cried out aloud, "By my soul, no!" and the match was thereupon broken off. Bevy adorned her speech with many proverbs, and she had an abiding faith in pow-wowing, and also in spooks, hexahemeron cats, and similar mysterious creatures. She had named the squire's dog "Whiskey" so that he could not be bewitched. She would as soon have thrown her cabbage plants away as to have planted them in any other planetary sign than that of the Virgin. She belonged, strangely enough, to a newly established religious sect in Millerstown, that of the Improved New Mennonites, who had no relation to the long-established worthy followers of Menno Simons in other parts of the Pennsylvania German section. It is difficult to understand how Bevy reconciled her belief in the orthodox if sensational preaching of the Reverend Mr. Hill with her use of such superstitious rhymes as

> "Dulix, ix, ux,
> Thou comest not over Pontio,
> Pontio is over Pilato" —

to which she had recourse when trouble threatened.

Sometimes Katy untied "Whiskey" and they scampered wildly, crazily away together. Katy did everything in the same unthinking, impetuous way. Both she and Whiskey were young, both were irresponsible, both were petted, indulged, and entirely care-free. Katy was the orphan child of her grandparents' Benjamin; it was not strange that they could deny her nothing. Of her mother and father she had no recollection; to her grandparents she owed anything she might now be or might become.

To-night there was no snow upon the ground. The stars shone crisply; in the west the young moon was declining; though it was December, the season seemed more like autumn than like winter. Millerstown lay still and lovely under its leafless trees; not in the quiet of perpetual drowsiness, — Millerstown was stirring enough by day! — but in repose after the day's labor and excitement. To the east of the village the mountain rose somberly; to the south the pike climbed a hill toward the church and the schoolhouse; to the west and north lay the wide fields. To the north might be seen the dim bulk of the blast furnace with the great starlike light of the bleeder flame.

"I wonder what it looks like now from the top of the mountain," soliloquized Katy. "I would like to climb once in the dark night to the Sheep Stable. I wonder if it is any one in all Millerstown brave enough to go along in the dark. I wonder what the church looks like inside without any light. I wonder — "

Awed by the quiet, Katy stood still under the pine trees at the gate. She heard Whiskey whine to be let loose; she heard Bevy open the door of the squire's kitchen.

"Katy, Katy Gaumer! Come here once, Katy Gaumer!"

Katy did not answer. Bevy had probably a cake for her or some molas-

I. The Great News

ses candy; she could just as well put it in the putlock hole in the wall of grandfather's house. A putlock hole is an aperture left by the removal of a scaffolding. It is supposed to be filled in, but either the builder of the old stone house had overlooked one of the openings, or the stone placed there had fallen out. It now made a fine hiding-place for Katy's treasures.

Katy had at this moment no time to give to Bevy. Her heart throbbed, her hands clutched the gate. She did not know why she was always so thrilled and excited when she was out alone at night.

"It is like Bethlehem," she whispered to herself, as she looked down the street, then up at the sky. "The shepherds might be watching or the kings might come."

Katy opened the gate.

"I love Millerstown," she declared. "I love Millerstown. I love everybody and everything in Millerstown."

The post-office was next to the store and on the same street as Grandfather Gaumer's. There are only three streets in the village, Main Street and Locust and Church, and all the houses are built out to the pavement in the Pennsylvania German fashion, so that the little settlement does not cover much ground. Perhaps that was why Katy, leaving Main Street and starting forth on Locust, came so soon to the end of her spasm of affection. There did not seem to be enough of the village to warrant any such fervent outpouring. At any rate Katy's mood changed.

"I am tired of Millerstown," she declared with equal fervor. "It is dumb. It is quiet. Nothing ever happens in this place."

The residents of Locust Street were especially dull to Katy's thinking. Dumb Coonie Schnable lived here and dumb Ellie Schindler, and Essie Hill, whom she hated. Essie was the daughter of the pastor of the Improved New Mennonites, of whom Bevy Schnepp was one. The preacher himself was tall and angular and rather blank of countenance, but Essie was small and pretty and pink and smooth of speech and by no means "dumb." Once, being a follower of her father's religious practices, Essie had risen in school and had prayed for forgiveness for Katy's outrageous impudence to the teacher, and had thereupon become his favorite forever. That Essie could really be what she seemed, that she could like to hear her father shout about the Millerstown sinners, that she could admire the silly, short-back sailor hat adorned with a Bible verse, which was the head-covering of the older female members of the Improved New Mennonite Church — this Katy could not, would not believe. Essie was a hypocrite.

Sometimes the Improved New Mennonites might be heard singing or praying hysterically. Katy had often watched them through the window, in company with Ollie Kuhns and Billy Knerr and one or two other naughty boys and girls, and had sometimes helped a little with the hysterical shrieking. To-night the little frame building was dark, and here, as down on Main Street, there was not a sound.

At the end of Locust Street, Katy went through a lane to Church Street, and there again she stood perfectly still, her eyes gleaming, her ears listening, listening, listening. On the mountain road above her, she could see dimly a little white house, which seemed to hug the hillside and to hold itself aloof from Millerstown. Here lived old Koehler, who was not really very old, but who was crazy and who was supposed to have stolen the beautiful silver communion service of Katy's church. The children used to shout wildly at him, "Bring it back! Bring it back!" and sometimes he ran after them. One sign of his lunacy was his constant praying in all sorts of queer places and at queer times that the communion service might be returned, when all he needed for the answering of his prayer was to seek the service where he had hidden it and to put it back in its place. The Millerstown children never carried their mocking to his house, since they believed that he was able to set upon them the swarms of bees that lived in hives in his little garden, among which he went without fear. They said among themselves — at least the romantic girls said — that he did not give his son, poor, handsome Alvin, enough to eat.

Suddenly Katy's heart beat with a new thrill. There was no instinct within her which was not awake or wakening. Her cheeks flushed, her scarlet mittens clasped each other. She liked handsome Alvin because she liked him — no better reason was given or required in Katy's feminine soul.

"I think Alvin is grand," exclaimed Katy to herself. "I am sorry for him. I think he is grand."

There was a sound, and Katy started. Suppose Alvin should come upon her suddenly! She went on a few steps, then once more she stopped to listen. Once more Millerstown was quiet, again she looked and listened.

Back in the shadows across the street stood a large, fine house, the home of John Hartman, Millerstown's richest man. There were in that house fine carpets and beautiful furniture. But in spite of their possessions the Hartmans were not a happy family. Mrs. Hartman was handsome and she had beautiful clothes and a sealskin coat to wear to church, but she was disturbed if leaves drifted down on the grass in her yard or if the coming of visitors made it necessary to let the sunlight in on her thick carpets. Her only child, David, was sullen and stupid and cross. Remembering the delightful bass singing of one Wenner in the church choir, Katy had run away from home when a mere baby to visit the church on a week day and from there John Hartman had driven her home. Her grandmother to whom she had fled had insisted that he had not been angry, but that he had only sent her back sternly and properly where she belonged. But the impression was not quite persuaded away. Katy used to pretend in some of her wild races that she was fleeing from John Hartman.

Suddenly there was another sound. Some Millerstonian had opened a window or had closed a shutter and Katy took to her heels. It amused her to pretend once more that she was running away from John Hartman. In a moment she had opened the door of the village store and had flashed in.

Round the stove sat four men, old and middle-aged; to the other three, Caleb Stemmel was holding forth dismally, his voice low, dreary as his mind, his mind dull as the dim room. Upon them Katy flashed in her scarlet attire, her thin legs in their black stockings completing her resemblance to a very gorgeous tanager or grosbeak. Katy had recovered from all her thrills; she was now pure mischief and impertinence.

"Nothing," complained Caleb Stemmel, "nothing is any more like it was when I was young."

"No, it is much better," commented the scarlet tanager.

"We took always trouble." Caleb paid no heed to the impertinent interruption. "We had Christmas entertainments that were entertainments — speeches and cakes and apples and a Belsnickel. But these children and these teachers, they are too lazy and too good-for-nothing."

Katy had no love for her teacher; she, too, considered him good-for-nothing; but she had less love for Caleb Stemmel.

"We are going to have a Christmas entertainment that will flax [beat] any of yours, Caleb Stemmel," she boasted.

"Yes, you will get up and say a few Dutch pieces and then you will go home."

"Well, everything was Dutch when you were young. You ought to like that!"

"Things should now be English," insisted Caleb. "But you are too lazy, all of you, from the teacher down. You will be pretty much ashamed of yourselves this year, that I can tell you."

Katy was already halfway to the door, her black legs flying. She would waste no words on Caleb Stemmel. But now she turned and went back. Katy was curious.

"Why this year?"

"Because," teased Caleb.

"That is a dumb answer! Why *because*?"

"Because it is some one coming."

"Who?"

"A visitor." Caleb pronounced it "wisitor."

"Pooh! What do I care for a 'wisitor'?" mocked Katy.

"This is one that you care for!"

"Who is it!"

"Don't you wish you knew?"

Katy stamped her foot.

"If you don't tell, I'll throw you with snow when the snow comes," she threatened. Katy had respect for age in general, but not for Caleb Stemmel.

Caleb did not answer until he saw that Danny Koser was about to tell.

"It is a governor coming," he announced impressively.

Katy drew a step closer, her face aglow. No eyes of tanager or grosbeak could have shone blacker against brilliant plumage.

"Do you mean" — faltered Katy — "do you mean that my Uncle Daniel is coming home once, my Uncle Daniel Gaumer?"

"The squire was here and he told us." Danny Koser was no longer to be restrained. "Then he went to your gran'pop. He got a letter, the squire did. What do you think of that now?"

"And what," jeered Caleb Stemmel, — "what will the governor think of Dutch Millerstown and the Dutch entertainment and Dutch Katy; what — "

Once more had Katy reached the door at the other end of the long room. She had a habit of forecasting her own actions; already she could see herself pounding at the teacher's door, then racing home to her grandfather's, her heart throbbing, throbbing, her whole being in the glow of excitement which she loved, and of which she never had enough.

Suddenly she stopped, her hand on the latch. She had a secret, the whole Millerstown school had a secret, but now it must be told. Every father and mother in Millerstown would have to know if the great project, really her great project, were to succeed. Since the news would have to come out, it might as well be announced at once.

"We are going to have an English entertainment, Caleb Stemmel," she cried. "It is planned this long time already; we have been practicing for a month, Caleb Stemmel. We will have you in it; we will have you say, 'A wery wenimous wiper jumped out of a winegar wat'; that will be fine for you, Caleb. Aha! Caleb!"

Outside Katy paused and stretched forth her arms. There was still not a soul in sight, there was still not a sound; she looked up the street and down and could see the last house at each end. Then Katy started to

I. The Great News

run. Ten minutes ago she had been only little Katy Gaumer, with lessons learned for the morrow and bedtime near, hating the quiet village, a good deal bored with life; now she was Katy Gaumer, the grandniece of one of the great men of the world.

"I wonder what he will look like," said Katy. "I want to do something. I want to be something. I want to make speeches. I want to be rich and learned. I want to do *everything*. If he would only help me, I might be *something*."

There was no one at hand to tell her that she was a vain child; no one to remind her that she was only one of twenty-odd grandnieces and nephews and that the governor of a Western State was after all not such an important person, since there were many still higher offices in the land. No Millerstonian would have so discounted Daniel Gaumer, who had made his own way and had achieved greater success than any of his Millerstown contemporaries. To Katy he was far more wonderful than the President of the United States. If she could do well at the entertainment — she, of course, had the longest and most important piece, and she had also drilled the other children — if it only turned out well, and if some one only said to the governor that success was due to her efforts, he might persuade her grandfather to send her away to school; he might —

But this was not the time to dream. With a fresh gasp for breath, Katy ran on and hurled herself against the teacher's door, or rather against the door of Sarah Ann Mohr, in whose house the teacher boarded. In an instant she was in the kitchen where Sarah Ann and the teacher sat together.

Sarah Ann was large and ponderous and good-natured. She was now reading the paper and hemming a gingham apron by turns. Sarah Ann loved to read. Her favorite matter was the inside page of the Millerstown "Star," which always offered varied and interesting items of general news. Sarah Ann was far less interested in the accounts of Millerstown's births and deaths and marriages than she was in the startling events of the world outside. Sarah Ann's taste inclined to the shocking and morbid. This evening she had read many times about a man who had committed suicide by sitting on a box of dynamite and lighting the fuse, and about a man whose head was gradually becoming like that of a lion. When she observed that the next item dealt with the remarkable invention of a young woman who baked glass in her husband's pies, Sarah Ann laid down the paper to compose her mind with a little sewing.

The teacher, who was small and slender and somewhat near-sighted, was going painstakingly over a bundle of civil service examination questions. He was only in Millerstown for a little while, acting as a substitute and waiting for something to turn up. He was a Pennsylvania German, but he would as soon have been called a Turk. He had changed his name from Schreiner to Carpenter and the very sound of his native tongue was hateful to him. He did not like Katy Gaumer; he did not like any young, active, springing things.

Now he listened to Katy in astonishment. Katy flung herself upon Sarah Ann.

"Booh! Don't look so scared. I will not eat you, Sarah Ann! And I am no spook! I am only in a hurry. Teacher, I have told the people about the English entertainment. It is out. I had to tell because the children must know their pieces better. Ollie Kuhns, he won't learn his until his pop thrashes him a couple of times, and Jimmie Weygandt's mom will have to make him learn with a stick, and then he will not know it anyhow, perhaps, and they won't leave us have the Sunday School organ to practice beforehand for the singing unless they know why it is, and everybody must practice all the time from now on. You see, I *had* to tell."

The teacher looked at her dumbly. So did Sarah Ann.

"But *why?*" asked they together.

"Why?" repeated Katy, impatiently, as though they might have divined the wonderful reason. "Why, because my Uncle Daniel is coming. Is n't that enough?"

Sarah Ann laid down her apron.

"Bei meiner Seel'!" said she solemnly.

The teacher laid down his papers.

"The governor?" said he. He had heard of Governor Gaumer. He thought of the appointments in a governor's power; he foresaw at once escape from the teaching which he hated; he blessed Katy because she had proposed an English entertainment. He blessed her inspired suggestion of parental whippings for Ollie and Jimmie. "Sit down once, Katy, sit down."

It gave Katy another thrill of joy to be thus solicited by her enemy. But now she could not stop.

"I must go first home and see my folks. Then I will come back."

At the squire's gate, Bevy Schnepp awaited her.

"Ach, come once in a little, Katy!"

"I cannot!"

"Just a little! I have something for you." Bevy put out a futile arm. People were forever trying to catch Katy.

"No," laughed Katy. "I'll put a hex on you, Bevy! I'll bewitch you, Bevy!"

Katy was gone, through her grandfather's gate, down the brick walk

I. The Great News

under the pine trees to the kitchen where sat grandfather and grandmother and the squire. Seeing them together, the two old men with their broad shoulders and their handsome heads and the old woman with her kindly face, a stranger would have known at once where Katy got her active, erect figure and her curly hair and her dark eyes. All three were handsome; all three cultivated as far as their opportunities would allow; all three would have been distinguished in a broader circle than Millerstown could offer. But here circumstances had placed them and had kept them. Even the squire, whose desk was frequently littered with time-tables, and who planned constantly journeys to the uttermost parts of the earth, had scarcely ever been away from Millerstown.

Upon these three Katy rushed like a whirlwind.

"Is it true?" she demanded breathlessly in the Pennsylvania German which the older folk loved but which was falling into disuse among the young.

"Is what true?" asked grandfather and the squire together. They liked to tease Katy, everybody liked to tease Katy.

"That my uncle the governor is coming?"

"Yes," said Grandfather Gaumer. "Your uncle the governor is coming."

CHAPTER II
THE BELSNICKEL

On the afternoon of the entertainment there was an air of excitement, both within and without the schoolroom. Outside the clouds hung low; the winter wheat in the Weygandt fields seemed to have yielded up some of its brilliant green; there was no color on the mountain-side which had been warm brown and purple in the morning sunshine. A snowstorm was brewing, the first of the season, and Millerstown rejoiced, believing that a green Christmas makes a fat graveyard. But in spite of the threatening storm nearly all Millerstown moved toward the schoolhouse.

The schoolroom was almost unrecognizable. The walls were naturally a dingy brown, except where the blackboards made them still duller; the desks were far apart; the distance from the last row, where the ill-behaved liked to sit, to the teacher's desk, to which they made frequent trips for punishment, seemed on ordinary days interminable.

This afternoon, however, there was neither dullness nor extra space. The walls were hidden by masses of crowfoot and pine, brought from the mountain; the blackboards had vanished behind festoons of red flags and bunting. Into one quarter of the room the children were so closely crowded that one would have said they could never extricate themselves; into the other three quarters had squeezed and pressed their admiring relatives and friends.

Grandfather and Grandmother Gaumer were here, the latter with a large and mysterious basket, which she helped Katy to hide in the attic, the former laughing with his famous brother. The governor had come on the afternoon train, and Katy had scarcely dared to look at him. He was tall, — she could see that without looking, — and he had a deep, rich voice and a laugh which made one smile to hear it. "Mommy Bets" Eckert was here, a generation older than the Gaumer men, and dear, fat Sarah Ann Mohr, who would not have missed a Christmas entertainment for anything you could offer her. There were half a dozen babies who cooed and crowed by turns, and at them cross Caleb Stemmel frowned — Caleb was forever frowning; and there was Bevy Schnepp, moving about like a restless grasshopper, her bright, bead-like eyes on her beloved Katy.

"She is a fine platform speaker, Katy is," boasted Bevy to those nearest her. "She will beat them all."

Alvin Koehler, tall, slender, good-looking even to the eyes of older persons than Katy Gaumer, was an usher; his presence was made clear to Katy rather by a delicious thrill than by visual evidence. It went without saying that his crazy father had not come to the entertainment, though none of his small businesses of bricklaying, gardening, or bee culture need have kept him away. When Koehler was not at work, he spent no time attending entertainments; he sat at his door or window, watching the mountain road, and scolding and praying by turns.

Upon the last seat crouched David Hartman, sullen, frowning, as ever. The school entertainment was not worth the attention of so important a person as his father, and his mother could not have been persuaded to leave the constant toil with which she kept spotless her great, beautiful house.

Millerstown's young bachelor doctor had come, and he, too, watched Katy as she flew about in her scarlet dress. The doctor was a Gaumer on his mother's side, and from her had inherited the Gaumer good looks and the Gaumer brains. Katy's Uncle Edwin and her Aunt Sally had brought their little Adam, a beautiful, blond little boy, who had his piece to say on this great occasion. Uncle Edwin was a Gaumer without the Gaumer brains, but he had all the Gaumer kindness of heart. Of these two kinsfolk, Uncle Edward, and fat, placid Aunt Sally, Katy did not have a very high opinion. Smooth, pretty little Essie Hill had not come; her pious soul considered entertainments wicked.

But Katy gave no thought to Essie or to her absence; her mind was full of herself and of the great visitor and of Alvin Koehler. For Katy the play had begun. The governor was here; he looked kind and friendly; perhaps he would help her to carry out some of her great plans for the future. Since his coming had been announced, Katy had seen herself in a score of rôles. She would be a great teacher, she would be a fine lady, she would be a missionary to a place which she called "Africay." No position seemed beyond Katy's attainment in her present mood.

Katy knew her part as well as she knew her own name. It was called "Annie and Willie's Prayer." It was long and hard for a tongue, which, for all its making fun of other people, could not itself say *th* and *v* with ease. But Katy would not fail, nor would her little cousin Adam, still sitting close between his father and mother, whom she had taught to lisp through "Hang up the Baby's Stocking." If only Ollie Kuhns knew the "Psalm of Life," and Jimmie Weygandt, "There is a Reaper whose Name is Death," as well! When they began to practice, Ollie always said, "Wives of great men," and Jimmie always talked about "deas" for "death." But those faults had been diligently trained out of them. All the children had known their parts this morning; they had known them so well that Katy's elaborate test could not produce a single blunder, but would they know them now? Their faces grew whiter and whiter; the very pine branches seemed to quiver with nervousness; the teacher — Mr. Carpenter, indeed!

— tried in vain to recall the English speech which he had written out and memorized. As he sat waiting for the time to open the entertainment, he frantically reminded himself that the prospect of examinations had always terrified him, but that he invariably recovered his wits with the first question.

Once he caught Katy Gaumer's eye and tried to smile. But Katy did not respond. Katy looked at him sternly, as though she were the teacher and he the pupil. She saw plainly enough what ailed him, and prickles of fright went up and down her backbone. His speech was to open the entertainment; if he failed, everybody would fail. Katy had seen panic sweep along the ranks of would-be orators in the Millerstown school before this. She had seen Jimmie Weygandt turn green and tremble like a leaf; she had heard Ellie Schindler cry. If the teacher would only let her begin the entertainment, she would not fail!

But the teacher did not call on Katy. No such simple way out of his difficulty occurred to his paralyzed brain. The Millerstonians expected the fine English entertainment to begin; the stillness in the room grew deathlike; the moments passed, and Mr. Carpenter sat helpless.

Then, suddenly, Mr. Carpenter jumped to his feet, gasping with relief. He knew what he would do! He would say nothing at all himself; he would call upon the stranger. It was perfectly true that precedent put a visitor's speech at the end of an entertainment, rather than at the beginning, but the teacher cared not a rap for precedent. The stranger should speak now, and thus set an example to the children. Hearing his easy *th's* and *v's*, they would have less trouble with their English. Color returned to the teacher's cheeks; only Katy Gaumer realized how terrified he had been. So elated was he that he introduced the speaker without stumbling.

"It is somebody here that we do not have often with us at such a time," announced Mr. Carpenter. "It is a governor here; he will make us a speech."

The governor rose, smiling, and Millerstown, smiling, also, craned its neck to see. Then Millerstown prepared itself to hear. What it heard, it could scarcely believe.

The governor had spoken for at least two minutes before his hearers realized anything but a sharp shock of surprise. The children looked and listened, and gradually their mouths opened; the fathers and mothers heard, and at once elbows sought neighboring sides in astonished nudges. Bevy Schnepp actually exclaimed aloud; Mr. Carpenter flushed a brilliant, apoplectic red. Only Katy Gaumer sat unmoved, being too much astonished to stir. She had looked at the stranger with awe; she regarded him now with incredulous amazement.

The governor had been away from Millerstown for thirty years; he was a graduate of a university; he had honorary degrees; the teacher had warned the children to look as though they understood him whether they understood him or not.

"If he asks you any English questions and you do not know what he means I will prompt you a little," the teacher had promised. "You need only to look once a little at me."

But the distinguished stranger asked no difficult English questions; the distinguished stranger did not even speak English; he spoke his own native, unenlightened Pennsylvania German!

It came out so naturally, he seemed so like any other Millerstonian standing there, that they could hardly believe that he was distinguished and still less that he was a stranger. He said that he had not been in that schoolroom for thirty years, and that if any one had asked him its dimensions, he would have answered that it would be hard to throw a ball from one corner to the other. And now from where he stood he could almost touch its sides!

He remembered Caleb Stemmel and called him by name, and asked whether he had any little boys and girls there to speak pieces, at which everybody laughed. Caleb Stemmel was too selfish ever to have cared for anybody but himself.

Still talking as though he were sitting behind the stove in the store with Caleb and Danny Koser and the rest, the governor said suddenly an astonishing, an incredible, an appalling thing. Mr. Carpenter, already a good deal disgusted by the speaker's lack of taste, did not realize at first the purport of his statement, nor did the fathers and mothers, listening entranced. But Katy Gaumer heard! *He said that he had come a thousand miles to hear a Pennsylvania German Christmas entertainment!*

He said that it was necessary, of course, for every child to learn English, that it was the language of his fatherland; but that at Christmas time they should remember that they had an older fatherland, and that no nation felt the Christmas spirit like the Germans. It was a time when everybody should be grateful for his German blood, and should practice his German speech. He said that a man with two languages was twice a man. He had been looking forward to this entertainment for weeks; he had told his friends about it, and had made them curious and envious; he had thought about it on the long journey; he knew that there was one place where he could hear "Stille Nacht." He almost dared to hope that this entertainment would have a Belsnickel. If old men could be granted their dearest wish, they would be young again. This entertainment, he said, was going to make him young for one afternoon.

The great man sat down, and at once the little man arose. Mr. Carpenter did not pause as though he were frightened, he was no longer panic-stricken; he was, instead, furious, furious with himself for having called on Daniel Gaumer first, furious with Daniel Gaumer for thus upsetting his teaching. He said to himself that he did not care whether the children failed or not. He announced "Annie and Willie's Prayer."

It seemed for a moment as though Katy herself would fail. She stared into the teacher's eyes, and the teacher thought that she was crying. He could not have prompted her if his life had depended upon it. He glanced at the programme in his hand to see who was to follow Katy.

But Katy had begun. Katy's tears were those of emotion, not those of fright. She wore a red dress, her best, which was even redder than her everyday apparel; her eyes were bright, her cheeks flushed, she moved lightly; she felt as though all the world were listening, and as though — if her swelling heart did not choke her before she began — as though she might thrill the world. She knew how the stranger felt; this was one of the moments when she, too, loved Millerstown, and her native tongue and her own people. The governor had come back; this was his home; should he find it an alien place? No, Katy Gaumer would keep it home for him!

Katy bowed to the audience, she bowed to the teacher, she bowed to the stranger — she had effective, stagey ways; then she began. To the staring children, to the astonished fathers and mothers, to the delighted stranger, she recited a new piece. They had heard it all their lives, they could have recited it in concert. It was not "Annie and Willie's Prayer"; it was not even a Christmas piece; but it was as appropriate to the occasion as either. It was "Das alt Schulhaus an der Krick," and the translation compared with the original as the original Christmas entertainment compared with Katy Gaumer's.

> "To-day it is just twenty years
>   Since I began to roam;
> Now, safely back, I stand once more,
> Before the quaint old schoolhouse door,
>   Close by my father's home."

Katy was perfectly self-possessed throughout; it must be confessed that praised and petted Katy was often surer of herself than a child should be. There were thirty-one stanzas in her recitation; there was time to look at each one in her audience. At the fathers and mothers she did not look at all; at Ollie Kuhns and Jimmie Weygandt and little Sarah Knerr, however, she looked hard and long. She was still staring at Ollie when she reached her desk, staring so hard that she scarcely heard the applause which the stranger led. She did not sit down gracefully, but hung halfway out of her

II. The Belsnickel

seat, bracing herself with her arm round little Adam and still gazing at Ollie Kuhns. She had ceased to be an actor; she was now stage-manager.

The teacher failed to announce Ollie's speech, but no one noticed the omission. Ollie rose, grinning. This was a beautiful joke to him. He knew what Katy meant; he was always quick to understand. Katy was not the only bright child in Millerstown. He knew a piece entitled "Der Belsnickel," a description of the masked, fur-clad creature, the St. Nicholas with a pelt, who in Daniel Gaumer's day had brought cakes for good children and switches for the "nixnutzige." Ollie had terrified his schoolmates a hundred times with his representation of "Bosco, the Wild Man, Eats 'em Alive"; it would be a simple thing to make the audience see a fearful Belsnickel.

And little Sarah Knerr, did she not know "Das Krischkindel," which told of the divine Christmas spirit? She had learned it last year for a Sunday School entertainment; now, directed by Katy, she rose and repeated it with exquisite and gentle painstaking. When Sarah had finished, Katy went to the Sunday School organ, borrowed for the occasion, on which she had taught herself to play. There was, of course, only one thing to be sung, and that was "Stille Nacht." The children sang and their fathers and mothers sang, and the stranger led them all with his strong voice.

Only Katy Gaumer, fixing one after the other of the remaining performers with her eye, sang no more after the tune was started. There was Coonie Schnable; she said to herself that he would fail in whatever he tried to say. It would make little difference whether Coonie's few unintelligible words were English or German. Coonie had always been the clown of the entertainments of the Millerstown school; he would be of this one, also.

But Coonie did not fail. Ellie Schindler recited a German description of "The County Fair" without a break; then Coonie Schnable rose. He had once "helped" successfully in a dialogue. For those who know no Pennsylvania German it must suffice that the dialogue was a translation of a scene in "Hamlet." For the benefit of those who are more fortunate, a translation is appended. Coonie recited all the parts, and also the names of the speakers.

   Hamlet: Oh, du armes Schpook!
   Ghost: Pity mich net, aber geb mir now dei' Ohre,
            For ich will dir amohl eppas sawga.
   Hamlet: Schwets rous, for ich will es now aw hera.
   Ghost: Und wann du heresht, don nemsht aw satisfaction.
   Hamlet: Well was is's? Rous mit!
   Ghost: Ich bin dei'm Dawdy sei' Schpook!

To the children Coonie's least word and slightest motion were convulsing; now they shrieked with glee, and their fathers and mothers with them. The stranger seemed to discover still deeper springs of mirth; he laughed until he cried.

Only Katy, stealing out, was not there to see the end. Nor was she at hand to speed little Adam, who was to close the entertainment with "Hang up the Baby's Stocking." But little Adam had had his whispered instructions. He knew no German recitation — this was his first essay at speech-making — but he knew a German Bible verse which his Grandmother Gaumer had taught him, "Ehre sei Gott in der Höhe, und Friede auf Erden, und Den Menschen ein Wohlgefallen." (Glory to God in the Highest and on earth, peace, good will toward men.) He looked like a Christmas spirit as he said it, with his flaxen hair and his blue eyes, as the stranger might have looked sixty years ago. Daniel Gaumer started the applause, and as little Adam passed him, lifted him to his knee.

It is not like the Millerstonians to have any entertainment without refreshments, and for this entertainment refreshments had been provided. Grandmother Gaumer's basket was filled to the brim with cookies, ginger-cakes, sand-tarts, flapjacks, in all forms of bird and beast and fish, and these Katy went to the attic to fetch. She ran up the steps; she had other and more exciting plans than the mere distribution of the treat.

In the attic, by the window, sullen, withdrawn as usual, sat David Hartman.

"You must get out of here," ordered Katy in her lordly way. "I have something to do here, and you must go quickly. You ought to be ashamed to sit here alone. You are always ugly. Perhaps" — this both of them knew was flippant nonsense — "perhaps you have been after my cakes!"

David made no answer; he only looked at her from under his frowning brows, then shambled down the steps and out the door into the cold, gray afternoon. Let him take his sullenness and meanness away! Then Katy's bright eyes began to search the room.

In another moment, down in the schoolroom, little Adam cried out and hid his face against the stranger's breast; then another child screamed in excited rapture. The Belsnickel had come! It was covered with the dust of the schoolhouse attic; it was not of the traditional huge size — it was, indeed, less than five feet tall; but it wore a furry coat — the distinguished stranger leaped to his feet saying that it was not possible that that old pelt still survived! — it opened its mouth "like scissors," as Ollie Kuhns's piece had said. It had not the traditional bag, but it had a basket, Grandmother Gaumer's, and the traditional cakes were there. It climbed upon a desk, its black-stockinged legs and red dress showing through the rents of the old, ragged coat, and the children surrounded it, laughing, begging, screaming with delight.

The stranger stood and looked at Katy. He did not yet realize how large a part she had had in the entertainment, though about that a proud grandfather would soon inform him; he saw the Gaumer eyes and the Gaumer bright face, and he remembered with sharp pain the eyes of a little sister gone fifty years ago.

"Who is that child?" he asked.

Katy's grandfather called her to him, and she came slowly, slipping like a crimson butterfly from the old coat, which the other children seized upon with joy. She heard the governor's question and her grandfather's answer.

"It is my Abner's only child."

Then Katy's eyes met the stranger's bright gaze. She halted in the middle of the room, as though she did not know exactly what she was doing. Their praise embarrassed her, her foolish anger at David Hartman hurt her, her head swam. Even her joy seemed to smother her. This great man had hated Millerstown, as she hated Millerstown, sometimes, or he would not have gone away; he had loved it as she did, or he would not have come back to laugh and weep with his old friends. Perhaps he, too, had wanted everything and had not known how to get it; perhaps he, too, had wanted to fly and had not known where to find wings! A consciousness of his friendliness, of his kinship, seized upon her. He would understand her, help her! And like the child she was, Katy ran to him. Indeed, he understood even now, for stooping to kiss her, he hid her foolish tears from Millerstown.

CHAPTER III
THE GREAT MAN

ON ordinary Christmas days, when only the squire and the doctor and Uncle Edwin and Aunt Sally and little Adam and Bevy Schnepp dined at Grandfather Gaumer's, Grandmother Gaumer and Bevy prepared a fairly elaborate feast. There was always a turkey, a twenty-five pounder with potato filling, there were all procurable vegetables, there were always cakes and pies and preserves and jellies without number. One gave one's self up with cheerful helplessness to indigestion, one resigned one's self to next day's headache — that is, if one were not a Gaumer. No Gaumer ever had headache.

It cannot be claimed for Katy that she was of much assistance to her elders on this Christmas Day, tall girl though she was. Grandfather Gaumer and the governor started soon after breakfast to pay calls in the village and her thoughts were with them. How glad every one would be to see the governor; how they would press cakes and candy upon him; how he would joke with them; how they would treasure what he said! What a wonderful thing it was to be famous and to have every one admire you!

"I would keep the chair he sat in," said Katy. "I would put it away and keep it."

Presently Katy saw Katy Gaumer coming back to her native Millerstown, covered with honors, of what sort Katy did not exactly know, and going about on Christmas morning to see the Millerstown Christmas trees and to receive the homage of a delighted community.

Meanwhile, Katy tripped over her own feet and sent a dish flying from the kitchen table, and started to fill the teakettle from the milk-pitcher. Finally, to Bevy Schnepp's disgust, Katy spilled the salt. She moved swiftly about, her little face twisted into a knot, profoundly conscious of the importance of her position as assistant to the chief cook on this great day, her shrill voice now breathing forth commands, now recounting strange tales. Grandmother Gaumer, to whose kitchen Bevy was a thrice daily visitor, had long ago accustomed herself not to listen to the flow of speech, and had thereby probably saved her own reason.

"You fetch me hurry a few coals, Katy. Now don't load yourself down so you cannot walk! 'The more haste the less speed!' Adam, you take your feet to yourself or they will get stepped on for sure. Gran'mom, your pies! You better get them out or they burn to nothing! Go in where the Putz is, Adam, then you are not all the time under the folks' feet. Sally Edwin, you peel a few more potatoes for me, will you, Sally, for the mashed potatoes? Mashed potatoes go down like nothing. Ach, I had the worst time with my supper yesterday! The chicken wouldn't get, and the governor was there. I tell you, the Old Rip was in it! But I carried the pan three times round the house and then it done fine for me. Katy, if you take another piece of celery, I'll teach you the meaning. To eat my nice celery that I cleaned for dinner! And the hard, yet! If you want celery, fetch some for yourself and clean it and eat it. I'd be ashamed, Katy, a big girl like you! You want to be so high gelernt, you think you are a platform speaker, yet you would eat celery out of the plate. Look out, the salt, Katy! Well, Katy! Would you spill the salt, yet! Do you want to put a hex on everything! I —"

"Bevy!" Katie exploded with alarm.

"What is it?" cried Bevy.

"Your mouth is open!"

"I — I —" Bevy gurgled, then gasped. Bevy was not slow on the uptake. "I opened it, I opened it a-purpose to tell you what I think of you. I —"

But Katy, hearing an opening door, had gone, dancing into the sitting-room, where on great days like this, the feast was spread. The room was larger than the kitchen; in the center stood the long table, and in one corner was the Christmas tree with the elaborate "Putz," a garden in which miniature sheep and cows walked through forests and swans swam on glass lakelets. Before the "Putz," entranced, sat fat Adam; near by, beside the shiny "double-burner," the governor and his brothers and young Dr. Benner were establishing themselves. The governor had still a hundred questions to ask.

Katy perched herself on the arm of her grandfather's chair, saying to herself that Bevy might call forever now and she would not answer. The odor of roasting turkey filled the house, intoxicating the souls of hungry men, but it was not half so potent as this breath of power, this atmosphere of the great world of affairs, which surrounded Great Uncle Gaumer. Katy's heart thumped as she listened; the great, vague plans which she had made in the night seemed at one moment possible of execution, at the next absolutely mad. Her face flushed and her skin pricked as she thought of making known her desires; her heart seemed to sink far below its proper resting place. She listened to the governor with round, excited eyes, now praying for courage, now yielding to despair.

The governor's questions did not refer to the great world, — it seemed as though the world had become of no account to him, — but to Millerstown, the Millerstown of his youth, of apple-butter matches, of raffles, of battalions, of the passing through of troops to the war, of the rough preachers of a stirring age. He remembered many things which his brothers had forgotten; they and the younger folk listened entranced. As for Bevy, moving about on tiptoe, so as not to miss a word, — it was a marvel that she was able to finish the dinner.

"He traveled on horseback," said the governor. "He had nothing to his name in all the world but his horse and his old saddlebags, and he visited the people whether they wanted him or not. At our house he was always welcome, — he stayed once a whole winter, — and on Sundays he used to give it to us in church, I can tell you! Everything he'd yell out that would come into his mind. One Sunday he yelled at me, 'There you stand in the choir, and you could n't get a pig's bristle between your teeth. Sing out, Daniel!'

"But he could preach powerfully! He made the people listen! There was no sleeping in the church when he was in the pulpit. If the young people did not pay attention, he called right out, 'John, behave! Susy, look at me!'"

"We have such a preacher here," said Uncle Edwin in his slow way. "He is a Improved New Mennonite. He —"

"They wear hats with Scripture on them, and they sing, 'If you love your mother, keep her in the sky,'" interrupted Katy.

"'*Meet* her in the sky,'" corrected Grandmother Gaumer. "That has some sense to it."

"He won't read the words as they are written in the Bible," went on Uncle Edwin, apparently not minding the interruption. He shared with the rest of Katy's kin their foolish opinion of Katy. "He says the words that are printed fine don't belong there, they are put in. It is like riding on a bad road, his reading. It goes bump, bump. It sounds very funny."

"He preaches on queer texts," said Katy. "He preached on 'She Fell in Love with her Mother-in-Law.'"

"Now, Katy!" admonished Grandmother Gaumer.

Bevy Schnepp had endured as much as she could of insult, to the denomination to which she belonged and to the preacher under whom she sat.

"Your Lutheran preachers have 'kein Saft und kein Kraft, kein Salz und kein Peffer' [no sap and no strength, no salt and no pepper]," she quoted. "They are me too leppish [insipid]. You must give these things a spiritual meaning. It meant Naomi and Ruth."

The governor smiled his approval at Bevy. "Right you are, Bevy!" Then he began to ask questions about his former acquaintances.

"What has come over John Hartman?"

"While he is so cross, you mean?" said Grandfather Gaumer. "I don't know what has come over him. It is a strange thing. He is so long queer that we forget he was ever any other way."

"Was he ugly this morning?" asked Grandmother Gaumer.

"He didn't ask us to come in and she didn't come to the door at all."

Bevy Schnepp, entering with laden hands, made sharp comment.

"She is afraid her things will get spoiled if the sun or the moon or the cold air strikes them. She is crazy for cleanness. She will get yet like fat Abby. Fat Abby once washed her hands fifteen times before breakfast, and if he (her husband) touched the coffee-pot even to push it back with his finger if it was boiling over, then she would make fresh."

"And do the Koehlers still live on the mountain?"

"There are only two Koehlers left," answered the squire, "William and his boy." The squire shook his head solemnly. "It is a queer thing about the Koehlers, too. The others were honest and right in their minds, but William, he is none of these things."

"Not *honest!*" said the governor.

"About fifteen years ago he did some bricklaying at the church and he had the key of the communion cupboard. The solid service was there and while he was working it disappeared."

"Disappeared!" repeated the governor. "You mean he took it? What could he do with it?"

"I don't know. Nobody knows. He goes about muttering and praying over it. They say his boy hardly gets enough to eat. I can't understand it."

"He!" Bevy now had the great turkey platter in her arms; its weight and her desire to express herself made her gasp. "He! He looks at a penny till it is a twenty-dollar gold-piece. And you ought to see his boy! He is for all the world like a girl. 'Like father, like son!' He'll do something, too, yet."

Katy slid from the arm of her grandfather's chair, her cheeks aflame.

"You have to look at pennies when you are poor," she protested. "You can't throw money round when you don't have it!"

Bevy slid the platter gently to its place on the table, then she faced about.

"Now, listen once!" cried she with admiration. "You can't throw money round when you don't have it, can't you? What do you know about it, you little chicken?"

Katy's face flushed a deeper crimson. If looks could have slain, Bevy would have dropped. Young Dr. Benner turned and looked at Katy suddenly and curiously. She would have gone on expostulating had not Grandmother Gaumer risen and the other Gaumers with her, all moving with one accord toward the feast. There was time only for a secret and threatening gesture toward Bevy, then Katy bent her head with the rest.

"'The eyes of all wait upon Thee,'" said Grandfather Gaumer in German.

"'Thou givest them their meat in due season.'"

Heartily the Gaumers began upon the Christmas feast, the feast beside which the ordinary Christmas dinner was so poor and simple a thing. Here was the turkey, done to a turn, here were all possible vegetables, all possible pies and cakes and preserves. To these Grandmother Gaumer had added a few common side-dishes, so that her brother-in-law might not return to the West without a taste, at least, of all the staple foods of his childhood. There was a slice of home-raised, home-cured ham; there was a piece of smoked sausage; there was a dish of Sauerkraut and a dish of "Schnitz und Knöpf," — these last because the governor had mentioned them yesterday in his speech. It was well that the squire lived next door and that Bevy had her own stove to use as well as Grandmother Gaumer's.

Bevy occupied the chair nearest the kitchen door. There are few class distinctions in Millerstown, though one is not expected to leave the station in life in which he was born. It was proper for Bevy to occupy the position of maid and for little Katy to go to school. If Katy had undertaken to live out, or Bevy to become learned, Millerstown would have disapproved of both of them. When each remained in her place, they were equal.

The governor tasted all the dishes serenely, and Grandmother Gaumer apologized from beginning to end, as is polite in Millerstown. The turkey might have been heavier — if he had, he would certainly have perished long before Grandfather's axe was sharpened for him! The pie might have been flakier, the sausage might have been smoked a bit longer — it would have been sinful to add a breath of smoke to what was already perfect.

"And then it would n't have been ready for to-day!" said the governor.

"But we might have begun earlier." Grandmother Gaumer would not yield her point. "If we had butchered two days earlier, it would have been better."

When human power could do no more, when Bevy had no more breath for urgings, such as "Ach, eat it up once, so it gets away!" or "Ach, finish it; it stood round long enough already!" the Gaumers pushed back their chairs and talked with mellower wit and softer hearts of old times, of father and mother and grandparents, and of the little sister who had died.

"She was just thirteen," said Governor Gaumer. "She was the liveliest little girl! I often think if she had lived, she would have made of herself something different from the other people of Millerstown. But now she would have been an old woman, think of that!" The governor held out his hand and Katy came across to him, her eyes filled with tears. Katy was always easily moved. "Did n't she look like this one?"

III. THE GREAT MAN 23

"Yes," agreed Grandfather Gaumer. "That I always said."

The governor laid both his hands on Katy's shoulders.

"And what" — said he, — "what are you going to do in this world, Miss Katy?"

Katy looked up at him with a deep, deep breath. She had thought that yesterday held a great moment, but here was a much greater one. She clasped her hands, she gasped again, she looked the governor straight in the face. Here was her opportunity, the opportunity which she had begun to think would never come.

"Ach," said Katy with a deep sigh, "when I am through the Millerstown school, I should like to go to a big school and learn *everything!*"

The governor smiled upon her.

"Everything, Katy!"

"Yes," sighed Katy.

"Listen to her once!" cried Bevy Schnepp with pride.

"Can't you learn enough here?"

"I am already in the next to the highest class," explained Katy. "And our teacher, he is not a very good one. He wants to be English and a teacher ought to be English, but he is werry Germaner than the scholars. He said to us in school, 'We are to have nothing but English here, *do you versteh?*' That is exactly the way he said it to us. He says lots of words that are not English I want to be English. I —"

"Just listen now!" cried Bevy again, her hands piled high with dishes.

"I want to be well educated," finished Katy with glowing cheeks.

"And what would you do when you were educated?" asked the governor.

"I would leave Millerstown," said Katy.

"Why?" asked the governor.

"It would be no use having an education in Millerstown," answered Katy with conviction. "You have no idea how slow Millerstown is."

"And where did you think you would go?"

"Perhaps to Phildel'phy," answered Katy. "Perhaps I would be a missionary to Africay."

Strange sounds issued from the throats of Katy's kin.

"You are sure you could do nothing in Millerstown with an education?" asked the governor.

"It is nothing to do here," explained Katy. "You can walk round Millerstown a whole evening and you don't hear anything and you don't see anything."

"Would she like *murders?*" demanded Bevy Schnepp.

"You go in the store and Caleb Stemmel and Danny Koser are too dumb and lazy even to read the paper, and Sarah Ann Mohr is hemming and everybody else is sleeping. The married people sit round and don't say anything, and —"

"Do you want them to *fight*?" Bevy was not discouraged by being ignored.

"You think it would be better to be a missionary?" said the governor.

"It would be better to be *anything*," declared Katy fervently. "I *cannot stand* Millerstown!" Katy clasped her hands and looked into the face of her distinguished relative. "Oh, please, please make them send me away to a big school! I prayed for it!" added Katy.

Over Katy's head the eyes of her elders met. The older folk thought of the little girl who might have been something different, the squire remembered the journeys he had planned in his youth and the years he had waited to take them.

But to Katy's chagrin and bitter disappointment, no one said another word about an education. Grandmother Gaumer suggested that Katy might help Aunt Sally and Bevy with the dishes. Afterwards, Katy was called upon to say her piece once more. When little Adam followed with his Bible verse and was given equal praise, Katy's poor heart, sinking lower and lower, reached the most depressed position which it is possible for a heart to assume. Her cause was lost.

Then the governor prepared to start on his long journey to the West. There he had grown sons and daughters and little grandchildren whom these Eastern cousins might never see. He kissed Grandmother Gaumer and his niece Sally and little Adam and Katy, and shook hands with Bevy Schnepp, then he returned and kissed Grandmother Gaumer once more. There was something solemn in his farewell; at sight of Grandmother Gaumer's face Katy was keenly conscious once more of her own despair. From the window she watched the three old men go down the street, the famous man who had gone away from Millerstown and the two who had stayed. It seemed to Katy that the two were less noble because of the obscurity of their lives.

"Why did gran'pop stay here always?" she asked when she and her grandmother were alone. "Why did uncle go away?"

"Gran'pop was the oldest, and he and the squire had to stay here. Uncle had the chance to go."

"But —" Katy crossed to her grandmother's side. Everything was still in the warm, pine-scented room. "But, grandmother, why do you cry?"

"I am not crying," said grandmother brightly.

"But you look — you look as if "— Katy struggled for words in which to express her thoughts — "as if everything were finished!"

III. The Great Man

Grandmother sighed gently. "I am an old woman, Katy, and your uncle is an old man. We may never see each other again."

"Oh, dear! Oh, dear!" cried Katy. "This is a very sad Christmas!"

It was not the sadness of parting which made Katy cry. It was unthinkable that anything should change for her. Everything would be the same, always — alas, that it should be so! She, Katy Gaumer, with all her smartness in school, and all her ability to plan and manage entertainments, would stay here in this spot until she died. Grandmother Gaumer, reproaching herself, comforted her for that which was not a grief at all.

"We will be here a long time yet. And you are to go away to school, and — "

Katy sprang to her feet.

"Who says it, gran'mom? Who says I dare go to school?"

"Your gran'pop said it, and your uncles said it when you were out with Bevy. You are to study here till you are through with the highest class, then you are to go away. Your uncle will find a school: he will send us catalogues and he will give us advice."

Katy clasped her hands.

"I do not deserve it!"

"You said you prayed for it," reminded Grandmother Gaumer.

"But I prayed without faith," confessed Katy. "I did not believe for one little minute it would ever come true in this world!"

"Well," said Grandmother Gaumer, "it is coming true."

Here for once was bliss without alloy, here was a rapture without reaction. Christmas entertainments, at which one did well, ended; there was no outlook from them, and it was the same with perfect recitations in school. But this was different. One had the moment's complete joy, one had also something much better.

"I must study," planned Katy. "I must learn. I must make" — alas, that one's joy should be another's bitter trial! — "I must make that teacher learn me everything he knows!"

It was dusk when Grandfather Gaumer came home.

"I told Katy," said Grandmother Gaumer.

"Daniel gave me two hundred dollars to put in the bank in Katy's name," announced Grandfather Gaumer solemnly. "It shall be spent for books and to start Katy. He and the squire and I will see her through."

Katy flung herself upon her grandfather.

"I will learn everything," she promised. "I will make you proud of me. Like it says in the Sunday School book, 'I will bring home my sheaves.' And now," said Katy, "I am going to run out to the schoolhouse and back."

In an instant she was gone, scarlet shawl about her, slamming the door. Perhaps the two old people sitting together were not sorry to have her away for a while. The day with its memories and its parting had been hard, and the mere youthfulness of youth is sometimes difficult for age to bear.

"Her legs fly like the arms of a windmill," said Grandfather Gaumer.

Then they sat silently together.

Already Katy was halfway out to the schoolhouse. The threatened snow had fallen and the sky had cleared at sunset. There was still a faint, rosy glow in the west, a glow which was presently dimmed by the brighter light which spread over the landscape as the cinder ladle at the furnace turned out its fiery charge upon the cinder bank. When that flame faded, the stars were shining brightly; Katy stood in the road before the schoolhouse and looked up at them and then round about her. The schoolhouse, glorified by her recent triumph, was further sanctified by her great hopes. Beside it on the hillside stood the little church, where she had been confirmed and had had her first communion, where during the long German sermons she had dreamed many dreams, and where she had been thrilled by solemn watch-night services. Millerstown was not without power to impress itself even upon one who hated it.

Now Katy raced down the hill. But she was not ready to go into the house. She shrieked into Bevy Schnepp's kitchen window; she almost upset Caleb Stemmel as he plodded to his place behind the stove in the store, wishing that there were not Christmases; she ran once more to the end of Locust Street and across to Church Street and looked through the thick trees at the Hartman house. David had surely some handsome Christmas gifts from his parents. Then, straining her eyes, she gazed up at the little white house on the mountain-side. There was not much Christmas there, that was certain, but Alvin was there, handsome, adorable. Alvin would pay heed to her if she was going away, the one person in Millerstown to be educated!

Then Katy stretched out her arms.

"Oh, dear Millerstown!" cried Katy. "Oh, dear, dumb Millerstown, I am going away from you!"

CHAPTER IV
THE KOEHLERS' CHRISTMAS DAY

At Grandfather Gaumer's house, where the governor dined; at the Weygandt farm where there was another great family dinner; at the Kuhnses, where Ollie still swelled proudly over yesterday's oratorical triumph; at Sarah Ann Mohr's, where ten indigent guests filled themselves full of fat duck, — indeed, one might say at every house in Millerstown, there was feasting. The very air smelled of roasting and boiling and frying, and the birds passing overhead stopped and settled hopefully on trees and roofs.

But in the house of William Koehler, just above Millerstown on the mountain road, there was no turkey or goose done to a turn, there were no pies, there was no fine-cake. Here was no mother or grandmother to make preserves or to compound mincemeat in preparation for this day of days. What mother there had been was seldom thought of in the little house.

Here the day passed like any other day, except that it was duller and less tolerable. There was no school for Alvin and no work for his father, and they had to spend the long hours together. Alvin did not like school, but to-day he would cheerfully have gone before daylight and have remained until dark. His father did not like holidays; they removed the goal, for which he worked and of which he thought night and day, a little farther away from him. He would have preferred to work every day, even on Sundays.

William was a mason by trade, but when there was no mason work for him, he was willing to turn his hand to anything which would bring him a little money. Another mason had recently established himself in the village, urged, it was supposed, by those who were unwilling to admit Koehler to their houses for the occasional bits of plastering which had to be done. There was no question that Koehler was very queer. Not only was he likely to kneel down at any moment and begin to pray, but he did other singular things. He had once worked until two o'clock in the afternoon without his dinner, because his watch had stopped and he had not sense enough to know it. It was not strange that thrifty Millerstown agreed that he was not a safe person to have about.

Between him and his son there was little sympathy; there was, indeed, seldom speech. Alvin was bitterly ashamed of his father, of his miserly ways, of his shabby clothes, and above all, of his insane habit of praying. William prayed incoherently about the communion service which he was supposed to have stolen — at least, that was what seemed to be the burden of his petition. Whether he prayed for grace to return it, or for forgiveness for having taken it, Millerstown did not know, so confused was his speech. Alvin's position was a hard one. He was humiliated by the taunts of the Millerstown boys; he hated the poverty of his life; he was certain that never had a human being been so miserable.

Early on Christmas morning the two had had their breakfast together in the kitchen of the little white house where they lived, and there Alvin had made an astonishing request. Alvin was fond of fine clothes; there was a certain red tie in the village store at which he had looked longingly for days. Alvin was given to picturing himself, as Katy Gaumer pictured herself, in conspicuous and important positions in the eyes of men. Alvin's coveted distinction, however, was of fine apparel, and not of superior education. He liked to be clean and tidy; he disliked rough play and rough work which disarranged his clothes and soiled his hands.

"Ach, pop," he begged, "give me a Christmas present!" His eyes filled with tears, he had been cruelly disappointed because he had found no way to get the tie in time for the Christmas entertainment. "Everybody has a Christmas present!"

"A Christmas present!" repeated William Koehler, his quick, darting eyes shining with amazement. His were not mean features; he had the mouth of a generous man, and his eyes were full and round. But between his brows lay a deep depression, as though experience had molded his forehead into a shape for which nature had not intended it. If it had not been for that deep wrinkle, one would have said that he was a gentle, kindly, humorous soul. "A Christmas present!" said he again.

Without making any further answer, he rose and went out the kitchen door and down the board walk toward the chicken house. He repeated the monstrous request again and again, like a person of simple mind.

"A Christmas present! He asks me for a Christmas present!"

When he reached the chicken house, he stood still, leaning against the fence. The chickens clustered about him with crowings and squawkings, some flying to his shoulders. Birds and beasts and insects loved and trusted poor William if human beings did not. It was possible for him to go about among his bees and handle them as he would without fear of stings.

IV. The Koehlers' Christmas Day

Now he paid no heed to the flapping, eager fowl, except to thrust them away from him. He stood leaning against the fence and looking down upon the gray landscape. It was not yet quite daylight and the morning was cloudy. The depression in his forehead deepened; he was looking fixedly at one spot, John Hartman's house, as though he had never seen it before, or as though he meant to fix it in his mind forever.

The Hartman house was always there. He had seen it a thousand times, would see it a thousand times more. On moonlight nights, its wide roofs glittered, on dark nights a gleaming lamp set on a post before the door fixed it in place. In winter its light and its great bulk, in summer its girdle of trees, distinguished it from all the other houses in Millerstown. William Koehler could see it from every foot of his little house and garden. It was before his eyes when he worked among his plants, which seemed to love him also, and when he sat for a few minutes on his porch, and when he tended his bees or fed his chickens.

Beyond the Hartman house he did not look. There the country spread out in a wide, cultivated, vari-colored plain, with the mountains bounding it far away. To the right of the village was the little cemetery where his wife lay buried, and near it the Lutheran church to which they had both belonged, but he glanced at neither. Sometimes he could see John Hartman helping his wife from the carriage when they returned from church, or stamping the snow from his feet before he stepped into his buggy in the stable yard. Often, at this sight, where there was no one within hearing, William waved his arms and shouted, as though nothing but a wild sound could express his emotion. He was not entirely free from the superstitions in which Bevy and many other Millerstonians believed, superstitions long since seared upon the souls of a persecuted generation in the fatherland. He recited the strange verse, supposed to ward away evil, —

> "Dulix, ix, ux,
> Thou comest not over Pontio,
> Pontio is over Pilato!" —

and he carried about with him a little spray of five-finger grass as a charm.

When John Hartman drove along the mountain road, his broad shoulders almost filling his buggy, William had more than once shouted an insane accusation at him. This Millerstown did not know. Koehler never spoke thus unless they were alone, and Hartman told no one of the encounter. One is not likely to tell the world that he has been accused of stealing, even though the accuser is himself known to be a madman and a thief. But John Hartman came presently to avoid the mountain road.

After a while William roused himself and fed his chickens and looked once more at the house of John Hartman. There was smoke rising from the chimney, and tears came into William's eyes, as though the smoke had drifted across the fields and had blinded him. Suddenly he struck the sharp paling a blow with his hard hand and spoke aloud, not with his usual faltering and mumbling tongue, but clearly and straightforwardly. William had found a help and a defense.

"I will tell him!" cried he. "This day I will tell my son, Alvin!"

All the long, snowy Christmas morning, Alvin sat about the house. He did not read because he had no books, and besides, he did not care much for books. Alvin was a very handsome boy, but he did not have much mind. He did not sing or whistle on this Christmas morning because he was not cheerful; he did not whittle because whittling would have wasted both knife and stick, and his father would have reproved him. He did not walk out because he was not an active boy like David Hartman, and he did not visit because he was not liked in Millerstown. He did not take a boy's part in the games; he was afraid to swim and dive; he whined when he was hurt.

He looked out the window toward the Hartman house with a vague envy of David, who had so much while he had so little. He watched his father's parsimonious preparation of the simple meal — how Grandmother Gaumer and Bevy Schnepp would have exclaimed at a Christmas dinner of butcher's ham!

"Oh, the poor souls!" Grandmother Gaumer would have cried. "I might easily have invited them to us to eat!"

"Where does the money go, then?" Bevy would have demanded. "He surely earns enough to have anyhow a chicken on Christmas! Where does he put his money? No sugar in the coffee! Just potatoes fried in ham fat for vegetables!"

All the long afternoon, also, Alvin sat about the house. He did not think again of the Hartmans; he did not think of Katy Gaumer, who thought so frequently of him; he thought of the red tie and wished that he had money to buy it.

All the long afternoon his father huddled close to the other side of the stove and muttered to himself as though he were preparing whatever he meant to tell Alvin. It must be either a very puzzling or a very long story, or one which required careful rehearsing. When the sun, setting in a clear sky, had touched the top of a mountain far across the plain, he began to speak suddenly, as though he had given to himself the departure of day for a signal. He did not make an elaborate account of the strange events he had to relate; on the contrary, he could hardly have

IV. THE KOEHLERS' CHRISTMAS DAY

omitted a word and have had his meaning clear. He said little of Alvin's mother; he drew no deductions; he simply told the story.

"Alvin!" cried he, sharply.

Alvin looked up. His head had sunk on his breast; he was at this moment half asleep. He was startled not alone by the tone of his father's voice, but by his father's straightened shoulders, by his piercing glance.

"I am going to tell you something!"

Alvin looked at his father a little eagerly. Perhaps his father was going to give him a present, after all. It would take only a quarter to buy the red tie. But it was a very different announcement which William had to make. He began with an alarming statement.

"After school closes you are to work at the furnace. I let you do nothing too long already, Alvin!"

"At the furnace!" Alvin's astonishment and alarm made him cry out. He hated the sight of Oliver Kuhns and Billy Knerr when they came home all grimy and black.

"I will tell you something," said his father again. "Listen good, Alvin!"

Alvin needed no such command to make him hearken. Alvin had not much will, but he was determining with all his power that he would never, never work in the furnace. He did not observe how his father's cheeks had paled above his black beard, and how steadily he kept his eyes upon his son. The story William had to tell was not that of a man whose mind was gone.

"You know the church?" said William.

"Of course."

"I mean the Lutheran church where I used to go, where my pop went."

"Yes."

"You go in at the front of the church, but the pulpit is at the other end. There were once long ago two windows, one on each side of the pulpit. They went almost down to the floor. From there the sun shone in the people's eyes. You can't remember that, Alvin. That was before your time."

Alvin sat still, sullenly. This conversation was, after all, only of a piece with his father's strange mutterings; it had to do with no red necktie.

"But now the Sunday School is there and those windows are gone this long time. One is a door into the Sunday School, the other is a wall. I built that wall, Alvin."

William paused as though for some comment, but Alvin said nothing.

"I was sitting where I am sitting now one evening and she [his wife] was sitting where you are sitting and you were running round, and the preacher climbed the hill to us and he came in and he said to me, 'William,' he said, 'it is decided that the big window is to be walled up. When can you do it?' That was the way he said it, Alvin. I said to him, 'I can do it tomorrow. I had other work for the afternoon at Zion Church, but I can put it off.' She could have told you that that was just what he said and what I said. I was in the congregation and there was at that time no other mason but me in Millerstown. It was to be made all smooth, so that nobody could ever tell there was a window there. Then the preacher, he said to me, — she could tell you that, too, if she were here, — he said, 'Come in the morning and I will give you the key of the communion cupboard,' the little cupboard in the wall, Alvin. There the communion set was kept. It was silver, real silver, all shiny." William's hands began to tremble and he moistened his dry lips. William spoke of objects which were to him manifestly holy. His son bent his head now, not idly and indifferently, but stubbornly. He remembered the names which the boys had shouted at his father; with all his soul he recoiled from hearing his father's confession. "There was a silver pitcher, so high, and a silver plate and a silver cup on the stem like a goblet. The preacher put it away there and he locked the door always.

"But he gave me the key and I went to my work. I thought once I would have to open the door and I stuck the key in the lock. It was a funny key.

"But I did n't need to open the door. I took my dinner along — she could tell you that. But I did n't need to open the door, and I took the key out again and put it in my pocket, and when I finished I swept everything up nice and locked the church door and came down the pike. It was night already and I went to the preacher and gave him the two keys, the church key and the other, and got my money. That quick he paid me, Alvin. He said to me, 'Well, I guess you had a quiet day, William,' and I said, 'Yes, nobody looked in at me but a little one.' That is what I said to the preacher *then*, Alvin, exactly that, but it was not true. But I thought it was true.

"Then I came home and I told her how nice and smooth I had made it — to this day, you cannot see it was a window there. Now, listen, Alvin!"

The sunset sky was darkening, a rising wind rattled the door in its latch. The little house was lonely on a winter night, even a bright night like this. The boy began to be frightened, his father looked at him with such dagger-like keenness.

"So it went for three weeks, Alvin, and then it was Sunday morning

IV. The Koehlers' Christmas Day

and here I sat and there she sat and you were running round, and it came a knock at the door and there was the preacher. I was studying my lesson for the Sunday School. It was about Ananias. I had learned the answers and the Golden Text, but it was not yet time to go. I always went to church; I liked to go to church. Then there came this knocking, Alvin, and it was the preacher. I thought perhaps he had come to give her the communion while she was n't very well and could n't go down through the snow. The preacher came in and he looked at me.

"'William,' said the preacher to me, 'do you remember how I gave you the key to the cupboard when you fixed the wall?'

"'Why, yes,' I said. 'Of course!'

"'William,' said he to me, 'did you open the cupboard?'

"'Why, no,' I said. 'I did n't have to, Para [Pastor].'

"'Were you away from the church?'

"'No,' I said. 'I took my dinner. She can tell you that.'

"'Why, William,' said he to me, 'the communion set is gone! The communion set is gone,' he said, 'gone!'

"I went with him to the church, Alvin, and I looked into the cupboard. Everything was gone, Alvin, bag and all. Then I came home and after a while they came. They wanted to talk, they wanted me to tell them everything that had happened all day. But I could n't tell them anything. I had built the wall and a little one had talked to me, that was all. There she sat and here I sat and it was dark. Then, Alvin, it came to me! When I got halfway up the window, it was too high to go farther, and I went out of the church to get boards and build a platform across chairs to that I could reach. I was gone some little time, and when I came back Hartman was going down the pike. It was Hartman that took the communion set."

Alvin moved toward the side of his chair, and away from his father.

"Then I got up and went down the hill, and into Hartman's house I walked. He was sitting by the table with his best clothes on to go to church and she was there, too. They were always rich; they had everything grand. I made tracks on her clean floor, and she looked sharp at me, but I did not care. I spoke right up to him.

"'When I was building the wall in the church,' I said, 'I went out for a few boards. In that time you were in the church and took the communion set.'

"He did not look at me, Alvin; he just sat there.

"'What would I do with a communion set?' he said after a while to me.

"'I do not know what you would do with it,' I said back to him, 'but you have it. You took it. God will punish you like Ananias.'

"Then, Alvin —" William laid a hand on his son's shrinking arm. "He went to the preacher, and the preacher came to me and said I must be quiet. That the preacher said to me! Then I went to church and prayed out loud before all the people that God would punish the wicked. I did not mention any names, Alvin; I obeyed the preacher in that! But God did not punish him. Everything gets better and better for him all the time. Now, I will punish him, Alvin, and you will help me. I have paid a lot to detectives, but I have not yet enough. He must be watched; we must have proof. I cannot save so much any more because I have not so much work. Now, if you work at the furnace you will make a dollar a day. It will take all we can earn, Alvin, *all*. I did without things that I need; I have saved all I can, but I cannot save enough."

William broke off suddenly. The room was quite dark; where no light was needed, none was made in William Koehler's house. William rose and went stumbling about and lit the lamp, the lamp which Katy saw gleaming against the dark side of the mountain. In its light poor William gazed at his son with yearning. He seemed now perfectly sane.

Then William spoke in a hollow, astonished voice, the lamp rattling in his hand.

"Don't you believe he took it, Alvin?"

"Why, no," stammered Alvin. "What would he want with it?"

CHAPTER V
ANOTHER CHRISTMAS DAY

In the Hartman house on Christmas Day there was feasting, but no rejoicing. Cassie Hartman was fully as able a cook as Grandmother Gaumer, and she roasted as large a turkey and prepared almost as many delicacies as Grandmother Gaumer and Bevy Schnepp prepared for their great party. On the kitchen settle were gifts, a gold breastpin set with a handsome diamond, a heavy gold watch-chain, a boy's suit, a gun, and a five-dollar gold-piece. There were on them no affectionate inscriptions, no good wishes. The breastpin was for Cassie, the watch-chain for John Hartman, the other articles for David. There were no gifts from outsiders — few Millerstonians would have ventured to offer gifts to the rich Hartmans. In the parlor windows hung holly wreaths, the only bought wreaths in Millerstown.

The Hartmans had asked no guests to their feast. John had long since separated himself from the friends of his youth; as for Cassie, the thought of the footprints of Christmas guests on her flag walk and her carefully scrubbed porches would have made the day even more uncomfortable than it was. Moreover, one could not entertain Christmas company in the kitchen, however fine that kitchen might be, and in this wintry weather fires would have to be made in the parlor and the dining-room.

"Company would track dust so for me," Cassie would have said if any one had suggested that some companions of his own age might do David good and might not be a bad thing for his elders. "When you have fires, you have ashes, and I would then have to clean my house in the middle of winter when you cannot clean the carpets right."

Cassie Hartman was a beautiful woman, how beautiful Millerstown, which set a higher value upon mere prettiness than upon beauty, did not know. Her figure was tall and full and she bore herself with grace and dignity. Her face with its even features and its full gray eyes was the face of an austere saint, although her eyes, lifting when you addressed her, seemed rather to hide her real character than reveal it. But her character was austere and reserved, of that you were sure.

If Cassie's soul was a consecrated one, the gods to whom one would have assigned her worship were Cleanliness and Order. The very progress of her husband and son about the house annoyed her because it was masculine and untidy. David knew better than to enter the kitchen with muddy shoes, but his father was not so careful; therefore both trod upon an upper layer of slightly worn rag carpet, superimposed upon the bright and immaculate lower layer. In all other details but one of the management of her house Cassie had her way. Her husband refused stubbornly to leave the great walnut bed and large room in which he slept for a smaller room at the back of the house, as Cassie wished, so that the great best bedrooms might be garnished day and night with their proper spreads and counterpanes and shams.

Each of Cassie's days and hours had its appointed task. She could have told how her time would be spent from now on until the last hour before her passing, when the preacher would come in the proper Lutheran fashion to give her the communion. The Church required no such ceremony, but Cassie was a formalist in religion and required it for herself.

So the three Hartmans ate alone in their broad kitchen, John Hartman at one end of the table, Cassie far away at the other, and David midway between them. John Hartman's eyes were hardly lifted above his food; he was an intolerably silent person. Cassie's eyes roved everywhere, from her stove, which she could scarcely wait to blacken, toward her husband who ate carelessly, and toward her son, who devoured his drumstick with due regard for the clean cloth. The cloth was spotless and would probably remain spotless, for an extra white cover had been laid beneath the plates of John and David. But to-morrow it would go into the tub, none the less. It was too good to be used every day, and it could not be put away bearing even the slight wrinkles produced by unfolding. Cassie had no more to say than her husband. There was really nothing for Cassie to say. Her mental processes involved herself and her house, they responded to no inspiration from without.

As for little David, he said nothing either. Katy Gaumer had been right when she said that David was a cross boy. David was cross and sullen. To-day, however, he was only solemn. David was deeply concerned about his sins. He was not only a sinner in general, but he had sinned in a very particular way, and he was unhappy. The turkey did not taste as a Christmas turkey should, and his second slice of mince-pie was bitter.

When John Hartman had eaten all he could, he rose and put on his coat and went out to his great barn to feed his stock. He went silently, as was his wont.

When David had finished the last morsel of pie which he was able to swallow, he, too, put on his hat and went toward the door, moving silently and slouchingly. There he stood and nervously kicked the sill. His eyes, gray like his mother's, looked out from under frowning, knitted brows; he thrust his hands deep into his pockets and looked down at the floor. This was Christmas Day; his parents had treated him generously; he was convinced that he ought to confess to them his great wickedness. He felt as though he might cry, and as though crying, if he had a shoulder to lean on, would be a soothing and healing operation. The assault of Katy Gaumer had sunk deep into his heart, as was natural since he thought of Katy night and day, since he saw her wherever she went in her red dress, now scolding, now laughing, and perpetually in motion. He had fled to the attic of the schoolroom yesterday because she had not spoken to him or looked at him, had even passed him with her weight planted for an instant heavily on his foot without even acknowledging his presence. And to the attic she had followed him and had there taunted and insulted him! She had no business to say that he was cross and ugly; he would be nice enough to her if she would return the compliment. As for Grandmother Gaumer's cakes, he had better cakes at home than Grandmother Gaumer could bake!

David's heart was sore, and David was inexpressibly lonely and miserable. He was now certain that he would be happy if he could confess his sins to his mother.

He forgot the last occasion of his appeal to her. Then his finger had been cut, and he had been dizzy and had seized hold of her, and the blood had fallen down on her new silk dress. He forgot her reproof; he remembered only that he needed some sort of human tenderness. His father did not often speak to him, but women were made, or should be made, of different stuff from men. He had seen Susannah Kuhns sit with her great Ollie upon her lap, and Ollie was older than he was by a year. He had heard Katy Gaumer, who had been so outrageously cruel to him, cry over a sick kitten, and Katy was herself often rocked like a baby on Grandmother Gaumer's knee.

David forgot now not only the cut finger, but other repulses. He had no claim on Grandmother Gaumer's embrace, and he would have hated to have to sit on Susannah Kuhns's knee, but upon this tall, beautiful person sitting by the table, he had a claim. Moreover, her embraces would have been pleasant.

"Mom!" said David.

Cassie's eyes were now on the dishes before her. She liked to plan her mode of attack upon a piece of work, and then proceed swiftly, keeping her mind a blank to everything but the pleasure of seeing order grow where disorder had been. Thus she liked to go through her fine house, sweeping the rich carpets, polishing the carved furniture, letting the sunlight in only long enough to show each infamous dust mote. Cassie was in the midst of such planning now; she saw the dishes neatly piled, the hot suds in the pan, her sleeves rolled above her elbows. She did not answer David, did not even hear him.

"Mom!" said David again. He did not know now exactly what he had meant to say. The necessity for confession had dwindled to a necessity for the sound of his mother's voice. It was dismal to live in a house with companions who seemed deaf and blind to one's existence. She *must* speak to him.

At the second call, Cassie looked at her son. Cassie recognized dirt and disorder, but she did not recognize any need of the human soul. The needs of her own soul had been, Cassie thought, cruelly denied. At any rate, its power of perception had failed.

"You stamp on that sill again and I'll have to scrub it, David! To spoil things on Christmas!"

Cassie's voice contained no threat of punishment; it was merely mildly exclamatory. The tone of it was not vibrant but wooden. It might have been rich and beautiful in youth; now it expressed no emotion; it was flat, empty. She did not ask David what he wanted, or why he addressed her; she did not even wonder why he stopped in the doorway and stared at her. She only frowned at him, until he closed the door, himself outside. David had all the clothes he could wear, all the food he could eat; he had the finest house, the richest father and the most capable mother in Millerstown; what more could he wish to make him happy? His mother did not speculate as to whether he was happy or not.

David crossed the yard in the freshly fallen snow and slammed the gate behind him. Then he went toward the mountain road, and started to climb, passing the house of the Koehlers, where William sat on one side of the stove and Alvin on the other, the one muttering to himself, the other half asleep. David kicked the snow as he walked, his head bent lower and lower on his breast. He could see Katy Gaumer like a sprite in her red dress with her flashing eyes and her pointing finger; he could see her smiling at Alvin Koehler, whom he hated without dreaming that in that son of a demented and dishonest father Katy Gaumer could have any possible interest.

As he started up the steepest part of the hill, he began to talk aloud.

"I want her!" said poor little David. "I want Katy! I want Katy!"

Presently David left the road, and climbing over the worn fence into the woodland, struck off diagonally among the trees. Still far above him, at the summit of the little mountain, there was a rough pile of rocks which formed a tiny cairn or cave. Before it was a small platform, parapeted by a great boulder. Generations past had named the spot, without any apparent reason, the "Sheep Stable." It was a favorite resort of David Hartman. Here, in secret, far above Millerstown, he carried on the wicked practices which he had meant to confess to his mother. From the little plateau one could look for miles and miles over a wide, rich, beautiful plain, could see

V. Another Christmas Day

the church spires of a dozen villages, the smoke curling upward from three or four great blast furnaces, set in the midst of wide fields, and could look far beyond the range of hills which bounded the view of William Koehler on his lower level, to another range. The Pennsylvania German made his home only in fertile spots. When other settlers passed the thickly forested lands because of the great labor of felling the trees and preparing the soil, he selected the sections bearing the tallest trees and had as his own the fertile land forever.

David did not look out over the wide, pure expanse upon which a few flakes were still falling and beyond which the sun would soon sink gorgeously, nor did he see the purple shadows under the pine trees, nor observe the glancing motions of a squirrel, watching him from a bough near by. He determined, desperately, firmly, that he would repent no more; he would now return to his evil ways and get from them what satisfaction he could.

He crept on hands and knees into the little cave and felt round under a mass of dried leaves until his hands encountered the instruments of his evil practices. Then David drew them forth, a stubby pipe, which he had smoked once and which had made him deathly ill, and a pack of cards, about whose mysterious and delightful use he knew nothing. He sat with them in his hands on the sloping rock, wishing, poor little David, that he knew how to be wickeder than he was!

Having fed his stock, John Hartman tramped for a little while round his fields in the snow, then he returned to the kitchen and sat down by the window with a newspaper. Cassie lay asleep on the settle. Custom forbade her working on Christmas Day, and she never read, even the almanac. At her, her husband looked once or twice inscrutably, then he laid his head on the back of his tall chair and slept also. It was a scene at which Katy Gaumer would have pointed as proof of the unutterable stupidity of Millerstown.

When her husband slept, Cassie opened her eyes and looked at him with as steady a gaze as that which he had bent upon her. Her mouth set itself in a firm, straight line, her eyes deepened and darkened, her hands, folded upon her breast, grasped her flesh. Surely between these two was some great barrier of offense, given or suffered, of strange, wounded pride, or insufferable humiliation! Presently Cassie's lids fell; she turned her check against the hard back of the old settle and so fell asleep also.

John Hartman owned four farms and a great stretch of woodland and a granite quarry on the far side of the mountain and two farms and two peach orchards and an apple orchard on this. A generation ago a large deposit of fine iron ore had been discovered upon a tract of land owned by his father. The deposit was not confined to his fields, but extended to the lands of his neighbors. But while they sold ore and spent their money, John Hartman's father, as shrewd a business man as his son, sold and saved, and laid the foundation of his fortune. In a few years the discovery of richer, more easily mined deposits in the West and the cheap importation of foreign ores made the Millerstown ore for the time not worth the mining. Hartman the elder then covered his mine breaches and planted timber, and the growth set above the treasure underground was now thick and valuable. John Hartman was also a director in a county bank; he owned the finest, largest house in Millerstown; he had a handsome and a capable wife, and a son who was strong in body and who had a good mind. Apparently his position in life was secure, his comfort certain.

John Hartman, however, was neither comfortable nor secure, The long-past accusations of a poor, half-crazed workingman filled his waking hours with apprehension and his nights with remorse. Of William Koehler and his accusation John Hartman was afraid, for William's accusation was, at least in part, true.

John Hartman had been walking away from the church on that bright November day years ago, when his own David and Alvin Koehler were little children and Katy Gaumer not much more than a baby. He had upon him, as William had said, an air of guilt; he had refused to reply to William's shouted greeting; he was at that moment rapidly becoming, if he was not already, what William called him, a thief.

On that November day, a little while before William had shouted at him, he had come down the pike and had seen William leave the church to get the boards for his platform, and had thereupon entered the church with no other impulse than the vague motions of a man sick at heart. A sin of his earlier youth had risen suddenly from the grave where he thought it buried, and now confronted him. In his pocket lay an accusing, threatening letter, written with pale ink upon poor paper in an ignorant way. The amount of money which it demanded, large as it was, did not trouble him, since he was already possessor of his inheritance and growing daily richer; it was the horror of the discovery of his sin. Once cured of his obsession he had become a devout man, had taken pleasure in the services of the church of his fathers, attending all her meetings and contributing to all her causes. He had married a good woman from a neighboring village, who knew nothing of the year he had spent away from Millerstown; he had had a son; he was wholly happy.

He had gone during the latter part of the year which he spent away from home, as a way of escaping from himself, to Europe. He had been only a few weeks ashore, but he had seen during that time civilizations different from anything he had dreamed of. He was most moved by great churches — he saw Notre Dame of Amiens and Notre Dame of Paris — and by the few great English estates of which he caught glimpses in his rapid journey to Liverpool. That was the way a man should live, planted in one place, like a great oak tree, the center of a wide group — a wife, children, dependents. He should have his garden, his woodland, his great house, his stables, his beautiful horses; he should pass the home place on to a son who would perpetuate his name. With such a home and with a worthy church to worship in, a man could ask for nothing else in the world.

Repentant, healed, John Hartman had returned to Millerstown. There he had married and had built his house, with great rooms at the front and smaller rooms at the back for the servants who should make his wife's life easy and dignified and should help to care for the little brothers and sisters whom David was to have. Cassie had had a hard youth; her father had been a disgrace to his children; she was quiet and stern and not hopeful, even though John Hartman had lifted her to so high a place, of very great happiness in this life. But Cassie's nature had seemed to change in the glow of John Hartman's affection and in the enjoyment of the luxuries with which he surrounded her. She became less silent; she met her husband at times with a voluntary caress, which opened in his heart new springs of happiness.

But here, into this blessed peace and security, into this great planning, fell, like a dangerous explosive, the threatening letter. Almost beside himself with fright, worn with three nights' sleepless vigil, confused with the numerous plans for ridding himself of his persecutor which he made only to reject, and aware that an immediate answer must be sent, John Hartman approached the church where William Koehler had been working.

The open door seemed to invite him to take refuge within. He kept constantly touching the letter in his pocket. He meant to destroy it, but it bore an address which he dared not lose. He had been sitting by the roadside on a fallen log, holding the letter in his hand and writing absent-mindedly upon it.

In the church he saw William's half-finished work and the curious key in the little cupboard. As an elder, he had a right to open the door and to take out the beautiful silver vessels, the extravagance of one generation which had become the pride of the next. It seemed for an instant as though a touch of the holy things might give him peace. Untying the cord of the heavy bag as he laid it on top of William's half-finished wall, he lifted out the silver chalice.

But the sight of the beautiful vessel gave him no relief, and the cool, smooth surface made him shiver. He grasped it suddenly and involuntarily cried out, "Oh, what shall I do! What *shall* I do!"

The grip of his hand was so strong that the cup slipped from his fingers and striking the top of William's wall, bounded into the dark aperture which the building of the wall had made. He reached frantically after it, and the gray bag, containing the pitcher and paten, struck by his elbow, followed the silver cup.

For an instant the accident drove the more serious trouble from John Hartman's mind. He had great reverence for the sacred vessels and he was afraid that the fall had bruised their beautiful surfaces. He tried to reach the bag, which lay uppermost, but it was just beyond the tips of his fingers at the longest reach of his arm. He would have to get William Koehler to help him, much as he disliked to confess to such carelessness. William would be shocked and horrified.

Then, suddenly, John Hartman gave a sharp cry. In his struggle to reach the gray bag, the letter had dropped from his pocket. He had not put it back into its envelope after his last anguished reading; he could see it now as it lay spread out below him in the darkness. His frantic eyes seemed to read each word on the dim page. "Your wife will know about it, and your little boy and all the country." If he called William to help him, William might read the letter. Even if William made no actual effort to decipher it, a single glance might reveal that some one was threatening John Hartman.

He thought that he heard William coming through the new Sunday School room and in panic, and without stopping to reason beyond the swift conclusion that if William's attention were not called to them, he would not see the bag and letter far down in the narrow pit, he turned and locked the cupboard door and went out the door of the church and down the road. He did not reflect that William might easily discover that the communion set was gone, that he might accidentally drop his trowel into the deep hole and in reaching it find the dreadful letter, and that he might give an alarm, and all be lost; his only thought was to get away.

He remembered dimly that he had brushed aside a little child in his rush to the church door. When he reached the door, he held himself back from running by a mighty effort and walked slowly down the pike, little Katy Gaumer toddling fearfully behind him. It was easy to pretend that he did not hear William call. Already he had planned how he would restore the silver to its place. He knew that William was engaged that afternoon to work at Zion Church; therefore the wall would not be closed that day.

At night he would go to the church with a hoe or rake and lift out the sacred vessels and the dreadful letter, whose very proximity to them was sacrilege. If the pitcher and the chalice and the plate had suffered harm, he would explain that he had taken them to the jeweler to be polished, and he would then have them repaired.

But William postponed his work at Zion Church, and that night, when John Hartman stole back to replace the silver, the wall was finished and the mortar set.

That night, also, John Hartman learned with absolute certainty that his persecutor was dead, and his persecution at an end.

"They do not know that the communion set is gone," thought he. "Tomorrow I will find a way."

But in a sort of stupor, from which he roused himself now and then to make wild and fruitless plans, John Hartman let the days go by. The blow he had received had affected him not only mentally, but physically, and he was slow to recover from it, past though the danger was. He went about his farms, he looked earnestly upon his wife, he clasped his little boy in his arms to assure himself that his two treasures were real.

But the more certain he became that the ghost of the past was laid, the more terribly did the present specter rise to harass him. Communion Sunday was approaching, the loss of the communion service would be discovered. There were moments when the distracted man prayed for a miracle. He had been delivered from that other terror by an act of Providence which was almost a miracle; would he not be similarly saved in a situation in which he was innocent?

He thought of going at night and tearing the wall down and restoring the service to its place, leaving the strange vandalism a mystery to horrified Millerstown. How happy he should be to pay for the rebuilding of the wall! But the task was too difficult, discovery too probable.

As the days passed, another way out of his trouble occurred to him. He would go to William Koehler and tell him all his misery. William was a good-natured, quiet soul, who could be persuaded to silence, or who might set a price upon silence, if silence were a salable commodity. William could easily find an excuse for doing his work over; it was well known that he was foolishly particular. It never occurred to John that suspicion of theft would probably fall upon honest, simple William, who had had the key of the cupboard and who had been the whole day alone in the church. He got no farther than his own terrible problem. He had dropped the silver into the wall; both letter and silver were there convicting him; he must find a way to get them both out and to put the silver in its place.

But he allowed day after day to pass and did not visit William. William was, after all, only a day laborer of the stupid family of Koehlers and John was a property owner and an elder in the church; it would be intolerably humiliating to make such a confession. Communion Sunday was still two weeks away; there would be time for him to make some other plan.

When Communion Sunday morning came, John had still no plan. Moving as in a trance, he went with his wife to church, to find the congregation gathered into wondering, distressed groups. The door of the little cupboard was open, and beside it was the smooth, newly painted wall. It was too late for John to ask William Koehler for help in his difficulty.

He did not realize that all about him his fellow church members were whispering about William; he did not hear that William was accused, he was so dazed by the fortunate complications of his own situation. They did not dream of his agency! He would replace the set with a much more beautiful one. This generation would pass away long before the wall would be taken down and then the letter would be utterly destroyed by age or dampness. He said to himself that God had been very good to him; he even dared to thank Him during the confused, uneasy service which the pastor conducted upon his return from the house of William Koehler.

And if William were accused, William had only to deny that he had seen the communion service or that he had even opened the door! He might, if worse came to worst, let them search his house. John wished patronizingly that he could give William a little advice. He pitied William.

By night this pity had changed to hate. For like the wildcats, whose leap from above he had feared as a child when he walked the mountain road, so William leaped upon him with his charge.

"You took it!" insisted William. "You stole the communion set!"

Here was ruin, indeed! But Cassie thought the man mad; she paid no attention to his frantic words; she was concerned only about the state of her snow-tracked floor. Hope leaped in the breast of John Hartman. No living soul would believe such an accusation against him!

When William had gone, John put on his coat and went to the house of the preacher. He even forced himself to use one of Millerstown's interesting idioms, one of the last humorous expressions of John Hartman's life.

"William Koehler came to me and accused me of stealing the communion service," said he. "There is one rafter too few or too many in his little house."

The preacher shook his head.

"There is something very wrong with poor William," said he sorrowfully.

V. Another Christmas Day

With a firm step John Hartman returned to his house. When it was time for the evening service he went to church as was his custom.

John Hartman's bank account increased steadily; he added field to field and orchard to orchard. His great safe in the dining-room held papers of greater and greater value; his great Swiss barns with their deep forebays and their mammoth haylofts were enlarged; his orchards bent under their weight of fruit. But John Hartman did not say to his soul, "Take thine ease, eat, drink, and be merry." With his soul poor John held a different sort of converse.

Desperately he tried to fix his mind upon his many affairs, so that he might shut out the recollection of William Koehler and the sound of his mad voice. He was afraid for a long time that he, John Hartman, might rise suddenly in church and make rash confession, or that he might point out to his fellow directors in the bank the black-bearded, sharp-eyed face, which he saw looking at him over their shoulders, or that he might shout out upon the street his secret.

Gradually he succeeded in thinking only of his work. The sudden appearance of William Koehler gave him a strange trembling of the limbs and an oppression about the heart, that was all. William made no further accusation for a long time, and encounters could be avoided. Long before William had begun to pray aloud, dropping down in front of the post-office or at a street corner, Millerstown had become certain that he was crazy. His unintelligible prayers betrayed nothing.

But, slowly, as his mind turned itself a little from its own wretchedness, poor Hartman became aware of an enemy in his own household. To his caresses his wife ceased to respond; she had become once more the silent, cold woman of their earliest married life, whom he had chosen because she and the woman who had victimized him were as far apart as the poles in character and disposition. At first poor Hartman thought that she felt his neglect of her during the weeks of his misery; he tried now to be all the more tender and affectionate. If he could only find here a refuge, if he could only lay before her his wretched state! But confession to Cassie was impossible; one had only to look upon her to see that!

Presently Hartman decided that she believed William's accusation, and he become enraged with her because she would believe that to which no one else in Millerstown would give an instant's credence. "Let her believe!" said he then in his despair. She became in his mind a partner of William against him. Let each do his worst; they could convict him of nothing.

In reality it was Hartman's earlier sin which was no more his secret. He had delayed too long in answering the demand for money and a letter had been written to Cassie also, and Cassie had hardened her heart against him, hardened her heart even against her child. Cassie had had a sad life; her heart was only a little softened as yet by her happiness.

"I will not care," cried poor Cassie. "I will henceforth set my heart on nothing!"

Cassie was a woman of mighty will; her youth had trained her to strength. When her child climbed her knee, she put him away from her; when she remembered John Hartman's hopes for the occupation of the many rooms he had built in his house, she shook her head with a deep, choking, indrawn breath. It could never, never be!

But the human heart must have some object for its care or it will cease to beat. Upon her possessions, her house, her carpets, her furniture, Cassie set now her affection. These inanimate things had no power to deceive, to betray, to torture. Gradually they became so precious that her great rooms were like shrines, into which she went but seldom, but to which her heart turned as she sat alone by her kitchen window and her sewing or lay awake by her husband's side in the great wonderfully bedecked walnut bed which, to her thinking, human use profaned.

Thus, in the same house, eating at the same table, sitting side by side in church, watching their son grow into a young manhood which was as silent as their middle age, the guilty man and the unforgiving woman lived side by side for almost fifteen years this Christmas Day. John Hartman had built no great church, rising like a cathedral on the hillside. He had not even presented the church with a communion service, being afraid of rousing suspicion. He had gathered great store for himself — an object in life toward which he had never aimed.

Millerstown suspected nothing, neither of the sin of John Hartman's youth, nor of his strange connection with the disappearance of the communion service, nor of Cassie's aching, hardening heart. Millerstown, like the rest of the world, accepted people as they were; it did not seek for excuses or explanations or springs of action. John Hartman was a silent and taciturn man — few persons remembered that he had been otherwise. Cassie was so unpleasantly particular about her belongings that she would not invite her neighbors to quiltings and apple-butter boilings, and so inhumanly unsocial that she would not attend those functions at other houses. There was an end of the Hartmans.

Gradually a second change came over John Hartman. His horror of discovery became a horror of his sin; he was bowed with grief and remorse.

"He has gone crazy over it!" he lamented. "William Koehler has gone crazy over it. I wish" — poor Hartman spoke with agony — "I wish he had proved it against me. Then it would all have been over long ago!"

When William Koehler's wife died, John Hartman struggled terribly with himself, but could not bring himself to make confession. From an upper window he watched the little cortège leave the house on the hill; he saw William lift his little boy into the carriage; he saw the cortège disappear in the whirling snow. But still he was silent.

When William in his insanity mortgaged his little house in order to pay dishonest and thieving men to watch John Hartman, John Hartman secured the mortgage and treasured it against the time when he would prove to William that had tried to do well by him. John Hartman also bought other mortgages. When Oliver Kuhns, the elder, squandered his little inheritance in the only spree of his life, John Hartman helped him to keep the whole matter from Millerstown and restored to him his house. When one of the Fackenthals, yielding to a mad impulse to speculate, used the money of the school board and lost it, John Hartman gave him the money in secret. Proud Emma Loos never knew that her husband had wasted her little patrimony before he died. Sarah Benner never discovered that for days threat of prison hung over her son and that John Hartman helped him to make good what he had stolen.

But John Hartman's benefactions did not ease his soul. He came to see clearly that he must have peace of mind or he would die. He no longer thought of the disgrace to his wife and son; his thoughts had been for so long fixed upon himself that he could put himself in the place of no one else.

"To-morrow I will make this right," he would say, and forever, "To-morrow, to-morrow!"

But the years passed and William Koehler grew more mad and John Hartman more rich and more silent, and the silver service lay deep in the pit between the church and Sunday School. The little building was solid, it was amply large, it would serve many generations. Katy Gaumer, brushed out of his path by John Hartman as he sought the door that November day, recalled nothing of the incident except that her childish dignity had been wounded. It was Katy herself who said that nothing ever happened in Millerstown!

Presently the beating of John Hartman's pulse quickened; it became difficult for him to draw a long, free, comfortable breath. Dr. Benner, whom he consulted, said that he must eat less and must walk more. John Hartman said to himself that now, before another day passed, he would go to the little house on the mountain-side and begin to set right the awful wrong of his youth. But still he planned to go to-morrow instead of to-day. Finally, one afternoon in May, he had his horse put into the buggy and drove slowly up the mountain road.

CHAPTER VI
THE MILLERSTOWN SCHOOL

The 24th of December, with its great Christmas entertainment, had closed a term of average accomplishment in the Millerstown school. Alvin Koehler and David Hartman, who composed the highest class, had been, the one as idle, the other as sullen, as usual. The children had learned about as much as the Millerstown children were accustomed to learn in an equal time, they had been reprimanded about as often. The teacher had roared at them with the vehemence usually required for the management of such young savages as Coonie Schnable and Ollie Kuhns and Katy Gaumer. Katy, in the second class, had not nearly enough to keep her busy; there remained on her hands too many moments to be devoted to the invention of mischief.

But now, suddenly, began a new era in the Millerstown school. Mr. Carpenter, recovering at happy ease in his home in a neighboring village from the strain put upon him by the stupidity and impertinence and laziness of his pupils, was to be further irritated and annoyed.

School opened on New Year's morning, and Mr. Carpenter rose a little late from his comfortable bed at Sarah Ann Mohr's and ate hurriedly his breakfast of delicious panhaas and smoked sausage. Haste at meals always tried the sybarite soul of Mr. Carpenter. He was cross because he had to get up; he was cross because he had to teach school; he was cross at Sarah Ann because she urged him to further speed. Sarah Ann always mothered and grandmothered the teacher.

"You will come late, teacher. You will have to hurry yourself. It is not a good thing to be late on New Year's already, teacher. New Year," — went on Sarah Ann in her provokingly placid way, — "New Year should be always a fresh start in our lives."

Mr. Carpenter slammed the kitchen door; he would have liked to be one of his own scholars for the moment and to have turned and made a face at Sarah Ann. He was not interested in fresh starts. Taking his own deliberate, comfortable time, he started out the pike.

Then, suddenly, the clear, sweet notes of the schoolhouse bell, whose rope it was his high office to pull, astonished the ears of the teacher. It was one of the impertinent boys, — Ollie Kuhns, in all probability, — who thus dared to reprove his master.

"It will give a good thrashing for that one, whoever he is," Mr. Carpenter promised himself. "He will begin the New Year fine. He will ache on the New Year."

VI. The Millerstown School

But the bell rang slowly, its stroke was not such as the arm of a strong boy could produce. Indeed, Mr. Carpenter never allowed the boys to ring the bell, because there responded at once to the sound the whole of alarmed Millerstown seeking to rescue its children from fire. The bell had, moreover, to Mr. Carpenter's puzzled ears, a solemn tone, as though it portended things of moment. Faster Mr. Carpenter moved along, past the Squire's where Whiskey barked at him, and he hissed a little at Whiskey; past Grandfather Gaumer's, where he thought of Grandfather's Katy and her ways with bitter disapproval, to the open spaces of the pike.

The bell still rang solemnly, as Mr. Carpenter hurried across the yard and up the steps.

In the vestibule of the schoolhouse, he stood still, dumb, paralyzed. The ringer of the bell, the inventor of woe still unsuspected by Mr. Carpenter, stood before him. During the Christmas holiday, Katy's best dress had become her everyday dress; its red was redder than Katy's cheeks, brighter than her eyes; it had upon her teacher the well-known effect of that brilliant color upon certain temperaments. Mr. Carpenter's cheeks began to match it in hue; he opened his lips several times to speak, but was unable to bring forth a sound.

Katy gave the rope another long, deliberate pull, then she eased her arms by letting them drop heavily to her sides. From within the schoolroom the children, even Ollie Kuhns, watched in admiration and awe. Katy was always independent, always impertinent, but she had never before dared to usurp the teacher's place.

"Say!" Thus in a terrible voice did Mr. Carpenter finally succeed in addressing his pupil. "Who told you you had the dare to ring this bell?"

To this question Katy returned no answer. With eased arms she brushed vigorously until she had removed the lint which had gathered on her dress, then she walked into the schoolroom, denuded now of its greens and flags and reduced to the dullness of every day. Her teacher continued his admonitions as he followed her up the aisle.

"I guess you think you are very smart, Katy. Well, you are not smart, that is what you are not. I would give you a good whipping if I did right, that is what I would do. I —"

To the amazement of her school-fellows, Katy, after lingering a moment at her desk, followed Mr. Carpenter to the front of the room. She still made no answer, she only approached him solemnly. Was she going, of her own accord, to deliver herself up to punishment? Mr. Carpenter's heavy rod had never dared to touch the shoulders of Katy Gaumer, whose whole "Freundschaft" was on the school board.

The Millerstown school ceased speculating and gave itself to observation. Upon the teacher's desk, Katy laid, one by one, three books and a pamphlet. Then Katy spoke, and the sound of the school bell, solemn as it had been, was not half so ominous, so filled with alarming import as Katy's words. She stood beside the desk, she offered first one book to the master, then another.

"Here is a algebray," explained Katy; "here is a geometry, here is a Latin book. Here is a catalogue that tells about these things. I am going to college; I must know many things that I never yet heard of in this world. And you" — announced Katy — "you are to learn me!"

"What!" cried Mr. Carpenter.

"I am sorry for all the bad things I did already in this school." The Millerstown children quivered with excitement; on the last seat Ollie Kuhns pretended to fall headlong into the aisle. Alvin Koehler looked up with mild interest from his desk which he had been idly contemplating, and David Hartman blushed scarlet. Poor David's pipe had not yet cured him of love. "I will do better from now on," promised Katy. "And you" — again this ominous refrain — "You are to learn me!"

"You cannot study those things!" cried Mr. Carpenter in triumph. "You are not even in the first class!"

"I will move to the first class," announced Katy. "This week I have studied all the first class spelling. You cannot catch me on a single word. I can spell them in syllables and not in syllables. I can say l, l, or double l. I can say them backwards. I have worked also all the examples in the first class arithmetic. The squire" — thus did Katy dangle the chains of Mr. Carpenter's servitude before his disgusted eyes — "the squire, he heard me the spelling, and the doctor, he looked at my examples. They were all right. It will not be long before I catch up with those two in the first class." Katy flushed a deeper red. Over and over she said to herself, "I shall be in the first class with Alvin, I shall be in the first class with Alvin!" Her knees began suddenly to tremble and she started back to her desk, scarcely knowing which way she went.

As she passed down the aisle, she felt upon her David Hartman's glance. He sat in the last row, his head down between his shoulders. As Katy drew near, his gaze dropped to the hem of her red dress. David's heart thumped; it seemed to him that every one in the school must see that he was in love with Katy Gaumer. He hated himself for it.

"Don't you want me in your class, David?" asked Katy foolishly and flippantly. Katy spoke a dozen times before she thought once.

David looked up at her, then he looked down. His eyes smarted; he was terrified lest he cry.

"I have one dumb one in my class already," said he. "I guess I can stand another."

Katy dropped into her seat with a slam. The teacher's hand was poised above the bell which called the school to order, and for Katy, at least, there was to be no more ignoring of times and seasons.

"Dumb?" repeated Katy. "You will see who is the dumb one!"

With the loud ringing of the teacher's bell a new order began in the Millerstown school. Its first manifestation was beneficent, rather than otherwise. It became apparent that with Katy Gaumer orderly, the school was orderly. The morning passed and then the afternoon without a pause in its busy labors. No one was whipped, no one was sent to the corner, no one was even reproved. A studious Katy seemed to set an example to the school; a respectful Katy seemed to establish an atmosphere of respect. Mr. Carpenter was wholly pleased.

But Mr. Carpenter's pleasure did not last. Mr. Carpenter became swiftly aware of a worse condition than that of the past. Mr. Carpenter had been lifted from the frying-pan and laid upon the fire.

To her teacher's dismay, Katy came early in the morning to ask questions; she stayed in the schoolroom at recess to ask questions; sometimes, indeed, she visited her afflicted teacher in the evenings to ask questions. Katy enjoyed visiting him in the evenings, because then Sarah Ann Mohr, sitting on the other side of the table, her delectable Millerstown "Star" forgotten, her sewing in her lap, her lips parted, burned before her favorite the incense of speechless admiration. Poor Mr. Carpenter grew thin and white, and his little mustache drooped as though all hope had gone from him. Mr. Carpenter learned to his bitter sorrow that algebra and geometry were no idle threats, and Mr. Carpenter, who had put his normal school learning, as he thought, forever behind him, had to go painfully in search of it. The squire was Katy's uncle, the doctor was her cousin; they are all on Katy's side; they helped her with her lessons; they encouraged her in this morbid and unhealthy desire for learning, and the teacher did not dare to refuse her. The difficulties of the civil service examination appalled him; he could never pass; he must at all costs keep the Millerstown school.

Occasionally, as of old, Katy corrected him, but now her corrections were involuntary and were immediately apologized for.

"You must not say 'craddle'; you must say 'crawl' or 'creep,'" directed Katy. "Ach, I am sorry! I did not mean to say that! But how"— this with desperate appeal — "how can I learn if you do not make it right?"

Sometimes Katy threatened poor Mr. Carpenter with Greek; then Mr. Carpenter would have welcomed the Socratic cup.

"My patience is all," he groaned. "Do they take me for a dictionary? Do they think I am a encyclopædia?"

Still, through the long winter Katy's relatives continued to spoil her. In Millerstown there has never been any objection to educating women simply because they are women. The Millerstown woman has always had exactly what she wanted. The normal schools and high schools in Pennsylvania German sections have always had more women students than men. If Katy wanted an education, she should have it; indeed, in the sudden Gaumer madness, Katy should have had the moon if she had asked for it and if her friends could have got it for her. Her grandfather and grandmother talked about her as they sat together in the evenings while Katy was extracting knowledge from the squire or from the doctor or from Mr. Carpenter, never dreaming that they were rapidly ruining the Benjamin of their old age. They had trained many children, and the squire had admonished all Millerstown, but Katy was never admonished by any of them. They liked her bright speech, they liked her ambition, they allowed themselves the luxury of indulging her in everything she wanted.

"She is that smart!" Bevy Schnepp expressed the opinion of all Katy's kin. "When she is high gelernt [learned] she will speak in many voices [tongues]."

Of all her relatives none spoiled Katy quite so recklessly as young Dr. Benner. There was not enough practice in healthy Millerstown to keep him busy, and Katy amused and entertained him. He liked to take her about with him in his buggy; he liked to give her hard problems, and to see to what lengths of memorizing she could go. Dr. Benner had theories about the education of children and he expounded them with the cheerful conceit of bachelors and maiden ladies. Dr. Benner, indeed, had theories about everything. It was absurd, to Dr. Benner's thinking, ever to restrain a healthy child from learning.

"Let 'em absorb," said he. "They won't take more than is good for 'em."

Dr. Benner was nearly enough related to Katy to be called a cousin, yet far enough removed to be stirred into something like jealousy at Katy's enthusiastic defense of the Koehlers. Katy should have no youthful entanglement — Dr. Benner remembered his own early development and flushed shamefacedly — to prevent her from growing into the remarkable person she might become. Dr. Benner decided that she must be got away from Millerstown as soon as possible; she had been already too much influenced by its German ways. Katy was meant for higher things. For a while young Dr. Benner felt that, pruned and polished, Katy was meant for him!

VI. THE MILLERSTOWN SCHOOL

Meanwhile, Katy was to be saved from further contamination by being kept constantly busy. It pleased him to see her devoted to algebra, and he was constantly suggesting new departures in learning to her aspiring mind. It was unfortunate that each new suggestion included a compliment.

"I believe you could sing, Katy," said he, one March day, as, with Katy beside him, he drove slowly down the mountain road.

The landscape lay before them, wide, lovely, smiling, full of color in the clear sunshine. Far away a bright spot showed where the sun was reflected from the spires and roofs of the county seat; here and there the blast furnaces lifted the smoky banner of prosperous times.

Katy's cheeks were red, her dark hair blew across her forehead; it was with difficulty that she sat still beside the doctor. Spring was coming, life was coming.

"Sing?" said Katy, "I sing? I would like that better than anything I can think of in this world. I would rather be a singer than a missionary."

There was really nothing in the world that Katy would not have liked to do, except to stay in Millerstown and be inconspicuous; there was nothing in the world which she questioned her ultimate ability to do.

The doctor chuckled at Katy's comparison, which Katy had not intended to be funny.

"A classmate of mine is coming to see me next week. He teaches singing, and I'm going to get him to hear your voice. Won't that be fine, Katy?"

"Everything is fine," answered Katy.

The doctor's classmate arrived; for him Katy *oh'd* and *ah'd* through an astonishingly wide range. The young man was enthusiastic over her vocal possibilities.

"But he says you mustn't take lessons for another year," said Dr. Benner.

Again he and Katy were driving down the mountain road. They had climbed this afternoon to the Sheep Stable, and from there had gazed at the glorious prospect and had counted through a glass the scattered villages and the church spires in the county seat.

Katy's blood tingled in her veins. She had never dreamed that she could *sing!* She had never seen a picture which was painted by hand or she would now have been certain that she could become a great artist. She determined that some day she would return to the Sheep Stable alone and there sing for her own satisfaction. She had not sung her best for the doctor's friend down in grandmother's parlor, her best meaning her loudest. At the Sheep Stable there would be no walls to confine the great sounds she would produce.

"I will sing so that they hear me at Allentown," she planned. "I have no time now, but when I have time I will go once. It is so nice not to be dumb," finished Katy with great satisfaction.

The winter passed like a dream. Presently an interesting change came about in the Millerstown school and in its teacher. Perhaps Mr. Carpenter was mortified, as well as driven into it, but there sprang up somehow in his soul a decent, honest ambition. Delving painfully after forgotten knowledge, he studied to some purpose, and it began to seem as though even civil service questions might become easy and Mr. Carpenter pass his examinations at last. For the first few weeks of the new régime, he was able to keep only a lesson or two ahead of his pupils, but, little by little, that space widened. As if in pure spite, Mr. Carpenter learned his lessons. Then he assumed a superior and taunting air. Katy at the Christmas entertainment had looked at him with no more disgust than his face now expressed when his pupils gave wrong answers.

"'Gelt regiert die Welt, und Dummheit Millerstown'" (Gold rules the world and stupidity Millerstown)! Thus Mr. Carpenter adapted a familiar proverb in comment upon mistakes which he himself would have made a month ago.

Mr. Carpenter's pupils followed him steadily. David Hartman was more mature than the others and kept without difficulty at their head. As for Katy, with the help which Katy had out of school hours, even a dull child might have done well. It was help which was not unsuspected by David, but David held his tongue. David felt a fierce, unwilling pride in Katy's spirit.

But there was another sort of help being given and received which David resented jealously and indignantly, hardly believing the evidence of his own ears and eyes. David had taken some pleasure in the winter's work. He sat daily beside Katy in class; it was not possible for her to be always rude and curt. David was also puzzled and moved by a change in his father. He often met his father's glance when he lifted his own eyes suddenly, and it seemed to him that his father had come to realize his existence. His heart softened; he was pathetically quick to respond to signs of affection. It seemed to him that each day brought with it the possibility of some new, extraordinary happening. Several times he was on the point of putting his arm about his father's shoulders as he sat with his paper. Without being conscious of it, John Hartman showed outwardly the signs of the inward struggle. Never had his yearning, repressed love for the boy so tortured him, never had it demanded so insistently an outward expression. But he repressed himself a little longer. When he should have made all right with William Koehler, then would he yield to the impulses of fatherhood. That bound poor Hartman had set himself.

Katy remembered all her life, even if Alvin Koehler did not, the day on which Alvin set to work with diligence. He often looked at her curiously, as if he could not understand her. But Alvin gave earnest thought only to himself, to his hopeless situation with a half-mad and dishonest father and the dismal prospect of working in the furnace. His father seemed to be becoming more wild. There were times when Alvin feared violence at his hands. He talked to himself all day long, making frequent mention of John Hartman. Sometimes Alvin thought vaguely of warning the squire or John Hartman himself about his father. He believed less and less his father's crazy story.

Sometimes Alvin stared at Katy and blinked like an owl in his effort to account for her alternate shyness and kindness. Alvin was not accustomed to being treated kindly.

"And what will you do when you are educated?" he inquired.

"What will I do?" repeated Katy, her heart thumping as it always did when Alvin spoke to her. "I will teach and I will earn a great deal of money and travel over the whole world and buy me souvenirs. And I will sing."

It was very pleasant to tell Alvin of her prospects. Perhaps he would walk home with her from church on Sunday. Then how Essie Hill, in spite of all her outward piety, would hate her! The secret of mild Essie's soul was not a secret from Katy.

"Will you teach in a school like Millerstown?" asked Alvin.

"Millerstown! Never! It would have to be a bigger school than Millerstown."

Alvin looked up at Mr. Carpenter. It was recess and Mr. Carpenter was hearing a spelling class which had not learned its lesson for the morning recitation. Mr. Carpenter did not appear at his best, judged by the usually accepted standards of etiquette; he leaned back lazily in his chair, his feet propped on his desk, his hands clasped above his head; but to Alvin there was nothing inelegant in his attitude. Mr. Carpenter was an enviable person; he never needed to soil his hands or to have a grimy face or to carry a dinner pail.

"Teaching would be nice work," said Alvin drearily. "But I can never learn this Latin. I am all the time getting farther behind. It gets every day worse and worse."

"Oh, but you can learn it!" cried Katy, her face aglow. If he would only, only, let her help! "I will show you. Here are my sentences for to-day. The doctor went over them and he says they are all right." And blushing, with her heart pounding more than ever, Katy returned to her seat.

There was a difficult sentence in that day's lesson, a sentence over which David Hartman had puzzled and on which he failed. Then the teacher called on Alvin, simply as a matter of form. The school had begun to giggle a little when they heard his name. But now up he rose, the dull, the stupid, the ordinary, and read the sentence perfectly! At him David Hartman stared with scarlet face. He expected that the teacher would rise and annihilate Alvin, but the teacher passed to the next sentence. Mr. Carpenter was at the present time angry at David; he was rather glad he was discomfited. Such was the nature of Mr. Carpenter!

To Alvin David said nothing, but upon the shoulder of Katy Gaumer, putting on her cloak in the cupboard after school, David laid a heavy hand.

"You helped Alvin!" David's hand quivered with astonishment and anger and from the touch of Katy's shoulder. "It is cheating. Some day I am going to catch you at it before the whole school."

Before she could answer, if she could have made answer at all, David was gone. She hated him; she would help Alvin all she liked until he had caught up, and afterwards, too, if she pleased. Alvin had had no chance, and David had everything, a rich father, fine clothes and money. It was perfectly fair for her to help Alvin. She hated all the Hartmans. She was furiously angry and it hurt to be angry. It did not occur to her to be ashamed of Alvin who would accept a girl's translation. With a whirl and a flirting of her skirts, Katy sailed through the door and down the pike.

"You will sit in Millerstown!" she declared to the empty air. "But I am going away! Nothing ever happens in Millerstown. Millerstown is nothing worth!" Then Katy stood still, dizzy with all the glorious prospect of life. "I am going away! I am going away!"

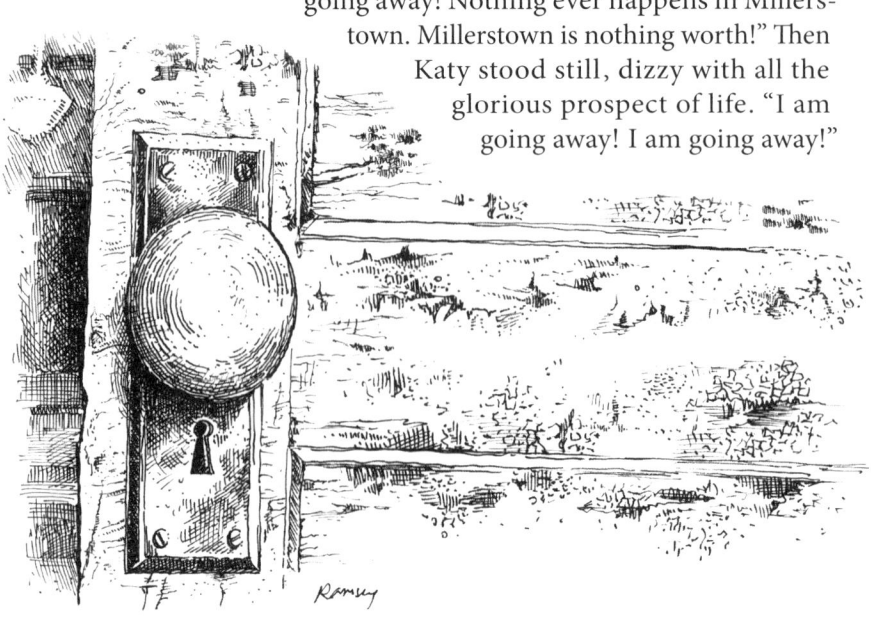

CHAPTER VII
THE BEE CURE

January and March and April passed, and still Mr. Carpenter and his pupils studied diligently. David Hartman did not carry out his threat to expose Katy; such a course would have been impossible. Day after day it seemed more certain that his father was about to say to him some extraordinary thing. He saw his father helping himself out of his buggy with a hand on the dashboard; he saw that hand tremble. But his father still said nothing. That May day when John Hartman would at last begin to right the wrong he had done had not yet arrived.

In spite of all Katy's efforts she could not pass above David in school. Alvin Koehler needed less and less help now that he was convinced that through learning lay the way to ease and comfort, to the luxurious possession of several suits of clothes, to a seat upon a platform. Mr. Carpenter would never have to do hard work; Alvin determined to model his life after that of his teacher. He scarcely spoke to his father now, and he grew more and more afraid of him.

In May the Millerstown school broke its fine record for diligence and steady attendance. The trees were in leaf, the air was sweet, the sky was dimmed by a soft haze, as though the creating earth smoked visibly. Locust blooms filled the air with their wine-like perfume, flowers starred the meadows. Grandmother Gaumer's garden inside the stone wall was so thickly set with hyacinths and tulips and narcissus that one wondered where summer flowers would find a place. Daily Katy gathered armfuls of purple flags and long sprays of flowering currant and stiff branches of japonica and bestowed them upon all who asked. Katy learned her lessons in the garden and planned for the future in the garden and thought of Alvin in the garden.

One day, unrest came suddenly upon the Millerstown boys; imprisonment within four walls was intolerable. Even Katy, yearning for an education, was affected by the warmth of the first real summer day, and Alvin Koehler wished for once that he had learned to swim, so that he could go with the other boys to bathe in Weygandt's dam. Alvin had not yet bought the red necktie; money was more scarce than ever this spring. Alvin's whole soul demanded clothes. He reflected upon the impression he had made upon Katy Gamer; he observed the blush which reddened the smooth cheek of Essie Hill at his approach; he was increasingly certain that his was an unusual and attractive personality.

All through the long May afternoon, Katy studied with great effort, wishing that she, too, had played truant, and had climbed to the Sheep

Stable as she had long planned, there to discover the full volume of her voice. She looked across at Alvin, but Alvin did not look back.

All the long afternoon Alvin gazed idly at his algebra, and all the long afternoon David Hartman and Jimmie Weygandt and Ollie Kuhns and the two Fackenthals and Billy Knerr and Coonie Schnable braved the wrath of Mr. Carpenter and played truant. First they traveled to the top of the mountain, then raced each other down over rock and fallen tree; and then, hot and tired, plunged into Weygandt's dam, which was fed by a cold stream from the mountain. When the water grew unendurable, they came out to the bank, rubbed themselves to a glow with their shirts, and hanging the shirts on bushes to dry, plunged back with shouts and splashing.

Mr. Carpenter did not greatly regret their absence. Upon him, too, spring fever had descended; he was too lazy to hear thoroughly the lessons of the pupils who remained. When the lowest class droned its "ten times ten iss a hundred," Mr. Carpenter was nodding; when they sang out in drowsy mischief, "'laven times 'laven iss a hundred and 'laven," Mr. Carpenter was asleep.

Mr. Carpenter planned no immediate punishment for his insubordinate pupils. The threat that he would tell their parents would be a powerful and valuable weapon in his hands for the rest of the term. The Millerstown parents had fixed theories about the heinousness of truancy.

But though Mr. Carpenter planned no punishment, punishment was meted out.

The stroke of the gods was curiously manifested. The next morning the disobedient seven ate their breakfasts in their several homes, in apparently normal health, unless a sudden frown or twist of lip or an outburst of bad temper might be said to constitute symptoms of disorder. One or two clung closely to the kitchen stove, though the day was even warmer than yesterday, and David Hartman visited surreptitiously the cupboard in which his mother kept the cough medicine with which he was occasionally dosed. With a wry face he took a long swallow from the bottle. Ollie Kuhns hung round his neck the little bag filled with asafœdita, which had been used in similar manner for the baby's whooping-cough, and Jimmie Weygandt applied to himself the contents of a flask from the barn window, labeled "Dr. Whitcraft's Embrocation, Good for Man and Beast."

All left their homes and walked down the street with the stiff uprightness of carriage which had prevented their families from realizing how grievously they were afflicted. But one and all, they forgot their household chores. Billy Knerr's mother commanded him loudly to return and to fill the coal bucket, but Billy walked on as calmly as though he were deaf, and turned the corner into the alley with a thankful sigh.

There his erectness vanished. He stood and rubbed his knee with a mournful "By Hedes!" an exclamation of unknown origin and supposed profanity much affected by him and his friends, and henceforth walked with a limp. A little ahead was Ollie Kuhns, who, when shouted at, turned round bodily and stood waiting as stiff and straight as a wooden soldier. It was difficult to believe that this was the supple "Bosco, the Wild Man, Eats 'em Alive," who rattled his chains and raised his voice in terrifying howls in the schoolhouse cellar.

"Where have *you* got it?" demanded Billy.

"In my neck. I cannot move my head an inch."

"I have it in my knee. Indeed, I thought I would never get out of bed. My mom is hollering after me yet to fetch coal, but I could not fetch coal if they would chop off my head for it."

"Do you suppose any one else has it like this?"

Billy did not need to answer. The alley through which they walked led out to the pike, where moved before them a strange procession. The vanquished after a battle could have worn no more agonized aspect, could not have been much more strangely contorted.

"Both my arms are stiff," wailed Coonie Schnable. "It is one side as bad as the other."

"I can't bend over," announced the older Fackenthal, woefully. "I gave my little sister a penny to tie my shoes and not say anything."

"Did any of you tell your folks?" demanded Ollie. "Because if you did we will all get thrashed."

A spirited "No!" answered the insulting question.

"I got one licking from my pop last week," mourned Billy Knerr. "That will last, anyhow a while." The pain in Billy's knee was so sharp that sometimes, in spite of all his efforts, tears rolled down his cheeks. "You'll never catch me in that dam again, so you know it!"

"It was n't the dam," said David Hartman, irritably. David could not indicate a spot on his body which did not ache. "We were too hot and we stayed too long. Ach! Ouch! I'll —" The other pupils of the Millerstown school had crowded about the sufferers and had jostled against them and David turned stiffly upon them with murder in his heart. But it was impossible to pursue even the nearest offender, Alvin Koehler. Instead David cried babyishly, "Just you wait once till I catch you!"

Not for the world would unsuspecting Alvin have jostled him intentionally. He knew better than to offer to any schoolmate a gage to physical conflict. They were too strong and there were too many of them. He saw the jostled David speak to Billy Knerr; he saw Billy Knerr approach him and he turned, ready for flight.

Then Alvin's eyes opened, his cheeks flushed. Billy called to him in a tone which was almost beseeching. "Wait, once, Alvin! Do you want to make some money, Alvin?"

At once the red tie, still coveted and sighed for, danced before Alvin's longing eyes. Money! He would do anything to make money! He stood still and let Billy approach, not quite daring to trust him.

"What money?" he asked, hopefully, yet suspiciously.

"Come over here once," said Billy.

With great hope and at the same time with deadly fear, Alvin ventured toward the afflicted crew.

"We have the rheumatism," explained Billy.

"Where?" asked Alvin stupidly.

"Where!" stormed Ollie, with a violence which almost ended the negotiations. "Where! In our legs and our backs and our arms and our eyelids." Ollie was not one to wait with patience. "We will give you a penny each for a bee in a bottle. Will you sell us a bee in a bottle, or won't you?"

Alvin's eyes glittered; fright gave place to joy. There has always been a tradition in Millerstown that the sting of a bee will cure rheumatism. The theory has nothing to do with witchcraft or pow-wowing; it seems more like the brilliant invention of a practical joker. Perhaps improvement was coincident with the original experiment, or perhaps the powerful counter-irritant makes the sufferer forget the lesser woe. Bee stings are not popular, it must be confessed; they are used as a last resort, like the saline infusion, or like a powerful injection of strychnia for a failing heart.

Strangers had often come to be stung by William Koehler's bees, but Alvin had never heard that any of them were cured. Alvin himself had tried the remedy once for a bruise with no good result. One patient had used violent language and had demanded the return of the nickel which he had given William, and William was weak enough to pass it over. But now the red tie fluttered more and more enticingly before Alvin's eyes. If he could earn seven cents by putting seven of his father's bees in bottles, well and good. It made no difference if the patients were deceived about the salutary effects of bee stings.

Then into the quickened mind of Alvin flashed a brilliant plan.

"I will do it for three cents apiece," he announced with craft. "I cannot bann [charm] them so good as pop. They will perhaps sting me."

Alvin's daring *coup* was successful.

"Well, three cents, then. But you must get them here by recess." Ollie Kuhns groaned. He was not used to pain, and it seemed to him that his agony was spreading to fresh fields. "Clear out or the teacher will get you and he won't let you go. He's coming!"

With a great spring, Alvin dropped down on the other side of the stone fence, and lay still until the teacher had shepherded his flock into the schoolroom. By this time not only the red tie, but a whole new suit dazzled the eyes of Alvin. Old man Fackenthal bottled his cough cure and sold it all about the county. Why should not bees be bottled and labeled and sold? If their sting was supposed to be so valuable a cure, they would be a desired commodity. Alvin had told a lie when he had said he could not "bann" bees as well as his father, for he had over them the same hypnotic influence. He saw himself spending the rest of his life raising them and catching them and bottling them and selling them. There would have to be air holes through the corks of the bottles so that they could breathe, and a few drops of honey within to nourish them, but with these provisions they could be shipped far and wide.

"They would be powerful mad when they were let out," said Alvin to himself, as he lay in the lee of the schoolhouse fence. "The people would get their money's worth."

Alvin saw suddenly all the old people in the world stiff and sore and all the young people afflicted like Ollie and his friends. He did not wish for any of them such a fate. He had various weaknesses, but a vindictive spirit was not one of them. He saw only the possibilities of a great business. Hearing the schoolhouse bell, and knowing that all were safely within doors, he started across the fields and up the mountain-side.

The bargain was consummated in the woodshed, a little frame building leaning against the blank wall of the schoolhouse. Alvin, hurrying back from his house, scrambling over fences, weary from his long run, thought that he was too early with the wares in the basket on his arm. Or could it be, alas! that he was late and recess was over? That would be too cruel! With relief he heard the sound of voices in the woodshed where his patients awaited him.

The truants had endured an hour and a half of torture. They anticipated punishment for yesterday's misdemeanor, and they had a deadly fear that that punishment would be physical. Anxiously now from the woodshed, where they could lie at their ease, they listened for Alvin.

"Perhaps he won't come back," suggested Billy Knerr. "Perhaps he cannot catch the bees."

Recess was all over but five minutes, and the disheartened sufferers were expecting the bell, when Alvin appeared. David Hartman had collected the money against such necessity for haste, and, indeed, had advanced most of it from his well-lined pocket. Only in such dire trouble would he have treated with Alvin Koehler; only in this agony would he have bought from any one such a pig in a poke. If he had been himself, he would have made Alvin open the basket and would have examined the contents to be sure that Alvin was playing fair. But now, with only two minutes to cure himself and his friends of their agony, there was no time for the ordinary inspection of the articles of trade.

The commodities exchanged hands; twenty-one pennies into Alvin's outstretched palm, the basket into David's. It took David not much more than one of his hundred and twenty seconds to open the basket lid, even though it fitted closely and needed prying. A low, angry murmur, which the boys had not heard in their pain, changed at once to a loud buzz, and suddenly the hearts of the most suffering failed them. But the basket lid was off, and with it came the lid of a fruit jar which stood within. The bees were not in separate bottles — Alvin maintained stoutly that separate bottles had not been stipulated — so that one sting could be applied at a time, like a drop of medicine from a pippette; they were, or, rather, they had been, in a broad-mouthed jar, whose lid, as I have said, came off with the basket lid.

Moreover, at this instant the door of the woodshed, impelled by a gentle May breeze, blew shut and the latch dropped on the outside. There were seven boys penned into the woodshed and there were at least a hundred bees. Alvin had been in too much of a hurry to count the precious things he sold. He had held the jar before the outlet of the hive and the bees had rushed into it. Granted that honey bees sting but once, and granted that thirty of these bees did not sting at all, there were still ten for each patient.

Wildly the frantic prisoners batted the bees about with their bare hands. There were no hats, there was nothing in the empty woodshed which could be used as a weapon. Piteously they yelled, from great David Hartman to the eldest of the Fackenthals.

The uproar reached the ears of Alvin, who was just entering the schoolhouse door and Alvin fled incontinently to the gate and down the road. It penetrated to the schoolroom and brought Mr. Carpenter rushing angrily out. He had rung the school bell; his pupils did not respond; he thought now that their yells were yells of defiance. Emboldened by yesterday's success they had arranged some new anarchy. Whatever may have been the faults of Mr. Carpenter, he was physically equal to such a situation, short and slender though he was. He tore open the woodshed door; he caught Ollie Kuhns and shook him before any one could explain. Then as he reached for the collar of David Hartman, one of the bees, which had not already committed suicide by stinging, lit on his hand. The pain did

VII. The Bee Cure

little to pacify the teacher. The boys, seized one after the other, had no shame strong enough to keep them from crying. Herded into the schoolroom, David at the tail end with the teacher's grasp on his ear, they forgot their rheumatism, they forgot the girls, they forgot even Alvin himself, who was by this time flying down the road. They laid their heads upon their desks, and Mr. Carpenter, dancing about, demanded first of one, then of the other, an explanation of this madness. Mr. Carpenter forgot his objections to Pennsylvania German; in this moment of deep anguish he was compelled to have recourse to his native tongue.

"What do you mean?" roared Mr. Carpenter. "What is this fuss? Are you crazy? You will catch it! Be quiet! Go to your seats! It will give an investigation of this! Ruhig!!"

In reality Mr. Carpenter himself was producing most of the confusion. The grief of those at whom he stormed was silent; they still sat with heads bent upon their desks. At them their schoolmates gaped, for them the tender-hearted wept.

As Alvin flew down the pike he began to be frightened. He was not repentant, not with twenty-one coppers in his pocket! He had a nickel already and now the beautiful tie was his. He could not go at once to purchase it for fear that the smitten army behind him might rally and pursue, nor did he wish to hide his money about the house for fear that his father might find it. He decided that he would get himself some dinner and then go walking upon the mountain. It would be well to be away from home until the time for his father's return. To his house the lame legs of his schoolmates might follow him, there their lame arms seize him, but to the Sheep Stable they could not climb. He did not realize that, as he crossed the fields above his father's house, he was for a moment plainly exposed to the view of the Millerstown school.

Tired, certain that he was out of reach of the enemy, Alvin lay down on the great rock which formed the back of the little cave. His heart throbbed; he was not accustomed to such strenuous exertion of body or to such rapid and determined operations of mind. He was even a little frightened by his own bravery and acuteness. He thought for a long time of himself and for a little time of Katy Gaumer and Essie Hill; then, deliciously comfortable in the spring sunshine, he fell asleep.

For three hours Alvin lay still on the great rock. Occasionally a chestnut blossom drifted down on his cheek, and was brushed drowsily away; occasionally the chatter of a squirrel, impatient of this human intrusion, made him open his eyes heavily. But each time he dropped into deeper sleep. The rock was hard, but Alvin was young and, besides, was not accustomed to a soft bed.

At the end of three hours he woke suddenly. It seemed to him that a dark cloud had covered the sun or that night had fallen. But a worse danger than storm or darkness was at hand.

Above him, almost touching his own, bent an angry face.

"Get up!" commanded a stern voice, and Alvin slid off the rock and stood up."

"Now, fight," David ordered. "I was stiff but I am not so much stiff any more. But the stiffness you may have for advantage. One, two, three!"

Even with the handicap of stiffness, the advantage was upon the side of David. He was strong; he was furiously and righteously angry; he had been shamed in the eyes of Millerstown. Katy Gaumer had seen his ignominy; she had whispered about him to Sarah Knerr. Alvin was a coward; he had long been cheating; he had accepted the help of a girl. Besides, Katy Gaumer was kind to him. For that crime his punishment had long been gathering.

Automatically Alvin raised his fist. Below them was the steep, rock-piled hillside; back of them was the rock wall of the Sheep Stable; and there was no help nearer than Millerstown, far below in its girdle of tender green. Even through the still air Alvin's cries could not be heard in the valley. He cried out when David struck him; he begged for mercy when David laid him on his back on the stony ground. He thought that there was now no hope for him; he was certain that his last hour had come. He expected that David would hurl him down over the edge of the precipice to the sharp rocks far below. He closed his eyes and moaned.

David had already determined to let his victim go. He was suddenly deeply interested in certain sensations within himself; he was distracted from his intention of administering to Alvin all the punishment he deserved. He felt a strange, uplifted sensation, a consciousness of strength; he was excited, thrilled. Never before in his life had he acted so swiftly, so entirely upon impulse. The yielding body beneath him, Alvin's fright, made him seem powerful to himself. The world was suddenly a different place; he wanted now to be alone and to think.

But David had no time to think. As unexpectedly as though sent from heaven itself arrived the avenger. Katy Gaumer had found time dull and heavy on her hands. Alvin had vanished; there would be the same lessons for the next day since one third of the class was absent and one third incapacitated. Katy was amused at the tears of David and his friends. A bee sting was nothing, nor yet a little stiffness! Katy had been once stung by a hornet and she had had a sprained ankle. Katy's heart was light; she had had recently new compliments from the doctor about her voice, and she had determined that this afternoon she would ascend to the Sheep

VII. The Bee Cure

Stable and startle the wide valley with song.

Katy was not lame or afflicted; she climbed gayly the mountain road. Nor was Katy afraid. She would not have believed that any evil could befall one so manifestly singled out by Providence for good fortune. She sang as she went; therefore she did not hear the wails of Alvin. Alvin cried loudly as he lay upon the ground; therefore he did not hear the song of Katy.

But Alvin felt suddenly the weight shoved from his body; he saw the conqueror taken unawares, thrust in his turn upon the ground; and he had wit and strength enough to scramble to his feet when the incubus was removed.

"Shame on you!" cried the figure in the red dress to the figure prone upon the ground. "Shame on you! You big, ugly boy, lie there!" Katy almost wept in her wrath. It was unfortunate for Katy that she should have been called upon to behold one toward whom her heart was already unwisely inclined thus in need of pity and help.

To Alvin's amazement the conqueror, a moment ago mighty in his rage, obeyed. The arrival of Katy, sudden as it was to him, was even more sudden to David. David was overwhelmed, outraged. He had not wit to move; he heard Katy's taunts, saw her stamp her foot; he heard her command Alvin to come with her, saw her for an instant even take Alvin by the hand, and saw Alvin follow her. His eyes were blinded; he rubbed them cruelly, then he turned over on his face and dug his hands into the ground. From poor David's hot throat there came again that childish wail. Conquered thus, David was also spiritless; he began to cry, "I want her! I want her! I want her!"

Aching, motionless, he lay upon the ground. With twitching tail the squirrel watched from his bough, chattering again his disgust at this queer human use of his abiding-place. The air grew cool, the blazing sun sank lower, and David lay still.

Meanwhile, down the mountain road together went Katy Gaumer and Alvin Koehler.

"He came on me that quick," gasped Alvin. He had brushed the clinging twigs from his clothes and had smoothed his hair. His curls lay damp upon his forehead, and his cheeks were scarlet, his chin uplifted.

Katy breathed hard.

"Well, I came on him quick, too!"

Alvin began to gasp nervously. Self-pity overwhelmed him.

"I have nothing in this world," mourned he. "This summer I will have to work at the furnace. I will have a hard life."

"But I thought you were going to have an education!" cried Katy.

"I cannot," mourned Alvin. "It is no use to try. I am alone in the world."

Katy turned upon him a glowing face.

"That is nonsense, Alvin! Everybody can have an education. There are schools where you can study and work, too. It is so at the normal school where they learn you to teach. I thought you were going to be a teacher, Alvin!"

"I was," said Alvin. "I would like to be a teacher."

"I will find out about those schools," promised Katy, forever eager to help, to plan. "I am going away; nothing would keep me in Millerstown. You must surely go, Alvin!"

"David Hartman can have everything," wailed Alvin, his aching bones making themselves felt. "He had no business to come after me. He has a rich pop. He — "

"He has a horrible pop," answered Katy. "He chased me once when I was little, and I never did him anything. Why, Alvin!" Katy stopped in the dusty road. "There is David's pop in his buggy at your gate!"

Alvin grew deathly pale, he remembered his father's madness, his threats, the crime which he had committed and which he blamed upon John Hartman.

"What is it?" cried Katy. "What ails you, Alvin? He would not dare to touch me now that I am big. Come!"

"No!" Alvin would not move. "Look once at him, Katy! Something is the matter with him!"

"I am not afraid," insisted Katy bravely. "I am — he is sick, Alvin; he is sitting quiet in his buggy." She went close to the wheel. "Mr. Hartman!" She turned and looked at Alvin, then back at the figure in the buggy. "His head hangs down, Alvin, and he will not answer me. I believe he is dead, Alvin!"

Slowly Alvin moved to Katy's side. He laid a hand upon her arm — Katy thought it was to protect her; in reality Alvin sought support in his deadly fear.

"I believe it, too, Katy!"

Speechlessly the two gazed at each other. When Alvin had shouted wildly for his father and Katy had joined her voice to his and there was no answer, the two set off, hand in hand, running recklessly down the mountain road.

CHAPTER VIII
WILLIAM KOEHLER MAKES HIS ACCUSATION FOR THE LAST TIME

Dusk was falling when David started down the mountain road. He did not walk rapidly; sometimes, in his weakness, he stumbled. Bad as his aches had been when he climbed the mountain hours before, they were worse now, and added to them was smart of soul. Every spot on his body upon which Katy had laid her hand burned; she was continually before his eyes in her kaleidoscopic motions, now running down the pike from school, now storming at him as he lay on the ground. He tried to hate her, but he could not. As he stumbled along, his feet kept time to a foolish wail, "I want her! I want her!" The glow of triumph had faded entirely; David was more morose, more sullen, more unhappy than ever. His anger with Alvin had changed to a sly intention to scheme against him until he could give him a greater punishment than a mere beating. He was not done with Alvin! His own father was a rich and powerful man; Alvin's father was a poor, half-witted thief. He thought for the first time with satisfaction of his father's wealth.

The young moon overhead, the scent of spring in the air, the gentle breeze against his cheek, all deepened his misery and loneliness. He said to himself that he had no one in the world. In spite of his vague conclusions about his father, his father was still the same. There are persons whose success depends wholly upon their relations with the human beings nearest to them. Given affection, they expand; denied it, their souls contract, their powers fail. It is a weakness of the human creature, but it is none the less real. Resentment was rapidly becoming a settled attitude of David's mind; his father was postponing dangerously that opening of his heart to his son of which he thought day and night.

David wished now that he need not go home; he wished — poor little David! — that he was dead. He would have his supper and he would go to bed, and to-morrow there would be another bitter day. He would sit in school and be conscious of Katy and Alvin and their knowing glances, and love and hate would tear him asunder once more.

Then David stood still and looked down upon his house. Even though the trees about it were thickly leafed, he could see lights in unaccustomed places. The parlor was lighted; in that room David could not remember an illumination in his lifetime. There were lights also in bedrooms — David forgot his aches of body and soul in his astonishment. He slept over the kitchen in one of the little rooms his father had provided for the day when servants should attend upon the wants of his children; except for his father's and mother's room the front of the house was never opened. Had some great stranger come to visit — but that was unthinkable! Was some one ill — but that would be no reason for the opening of the house! David did not know what to make of the strange sight. He hurried down the road, almost falling as he ran.

Then David stood still, looking stupidly at a dark wagon which stood before the gate. He knew the ownership and the purpose of that vehicle, but he could not connect it with his house. There dwelt only his father and his mother and himself, and all of them were alive and well.

A group of children lingered near by, silent, staring at the dark wagon and the brightly lighted windows. The Hartman house with its illumination was as strange a phenomenon as the Millerstown children had ever seen. To them David, still standing at his gate, put a question.

"What is the matter?"

Instantly a small, excited, feminine voice piped out an answer.

"Your father is dead."

"He was sitting in his buggy in the mountain road," another excited voice went on. "They brought him down here and carried him in."

David went into the yard and along the flag walk, and for the first time in his life entered his father's house by the wide-open front door, through which various Millerstonians were passing in and out. This was a great opportunity for Millerstown. Some one came out of the parlor, leaving the door ajar, and David saw a long dark figure lying on a low couch in the middle of the room. What there was to be known about his father's death he gathered from the conversation of those about him. He heard pitying exclamations, he felt that in a moment he would burst into cries of shock and terror. Bitterness fled, he was soft-hearted, weak, childlike. His father was gone, but there remained another person. He must find her; in her lay his refuge; she must be his stay, as he must henceforth be hers. Stumbling back through the hall toward the kitchen, he sought his mother. He was aware of the kind looks of those about him; his whole being was softened.

"Mother!" he meant to cry. "Oh, mother! mother!"

He felt her grief; he expected to find her prostrate on the old settle, or sitting by the table with her head on her arm, weeping. He would comfort her; he would be a good son to her; he truly loved her.

From the kitchen doorway he heard her voice, clear and toneless, the voice of every day. She was giving orders to the Millerstown women who had hastened

VIII. William Koehler Makes His Accusation For The Last Time

in with offers of help, — to Grandmother Gaumer and Sarah Knerr and Susannah Kuhns. She indicated certain jars of canned fruit which were to be used for the funeral dinner, and planned for the setting of raised cake and the baking of "fine cake." In Cassie's plan for her life, she had prepared for this contingency; even now her iron will was not broken, nor her stern composure lost. She moved about as David had always seen her move, quiet, capable, self-centered. She shed no tear; she seemed to David to take actual pleasure in planning and contriving.

The frantic cry, already on David's lips, died silently away, his throat stiffened, he drew a long breath. For an instant he stood still in the doorway; then, with a bent and sullen head, he turned and crept back through the hall to the front stairs, which had scarcely ever been touched by his foot, and thence to his tiny room, where he knelt down by his narrow bed. How terrible was the strange figure under the black covering, with the blazing lights beating upon it, and the staring villagers stealing in to look! It seemed incredible that his father could lie still and suffer their scrutiny. He wished that he might go down and turn them out. But he did not dare to trust his voice, and besides, his mother accepted it all as though it were proper and right. Then David forgot the intruders, forgot his mother. His father was dead, of whom he had often thought unkindly, and his father was all he had in the world. He would never be able to speak to him again, never be able to lay a hand upon his shoulder as he sat reading his paper, never meet again that sudden glance of incomprehensible distress. Death worked its alchemy; now at last the poor father had his way with his son's heart.

"He was my father!" cried David. "I have no father!"

His breath choked, his heart seemed to smother him; he felt himself growing light-headed as he knelt by the low bed. He had had nothing to eat since noon; he had had since that time many things to suffer; he thought suddenly in his exhaustion that perhaps he, too, was about to die.

Presently there was a step in the hall and his heart leaped. Perhaps his mother had come, perhaps she did not wish to show her grief to these curious people. But the person outside knocked at the door and his mother would not have knocked.

"What is it?" asked David.

"It is me," said Bevy. "I brought you a little something to eat."

Bevy waited outside, plate and glass in hand. She had seen David's entrance and exit. Prompted now partly by kindness and sympathy, and partly by an altogether human and natural curiosity to see as much of the house and the bereaved family as she could, Bevy had carried him his supper. But Bevy was not rewarded, as she had hoped.

"Put it down," commanded a voice from within. "Thank you."

Bevy made another effort.

"Do you want anything, David?"

"No, thank you," said the voice again.

"Yes, well," answered Bevy and went down the front steps. If Bevy could have had her wish, her whole body would have been one great eye to take in all this magnificence of thick carpets and fine furniture.

Then, while the mother for whom he hungered made her plans for the great funeral feast, still customary in country sections, where mourners came from a long distance, and while Katy Gaumer recounted to curious Millerstown how she had found John Hartman sitting in his buggy by the roadside, David ate the raised cake and drank the milk which Bevy brought him. Then he sat down by the window and looked out into the dark foliage which on this side touched the house. It had not been John Hartman's plan to have his house grow damp in the shadow of overhanging branches, but John Hartman had long since forgotten his plans for everything.

Sitting here in the darkness, David thought of his father. The puzzle of that strange character he could not solve, but one thing became clear to his mind. He saw again that yearning gaze; he remembered from the dim, almost impenetrable mist which surrounded his childhood, caresses, laughter, the strong grasp of his father's arms. Finally he lay down on the bed and went to sleep, a solemn, comforting conclusion in his heart.

"My father loved me," whispered David. "I am sure my father loved me."

A little later David's mother opened his door softly and entering stood by his bed. She had not seen him in the kitchen; some one had told her that he had come in and had gone to his room. She saw that he was covered and that the night air did not blow upon him, and then she took the empty plate and glass and went back to the kitchen.

Alvin Koehler need not have suspected his father of having had any hand in the death of John Hartman. William Koehler was in the next village, where he had half a day's work. While he worked he plotted and planned and mumbled to himself about his wrongs. It was apoplexy which had killed John Hartman as he drove up the mountain road; Dr. Benner told of his warnings, recalled to the mind of Millerstown the scarlet flush which had for a long time reddened John Hartman's face. If he had taken the path so long avoided by him in order to confess his crime to the man he had wronged and thus begin to make his peace with God, he had set too late upon that journey, for his hour had been

VIII. William Koehler Makes His Accusation For The Last Time

appointed. When William, walking heavily, with his eyes on the ground, came home from Zion Church, John Hartman lay already in the best room of his house, his earthly account closed. When he heard the news of John Hartman's death, William seemed stupefied; it was hard to believe that he understood what was said to him.

It was not necessary that any provision should be made beyond the great dinner for the entertainment of guests at the Hartman house. Nevertheless, the house was cleaned and put in order from top to bottom for its master's burying. Fluted pillow and sheet shams and lace-trimmed pillow cases were brought forth, great feather beds were beaten into smoothness, elaborate quilts were unfolded from protective wrappings and were aired and refolded and laid at the foot of beds covered with thick white counterpanes. There was dusting and sweeping and scrubbing, and, above all, a vast amount of cooking and baking. The funeral was to be held in the morning, and afterwards there would be food at the Hartman house for all those who wished to partake.

Cassie was fitted with a black dress, various bonnets were sent out from the county seat for her to try, and over each was draped the long black veil of widowhood, — this, to Cassie, in the opinion of Millerstown, a crown of independence. Millerstown could form no judgment of Cassie's feelings. If she had, like William Koehler, any moment of stupefaction, or, like David, any wild outburst of grief, that fact was kept from a curious world.

David also was fitted with a suit of black, and together he and his mother rode in a closed carriage, sent from the county seat, down through pleasant Millerstown in the May sunshine and out to the church on the hill.

The service was long, as befitted the dignity of a man of prominence like John Hartman who had always given liberally to charitable objects, though he had become of late years an infrequent attendant at church meetings. The preacher who had heard the accusation of William Koehler was long since gone; the present pastor who lauded the Christian life of the dead man knew nothing of any charge against him. He would scarcely have known William by sight, so entirely had William separated himself from the life of the village. The preacher had a deep, moving voice, he spoke with feeling of the death of the righteous, and of the crown laid up for them in heaven. Many of the congregation wept, some in recollection of their own dead, some in sad anticipation of that which must some day befall themselves, and some in grief for John Hartman. Two men, sitting in opposite corners of the gallery, bowed their heads on the backs of the benches before them so that their tears might drop unseen. Oliver Kuhns, the elder, stayed at home from the funeral and at home from his work, and watched from the window the procession entering the church, and wept also. John Hartman was not without mourners who called him blessed!

David and his mother sat in the front pew, near the body, which had been placed before the pulpit. Upon David had settled a heavy weight of horror. He had not yet accustomed himself to the fact of his father's death. Only a few days before he had seen his father moving about, had sought to read the enigmatic expression in his eyes. But here his father lay, dead. Living he would never have suffered these stares, this weeping. Upon David, also, rested the interested, inquisitive eyes. From the gallery Katy Gaumer looked down upon him; from a seat near her Alvin Koehler stared about. The smothering desire to cry rushed over David once more; he slipped his hand inside his stiff collar as though to choke off the rising sob. Beside him rose the black pillar of his mother's crape; on the other side was the closed door of the old-fashioned pew. He was imprisoned; for him there was no escape. The service would never end; here he would be compelled to sit, forever and ever.

Then, suddenly, to the startled eyes of David and of Millerstown, there rose in the right-hand gallery the short, bent figure of a man. The preacher did not see; Millerstown sat paralyzed. They had never been really afraid of William Koehler, queer as he was, but now there was madness in his face. His eyes blazed, his cheeks were pale, he had scarcely touched food since he had heard of the death of his enemy. He had not gone to work; he had sat in his little house talking to himself, and praying that he might, after all, have some sort of revenge upon the man who had wronged him. Several weeks ago he had consulted a new detective, who, in the hope of getting a fee, or wishing to have an excuse for getting rid of him, had given him fresh encouragement. The sudden ending of his hopes was all the more cruel.

"I have something to say," he announced now in his shrill voice. "This man lying here is not a good man. I have this to say about him. He — he —"

Then poor William paused. Already, to his terror, in spite of his practicing, the words were slipping away from him. He had planned to tell the story carefully, impressing each detail upon the large congregation which would gather at the funeral. They *must* listen to him. It would be useless to cry out suddenly the whole truth, that John Hartman was a thief — he had tried that once, and had been silenced by the preacher.

VIII. William Koehler Makes His Accusation For The Last Time

The detective had said that he must get all his proofs carefully together. He had arranged them in his poor, feeble mind; he meant to speak as convincingly as the preacher himself. His eyes were fixed on the smooth gray wall beside the pulpit cupboard; the sight of it helped to keep his mind clear. There he had been working on the day when the communion set was taken.

He rubbed his damp hands down the sides of his dusty suit, and a flush came into his cheeks. He remembered clearly once more what he had to say.

"I was building up the wall," he said with great precision. "I —"

Stupidly he halted. He began to grow frightened; the unfriendly faces paralyzed his brain; the words he had planned so carefully slipped all at once away from him. He pointed at the still figure lying in the front of the pulpit and burst into vehement, frantic speech.

"He stole the communion set!" he cried shrilly. "He stole it! He —"

Poor William got no further. Many persons rose. The two men in opposite corners of the gallery who had wept started toward him; one of them opened his lips, as though, like crazy William, he was about to address the congregation. The paralyzed spectators came to their senses. Hands were laid upon William. The deacons and elders of the church went toward the gallery steps, Grandfather Gaumer among them. Even Alvin in his mortification and shame had still feeling enough to go to his father's side.

"Come away, pop!" he begged. "Ach, be quiet, pop, and come away!"

"He tells me to be quiet!" cried William in the same shrill tone. "My son tells me to be quiet!"

Grandfather Gaumer laid a firm hand on his shoulder.

"Come with me, William."

But William was not to be got so quietly away. In the front pew young David had risen. Was his father not now to have a decent burying? David's face was aflame; he did not see the madness in the shivering figure and the bright eyes of William Koehler. William belonged with his son Alvin, and both were hateful.

But David had no chance to speak. The preacher foolishly held up a forbidding hand to poor William.

"You cannot say such a thing at this time and not confess that it is not true. The accused cannot answer for himself."

Poor William rubbed his hands over his eyes. He still had great respect for the authority of preachers. Besides, he saw John Hartman suddenly as a dead man, and since his trouble he had always been afraid of death. No revenge could be visited upon this deaf, impassible object, that was sure!

"Ach, I forget my mind!" wailed poor William. "I forget my mind!"

Then William could have been led unresisting away. But the preacher, stupidly insistent, held up his hand again.

"Do you confess that your accusation is not true?" said he.

William placed a hand on either side of his forehead. It seemed as though his head were bursting and he must hold it close together. There was now a murmur of speech in the congregation. This terrible scene had gone on long enough; John Hartman did not need defense from so absurd an accusation. Then the murmur ceased.

"No!" cried William. "It is not true. I took the communion set myself!"

William was now led away, a final seal put upon the pit in which his honesty and sanity lay buried. Another unforgivable offense was added to the sum of unforgivable offenses of the son of William Koehler toward young David. The confession did not help the Millerstown church to recover its beautiful silver. William's insanity, the congregation thought, was the only bar to its recovery.

John Hartman was laid in the grave which had been walled up by the mason who had taken William Koehler's place in Millerstown, and which had been lined with evergreens and life everlasting according to Millersown's tender custom. Over him prayers were said and another hymn was sung, "Aus tiefer Noth shrei ich zu dir" (Out of the depths I cry to thee), familiar to generations of Millerstown's afflicted. Then the procession returned to John Hartman's great house, whispering excitedly.

David sat in his room during the funeral dinner. David was queer; he was not expected to do as other people did. His fury with the Koehlers took his thoughts to some extent away from his grief.

That night Cassie did not sleep in the great, comfortable room at the front of the house which she had shared with her husband, but in a room even smaller than David's at the back. It contained, instead of the great walnut four-poster, with its high-piled feather bed to which she was accustomed, a little painted pine bedstead and a chaff bag; it was on the north corner of the house and was cold in winter and deprived of the breeze by the thick foliage in summer. Her husband's fortune was left to her while she lived; afterwards it was to go to David. Cassie was amply able to manage it, the investments were safe, the farmers had been in her husband's employ many years; it was not likely that anything would disturb the smooth, dull current of Cassie's life.

There was much discussion in Millerstown about whether it was safe for the community to allow William Koehler to be at large; there was some comment upon the cooking at the Hartman funeral dinner; then Millerstown turned its attention to other things. Cassie had behaved just

VIII. William Koehler Makes His Accusation For The Last Time

as she might have been expected to behave. It was surprising, however, that she had let Millerstown go so thoroughly through her house.

The day after the funeral David went back to the Millerstown school. He did not glance in the direction of Katy and Alvin, though he could not help realizing that Katy's skirts did not flirt so gayly past. Katy was sorry for him, though she did not repent her treatment of him. Her dresses had suddenly dropped several inches, her flying curls were twisted up on her head, her eyes were brighter than ever. She was filled with herself and her own concerns and opinions; she grew daily more dictatorial, more lordly.

"I am going away!" said she, upon rising.

"I am going to be educated!" said she at noon.

"I can take education," said she at night. "I thank God I am not dumb."

She and Grandmother Gaumer were increasingly busy with dressmakers' patterns and with "Lists of Articles to be provided by Students." Life was at high tide for Katy Gaumer.

Still David kept at the head of his class. In his mind a slow plan was forming. He would think of Katy no more, of that he was determined, and he would, as a means of accomplishing that end, leave Millerstown. His mother was a rich woman; he could do anything in the world he liked. He would first of all go to college. Afterwards he would study law.

In June he started late one Sunday afternoon to walk to the Sheep Stable. Overwhelmed as he had been upon that spot, he loved it too well to stay away. The heavenly prospect was part of his life's fabric and would continue to be all his days.

As he passed the Koehler house, he heard a strange sound, apparently an unending repetition of the same phrase. It was William Koehler at his prayers — Millerstown knew now for what William prayed!

"God will punish *him!*" said David with a hot, dry throat. "If there is a God" — thus said David in his foolish youth — "if there is a God, he will punish him! Oh, I wish, I wish I could see my father!"

At the Sheep Stable, as one who opens the book of the dim past, David took his pipe and cards from their hiding-place and hurled them far down the mountain-side. He even managed to smile a little sorely at himself.

It was dark when he returned to the village. He did not like to walk about in the early evenings, past the groups of Millerstonians on the doorsteps; they talked about him, and he did not like to be talked about. Now almost all Millerstown had gone to church. The pastor of the Improved New Mennonites was conducting a meeting in a neighboring village, but there was service in all the other churches. A few persons sat on their doorsteps, listening quietly to the music which filled the air, — the sound of the beautiful German hymns of the Lutherans and the Reformed, and the less classic compositions of the New Baptists. Millerstown was like a great common room on summer evenings, with the friendly sky for ceiling.

Again the young moon rode high in the heavens; again David's young blood throbbed in his veins; again the miserable, unmanly desire for the girl who would have nothing to do with him began to devour him. He bit his lips, wondering drearily where he should go and what he should do. The night had just begun; he would not be sleepy for hours. Nothing invited him to the kitchen or to the two little bedrooms to which Cassie had restricted their living. He had no books, and books would have been after all poor companions on such a night as this.

David was not an ill-looking boy; he had indeed the promise of growing handsome as he grew older; he was many times richer than any other young man of Millerstown. There were probably only two girls in the village to whom these pleasant characteristics would make no appeal. The first of these was Katy Gaumer. The second was smooth, pretty, blue-eyed Essie Hill, the daughter of the preacher of the Improved New Mennonites, who sat now demurely on her father's doorstep. Beside her David suddenly sat himself down.

CHAPTER IX
CHANGE

It sometimes happens that death gathers from a single spot a large harvest in a year. We seem to have been forgotten; we learn to draw once more the long, secure breath of youth; we almost believe that sorrow will no more visit us.

For many months Millerstown had had scarcely a funeral. In security Millerstown went about its daily tasks. Then, in May, John Hartman was found dead along the mountain road.

In June there came a letter from the Western home of Great-Uncle Gaumer, telling of a serious illness and the rapid approach of the end of his life. A few days later, when a telegram announced his death, Grandfather Gaumer himself dropped to the floor in the office of his brother the squire and breathed no more. Dr. Benner, who was passing, heard from the street the crash of his fall and the squire's loud outcry, and Bevy rushed in from the kitchen. The doctor and the squire knelt beside him, and still kneeling there, regarded each other with amazement.

Bevy Schnepp lifted her hands above her head and cried out, "Lieber Himmel!" and stood as if rooted to the floor. "Who will tell her?"

The squire rose from his knees, pale and unsteady, and stood looking at his brother as though the sight were incredible.

"Is there no life?" he asked the doctor in a whisper.

The doctor shook his head. "He was gone before he fell."

Bevy began to cry. "Ach, who will tell her?"

"I will tell her," answered the squire. Then he went round the house and across to the other side of the homestead where Grandmother Gaumer and Katy sat at their sewing.

There was a quantity of white material on Grandmother Gaumer's lap, and her fingers moved the needle swiftly in and out. Katy was talking as she hemmed a scarlet ruffle — Katy was always talking. She had been shocked by the news of the governor's illness, but she believed that he would get well. Besides, she had seen the governor only once in her life, and her grandfather had assured her that her plans for her education need not be changed. She could not be long unhappy over anything when all these beautiful new clothes were being made for her and when she was soon to leave dull Millerstown, and when Alvin Koehler had twice sat on the doorstep with her. She had journeyed to the county seat with her grandmother and they had made wonderful purchases.

"And the ladies in the stores are so fine, and so polite, and they show you everything," said Katy. "When Louisa Kuhns went to Allentown she said, 'the people are me so impolite, they go always bumping and bumping and they don't even say *uh!*' That is not true. I do not believe there is anywhere in the world a politer place than Allentown."

"Louisa —" No gap between subjects halted Katy's speech; she leaped it with a bound. "Louisa is very dumb. Now I do not believe myself that a person can learn everything. But you can train your mind so that you can understand everything if it is explained to you. You must keep your mind all the time busy and you must be very humble. Louisa said that poetry was dumb. Louisa cannot even understand, 'Where, oh, where are the visions of morning?' Louisa thinks everything must be real. I said to her I would be ashamed to talk that way. The realer poetry is the harder it is. But Louisa! Ach, *my*! Gran'mom! The teacher said Louisa should write 'pendulum' in a sentence, and Louisa wrote 'Pendulum Franklin is dead'!"

"Do you like poetry, Katy?" asked Grandmother Gaumer.

"Some," answered Katy. "It is not the fault of the poetry that I cannot understand it all. I want to understand everything. I do not mean, gran'mom, that you cannot be good unless you understand everything. But there is more in this world than being good. Sarah Ann is good, but Sarah Ann has a pretty slow time in this world."

"Sarah Ann does many kind things."

"But the squire and gran'pop do more because they are smarter," said Katy triumphantly. "When the people want advice, do they go to Sarah Ann? They come to the squire or to gran'pop!"

Grandmother Gaumer smiled. Sometimes Katy talked in borrowed phrase about a "larger vision" or "preparation for a larger life."

"Millerstown!" said Katy with a long sigh and a shake of the head. "I could not stay forever in Millerstown, gran'mom. Think of the Sunday School picnics with the red mint candy on the cakes and how Susannah and Sarah Knerr try to have the highest layer cakes, and each wants the preacher to eat. Think of the Copenhagen, gran'mom, and the Bingo and the Jumbo, gran'mom!" In derision Katy began to sing, "A certain farmer."

Grandmother Gaumer leaned forward in her chair. A sense of uneasiness overwhelmed her, though Katy had heard nothing. "Listen, Katy!"

There was nothing to be heard; Grandfather Gaumer had fallen; beside him knelt his brother and the doctor; aghast Bevy flung her arms above her head; all were as yet silent.

"It is nothing, gran'mom," said Katy. Katy began her chattering again; she laughed now because Bevy had said that it brought bad luck to use black pins on white material or to sew when the clock struck twelve.

IX. Change

Grandmother Gaumer went on with her stitching. A boy ran down the street; the sound disturbed her.

"I will go and see," offered Katy, putting the scarlet ruffles off her lap. She did not move as swiftly as she would have moved six months ago. Then the sound of rapid steps would have drawn her promptly in their wake. But the affairs of Millerstown had ceased to be of great importance. She did not even hate Millerstown now. "I guess it is just a boy running, gran'mom. I guess —"

The squire had thought that he would go bravely to Grandmother Gaumer and put his arm round her and break to her gently the terrible news. He did not realize that his lips and hands grew each moment more tremulous and his cheeks more ashen. He saw his sister-in-law sitting beside her lovely garden in security and peace, and his heart failed him.

Katy had risen to her feet, and she stood still and regarded him with astonishment. She had forgotten for the instant that he was awaiting news of Governor Gaumer's death. Now she remembered it and was disturbed to the bottom of her soul by the squire's evident grief. Grief was new to Katy.

Grandmother Gaumer laid down her needle and thread. "Ach, the governor is gone, then!" said she. "Did a letter come?"

"Yes," answered the squire. "A message came. He died in the night."

Tears came into Grandmother Gaumer's eyes. "Where is William? I thought he was by you."

The squire sat down in the chair beside Grandmother Gaumer and took her hand. The heap of white stuff slid off her lap to the floor of the porch and lay there unheeded until hours later when Bevy gathered it up, weeping, and laid it away.

"I have bad news for you," said the squire.

"Well," said Grandmother Gaumer, bravely.

"When William heard that Daniel was gone, he dropped to the floor like one shot."

"William!" cried Grandmother Gaumer.

"Yes," answered the squire. "He suffered no pain. The doctor said he knew nothing of it."

"Knew nothing of it!" repeated Grandmother Gaumer. "You mean that he fell *dead?*"

"Yes."

"Where is he?" asked Grandmother Gaumer in a quieter tone.

"In my office. They will bring him home."

"Then we will make a place ready for him. Come, Katy."

Katy followed into the kitchen. Grandmother Gaumer stood looking about her and frowning, as though she were finding it difficult to decide what should be done. Katy thought of John Hartman and of his strange attitude and his staring eyes. Would Grandfather Gaumer look like that? Katy was about to throw herself into the arms which had thus far opened to all her griefs.

"Ach, gran'mom!" she began, weeping.

Then, slowly, Grandmother Gaumer turned her head and looked at Katy. Her eyes were intolerable to Katy.

"What shall I do?" she asked. "I am old. I cannot think. We have lived together fifty years. I cannot remember where my things are. There are things put away in the bureaus all ready for such a time. What shall I do, Katy?"

With a gasp Katy drove back the tears from her smarting eyelids. Katy was confused, bewildered; she still lacked the education with which she expected to meet the problems of life. But Katy, whose forte was managing, did not fail here.

"You will sit here in this chair, gran'mom. I will get a white pillow to put on the settee and they can lay gran'pop there. Then we will find the things for them." She guided her grandmother to the armchair and helped her to sit down. Even the touch of her body seemed different. "It will take only a minute for me to go upstairs. I will be back right away. You know how quickly I can run."

When Katy returned, the feet of the bearers were at the door. With them Millerstown crowded in, weeping. Grandmother Gaumer had wept with them, Grandfather Gaumer had helped them in their troubles. Grandfather was laid in state in the best room and presently the house settled into quiet. In this house five generations had met grief with dignity and death with hope; thus they should be met once more.

Preparations were begun at once for the laying away of the body in the little graveyard of the church which the soul had loved. At the feet of his mother, beside his little sister, a grave was dug for William Gaumer and was lined with boughs of arbor vitæ and sprays of life everlasting.

In the Gaumer house there was little sweeping and cleaning; the beds were not made up for show, but were prepared for the gathering relatives. Grandfather Gaumer did not lie alone in the best room as John Hartman had lain; his children and his grandchildren went in and sat beside him and talked of him.

When the funeral was over and the house was in order and the relatives had gone, Katy sat on her little stool at her grandmother's knee and cried her fill. Grandmother Gaumer had not given way to grief. She had moved about among her kin, she had given directions, she had wept only a little.

To Katy there was not now a ray of brightness in the world.

"Nothing is certain," she mourned. "My gran'pop brought me up. I was always by him, he was my father. I cannot get along without him."

"You will feel certain again of this world, Katy," her grandmother assured her. "You must not mourn for grandfather. He had a long, long life. You would not have him back where he would get lame and helpless after while. That is worse, Katy."

"But there are many things I would like to say to him. I never told him enough how thankful I was to him."

"He knew you were thankful. Now you are to go to school. Everything is to be just as it was planned."

Katy burst into tears once more.

"Ach, I do not think of school!"

Nevertheless, her heart beat a little faster. There was, after all, something right in the world. Moreover, she still had another person to think of. That day Alvin Koehler's dark eyes had looked down upon her as she sat by her grandmother in church. She had promised to help Alvin; his eyes reminded her consciously or unconsciously of her promise.

"Your Uncle Edwin and I talked this over," went on Grandmother Gaumer. "You have two hundred dollars from the governor in the bank in your name and the squire and Uncle Edwin and I will all help. You are to go right on, Katy."

"I was n't thinking about school," persisted Katy. "I was thinking about my grandfather."

Grandmother Gaumer laid a trembling hand on Katy's head.

"He was always good and kind, Katy, you must never forget that. He was first of all good; that is the best thing. He did what he could for everybody, and everybody loved him. You see what Millerstown thought of him. See that Millerstown thinks that well of you! You must never forget him, never. He loved you — he loved you — "

Grandmother Gaumer repeated what she had said in a strange way, then she ceased to speak, and Katy, startled, lifted her head. Then she got to her feet. She had become familiar in these last weeks with the gray pallor of a mortal seizure.

"Gran'mom!" shrieked Katy. "Gran'mom!"

Only the gaze of a pair of bright, troubled eyes answered her. Grandmother's face was twisted, her hands fell heavily into her lap.

Katy threw her arms round her and laid her cheek against the white hair.

"I will be back, dear, dear gran'mom," said Katy. "You know how I can run!"

An instant later, Katy had flung open the door of the squire's office where sat the squire and Dr. Benner. Her grandmother had insisted upon her putting on her red dress after the funeral. She paused now on the sill as she had paused in her birdlike attitude to call to Caleb Stemmel in the store at Christmas time. But this was a different Katy.

"Oh, come!" she cried. "Oh, come, come quickly!"

CHAPTER X
KATY MAKES A PROMISE

Grandmother Gaumer was not dead. When the squire and the doctor reached her side, she sat just as Katy left her, erect, motionless, bright-eyed. They put her to bed and there she lay with the same bright, helpless gaze.

"Can you understand me?" asked the doctor gently.

The expression in the brown eyes changed. The flash of perception was almost invisible, but it was there; to the eyes of Katy who stood by the bed, breathless, terrified, it was as welcome as the cry of a first-born child to its mother.

"She is conscious," the doctor assured them.

Uncle Edwin and Aunt Sally, whom Katy considered so dull, returned presently in tearful haste from their farm at the edge of the town. They sat with grandmother while the doctor gave directions for the night to Katy in the kitchen.

Katy looked at the doctor wildly. The lamp cast dark shadows into the corners of the room; it surrounded Katy with a glare of light. Her hands clasped and unclasped, tears rolled down her cheeks.

"Will my grandmother die?" asked Katy in a hollow voice.

Young Dr. Benner looked down upon her. He had not given so much thought of late to the development of his protégé. He had met in the county seat an older lady who had taken his fancy, who needed no improvement, and whose mind was already sufficiently developed to suit his ideas. He looked now at Katy through narrowed eyelids. He suddenly remembered the great plans he had had for her and the greater plans she had had for herself. He began to wonder what Katy's life would be like, he who had just a little while ago been planning it so carefully! He heard in that instant's pause a clear whistle from the direction of the garden, and he decided without knowing the identity of the whistler that there would sooner or later be that sort of complication in Katy's life which would end her education, even if her grandmother's need of her did not. He was so busy with his speculations that he did not answer Katy's question until she was faint with apprehension.

Katy was a sensitive creature; she was suddenly aware of the changed, absent way in which he regarded her. She remembered that it was a long time since the doctor had invited her to ride with him, a long time since he had said anything to her about singing.

"My gran'mom is all I have in this world," she reminded him with piteous dignity.

"No, Katy." The doctor came back to reality with a start. "She will not die."

His expression terrified Katy.

"Then, when will she be well again?"

"I cannot say."

The whistle sounded again from beyond the garden wall. This time it penetrated to the consciousness of Katy, who, hearing it, blushed. No one but Alvin Koehler could produce so sweet and clear a note. For the first time he had called her. The night was warm and bright, and the breeze carried the odor of honeysuckle and jasmine into the kitchen. The beauty of the night seemed mocking. Katy's heart cried out angrily against the trouble which had come upon her, against the greater grief which now threatened.

"You mean that she will be sick a long, long time?"

"Possibly."

Katy clasped and unclasped her hands.

"You do not mean that perhaps she will never be well?"

"I do not believe she can ever be well, Katy." The doctor now laid his hand on Katy's shoulder.

Katy moved away, her hand on her side, as if to sustain the weight of a heavy heart.

"What am I to do for her?"

The doctor gave directions about the medicines, and then went across the yard to sit with the squire in his office. When he had gone, Katy stood for a moment perfectly still in the middle of the room. The whistle did not come again; Alvin, approaching the house without knowing anything of Grandmother Gaumer's illness, saw suddenly that the house was more brightly lighted than usual and stole away.

For an instant Katy stood still, then she crossed the room and opened the door which led into the dim front of the house, and went into the parlor. There she sat down on the high, slippery haircloth sofa. Presently she turned her head and laid her cheek against the smooth, cool surface of the arm. Overhead she could hear the sound of Uncle Edwin's soft, heavy tread, the sound of his deep voice as he spoke to Grandmother Gaumer or to Aunt Sally. Uncle Edwin was a good man, Katy said to herself absently, her mind dwelling upon a theme in which it took at that moment no interest; Uncle Edwin was a good man, but he was not a very smart man. He had never gone to school — to school — Katy found herself repeating that magic word. It brought fully into the light of consciousness the dread question which had been lingering just outside. If Grandmother Gaumer were to be a long time sick, who would take care of her?

Uncle Edwin and Aunt Sally were kind, but they had their farm on the outskirts of Millerstown; they could not leave it.

"But I must have my education," whispered Katy to the smooth surface of the old sofa. "This is my time in life for education. Afterwards the mind gets dull, and you cannot learn. It is right that I should have a chance to learn."

Then Katy sat up; from the room above Uncle Edwin called her. "Ach, Katy, come once here!"

"I am coming," answered Katy as she flew.

In the sick-room her uncle and aunt welcomed her with relief. To them Katy was always a sort of wonder child. They had wanted to adopt her when she was a little girl; they had always loved her as they loved their own little Adam.

"We cannot make out what she wants, Katy. Perhaps it is you she wants."

Katy looked about the room, at the stout, disturbed uncle and aunt, then at the great bedstead, with its high feather bed, its plump pillows. Grandmother Gaumer's hair had been covered by a close-fitting cap; the sheet was drawn up under her chin; she seemed to have shrunk to a pair of eyes. But they were eyes into which the life of the body was concentrated. Katy almost covered her own as she met them, her throat contracted, all emotions combined into the one overwhelming sensation.

"I will stay here now," announced Katy. "Aunt Sally, you can go home, and Uncle Edwin, if he is to stay all night here, can go to bed, and if I need anything I will call him."

Thus Katy, the dictator. When they had obeyed, Katy crossed the room to her grandmother's side. To such an interview as this there could be no witnesses.

"No one else is going to take care of you, gran'mom," promised Katy. "No one can travel so fast and talk so much." She leaned over and laid her hand on her grandmother's cheek. "I am going to stay with you to-night and to-morrow night and always. I am never going to leave you. I care for schooling, but I care more for you. You raised me from little when I had no father and mother to take care of me. I will remember what you said about gran'pop, and I will try to be like him. *Do you understand me?*" besought Katy in a sudden agony of fright.

The brown eyes answered, or Katy thought they answered.

"Well, then," said Katy. "Now I will read you a chapter and then you will go to sleep."

CHAPTER XI
KATY FINDS A NEW AIM IN LIFE

It was on Tuesday evening that Grandmother Gaumer was smitten and Alvin Koehler whistled in the garden. On Wednesday Millerstown flocked to the Gaumer house with inquiries and gifts. They all saw Grandmother Gaumer, according to Millerstown's custom in sickness, then they went down to the kitchen to hear from Bevy an account of this amazing seizure. Sarah Ann Mohr, who was one of grandmother's oldest friends, brought fresh pie and many tears. Susannah Kuhns promised fresh bread in the afternoon, and Sarah Knerr carried off the washing.

Then Sarah Ann, accustomed to hear with admiration and wonder the problems which Katy put to a puzzled Mr. Carpenter, and expecting, with the rest of the community, that she would bring extraordinary honor to Millerstown, asked Bevy Schnepp a question.

"My mom was taken that a way," she explained, tearfully. "For seven years she laid and did n't speak and toward the end she had n't her mind any more. Who will take care of gran'mom? Will Edwin and Sally move home or will they get some one from outside?"

Bevy stood beside the sink, her arms akimbo.

"Gran'mom is n't sure to lie seven years," said she. Bevy had in her possession the seventh book of Moses, which contained many powerful prescriptions; she meant to see what pow-wowing could do before she despaired of Grandmother Gaumer. "But if she does lay, Edwin won't come home and they won't get anybody from outside. It was never yet a Gaumer what had to be taken care of by one from outside. Katy will take care of her gran'mom."

"Katy will take care of her gran'mom!" repeated Sarah Ann. "But she won't be well till [by] September! How will Katy then be educated? Carpenter has learned her everything he knows in this world. I could easy hear that!"

"Katy does not think of education," answered Bevy. "She thinks of nothing but her gran'mom. She is with her night and day."

Solemnly Sarah Ann and Bevy regarded one another. Then solemnly they nodded.

"That is what I said to Millerstown!" Thus Sarah Ann in triumph. "There are those in Millerstown who will have it that Katy will let her gran'mom stick. There are those in Millerstown who say that when people get education, they get crazy. Did she cry, Bevy?"

"Not that I saw," answered Bevy, proudly. "Or that any one else saw, I guess."

XI. Katy Finds A New Aim In Life

"I will tell Millerstown," Sarah Ann made ready to depart. "It is three places where I will stop already on my way home."

Ponderously, satisfied with her darling, Sarah Ann moved through the door.

Among the numerous visitors was Essie Hill, who had recently experienced the sudden and violent change of heart which admitted her to full membership in the Improved New Mennonite Church. She wore now a little short back sailor like the older women, with an inscription across the front to the effect that she was a worker in the vineyard. Essie was sincere; she was good, but Katy hated her. When she told Essie, not without a few impertinent embroideries, that her grandmother was asleep, Essie departed with a quiet acceptance of the rebuff which no Millerstonian would have endured without resentment. Essie's placid soul, however, was not easily disturbed. She performed her duty in offering to sit by Grandmother Gaumer and to read and pray with her; further she was not obligated.

Katy heard no more Alvin's clear whistle in the garden. She said to herself, in a moment of physical and mental depression, that he might easily have made a way to see her by coming with the rest of Millerstown to inquire for the invalid; then she reminded herself that the Koehlers went nowhere, had no friends.

"He is ashamed of his pop," said Katy to herself. "His pop is a black shame to him."

On Thursday she left her grandmother while she went on an errand to the store and her eyes searched every inch of Main Street and the two shorter streets which ran into it. But Alvin was nowhere to be seen. She answered shortly the questions about her grandmother, put to her by the storekeeper and by all other persons whom she met, and returned to the house in despair.

"If I could only see him," she cried to herself. "If I could only talk to him a little!"

On Sunday evening Bevy drove her out, almost by force, to the front porch. Bevy's preacher was again holding services in the next village, and Bevy was therefore free to care for the invalid. She had sought all the week an opportunity to sit by Grandmother Gaumer and to repeat the pow-wow rhymes which she firmly believed would help her. Now, sitting at the head of the bed in the dusk, she made passes in the air with her hands and motions with her lips. When she was certain that Grandmother Gaumer slept, she slid down to her hands and knees and crept three times round the bed, repeating the while some mystic rhyme. In reality, Grandmother Gaumer did not sleep, but lay amusedly conscious of the administrating of Bevy's therapeutic measures.

Meanwhile Katy was not alone. Had Bevy suspected the company into which she was sending her beloved, it is probable that one spring would have carried her down the steps, and another to the porch.

Katy sat for a long time on the step with her chin in her hands. She was thin, her eyes were unnaturally large, the hard work of nursing had worn her out. Her gaze searched the street, and she shrank into the shadow of the honeysuckle vine when couples paraded slowly by, arm in arm.

"I have nobody," mourned Katy, weakly, to herself. "Nobody in all the world but my gran'mom, and she cannot even speak to me."

After a long time Katy's sharp gaze detected a lurking figure across the street. Her heart throbbed, she leaned forward out of the shadow of the vine. Then she called a soft "Alvin!"

Alvin came promptly across and Katy made room for him beside her. He wore his new red tie, but his face as the light from the street lamp fell upon it was far from happy.

"Is your gran'mom yet sick?" he asked.

"Yes." Katy could answer only in a monosyllable. Alvin was here, he sat beside her, the skirt of her dress rested against him.

"I was here once in the garden, and I whistled for you. I did not know your gran'mom was sick."

"I heard it, but I couldn't come." The two voices had all the tones of deep tragedy. "It was when my gran'mom was first taken sick." Katy felt suddenly tired and weak. But she was very happy. She noticed now the odor of honeysuckle and the sweeter jasmine out on the garden wall. It was a beautiful world.

After a long time Alvin spoke again, still unhappily.

"David Hartman is going away to school."

Katy's heart gave a jealous throb. It was not fair for any one to have an education when she could not.

"He is going right away to the real college."

"He cannot!" said Katy. "He cannot pass the examination. He is no farther than I and I couldn't get in the real college. I guess we have catalogues that tell about it!"

"But there is a young fellow here to teach him this summer, so he can get in. His mother is willing for him to go. Some say that David has already his own money. It costs a lot of money to get such a young man. He gets more than Carpenter got, they say. He is living at the hotel because it is too clean at the Hartmans' for strangers. David goes to him at the hotel. They say he will learn to be a lawyer so that he can take care of his money. And the tailor" — the spaces between Alvin's words grew wider and wider, his voice rose and fell almost as though he were chanting — "the tailor is making new clothes for him, and his mom bought him a trunk in Allentown!"

"So!" said Katy, scornfully, the blood beating in her temples. She did not envy David his clothes, but she envied him his learning. Katy was desperately tired; a noble resolve, though persisted in bravely, does not keep one constantly cheerful and courageous.

"And he sits on the porch in the evenings sometimes with Essie Hill."

"He has good company! It is queer for such an educated one to like such a dumb one! Perhaps Essie will get him to convert himself. She was here to get me to convert myself. She says it is while I am wicked that this trouble comes upon me. She wanted to sit by my gran'mom and talk about my gran'mom's sins, and I told her my gran'mom hadn't as many sins in her whole life as she had already." Katy could not suppress a giggle. "That settled her. I wouldn't even let her go up. I wanted to choke her."

Again Katy sat silently. Alvin was here, she was consuming the time in foolish talk; at any minute Bevy might descend from above or they might be interrupted by a visitor. Alvin moved uneasily. Perhaps he, too, felt this talk to be foolish. The light fell full upon his red tie and the beautiful line of his young throat. A more mature and experienced person than Katy Gaumer would have been certain that there must be good in a creature so beautiful.

"David can go to college," he said mournfully. "But I cannot go anywhere, not even to the normal school where I could learn to be a teacher. I thought I would surely get that much of an education, but there is no hope for me."

Katy turned and looked at him. "Why no hope?"

"Why, they say in Millerstown that you are not going to school. You said that when you went to school you would find a way for me to go. But if you are not going, then there is no one to help me. And pop" — Alvin's lapses into the vernacular were frequent — "pop gets worse and worse. He is going very fast behind. He is getting so he has queer ideas. He was making him shoelaces with the ravelings of the carpet. And he thinks there is now a woman with horns after him. He talks about it all the time. I have nothing in this world. When he was so bad I came to tell you. It was then I whistled."

"You do not need any one at the school to help you," said Katy in a clear voice. "If I am not going, I can all the better help you to go; don't you see that, Alvin? If you are going to teach, you do not have to pay anything except for board and room. I have two hundred dollars in the bank, and I can lend you some to begin with and then you can get something to do. I will give you fifty dollars" — poor Katy planned as though she had thousands. "There is a little hole round the corner of the house in the wall, where Bevy used to put the cakes for me. There I will put the money for you, Alvin."

Alvin's lips parted. He felt not so much gratitude as amazement.

"Are n't you going to school *ever?*"

Katy did not answer.

"Millerstown will be crazy when it finds I am going away!" cried Alvin with delight.

"They must never know how you go!" said Katy in alarm. "You must not tell them how you go!"

"They think my father has money." Here was a solution. "They do not know he has given it all to detectives. They think he has it hidden away. Millerstown is very dumb."

"You must get a catalogue from the school, Alvin, and you must send in your name. That is the first."

"I will," promised Alvin. "I will do it right away. It is a loan, Katy, and I will pay it back!"

The sound of a descending footstep on the stairway frightened them, as though they had been plotting evil. Alvin went swiftly and quietly out the brick walk, and Katy sat still. When Bevy came to the kitchen door, Katy sat on the lowest step, where Bevy had left her, her elbows on her knees, her chin in her hands.

"You are not to come in yet," said Bevy. "I just came to get a drink. Your gran'mom is sleeping."

"Yes, well," answered Katy, keeping her voice steady by great effort. She did not wish to move. She wished to think and think. If Alvin had omitted an expression of thanks, she held no grudge against him, had not, indeed, even observed the omission. Here was an outlet from prison; here was something to be, to do! She would cheerfully have earned by the labor of her hands enough to send Alvin Koehler to school. After such a foolish, generous pattern was Katy made in her youth; thus, lightly, with a beating, happy heart, did she put herself in bondage.

"I will educate Alvin," said Katy. "If I cannot do one thing, I can do another."

Alvin Koehler climbed the hill. His heart did not throb as rapidly as Katy's, but Alvin, too, was very happy. Alvin was not yet possessed by an overwhelming desire for an education; but he saw a new suit and at least three neckties. Above that delectable goal, his ambition did not rise.

When he reached the little white house on the hillside and lifted the

XI. Katy Finds A New Aim In Life

latch of the door, he could not get in. After he had pounded and called, his terror growing each moment greater, he tried the window. From there his father's strong hands pushed him so suddenly that he fell on his back into the soft soil of the garden. Poor William Koehler had come to confuse the woman with horns with his harmless son.

Terrified, Alvin retraced his steps to the village and sought the squire. In the morning, the squire, with gentle persuasion, carried poor William to the county home. There William was kept at first in a cell, with a barred window; then he was allowed to work in the fields under guard. Gradually, the woman with horns vanished; his work with his familiar tools and with the plants which he loved seemed to have a healing effect. He grew more and more quiet; presently he ceased to pray aloud in his frantic way. He said after a while that God had told him to be quiet. He seemed to have forgotten his home, his child, his old life, even his enemy.

CHAPTER XII
KATY BORROWS SO THAT SHE MAY LEND

In June Grandmother Gaumer was smitten; in September Alvin was to go away; the months between were not unhappy for Katy. Occasionally Alvin came and sat with her on the porch in the darkness. It was tacitly agreed that they should not be seen together. Public opinion in Millerstown was less favorable than ever to Alvin since his father's removal to the poorhouse was coincident with Alvin's elaborate preparations for school. Alvin could not wait for the slow operations of a tailor; he went at once to Allentown and purchased a suit; the fifty dollars which he found at the time appointed in the putlock hole remained intact no longer than the time consumed in making the journey. Millerstown was certain that Alvin had found his father's hoarded wealth, and speculated wildly about its possible size.

"Koehler was working all these many years," said Susannah Kuhns. "He had all the time his place free on the hill. Alvin will have enough money for education, of that you may be sure."

"But can he take education?" asked the puzzled Sarah Ann. "The Koehlers were always wonderful dumb. There was once a Koehler whose name was Abraham and he wrote it always 'Aprom,' and one made a cupboard and nailed himself in and they had to come and let him out. They are a dumb Freundschaft. They are bricklayers and carpenters; they are not educated men. Now, with Katy it is different. She has a squire and a governor in her Freundschaft."

"I don't believe he got all this money from his pop," protested Bevy. "There are other ways of getting money. It says in the Bible, 'Like father, like son.'"

"He parades up and down like a Fratzhans [dude] in his new clothes," said Susannah.

"Ach, Susannah!" reproved gentle Sarah Ann, in whose judgment criticism had now gone far enough.

Such speculations and accusations Katy had more than once to hear. Then Katy clenched her hands. They would see Alvin come back to Millerstown some day a great man. She hated Susannah and Bevy and all Alvin's detractors. Never was Katy doubtful for an instant of her undertaking; she had succeeded with the Christmas entertainment; she had succeeded in compelling Mr. Carpenter to teach her; she was succeeding now in doing all the work in her grandmother's house; she would succeed in educating Alvin.

"Sarah Ann is a great, fat worm," said Katy with scorn. "When the brains were given out, Sarah Ann was missed. And Bevy is a little grasshopper and she, too, is dumb. It is a great pity for them."

She wished that she might see Alvin oftener, but that was impossible. He was near at hand; she could get occasional glimpses of him, and she could sit by her grandmother's bed and think of him. She had put her precious fifty dollars in the putlock hole and Alvin had removed it. It must be confessed that between the time Katy promised and the time that she deposited the money, Alvin came more than once after night to feel round in the improvised bank. The gift constituted now in Katy's mind an unbreakable bond between them. Such largess would have inspired her to lay down her life for the giver, and Alvin was endowed in her mind with gifts and graces far greater and nobler than her own. At the garments which he bought she looked with tender approval. Certainly he could not go to the normal school without suitable clothes!

Besides Katy's clearly expressed conviction that it was unwise for Alvin to come to see her, there was another reason why Alvin did not turn his steps oftener to Grandmother Gaumer's gate. Alvin's new clothes put him temporarily into a condition bordering upon insanity. He must show himself in his fine apparel. He would have liked to appear in it each evening, but such a performance was unthinkable. Only on Saturday and Sunday did Millerstown wear its best.

On Saturday and Sunday, therefore, Alvin lived. He attended ice-cream festivals and Sunday School picnics; he went diligently to church, selecting each Sunday the one of Millerstown's churches which was likely to have the largest attendance. When the Lutherans had a Children's Day service, Alvin went early to get a good seat. Often he sat in the Amen corner, close to the little cupboard with the space of smooth, gray wall beside it. Upon the smooth, gray wall his profile and curly head cast a beautiful shadow. When there was a revival service at the church of the Improved New Mennonites, Alvin was in the congregation. There he was conscious of the demure eyes of Essie Hill. Essie was always alone. David Hartman, who sat with her on the doorstep, never was seen inside her church. To David revivals, such as enlivened many of the meetings of the Improved New Mennonites, were intolerable; they made him feel as he had felt at his father's funeral with the gaze of all Millerstown searching his soul. Between Essie and her father there had occurred a short conversation about David and his worldly ways.

"You can never marry outside your church, Essie," said grave, sober Mr. Hill.

"No, pop," agreed Essie. "Such a thing I would not do."

Alvin Koehler would have had no objection to a scrutiny of his soul.

To Alvin, all of himself was interesting.

Alvin did not think often of his father. By this time William was trusted to work in the almshouse fields, and was allowed to talk from morning till night of his wrongs.

Early in September Alvin went away. He came on the last Saturday evening to say good-bye to Katy and they sat together on the dusky porch. The porch was darker than it had been in the springtime, since the hand which usually pruned the vines was no longer able to hold the shears. There were still a few sprays of bloom on the honeysuckle and the garden was in its greatest glory. There bloomed scarlet sage and crimson cock's-comb and another more brilliant, leafy plant, red from root to tip. Among the stalks of the spring flowers twined now nasturtiums and petunias, and there was sweet alyssum and sweet William and great masses of cosmos and asters. In the moonlight Katy could see a plant move gently; even in her sadness she could not resist a spasm of pleasure as a rabbit darted out from behind it. On the brick wall between the porch and the garden stood Grandmother Gaumer's thorny, twisted night-blooming cactus with great swollen buds ready to open to-morrow evening. The air had changed; it was no longer soft and warm as it had been the night when Katy first planned to educate Alvin.

Sitting by her grandmother's bed Katy had finished her red dress with the ruffles. It had been necessary to make the hem an inch longer than they had planned in the spring. Grandmother Gaumer's patient eyes had seemed to smile when Katy showed her. Grandmother Gaumer was shown everything; to her bedside Bevy bore proudly Katy's first successful baking of bread; thither to-morrow, Uncle Edwin would carry the great cactus in its heavy tub.

Katy sat for a long time on the step before Alvin came. Her body softened and weakened a dozen times as she thought she heard his step, then her muscles stiffened and her hands clenched as the step passed by. Presently it would be time for Bevy to go home and for Katy to go into the house, or presently some one would come, and then her chance to see Alvin would be gone. It seemed to her that Bevy looked at her with suspicion when Alvin's name was mentioned; the later it grew the more likely Bevy was to interrupt their interview.

XII. Katy Borrows So That She May Lend

The grip of Katy's hands, one upon the other, grew tighter, her cheeks hotter, the beating of her heart more rapid. He must come; it was incredible that he could stay away. Her throat tightened; she said over and over to herself, "Oh, come! come! come!"

Presently down the dusky street approached Alvin with his swinging walk. Now Katy knew at last that she was not mistaken. He was here; he was entering the gate which she had opened so that its loud creak might not be heard by Bevy; he was walking softly on the grass as Katy had advised him.

Alvin sat down a little closer to Katy than was his custom. A subtle change had come over him. Though the Millerstown boys looked at him with scorn, the Millerstown girls, smiling upon him, had completed the work which Katy's attentions had begun. Alvin had not attended Sunday School picnics, with their games of Copenhagen and their long walks home in the twilight, for nothing. Alvin had less and less desire for learning; he still thought of education as a path to even finer clothes than he had and greater admiration and entire ease. He had come now from service at the Lutheran church, and from his favorite corner he had been conscious of the notice of the congregation. He had asked Katy for twenty-five dollars more than she had given him; this, Katy told him, lay now in the putlock hole in the house wall. His spirits rose still more gayly as he heard of it.

"I will pay it back in a year or two," he assured Katy lightly. "Then I will tell you how to do when you go to school."

"Yes," said Katy. She would have liked to say, "Oh, Alvin, keep it, keep it forever!" But how then should she attain to an equality with Alvin? She realized now fully that he was going away. The long, long winter was fast approaching, and she would be here alone in this changed house. There would be no more entertainments; there would be no more frantic racing with Whiskey; there would be no more glorifying, sustaining hope.

Slowly the tears rolled down Katy's cheeks. She knew that the minutes were passing rapidly, and that she and Alvin had said nothing. But still she sat with her hands pressed against her eyes.

Almost immediately, alas! there was an alarming sound. The step of Bevy was heard descending the stairway. Poor Katy could cheerfully have slain her. A hundred confused thoughts filled her mind, the tears came faster than ever; she rose, and Alvin rose with her and they looked at each other, and then Alvin was gone. In his excitement he closed the gate noisily behind him. Katy sank down again on the step from which she had risen. When Bevy looked out from the doorway, Katy sat motionless.

"You ought to come in, Katy," advised Bevy. "It is cold."

"I am not cold," said Katy.

"It is damp and cold," insisted Bevy. "I thought I heard the gate slam."

Katy made no answer.

"Did it slam?" asked Bevy.

Katy looked round. Her eyes were bright; her voice, if it trembled, did not tremble with grief. "If you heard it, I guess it slammed," said she.

"The night air is bad." Bevy was losing patience. "*Will* you come in?"

"No," said Katy.

Bevy snapped the screen door shut.

"Je gelehrter, je verkehrter" (The more learned, the more perverse), she declared.

When Bevy had reached the upper hall, Katy rose from her place on the lowest step, and stretched out her arms as though to embrace the garden and Millerstown and the world. Mist was rising from the little stream below the orchard; it veiled the garden in a lovely garment; it seemed to intensify the odor of the honeysuckle and the late roses. Again Katy sank down on the step and hid her face in her arms.

"He kissed me!" said Katy shamelessly.

Now Katy's winter was guarded against unhappiness.

A little later in September David Hartman went to school also, not to the normal school where tuition cost nothing, but to college as befitted the heir of a rich man. His tutor had prepared him thoroughly for his examinations; he had an ample allowance; there was no reason why the gratification of any legitimate desire should be denied him. His mother had spared no pains with his outfit; she had bought and sewed and laundered and packed a wardrobe such as, it is safe to say, no other student in the college possessed. During the long summer she and David had had little to say to each other. David had been constantly busy with his books; he had had little time even to think of his father, whom he so passionately regretted. Death continued to work its not uncommon miracle for John Hartman; it dimmed more and more for his son the character of his later years, and exaggerated greatly the vaguely remembered tendernesses of David's babyhood. John Hartman had to an increasing degree in his death what he had not had in life, the affection and admiration of his boy. How was it possible for him to be anything else but silent with a wife so cold, so immovable, so strange? David was certain that he had solved his father's problem. Sometimes David could not bear to look at his mother.

But now that he was going away, David's eyes were somewhat sharpened. His mother looked thin and bent and tired; she seemed to have grown old while she sewed for him.

XII. Katy Borrows So That She May Lend

"You ought to get you a girl," he said with the colossal stupidity of youth and of the masculine mind.

Mrs. Hartman looked at him, as though she were suddenly startled. He seemed to have grown tall overnight; his new clothes had made a man of him. Then a film covered her eyes, as though she withdrew from the suggestions of lunacy into some inward sanctuary where burned the lamp of wisdom.

"A girl!" cried Cassie, as though the suggestion were monstrous. "To have her spoil my things! A girl!"

David's trunk was packed in the kitchen, thither his hat and satchel were brought also. When his breakfast was over he went down the street to the preacher's for a letter recommending his character. When he returned, his trunk and satchel had been sent to the station; he had now only to take his hat and say good-bye to his mother who was at this moment in the deep cellar. For her David waited awkwardly. He remembered how he had stood kicking his foot against the door sill on Christmas Day — how many years and years ago it seemed!

Now, as then, David experienced a softening of the heart. He forgot his resentment against his mother's coldness, against her strange passion for material things. She was his mother, she was all he had in the world, and he was going away from her and from his home. He heard her ascending the cellar steps, and he turned and went up to his room as though he had forgotten something, so that he might hide his tears.

At the entrance of the little hall which led to his room, David stood still, the lump hardening in his throat, his breath drawn heavily. His errand to the preacher's had not taken half an hour, but in that half-hour his room had been dismantled. The cheap little bed had been taken apart and had been carried into the hall; the carpet had been dropped out of the window to the grass below; broom and scrubbing-brush and pail waited in the corner. The door of his mother's room opposite his own was closed; a dust cloth was stuffed under it so that no mote could enter. Now, all the rooms in Cassie's house except the kitchen and her own could be immaculate.

For a long moment David stood still. He looked into his room, he looked at his mother's closed door, he looked at the door which shut off the deep front of the great house. He felt the same mysterious impression which Katy Gaumer felt when she looked at the outside of the Hartman house, as though it held within it strange secrets. It seemed now as though it thrust him forth as one who did not belong, as though its walls might presently contract until there should be no space for him to stand. It was a cruel suggestion to a boy about to leave his home!

David breathed deeply as though to shake off the oppression, and then went down the steps.

Without apparent emotion he bade Cassie farewell, then strode briskly toward the station. Essie Hill, who let him sit beside her on the doorstep and who argued prettily with him about his soul, was nowhere to be seen; his companions, Ollie Kuhns and Billy Knerr and the Fackenthals, were at work or at school; Bevy Schnepp, whose great favorite he was, was busy with her washing in the squire's yard far up the street. In the door of the store stood Katy Gaumer. Her, with Alvin Koehler, he hated. David had with his own eyes beheld one of Alvin's hasty departures from Grandmother Gaumer's gate. Persons found their levels in this world and Katy had found hers.

But on the corner David hesitated. How tall she had grown! How large her eyes were, and how lacking in their old sparkle! Cheerfully would he have returned in this final moment of madness to the dullness of the Millerstown school to be near her once more, cheerfully would he have continued his abode in Millerstown forever. He determined to go to speak to her, to say, "Let us be friends." Essie Hill was pretty and sweet, and her anxiety about his soul was flattering, but Essie was like a candle to a shining star. He saw the flirt of Katy's red dress as she sailed up the schoolroom aisle; he heard her saucy answers to the teacher; he admired her gayety, her great ambition. She had planned by now to be at school, learning everything; instead, she wore a gingham apron and stood in the Millerstown store buying a broom!

A single step David had already taken, when Katy turned from her bargaining and their eyes met. Katy knew whither David was bound; already his train whistled faintly at the next station. It seemed to her that he looked at her with pity. He was to go, and she was to stay — forever! With bitterness Katy turned her back upon him.

For a year Grandmother Gaumer lay high upon her pillows, her patient eyes looking out from her paralyzed body upon her friends and her quiet room. Presently she was able to lift her hands and to say a few slow and painful words. Her bed had been moved to the parlor; from here she could look up and down the street, and out to the kitchen upon Katy at her work. A trolley line was being built to connect Millerstown with the county seat; she could see the workmen approaching across the flat meadows, and after a while could watch with a thrill a faint, distant gleam of light broaden into the glare of a great headlight as the car whizzed into the village. Her face grew thinner and more delicate; her survival came presently to seem almost admirable. But still she lay patiently, listening to the storms and rejoicing in the sunshine. To her Katy read the Bible, hour after hour, a dull experience to the mind of Bevy, devout Improved New Mennonite though she was.

"You are an old woman," protested Bevy. "You are older than I in your ways. Run with Whiskey a little like you used to run! I could be much oftener here, and the other people would be glad to sit with gran'mom. I even put cakes for you in the hole and you don't take them out any more!"

Katy was really very happy during the long winter. Housekeeping had become easy; she would accept no help even with washing and cleaning. As for going about in Millerstown, Katy laughed, as neat, aproned in housewifely fashion, she sat by her grandmother's bed.

"Shall I go now to quiltings and surprise parties when I would not go before? I am not interested in those things."

Often there was time in the long afternoons for Katy to sit with her books. She knew what Alvin was studying; it was easy at first to keep up with him. She enjoyed the sense of importance which her position as head of the house gave her. Sarah Ann dissolved in tears as she praised her; Uncle Edwin and Aunt Sally made much of her. And how much more important was she than any of them knew! Alvin was doing well at school, at least so Alvin wrote. When trouble came, she would have Alvin to fly to. When her tasks seemed a burden, or when studying without a teacher became difficult, or when the winter storms shook the house, she remembered how he had kissed her. The complication which Dr. Benner had feared for Katy had arrived. Dr. Benner was by this time married; in the glamour in which he lived, he was unconscious of the existence of Katy except as a person of whom questions must occasionally be asked, to whom directions must sometimes be given. His wife was not pleasant and "common"; she was "proud"; she gave Millerstown to understand that as soon as she could persuade her husband to buy a practice in a more cultivated community, they would leave.

At Christmas time Alvin did not come home, but went instead to visit a schoolmate. If he had come, there would have been no place for him to stay. The little house on the mountain-side was cold and deserted; it would probably never be occupied again. Alvin wrote occasionally to Katy and Katy wrote regularly to him. It was not to be expected that he should neglect his work to write letters. Fortunately the Millerstown post-office was presided over at present by old man Fackenthal, who did not scrutinize addresses with undue closeness. Nevertheless, Katy disguised her own hand and dropped her letters into the slit in the door at night.

David returned at Christmas time with an added inch of height, with straighter shoulders and a sterner glance. David moved swiftly, answered questions directly, walked alone upon the mountainside, or sat with his books in his mother's kitchen. He seemed to have had some improving, enlightening experience; college had already done a great deal for him. Him Katy did not see.

Nor did Alvin appear in the summer time, except for a few days at the end. He had asked Katy for another fifty dollars in the spring, and she had sent it to him without stopping to consider that now more than half of her money was gone. Alvin meant to work in a drug store this summer, at least so Alvin said, in order to pay part of his debt. But the dispensing of soda water did not appear to have been as profitable as he expected, for in August, when he came to Millerstown, he borrowed another fifty dollars. He promised certainly now that he would come for Christmas. He put his arms boldly round Katy and kissed her many times. It seemed that Alvin, too, had had illuminating experiences.

David spent the summer in his little room and on the mountain-side. David sometimes lay for hours together on the plateau before the Sheep Stable. Sometimes he carried thither the books which he continued to study diligently. Sometimes he walked about, climbing among rocks, tramping along the arched back of the little range of hills, — mountains, to Millerstown. David sighed contentedly and breathed deeply. He noted the dappled shadows, the wreathing clematis, the tall spikes of lobelia, the odor of slippery elm, the first reddening branch of the gum trees. He looked down upon the fertile fields, upon the scattered villages, and he was almost happy. Then David returned to his books. It was strange that he should study so earnestly during the long summer. Surely David with his good mind had not fallen behind his fellows!

XII. Katy Borrows So That She May Lend

David's illuminating experiences had not been entirely those which study and knowledge bring. David's arrival in the college town had been at once observed and marked. He towered above his fellows; he had a look of greater maturity than his years would warrant; he had apparently large means at his command. Upper classmen are not so entirely devoted as is supposed to the abuse of the entering novice. Upon the novice depends the continued existence of the college society which is so important a part of the college's social structure. You cannot very well urge a man to join an organization of which you are a member after you have beaten him or held his head under an icy hydrant! David's college made a tacit but no less real distinction between the youth who was likely to prove valuable society material and the youth who would likely prove to be merely a student. David's clothes were of the best, he had many of them, he occupied an expensive room; it was evident that he need not have recourse to the many shifts by which the poor boy in college provides himself with spending money. David was overlooked in the disciplinary measures by which many of his classmates were trained to respect their betters. His discipline was, alas! much harder to endure!

He accepted in his silent way the attentions which were showered upon him, the drives, the treats, the introductions to foolish young ladies whose eyes spoke their admiration. David was bewildered and embarrassed, and David for a time wisely remained silent. There was no reason to think that David had not been brought up in the politest of society. But, finally, alas! David spoke.

It was not often that a student had a party given especially for him. But, as the seven villages struggled for the honor of the birth of Homer, so the college societies longed for the honor of possessing David. Finally all but two dropped out of the race. David had not committed himself to either, but it was understood that in accepting the proffered entertainment he was practically making his decision.

The great evening approached; the great guest in his fine apparel, another new suit, now a dress suit made by the college tailor, appeared at his party. The prettiest girl of all appointed herself his companion, and to him addressed a pretty remark.

"We are glad to have you here at college, Mr. Hartman."

Then David spoke. The prettiness of the girl, the formality of her address, the bright lights, his conspicuous position — all combined in David's downfall. David did not speak naturally as he spoke now; David had no trouble with *th*, David knew the English idiom; David knew better, oh, much, much better. But poor David reverted to type.

"I sank myself," said David amid a great and growing hush. Then David walked out, away from the pretty girl, away from the bright lights, away, forever, from the organization which had sought him. Overwhelmed with embarrassment, outraged, David sought his room and his books. David could never be persuaded to return to the society in which he had been thus humiliated; he never emerged again from his room or his books except to recite or to walk or to go to his meals or to church. He henceforth lived alone. He discovered that by diligent study he could accomplish in three years what he had expected would require four. The sooner he was out of this place the better. He went weekly to a neighboring city, and there, finding a teacher of elocution, conquered, he was sure forever, that damning trick of speech. He grew handsomer; he filled his room with beautiful furniture and many books; his allowance assumed in the eyes of his college mates the proportions of a fortune in itself. But David could not be induced to forget. David lost much, but David in his sullen hermitage remained decent and unspoiled.

Once or twice in the summer he sat with Essie on her doorstep. Essie was prettier than ever; she still besought him to be "plain." David laughed at her and teased her; she was really the only person in the world with whom he laughed. His mother's strength seemed to have failed; often she lay down on the settle before it was dark, but only when she fell asleep did David find her in this ignominious position. If she heard a step she sprang up, as though she had committed a crime.

Once more Christmas approached and passed. This time again there was no visiting governor, no great feast, no entertainment. Again Alvin did not come home; he did not now write a letter or send a gift. Grandmother Gaumer was worse; the patience in her eyes had changed to a great weariness; she had ceased to be able to move or to speak.

In March there came a great storm. It extinguished all the village lamps; it whirled across the broad breast of the mountain, sending to the ground with a mighty crash, unheard of man, many trees; it beat against the Gaumer house, which seemed to tremble. In spite of the storm, however, Katy put on her scarlet shawl and went to the post-office, as of old. But in those days there had been no such feverish haste as this!

Her grandmother looked at her for a moment as she stood by the bed and tried to smile. Then Katy went out, her skirts flying in the wind, the rain beating in her face. She plodded along as best she could, without the old sensation of a viking breasting an angry sea.

At the post-office she found a letter, and there stopped to read it because she could not wait.

"Dear, dear Katy!" With what a wild thrill Katy beheld the opening words. Then Katy read on. "I am in great trouble, Katy. For some time I

XII. Katy Borrows So That She May Lend

have not had enough money to get along, and now I must have fifty dollars. Oh, Katy, try and get it for me! Oh, I don't know what will happen, Katy. Oh, please, Katy!"

Katy read the letter through twice; then she stood gaping. Old man Fackenthal spoke to her and she answered without knowing what she said; then she went out and stood in the rain, trying to think. She had no money; her last cent had been given to Alvin in the fall. But Alvin had appealed to her to help; it was — oh, poor Katy! — an honor to be thus solicited. No one else could help him; he would go to no one else in the world.

Like a shock of cold water upon an exhausted body, fell Alvin's request upon Katy's weary, tired soul. When the necessity for an English entertainment was made clear to Katy, plans were immediate, execution prompt. Katy had known at once what she would do. She forgot now that she had no way of earning money; she did not anticipate that to her honest soul the burden of a debt would be almost as great as the burden of remembered theft. Boldly she presented herself to the squire in his office and there made her request. Nothing was plain to Katy except Alvin's bitter need.

The squire looked at her in astonishment.

"That is a good deal of money, Katy!" But the squire had seen Katy at her books. "You need books, I suppose, and things to wear. I see you studying and sewing, Katy. You are not to slip back in your studies before you go away."

"I will give you a paper and I will pay interest," promised Katy, who did not wish to discuss the spending of the money.

The squire went slowly to his safe. It must be very dismal for the child. His poor sister-in-law was not likely to improve, and she might, alas! be a long time dying. If the situation were not changed by fall, the child must be sent away and Edwin must come home to live. He remembered his own bright little sister; he remembered the plans of all the family for Katy. A sudden remorseful consciousness that they had forgotten Katy, and that they had left a good many burdens on her shoulders, moved him to give her the foolish sum for which she asked.

"This I *give* you, Katy," said he as he counted the money into her hand. It was not strange that the squire had taken so few journeys.

"No," protested Katy with a scarlet face; "it is a debt."

Recklessly Katy slipped the money into an envelope and mailed it, and Alvin, receiving it, wept for joy and thought with gratitude of the sender. The small part of it which he did not have to use to pay his most pressing debts he spent upon a girl from the county seat, one Bessie Brown, who had visited a friend at the normal school, and for whom he had great admiration.

CHAPTER XIII
EMPTINESS

The great March storm seemed to clear the way for an early spring. The winter had been unusually cold and long; even honeysuckle and ivy vines were winter-killed. The great old honeysuckle vine on the Gaumer porch died down to the ground and hung a mass of brown stems, through which the wind blew with a crackling sound. Day after day Millerstown had had to thaw out its pumps. To Sarah Ann Mohr, who had once read an account on the inside pages of the Millerstown "Star" of the delicate balance of meteorological conditions, the signs were ominous.

"It means something," insisted Sarah Ann. "Once when my mom was little they had such a winter and then the snow fell in June on the wheat. The wheat was already in the head when the snow fell on it. If it gets only a little colder than that, the people die."

But spring returned. Sarah Ann beheld with a thankful heart the hyacinths and narcissus in her flower beds pushing their heads through the soil, the rhubarb sprouting in her garden; she breathed in with unspeakable delight the first balmy breeze. Sarah Ann's friends were slipping rapidly away from her; she was one of the last survivors of her generation but her appetite was still good, her step firm, her eye bright. Sarah Ann was a devout and trustful Christian, but she had never been able to understand why a heaven had not been provided on the beautiful earth for those who were worthy.

The dogwood put out earlier than usual its shelf-like boughs of bloom; before the end of April bluets starred the meadows round the Weygandt dam, and everywhere there was the scent of apple blossoms. Grandmother Gaumer's garden, with its vine-covered wall, its box-bordered paths, its innumerable varieties of flowers, was a place of magic. Though its mistress was away, it had never been so beautiful, so sweet.

In it Katy walked up and down in the May twilight. She moved slowly as though she were very idle or very tired, or as though no duties waited her. Her face was white; in the black dress which she had made for her grandfather's funeral and which her grandmother had persuaded her to lay away, she seemed taller and more slender than she was.

Each time she turned at the end of the garden walk, she looked at the house and then away quickly. She did not mean to look at all, but involuntarily she raised her eyes. The parlor windows behind which Grandmother Gaumer's lamp had shone so long were blank. In the room above, which had been Grandfather and Grandmother Gaumer's there was now a light. Every few seconds the light was darkened by the shadow cast by

XIII. Emptiness

the passing to and fro of a large figure. From the same room came the sound of a child's voice, the little voice of "Ehre sei Gott" in the Christmas entertainment long ago. Now it was raised in cheerful laughter. In the kitchen, Edwin Gaumer sat by the table, a page of accounts before him. There were now more persons in the house than there had been since Katy had been taken there as a baby, but the house was, nevertheless, intolerably lonely. Grandmother Gaumer's life was ended; she had been laid beside her husband in the Millerstown cemetery. She had had a long life; she had outlived almost all those whom she had loved, even all her children but one; she needed no mourning.

But Katy sorrowed and would not be comforted.

"She was all I had. I have a few other friends like the squire and Sarah Ann, but these are old, too."

Katy walked more and more slowly along the garden path. Even her grandmother's death had brought from Alvin no letter.

"I cannot understand it," whispered Katy to herself; "I cannot understand it!"

It seemed to Katy that there was no subject in the world upon which her thoughts could rest comfortably, no refuge to which her weary, sorrowful soul could flee. During her grandmother's illness, she had dreamed of Alvin, of his progress at school, of the time when he should come home and they should plan together. He had kissed her again and again; she belonged to him forever. But why, oh, why did he not write? There was for poor Katy only anxiety and humiliation in the world.

"And I am in debt!" she mourned. Her constant reading of the Bible to her grandmother had furnished her with quotations for all the experiences of life. It was a textual knowledge which many preachers would have envied her. It gave her now a vehicle with which to express her woes. "I am like David in the cave," said she. "I am in distress and in debt."

"Fifty dollars!" whispered Katy as she walked up and down the garden paths. "I am fifty dollars in debt!"

It was true that the squire had insisted that the money must be a gift. But the squire had not the least suspicion of the purpose to which his gift had been devoted.

"They have nothing for Alvin," said Katy to herself. "Alvin has had no chance. He will surely pay it back to me. I am certain he will pay it back!"

The dew fell damp about her, but still Katy walked on and on, up and down the garden paths. When, finally, she went into the kitchen, her Uncle Edwin looked up at her blinking. In his rugged face was all the kindness and sober steadfastness of the Gaumers.

"Sit down once, Katy," said he, neither in command nor in request, but with gentle entreaty. "I want to talk to you a little."

Katy sat down on the edge of the old settle. She would listen to no condolences; every fiber in her body bristled at the first sign of sympathy. Sympathy made her cry, and she hated to cry. Katy hated to be anything but cheerful and happy and prosperous and in high hope.

Several minutes passed before Uncle Edwin began upon his subject. Though he loved Katy, he stood in awe of her, gentle and weak though she appeared in her black dress.

His first question was unfortunately worded.

"What are you going to do now, Katy, that gran'mom is gone?"

Katy looked at him sharply. She was not well; she was worried and unhappy; she found it easy to misunderstand.

"For my living, you mean?" said Katy, cruelly.

Uncle Edwin gazed, open-mouthed at his niece. He would have been ludicrous if he had not been so greatly distressed.

"Ach, Katy!" protested he, in bewilderment.

"What do you mean, then?"

Uncle Edwin had at that moment not the faintest idea of what he meant. He hesitated for an instant, then he stammered out an answer.

"I mean, Katy, when are you going to school?"

The room swam round before Katy's dull eyes. School! She was never going to school; she could not go to school. But a more acute anxiety threatened; the moment when she must give an account of her two hundred dollars was probably at hand. Katy's very heart stood still.

"I am not going to school," said she.

Again Uncle Edwin's mouth opened.

"Why, you are, Katy!"

"Do you mean" — wildly Katy seized upon any weapon of defense she could grasp: it was easy to confuse Uncle Edwin's mind — "do you mean when am I going away from here?"

Now Uncle Edwin's blue eyes filled with tears.

"Ach, Katy!" cried he. "We are only too glad to have you. You know how I wanted to take you when you were a little baby, and Aunt Sally wanted you. This is your home forever, Katy. But you always talked so of school and education!"

"I do not care for education."

Uncle Edwin's head shook with the activity of the mental processes within it.

"What!" he exclaimed, incredulously. Then he took a fresh start. Katy's ill-temper was incomprehensible, but when she heard what his plans were, she would be cross no longer.

"You have two hundred dollars in the bank, Katy. The two hundred that the governor sent you a while back, have n't you Katy?"

He did not ask the question for information, but to establish the points of his simple discourse.

"Well," said Katy, faintly, from her agitation.

"That is a good start. Now the squire will help and I will help. We have this all arranged between us. Then, when you come of age you will get the money your gran'mom left you. But that you are not to touch for your education. That you will leave by me, because I am your guardian in the law. You were faithful to your gran'mom till the end, and you are not to spend your own money for education. The squire and I will look after that."

The muscles of Katy's face had stiffened and utterance was impossible. All the old, dear, eager hope filled her heart. But Alvin was still precious to her; her sacrifice had been made for him; the sacrifice whose extent she was just beginning to understand. This, however, was no time to think of Alvin. She forced herself to say again quietly that she was not going to school.

"Not — going — to — school!" cried Uncle Edwin with long pauses between his words.

"No," repeated Katy. "I am not going to school."

Then Katy sought her room and her bed.

When Uncle Edwin reported his interview with Katy to the squire, the squire laughed.

"Ach, she just talks that way! She is a little contrary, like all the women when they are tired or not so well. Of course she is going! She was in here not long ago talking about it and I gave her some money for books and other things."

The next day the squire himself spoke to Katy.

"Are you getting ready for school, Katy?"

"I am not going to school."

"Since when have you changed your mind?"

"This long time."

The squire turned and looked at Katy over his glasses.

"Why, it is only a little while since I gave you money for books!"

"You did n't give me money," corrected Katy, stammering. "It was a loan; I said it was a loan. Else I would n't have taken it."

"Humbug, Katy!"

If the squire had been Katy's guardian, she would have gone promptly to school. But Uncle Edwin held that office and he could not have brought himself to compel Katy to do anything. The squire argued and coaxed and cajoled and Katy looked at him with a white face and stubborn eyes.

"It was n't right to take the two hundred dollars from Daniel in the beginning if you did n't intend to use it for schooling, Katy. What *are* you going to do?"

"I am going to earn my living," answered Katy. Her debt to the squire was swelling to tremendous proportions; and there was also the much greater sum for which she could give no account. Katy was sick at heart. But she managed to end the interview lightly. "I'm going to earn money and save it, and be a rich, rich woman."

Once safely out of the squire's office, Katy walked up the mountain road. She must be alone, to think and plan what she must do. School? Her whole body and mind and soul longed for school. But she could never go to school. She must pay the squire his fifty dollars. Suppose he should ask her to show him the books and dresses she had bought! She must also replace the whole two hundred before they found her out. She could see the expression of amazement and disgust on the face of the squire at the mere suspicion of any close friendship between a Gaumer and a Koehler. People despised Alvin.

"But they have no right to," cried Katy. "I want to see Alvin. He will make it right, I am sure he will make it right. He is older than I!" Katy spoke as though this fact were only now known to her. "He has no right —" But Katy went no further; her love had been already sufficiently bruised and cheapened. "I have tied myself up in a knot! I have done it myself!"

Katy looked down upon the Hartman house. Rumor said that Mrs. Hartman was failing; the rare visitors to her kitchen found her on the settle in midday.

"It is nothing but dying in the world," mourned Katy. "We grow up like grass and are cut down."

But Katy had now no time to think of the Hartmans. She went on up the mountain road until she reached the Koehler house. The walls needed a coat of whitewash, the fences were brown, the garden was overgrown. It was a mean little place in its disorder.

"He never had a chance," protested Katy in answer to some inward accusation. Then Katy went drearily home.

By the first of June Alvin had still not written; by the end of June Katy was still looking for a letter. The term of the normal school had closed; it was time for him to be at home. Surely he could not mean to stay away forever!

Day after day Katy's relatives watched her solicitously, expecting her grief to soften, her old spirits to return; day by day Katy grew more silent, more depressed. Uncle Edwin now attacked her boldly.

"Do you forget how smart the governor thought you were, Katy?" Or, "It was bad enough for your gran'mom that you could n't go to school for two years, Katy, but this would be much worse for her."

In July Uncle Edwin took fresh courage and began to reproach her. If she was going to school, no time must be lost, they must make plans, she

XIII. Emptiness

must have an outfit.

"David Hartman is at home," said he. "He will be very learned. He is smart. But he is not so smart as you, Katy. Do you forget how you were up to him in school and he is older than you?"

Katy swallowed her coffee with a mighty effort.

"And Alvin Koehler was here to-day," went on Uncle Edwin. "He wants that the directors should give him the Millerstown school, now that Carpenter is no longer here. We think he should have it while he comes from Millerstown. He has made a good deal of himself. You would be surprised to see him. But you are much smarter than he, Katy!"

Katy put up her left hand to steady her cup.

"If he gets the school, he is going to get married," went on Uncle Edwin placidly. "It is a girl from away. I am surprised that Alvin had so much sense as to study good and then settle down and get married. He said he had such an agency in the school for hats and neckties and such things. That was how he got along. There is, I believe, a good deal more in Alvin than we thought. But you, Katy — Why, *Katy*!"

Katy had risen from the table, her face deathly pale.

"I have burned myself with coffee," said she.

Simultaneously Uncle Edwin and Aunt Sally and little Adam pushed back their chairs.

"Ach, Katy, here; take water, Katy!"

"No," protested Katy, "it is not so bad as that. But I will go and lie down a little. My head hurts me, too. I am tired and it is very hot. I will go to my room."

Stammering, Katy got herself to the stairway. There, having closed the door behind her, she started up the steps on hands and knees. At the top she sat down for a moment to rest before she crept across the room to her bed. Again it was an advantage to be "Bibelfest," she had once more an adequate vehicle for the expression of her woes.

"I am like Job," wept poor Katy. "I am afflicted. I am a brother to jackals and a companion to ostriches."

Once when Katy opened her eyes, she saw opposite her window a single, pink, sunset-tinted cloud floating high in the sky. Somehow the sight made her agony more bitter.

Down in the kitchen Uncle Edwin, alarmed, confused, distressed, found himself confronted by an irate spouse. He could not remember another occasion in all their married life when his Sally had lost patience with him.

"Now, pop," said she, "it is enough. You are to leave poor Katy be."

CHAPTER XIV
KATY PLANS HER LIFE ONCE MORE

For a long time Katy lay motionless upon her bed. The shock of Uncle Edwin's announcement was overwhelming; it robbed her of power to move or think. When an hour later Aunt Sally tiptoed into the room, she found her still upon her bed, her face buried in the pillow, relaxed in what seemed to be a heavy sleep. Aunt Sally gathered her clothes from the untidy heap into which they had been tossed, and laid them on the back of a chair and drew down the shade so that the sun should not shine directly into the sleeper's eyes; then she closed the door softly and went down the steps.

Katy did not stir until the sun had vanished behind the western hills and the stars were shining. Then she rose and bathed her face and sat down by the window.

"I must think," said Katy. "I must now plan out my life in a new way."

Stubbornly she forced herself to face the event which made necessary this fresh planning of her life. Beyond the event itself she did not at this moment proceed. She beheld Alvin with his red tie, Alvin with his dark curls, Alvin with his beautiful olive skin, Alvin with his great, expressive eyes. Sitting by her window with the soft evening air blowing in her face, the odors of the garden rising sweetly about her, Adam's gentle, laughing voice, and all the other pleasant sounds of the Millerstown evening in her ears, Katy wept.

"Oh, Elend (Misery)!" cried she, after the manner of Millerstown in trouble.

After a while, the voice of pride made itself heard. It was not Alvin whom she defended, but herself.

"No word of marrying was said between us."

"But he kissed you," reminded the inward voice. "You thought he would marry you."

To this Katy could return only the answer of flaming cheeks and a throbbing heart.

"And there is all the money you gave him!" reminded the voice within her.

"I said he need n't pay it back!"

"But you expected him to pay it back!"

"But he need n't!"

"An honorable person would pay it before he got married."

"He has no money! He has nothing to pay it with!"

"He had an agency for neckties! He has enough to get married!"

It seemed to Katy that a ring of queer faces mocked her. She had eaten only a mouthful of supper, and she was a little light-headed. She seemed to see clearly the "lady from away" of whom her uncle had spoken. Imagination, helped by recollection of the beautiful ladies in the Allentown stores, pictured her clearly. She was brilliant and beautiful and learned, and she dressed marvelously. She was probably an acquaintance whom Alvin had made at school; she was all that Katy longed to be.

Now there rushed upon Katy a new and terrible sensation. She had been envious of David Hartman because he was going away to school, but here was a new kind of envy which affected not only the mind but the whole being. She threw herself down on her bed once more and hid her face in the pillow and wept with deep, sobbing gasps.

Presently, the paroxysm of crying over, Katy rose once more and once more dashed cold water over her burning cheeks.

"I will not cry another tear," said she with stern determination. "I will now plan my life. I must first earn the fifty dollars to pay back the squire; that is certain. Beyond that is nothing — nothing — nothing in this world. My young life is ruined."

For an hour Katy sat by the window, her chin in her hands. Frequently tears dropped to the window sill, but she gave way to sobs no more.

"My heart is broken," declared Katy. "But I must live on. I will probably live to be a thousand years old. I wish I was with my good gran'mom in heaven. I wish" — said Katy presently, with a long sigh — "I wish I had been born into this world with sense."

By the time that the house had quieted for the night and the sounds of Millerstown's going about had ceased, Katy, too, was asleep. She stirred uneasily on her pillow, her hands now clasped under a scarlet cheek, now flung above her head. But she had outlined her working theory.

In the morning she appeared in good time for her breakfast. She had not been refreshed by her restless sleep, but the first sharpness of the blow was past. In the doorway of the kitchen stood Bevy, her bright eyes sparkling with curiosity.

"What is this I hear about Kohler's boy?" she asked Edwin Gaumer. "Is it so that he will have the Millerstown school?"

"It looks that way," answered Uncle Edwin. "He is a normal, and he had good letters from the normal about his work, and he comes from Millerstown and we should help our own; and besides nobody else wants the Millerstown school."

"A Koehler teaching!" Bevy raised her hands in an astonished gesture. "He is the first Koehler that ever knew more than A B C. The school board will get into trouble. This will never go. Where will he live?"

"He will rent a house. He is getting married after school takes in."

"Married!" shrieked Bevy. The suspicion that friendly relations existed between Katy and Alvin had grown to certainty. Now, furious as Bevy had been because Katy had so lowered herself, she resented Alvin's daring to attach himself to any one else. "What cake-not-turned will have him?"

"A lady from away. I think she comes from Allentown."

"You have right to say from away," sniffed Bevy. "No girl from here would look twice at him."

Katy turned her back upon Bevy as she lifted the breakfast from the stove to the table. Sharp stabs of pain pierced her. She would have to hear a dozen times that day that Alvin was to be married. The strain of listening to Bevy's comments was almost more than she could endure. It had been important before that no one should suspect that she was helping Alvin; now it had become absolutely imperative.

When breakfast was over, Katy started down the street to carry out her plan of life. Her dress was longer than was becoming, the spring had gone out of her step. She passed the store and the post-office and turned up Church Street, and there beheld approaching the object of her journey, who started visibly at sight of her. David had grown still taller; he wore still more elegant clothes; he would have found an even more cordial welcome to the societies of his college than would have been extended to him upon entering. He was certain that he could be graduated in June of the next year, and he was pleasantly aware of his position as the most wealthy and the most reserved student in college. David liked the distinction. His speech was now entirely English; he was certain that it would be impossible for him to blunder again. He had determined that when he had graduated he would travel; he would never live for many months at a time in dull Millerstown. David added another adjective to Katy's characterization of that busy, tidy village; he called it *bourgeois*. David had, indeed, soared high above the low plane of his origin! He had found among the few books in the Hartman house the pictures of Paris and Amiens and Canterbury, and had learned for the first time that his father had been abroad. The mystery of his father was thereby deepened. There was only one portion of David's heart which had not hardened; in that his father was enthroned. His father, he was convinced, had had great powers, but he was held to earth and to Millerstown by a cruel fate which had linked him forever to an unworthy companion. Thus had Cassie's son decided against her.

David was astonished to hear Katy call to him.

"Come here, please, David. I want to talk to you."

He crossed the street at once and stood looking down at her. He could

XIV. Katy Plans Her Life Once More

not help seeing, even though he had relegated Katy forever to obscurity in Millerstown, that Katy had not become altogether unattractive. Her eyes no longer sought his brightly, she looked down or past him as he came toward her. He wondered what possible errand she could have with him. He felt his face flushing and he was furious with himself.

"How are you, Katy?" said he, his voice sounding strangely in his ears.

Katy did not hear his question. Her thoughts were fixed upon the plan of life.

"I want to speak to you about something, David. I was going to your house. The doctor said your mother was not well. I heard him say to the squire that she would have to have a girl to live with her when you went back to school. I would like the place, David."

David's eyes nearly popped from his head. It was true that his mother seemed feeble and that he had been making inquiries about a maid for her. But by such an offer as this he was dumbfounded. Had Katy lost her mind? No Gaumer had ever worked out. Her relatives were comfortably fixed; she would doubtless have some money of her own when she came of age. Where was Alvin Koehler, the despicable, to whom Katy had seemed attached? Had he heard her aright? He could only look at her and gasp out a foolish, "*You!*"

"I can work," said Katy, with a scarlet face. "I did all the work when my grandmother was sick for so long."

"Are you not going to school?" David grew more and more astonished as he became convinced that Katy was in earnest.

"I am not going to school," said Katy. "If I cannot get a place to work at your house, I will get a place somewhere else, that is all."

"Are you in any trouble, Katy?" asked David. "Can I do anything for you?"

Katy's head lifted. David Hartman was pitying her, asking to be allowed to help her. It was intolerable. She realized now how tall he was, how deep his gray eyes, how fair his white skin; she remembered her gingham apron, her debt, her disappointed hopes, every embarrassment and pain that had befallen her.

"There is nothing wrong, of course," said she coldly as she turned away. "That is all I wanted of you."

"Oh, but wait!" David went to her side and kept pace with her. He did not proceed with his speech at once. The old vision dazzled him, Katy in a scarlet dress, Katy laughing, Katy racing down the pike. It was abominable for her to become a servant — upon this subject, also, David's opinions had advanced. What in the world were her relatives about? But if she must live out, it would be better for her to work for his mother than to work at the hotel — the only other establishment in Millerstown which required the services of a maid. He would then have her in his house; the notion set David's cheeks suddenly to burning, his heart to throbbing. He wondered what room his mother would give her, where she would sit at the table, what she would do in the evenings when her time was her own.

"Do you want to engage me?" asked Katy, sharply; "or don't you want to engage me?"

"My mother will be only too glad to have you," said David, eagerly.

"I will come when your school opens," promised Katy, as she turned the corner.

"If I get a dollar and a half a week," — the standard of wages in Millerstown was not high, — "it will take me thirty-three and a third weeks to save fifty dollars," reckoned Katy. "That will take from September till June. After that I do not think of anything. Perhaps by that time I will die. Then I do not care if they find out that I have n't my two hundred dollars any more."

Katy at home went on with her accustomed tasks. She was silent; she avoided her aunt and uncle, since any sudden, gentle address made her certain that she was going to cry. She put little Adam down whenever he wished to climb up beside her on the settle; she was to every one a trying puzzle. In her nervousness she had often a desire to stand still and scream.

One evening the squire came into the Gaumer kitchen. Edwin lay on the settle asleep, his wife sat by the table sewing, little Adam was long since in bed. Katy, too, had gone upstairs. Forgetting now that she had announced her intention of going to bed immediately, she left her place by the window to go down for a drink, and came face to face with the squire who was entering. The squire looked grave; he seated himself in Grandfather Gaumer's armchair as though he meant to hold court. In a flash Katy knew what he had come to say. Uncle Edwin sat up blinking, Aunt Sally dropped her sewing into her lap. The squire did not often pay calls so late in the evening.

"Katy," began the squire in a stern voice, "what is this I hear about you?"

Katy's hand was still upon the latch of the stairway door; she grasped it for support. She had thought that she was prepared for the coming interview, but she was now badly frightened. Never before had the squire spoken to her with anything but gentleness and affection.

"What do you hear about me?"

"Benner came in just now on his way from Cassie Hartman's. He had been trying to find a girl for her. She said that now she would not need one, that you were going to hire out to her in September."

Uncle Edwin blinked more rapidly. Aunt Sally's lips parted.

"Well?" said Katy.

"Is this thing so?"

"Yes," answered Katy bravely. "There is nothing wrong in it. It is honest."

"You are going to hire out!" cried Edwin.

Aunt Sally began to cry. These tears were not the first she had shed on Katy's account.

"What *for?*" demanded Uncle Edwin. "You have a home. I told you we would send you to school. You need not even touch your money. What is this, Katy?"

"I want to earn my living, that is all." Katy's voice was dry and hard. "It is surely my right to earn my living if I want to!"

"Earn your living if you must!" said the squire, gruffly. "Of course you can earn your living if you want to. But go to school and learn to earn it right!"

"I do not want to go to school."

The squire looked at her helplessly. Then he crossed the room and took her by the shoulders and seated her on the settle between Edwin and himself. He was a persuasive person; it was hard for any one to deny him what he commanded or what he requested.

"Katy, dear, are you in any trouble?"

Katy actually prayed for help in her prevarication.

"No."

"There is Edwin and here am I," went on the squire. "We are strong enough to do up anybody. Now, what is the matter, Katy?"

"Nothing," insisted Katy.

"You once wanted to sing," Aunt Sally reminded her. "You were wonderful strong for singing."

"Sing!" echoed Katy. "I, sing? I can only caw like a crow."

"You had such plans," said Uncle Edwin. "You were going to be so educated. You were going to bring home your sheaves!"

"I have more sense now," explained Katy.

She looked at them brightly. Her eyes measured their broad shoulders — how she longed to lay her heavy burden upon them! She no longer belonged to her kin, she was an alien; she had allied herself with Koehlers, with William Koehler who was a thief, with Alvin Koehler who scorned her. She would sooner die than tell what she had done. The Gaumers were not niggardly, but they knew the value of money. Even Katy had learned that it took thirty-three and one third weeks to earn fifty dollars!

"You must let me be!" she burst out wildly. "I am not a child. I have no father and mother and my dear grandfather and grandmother are dead. You must let me be! You are persecuting me!"

In an instant the stairway door closed in the faces of her astonished elders. Uncle Edwin got out his handkerchief and wiped his eyes.

"Millerstown will think we are ugly to her," he said.

"I do not care what Millerstown thinks," declared the squire as he rose to go. "It is what *I* think. In the name of sense what has come over the girl?"

In her room Katy threw herself once more upon that oft-used refuge, her bed.

"If I could forget him," she moaned. "If I only could forget him. It is not right to think of him. I cannot be learned, but I can be good. It is wrong to think all the time of him." She remembered various women in the village who loved inconstant, unfaithful men. "I am a Mary Wolle! I am Sally Hersh! I am a shame to myself!"

Three times before September the squire reasoned with her. Even the doctor ventured to remonstrate.

"No Gaumer has ever done such a thing before, Katy."

"Well, you," said Katy with spirit, "are not a Gaumer, so you do not need to care."

At her Bevy stormed.

"You surely have one rafter too few or too many, Katy. There is something wrong with your little house! *Are* you crazy, Katy?"

"Yes," answered Katy, thus nearly paralyzing Bevy Schnepp. "I am."

In September Katy took up her abode at the Hartmans'. Millerstown saw her go with wonder. She carried a little satchel and walked with her chin in the air. Millerstown gazed out doors and windows to see whether the thing it had heard could be true.

"Ach, Katy!" protested Sarah Ann, "are you not going to be high gelernt?" Sarah Ann suspected some difficulty at home; her sympathetic soul was distressed for Katy. "You can come any time and live with me."

"Won't you ever go to your uncle any more?" asked Susannah Kuhns, her frank inquiry voicing the curiosity of Millerstown.

Katy turned and faced them.

"Why, certainly I will. I will go there every day."

Alvin Koehler had opened the Millerstown school and had already rented a house from William Knerr the elder. Katy saw him almost daily; he had even stopped her on the street to tell her that he had not forgotten her. He exuded satisfaction with himself from every pore; he would even have told her about his Bessie if Katy had lingered for an instant.

XIV. Katy Plans Her Life Once More

"She is not so good-looking as she once was, Katy is n't," said Alvin as he looked after her.

David Hartmen had gone when she reached his mother's house. Mrs. Hartman lay upon the settle in the kitchen. Her face was pale; she sat up with difficulty when Katy came in. She knew little of the affairs of Millerstown; she did not speculate about the reasons for Katy's presence in her house.

"It is a long time since my house was cleaned right," she complained. "We must begin at the top and clean everything. To-day, though, we will clean David's room. That is where you are to sleep. You can first scrub the cupboards and dust the books and put them away in the cupboard. He has many, many books and they gather dust so. Then stuff a dust-cloth tight under the door while you clean the rest. And take the bed apart so you can dust it well."

Mrs. Hartman lay down, breathless. The Gaumers had the reputation of being fine housekeepers; she hoped that her house would again be restored to cleanliness. Her son, with his untidy, mannish ways, was gone; peace had returned.

By Saturday Katy had become acquainted with the attic of the great house, the house which in her childhood had been to her the abode of Mystery. The attic, with its store of discarded but good furniture, its moth-guarded chests, was clean; it had been swept, whitewashed, aired, scrubbed, made immaculate. Each garment had been carried down to the yard, had there been beaten and sunned, and then had been restored to its proper place. Cassie, making her painful way to the third story, pronounced the work good. The next week the bedrooms were to be similarly treated. Into their magnificence Katy had peered, round-eyed. Here was no mystery, here was only grandeur. Thus Katy would have furnished her house.

On Saturday evening when work was done, Katy went down to sit with Aunt Sally. She was desperately tired; such toil as Cassie Hartman directed had not come within the Gaumer experience. But Katy was happier; that was plain even to the eyes of Aunt Sally, who shook her head over the strange puzzle. Katy had had no time for thinking. And into the putlock hole she had dropped a dollar and a half. The putlock hole was a safe bank; only a small hand like her own could reach into the inner depths into which she thrust her precious earnings.

CHAPTER XV

AN OLD WAY OUT OF A NEW TROUBLE

O<small>N</small> the morning of the 1st of September, Alvin dressed himself handsomely and went out the pike to the schoolhouse. The school board had, at his request, advanced his first month's salary, and with a part of it, though he was not to be married until January, he had paid the rent of the little house on Main Street, and with the rest he had bought a present for Bessie. It must be confessed that no generous spirit dictated Alvin's giving of gifts. It was a proper thing to give girls presents, thereby one made an impression upon them and upon their friends. But it also deprived the giver of luxuries. Alvin had begun to anticipate eagerly the time when he would no longer need to make presents to Bessie.

Bessie was a saleswoman in a store in a county seat; she received good wages and lived at home.

"What I earn is mine," she explained. "My pop buys even some of my clothes for me. I need only buy my fancy clothes. I have a nice account in the bank."

Bessie was a thrifty soul; she had made Alvin persuade his landlord, Billy Knerr, the elder, to take two dollars a month less than he had asked at first for the little house. She had planned already the style of furniture she wished for each room.

"It is to be oak in the dining-room," Alvin explained to Sarah Ann Mohr, with whom he took his meals. Alvin had reached that point in his self-satisfaction when he would have bragged to stones and trees if there had been no human creature at hand to listen. In Sarah Ann he had an eager hearer. Sarah Ann sat at close attention with parted lips and shining eyes. Sometimes she cried out, "Du liefer Friede" (Thou dear peace)! Or, "Bei meiner Seele" (By my soul)!

"There is to be a sideboard and a serving-table to match," went on Alvin.

Sarah Ann opened her mouth a little wider.

"What is a serving-table, Alvin?"

"A serving-table is a — it is — a — a table," explained Alvin. "You serve on it."

"Oh, of course," said Sarah Ann, without understanding in the least. "I am astonished, Alvin!"

"We are just going to furnish two bedrooms now. When we have a servant, then it will be time enough to furnish the other room."

Sarah Ann's eyelids fluttered up and down.

"A servant! Ach, Alvin, I hope you are not going to marry a sick one!"

XV. An Old Way Out Of A New Trouble

"Of course not," protested Alvin. "Of course not, Sarah Ann!" Alvin's chest expanded, he breathed deeply. "Ladies in the city do not do their own work, Sarah Ann!"

"Ladies!" repeated Sarah Ann. Here was the capstone of Alvin's grandeur. A lady was to Millerstown almost a mythical creature. "Are you, then, marrying a lady, Alvin?"

"To be sure," answered Alvin. "She never yet had to work in a kitchen. She is in the store just because she likes it. Her pop is rich."

"Do you mean she cannot cook, Alvin? Or wash? Or bake?"

"She could," said Alvin. "She could if she wanted to. But she does n't like it."

"Does n't like it!" As well might one say that Bessie did not like to sleep or eat or breathe! Sarah Ann's own breath was quite taken away. She shook her head ponderously, certain that either she or Alvin was going crazy. Then a question occurred to Sarah Ann. She had really a delicate sense of propriety; if she had stopped to think, she would not have asked the question. But it was out before she could restrain herself. "You will then bring your pop home from the poorhouse, I suppose, Alvin?"

Alvin blushed. He did not like to have any one mention his father.

"Father is not in the poorhouse because he is poor. He is there because he has lost his mind."

"Ach, Alvin, he is better, *indeed*, he is better! I was at the poorhouse to help with a prayer meeting, and, indeed, he is almost himself, Alvin."

Alvin rose from his seat on Sarah Ann's bench. The conversation had taken a turn he did not like.

"I could not have pop with Bessie," he insisted. "Pop could easily become violent."

When he had left her, Sarah Ann sat paralyzed. Her whole soul longed for the listening ear of Susannah Kuhns, but as yet her body had not gathered strength enough to transport itself to Susannah's house. Mercifully, the fates arranged that Susannah should observe the departing Alvin and should hurry over as fast as her feet could carry her. Susannah liked to hear Sarah Ann tell of the strange events of which she read, of the man whose head was turning into the head of a lion, of the dog who had learned to talk, of the woman who put glass into her husband's pies. But Susannah loved better to hear Sarah Ann tell of Alvin.

Now Susannah stood with arms akimbo, with shakes of head, with astonished clapping of lips together.

"This makes the understanding stand still," declared Susannah as she listened.

"He gave her a ring already," went on Sarah Ann. "He has a wedding present ready for her. He let himself be enlarged from a photograph and he has a big picture. He carries a cane in the picture. He has it hung up already in his house. He said I should come over once and he would show it to me."

In Alvin's course at the normal school he had studied not only pedagogy and psychology, but he had had practical experience in teaching. Connected with the normal school was a model school. There, in a light and airy room whose windows were filled with blooming plants and whose walls were decked with pictures, Alvin had given the "May lesson," a half-hour of instruction in the blossoms and birds of spring. Vases of snowballs and iris and dishes of bluets and violets served as illustrations for his remarks; he had also pictures of flickers and robins. His class was orderly and polite. For a month he had prepared for this half-hour of teaching; he had even reviewed with the superintendent of the model school what he meant to say and had received her advice and approval. Alvin thought so much about himself and so little about any other subject that he had by this time forgotten the ways of the Millerstown school. The Millerstown school and the model school were not much alike.

He received after his lesson was over a commendatory letter from the superintendent, the same letter which he had proudly exhibited to Edwin Gaumer and the other directors. The superintendent said that he was a young man of good presence, that he had thoroughly mastered his subject, that he had held the interest of his pupils throughout his teaching period, and had maintained perfect discipline. The superintendent did not say that she herself was a stern person, whom no child would disobey, and that she had remained in the room while the lesson was in progress. The model school superintendent could, to be sure, have conducted the lesson no differently. It would hardly have been wise to train the model school children to test the disciplinary powers of the teachers by insubordination, in order that the teachers might be trained in the various methods for quelling riots!

On the 1st day of September, Alvin put on his best suit and went to school. He had been carefully instructed in the importance of first impressions, the necessity for brightness and cheerfulness of hue as well as of disposition in the schoolroom. He had quite forgotten that the Millerstown teachers were expected to dust and sweep the room in which they taught.

He looked for his scholars along the road, but could see none of them. He had forgotten also the custom which awarded the best seat, which was always the rear seat, to the first comer. In his own day he had frequently arrived at the schoolhouse at seven o'clock of the opening day to discover that there were half a dozen boys ahead of him.

XV. An Old Way Out Of A New Trouble

The children, trained finally by Mr. Carpenter into some respect for the office of teacher, answered politely the good-morning with which Alvin had been instructed to begin the school day. They sang with gusto the familiar, —

> "O the joys of childhood,
> Roaming through the wild wood,
> Running o'er the meadows,
> Happy and free," —

a favorite for several generations, since it gave full opportunity for the use of the human voice. Then the children set themselves with gratifying diligence to a study of the lessons which Alvin assigned them. Alvin had notebooks in which were Outlines of Work for Primary Schools, Outlines of Work for Secondary Schools, Outlines of Work for Ungraded Schools, and the like. Here also were plans for Nature Work and Number Work, and various other kinds of Works whose names at least were new in the curriculum of the Millerstown school. The children took kindly enough to them all; they went quietly about their tasks. The discipline of school was pleasant. The older girls smiled at Alvin and blushed when he spoke.

To Sarah Ann, Alvin imparted daily fresh plans made by him and his Bessie for the furnishing of their house.

"We have changed to mahogany for the dining-room. Oak is not fashionable any more. People are getting rid of their oak." In these statements Alvin quoted from the clerk in a furniture store who had showed to him and Bessie a new mahogany set of dining-room furniture. "We have picked out our things already."

Sarah Ann did not know much about the various kinds of wood, but mahogany was a longer word than oak, and the furniture made of that wood was probably the finest that could be had. As a matter of fact, Sarah Ann had in her house without knowing it several fine pieces of mahogany. Sarah Ann told Susannah about Alvin's plans and they spread promptly over Millerstown.

"It is a rich girl, for sure," said Millerstown.

Once the young lady herself appeared to inspect Alvin's house. Millerstown saw the two step from the car and appraised the furs and the feathered hat as well as they could, considering that furs and feathers were not in general use in Millerstown except upon the backs of the creatures who wore them naturally. Millerstown was astonished and Millerstown admired. Katy Gaumer, returning from an hour spent with her Aunt Sally, her feathers a scarlet nubia, her furs a crimson shawl, blushed first scarlet and then crimson as she came upon Alvin and his lady, and went on her way choking back something in her throat. Alvin took his Bessie directly to Sarah Ann's house, and Sarah Ann, embarrassed and silent, accompanied them upon their tour of inspection. Sarah Ann could not explain exactly why she was invited.

"It is something about fashion," she explained to Susannah. "The young folks are nowadays not to be alone."

Susannah laughed a scornful laugh.

"These must be fine young folks nowadays, if they cannot be trusted fifteen minutes to walk alone through a cold house!"

Upon the strength of Alvin's good position, and of Sarah Ann's account of the riches of the young lady's father, and of a dazzling glimpse of the young lady herself, Billy Knerr trusted Alvin for the second and the third and the fourth month's rent of his house, the school board continued to pay Alvin in advance, and the coal dealer let him have three tons of coal on credit. An Allentown tailor made him a new winter suit on the same terms, and Sarah Ann let him stay on without reminding him of his board bill. Alvin hated to pay for commodities which could be eaten, like potatoes, or which could be burned up, like coal. When the coal was in the cellar, he forgot entirely that presently there would be a bill. Alvin was wholly happy; there were moments when the contemplation of his good fortune made him dizzy.

On Sunday evenings Alvin continued his attendance at the Millerstown churches. He meant to ally himself finally with one of them, the Lutheran, probably, since the Weygandts and Gaumers and Fackenthals were Lutheran. He still visited, however, the church of the Improved New Mennonites where Essie Hill blushed deeply under her plain hat as he approached. There was a new legend upon Essie's hat. Instead of being a worker in the vineyard, she was now a soldier in the kingdom. David Hartman still sat occasionally with her upon her doorstep. Again her father spoke to her about him.

"You can't marry anybody outside the church, Essie."

"No, pop."

Into the Reverend Mr. Hill's somber eyes there came for an instant a hopeful gleam.

"Perhaps we could get him in the church?"

"Perhaps," agreed Essie. "I talk to him sometimes."

It was in December when Fate turned against Alvin. Alvin had now burned his supply of coal and was angrily refused more. Alvin's Allentown tailor, failing to receive replies to his letter, sent a collector to interview Alvin, an insistent person who, failing to find him at home, visited him at the schoolhouse. Even Sarah Ann, who was patience personified, reminded her boarder gently that she had fed him for four months without any return.

"I did it to earn a little extra missionary money, Alvin," explained Sarah Ann. "We have at this time of the year always a Thank Offering. I thought I would earn this to put in my box."

In December, the spirit of evil entered the Millerstown school. The familiar sound of twanging wires, of slamming desk lids, the soft slap of moistened paper balls striking the blackboards, were the first warnings of the rise of rebellion. The Millerstown children had not enough to do. Their teacher had reached the end of his outlines and knew not how to make more. He was desperately tired of teaching; he could not understand how he could ever have supposed that Mr. Carpenter had an easy or a pleasant time.

One morning when he entered the schoolroom, he found the blackboard decorated with a caricature of himself, labeled with the insulting appellation which Susannah Kuhns had once bestowed upon him, "Der Fratzhans." There were only two pupils who were skillful enough to have drawn so lifelike a representation of their teacher; they were two of the four large girls in the upper class, of whose admiration Alvin had been certain. It was a cruel blow for poor Alvin.

Again the collector who represented the tailor visited him. This time he met Alvin on Main Street, in front of the post-office, and at the top of his loud and unfeeling voice, demanded instant payment.

"I will get it," promised Alvin. "Till Monday I will have it for sure."

It must be said in justice to Alvin that he did not think at once of making application to Katy Gaumer for succor in his financial situation. To his Bessie he offered no such slight as that. But succor Alvin must have. He knew so little about the law that he feared he might be cast into prison. When he had got rid of the insulting creature and his demands, he dressed himself in the suit under discussion and at once sought Bessie at her father's house in the county seat.

There, alas! Alvin did not behave in a manner befitting one whose education and manners were so fine. He asked Bessie plainly and frankly for a loan, having been led by Miss Katy Gaumer to expect an immediate and favorable response from any female whom he honored with such a request. To his astonishment Bessie stared at him rudely.

"Why do you want money?"

"To pay a few things."

"Don't you have any money?"

"It is n't time yet for my salary." In reality Alvin had been paid as at first, in advance.

"Don't you have any money in the bank?"

"Why, no!" It had never occurred to Alvin to do anything with money but spend it.

"Have you paid for the furniture?"

"The furniture?" repeated Alvin weakly.

"Yes, the furniture." Bessie was growing redder and redder, her voice sharper. "The furniture you and I picked out this long while!"

"Why, no," confessed Alvin, "I thought that you — that you would — would —"

"You thought *I* would pay for it!" Bessie's voice rose so high that her whole family might have heard if they had not considerately left the house to her and her beau. "Well, you were mistaken!" — Bessie was a slangy person, she said that Alvin was "stung." "And here" — Bessie ran upstairs and returned with a letter — "here is this. I thought, of course, this was a mistake. I paid no attention to it. Open it!"

Alvin grew pale. He recognized, before the envelope was in his hand, the business card on the corner. The bill for Bessie's ring had come to him many times. Now upon the bill Bessie laid the ring itself.

"There!" said she.

Alvin remembered suddenly how David Hartman had appeared on the mountain long ago and had hurled himself upon him. He had now much the same sensations.

"Do you mean that it is over?" he faltered in a dazed tone.

"Yes," answered Bessie in a very firm, decided tone; "I mean just that."

After Alvin had carried the ring back to the jeweler, a way suggested itself of paying the tailor. He returned his beautiful best winter suit, worn but a very few times, and received some credit on his bill. The balance, alas! remained, and the tailor seemed but slightly mollified by his humility. The coal bill remained also, but the coal had been burned and could not be restored to the dealer. The landlord had also been deprived of the rent for his house, the food had been eaten. What Alvin should do about the landlord and about Sarah Ann he did not know. Alvin had a sad Christmas.

January and February passed slowly. Alvin was still too proud to confess to Millerstown that Bessie had jilted him; he paid a little on his great rent bill as means of staving off the discovery a little longer. The children in school became entirely ungovernable, their invention more brilliant and demoniacal. The stovepipe fell with a crash to the floor, the flying soot blackening the faces of teacher and pupils alike. Alvin found his overshoes filled with powdered chalk and damp sponges; he met fresh pictures of himself when he opened the door. When he undertook in

XV. An Old Way Out Of A New Trouble

midwinter to raise a mustache there appeared promptly upon the upper lip of most of his pupils a dark and suggestive line. The children grew more impertinent, the bills more pressing. In despair Alvin climbed the hill and ransacked the little house where he had lived with his father. He thought bitterly of William, who had squandered his money on madness, and who had given his son so unpleasant a life.

He found nothing in the little house. As he shut the door behind him, he remembered how John Hartman had sat dead in his buggy before the gate as he and Katy came down the mountain road.

At once a warm glow flooded the soul of Alvin. How comforting had been the touch of Katy on that frightful day, how brave she had been! How kind Katy had been to him always, how freely she had granted all he asked! And now Katy was rich, she had doubtless inherited a good deal of money from her grandmother, and she was earning dear knows what liberal salary at the rich Hartmans'. She had come to take a sensible view of education; she had decided, Alvin was certain, that it counted for nothing. To Katy his heart warmed. He remembered her with tears.

At once Alvin hastened back to his little house, and there, sitting straightway down at his table, indited a letter. Composition was easy; he had long ago written a model.

> "Dear, dear Katy, — I am in great trouble. I need a little money. If you have any, Katy, say about $25, put it in the hole in the wall. Katy, say you will." Then Alvin added a postscript. "I am not going to marry, Katy. I have broken it all off."

But Alvin did not present his letter. Instead, he held it until he should have made trial of another expedient. Perhaps some fragment of Katy's earlier largess still remained in the putlock hole!

That evening Alvin attended service at the church of the Improved New Mennonites. He was so unhappy that he dared not be alone, and in the church of the Improved New Mennonites he would meet none of his creditors, all of whom belonged to the larger, longer established churches. Here, too, Essie smiled at him. Essie was a comfortable person; she was neither ambitious for learning nor scornful of those who had no money. The preacher exhorted his congregation to make a fresh start; this Alvin determined to do.

On the way home he made a détour through the open fields until he reached the back of the Gaumer garden. Through the garden he crept softly. The night was dark, the wind whistled mournfully through the doors of the Gaumer barn. Alvin slipped and fell when his foot sank into the burrow of a mole. But Alvin pressed on.

When he put his hand into the putlock hole and his fingers touched the hard stone, he could have sunk to the ground with disappointment. Again he thrust in his hand and could find nothing. A third time he tried, pushing his cuff back on his arm so as to insert his hand as far as possible. A fourth time he reached in vain. In the old days when Katy had laid there for him the fat bills, they had always been within easy reach. Finally, in the last gasp of hope, he took from his pocket a long lead pencil and felt about with its tip. The broad stone which formed the floor of the putlock hole sloped; there, in the little pit at the back, Alvin's pencil touched an object which he could move about.

After much prying he drew it forth, a round half-dollar, a part of the last wages which Katy had received from Mrs. Hartman.

He held it in his hand and tried desperately to reach its fellow. Surely the Fates would not mock him with a half-dollar when his needs were so great! To-morrow evening he would bring a bent wire and see what he could do with that.

With the blessed coin in his hand, Alvin turned his steps homeward.

CHAPTER XVI
BEVY PUTS A HEX ON ALVIN

AFTER Katy had cleaned the Hartman attic, she cleaned one by one the Hartman bedrooms. Cupboards and closets were emptied of their contents; clothes, blankets, great, thick comforts were carried to the yard and there were beaten and aired and restored to their places. Carpets were taken up to be put through the same process and then were nailed down once more to the floor, with mighty stretching of arms and pulling of fingers. Floors were scrubbed, paint was wiped, windows were polished; even the outside of the house was washed, the walls being approached by a leaning down from the upper windows, long-handled brush well in hand, and a stretching up from the lower windows. Any well-trained Pennsylvania German housewife is amply able to superintend the putting in order of an operating-room in a hospital.

Mrs. Hartman superintended the cleaning, though she was able to take no part. She lay day after day on the old settle in the kitchen and was helped night after night to her bed. She did not like to be helped; if she could make the journey herself while Katy was for a moment busy elsewhere, or when Katy had run down to sit for a few minutes with her Aunt Sally, she was well pleased. As the hoard in Katy's bank grew, Katy's heart became lighter, her tongue moved with some of its old gayety. But Cassie made no answer; she said nothing, indeed, from day's beginning to day's end, except to give Katy directions about her work. Dr. Benner came occasionally to see her, rather as one who watches the progress of an incurable disease than as one who hopes to stay its course. The Lutheran preacher visited her and was received with all appropriate ceremony. Then, according to the old German custom, all work ceased and family waited upon its guest. In nothing outside her house was Cassie interested. It seemed that for Cassie the springs of life had at last run dry.

When her day's work was done, Katy went to her room and read half the night away. David had brought home the sets of standard works in beautiful bindings which he had bought from agents who visited the college; and now into the stories of Scott and Dickens and Thackeray, stored by Cassie's command in David's cupboard, Katy plunged as a diver plunges into a stream. The books had not been packed away in any order of author or subject; upon them Katy seized as they came to hand. When she could not understand what she read — and there were many poems and essays at which Katy blinked without comprehension — she cried, thinking with bitter regret and heartache that now she might have been in school.

"And I am a servant girl!" sighed Katy. "It is no shame to be a servant girl, but it is a black shame for me!"

Daily she made mental reckoning of the silver dollars and half-dollars accumulating in the putlock hole.

"But there are the two hundred dollars!" she cried. "What shall I say to them about the two hundred dollars! Perhaps when I have paid the squire his fifty dollars, I could tell him that the two hundred dollars was gone and he could get uncle to give me some of my money. Perhaps I can sing again!" The pictures of foreign places in a beautiful book of David's made her heart throb. "Once I thought I could see all such places!"

Then Katy hid her face in her hands and David's beautiful book slid from her lap to the floor.

At Christmas time David Hartman came home. He had attained his full height; his gray eyes looked clearly into the eyes of those who spoke to him. He stood at the head of his class; he had gained confidence in himself. He had asked his mother for a larger allowance and had received it promptly. It amused him to flaunt his money in the eyes of the college, to spend large sums as though they were nothing. He brought his mother handsome presents, and his mother had handsome presents for him. It seemed as though he and she finally understood each other. Of resting his head on any one's shoulder, David thought no more; into his throat came no choking sensations as of old. At Millerstown's pronunciations and Millerstown's customs David laughed. When it was necessary for Katy to be with him, she recounted to him the Millerstown news and David listened politely. Presently it seemed to Katy that he was laughing at her; then she said no more. It was not necessary for them to have much speech together; Katy went down to her Aunt Sally's to sleep while David was at home, leaving the Hartman house soon after supper. During the day she did not see him except in his mother's presence.

"I have read some of your books," she told him one afternoon when she sat at the window sewing and he sat on the opposite side of the kitchen with a book, and Cassie lay asleep on the settle between them.

"That is right," said David. "I hope you have enjoyed them."

"I did." Katy laid down her sewing. If she could talk about these books with David! "I read first of all Wanity —" oh, terrible slip of a tongue which knew better! "I mean Vanity Fair!"

A flash came into David's eyes, a flash of bitter reminiscence. To Katy it was a flash of amusement.

"Vanity Fair is a fine book," said David. But David's tongue betrayed him again. David, too, said "Wanity." To Katy the tone was mocking.

XVI. Bevy Puts A Hex On Alvin

Katy said no more. Katy went to visit her Aunt Sally even in the afternoons.

"I am brutish as the ox and the ass," quoted Katy.

When the preacher came to see David she could not slip away, though she tried hard. She had to listen to the two discussing David's work. She was even unfamiliar with the names of some of his studies.

David, to the awe and envy of his college mates, had for some time kept a riding-horse. He rode while he was at home on a young horse of the Weygandts' which Jimmie had trained to the saddle. Millerstown watched him with admiration as he galloped along the village streets in curious riding-clothes; the squire shook his head over him. The squire was Cassie's adviser; he knew the extent of the fortune which David was to inherit; he was well acquainted also with the curious mental inheritance which was David's. He could not get on with David, who was as taciturn as his parents.

David rode about to all his mother's farms and orchards and to the fine woodland on the mountain with its precious soil. Many persons were dependent upon the Hartman estate for their livelihood, more would be dependent when the mines could be opened again. There came into David's mind as he rode homeward a dim vision like the vision his father had seen of a happy community of which he should be the head. But David did not try to make his vision clear to himself. He was passing the poorhouse and his thoughts turned to the Koehler family. Alvin he hated; with Alvin he still owed the settlement of a debt, even though Katy Gaumer seemed to think of him no more. William Koehler himself had been punished; he was praying and gibbering somewhere behind the walls of the poorhouse. David thought of his father, and the rage of his youth against the Koehlers swelled his heart again almost to bursting. Without exception he hated Millerstown.

Nevertheless, David went once or twice to see the little Improved New Mennonite, a proceeding which amazed and disgusted Millerstown. Susannah Kuhns expressed to Katy Millerstown's opinion that that connection would "give a match"; then she recounted to Katy at great length the ambitious plans of Alvin and his bride.

When David returned to school, Katy went back to her room in the Hartman house. Christmas had been dreary with its memories and its contrasts with the past; Katy was not sorry to have again constant occupation for her mind and her hands. She straightened out the slight disorder caused by the presence of David; she got the meals as usual; she exchanged a few words with the invalid; and when the quiet of night had settled upon the house, she lit the lamp in her room and opened the beautiful illustrated book at the page upon which she had closed it. But Katy did not proceed with the account of the Coliseum. Katy closed the book, and drawing her scarlet shawl a little closer about her shoulders, laid her cheek down on the bureau. Katy was again obsessed. She saw David's clear, gray eyes, looking at her in astonishment as she applied for a servant's place in his mother's house. She heard his speech, so unlike her own; he seemed to stand close beside her. She saw again that flicker of amusement in his eyes, heard again that unconscious mockery. David was a part of the great world into which she had expected to fare forth. David was English. David was as far above her as the stars.

"He was n't in the beginning!" cried Katy. "I have made myself what I am. I am mean and low and ignorant."

Then Katy rose from her chair and clasped her hands across her heart.

"Am I to have *this* again?" cried Katy. "Alvin is only just out of my mind. What am I to do? What *am* I to do? What am I made of? I am worse than Mary Wolle and Sally Hersh. If I cannot have one in my mind to worry me, then I must have another. Am I to have no peace in this world?"

Katy looked about the little room with its narrow bed, its little bureau, its single chair, its cupboard crowded with books. Katy remembered that this was David's room, that here he slept, had slept only last night. Katy knelt down by the bed and began to pray, not for David, but for herself.

By morning Katy had made a firm resolution.

"I will think only of this money. I have twenty-four dollars saved. In four months I will be free of my debt."

January, February, and March saw poor Cassie growing weaker and more silent, saw Katy's hoard swelling.

"It is thirty dollars!" said she. "Now it is thirty-six dollars!" "Now it is forty-two dollars!" Frequently Katy thanked God. A little lighter grew her heart.

One evening in March a sudden uneasiness overwhelmed her.

"I will go down and count it," said she. "Perhaps I should put it in a safer place. But no one knows that the hole is there but a few people, and no one could get a hand into the bottom but me."

It was not Saturday; Katy had no sum to add to the deposit; but she wrapped her shawl about her and went down to the Gaumer house. There, laughing at herself for her uneasiness, she rolled back her sleeve and thrust her arm deep into her hiding-place. Then she stood perfectly still and with a moan began to feel about. The little pit had no outlet; it was still safe and dry, a capital hiding-place, provided one kept its existence to one's self, but it was empty.

XVI. Bevy Puts A Hex On Alvin

At first Katy could not believe the evidence of her senses. Frantically she thrust in her hand, reluctantly she drew it out and felt of it with the other hand and even laid it along her cheek. It was not until she had repeated this process several times that she was able to appreciate the truth. The putlock hole was empty, her hard-earned hoard was gone, freedom from debt cruelly postponed.

Then Katy, who had so bravely hidden her various troubles from Millerstown and from her kin, began to cry like a crazy person. She struck at the hard stone wall until her hands bled; she ran, crying and sobbing, to her Uncle Edwin's door, and burst it open, frightening him and Aunt Sally nearly out of their wits as they sat by the kitchen table.

"My money is gone!" she cried, seizing Uncle Edwin by the arm. "I tell you my money is gone! It is stolen! It is not there! Somebody has run away with it!"

"Your money!" gasped Uncle Edwin, struggling to his feet. "What money? Where had you money, Katy? Who stole it? In Heaven's name, Katy, what is wrong?"

Katy sank down on the old settle and stared at them wildly.

"I had money in the hole in the wall."

"What hole in the wall, Katy?"

"Right here in this wall, where Bevy put cakes for me when I was little and lived with my gran'pop. I had all my money that I ever earned there — it was forty-two dollars. Cassie would tell you that she gave me forty-two dollars already, or you could count it up by weeks. On Saturday evening it was there, and now it is gone. Oh, what shall I do, what shall I do?"

Katy began to wring her hands; Aunt Sally besought her, weeping, to lie down; Uncle Edwin reached to the high mantel-shelf where he had laid his gun out of little Adam's reach.

"There is no one there now!" cried Katy. "It is no use to go now! I can reach to the bottom of the hole and there is not a penny there." She began to repeat what she had said. "My money is gone! My money is gone!" William Koehler when he was accused of stealing the communion service had behaved no more crazily.

"I will go for the squire," said Uncle Edwin, moving toward the door, gun in hand. "That is the first thing to do."

Then Uncle Edwin paused. From without rose a fearful uproar. There were loud cries in a man's voice, there were shrill reproaches and commands in a woman's. There were even squeals. Aunt Sally added her screams to those which proceeded from without. Uncle Edwin advanced boldly, his empty gun lifted to his shoulder.

"It is Bevy!" cried Aunt Sally. "Some one has Bevy!"

Bravely Aunt Sally followed Uncle Edwin; weeping Katy followed Aunt Sally. At the corner of the house they paused in unspeakable amazement.

The squire had opened his door; from it a broad shaft of light shot out across the lawn which separated the two houses. It illuminated brightly the opening of the putlock hole and its vicinity. There an extraordinary tableau presented itself to the eyes of Katy Gaumer and her kin. The center of the stage was occupied by Bevy and a struggling man. Over his head Bevy had thrown her gingham apron; she twisted it now tightly like a tourniquet and screamed for help.

"Thief! Thief!" shouted Bevy.

"My ear! My ear!" cried a muffled voice from beneath the apron, a voice recognized immediately by one at least of the astonished spectators.

"I do not care for your ear," screamed Bevy. "Your ear is nothing to me. You were stealing! What is that you have stolen?"

Wildly Alvin tried to free himself; frantically Bevy clung to him. Bevy now found an ally in Uncle Edwin, who seized the prisoner in a firm grasp.

"Whoa, there!" cried Uncle Edwin. "I have him, Bevy. I have him by the arm. You can let him go."

There was the sound of approaching footsteps, of opening doors, there were questions and outcries.

"What is it?"

"I heard some one yelling."

"Shall I bring a gun?"

"It was a pig that squealed!"

"What is wrong with everybody?"

The squire came flying across the lawn. He saw as he opened the door the struggling Alvin and the excited Bevy and Edwin Gaumer armed here on this peaceful night with a gun. He saw also his grandniece with her flaming cheeks, her swollen eyes, her disheveled hair. The squire did not know what had happened, but he closed his door behind him so that the scene should be no longer illuminated.

"Nothing is wrong," he declared sternly. "Nobody shall bring a gun."

With a gesture he ordered his kinsfolk and Bevy and her prey into his office; with an arm thrown across her shoulders he protected his niece from further observation. Then, cruelly, upon Millerstown he shut his office door. For a while Millerstown hung about; then having recognized no one but the squire, and neither able to see nor to hear further, departed for their several homes.

XVI. Bevy Puts A Hex On Alvin

Inside the squire locked the door and motioned his excited guests to seats. If Katy had had her way she would have died on the spot, she would have sunk into the earth and would have been swallowed up. But with the squire's arm about her she could do nothing but proceed to his office with the rest.

The squire looked from one to the other, from Edwin with his gun to Aunt Sally with her round and staring eyes; from Bevy to Alvin, who smoothed his hair and laid a protecting hand over his suffering ear.

"What on earth is the matter with you people?" he demanded. "Has war broken out in Millerstown?"

At once began an indescribable clamor.

"I was going over to Sally a little —" this was Bevy. "I saw him." Bevy indicated her prisoner with a contemptuous gesture. "He was digging in the hole, and I —"

"You did n't!" contradicted Alvin. "You did n't!"

"What hole?" asked the squire.

"Do you dare to say I did n't take you by the ear?" cried Bevy with threatening fingers lifted toward that aching member.

"The hole where Katy had her money," explained Edwin.

"It was stolen," cried Aunt Sally.

"I did n't!" protested Alvin again, his face green with fright. He blamed his own greediness for the discovery. On Sunday evening he had taken all Katy's hoard; why had he been so mad as to return to seek more?

"A mule is a mule," proclaimed Bevy Schnepp. "A Koehler is a Koehler. They steal; you cannot better them by education; they are all the time the same, they —"

"Be still, Bevy!" commanded the squire.

But Bevy would not be still. She gave another scream and began to dance up and down in her grasshopper-like fashion.

"Look at him, once! He says he did n't, does he? Look once what he has in his hand!"

At once all eyes turned with closer scrutiny upon Alvin. He still held in his hand the implement with which he had coaxed Katy's dollars and half-dollars from the depths of the putlock hole. It was only a bit of twisted wire, but it had done its work well.

"Like father, like son!" screamed Bevy again. "What did I say? Where did he get the money to get educated? Where —"

"Bevy, be still!" commanded the squire in a sterner tone. "Katy, did you keep your money in the putlock hole?"

"Yes," answered Katy in a low voice. Here, face to face with Alvin, she remembered all the past, her long vigils on the porch when she watched for him, his kiss in the shadow, his later, different kisses, his ingratitude, her shame. Katy's head sank lower and lower on her breast.

"Why did you select such a place for a bank, Katy?"

"I used to keep things there when I was a little girl. Into the deep part nobody could put a hand but me. That is why I thought it was safe."

The squire looked more and more angry. His voice sank deeper and deeper in his throat.

"You did n't count on bent wire, did you? How much money did you have there, Katy?"

Katy answered so faintly that the squire could not hear.

"She said forty-two dollars," answered Uncle Edwin for her. Uncle Edwin had now stationed himself behind Alvin; at Alvin's slightest motion he put forth a hand to seize him. The Gaumers had not been able to defend their kinswoman from her own incomprehensible foolishness, but from such bold assault from without they were amply able to protect her.

"Is this so, Katy?" asked the squire.

Katy's head sank on her breast. "Yes, sir."

"Alvin, look at me!"

Alvin lifted his head slowly. He saw jail yawning before him. If they searched his house, they could still find a few of Katy's silver coins. Then under the pressure of fear — Alvin as yet felt no shame — his mind worked to some purpose. There was one possible defense to make; this he offered.

"Katy often gave me money and put it in that place for me," he said, boldly. "There I got it many times. Ain't —" Alvin's normal school training suddenly forsook him — "ain't it so, Katy?"

"You must be wandering in your mind, Alvin," said the squire, scornfully.

"There he will not wander far," cried Bevy with a shrill laugh.

Alvin rose from his chair and approached Katy. Color returned to his cheek, his eyes brightened.

"Ain't it so, Katy, that you often put money in that hole for me?"

"Humbug!" cried the squire.

But Alvin persisted. He went nearer to Katy, and with single united motion Katy's relatives sprang toward him. Aunt Sally put her arm round her niece, Bevy made a threatening motion toward Alvin's ear, Uncle Edwin seized him by the arm. But Alvin grew ever bolder. Despite the threats of Bevy and the hand of Edwin, he took another step toward Katy.

"Say you gave money to me often, Katy?"

XVI. Bevy Puts A Hex On Alvin

Katy answered in a low voice. She was too confused to think of any expedient; she answered with the truth. Perhaps that would put an end to this intolerable scene. It would be bad enough to have them know, but it was worse to stand here in misery with them all staring at her.

"Yes," she answered Alvin, "I did give you sometimes money."

"What!" cried the squire.

Uncle Edwin and Bevy each gave a kind of groan.

Katy lifted her head.

"I said 'yes.'"

Now Bevy began to cry aloud.

"Next time I will not take you to the squire, you lump! Next time I will twist your ear quite off. I will settle you right!"

"Bevy, you had better go," suggested the squire; and meekly Bevy departed.

"Edwin, suppose you and Sally leave these young people here."

Together Uncle Edwin and Aunt Sally approached the door. Aunt Sally was wiping her eyes on her apron; Uncle Edwin walked with bent head as though the name of Gaumer was disgraced forever. Them the squire followed to the door, and outside, wishing to be certain that no curious Millerstonians lingered. With his hand on the outer knob, he closed the door while he promised to see Edwin later in the evening. Edwin stopped to express his horror at this strange situation; their conversation consumed a few seconds at least.

Behind the closed door Alvin approached Katy as she stood by the squire's desk, numb, smitten, unable to raise her head.

"Katy," said he, softly, "I do not care if you have worked out, Katy. That is less than nothing to me. I am never going to marry that other one. She is no good. I will marry you, Katy. I did not know" — Alvin's voice shook — "I did not know till this time how I love you, Katy."

At this point Alvin laid his hand upon Katy's arm and applied a tender pressure.

Then, suddenly, furiously, Alvin was flung aside, back against the sharp point of the squire's desk. Young women do not keep house in the Pennsylvania German fashion, with sweeping and scrubbing and beating of carpets, without developing considerable muscular power. Terrified, bruised by contact with the sharp corner of the desk, Alvin lifted hands to defend himself from Katy, whose worth he had learned so suddenly to value.

Katy, however, stayed to punish him no further. Instead, she rushed across the room and threw herself into the arms of the squire. She spoke shrilly, she sobbed and cried.

"Send him away and let me talk to you alone! I must talk to you! Oh, please send him away!"

Alvin needed no orders. He read in the squire's expression permission to depart, and he slipped sidewise out the door, making himself as small as possible for the passage.

When the door had closed behind him, the squire put Katy into a corner of the sofa in his back office and sat down beside her.

"Now, Katy, begin."

With tears and hysterical laughter, Katy began her story.

"I thought I was so fine and powerful when I helped him. I thought I was rich with my two hundred dollars and that I could do anything. I thought he had no chance and I would help him. I pitied him because he had a bad name from his father. The worst thing was I liked him. Oh, dear! Oh, dear!"

The squire's frown grew blacker and blacker.

"He took the money and never paid any of it back, and then stole this from you yet! Money you were saving to pay me! Money you had borrowed for him! Oh, Katy, Katy!" Then, suddenly, the squire laughed. "Katy, dear, I bought a gold brick like this once. It wasn't just like this, but it cost me much more. We've got to learn, all of us! Oh, you poor soul! And my gold brick was not bought for the sake of charity, Katy!" The squire laughed and Katy cried and cried as her head rested upon the broad shoulder which had been offered to her earlier. "Now, Katy, it is late and I will take you home."

The squire put Katy's scarlet shawl about her and took her by the arm, and together they went up the misty street. At the Hartmans' gate the squire left his companion. Then, with a quicker stride he sought the house of Alvin Koehler.

CHAPTER XVII
ALVIN DOES PENANCE AND IS SHRIVEN

THE squire stayed for fifteen minutes with Alvin Koehler; when he left, Alvin was limp; he sat in his little house and wept. Hitherto in his life Alvin had had grave difficulties; he had been unhappy in his poverty; he had been embarrassed by the queerness of his father; he had been disturbed when he feared that Katy Gaumer would not keep her promise and help him go to school; he had been terrified by the behavior of the Millerstown children and by the overshadowing cloud of his unpaid bills.

But now a new emotion filled his heart and weighed down his spirit. He was now, for the first time, bitterly ashamed. He had told the squire all his misery; his debt to the storekeeper, to the landlord, to Sarah Ann, to Katy, to the coal dealer, to the jeweler, to the tailor. He had a notion that in thus confessing he was doing penance. He had also a vain and foolish hope that the squire might offer to help him.

"I am turned inside out," he mourned when the squire had gone. "There is nothing to me any more."

It was on Friday that Alvin was caught, wire in hand, investigating the contents of Katy's putlock bank. That night he did not sleep. He sat by his table, pencil in hand, contemplating the problem which confronted him and trying to work out a sum in proportion. If he owed Katy two hundred and fifty dollars, and Sarah Ann Mohr twenty dollars, and the landlord fifty-eight dollars, and the coal dealer fifteen dollars, and the tailor thirty dollars, how much of his next month's salary should justly go to each — provided, of course, that he were not summarily dismissed from his position and thus deprived of his salary? Over the difficult problem he fell asleep toward morning.

He did not go to Sarah Ann's for breakfast, a fact which caused Sarah Ann no uneasiness, as he usually took advantage of the Saturday holiday to sleep late and thus make a good recovery from the exhaustion following his arduous association with the Millerstown children. Besides, another subject had this morning the whole of Sarah Ann's attention and the attention of Millerstown. Cassie Hartman had died suddenly in the night.

Nor did Alvin go to Sarah Ann's for dinner, but supported life with some crackers and apples which were in his house. It seemed to him that the passersby looked curiously at his dwelling; he was certain that the story of his difficulties had spread over Millerstown. Who could ever have dreamed that Katy would treat him so shabbily?

Late in the afternoon there came a ponderous step along his board walk and a knock at the door. Terrified, Alvin sat still until the rap was repeated, then he opened the door a tiny crack. Without stood a no more terrifying person than Sarah Ann.

At sight of Sarah Ann, however, Alvin trembled. Sarah Ann had again reminded him, gently but with firmness, that her Thank Offering was long overdue.

"I made it up out of the money I keep for regular collections, Alvin," Sarah Ann had explained. "I keep that money in a little can. But now that little can is empty. I have nothing for General Fund."

"I cannot pay you." Thus Alvin greeted her miserably through an inch-wide crack. "I will try to pay you sometime, Sarah Ann, but I cannot pay you now."

"I am not here for pay," protested Sarah Ann, weeping. "It is not a day for collecting money in Millerstown. Poor Cassie is gone."

"Cassie?" repeated Alvin, vacantly. So engrossed was Alvin with his own joys in time of joy, and with his own sorrows in time of sorrow, that persons not immediately associated with him disappeared entirely from the circle of his consciousness.

"Why, yes, Cassie Hartman, David's mom. David is now an orphan."

Alvin shook his head solemnly at this intelligence, remembering that he was practically an orphan, too. Beyond that he did not consider the situation. He felt no satisfaction at the Hartmans' misfortune; he had never cherished any animosity toward them, but only a vague envy of their worldly possessions.

"I am here now to see why you did not come to your dinner," went on Sarah Ann. "The folks say you are not going to get married, after all, Alvin. Is it so, Alvin? I thought you were sick. I had Sauerkraut for dinner, but still you did not come. I can heat it for supper. Ach, there is nothing but trouble in this world!"

Alvin desired to tell Sarah Ann all his woes. Like the Ancient Mariner, he would find relief in recounting the story of his griefs. But he was now too weak to do anything but select a hat from the row hanging behind the door. So low was he in his mind that he chose the shabbiest one of all. Then he followed Sarah Ann down the street. It seemed to him that there were many inches between the front of his body and his vest. He was certain that he had lost many pounds, and he thought that perhaps he would waste away. That, he decided gloomily, would be one solution of his troubles.

Once fed, Alvin felt his spirits rise. There was that in Sarah Ann's substantial victuals which was calculated to put heart into a man, there was

XVII. Alvin Does Penance And Is Shriven

tonic in her urging, tearful though it was.

"Ach, a little pie, Alvin, if it is you good enough! It is not to-day's pie, but yesterday's pie, but it is not yet soft. Some pies get softer than others quicker. Ach, a little rusk, too, Alvin! It stood round long enough already. Take jelly for on it, Alvin. Rusk is not good without a spread. It is too dry."

When Alvin had finished the first course, he no longer felt physically shrunken; when he had finished the second, he had ceased entirely to be conscious of the deadly twist of Bevy's grasp upon his ear. Of Katy and the squire no amount of food could hearten him to think.

But when he had finished his supper and had thanked Sarah Ann and had shut himself out of her pleasant kitchen into a cold damp night, he remembered that he had no place to go. On other Saturdays he had sought the home of Bessie in the county seat, but he could not go there now.

"I have no father and no mother and no friends," mourned Alvin to himself. "I am an outcast. I must go back to my cold house."

The wind made the limbs of the trees creak above his head; loose bricks sank sloppily under his feet, splashing his ankles; his heart sank lower and lower. The street lamps burned dimly; as most of the citizens of Millerstown sat in the kitchens, the fronts of their houses were dark and inhospitable. For his own lamp at home he had no oil and no money to buy oil. But home he must go. He saw ahead of him two men, one tall and young, the other broader of shoulder, and not so tall. He recognized them as the squire and David Hartman; he realized dully that David had just come home to his empty house, but his thought accompanied the two men no farther than the next street lamp.

There, mental as well as physical light flashed into Alvin's gloom. The Improved New Mennonites were in the midst of a series of meetings; into the misty darkness of the street their light shone pleasantly, into the lonely quiet their song poured cheerfully. Here was an invitation.

At once Alvin turned his steps toward their little church. He remembered with a thrill, a weak thrill it is true, but none the less a thrill, Essie's pretty face, her curly hair, her friendly glance. To a church every one was welcome. He went in and sat down humbly in the last pew, — no high seat for Alvin in his present state of mind! He saw in the front row no little, round head of Bevy Schnepp with its tight knot of hair at the back. Involuntarily and with great relief Alvin lifted a hand to his own head.

The preacher either directed his sermon toward Alvin, or else happened accidentally upon a text applicable to that young gentleman's condition. He reproved those whose hearts were set on worldly possessions, and Alvin groaned within himself. Doorknobs were a sign of pride — Alvin had himself set a glittering knob upon the jamb of his front door. Organs in the parlor were a snare — Alvin had long since discussed the purchase of a piano with a piano dealer. Fine clothes spelled perdition.

Poor Alvin began to wish himself out upon the dark street. If what the preacher said were true, then he was lost. It is hard to say what Alvin's views of the preacher's discourse would have been if he could have continued to call his own his dear belongings. Now that they were to be taken from him, he felt that it was wrong ever to have had them.

Then, in the depths to which he sank, Alvin longed again more desperately than ever to make confession and to be absolved. He could not endure another listener so hard-hearted as the squire; he craved a sympathetic ear, a tender eye, — a feminine eye and ear, in short.

The sermon ended, pretty Essie went to the organ. Facing the audience she looked at each one, sighing a little at the fullness of life. Then Essie's lovely eyes brightened. Alvin Koehler was here! Alvin's gaze was upon her; Alvin, in spite of the unusual disarray of his clothes, was still handsome; his eyes responded to her glance before she looked down at her music. During the course of the hymn Essie looked at him again; gradually her eyes narrowed; into them came a startled expression. She could see the change in his appearance; his jauntiness was gone; he was no longer the accepted lover. Into Essie's eyes came an intent expression like that which brightens the eyes of a hunter as he sees the approach of his game. Alvin was not himself; he was in trouble. Unconsciously Essie quickened the time of her hymn so that it changed from a dirge, intended to soften the hearts of the impenitent, to a gay, triumphant measure. Fortunately, the hymn was already near its end; there was no chance for the preacher to observe the quickening of the tune.

Waiting outside the door, Alvin joined Essie as she came from the church. Her father lingered within to talk to some of his members; there was opportunity for long and earnest discourse as Alvin walked by the side of Essie.

"You see how it was," said Alvin from time to time. Or, "That was why I did it!"

"She made me get everything ready," complained Alvin, bitterly. "Then, when I had gone to all this expense and was in debt to it yet, she wouldn't have me, and I had used my salary ahead, and I — I took a little money to help myself out. It was money I might have had if I had asked. But I didn't like to ask. It was in a way, you might say, mine. But I meant to put it back, Essie!"

Wisely Alvin entered into no further particulars, nor did he tell the name of the person from whom he had taken the money. Somehow Essie got the impression that it was the squire. That impression Essie was

XVII. Alvin Does Penance And Is Shriven

allowed to keep.

"Then you have sin on your mind." Thus with glowing cheeks Essie diagnosed Alvin's case. In reality Alvin had no sin, but the fear of punishment on his mind.

"Yes," he said.

Essie's cheeks glowed more brightly; she clasped her hands. She was not only curing the invalid, she was binding him to his physician forever.

"You must make everything right," she declared. "Everything down to the last penny. Then you will have peace, Alvin, and not before. You must go back to your childhood. Can you remember anything else you did?"

"I took cherries from trees already," confessed Alvin. "I put once five cents in the church collection and took six cents change out. I took often the cakes that Bevy Schnepp baked and put in a hole for — for" — here Alvin had the grace to gulp mightily — "for other children. Ach, Essie!" Alvin was terrified by the stern gaze bent upon him. He had expected to take her hand, to lay his head on her shoulder, to touch her soft cheek. It was a long time, or it seemed a long time, since Alvin had touched a soft cheek. But instead of soothing him, Essie grew each moment colder and more distant. "Don't turn away from me! I will do everything you say. What shall I do?"

"You must make all these things right," commanded the young judge. "That is the only way."

"Dare I, then, come to see you, Essie? You will not turn me off?"

"You must make it right with all these people," insisted Essie again. She had taken Alvin into the little sitting-room of her father's house. She rose now and moved to the back of her chair as though to put a barrier between herself and Alvin.

Alvin went home and sat him down at his table. The March wind had begun to blow again; Alvin's fire was pitifully small; he anticipated the dreary Sunday with horror.

"Oh, my soul!" wailed poor Alvin. "Oh, my soul!"

Once more he set himself to work with paper and pencil. There was Sarah Ann — he had often picked raspberries as he passed along her fence, but Sarah Ann would willingly forgive him. It would be ridiculous even to ask Sarah Ann. Mom Fackenthal would forgive him also for the cherries he had taken. There was Bevy — to banish this gnawing misery from his heart he could approach even Bevy.

When he had determined upon a course of action, he went to bed and slept soundly. The course of action, it must be confessed, would seem very strange to a person of common sense. But Alvin did not have common sense.

In the morning he slept late; in the evening he went to the church of the Improved New Mennonites. He would walk home with Essie, he would talk over his plans with her. Even a medical clinic involving the shedding of blood would not have been altogether unpleasant to Alvin if he could have been the subject.

But Essie would scarcely speak to him. She wore under her chin a blue bow, about as much of a decoration as her principles would allow, and she was an alluring spectacle. When Alvin stepped to her side, she asked him a single question, her eyes narrowing again like a fisherman's.

"Have you made everything right?"

"This was Sunday!" Alvin reminded her.

Essie made no friendly motion, but shook her head solemnly and went on alone.

In the morning before school Alvin visited Mom Fackenthal.

"Cherries!" said that pleasant old lady. "It is not time yet for cherries. You want to pay for cherries?" Mom Fackenthal was slightly deaf. "You don't owe me anything for cherries. Cherries that you *stole?* When did you steal cherries? When you were little! Humbug! Not a cent, Alvin. Keep your money. Why, all the boys take cherries, that is why there are so many. Are you *crazy*, Alvin!"

With Sarah Ann the result of his interview was the same.

"You took my raspberries, you say? Why, I planted those raspberries near the fence for the children. You were welcome to them, Alvin."

But the way of peace was not always so easy.

"What!" roared Bevy, furious because he dared to approach her. "You stole cakes off of me! I bet you did, Alvin. You want to pay me? Nothing of the kind. You pay Katy what you owe her. Get out of here!"

Threatened with the broom, Alvin stood his ground bravely. As a matter of fact, Bevy had been strictly charged by the squire to let no word of what had happened escape her. But there was no reason why she should not give Alvin a piece of her mind.

"You are good-for-nothing, Alvin. I should think you would be ashamed of yourself. I should think you would go and hide!"

Then upon the angry fire of Bevy's rage, Alvin undertook to pour the water of a pleasant announcement.

"I am going to join your church, Bevy."

"Nonsense!" shrieked Bevy. "Humbug! They would n't have you!"

Alvin grew maudlin in his humility.

XVII. Alvin Does Penance And Is Shriven

"I wish you would like me a little, Bevy."

"The farther away you are the better I like you," shrieked Bevy like a fury.

The news of Alvin's strange seeking for forgiveness followed close upon the rumor that the lady of his choice had rejected him. Millerstown looked at him with interest and pity. Even the landlord and the coal dealer felt a slight softening of the heart. The children in school were obedient for the first time in months.

But there still remained several persons for Alvin to see. He had as yet not approached the coal dealer and the landlord. Nor had he yet interviewed his chief debtor. Her Alvin did not dare to visit. Nor did he wish to approach the landlord and the coal dealer until he had a little money. But until things were made right, Essie would have none of him. Monday evening Alvin devoted to thought. On Tuesday evening he paid a mysterious visit to the editor of the Millerstown "Star." On Wednesday evening he attended the prayer-meeting of the Improved New Mennonites. He was a little late because he had stopped at the post-office. From his pocket protruded a newspaper.

Without asking permission, he joined Essie on the homeward way; without invitation he followed her into the house. He drew the paper from his pocket and offered it to Essie. No one but an Improved New Mennonite or an acolyte of the Improved New Mennonites could have manufactured so remarkable a document.

"What is it?" said Essie as she took the paper.

"There," answered Alvin, pointing.

Essie's eyes followed his finger down the first column of the first page. Sarah Ann Mohr would find this week more food for thought and discussion in the Millerstown local news than in the account of men turning into lions.

"If I have done injury to any one," read Essie, "I ask that they forgive me. Alvin Koehler."

Essie's eyes did not lift from the page for a long time. When they did, they had ceased to burn. Since her first advent into Millerstown, Essie had longed for a possession which she considered precious. Now, at last, it was hers. Now, at last, also was there hope for Alvin.

CHAPTER XVIII
A SILVER CHALICE

With knees trembling and lips quivering, Katy hastened across the Hartman lawn. She was still smarting too hotly from the shock of her loss and the shame of discovery to realize how great a burden had been lifted from her shoulders by the mere sharing of her secret. Poor Alvin seemed meaner than he was, her association with him criminal, herself imbecilic. She remembered his touch with loathing, his beseeching gaze with disgust. She thought of his father, with his queer, glancing eyes, his muttering, his praying. It was no wonder that David Hartman despised them. She saw herself through David's scornful eyes; she remembered the outrageous struggle at the Sheep Stable; she could have sunk through the ground in her distress.

But David had been avenged. Against her new madness of affection Katy was still struggling. By night she dreamed of David, by day she thought of David. Her care of Cassie, her sweeping and cleaning of the great house, had become labors of love.

"I do not think even any more of education," mourned Katy in her alarm. "I am at last quite crazy."

She hurried now into the Hartman kitchen, alarmed because she had been so long away. Cassie grew daily worse, a little less able to make the journey from her bed to the settle in the kitchen, a little more preoccupied, a little more silent. Katy's attentions troubled her, she did not like to have a hand laid upon her shoulder or an arm thrown round her. Once, when she had insisted upon going about the house, she had fainted, and Katy had sent in terror for the doctor, and Cassie had been put to bed in her little room. When she had recovered in a measure, she told Katy where she would find in the drawers of one of the great bureaus certain clothes for her laying away. It was not a cheerful position which Katy held!

To-day Cassie had stayed in her bed, her cheek on her hand, her eyes closed. Often she lay thus for hours. She did not seem to think, often she did not seem to breathe. The atrophy of Cassie's mind and heart were almost complete.

Katy, opening the door softly, so as not to rouse Cassie if she slept, found the kitchen as she had left it, dark and silent and warm. She did not stop to take off the scarlet shawl which she had worn when she went to satisfy herself that her hoard was still in the putlock hole, but climbed at once the steep, narrow stairway which led to the rooms above. Her body ached for rest, but there was still bread to be set and the fire to be fixed for the night. There awaited Katy, also, a more difficult experience than these.

Upstairs, also, all was dark and quiet. Katy tiptoed across the hall to look in upon the invalid. With hands resting on the sides of the door, she peered in. She could see the outlines of the bureau and the narrow bed; she thought that she heard the even, regular breathing of the sleeper, and she was about to turn and go down the steps. Then a startling suspicion halted her. The bedcovers seemed to hang straight and even to the floor, the pillows to stand stiffly against the headboard; there was, after all, it seemed suddenly to Katy, no sound of breathing. For an instant she clung to the door frame, her back to the room, then she turned slowly and compelled herself to take the few short steps to the bed. There she felt about with her hands. The covers were smooth; instead of the hand or cheek of Cassie Hartman, she touched the starched ruffles of a fresh pillowcase.

"Cassie!" cried Katy in wild alarm.

There was no answer. Striving to make her voice sound louder, but only succeeding in uttering a fainter whisper, Katy cried again.

"Cassie! Where are you?"

Still there was no answer.

Frantically Katy fumbled about for a match. The room was in order, a smooth towel covered the bureau, the bed was freshly made as though for a stranger. Katy stared stupidly about her until the match burned her fingers and she was left in the darkness which seemed to close in upon her and smother her. The great house with its tremendous length and breadth, its many rooms, their blackness, the dark closets in the eaves into which one could accidentally shut one's self and die — the great house took shape about her, dim, mysterious, terrible. Strange forms seemed to be here in the room crowding upon her. Though she was aware that it threatened her, and though she tried desperately not to yield it entrance to her consciousness, the horrible recollection of John Hartman's face as he sat in his buggy on the mountain road, of the still whiteness of the faces of her own dead, crept slowly upon her. Must she go through this house searching for her mistress? She dared not go for aid, when Cassie might be lying in some corner helpless or dying. Cassie could scarcely get out of her bed alone. Where had she gone? Who had made up this bed?

Then, in time to save her reason, Katy heard a faint voice addressing her from a distant corner of the great house.

"Katy!"

Katy moved slowly along the dark hall.

"Ach, where are you?"

"Here," answered the faint voice.

Supporting herself against the wall, Katy crept along. At the end a door opened into the house proper, that seldom visited temple to the gods of order and cleanliness. The door now stood open.

"Are you sick?" gasped Katy. "Where are you? Did you fall?"

"No," came the slow answer. "I am here. You can make a light."

Falteringly Katy obeyed. On a bracket at the end of the hall hung a lamp; this she lighted with a great clattering of globe against chimney. Then, lifting the lamp, she carried it into the room from which the voice proceeded. Her scarlet shawl was still about her, her hair was disorderly from the squire's embrace, her eyes were wild and startled. She was a strange contrast to the room in which she stood.

Here was the great high bed with its carved posts, each terminating in a pineapple; here the interesting steps on which one mounted to the broad plateau of repose; here the fine curtains and the rich carpet, — all as Katy had left them after the last careful sweeping and dusting and polishing. But the bed had been disturbed; in it lay the mistress of the house, white and sick, but full of satisfaction over having accomplished her pitiful purpose.

Katy's wild eyes questioned her.

"It was time for me to come," announced Cassie, solemnly.

"It was time for you to come!" repeated Katy. "What do you mean?"

"My time has come," explained Cassie. "You are to go for the preacher."

Katy clasped her hands across her breast. She remembered now the bureau in which the white underclothes and the black dress were kept. She began to cry.

"Oh, no! I will go for the doctor! You shouldn't have done this! You have made yourself worse! I will get you the medicine the doctor gave you, then I will run for him."

"You will go for the preacher," directed Cassie, wearily. "My time has come."

Katy looked wildly about her, but found no help either in the thick carpet or the heavy hangings. She was afraid to go, yet she did not dare to stay. Cassie sank a little deeper into her pillows, the shadows under her eyes seemed to darken, the covers moved with her throbbing heart.

"Go!" she commanded thickly.

Katy ran down the steps through the kitchen and out to the gate. The preacher lived nearer than the doctor; a single knock and his window was lifted.

"Cassie Hartman must see you!" cried Katy. "She is very low. Bring the doctor and come quickly."

XVIII. A Silver Chalice

Without staying to hear whether there were any questions to be answered, Katy flew back into the dark kitchen and up the narrow stairs. Cassie lay with her eyes closed, her hands folded across her breast.

"The front door should be opened, and there should be a light," she gasped.

"I cannot leave you!"

"Go!" said Cassie.

Again Katy flew to obey. David should be sent for; must she remind them that David should be sent for? It seemed to Katy that any observer could see her obsession in her face.

"You know where my things are, Katy," whispered Cassie.

"Yes, I know! But you are not going to die!"

"My time has come," said Mrs. Hartman. "Everything is attended to and written out in the desk. You can tell the squire."

"I will," faltered Katy, standing between the tall pillars at the foot of the bed. She remembered the squire's face as he came to tell her grandmother that Grandfather Gaumer was dead; she thought of David and David's face when he should be told. David would be alone in the world; surely, though he had all its riches, he would care! Surely his mother had a message for him. The preacher was a newcomer; he did not know David; he should give him no message from his mother! And Dr. Benner should give him no message from his mother. Katy clasped her hands a little more closely and looked down upon Cassie.

"And David?"

Cassie's eyelids quivered, but she made no reply.

"Some one must send for David!"

When Cassie still made no answer, Katy came round the corner of the bed and stood by the pillow.

"Suppose" — Katy stammered and faltered — "suppose — shall anything be said to David if — if"

"David will find everything ready," said Cassie, wearily. "He will find everything in order."

Katy leaned over the pillow. Cassie could not know what it was to die, to go away forever; Cassie could not know how one wept and mourned when those whom one loved had died; could not know how one remembered every word, cherished every caress. David had no one else, and David was young; David could not be so hard of heart as he seemed or Cassie so stony. There was hardly a person in Millerstown who would have ventured to oppose Cassie, or to persuade her against her will. But all the characteristics of Katy's youth had not vanished; still, seeing a goal, she moved toward it, disregarding obstacles. It seemed to her that she heard the gate swing open and shut, heard the sound of voices, of rapid footsteps. The preacher and the doctor were coming, and probably other Millerstonians would come with them. She took Cassie by the hand and was terrified by its chill.

"Do you not leave your love for David?" she asked, crying.

Cassie looked up at her with no other expression than slight astonishment, as though Katy's language were strange. Cassie loved nothing that could turn and rend her. John had turned and had rent her, but in David's case she had had a care for herself, from misery there she had sternly and bravely defended herself. This bright-eyed Katy with her light step and her pretty ways had disturbed her, had set her to dreaming at night of a house filled with children, of growing boys and girls who would have loved their mother and cherished her.

And here this same Katy hung above her, clung to her, would not, thought poor Cassie, would not let her die as she had planned! She did not know that hardness of heart was in her a more terrible hurt than any offense which love could have brought. In her weakness she felt a sudden quiver of life in that heart of stone; it seemed as though it melted to water.

But she would not yield. She tried to draw her hand away from the grasp which held it; she closed her eyes; she remembered how she had defended herself against grief. But she could not get her weak hand away, could not shut out the sound of Katy's voice.

"What shall I tell David? Let me tell David something from his mother. Why, David loves you! David will grieve for you! Oh, please!" She lifted Mrs. Hartman's white hand and held it against her cheek, as though she would compel a blessing. "Oh, please let me tell David something!"

But no word was spoken, no tears stole out from under the closed lids. The lids quivered, opened and closed; beyond that slight motion there was nothing. Already the preacher and the doctor were ascending the steps. To both the serious condition of the invalid was evident. The doctor told Katy in his dictatorial way that she should not have allowed Mrs. Hartman to leave her bed. The doctor always spoke to Katy with irritation, as though he could not quite escape the recollection of promises made and forgotten.

Cassie lay quietly with her hands clasped once more on her breast. Her eyes were open now; she spoke clearly in a weak voice, the self-control, fostered through years, serving her still. She signified that she wished her pastor to give her the communion, for which purpose he had brought with him his silver flask and chalice and paten. These he spread out on the little table at the head of Cassie's bed.

XVIII. A Silver Chalice

On the other side of the bed stood Katy, with wide, tearful eyes and white cheeks. The scene was almost too solemn for endurance; the great catafalque of a bed with its white valances and draperies, the dark shadows in the corners of the room, the deep silence of the night, the brightly illuminated, earnest faces of the doctor and the preacher. But all seemed to make Katy's eyes more clear to see, her heart more keen to remember. Her thoughts went back over all the solemn services she had witnessed, the watch-night services of her childhood, the communion services, the hour of her grandmother's passing. She remembered the clear nights when she had run through the snow with Whiskey and had been at once so unhappy and so happy. How foolish to be unhappy then when she had everything! She remembered even that morning, long, long ago, when John Hartman had frightened her. Surely, as her grandmother said, she must have imagined that rage! She was nothing to John Hartman.

The minister had poured the wine from the flask into the chalice, and had broken the bread. He lifted the chalice and the light flashed from its bright surface.

"Drink ye all of it," he began gravely in his deep voice.

Then Katy heard no more. She put her arm tightly round the tall post of the bed and clung and clung to it as though a great creature or a great wave threatened to drag her from her feet. She looked far away across the wide bed, through the walls of the great house, over the village and the fields to the church on the hill. She was a child again in a red dress, and she had run unsteadily out the brick walk from her grandmother's kitchen door to the gate, out to the blessed, free, forbidden open road. She had talked to herself happily; she had stopped to pull leaves which still lingered on the Virginia creeper vines on the fences.

Presently, when she had trotted past the first field, the open door of the church had attracted her. She had been taken to church a few times; she remembered the singing — even that early had the strange performance of Henny Wenner fascinated her; she now turned her steps toward the delightful place. In the church an interesting man was at work with a little trowel and beautiful soft mortar, and she had watched him until she had grown sleepy, whereupon, with that feeling of possession in all the world which had been hers so keenly in her childhood, she had laid herself down on the soft cushion of a pew.

When she woke the interesting little man with his trowel was no longer in the church. Another man had taken his place before the hole in the church wall, and spying her suddenly had driven her out with anger. She had not thought of it for years; they had persuaded her that she had dreamed it; had told her that if John Hartman had ever spoken to her sharply, it was only to send her home where she belonged, that he could have against her no unkindly feeling.

But now it came back, strangely illumined. John Hartman had driven her away angrily, and John Hartman had held in his hand a silver cup, the shape of the one which the preacher held to Cassie's pale lips, but larger, handsomer. Upon it the sun had flashed as the lamplight flashed now upon this smaller cup.

At first Katy only remembered vaguely that there had been trouble about the communion service, that it had disappeared, that dishonest Alvin's dishonest and crazy father had taken it. The thought of Alvin brought to her mind a new set of sensations, confusing to her.

"He held it in his hand," whispered Katy to herself. "Then he pushed it into the hole, quickly. I saw him do it!"

She leaned her head against the tall bedpost, and did not hear the command of the doctor to bring water.

"Katy!" said he, again, a little more loudly.

Still Katy did not stir. The preacher looked up also, and his communion service now over, came quickly with an alarmed glance at Katy round the great bed and took her by the arm. Her muscles were stiff; she had only one conscious thought — to cling to the thing nearest to her. The minister unclasped her hand and half carrying her, half leading her, took her down to the kitchen and laid her upon the settle. When he had taken the water to the doctor, he came back, to find Katy sitting up and looking about her in a dazed fashion.

"You had better lie down," bade the preacher.

Katy shook her head. "I cannot lie down."

"This has been too much for you," went on the preacher kindly. "My wife is coming now to stay. You cannot do anything more for poor Mrs. Hartman. If I were you I would go home. When the rest come I will walk down the street with you."

Katy looked at him with somber eyes and did not move.

"This house is no place for you, Katy."

Katy shivered; then she got to her feet. She remembered her aching desire to console David, her vague plans; she saw again the shining, silver chalice, the startled, terrified face of David's father as she tugged at his coat.

"No," agreed Katy with a stiff tongue. "You have right. This house is no place for me."

CHAPTER XIX
THE SQUIRE AND DAVID TAKE A JOURNEY BY NIGHT

On Saturday evening David returned to Millerstown and for the second time in his life entered his father's house — his house now — by the front door. There were friendly lights here and there; the squire, who had met him at the train, slipped a kindly hand under his arm as they ascended the steps and crossed the porch. To the squire the Hartmans were queer, unhuman. But David looked worn and miserable; perhaps they suffered more than one thought. In his first confusion after the disappearance of the communion service, John Hartman had behaved so strangely toward his old friend that the squire had avoided him as a burnt child avoids the fire. But that was long ago, and here was this boy come home to his mother's funeral. The squire patted David's shoulder as they entered the door.

David glanced with a shiver toward the room on the left where he had caught the first glimpse of the bed upon which his father lay. But the door was closed; Cassie had not been moved from the catafalque upon which she died.

From the dim end of the long hall, a short figure advanced to meet the two men. It was not Katy, who had resigned her place, but Bevy, who had come to stay until the funeral was over. Bevy shook hands with David solemnly, looking up at him with awe, as the owner of farms and orchards and this great house and unreckoned bank stock. She had spread his supper in the kitchen, and the squire sat with him while he ate. Then the two men went upstairs together.

In Cassie's room a light burned faintly. The squire turned it higher and then looked at David.

"Shall I go down, David?"

"No," said David.

The squire crossed the room slowly and laid back the cover from Cassie's face; then both men stood still, looking first at the figure on the bed, then at each other. Cassie had always been beautiful, but now an unearthly loveliness lighted her face. Her dark hair was braided high on her head; her broad forehead with its beautifully arched brows seemed to shed an actual radiance. David had never observed his mother's beauty, but now, in the last few months, he had wakened to aspects to which he had been blind. He had seen beautiful women; he could compare them with his mother as she lay before him. He looked at her hands, still shapely in spite of the hard toil of her life, folded now across her quiet breast; he noted the shape of her forehead; he saw the smile with which she seemed to be contemplating some secret and lovely thing.

Upon the squire the sight of Cassie made a deep impression. Tears came into his eyes, and he shook his head as though before him lay an unfathomable mystery. He felt about her as he might have felt about some young person cut off in youth. Here was extraordinary promise, here was pitiful blight. The squire had observed human nature in many unusual and pathetic situations, here was the most pathetic of all. The Hartmans could not be understood.

Then the squire, glancing at David, went out and closed the door and left him with his mother.

In dumb confusion, David stood by the great bed. More vaguely, the squire's puzzle was his also. His mother had had an empty life — it should not have been empty. He could not understand her, he could not understand his father. They had put him away from them. The old resentful, heart-breaking misery came back; he had no people, he had no one who loved him. Like a lover, refused, rejected, he knelt down beside the great bed.

"Oh, mother!" cried David, again and again. "Oh, mother, mother!" Then the old, unanswered, unanswerable cry, "Speak to me!"

From the great bed came no sigh. David rose presently and laid back the cover over the smiling lips and turned the light low and went down to join the squire. Composedly he made plans with him for the funeral. The squire announced that he and Bevy had come to take up their abode unless David wished to be alone. The squire looked at David, startled. In the last year David had grown more than ever like his parents; he had his mother's features and his father's deep gray eyes and thickly curling hair.

"When you are through your school, you must settle down in Millerstown," said the squire. "There ought to be little folks here in this house."

David's heart leaped, then sank back to its place. He had cured himself of Katy Gaumer; such flashes were only meaningless recollections of past habit.

"I am thinking of studying law," he told the squire. "That will keep me in school three years more. And then I couldn't practice law in Millerstown."

"The Hartmans are not lawyers," said the squire. "The Hartmans are farmers. You would have plenty to keep you busy, David."

If old habit caused David to look for Katy Gaumer, David's eyes were not gratified by what they sought. Neither before his mother's funeral nor afterward did she appear. Bevy had removed her few belongings from David's room before he returned; there remained in the Hartman house no evidence of her presence. Bevy said that Katy was tired, that she lay all

XIX. The Squire And David Take A Journey By Night

day on the settle in her uncle's kitchen. Bevy longed to pour out to David an account of Katy's treatment at the hands of Alvin Koehler, prospective church member though he was. But she had been forbidden by the squire to open her lips on the subject; and, besides, David Hartman, the heir to all this magnificence, could hardly be expected to take an interest in one who had demeaned herself to become his mother's servant. Nevertheless, a wild scheme formed itself in Bevy's mind.

"Sometimes Katy cries," reported Bevy sentimentally to David. "It seems as though this brought back everything about her gran'mom and everything. Yesterday she was real sick, but to-day she complains better again. Katy has had a good deal of trouble in this world."

David frowned. He was going back to college in the morning; his bag was already packed. Katy had been in the house until the time of his mother's death; she should have asked him to come to see her. Old habit tempted him to play once more with fire.

"I would like to see Katy," he said now to Bevy.

"Well!" Bevy faced him with arms akimbo, her little eyes sparkling. "I will tell Katy that she shall come here once this evening."

"No," answered David, who had got beyond the simple ways of Millerstown. "Ask her whether I may come to see her this evening."

"Of course, you can come to see her!" cried Bevy. "I will just tell her you are coming."

But Bevy returned with an astonishing message. Bevy was amazed at Katy's temerity. She had planned that she would suggest to Edwin's Sally that she and Edwin go to bed and leave the kitchen to David and Katy.

"She only cried and said you should not come. Sally said I must leave her alone. She said the squire and Edwin said that Katy must be left alone. Katy is not herself."

In June David returned to Millerstown with trunks and boxes to stay for the summer, at least. Upon his face a fresh record was written. He looked older, his lips were more firmly set. His last term had been easy; he had permitted himself holidays; he had visited New York, had seen great ships, had climbed great buildings, had learned, or thought that he had learned, that money can buy anything in the world. He had talked for defiance' sake with the pretty girl who had told him so sweetly long ago that the college town was glad of his presence. The pretty girl smiled upon him even more sweetly; it was clear to David's eyes that his blunder was nothing to her. He talked to other girls; it was equally clear that they were glad to forget any blunders of the past. He had not yet made up his mind what he would do with this great world which he could buy. Its evil was as plain to him as its good, but he meant to have all of it. It was as though David gathered together the pipe and cards flung into the tree-tops from the Sheep Stable.

It was late in the afternoon when he arrived in Millerstown. Main Street lay quiet and golden in the sunshine. It was supper time and the Millerstonians were indoors. Few persons saw him come, and those few stood in too great awe of him to invite him to their houses. He met Katy Gaumer as he turned the corner sharply, and Katy gasped and looked at him somberly, standing still in a strange way to let him pass. She answered his greeting without lifting her head. Old habit made David grit his teeth.

Upon her doorstep sat the little Improved New Mennonite, her supper finished. She was prettier than ever. By nature a manager, she had reduced Alvin's financial and other troubles to their simplest terms, and there was now hope of a happy issue from them. Alvin himself, though at peace, was not exactly happy. He had been held so diligently to his work, he had been compelled to dress so plainly that he was much depressed in spirit. Red neckties were now anathema; masculine adherents of the sect of the Improved New Mennonites, indeed, abjured neckties altogether, and Alvin feared that the black one to which he was reduced would presently also be taken from him. In her practical way Essie had long since decided that the rented house in the village could not be considered as an abode, but that the little house on the mountain-side must be returned to.

To the side of the little Mennonite came David when he had opened the windows of his house. The place was desolate. The baffling sense of his mother's presence, even the consciousness of his father's, so long past, were intolerable. He would not endure this discomfort. He was young, ought to have happiness, would have it. Essie Hill was lovely to look at, she admired him, she was a woman; he would go and talk to Essie. He wished that he had brought her a present, but he could order one for her. If he stayed in Millerstown this summer Essie would be a pleasant diversion.

From the doorstep Essie looked up at him. Then, as he prepared to sit down beside her, she drew away, blushing primly.

"I am going to be married," said she. "I think I ought to tell you."

David grew suddenly pale. If a pigeon had turned from his caress to attack him with talons, if a board from his walk had arisen to smite him, he could not have been more astounded.

"To whom?" said he.

"I am going to marry Alvin."

"Alvin who?" asked David, bewildered.

"Alvin Koehler."

XIX. The Squire And David Take A Journey By Night

Then was David's pride wounded! He wished Essie well with a steady voice, however, and went on to the post-office and back to his house and sat down on the dark back porch. How he hated them all, these miserable people, but how he hated most of all Alvin Koehler. It was not, he remembered, the first time that Alvin had been preferred to him. He thought again of William, gibbering and praying in the corner of the almshouse garden. God had put him there. It was a proof that God existed that he had punished Alvin's father. And Alvin should be punished, too. David knew of the mortgage among his father's papers. It was only by his father's grace that the Koehlers had been allowed to live so long on the mountainside. That house should continue in their possession no longer. Other schemes for revenge came into his mind. He sat miserably, his head buried in his hands as though he were a tramp waiting for food instead of the heir of the house come home to take possession.

He did not hear the sound of a step on the brick walk. Suddenly, a girl screamed lightly and he lifted his head, then spring to his feet.

"What is it?" he cried to the ghostly figure. "Who are you?"

"I didn't mean to scream," said Katy Gaumer. "I didn't see you at first and I was frightened. I thought it was some stranger."

"It is I," said David, gruffly. Katy's figure had seemed like an apparition in the dim light; he had been horribly startled.

"I want to see you, David," said Katy, hesitatingly. "I have something I must talk to you about."

"I'll make a light inside."

"I'd rather talk here," said Katy. "I'll sit here on the step. I don't believe any one will come."

David offered her a chair. The blood was pounding in his temples, his wrists felt weak.

Katy had already seated herself on the low step. David sat on a chair on the porch; he could see her as she propped her elbows on her knees and made a cup for her chin with her hands. David breathed deeply; old habit was reasserting itself. Then he saw that Katy was trembling; to his amazement he heard her crying.

"You aren't well, Katy!"

"Yes," said Katy. "But I have a duty to do. It is hard. It nearly kills me."

David's thoughts leaped wildly from one possibility to another. What had she done? What could she have done? Here was Katy in a new light, weeping, distressed.

"What is it, Katy? Don't be afraid to tell me."

"I am afraid to tell you." Katy turned her white face toward him. "But I must tell you. It has been on my mind day and night. I have tried to think of another way, but I cannot."

"But what is it?"

"When I was a little girl and lived with my grandfather and grandmother, I used to run away, and one day I ran away to the church. Alvin Koehler's father was there plastering the wall, and I watched him, and after a while I went to sleep in a pew. When I woke up Alvin's father was gone, but your father was there, David."

David gave a great start.

"You cannot say anything to me against my father!"

"But I must tell you, David. You will have to decide what is to be done. I have n't told the squire or any one, but you must know. It has been on my mind all this time. I can't rest or sleep any more. I went up to your father and he spoke roughly to me, and then I ran out and went home to my grandmother. She laughed at me and said your father was only chasing me home where I ought to be. After a while I believed it. Then Alvin Koehler's father got up at the funeral and talked about the communion set and I did n't believe such a thing for a minute, not a minute. Alvin is not — is not — very honest — and I never believed it."

"You did n't believe what?" said David with a dry throat. "What in this world are you talking about?"

"I did n't believe for a minute that your father would have anything to do with taking the communion set. I —"

"He did n't have anything to do with it," cried David. "What nonsense is this?"

Katy covered her face with her hands. She went on mechanically as though she had prepared what she had to say.

"Before your mother died and the preacher came to give her communion, he lifted the cup high in the air and the light shone on it. Then I remembered everything that I had forgotten, how I had run away to the church and everything, and I knew that your father had the shining cup in his hand when I ran up to him. That was what I wanted — the shining cup. He was there with it in his hand; it is as plain as if it were now."

"I do not believe you!"

To this Katy returned no answer.

"Why did n't you tell it long ago?"

"I did n't remember this part till that night," said Katy, patiently. "But I could n't come and tell you then! I have thought over this and prayed over it. If I could bear it for you, I would, David. But I can't."

"I do not believe you," said David. "You imagined it. What could my father have wanted with the communion service? What could he have done with it?"

XIX. The Squire And David Take A Journey By Night

"There was a hole in the wall and he pushed it in quickly."

"A hole in the wall!"

"Alvin's father was mending the wall. There used to be a window there. I asked the squire about the window. Alvin's father was closing it up."

Into David's mind came a sickening recollection of the wild-eyed, desperate figure which had risen to shout out the terrible accusation.

"I do not believe it," he said again. "You have always helped Alvin Koehler. You helped him dishonestly in school. You are trying to help him now."

Katy's head bent a little lower over her knees.

"He does not even have sense enough to care for you or to be grateful to you."

Katy rose from her place on the low step. With a gasp she started down the walk.

"What are you going to do about it?" cried David, hoarsely.

"Nothing," answered Katy.

"You are going now to tell the squire!"

"No," said Katy, "I am not going to tell any one."

"Then why did you come here?" David followed her to the gate. "You have made trouble, you are always making trouble. If you are not going to do anything about it, why did you come here?"

"I had to tell you," insisted Katy, woefully. "Can't you see that I had to tell you?"

"It is not true," said David again. "If you think I will do anything against my father's name you are mistaken. You —"

But Katy had gone. He heard the familiar click of the gate, he heard her steps quicken. She was running away as from a house of plague.

Then David hid his face in his arms and sat long alone on the porch. He saw his father's stern face. His father had gone about — this there was no denying — like a man with a heavy load upon his heart. But that he should have had anything to do with the theft of a communion service, that he should even have touched it, that he, himself, knowing the truth, should have allowed another to be suspected — this was monstrous.

With rapid step David went up and down the porch. He would go away from Millerstown forever, that was certain. He would sell his house, his farms; he would shake the dust of the place from his feet. But first he would clear the mind of Katy Gaumer from this outrageous suspicion and make it impossible for the slander to travel farther. As he made his plans, he stood still at the top of the porch steps, his head bent. Then he lifted his head with a sudden motion. There was for an instant a strangeness in the air, a sense of human presence. David felt blessed in his endeavor.

A few moments later he opened the door of the squire's office.

The squire, busy with his favorite occupation, the planning of a journey, sat with his feet comfortably elevated on the table. He let his chair slam to the floor and came forward to meet his guest.

"Well, David, now you are a graduate! Let me look at you! Now you are to stay with us. Why, David!" The squire stared at the countenance before him. "Are you in trouble?"

"Yes," answered David.

With the squire in his chair behind the desk, himself on the old settle, David told his story.

"Katy Gaumer came to the house this evening and told me a strange thing. She says that she saw my father with the communion cup in his hand the day that the service disappeared from the church."

"The communion cup?" repeated the squire, startled almost out of his wits. "What communion cup?"

"The one that disappeared."

The squire gasped.

"Katy saw him!" Here was Katy again, Katy who had seemed to them all to be such a promising child, Katy who was determined to go away to school, Katy who helped young rascals from her poverty, Katy who now would not study, who refused to do anything but sit dismally about! "Katy Gaumer," he repeated. "Our Katy?"

"Yes, Katy Gaumer," said David. "She says she was a little child and that she ran away from her grandmother to the church and saw my father put the silver cup into a hole made by plastering up the window."

"Impossible!" cried the squire. "Nonsense! Humbug! The girl is crazy. It could n't be!"

David looked at him and drew a deep breath.

"That was what I said. Then I thought of Koehler, and of how he had gone mad, and I knew my father would wish it investigated."

An electric shock tingled the squire's sensorium. He remembered the contorted face, the trembling hands, the terrible earnestness with which Koehler made his attack upon the dead man.

"What is your plan, David?" he asked.

"I thought we might get the key of the church and go out there and look about. It's bright moonlight and I believe we can see without making a light. I don't believe I can sleep until I have been out there and have looked about. I suppose we will have to get a key from the preacher."

"I have a key," said the squire. "But let us wait till to-morrow, David."

XIX. The Squire And David Take A Journey By Night

"I must go to-night," insisted David.

Only once were words exchanged on the journey. The two men went out the village street, past Grandfather Gaumer's, where a hundred sweet odors saluted them from the garden and where Katy lay weeping on her bed, to the path along the pike, between the open fields.

"You knew my father," said David. "Such a thing could not have been possible."

"I knew him from a boy," answered the squire heartily and honestly. "Such a thing could not have been possible."

"Had Koehler ever made this accusation before the time of my father's funeral?"

"He made it to the preacher after the service disappeared, but the preacher told him he must be still."

"Could Koehler have had any motive for taking it himself?"

"He was a poor man," answered the squire. "But he was simple and honest — all the Koehlers were."

"What do you suppose became of it?"

"I have always supposed that some one sneaked in while Koehler was away for a minute. A tramp could easily have walked in."

"Did my father never say that he had been in the church that afternoon?"

"Not that I know of."

The church door opened easily and quietly, the church was dim and silent. The tall, narrow windows, fitted with clear glass, let in the light of the moon upon the high pulpit, the oaken pews, the bare floor. The pulpit and the Bible were draped with protecting covers of white which made the church seem more ghostly and mysterious. Katy Gaumer in certain moods would have been enchanted.

Together the two men looked at the smooth wall beside the pulpit.

"It does n't seem as if that wall could ever have been broken," said David in a low voice. "Was the window there?"

"Yes," answered the squire. "There was a window there. But William Koehler was a fine plasterer. The window went almost from ceiling to floor."

"We would have to have a pickaxe and other tools. And we would have to ask for permission to open it. And all Millerstown would have to know," said David.

The squire pondered for an instant. "We would if we opened it from this side. But the Sunday School is built against the other side, and there there is only a little thin wainscoting to break through. It could be taken out and put back easily. There are tools here in the church somewhere."

The squire returned to the vestibule and opened the door of a cupboard.

"Here is a whole basket of tools. I do not like to make a light or every one will see. Millerstown is wonderful curious." The squire's light tone sounded strangely in the silence of the church, strangely to David and strangely to himself. "Don't you think, David" — the squire had his hand on the knob of the Sunday-School room door — "don't you think we had better wait till to-morrow?"

"No," answered David.

The squire passed on into the little Sunday-School room and David followed him.

"It's brighter here." The squire measured the wainscoting with his eye. "The old window ought to be about here. Sit down, David."

David obeyed, trembling.

"I don't believe I could open it," said he.

"Of course not!" answered the squire, cheerfully. "Do not worry, David. That silver has been melted this long time."

The squire thrust a chisel into a crevice and lifted out a section of wainscoting, then another. When three or four narrow strips were removed, he thrust his hand into the aperture. The moonlight grew brighter as the moon cleared the upper boughs of the old cherry trees outside the Sunday-School building; it shone upon a curious scene, the old man at his strange task, the young man watching so eagerly.

"There can't be anything here," said the squire, cheerfully. "There can't be. This might just as well be made into a book cupboard for the Sunday School; it is wasted space. It's queer we never thought of that. You see the church wall is four bricks thick here, and William's wall only one brick. It — "

The squire ceased suddenly to speak. His exploring hand had only now reached the bottom of the deep hole; it came into contact with a substance different from the fallen rubble which he expected to touch. David heard his voice die away, saw him start.

"What is it, sir?"

"There is something here," answered the squire.

David looked at the yawning hole with what courage he could muster. The squire thrust in his hand a little deeper, and groped about. Then, from the pit from which John Hartman might have lifted them easily had not all thought been paralyzed, he drew in their gray bag a pitcher, black with tarnish, and a silver plate, and set them on the floor beside him, and then a silver chalice. Still feeling about, he touched a paper and that, too, he lifted out and laid on the floor with the silver vessels.

Then, silently, he and David looked at each other.

CHAPTER XX
THE MYSTERY DEEPENS

For a long time neither the squire nor David spoke or moved. David sat on the bench where he had sat, a little boy at Sunday School, and the squire remained kneeling, forgetting his aching bones. When sharp pain reminded him of his years and his rheumatism, he rose and sat by David on the low, shallow bench.

"I can't understand it," said he again and again. "One cannot believe it. There was n't any motive. He could n't have wanted to steal it — such a thing would be entirely impossible. He was already rich; he was always well-behaved from his childhood up."

David did not answer. His face was in the shadow, only his tightly clasped hands were illuminated by the bright moonlight. His mind was confused, he could not yet coördinate his impressions. There was Katy Gaumer's story, there was Koehler's terrible accusation; here was this damning proof of both. He felt again that rising, protesting pride in his father, he felt a sickening unwillingness to go on with this investigation, which seemed to mean in his first confusion only an intolerable humbling of himself before Alvin Koehler, the effeminate, the smiling, the son of a madman and a thief. Poor David groaned.

At once the squire rose with a troubled sigh.

"We'd better put these things back and drive in a few nails to hold the wainscoting. We'll surely meet some one if we carry them into town and then the cat would be out of the bag."

David agreed with a nod.

"And here is this paper!" The squire started. Perhaps they were nearer an explanation than they thought. "Put it in your pocket, David."

David thrust the paper into his pocket with a sort of sob. The squire laid the precious vessels back on the rough floor of the little pit and put the wainscoting in place. A few light taps with a hammer and all was smooth once more as it had been for fifteen years. Then he led the way into the dim church.

"Come, David!"

David did not answer. He had sat down once more on the low bench. His thoughts had passed beyond himself; he sat once more beside his father's body here in the church. He experienced again that paralyzing horror of death, the passionate desire to shield his poor father from the curious eyes of Millerstown, his rage at the wild, dusty figure in the gallery. He remembered William Koehler as he had seen him later in the corner of the poorhouse garden, waving his arms, struggling like some frantic creature striving to break the bonds which held him. He saw the face of Alvin, empty, dissatisfied, vain. He remembered the little house, its poverty, its meanness. He remembered how he had called upon God to prove Himself to him by punishing Alvin Koehler's father. David was proud no more.

"Come, David!" urged the squire again, returning; and this time David followed him, through the church, out into the warm June night. Cinder was being dumped at the furnace, the sky flushed suddenly a rosy red, then the glow faded, leaving only the silvery moonlight. It was only nine o'clock; pleasant sounds rose from the village, the laughter of children, the voice of some one singing. Millerstown was going on its quiet, happy way. At Grandfather Gaumer's all was dark; the house stood somberly among its pine trees; the garden still breathed forth its lovely odors. The two men proceeded into the little office of the squire, and there the squire lit his lamp and both sat down.

Trembling, David drew from his pocket the paper which the squire had found with the silver vessels. John Hartman had expected that long before the silver service was discovered the threatening letter would be destroyed. But here it lay in his son's hand, its fiber intact. It had caused John Hartman hideous suffering; it was to hide it that he had given his life's happiness; here now it lay in the hand of David. Slowly David unfolded the yellowed sheet and looked at it.

The squire, startled by a cry, turned from the door he was locking against possible intruders. David's blond head lay on the squire's desk, the paper beside it.

"What is it, David?"

David held out the paper, his face still hidden. The squire felt for his spectacles, his hand shaking. Here now was the explanation of this strange mystery, a mystery thought to be forever inexplicable. Why had John Hartman done this thing? The squire held his breath in suspense.

But the squire read no answer to his questions. The paper, old and yellowed and flabby to the touch, could be scrutinized forever, held to the light, magnified, but it told nothing. On it only a few words were legible, a portion of those written by John Hartman as he sat by the roadside in his misery long ago.

"My dear little boy." "My poor Cassie." There was one fragment of a sentence. "What shall I —" and there all ended.

The squire looked at the paper solemnly. The mystery had only thickened.

"He was in some trouble, poor Hartman was," said he. "He was in great trouble. I wish he had come to me in his trouble." Again and again the

XX. The Mystery Deepens

squire turned the paper over in his hand, still he found nothing but the few, scattered words.

"I think I will ask Katy to come over," said he. "Perhaps she can remember something more of this."

David did not lift his head to answer; he did not hear what the squire said. He tried desperately to control himself, to decide what must next be done. When Katy came in with the squire, he was startled almost out of his senses and sprang up hastily. Of all the ignominy of his life Katy had been a witness.

Katy had not gone to bed to stay, but had only hurled herself down once more upon her oft-used refuge. It was evident that she had shed many tears. The squire drew her to a seat beside him on the settle and kept hold of her. It was always natural for any one who was near Katy to find her hand or to touch the curls on her neck or to make her more comfortable with one's arm. To David, as she sat by the squire, she was an impregnably fortressed and cruel judge.

Again Katy told her story — all her story, her running away, her talking with William Koehler, her falling asleep, her sight of the shining cup.

"You say he *pushed* it in, Katy?"

"He had it in his hand and he dropped it in quickly. Then he — he sent me away. I am sure I ought not to have been in the church; it was all right for him to send me away. I remembered it all but the shining cup. If gran'-mom was alive, she could tell you how I came running home."

"And you never told any one?"

"I spoke often of his having sent me home," explained Katy. "But I never remembered about the shining cup until the preacher came to see David's mother. Then I could n't tell David, — I *could n't* tell him! But perhaps it is n't there; perhaps even if he had the cup in his hand he had n't anything to do with the other; perhaps —"

"The silver is there," said the squire sadly. "We found it in the bottom of the pit."

"Oh, dear! oh, dear!" cried Katy.

David looked at her coldly. She sat with her curly head hidden against the squire's shoulder. David wished that she would go, that she would remove herself far from him forever. He had suffered this evening to the limit of endurance.

"You did your duty," said he in the tone learned at college. "You need n't feel any further responsibility."

Thus propelled, Katy rose and checked her tears and passed out of the squire's office.

When she had gone, David took up his burden manfully, though somewhat savagely. David was proud once more, but the pride was that of honor, not of haughtiness. John Hartman had had a code of honor; it was that which had broken his heart. Millerstown had a similar code of honor. By inheritance or by observation had David learned the way of a just man.

"Now," said he, "we will find Alvin."

"To-night, David?"

"Yes, to-night."

"But Alvin will know nothing!"

"But we will find Alvin."

CHAPTER XXI
THE SQUIRE AND DAVID TAKE A JOURNEY BY DAY

DAVID and the squire had not gone far in their search for Alvin before David's mind changed. He did not care to seek him at the house of the little Improved New Mennonite or to ask the squire to take the long walk to Alvin's house on the mountain-side. It would be better to follow the squire's suggestion and wait until morning.

"Then we will drive out to the poorhouse and see Koehler himself. He is the one to see. You'd better stay here to-night with me."

David shook his head. He wished to be alone; he had set a task for himself. Perhaps some letter or document had escaped him among those in his father's safe, some letter or document which could throw light on the strange past.

But David found nothing. He entered again into his great house, locked its doors, and opened the iron safe. There he read through ledgers and day books and mortgages and deeds in vain. He found nothing but the orderly papers of a careful business man. He looked again at the letter upon which the secret had been written, he held it up between him and the lamp, but the original writing was gone forever. It had been a letter, — of that there was no doubt, — his father's writing followed the spaces of a margin, but the text of the letter was gone.

In the morning the two men drove out the country road to the almshouse. The fields were green, wild roses and elder were in bloom, the air was sweet. A man could ask nothing better of fate than to be given a home and work in such a spot.

"They say Koehler has grown quieter," said the squire. "He does n't rave and pray this long time."

David did not answer. If another had visited such a shame upon him, it would have been a long time before he would have grown quiet. David was now pale, now scarlet; he moistened his lips as though he were feverish. Reparation must be made, but what adequate reparation could be offered? Of money there was plenty, and Alvin, alas! could be satisfied with money; Alvin would probably never understand the awful hurt which had been done him. But his father — how could reason be returned to him?

In his corner in the almshouse garden they found William. The almshouse was a pleasant place with shady lawns and comfortable porches upon which old men could smoke their pipes and old women could sit knitting or shelling peas, or helping in other ways with the work for the large family. William Koehler never sat with the rest. He worked all day and then went back to his room like any self-respecting laborer. He was disinclined to speak; he was happiest on long, sunny days when he could be in the garden from dawn till twilight.

Now he was on his knees, weeding his cabbage plants. Another man would have done the work quickly with a hoe, but not so William. The delightful labor lasted longer if he pulled each weed by hand. Frequently he paused, to press down the soil a little more solidly about the roots of a plant or to say what sounded like an encouraging word. Thus had he been accustomed to talk to his chickens and his bees.

When the squire and David approached, he looked up from his work with a frown. At David he merely glanced; at the squire he stared. When he recognized him, he smiled faintly and rose from his knees.

"Well, William," said the squire, cheerfully. "Do you know me?"

"To be sure I know you."

"Come over here and sit down, William."

"I am very busy this morning," objected William, uneasily.

He answered the squire in Pennsylvania German. The years which had almost anglicized Millerstown had had no educating effect upon the residents of the county home.

"But I want to talk to you a little."

The squire took him in a friendly way by the arm, at which an expression of terror came into William's eyes, and he jerked away from the squire's grasp.

"I will come," he promised. "But I will come myself."

The squire led the way across the lawn to the shade of a great tree where two benches were placed at right angles. Upon one the squire and David sat down, upon the other William. The line between William's eyes deepened, his lips trembled, he pressed his hands, palm to palm, between his knees. The squire and David looked at each other. The squire, too, had grown pale; he shook his head involuntarily over the task which they were beginning. He, too, had had a share in William's condemnation, as had all Millerstown. The squire felt helpless. He remembered the mocking boys, the scornful, incredulous people; he recalled the gradual taking away of William's business by the new mason whom Millerstown imported and encouraged. The squire thought as David had of the years that could never be returned, of the reason which could never be restored. He took a long time to begin what he had to say. When William half rose as though to escape back to his garden, the squire came to himself and his duty with a start.

"William, do you remember anything about the window that you plastered shut in the church and about the communion set?"

William lifted his hands, then joined them on his breast. He shook

XXI. The Squire And David Take A Journey By Day

now as with palsy. David, watching him, looked away to hide his tears. David was young, the wreck of William Koehler seemed a unique, horrible case.

Presently William answered in a low voice.

"God told me to be quiet. I prayed and prayed and God told me to be quiet. I am quiet now."

"But, William, you must tell us what you can remember. It will be for your good."

William opened his arms in a wild gesture, then clasped his hands again.

"A voice told me to forget it. I prayed till I heard a voice telling me to be quiet. You are tempting me! You are tempting me to disobey God. God said to be quiet about it!" He covered his face with his hands and began to weep aloud in a terrible way.

David crossed the little space between them and sat down beside him.

"You didn't take the communion set," he said. "We know you didn't take it."

William Koehler drew his hands away from his eyes and looked round at the young face beside him. Some tone of the voice startled him.

"Who are you?" he asked in astonishment. As he put the question he moved slowly and cautiously away, as though he planned to flee. "What do you mean to do with me?"

Together David and the squire rose. It was clear that William had heard as much as he could endure. His hands twitched, his eyes were as wild as any lunatic's.

"It doesn't make any difference who I am," said David, steadily. "You are to remember that all the people know you did not take the communion set. You are to think of that all the time."

Again William began to weep, but in a different way.

"I cannot think of it," he sobbed. "God told me not to think of it. God told me to forgive him. I have forgiven him."

As the squire and David drove through the gate, William was kneeling once more among his cabbages. Sometimes he stopped and rubbed his head in a puzzled way, then his hands returned to caress the young plants.

Almost silently the two men drove back to Millerstown and up to the little white house on the mountain road. Standing before the door, David saw once more its littleness, its meanness. It seemed as though it could never have been altogether proof against the storms of winter. Looking back at his own great mansion among the trees he shivered. Imagination woke within him; he comprehended something of the lonely misery of poor William. It was a salutary though dreadful experience for David.

Alvin answered their knock at once. In a half-hearted, inefficient way he was trying to put the house into habitable condition. For the first time in his life he thought with respect of his father and of his father's work. His father could have applied the needed plaster and boards skillfully and quickly.

When Alvin saw who stood without he looked at them blankly. The difference between his worn clothes and David's fine apparel hurt him. He was always afraid of the squire. Together the three sat down on the porch. Here David was the spokesman. To him the squire listened with admiration and respect.

"Alvin, the communion service has been found."

Alvin looked at them more blankly than ever. The affair of the communion service belonged to the dim past; since he had thought of the communion service he had been away to school, and had been educated and jilted, and cruelly maltreated by Bevy Schnepp, and had become engaged once more. It was a long time before Alvin could remember the very close relation he bore to the communion service. When he remembered, his heart sank. He recalled clearly his father's trying, desperate appeal on Christmas Day so long ago. Had they come to make him pay for his father's theft?

"Your father insisted that my father had been in the church and had taken it," explained David.

"I never believed it," cried Alvin at once. He was now terrified. Were they going to make him suffer for his father's madness. "I never believed it! Pop could never get me to believe it," he assured them earnestly.

"But it is true, Alvin," insisted David. "Your father had nothing to do with it. He spoke the truth when he said that he knew nothing about it. A great wrong was done your father. I want to try to make part of it right with you and him."

Alvin gaped at them. It was difficult to comprehend this amazing offer.

"I have been to see your father, Alvin," David went on. "I hope you will forgive my father and me."

David spoke steadily. The request was easy to make now; even greater humbling of himself would have been easy.

Alvin responded in his own way. He remembered his long poverty, his lack of the things he wanted, the cruel price he had had to pay for his first beautiful red necktie.

"My father spent a great deal of money for detectives," he said, ruefully.

"That will be restored to him," said David. "Everything that I can do, I will do, Alvin."

XXI. The Squire And David Take A Journey By Day

When their errand was made perfectly clear to Alvin, he was terrified again, now by his good fortune. He was to have money, money to do what he liked with, more money than he actually needed! The mortgage was to be destroyed — the mention of that instrument had alarmed him for the moment. Was he only to be relieved of a burden of whose existence he had been to this time unaware? But there was more to come! The sum his father had spent was to be guessed at liberally and was to be put on interest for his father's support, and Alvin himself was to have recompense.

"Do you like teaching?" asked David. "Is there anything you would rather do?"

Alvin clasped his hands as though to assure himself by physical sensation that he was awake and that the words he heard were real. He cherished no malice, hoarded no hatred — that much could be said for Alvin who failed in many other ways.

"Oh, how I would like to have a store!" he cried. "If I could borrow the money from you to have a store, a store to sell clothes and shoes and such things! I do not like teaching. I am not a teacher. The children are naughty all the time for me. I — " Suddenly Alvin halted. No more in this world could he go his own sweet way; liberty now offered was already curtailed. A fixed star controlled now the steady orbit of his life. His bright color faded. "We would better talk to her about it," said he.

David Hartman forgot for an instant the Pennsylvania German idiom. It is an evidence of the monogamous nature of the true Pennsylvania German that the personal pronoun of the third person, used alone, applies but to one human being.

"To her?" repeated David, puzzled.

"Yes, to Essie Hill. I am going to be married to Essie Hill." Alvin rose. "Perhaps we could go down there," he proposed hesitatingly.

Together the trio went down the mountain road. The squire drove the buggy, Alvin and David walked. The squire kept ahead, so that the curtains on the back of the buggy sheltered him from the view of his companions. Thus hidden, he laughed until the buggy shook. To the squire Alvin could never be a tragic figure; he belonged on the stage of comedy or broad farce.

When the squire reached the house of the preacher of the Improved New Mennonites, he dismounted, tied his horse, and awaited the arrival of the young men. Then the three went in on the board walk to the kitchen, where Essie was singing, "They ask us why we're happy." Again the squire's face quivered.

Essie received her three guests in her calm, composed way. She put the interesting scallops on the edge of her cherry pie with a turn of her thumb, and invited the three gentlemen to have seats. Essie was neither an imaginative nor an inquisitive person. Her life was ordered, her thoughts did not circle far beyond herself. The tragedy suggested by the juxtaposition of these three persons did not occur to her. She sat primly with her hands folded and heard her visitors for their cause. Her eyes narrowed as she listened to David's statement of Alvin's desire for a store. It was true that Alvin did not like teaching, was not a success as a teacher. Essie had intended to think out some other way for him to earn the family living. Selling fine clothes would not be a sin like wearing them; indeed, one could preach a sermon by refraining from what was so near at hand and so tempting. That such a policy might be damaging to the family pocketbook, Essie did not realize for the moment. Essie was always most anxious that the sermon should be preached. Millerstown, however, fortunately for Alvin's success as a haberdasher, was set in its iniquity as far as the wearing of good clothes was concerned.

"I think it would be a very good thing for Alvin to have a store," said she.

"I want to do everything I can to make up for the past," explained David. "I can't make it right entirely. I wish I could."

To Essie the balancing of accounts always appealed.

"That is right," said she.

"But there is Alvin's father," David went on. "We cannot leave him where he is if he can be persuaded to come away. He does n't understand yet that we have discovered that he was not guilty, but we hope he may."

Essie answered without pause. Essie had as clear an idea of her own duty as she had of other people's — a rather uncommon quality.

"We will take him home to us," said she.

When the interview was over, David went with the squire to partake of Bevy's dinner. The squire and his two companions had not been unobserved in their progress through Millerstown. Sarah Ann Mohr, on her way to David's house with a loaf of fresh bread and a Schwenkfelder cake and two pies and a mess of fresh peas from her garden and with great curiosity in her kindly heart about David's future movements, saw the three, and stood still in her tracks and cried out, "Bei meiner Sex!" which meaningless exclamation well expressed the confusion of her mind. When they vanished into Essie's kitchen, she cried out, "What in the world!" — and, basket in hand, plates rattling, instant destruction threatening her pies, she flew back to the house of Susannah Kuhns. Susannah hurried to the house of Sarah Knerr, and

XXI. The Squire And David Take A Journey By Day

together all sought Bevy, as the only woman connected with any of the three men. Other Millerstonians saw them assembled and the conference grew in numbers.

"The squire and David and Alvin Koehler together at the Mennonite's!" cried Susannah.

"Perhaps he is to marry her and Alvin," suggested a voice at the edge of the crowd.

"David used to sit with her, too, sometimes," Sarah Knerr reminded the others. "Perhaps there is trouble and it will give a court hearing."

"Humbug!" cried Bevy. "You don't know anything about it!"

Bevy, of course, knew nothing about it either.

Almost bursting with curiosity, Bevy made her noodle soup. It was only because she was not a literary person that the delicious portions of dough which gave the soup its name were not cut into exclamation points and question marks. Bevy was suffering; when the squire brought David home with him, her uneasiness became distressing to see. Presently she was thrown into a state bordering on insanity.

David laid down his fork and looked across the table at her restless figure.

"Bevy," said he in an ordinary tone, "the communion set has been found."

"What!" screamed Bevy.

All her speculations had arrived at no such wonderful conclusion as this. The squire looked startled; he had wondered how the report would first reach Millerstown.

"Did Koehler tell?" demanded Bevy. "Did he tell where he put it? Is it any good yet? Will they use it? Did you come to it by accident? Did —" Bevy's breath failed.

"Koehler had nothing to do with it," said David. "My father put it into the hole made by plastering up the window in the church. There it lay all these years."

"He never meant to take it!" screamed Bevy.

"No," agreed David; "I do not believe he meant to take it."

"What *did* he mean?"

"I do not know."

"Does n't anybody know?"

"Nobody knows," interposed the squire. "Now, Bevy, get the pie."

Immediately Bevy started for her kitchen. When after a few minutes she had not reappeared, the squire followed her. The kitchen was empty, no Bevy was to be seen; but from across the yard a loud chattering issued from Edwin's Sally's kitchen.

In the evening the squire and the preacher came and sat with David on his porch. The communion set had been taken from its hiding-place and the preacher's wife had polished it until it was once more bright and beautiful. Millerstown dropped in by twos and threes to behold it, each with his own eyes. The squire and the preacher and David talked about many things of interest to Millerstown and to the world at large. When the two men went away together, they said that David had astonished them.

Later in the evening another man entered the gate and came up to the porch. Oliver Kuhns, the elder, sat down in the chair which the squire had left.

"I heard a strange thing to-day," said he, brokenly. "I cannot understand it. When I was in great trouble, your father helped me. If you want I shall tell Millerstown, I will. I took my money when my father died and went to New York and bad people got me, and when I came home to my wife and little children, I had nothing. Your father lent it to me so she should not find it out, and he would never take it again."

"He would not want you to tell Millerstown," said David.

As Oliver Kuhns, the elder, went out the gate, Jacob Fackenthal came in. He would not sit down.

"Your pop saved me from jail, David," said he. "Anything I can do for you, I will. Nobody in Millerstown believes that he meant to take the communion set. If you will stay in Millerstown, Millerstown will show you what it thinks."

After a long time David went into the great house, through the front door, up the broad stairway to the handsome room which he had selected for his own. He could not understand his mother and father; still, in a measure, they put him away from them. Dimly he comprehended their tragedy, error on one side, refusal to forgive on the other, and heartbreak for both. He thought long of his father and mother. But when he went to sleep, he was thinking of William Koehler and his son Alvin and planning the fitting-out of a little store and the planting of a garden and the purchasing of a flock of chickens and several hives of bees. Old ghosts were laid, old unhappinesses forgotten; from David's consciousness there had vanished even Katy Gaumer, who in a strange way had brought him a blessing.

CHAPTER XXII
KATY IS TO BE EDUCATED AT LAST

Two months passed before Millerstown settled down, from the excited speculation which followed Katy Gaumer's flash of memory and its remarkable effects, into its usual level of excitement. Millerstown was usually excited over something. By the end of two months Sarah Ann and Bevy and Susannah Kuhns had ceased to gather on one another's porches or in one another's houses to discuss the strange Hartmans. By the end of three months all possible explanations had been offered, all possible questions answered, or proved unanswerable. Had Cassie known of the hiding-place of the silver service? Had Cassie died of a broken heart? Did persons ever die of broken hearts? Why, and again why, why, why, did John Hartman push the silver service into the hole? And why, having pushed it in, did John Hartman not take it out? Why had not Katy remembered the strange incident long before this?

"My belief is it *was* to be so," said Susannah Kuhns, a vague conclusion which Millerstown applied to all inexplicable affairs.

In all their speculations, no one ever thought of John Hartman or alluded to John Hartman as a thief. For once, Millerstown accepted the incomprehensible. Of the sad causes of John Hartman's behavior Millerstown knew nothing, could never know anything.

Sarah Ann, being more tender-hearted than the rest, and seeing a little more deeply into the lives of her fellow men and women, thought longest about the Hartmans. Sarah Ann's husband had been a disagreeable and parsimonious man and Sarah Ann knew something of the misery of a divided hearthstone. She often laid down the Millerstown "Star," fascinating as it was with its new stories, of a man driven by house cleaning to suicide in a deep well, of a dog which spoke seven words, or of a snake creeping up a church aisle, and took off her spectacles and thought of the Hartmans and of the Koehlers and of Katy Gaumer's strange part in their affairs.

Millerstown was not entirely deprived of subject-matter by its exhaustion of the Hartman mystery. David Hartman had employed a housekeeper and had opened his great mansion from top to bottom. All Millerstown walked past during the first few days of his occupancy to see whether it was true that there were lights in the parlor and that the squire and the preacher went in and out the front door to visit David. David had been carefully inspecting his orchards and farms, had visited again the land on the mountain-side with its double treasure. David had brought his riding-horse to Millerstown and Millerstown flew once more to doors and windows to see him pass. David consulted with his farmers; David asked a thousand questions of the squire; David was busy from morning till night.

"And David is nice and common," boasted Bevy Schnepp, who behaved as though she were David's mother and grandmother and maiden aunt in one. "He is never proud; you would never know he was so rich and educated."

David had gone himself in midsummer to bring William Koehler home to his house on the mountain-side. William seemed to understand now the startling information brought him by the squire and David. At last he realized who David was, and all the kindliness of his intentions. As he drove up the street, his old neighbors came out with pitying looks to speak to him and at his home his daughter-in-law received him with her placid kindness.

An addition had been built to the little house, but otherwise all was as it had been. The garden had been restored, onions and peas and tomatoes had been planted, though July was at hand, so that William might find immediate occupation. Back in the chicken house were cheerful cluckings and crowings, and about the hives the bees buzzed as of old.

At first William tended his garden and sat on the porch in the sunshine and was satisfied and happy. Then he grew restless; the line deepened again in his forehead. It was plainly to be seen that all was not right with William.

But all was made right. One afternoon Sarah Ann Mohr put on her sunbonnet and donned a white apron over her immaculate gingham one and took a basket on her arm and an umbrella in her hand, to be used now for sunshade, now for staff, and climbed the mountain road. She talked with William and gave Essie a little housewifely advice about the making of soap, in which occupation Essie was engaged; she emptied her basket, then she rose to go.

"William," said Sarah Ann, "I have a little plastering that should have been done this long time. I wonder if you would have the time to do it for me?"

It was not every one, Bevy Schnepp said proudly afterwards, who would ride on horseback to Allentown to fetch a mason's white suit and the best kind of trowel, but David had them ready for William in the morning. William accepted them eagerly and began to work at once. Presently he went all about Millerstown. Sometimes he even ventured to the Hartman house to speak to David. David learned after a long while to see him and talk to him without heartache. One day William made in a whisper an astonishing confidence.

XXII. Katy Is To Be Educated At Last

"People talk too much about themselves," said William. "I was queer once, out of my head, but I never let on and the people never found it out."

Thus mercifully was the past dulled.

By September Alvin was settled in his store in what had once been a little shoemaker's shop next to the post-office. Like the good housewife she was, Essie made the place all clean and tidy and banished all odor of leather. Then the little shop was painted and Alvin's glass cases for ties and collars and the low chairs for the trying on of shoes were put in place. Millerstown was curious, and went to see and remained to buy, and upon them waited Alvin in immaculate if sober clothes. Sometimes, alas! when there was no danger of Essie's coming into the shop, he wore a red necktie!

Alvin had paid his debt to Katy, and in the paying had achieved a moral victory worthy of a braver man. When the little store was planned and the fittings all but bought, he had gone to David Hartman and had confessed his debt.

"She helped me, she was the only one who ever helped me. She thought perhaps something could be made of me. And I could never pay her back."

"She helped you," repeated David. "You could never pay her back."

"That was it," explained Alvin. "When she could not go to school and had all this money she thought somebody should use it and she helped me."

David blinked rapidly. Then he went to the safe and counted a roll of money into Alvin's hand.

"Go pay your debts, Alvin. The store will be all right."

Alvin started briskly down the street, but his step grew slower and slower. He was, to tell the truth, desperately afraid of Katy Gaumer. Instead of going on to Grandfather Gaumer's he stopped in at the squire's, awful though the squire always seemed.

"Here is Katy's money," said he.

The squire put out a prompt hand and took the money, counted it, and put the roll into his pocket. It was just as well for the development of Alvin's soul that it had not been offered to Katy, who might not have accepted it.

"Thank you," said the squire. "I'll give you a receipt, Alvin. I am coming to your shop to get me a pair of shoes," added the squire with twinkling eyes.

July changed to August and August to September. The cock's-comb in Grandmother Gaumer's garden — it is, to this day, Grandmother

Gaumer's garden — thrust its orange and crimson spikes up through the low borders of sweet alyssum, the late roses bloomed, the honeysuckle put out its last and intensely fragrant sprays. In Millerstown busy life went on. Apple-butter boiling impended; already Sarah Ann and Bevy Schnepp saw in their minds' eyes a great kettle suspended from a tripod at the foot of Sarah Ann's yard, from which should presently rise into Sarah Ann's apple tree odors fit to propitiate the angry gods, odors compounded of apples and grape juice and spices. Round this pleasant caldron, with kilted skirts and loud chatterings, the women would move like energetic priestesses, guarding a sacred flame.

There came presently occasional evenings when it was not pleasant to be out of doors, when mothers called their children earlier into the warm kitchens and when men gathered in the store. Fall was at hand; Millerstown became quieter — if, an unobservant, unappreciative stranger would have said, Millerstown could have become any quieter than it was!

But Millerstown was still talking. Millerstown was now interested in another amazing event. Katy Gaumer was going away! The Millerstonians imparted it, the one to the other, with great astonishment.

"She will have her education now," said Sarah Ann with satisfaction. Then Sarah Ann's eyes filled with tears. Katy seemed to her to belong to the past; sometimes, indeed, to Sarah Ann's own generation. "I will miss Katy."

"Going to *school!*" cried little Mary Kuhns, who was now Mrs. Weimer. "Going to school when we are of an age and I have two children!"

"But I am not so fortunate as you, Mary," answered Katy.

Katy spoke with the ease of the preacher or the doctor; she seemed older than all her contemporaries.

"Going to school!" cried Susannah Kuhns. "You will surely be an old maid, Katy!"

"There are worse things to be," said Katy.

"Going to school!" Bevy's outcry was the loudest of all. "*Now! Are* you crazy, Katy?"

"Yes," laughed Katy as of old.

"Do you remember what learning you had?"

"Yes," indeed!"

"Pooh! I forget this long time everything I learned in school. It was mostly A, B, C, I guess. But there are better things than learning. I can cook. Was that why you went so often to the preacher this summer? Were you studying again?"

"Exactly," said Katy.

XXII. Katy Is To Be Educated At Last

Bevy looked at her half in admiration, half in disapproval. Katy had reached her full height; her dresses almost touched the floor, her curly braid was coiled on the top of her head; her eyes had darkened. But Katy's mouth smiled as it had smiled when she was a little girl. Bevy felt dimly that here was a different person from Mary Weimer with her babies and Louisa Kuhns, who, married a month, came to the store without having curled her hair.

"But you ought to get married sometime, Katy!" exploded Bevy. The wild dream which Bevy had cherished for her darling had faded. "What will you do in this world all alone?"

Presently Katy's new dresses were finished, her work with the preacher was concluded, and her new trunk was sent out from the county seat. Edwin's Sally and little Adam wept daily. Edwin shook his head solemnly over the impending separation.

In the few days which remained before her departure, the affairs of David Hartman and the Koehlers and the prospective apple-butter boilings were entirely forgotten. The gifts of friends who came to say good-bye would have filled two trunks, if Aunt Sally had not wisely discriminated between them.

"What will you do with three woolen quilts, Katy, when I gave you already nice blankets? These we will put in a chest in the garret. It will go for your Haus Steir [wedding outfit]."

Susannah Kuhns brought two jars of peaches and a glass or two of jelly, being firmly of the conviction that boarding-schools and colleges were especially constructed for the starving of the young.

"The English people do not eat anyhow like we do. I was once to some English people in Allentown and they had no spread at all for on their bread. Now you will have spreads, Katy."

Finally even Alvin Koehler caught the spirit and brought a present for Katy, a tie from his store. Alvin allowed no cloudy recollections of the past to darken his sunshine.

Sarah Ann came, too, with a silk quilt and a silk sofa pillow of the "Log Cabin" pattern, the product of long saving of brightly colored scraps.

"You are to have these things, Katy," said she. "You would 'a' had them anyhow when I was gone, and —"

"Now, Sarah Ann!" laughed Katy. "That will be years to come, Sarah Ann!"

Thus cheered, Sarah Ann dried her tears.

"Everybody in Millerstown is sorry you are going away," said she. "You are like the church or the schoolhouse, you are ours."

"I love Millerstown," said Katy: "I love Millerstown dearly."

Presently the trunk was packed, the last day was at hand. The squire came to a dinner such as Grandmother Gaumer used to prepare on holidays. He was as excited as a child over the prospect of his journey with Katy in the morning. He would see her established; it was almost as though he were going to school himself!

Aunt Sally refused any help with the dishes. Katy must not work; she might read, she might sew, she might go to see Sarah Ann, she might walk with little Adam to the schoolhouse, but she should not lay hand to dish-towel on her last day in Millerstown!

Katy chose the taking of little Adam to school. With his hand held tight in hers, she went out the gate, past the garden, and along the open fields toward the church and the schoolhouse set on the hill together. She glanced into the schoolroom, a dull place now, no longer the scene of the prancings of a Belsnickel or the triumphs of a studious Katy; then, leaving Adam, she set off toward the mountain road. From the first ascent she looked down at the house of David Hartman. The foliage about it was thinning; she was near enough to see the golden and scarlet flowers in the garden and a cat sleeping comfortably on the wide porch. She saw David almost daily, taking the two steps into the squire's office at a bound, sitting in his father's pew at church, riding about on his tall gray horse. She could not help hearing Millerstown's discussions of his doings, of his generosity to the Koehlers, of his subscriptions to the church, of his free-and-easy ways.

Presently there was a sudden motion on the Hartman porch; a tall figure appeared, the cat rose and went with arched back to meet her master, a clear whistle lifted to the ears of Katy. She started and went on her way, angry with herself for watching. She meant to climb to the Sheep Stable and sit there upon the great rock and look down upon the valley. There she could be alone, there she could look her fill upon Millerstown, there she could fortify herself for the future.

Before the Koehler house, William was puttering about in the yard. He called to her and gave her some flowers. He had been told of Katy's part in his deliverance, and though he seemed to have forgotten the specific reason for his kindly feeling toward her, he was more friendly only with David Hartman. He seemed not so much to have lost his mind and found it as to have harked back to his childhood.

Walking more rapidly after this delay, Katy went up the mountain road. The afternoon would pass all too quickly.

"I cannot make many plans," said Katy, soberly, as she went along. "If I make plans there is a hex on them. I must educate myself for whatever comes. It would be easier to educate myself if I were sure that something would come!" cried Katy, with sudden passion. "But there is nothing any more before me!"

The woods thickened; there was the chatter of an angry squirrel, a flash of gold as a flicker floated downward through the sunshine, showing the bright lining of his wings; there was the rich odor of ripening nuts, of slippery elm. On each side of the road and arching above rose the flaming trees, the golden brown beeches, the yellow hickories and maples, the crimson oaks. It was a beautiful, beautiful world, though one's heart was sad.

At the Sheep Stable Katy climbed out on the rocky parapet and sat with half-closed, half-blinded eyes. There was not a cloud in the sky; all was clear and bright. Far to the right lay the county seat; in the middle distance stood the blast furnace, the smoke rising lazily from its chimney; far away against the horizon rose the Blue Ridge with its three gaps where the Lehigh and the Schuylkill and the Delaware Rivers made their way through its barrier to the sea.

Directly below lay Millerstown, thickly shaded, still. Looking upon it, Katy felt her eyes fill with tears. She could see the golden light which the maples cast now upon its streets; she could see also the blanket of snow which would presently cover it, the moonlight which would light it enchantingly.

"But I will not be here!" mourned Katy. "Everything will go on in the same way, but I will not be here. I will be far away with those who do not know me. But I will not forget!" cried Katy. "I will not forget anything. I will have Millerstown graven on my heart!"

Then Katy bent her head. She was still cruelly obsessed. She thought of David Hartman, of his steady, gray eyes; she thought of his great house, of his fine mind, of his great prospects. Katy had grown up; remembering now the affection of her youth, she set her teeth and wept. Life and love were not devotion to a pair of dark eyes; life and love meant growth of one's heart and soul and mind, they meant possessions and power and great experiences which she could not now define. David was them all. Katy was not worldly or calculating, she had only learned to understand herself aright.

"I would like to talk to him," said Katy. "I would like him to know that I have some sense at last. Then I could be more satisfied to go away."

Then Katy turned her head and looked round at the little path which led through the woodland to the parapeted rock. The winding mountain road was out of sight from the Sheep Stable; a person could approach close to the little plateau without being seen. A rustle of the leaves betrayed a visitor. He walked briskly, leaping over rocks, thrusting aside branches like one whose mind is not upon the way but upon the goal. From the porch of his house he had seen Katy climbing the hill.

He lifted himself to a seat on the great rock beside Katy and raised his hand to shelter his eyes while he looked over the wide prospect.

"It is beautiful up here, isn't it, Katy?"

Katy caught her breath. Her chance to talk had come; she seemed to be filling her lungs to make the best of it. "Yes," said she.

"I'm sorry I frightened you." David did not speak very earnestly; his apology was perfunctory, as though he would just as soon have frightened her as not.

"It's all right," said Katy.

David looked about the little plateau. There was the little cairn; he wondered with amusement whether he had taken all evidences of his early wickedness away. Then he looked smilingly down upon his companion, who seemed unable to make use of the air which she had taken into her lungs, but sat silently with scarlet cheeks. The cheeks flushed now a still more brilliant color.

"We've met here before," said David, still smiling.

Katy filled her lungs with air again.

"I was *abominable*," she confessed, trembling. She began to be a little frightened. Here she had laid hands on David, had taken sides with his enemy, had thrust him violently down upon the ground, had screamed insulting things at him. She had a cold fear that he might be going to punish her for that miserable, compromising episode.

But David's tone was fairly pleasant.

"Yes," he agreed, "you were."

XXII. Katy Is To Be Educated At Last

Katy's head bent a little lower. She said to herself that all the education in the world would not remove the hateful stain of her association with poor Alvin. There was nothing she could say, though she had now ample opportunity; all she could do would be to remove herself as soon as possible from close proximity to this tall, gray figure, to the amused smile of these gray eyes. A moth on a pin could flutter no more feebly than Katy fluttered inwardly.

"I wish you would forgive me," said she, by way of preparation for a humble departure.

"But I won't," replied David. "I won't forgive you ever."

Katy's heart beat more and more rapidly. Was he really going to punish her in some strange way? Was he — she glanced rapidly about, then remembered how firmly that hand beside her controlled the great horse. There was no escape unless he let her go.

Then, in spite of herself, Katy looked up, to find David looking down upon her. An incredible notion came into her mind, an astounding premonition of what he meant to say. If she had waited an instant David would have spoken, would have mastered the overwhelming fear that, after all, the hunger of his heart was not to be satisfied. But being still Katy, she could not wait, would not wait, but rushed once more into speech, broken, tearful.

"I was crazy in my youth," gasped Katy. "I was *wild*. I cannot understand myself. Perhaps there are years when we are crazy. But I got over it. I got some sense. I was made to have sense. Trouble came upon me. I was tamed. Then I went to live at your house and I read your books, and you used to come home, and you were so wise and — and — so — so different from *everybody* —" Did any one think for an instant that Katy's day of romance was past? — "I thought it would kill me because I had been such a fool and you knew it. I thought you must do worse than hate me, I thought you must despise me. I thought —"

David put out his arm. With shaking voice he laughed.

"Oh, foolishness!" said David. He bent his cheek upon her forehead. "I have loved you as long as I can remember, Katy."

Katy clasped her hands across her beating heart, and closed her eyes.

"I am not prepared," said she in a whisper. "I am not educated! I am nothing! But, oh!" cried Katy Gaumer in the language of the Sunday-School book, "If you will give me a little time, I will bring home my sheaves!"

The End

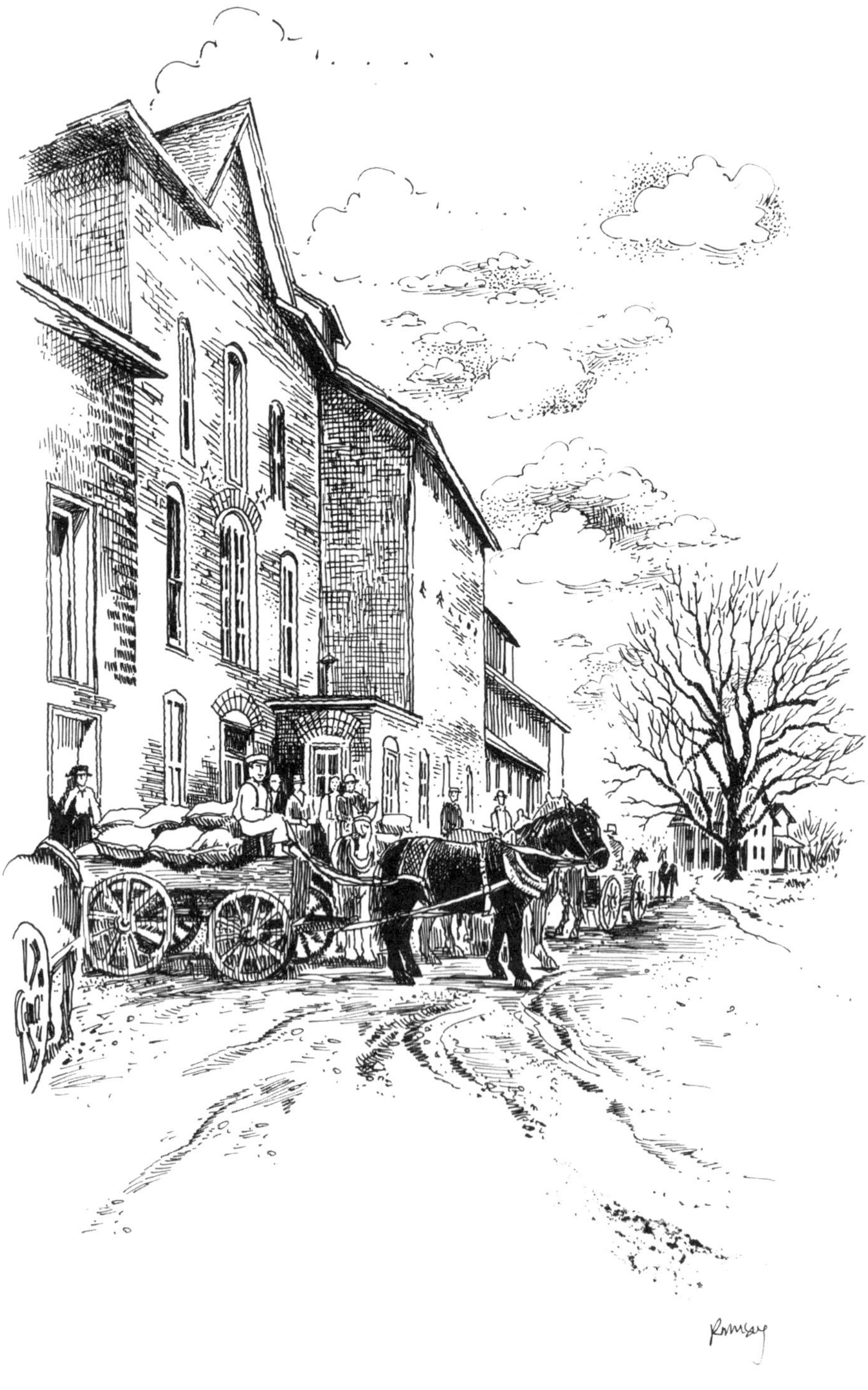
Ramsay

Short Stories of Millerstown

by

Elsie Singmaster

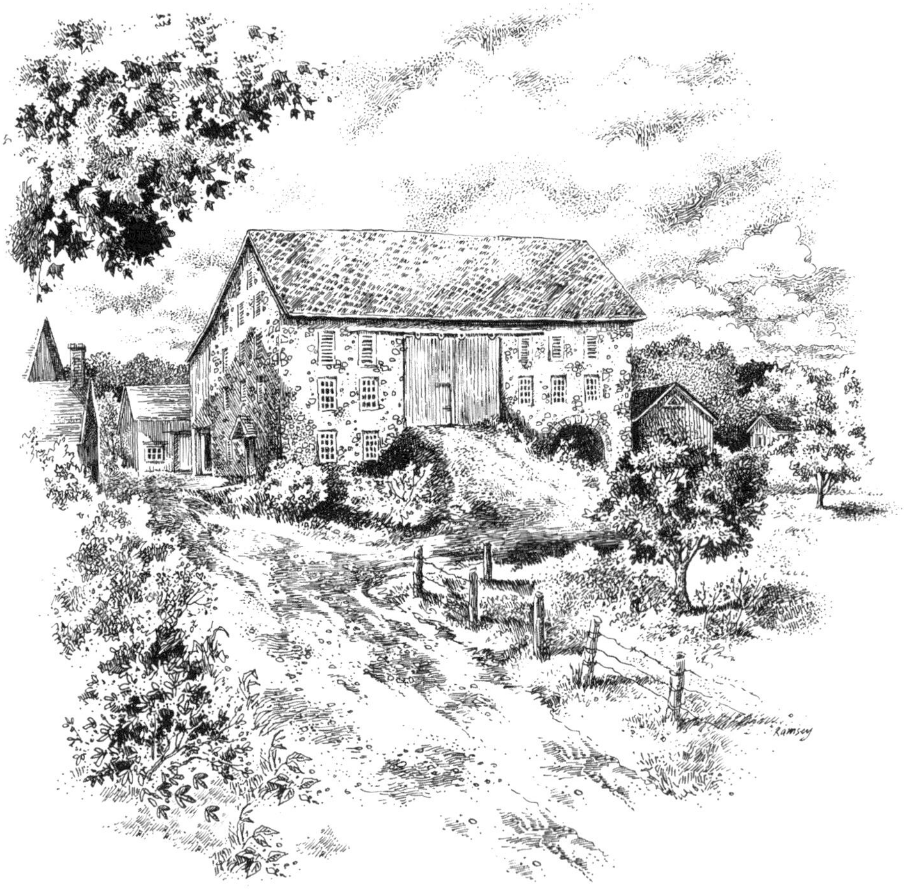
Ramsey

BIG THURSDAY

Originally published in the January 1906 issue of *The Century Magazine*

From Slatington down to Hosensack, from Stinesville across to Centre Valley, Lehigh County was astir, though it was just dawn of a clear September morning. For this — an ecstatic thrill ran down one's spine at the mere mention — this was Fair Week; and, moreover, this was Big Thursday. There were other holidays, of course. Christmas was well enough in its way, and gaily celebrated in the county-seat. Out in the country, however, where purses were not so deep, they did not expect so much from Santa Claus. Fourth of July came in the midst of the busiest season of the year, and only faint echoes of the city's boom of cannon and blare of bells reached the farm. But Big Thursday! It was not alone because of his Jersey or Durham cattle in the sheds or his wife's pies or preserves upon the shelves of the exhibition buildings that the Pennsylvania German looked forward, from September to September, to Big Thursday. It was because he himself was part of the exhibit, he was the fair. He toiled all year on the farm or in the wire-mill or the cigar-factory in order that his family might hold up their heads among their neighbors; and now on this day he meant to lose his own individuality in that of the crowd — the biggest crowd, if you please, at the biggest fair in the finest State in this great and glorious country! If he had consulted the wish which hid itself down in the bottom of his heart, he would have gone to the fair alone. There was the wife, however, who had looked forward to this day as eagerly as he, and there were the children, — six, seven of them, — and there was the grandmother, who had not missed a Big Thursday for years and years. He could not for the world disappoint them, though he did have to engineer their slow progress through the crowd instead of cheerfully elbowing his own way alone. Besides, after dinner he could easily get away to lean on the race-track fence, and with thrills which caught his throat even now watch Prince Alert break the record. And last year he had seen among the signs in the Midway one which read: "Homo Bovino. Walk in! The Greatest Curiosity of the Age!" That creature he meant to inspect. The children were too young to see such things, and the wife — *ach!* she would not be interested. Besides, he could tell her about it afterward. He had caught a glimpse of the Homo Bovino, and was sure that he detected through the boy's thin clothing the straps by means of which hoofs had been attached to his poor crippled limbs.

The great trolley system, which, like a huge octopus, reached from the county-seat far into the next counties, could not, for all its doubling of forces and speed, gather in all those who wished to come. The foresighted started early; they arose at four o'clock, packed their luncheon, and hastened to catch the five-o'clock car, when, lo! they discovered that the whole village shared their prescience. Even the first car was crowded far beyond the minimum of safety.

The country through which they sped lay like a vast garden, well watered, well tilled, fertile. Here and there on the hills, a single scarlet beech-limb or faintly yellowed hickory flung out a gay reminder that summer was almost gone. In the fence-corners the asters nodded gently, and the ironweed lifted its head proudly from the lush meadow-grass. There was a faint mist in the lowlands, and the morning breeze blew cool. Otherwise it was still summer.

The cars that day did not run straight to the Fair Grounds, as was their usual custom. Instead, in spite of loud objections, they emptied their passengers at Sixth and Washington streets, in the middle of the city, and twelve squares from the fair. Then with a loud clanging of gongs they started back whence they came, to Emaus and Millerstown, to Siegfried's and Coplay, to East Texas and Egypt, to gather in other waiting thousands.

Presently, in long trains which thundered down from the coal-regions or across from Berks County or "Chersey," came the visitors from other counties, eager to find some flaw in the management which might compare unfavorably with their own fair.

"It ain't so many side-shows like ours," Berks County would remark when once within the gates.

"I'd like to see them beat our record at the races," Northampton would rejoin proudly.

From the coal-regions came the miners. Encumbered with no womenfolk or children, with the wages of a month in their pockets, they determined to forget for twenty-four long, glorious hours the blackness and heaviness of their toil. They pinned their return tickets in their pockets, and now for a day of it!

For several hours it seemed as though the fair itself were crowded into the space at the intersection of Sixth and Washington streets. And here, where the great arms of the octopus dropped their prey, in the midst of farmers from her own county, of envious kinsfolk from Berks and Bucks and Northampton, of miners from Mahanoy City, Shenandoah, Centralia, and riot-stained McAdoo, of city reporters who had quarreled among themselves for the privilege of reporting the "Dutch Fair," and of sportingmen who came to see the races, stood pretty Mary Kuhns, the prettiest girl in Millerstown, a little village ten miles away. And Mary, who was usually accompanied by a train of gallants, was alone, and therefore a little frightened.

Until the evening before she had expected John Weimer, to whom she was to be married the next summer, to be her escort. Then, however, he had come to make his daily call, with a distressed expression on his round and rosy face.

"We cannot go to-morrow in de fair," he announced. "Pop's cousint at Oley he died, an' I must go to de funeral."

"An' miss de fair!"

"It iss no oder way, Mary. We can go Fridays in de fair."

"Fridays! You know it ain't no good Fridays. Were you, den, such good friends wis your pop's cousint?"

"No, I nefer once saw him. But pop he can't go because he has it so bad in his foot, an' mom she can't go because she has to stay by pop, an' it iss nobody left but me."

"Your pop's cousint, an' you nefer saw him, an' you must go all de way to Oley down to de funeral!" Mary's eyes blazed, and she sat up very straight in the rocking-chair.

"Now, Mary," he said soothingly, "you know how it iss wis funerals. We can go Fridays in de fair."

"*You* can when you want. *I* am going to-morrow. It iss me Fridays too slow."

"But, Mary, wis who den will you go?"

"Oh, I guess I can pick somebody up who does not haf to go to his pop's uncle's funeral. I get some one. I can sink already of somebody what would be glad to go, efen if his pop's aunt wass going to haf to-morrow her funeral. Or I can go alone. I sink dat would be, anyhow, de nicest. It iss me anyhow a boder to haf a man always along."

"Mary, when you would go alone in de fair I nefer forgive you."

"I sink I get along," she responded saucily. "Oh, dear, I am getting already sleepy. I sink it iss getting pretty late."

"But, Mary, all de people!"

"Where?" said Mary, as she craned her neck to see out beyond the honeysuckles.

"*Ach*, Mary, don't be so ugly! At de fair, of course."

"What do I care for de people? I am not afraid of people. When I haf trouble, I can ask de police. Dey will be dere, I guess."

"Mary!"

The creak of her rockers suddenly ceased.

"Chohn, tell me once dis: When a policeman's second cousin dies, dare he get off to go to de — "

"You da's n't go alone, Mary Kuhns! Why, I rader ask Bench an' Chovina Gaumer to take you dan haf you go alone in de fair."

At this Mary rose stiffly. Benjamin Gaumer, who had been one of her own most devoted admirers, had the month before married Jovina Neuweiler; and though Mary was at the time engaged to John, Benjamin's defection had hurt her vanity more than she allowed any one to suspect.

"You can go right aways home," she said. "If you wass de only one in all de world what could go wis me to-morrow in de fair, yet I would go alone."

"Mary — "

But Mary had vanished within doors. He waited for a few minutes in sore distress.

"She had no business to get so mad. I can't help it pop's cousint had to die."

That she would venture to the fair alone he did not for a moment seriously consider. If she were independent like Jovina Neuweiler, he might believe her. But Mary was afraid of Weygandt's mildest cow.

Whether she was braver than he knew, or whether anger and disappointment had bestowed upon her a temporary courage, the next morning found her alone in the great crowd at the county-seat. She wore her best white dress, laundered to a smooth stiffness which would have supported its own weight without the four stiffer petticoats beneath. Although she was uncomfortably cool, she would not for the world have hidden any of the glories of her white dress under the jacket which her mother had bade her take, and which she carried on her arm. A sash of ribbon as blue as her eyes encircled her waist, and the frill of lace around her neck stood out like a little ruff of the Elizabethan period. Under her best hat — a white Leghorn trimmed with buttercups — her fair hair was brushed back as smoothly as its curly nature would allow. On her hands were her white mitts, drawn carefully back from her fingers so that John's ring, a garnet with two emeralds, should show. If the tears did threaten to start when she realized that she was alone, or remembered that she had not told her mother that John was not coming with her, her face wore a most deceptive mask of cheerfulness, so that many older eyes that day gazed with pleasure upon so much youth and innocence enjoying itself.

There had been many Millerstonians on the car by which she came — Billy and Sarah Knerr and their brood of six, Jimmie Weygandt and Linnie Kurtz, the young Fackenthals, and her own brother Oliver and his wife. Mary succeeded, however, in climbing aboard without being seen by any of them.

"Dey will sink it iss mighty funny dat he did n't come along," she said to herself.

As she listened to the gay chatter in the car her spirits rose. One could have a good time even by one's self. Any time that she got tired of being alone she could join the Knerrs or Ollie and his wife. Presently the fields gave place to long rows of suburban houses built close together, with tiny yards, as though there were no wide fields behind them. Their progress through the streets was slow, with long waits on the switches, then a sudden mad dash where there were double tracks. When they reached Sixth and Washington streets, Mary did not follow her fellow-townsmen through the crowd to the other car, but, mounting the steps which led into a store, she stood head and shoulders above the throng and looked out over them. Then she permitted herself an exclamation for which she had often reproved her brother Oliver.

"*Harrejä!*" she said; "it iss no end of people!"

Car after car added its quota to the multitude, then sped with clanging gong back whence it came. Bewildered-looking women pressed their way through the crowd, the balloon-man and the peanut-vender cried their wares at its edge, and round-faced, tanned youths, with bright ties, and flowers in their buttonholes, jostled one another with rough gaiety. Once the sound of a child's cry rang clear and sharp above the din, but was quickly lost in the shouting, the creak of the car-wheels, and the loud bells.

Presently Mary's eyes fell upon a group of men standing near her. She caught snatches of their conversation, — mentions of Prince Alert and Myrtle Peak, — and she watched admiringly the gleam of the huge diamonds in their shirt-bosoms.

"Well, I bet it 'll be the biggest thing this county ever saw," one of them exclaimed. "How much you got on it?"

She did not hear the man's answer, but suddenly the group turned and looked at her. She was not unaccustomed to admiring glances, but there was something about the rudeness of their stare which troubled her.

"I — I sink I go on," she said to herself, her cheeks afire, as she started up the street.

The Fair Grounds lay twelve long squares to the west, but Mary preferred the walk to the wild scramble necessary to secure a seat in a car. Besides, there were many interesting things to see — the shop-windows, the great white bear in front of the fur-store, the huge horse at the saddler's, and the dummies at the tailor shops, which were so natural that once, on a previous visit to the county-seat, she had asked some directions of one and had been much astonished that he did not reply. There were also hundreds of people, old and young, by threes or fours or in family groups of six or seven, and many couples, sweethearts evidently, whose air of gaiety sent a sharp stab of envy to Mary's heart.

"He might 'a' come," she thought; "but what do I care? I am hafing chust so good a time as when he wass along."

She bought her ticket at the gate of the Fair Grounds, and then —

"But dis iss me first grand!" she said rapturously at her first glimpse of the enchanted country, bigger, more beautiful, noisier, and more crowded than ever before.

The grounds covered about eighty acres in the form of a square, inclosed by a tall fence. They had originally been covered by a thick grove of trees, half of which had been cut down; and it was there, on the wide, open space, that the chief business of the fair was conducted. There stood the exhibition buildings, — the main building, the agricultural building, the flower-house, and various other frame structures designed to shelter the treasures of the county, — and beyond them the long sheds whence came sounds which made the farmer feel at home at once — the low of cattle, the crow of roosters, and the long *baa–a–a* of sheep. Above them towered the grand stand, and beyond curved the race-track — "the best in the State," if you please, you Berks and Northampton county people. Near the entrance gate lay the Midway, "the size of which, ladies and gentlemen, we cannot guarantee, of course, to be equal to that of the great and only original Midway, but whose quality, we can assure you, is, if anything, superior." It consisted of two parallel rows of tents, their doors, before which platforms had been erected, facing each other, and the ground between beaten as hard as that of the much-vaunted race-track. At one end stood the tent of the famous Georgiana and her company of trained entertainers, "warranted, ladies and gentlemen, not to offend the most refined taste." Across the narrow alley, Penelope, — her manager pronounced her name in three syllables, — the Petrified Lady, exhibited her adamantine charms, and next door Bosco the Wild Man of the Siberian Desert rattled his chains, so that even the crowd outside, who had not money enough to pay the admission fee, could share the horror of his close proximity. The Homo Bovino — a favorite for years — was in his place, and the snake-charmers and the Rubber Man. If one only had money enough to see them all!

In the lower half of the grounds, under the trees, were the shooting-galleries, the merry-go-rounds, the great swings, the tents of the fortune-tellers, and, far beyond them all, stretching its length along the whole side of the great inclosure, a huge bar, where the sporting-man from New York clinked glasses with the Irishman from Hazleton, and the reporter who watched them planned to end his article on the Pennsylvania-German County Fair with this sentence, "The Pennsylvania Dutchman goes to his fair to see and be seen, but the dearest of all to his heart is the mammoth bar, at which, although it extends for the length of two city squares, it is hard to get standing-room."

And over all, from the entrance gate to the race-track, from the cattle-sheds down to that other long shed at the very bottom of the grove, hung Noise like a tangible thing. At a little distance not one of its elements could be distinguished. The cries of the managers of Bosco, of Penelope, of the Rubber Man, the weird fanfare before the tents of the snake-charmers, the shriek of tin whistles, the loud reports at the shooting-galleries, the blare of a band down toward the bar, the bucolic echoes from the cattle- and poultry-sheds, the blasts of the calliope, the jingle of the mechanical piano at the merry-go-round, the sound of ten thousand voices — all blended into one great vociferation, indescribable, elemental.

It was small wonder that little Mary Kuhns should stand for a moment bewildered. It was hard to decide where to go first. Presently, however, she climbed the steps of the main building and went slowly down the broad aisle. Here hung a quilt composed, so its tag stated, of four thousand, four hundred, and seventy-six pieces, and beside it an elaborate crocheted spread. There were wax-works, and hair-works, and paper flowers, rolls of crocheted or tatted lace, embroidered doilies, pincushions of unique design — one representing a huge carrot, another a tomato. After admiring them all, Mary hastened on to the food exhibit. There she found Linnie Kurtz's preserved peaches, Savilla Arndt's canned pears, and, standing proudly above them, Jovina Gaumer's cake, five layers high, with an elaborate scroll design in tiny pink wintergreen drops on its white icing. In its side yawned a huge wedge-shaped orifice from which the judges had cut the generous slice from which to test its quality. That it was satisfactory the blue tag, emblem of the first prize, declared.

Mary, however, was not thoroughly appreciative of this evidence of her towns-woman's skill.

"Pooh! What do I care?" she said to herself. "He nefer would 'a' married her when it had n't been for her cake. Now I am going to look once for Ollie's chickens and Chimmie Weygandt's cows."

She found them both, each with a blue tag above their stalls, then she laid her hand for an instant on Bossy's broad face.

"You know me, don't you, Bossy?" she said.

She wandered forth again past the side-shows and the race-track to the cool shadow of the grove, now transformed into one vast dining-room. The tomtoms had ceased to beat, the calliope blew out its last despairing note. Even the fortune-teller, with her prosaic husband by her side, partook of huge hot rolls and frankfurters in the doorway of her tent. The tents of Bosco and Penelope and the Homo Bovino were closed; and did not one's imagination halt before the abode of so much mystery, one might guess that they, too, were dining.

At the eating-stands there were several menus offered. For fifteen cents one could get a huge plate piled with sauerkraut and mashed potatoes; or, for a quarter, a large helping of stewed chicken and three or four waffles. Were one so lacking in discrimination as to care for neither of these delicacies, one might have fried oysters, or sandwiches—ham, chicken, beef, or tongue between thick slices of bread, or oysters or frankfurters between the halves of a long roll.

Mary hesitated for an instant between the chicken and waffles and fried oysters. Of the sauerkraut she would have none. She liked it well enough, to be sure, but one could get sauerkraut any day at home. Chicken and waffles were much more appropriate to high days and holidays, but fried oysters were rarest of all; and presently she sat with a plate of sizzling-hot oysters before her, and a huge saucer of cole-slaw beside the plate. She ate them both, down to the last crumb of oyster and the last bit of slaw. Then deciding that a glass of lemonade would be suitable dessert, she rose and sought the nearest lemonade-stand.

"A three-cent glass or a five-cent glass, madam?" asked the vender.

"Oh, a fife-cent glass," she answered; "an' pink."

She drained the glass, her blue eyes peering over its edge in anticipation of all the delights to come.

"It iss more an' more people coming all de time," she said to herself. "It seems as when all de world wass already here, an' dey are yet coming."

The crowd had trebled since her arrival. The newcomers halted to look for an instant over the vast throng and listen to the thousand sounds which, after the temporary lull at noon, grew each moment louder and less distinguishable; then, pressed by those behind, they hastened away toward the exhibition buildings, the race-track, the cattle-sheds, or the Midway. Mary, too, was tempted to investigate the Midway. The mysterious Penelope, especially, fascinated her, and she wished to get near enough to the Circassian beauty to see whether her serpentine bracelets and necklaces were really alive. She walked over to the edge of the crowd gathered about the tent of Penelope, and then, when she had listened only a moment, walked quickly away, her cheeks scarlet.

"I don't belief it iss a nice place, dat one. I sink—" and a sudden loneliness overwhelmed her— "I sink he might 'a' come, dat iss what I sink."

Suddenly the timbre of the great chord was altered. The calliope ceased its sepulchral piping, one heard no more the *pop-pop* at the shooting-gallery, and the piano at the carrousel jingled slowly into silence. The noise became vocal, human. The calliope, the merry-go-round, and the shooting-gallery charmed no more: it was time for the races.

Mary found herself carried with the crowd toward the race-track—not, however, without some reproaches of conscience. Her church, the Jonathan Kuhns Baptist, founded by, and bearing the name of, her grandfather, did not approve of horse-racing, and Mary knew well that if any of the members saw her, they would be shocked and grieved. However, she had seen no one from Millerstown since she left the car, and who would be the wiser if she went across to the fence and discovered for herself the secret of the mad shouts which had, during other visits to the fair, excited her curiosity? It did not occur to her to seek a seat on the grand stand. In the first place, that would have been too conspicuous a defiance of Jonathan Kuhns Baptist traditions; in the second, it would have been a shameful waste of money, when there was half a mile of low fence upon which one could lean comfortably. She saw them leading out the horses, and she watched in astonishment the upward toss of their heads and the proud fling of each slender hoof.

"Gee-oh!" she heard some one say; "ain't he a beaut!"

"I wish dey could see once Chimmie Weygandt's Bessie," thought Mary. "She iss me once a pretty horse; she has some fat on her. Dese horses haf surely not enough feed."

She found that the fence was rapidly filling with those who, either for fear of wickedness in high places or else for lack of the admission fee, avoided the grand stand. She found a place between a stout woman who glanced at her pleasantly, and a tall man in a silk hat who obsequiously made room for her.

"Well," he queried, with smooth pleasantry, "come to see the show? You'd better come up on the grand stand with me. We can see much better from there."

"No, sank you."

All day people had looked at Mary as she walked about alone in her white dress, and her blue eyes had looked back, unaware of the impudence of their scrutiny. This man, however, was the first who had spoken to her. Had his accent been that of her own people, she would have answered him with frank friendliness; but he was "English," and she feared him.

"Oh, come on." He moved a step toward her.

"No; *ach!* no," she said, and started away. Suddenly the stout woman took a hand.

"Will you leaf once my girl alone?" she questioned sternly. "Ain't you got den no politeness?"

"Oh," the man answered in confusion, and in a moment was gone.

"I am for sure much obliched," said Mary. "I can't sink for why he should talk to me. I nefer once saw him."

"You are for sure welcome," the kind voice answered. "But dis iss a bad place for girls alone. Where are den your folks?"

Mary hesitated. "I don't know," she faltered.

"You did n't come all by yourself in de fair?" There was amazement and reproof in every word.

"No," responded Mary. Were not Jimmie Weygandt and Linnie Kurtz and the Fackenthals and the Knerrs all there, and her own brother Ollie? "Dere are lots a folks here what I know."

"Well, when I wass you I stay by my folks."

"I guess nobody would dare touch me. Chohn would pretty soon gif dem one."

"Who iss den Chohn?"

"Ay, Chohn Weimer." Mary's tone was sufficiently expressive for the dullest comprehension.

"Why ain't Chohn den here wis you?"

"Ay, his pop's cousint died, an' he had to go to de funeral."

"Could n't you come Wednesdays or Fridays?"

"No."

"Well, could n't he stay away from de funeral?"

"Ay, of course not. Funerals come first, I guess."

"Well, you stay now here by me, an' we watch de races." The woman divined some lover's tragedy in Mary's indignant response. "Den you must find right away your folks. Look out once, you get your nice dress against de fence. See, dey are starting. See once! Look at de funny carts. It iss de brown one what iss de best. My man he saw him race already."

In the excitement she grasped Mary's arm. The roar of the crowd around them settled into a dull murmur, then into silence. There was a false start, then the horses were off again, four of them, almost neck to neck.

"Iss dat all?" cried Mary in bewildered disappointment of something, she knew not what. "Chust horses running?"

"You wait once," said the stout woman. "Twice around iss a mile. Chust watch once how dey fly!"

In a second Mary was holding her breath with the rest. She had never seen a race before, she had no preference among the horses, she knew nothing of the mad excitement of those whose money is staked upon the outcome of the race, to whom victory may mean plenty, defeat ruin. Nevertheless, a strange thrill shot through her, born of the sight of the clean-limbed, glossy-coated racers — which, she began to feel, were vastly superior even to Jimmie Weygandt's Bessie — and the consciousness of the strain and excitement in the crowd about her. In six seconds over two minutes the race was over, and Mary, her cheeks flushed and her eyes shining, leaned out across the fence, hurrahing with the rest.

Presently, when the shouts of the multitude were dying slowly away, she looked around for the stout woman, to find that in some way the crowd had pressed between them. Fearing that the big man might come back and speak to her again, she walked away. The side-shows were deserted except for their proprietors, and she wandered slowly down between the dirty tents. The snake-charmers, deprived of their audience for a while, watched her with curious wistfulness. There was an air of the woodland about her. One thought instinctively of wide meadows and the sound of softly flowing water bubbling from the cool edge of the woods, and of all manner of pleasant country things. The famous Penelope, who now sat in the tent door indulging in a little talk of the trade with her manager, eyed her curiously.

"Seems to me," she was saying, "if I was a man, I wouldn't be fooled so often. Once let a woman into this tent, and she'd be on to my petrifactions in less 'n no time. Gracious, Bill! Look at this a-comin'!"

Bill turned and regarded Mary as though she were a visitor from another world.

"They don't make 'em like that in New York, do they, Mamie? Can't you just see the hay growin' and hear the lambs bleat?"

"Well, I guess!" responded the fair Penelope. "But that girl ought n't to be wandering round here by her lonely — that she ought n't. I 've half a mind to tell her."

The manager grinned. "Set down, Mamie. You 'd be a fine one to march up to that sprig o' youth and beauty and warn her against the ways of the wicked world, now!"

The woman drew the shawl which half concealed her shoulders a little closer.

"Sometime we're going to get out o' this business, Bill. It makes me sick."

"Nonsense!" he rejoined cheerfully. "You 'd be back in a week, Mamie. You know you would."

For the space of a second her eyes followed the white figure. Then she rose.

"Come on, git up and sing your little song," she said with a gaiety that was half real. "There's more galoots a-comin' to see Penelope. Make hay while the sun shines, for there is rain comin', or my name's not Mamie Bates, alias the Petrified Lady."

It was a tradition that Big Thursday was always fine. Now, however, in spite of the fair promise of the morning, low clouds began to gather in the west, hid from the crowds by the grove, and a low rumble, indistinguishable from the thunder of hurrahs, presaged the coming of an unseasonable thunder-storm.

Mary, as oblivious as the rest to the ominous sound, started slowly down through the grove. She had always wished to know what attraction at the lower end of the Fair Grounds drew so many people in that direction, and now she meant to find out. She looked lovingly at the merry-go-round as she passed. The manager had gladly started it at the appeal of a number of young people for whom the races seemed to have no attraction, and it ground out gaily "The Carnival of Venice," while its wooden horses curveted and lions pranced. Mary watched the riders enviously. Last year—

"I sink he need n't 'a' gone to his pop's cousint's funeral," she thought, her lips quivering like a child's. She began, alas! to be tired. She had been walking or standing since seven o'clock that morning, and it was now past four. There was no place to sit down, however, save the beaten, dusty ground, and she walked on down toward the great shed. As she approached it, the multitudinous shouts from behind gave place to another sound, akin yet different—the loud voices of men and women, raised now in heavy laughter, now in shrill dispute. Mary drew nearer. What could they be doing? Suddenly another sound, fainter but as continuous, reached her ear—the clink, clink of glass against glass, and Mary knew. For an instant she was too astonished to move. They did not come and go, these men and women crowded together. They stood and drank and drank, and quarreled or laughed, and drank again. Mary, who, with all her kith and kin, was "strictly temperance," fled, fearful lest the fate of Sodom and Gomorrah should suddenly encompass her. She would go home, straight back to Millerstown. As she passed the exhibition building, the wide, dusty steps, almost deserted, looked so inviting that she sat down for an instant. A man reeled by and she caught her breath in a sob. Suddenly her fright became terror. A stream of something wet and cold struck her in the neck, and she sprang up and looked fearfully around. At her side stood a young man who held in his hand a small squirt from which the water had evidently come.

"What do you mean?" demanded Mary, angrily. "I did n't do you nossing."

For reply, he pointed the little toy at her again. The conviction dawned slowly upon her that he had sprinkled her on purpose. For a second she was speechless.

"W-when Chohn Weimer wass here, you get de worst srashing you efer had, dat I can tell you!"

The boy laughed.

"Or our Ollie or Chimmie Weygandt or Bench Gaumer!"

"You must haf a lot of fellers," he said impudently. "Come on; you be my girl for a while. We go an' get some lemonade wis a straw in it."

Suddenly Mary's deliverance came in the shape of a girl of about her own age, who, squirt in hand, deluged the young man's celluloid collar and purple tie with a well-aimed jet of water. Mary, more horrified than ever, started rapidly away.

The races were over, and she found herself suddenly pressed on all sides by the crowd. If she could only find Ollie, or the Fackenthals, or the stout woman, or some one to take care of her! Her taste of independence, at first sweet, had turned bitter. Oh, to be home getting supper, or sitting on the porch with John! But would John ever care for her again? The Weimers were all easy-going until they were roused. Then look out! Old John Weimer, her John's uncle, had not spoken to his wife for thirty years, although in all that time they had lived in the same house, eaten at the same table. Suppose her John should never speak to her again! At any rate, she would go straight back to Millerstown and tell him that she was sorry. She started toward the wide gate marked "Exit," her aching feet a little less painful now that they were set toward home, and her blue eyes bright again. Suddenly she felt a splash of water on her hand. She glanced around piteously. Why could they not let her alone? Then Mary's eyes, with more than fifty thousand other pairs of eyes, sought the sky. The storm was almost upon them. The loud rumble needed not the sudden hush to make itself heard. She was caught and whirled along in the mad rush for shelter. She tried at first to struggle out to the edge of the crowd toward the exit gate, but she could not move. Once she slipped and fell on one knee, and a man's strong hand lifted her from the ground. She looked up gratefully from under her broad hat, to meet a pair of sharp eyes and a sarcastic smile.

"Where's your mother, my dear?"

Mary gasped. It was the big man! She ducked her head under the arm of another tall man on the other side, and elbowed her way frantically through the crowd. Her blue sash became untied and trailed behind her; but she heeded it not until, caught under a heavy foot, it held her back;

then she gathered it around her. The rain came no longer in huge drops, but in wind-driven sheets which in a moment washed all semblance of stiffness from her hat and set it flapping about her face. She slipped into her jacket, which only made her shiver as it pressed her wet sleeves against her arms. Great red stains from her leather purse marked her white mitts. A woman pinched her arm spitefully as she rushed against her in her mad flight, and once a man swore, but she paid no heed. She was afraid to stop; she expected each moment to see that sarcastic smile and hear that smooth voice, "Where 's your mother, my dear?" Suddenly the crowd gave way about her, and she caught a glimpse of the exit. One more determined shove, a ruthless stepping on her neighbor's feet, and Mary was out in the wide street, where thousands of people, rain-soaked and tired like herself, struggled for places in the street-cars. She tried in vain to climb up the steps of a car. As soon as she secured a foothold, she was pushed back. The crowd was no longer a good-natured holiday throng: it was a vast mob of selfish beings, worn out by the day's pleasuring, and angry at the storm which put an end to it.

As she looked about her she was astonished at the bedraggled appearance of the hundreds who started with her down Washington street. The men turned their collars up and their hats down, and thus tramped along in comparative comfort. But the women! Their skirts hung about them limp and soiled, their hats retained not a vestige of the gay jauntiness which had that morning delighted both the wearer and the beholder. One woman, who looked the more bedraggled because her dress had, like Mary's, once been white, tried to make friends with her.

"Dis iss once a surprise, ain't it — dis rain?" she remarked cheerfully. "Haf you den far to go till you get home?"

Mary looked at her, from the dripping roses on her hat to the soiled ruffles above her muddy shoes.

"I sink I do not know you," she responded with dignity.

"Nor I you," the woman answered sharply. "An' when you would see yourself once you would n't want to know yourself."

With which remark, she hurried on, leaving Mary dumfounded. How did she dare to talk to her like that? Was not this her best hat, her best dress, and her new blue sash? All at once Mary realized how she herself must look, and was properly punished then and there for her haughtiness. She had forgotten, in the blessed prospect of getting home, how her hat flapped against her face. She became suddenly aware of every wet stroke. She realized that her blue sash trailed behind her as she walked, and that her white dress was mud-splashed to her knees.

She plodded on. The west wind, which grew stronger as the rain ceased, was cold, even through her coat, against her wet arms; the water which had soaked through her thin shoes made curious noises as she walked. For a while she had lifted her skirts carefully; now she let them drop. They could not be any wetter or more soiled than they already were. In sudden hopelessness, Mary doubted whether she should ever reach Millerstown again.

The street seemed suddenly dark, then there twinkled out at the corner a faint blue light, then farther down another and another. When she finally came to Sixth and Washington streets her fright was augmented by bewilderment. The crowd of the morning seemed to have increased a hundredfold. It was not yet time for the excursion trains to leave, and the visiting thousands lingered here, waiting for any excitement which might befall. The car-despatcher shouted madly at his subordinates, who would not hear or heed; he cursed the people, who stood constantly between the tracks and, overestimating the patience of the motormen, were dragged almost from under the wheels of the cars by their friends.

Tears of relief started to Mary's eyes as she saw on the front of a car about to start the single charmed word, "Millerstown." She started forward and tried to climb aboard. The conductor, however, took her gently but firmly by the arm and moved her down from the running-board.

"No more room."

"*Ach!* take me along—please take me along!" she cried, but the car had gone.

How she spent the next hour she did not know. She was aware that several persons spoke to her as she hung about the edge of the crowd, but she could not remember what they said. Once she thought she saw the tall man coming toward her, but she did not move.

When the next car started, however, Mary was aboard. She knew there had been a wild scramble for seats, and she remembered a curious ripping sound which seemed to come from under the feet of the man next to her, and which probably marked the separation of the ruffles on her gown, but she did not care. She was going home.

The evening wind, damp and cold, sent shivers up and down her arms and across her shoulders. She would die of consumption. As well that, however, as anything else, since John Weimer no longer cared for her.

When they reached the little village between the county-seat and Millerstown, the car was emptied of all its passengers save her. Evidently the other Millerstonions, the Fackenthals, the Knerrs, and the Weygandts, had caught the earlier car. As they sped on, she could tell each foot of the way, though she sat with her eyes closed. The smell of tar at the pipe-foundry, the rush of dampness as they dashed through the little valley which Trout Creek makes for itself in the meadows, the grinding of the wheels as they climbed the slope on the other side, the mad leap of the car as they reached the long, level stretch where the conductor bade the motorman "Let her go," the sickening twist as they turned the sharp curve at the end, the blaze of the flaring bleeder at the furnace, and then — home!

Mary rose stiffly as the car stopped. Her teeth chattered.

"*Ach!*" she thought, "I can nefer again be happy so long as I lif!"

The conductor helped her down. Millerstown had gone to bed. There were lights here and there in the second stories, but beneath all was dark.

"Oh, dear! Oh, dear!" sighed Mary. "If only —"

A pair of strong arms infolded her, and the rest of the sentence was lost in a sob.

"*Ach*, Chohn!" was all she could say over and over again. Then: "But how could you get so soon home from your pop's cousint's funeral?"

"I did n't stay for de funeral," he said. "I went, an' I came wis de first train back. It made me sick. I wass so afraid because you might go alone in de fair, Mary. And de train wass late, an' I only chust got here. I haf been worried crasy, Mary. Were n't you scared, all alone?"

For answer she laid her cheek against his hand.

"I nefer, nefer, nefer will again do anysing what you say I da's n't," she answered.

IN DEFIANCE OF THE OCCULT

Originally published in the February 1906 issue of
Appleton's Booklover's Magazine

Young Oliver Kuhns, who was slag man at the Millerstown furnace, went slowly across the meadow, his lunch pail in his hand and misery in his heart. Across at the station, half of Millerstown was gathered to await the arrival of the six o'clock train, which would bring the paraphernalia of the noted Professor Van Deusen, magician, animal trainer, hypnotist, and lecturer, who would give an entertainment that evening in Guth's Hall.

It was springtime and the meadow across which he went was gay with clover and daisies and wild primroses, whose yellow corollas were just now unfolding. Except for the faint, steady murmur of the bleeder, from which a soft purple exhalation flamed against the sunset, there was not a sound in the evening air.

The clover and primroses grew almost to the walls of the plant itself, the laboratory was shaded by a growth of oaks, and in the marshy pond at its side the children waded for cat-o'-nine-tails. The noise and grime inseparable in one's thoughts from the manufacture of iron seemed to have here no place; all about it was peaceful and still. As the dusk deepened, the great plant seemed like some huge monster lying lifeless in the fields. There was no shapeliness about it. Its various parts had varying heights, from the little one-story laboratory, the low boiler house, and the great outlying piles of cinder and slag, which in the dusk seemed to become part of the plant itself, to the tall cylindrical stack which towered above them all.

Yet the monster lived. The bleeder flame, which in daylight was a faint purple, blazed out suddenly, a flaming, splendid orange, then with a deep roar was as suddenly imprisoned; an engine lumbered slowly down the track beside the furnace, and having fastened to itself a train of cars loaded with pig iron, pulled slowly and noisily away.

Other men besides young Oliver appeared, some along the track, some across the meadows, and some down the road which led to the village, to take the places of those who, blackened and begrimed, came from the furnace.

"Hello, Ollie," they called gayly.

Young Oliver did not respond, and the men laughed and went on.

"I guess Susannah iss perhaps once ugly to him," some one said carelessly.

Oliver went slowly into the cast house. He could see in the flaring light of a torch fastened against the wall at the front of the great building, the thickly sanded floor, half of which was shaped into a pattern as though a huge grid-iron had been pressed down upon it, and overhead the arched ceiling far above him. It was almost like a church in its silence and dimness. The huge stack vanishing upward like a great organ completed the illusion.

He placed his lunch pail beside a row of other pails against the wall, and flung down his coat and hat beside it.

"Kuhns!"

He straightened up before he answered, and his hands closed.

"Yes, sir."

A man tall as Oliver himself came around the curve of the stack. His hands were in his pockets, and there was a gay lilt in his voice, as though he might whistle or sing the next moment. One could guess that he was Irish without knowing his name.

"I've changed my mind about having you dump the cinder on the old pile. You can keep on where you are."

Oliver did not answer.

"Do you hear me, Kuhns?" The voice was still as gay.

"Yes," Oliver said sullenly.

The superintendent jumped nimbly over the runner which led from the mouth of the furnace down to the molds, and went out the door at the upper end of the house, whistling gayly.

Did he dream for one mistaken instant that Oliver did not know why he had countermanded his order that the slag be run out on the old dump? Had he forgotten that the cinder as it ran from the car down over the pile lit up the country for miles? Did he suppose that Oliver had not seen him over on the old dump with Susannah Kemerer? Oliver knew well enough why they were there. The superintendent had an unaccountable but none the less real interest in birds. Oliver himself had seen him stand for half an hour almost without moving, to watch a pair of nesting orioles over in the tall oaks beside the laboratory. Up on top of the old dump the night hawks had nested for years, and no one had known it but Oliver himself, until the week before when he had showed them to Susannah. What business had she to show them to the superintendent? What business had she to know him at all? Oliver had not forgotten how he himself had helped her up and almost carried her down, the pile was so steep. And the superintendent — He bit his lip savagely.

Since that illuminating moment the night before, Oliver had counted up all the things he had against Murphy. He was not a Pennsylvania German, therefore he was to be somewhat distrusted. He was stuck up; he wore fine clothes, outlandish clothes. Oliver had met him hurrying along in the summer dusk the week before wearing a curious short coat which opened over an expanse of shirt-bosom at which Oliver stared. Several hours afterwards Murphy had come into the cast house with a party of men and girls who were staying at the only house in the village to which he ever went, the Masons', who were as English as he himself was Irish, and whose property the furnace was.

Oliver had watched them as the girls had delicately lifted their skirts and had admired and exclaimed. Murphy never left Miss Mason, who was a little thing as straight and slender as Susannah Kemerer. It was small wonder that he stared down at her brown eyes and the rosy reflection from the molten iron on her bare arms and the glimpses of white throat which one caught through her gauzy wrap. To the men toiling over the scorching exhalation they had seemed like beings from another world, with whom they were connected only by the superintendent's gay laugh.

Oliver had not hated him then. Instead, he had looked on admiringly when Murphy, leaving Miss Mason, had taken into his own hands a heavy sledge, and with one blow against the bar had pierced the hard-baked clay which closed up the outlet of the furnace, which the men had been trying vainly to open. Then, however, he had not known that Murphy was meeting Susannah in the country at night.

Now, sitting there with his back against the cast-house wall, he frowned savagely. The entertainment of Professor Van Deusen was another grievance. Long before, Susannah had accepted his invitation to attend. Then a week ago he had been unexpectedly transferred to the night shift. Nor had Susannah received his explanations in a manner which was calculated to soothe him.

"I can go wis Chimmie Weygandt," she had said. "I guess he will ask me."

The missing of the entertainment itself was a keen disappointment. The advertisements promised that Professor Van Deusen would reveal the secrets of the future; he would reveal the past. He would perform a variety of card tricks. He would allow them to tie him into a chair and he would get out without untying the knot. He would exhibit his trained animals. He would show his skill as a hypnotist, the subject to be his wife, who traveled with him. His wife was not only a good hypnotic subject, she was also a medium. The fact that Millerstown had never before heard of a medium only added to their curiosity.

Old Elias Bittner was the only one who ventured an explanation.

"Dis hypnotism iss a kind of powwowing," he said. "An' a medium iss a kind of fit. She gets a kind of fit."

Oliver had heard them talking all the week, too sick at heart to join in the discussion himself. He thought of Jimmie Weygandt with his arm across the back of Susannah's chair, and gritted his teeth. Was it any wonder that he did not care to watch the arrival of Professor Van Deusen?

Presently Billy Knerr came in and threw himself down on the sand pile.

"Why don't you ask him if you dare go in de show, Ollie?" he asked. "I ask him when I wass you. You can get easy off."

"I don't want to go," said Oliver sullenly.

Then he got up and walked away. It was almost time for the final flushing of the cinder before the cast. Billy Knerr watched him, smiling. The oldest of his three children was four years old, but Billy had not forgotten the days when Sarah led him a chase.

"It iss somesing about Susannah," he said to himself.

Oliver crossed to the other side of the stack. The little engine, after having shoved the heavy car under the cinder runner, puffed slowly away. Then Henny Kleibscheidel withdrew the plug which closed the cinder notch. Out poured the cinder, a molten fiery mass, its heat driving out before it the cool night air. Henny Kleibscheidel sprang back, his arm before his face. When the flow had almost ceased, he inserted the plug. The little engine came slowly back, and after coupling it to the car, Oliver climbed aboard.

The engineer got no answer to his cheerful questions as they rumbled slowly across the yard and then slowly climbed the cinder tip. Oliver was there bodily, with his hand resting unmindfully on the hot window pane in the little cab. Mentally, however, he was with Susannah. The entertainment must have begun, and Susannah was laughing and talking with Jimmie Weygandt as she laughed and talked with him.

When the car stopped with a lurch at the end of the uneven track, he sprang out and, going to the side of the car, turned the hand wheel. The great ladle swung over, and the cinder rushed out hissing, the dark non-luminous crust which had formed on the top broken into a thousand pieces before the rush of the seething mass beneath. In the brilliant glow Oliver could see the great wheel at the Weygandt sawmill half a mile away. Even the trees on the mountain side seemed to stand out, one from the other. Then, suddenly, his hands clinched.

Down along the furnace road came a man and a girl, the man very tall, the girl short. It was the superintendent and Susannah.

He stood still until they had vanished into the shade of the furnace woods and presently came slowly out on the other side. There he saw their hands, clasped as though they were children, swing apart.

Afterwards he did not remember whether or not he had uncoupled the car. He would go along the road to meet them, and take Susannah away. She had lied to him — she had said that she would go to the entertainment with Jim Weygandt. The superintendent meant no good. Afterwards he would fight him.

As he strode across the cast house, they were opening the tapping hole. Henry Kleibscheidel held a bar against the clay, and Jacob Neuweiler and John Bittner swung their heavy sledges in a wide and apparently reckless sweep. Down along the sides of the great gridiron of sand the others waited with cutters to direct the flow of iron when it should come.

Oliver rushed out into the night. He could see the two figures coming toward him. How did Susannah dare to come so near the furnace? They were evidently coming in to watch the cast. He started toward them. Then suddenly as the iron left the hole, the night was again lit up. A shaft of light from the long windows of the cast house struck across the two figures. One was the superintendent, smiling, happy as always, the other was — the Mason girl.

The superintendent called to him a little sharply.

"What is it, Kuhns?"

"I — I wass looking for you," Oliver began. He did not know what to say. The sudden mad relief sent his tongue stammering. It must have been the Mason girl who was up on the cinder dump with the superintendent. Then Billy Knerr's question came to save him. "Dare I go a while up in de show?"

"Yes, I guess so, for a while." The superintendent's present mood found happy expression in the granting of a favor. "Get Knerr to take your place."

A moment later Oliver started off through the wet meadow grass. He would go to the show. He must see Susannah, even though it would be only to watch her from the back of the hall.

He listened outside the door before he turned the knob. There was no one there to take tickets. Evidently the doorkeepers had joined the audience within.

Though he stumbled over the doorstep, not a head turned to look. The lamps had been moved to the platform, where sat the magician's wife. The card tricks had been performed. Professor Van Deusen had struggled out of every knot which Millerstown could tie. His trained animals had proved to be but one trained pig, which, however, had given such remarkable evidence of intelligence that Millerstown did not miss the trained dogs and monkeys which the playbills had advertised. Millerstown, indeed, was dazed and breathless.

Beside Madame Van Deusen stood her husband, a black cloth in his hand. He was a tall man with a pointed beard and a mysterious eye.

"Now any of you can examine this cloth if you want to," he was saying as Oliver entered. "You can see that it is simply a thick black cloth."

"Why for do you haf such a clos?" demanded old Elias Bittner. No one else would have dared a question.

"So that she may not be disturbed by anything outside," he explained. "Now my assistant, whom I call Phosphorescence, because he is so bright" — the witticism was lost on Millerstown — "will go among you with this little tablet and this lead pencil, and anyone who so desires may write a question. Then tear the paper off and put it into your pocket. Let no one see it, and tell no one what you have written. Madame Van Deusen, the medium, will answer the questions for you, first telling you what they are."

Phosphorescence moved softly among them, his black face smiling. The more astute, who watched him narrowly, swore afterwards that he did not look at what anyone wrote. Besides, he could not have read in that dim light what they had written with difficulty. Millerstown did not notice that the pencil was very hard and the tablet very soft, and that each time the writer removed his little sheet of paper, Phosphorescence slipped the next one up his sleeve.

He came last of all to Oliver, who stood behind the last row of seats.

"Gem'man write?" he asked.

For an instant Oliver hesitated. He found that he could look upon Susannah with Jimmie by her side with less equanimity than he expected. He could see her curly head from where he stood. He had not been there to be impressed by the earlier part of the entertainment. He did not believe there was anything in the performance.

"Gif it here," said a voice at his elbow. Oliver looked down to see Clara Kleibscheidel scribble something hastily on the paper. She appeared amused.

Then while Phosphorescence went back to the platform, his master began to explain his wife's power, or rather to explain that it was inexplicable.

"There are more things in the world, Horatio, than your philosophy dreams of," he said solemnly, and Millerstown wondered what he meant.

After he had talked very loudly and rapidly for a few minutes, he turned to the veiled figure beside him.

"Madame Van Deusen will speak," he said. For the fragment of a second there was silence. Millerstown felt the chills creep up its back.

"I see the question, 'Will my crops turn out good?'" said Madame Van Deusen in a faint voice. "The answer is" — there was a long pause — "the answer is 'Yes.'"

"Did anyone ask that question?" demanded the professor loudly. There seemed to be faint voices around him, above him.

"I did," answered Jimmie Weygandt.

"The next," said the professor triumphantly.

"I see the question, 'Will Billy Trostle pay me what he owes me?' The question is signed 'Peter Guth.' The answer is 'No.'"

Millerstown shouted aloud. Billy Trostle never paid anyone. Peter Guth, however, could compass no more than a smile. Had he known that Professor Van Deusen would fold his tent like the Arab and leave him only the trained pig as an equivalent for the rent of the hall, even that would have died speedily away.

Again there came those mysterious whispers.

"The next," called the professor.

"'Will the new Baptists get a good preacher?' The answer is 'Yes.'"

"Dat wass my question," said Elias Bittner, his eyes staring.

"The next?"

"'If I give up Dr. Bender and get me the powwow doctor, will I get well?' The answer is 'Yes.'"

Then the medium told them that Sarah Ann Mohr's night-blooming cactus would have more than twenty flowers. The trolley road would come to Millerstown, and the Democrats would carry the borough election.

"Dis iss for sure sonderbar [wonderful]," said Jimmie Weygandt to Susannah. Susannah had not been pleasant to him that evening. She was restless and unlike herself. He had laughed at her and teased her, but she only grew the more surly. Now she looked at him angrily, her black eyes sparkling. Her father was a Republican.

"She don't know nosing," she said scornfully. "I bet de Republicans get it."

The answer to the next question, which was her own, angered her still more.

"'Will I go this year in the Fair?' The answer is 'No.'"

"She iss me too dumb," she said, and Jimmie laughed.

"And now," went on Professor Van Deusen, "we have reached the last question. I want to tell you first that I have learned to put implicit faith in the medium. The voices which answer your questions are unheard by you, but they are omniscient. They see all, know all. The last question is —" He paused. Oliver Kuhns caught his breath. His eyes had wandered from the shrouded figure on the platform to the figure of Susannah, outlined clearly in its white dress against Jimmie Weygandt's dark coat. He saw that that coat bent protectingly toward her.

"The question is," interrupted the medium's voice suddenly, "'Will O. K. get Susannah?'"

There was no one in the audience who did not know who was "O.K." and who was "Susannah." But Millerstown was too smitten with terror of the occult to laugh. Only Clara Kleibscheidel snickered.

"The answer is 'No.'"

There was a long silence. Then in Susannah's voice there came to Oliver's ears, "A lie! Who tole you?"

The medium, half hidden by the screens with which Phosphorescence was enveloping her, did not hear. Nor did Millerstown, deafened by the sudden scraping of chairs. To Jimmie Weygandt, however, the words came clearly, and he laughed aloud. No one could ever tell whether Jimmie really cared for Susannah. Then lifting up his eyes, he saw young Oliver close to him.

"I haf off till elefen o'clock," said Oliver meaningly.

"Well?" demanded Jimmie provokingly as he rose.

Then Susannah turned her head. Her eyes, cool, composed, met Oliver's.

"Hello, Ollie," she said calmly. She did not dream that he had heard her defiant remark, which she had made chiefly to tease Jim Weygandt. Then, feeling his hand on her arm, she looked at him in amazement.

"What iss den wrong wis you?" she said with stately reproof.

Oliver only tightened his grasp.

"I said I had off till elefen o'clock," he repeated.

Jimmie turned to Susannah.

"It iss de lady what shall haf de say. Shall I go, Susannah?"

"Why should you go?" said Susannah with well-feigned mystification. Underneath it, however, was a sharp amazement. Could this red-shirted, masterful Oliver be the same Oliver who sat on her doorstep in his best clothes, who was always so fearful, so doubtful of what privileges he might take, who lifted her hand so lightly in his own that for very shame's sake she had to pull it away, and who then made no effort to regain it? She realized suddenly that she had always liked him best. But Jim was nice, too, and John Weimer.

"I guess — " she began.

Then again she felt his hand on her arm. It crushed the ruffles of her sleeve in its careless grasp, it pressed into her flesh, it hurt her. She caught her breath suddenly.

"I don't care if you do, Chimmie Weygandt," she finished weakly.

THE VACILLATION OF
BENJAMIN GAUMER

Originally published in the March 1906 issue of *The Century Magazine*

"When I wass young —"

"Dat wass a good many years back, Sarah," interrupted old Peter Gaumer, ungallantly.

"When I wass young," Sarah Arndt went on, — "and dat wass n't so many years back as when *you* wass young, Pit Gaumer, — de girls had more spunk as dey haf nowadays. Nobody would 'a' taken it from a feller dat he went one Saturday wis one girl and de next wis anoder girl."

"Perhaps de girls wass more anxious to get de fellers den as dey are now," said Peter, slyly.

"Nosing of de kind," old Sarah answered sharply. "It wass dat dey had more spunk."

"Well, who has n't now no spunk?" queried Peter, balancing a little more comfortably on the hind legs of his chair as he leaned against the tree in front of the Fackenthals' house. "Sit once down on de bench, Sarah, an' tell us from dese girls what haf n't no spunk."

Sarah sat down on the wide bench. She was a little old woman with sharp black eyes, which peered forth uncannily from under her black silk sunbonnet.

"Why, it iss Chofina Neuweiler and Mary Kuhns what are me too soft. Benj Gaumer he —"

"Now look a little out, Sarah! Benj iss my nephew."

"I don't care what he iss. He goes wis bos de girls."

"Well, I gif him right. Two girls are for sure better dan one, Sarah."

"Well, I sink it iss a sin an' a shame. When I wass Mary, I srow him ofer, or make him pretty quick srow Chofina ofer; or when I wass Chofina, I do de same sing. He would n't go twice wis anoder girl when he had once started to keep company wis me, dat I can tell you! We will easy see which one has de most spunk."

"Perhaps he don't know yet for sure which one he wants."

"Den I gif him notice he must pretty quick find out, dat iss what I would do." Old Sarah rose with a nimbleness which belied her seventy-five years, and went briskly away, and Peter gazed meditatively up the street to where, on the Neuweilers' door-step, sat Jovina, the daughter of the house, with his nephew, Benjamin Gaumer, by her side.

Benjamin was in reality the most miserable young man in the Pennsylvania-German village of Millerstown; for Benjamin halted between two opinions, or, to speak more correctly, between two girls, and though most of his waking thoughts for a year had been devoted to an effort to decide between them, he seemed to grow each day farther from a solution of the difficulty.

Mary Kuhns was the prettier of the two. She was short and plump, with light, fluffy hair, blue eyes, and a skin which no amount of exposure to the wind or sun could harm. Her voice, as Benjamin often said to himself, was "like old man Fackenthal's pigeons what coo so pretty." The women, alas! called her "flirty," which, translated into the masculine vocabulary, meant that direct glances were not the only method by which Mary beheld her fellow-man. She was so short that she could stand under Benjamin's outstretched arm, and he often remembered with delight how she fled to him for protection when Weygandt's old mooly looked at her in the lane. He had encouraged her with shameless deceit to think the mild beast dangerous, and she clung to him helplessly. Fortunately, he was not at hand the next day to see her walk through Weygandt's meadow, where there were thirty cattle, and switch them, even savage old Tom, with a willow switch as she passed.

There were times when Benjamin was positive that Mary was his choice. Then he grew hot with jealousy of John Weimer and Jimmie Weygandt, to whom she freely dispensed her favors, and he made up his mind that, before another day passed, Mary should be his. But — and in this hesitation lay his undoing — before he decided finally, it would be well to see Jovina once more.

Jovina was not pretty, except for her dark eyes. She was tall and spare and sallow, and her hair was a dull brown. Jovina, however, could cook, and for that reason her popularity was equal to Mary's. Plain cooking is not counted much of an accomplishment in Millerstown, for every woman is a good plain cook. There were a few, however, — Jovina, Savilla Arndt, and Linnie Kurtz, — in whose skilful hands cooking had become a fine art, and Jovina perhaps excelled all the others.

"Chofina can bake sirty-sefen kinds cake," her mother claimed proudly. "And she need n't look once in de receipt-book. She can make, of course, pancakes an' funnel-cakes an' *schwingfelders* an' waffles, besides. De sirty-sefen means fancy cakes."

Beside this, Jovina could make yeast-beer and root-beer and half a dozen fruit-vinegars. Her chicken and waffles, her *schnitz und knöpf*, her *latwerk* (apple-butter), were the envy of all the other women. Her soap was always the whitest, her dried peaches and corn were the most tasteful, her liver-pudding, sausage, and *pan-hass* (scrapple), the best in the village. Was it any wonder that the delicious flavors of the products of her skilful hands veiled for a while Mary Kuhns's saucy face and dimmed the tender glances of her blue eyes?

Had Benjamin been more sophisticated, he might have ascribed the duality of his love-affairs to the naturally polygamous instincts of man. So advanced a theory, however, had not yet become part of Millerstown's ethics. Each man was expected to love, cherish, and, in many cases, obey one woman, be she sweetheart or wife. Girls were allowed, on account of their natural fickleness, to change their minds. Any masculine wanderings from the narrow path of single-hearted devotion, however, were considered evidences of woeful weakness of character. Hence Benjamin, who had once shared Millerstown's old-fashioned opinions, and who had no new theories with which to console himself for his inconstancy, was thoroughly miserable.

"It iss n't any oder way about it," he would say despairingly to himself. "I must pretty soon decide. When I don't, den John Weimer or Jimmie Weygandt will perhaps get her. But perhaps it iss n't *her* what I want, but Chofina. An' den when it *iss* Chofina, she iss pretty spunky, an' perhaps she won't haf me when I put it much longer off."

As he ate Jovina's crullers and molasses-cake, he looked with eager anticipation down a long line of years during which crullers and "finecake" should be his daily fare. When he had thoroughly satisfied his hunger, he decided to ask her to be his. Then, as he ate still more, he began to think that perhaps he had better see Mary once again before taking so irrevocable a step. Mary's eyes were so blue, and there was such an alluring dimple in her chin! Mary was always so sweet-tempered, and Jovina — well, Jovina had a mind of her own.

Ten minutes on the Kuhns's dim, vine-shaded porch with Mary by his side convinced him that it was not Jovina that he wanted at all. Poor, desolate Jovina, she would probably be heartbroken when she heard he was to marry Mary, but that, of course, could not be helped.

In another ten minutes he had again changed his mind; for Mary gave him a piece of chocolate-cake, "which I myself baked," she explained. Now Mary's was the exception which proved the rule of Millerstown's good cooking. Even everyday necessities, such as pie, bread, and fried potatoes, grew into strange things in her hands. When she attempted anything as ambitious as chocolate-cake, the result was sad to behold and worse to taste. At the first bite, Benjamin's lips puckered over a huge lump of baking-soda, and he said fervently to himself: "*Nay, bei meiner Seele! Des du ich net!*" ("No, by my soul! This I will not do!") Again the star of Jovina was in the ascendant. Should he ever get the taste of that soda out of his mouth? Certain delicious crullers suggested themselves as an antidote, and firmly convinced that "good cooking iss more dan good looks, for cooking lasts, and looks don't," he determined to seek Jovina the next day and offer her his heart and hand.

Jovina, however, to whose ears had penetrated some gossip concerning her willingness to share the attentions of her lover with another, was, naturally enough, in a bad humor, and the sharpness of her voice and the angry flash in her black eyes reminded Benjamin by force of contrast of another voice which was always soft, and other eyes in which he never saw aught but tenderness. Mary Kuhns was the girl who should be the future Mrs. Benjamin Gaumer. Mary, however, again fed him cake, with results disastrous to her prospects.

Thus it went on all the long summer. Millerstown did not for a moment appreciate Benjamin's situation, and undertook to tell the girls plainly what it thought. For its pains it got only a laugh from Mary and a scathing "It would be a fine sing for Millerstown when de folks would learn once to mind deir own business," from Jovina. Evidently the girls did not purpose to take any one into their confidence. No one thought of admonishing Benjamin. He had always been too ready with his fists to make that an inviting task.

The girls, meanwhile, who lived near each other on Church street, continued to be good friends.

Then one day Mary, coming out of Jovina's gate, met Sarah Arndt. The old woman greeted her with a sly smile.

"Well," she began, "did n't she do you nosing?"

"Who?" Mary asked in frank amazement.

"Ay, Chofina."

"Why, of course not. Why should Chofina do me anysing?"

The old woman laughed shrilly.

"Sure enough! You need n't act as when you did n't know what she said from you and Benj."

"From me and Benj?" A faint color began to show on Mary's cheek.

"Yes. She said dat you wass trying to get Benj Gaumer away from her, and dat she would settle you once."

"What will she do?" Mary spoke in angry haste.

"I don't know; but you better look a little out."

"I guess I can take care of myself; you can tell her dat once." Mary slammed her own gate defiantly.

That evening old Sarah stopped for a moment at the Neuweilers' to tell Jovina's mother that Mary said that she "would 'a' srown Benj long ago ofer, only she liked to tease Chofina." Both Jovina and Mary might have known better than to believe Sarah's tales, but the subject of their common love had, through long teasing, become a sore point. So Mary walked by Jovina one day on the street without speaking to her, only to realize a second later that her trouble was unnecessary, as Jovina had turned her head the other way. After this there was openly declared rivalry between them for Benjamin's attentions. Whether they wanted his love was another question. Mary was just as cordial to John Weimer and Jimmie Weygandt as she was to Benj, and whether Jovina would ever really accept him was doubtful.

"Perhaps he gets after all left," said old Sarah. "Perhaps Mary will take one of de oders, and perhaps Chofina will at last get her spunk up and not haf him. When I wass young, girls had more spunk, dat iss what dey had. No man could fool so long round and yet mean nosing by it."

Meanwhile poor Benjamin grew more puzzled as each day went by. Mary's smiles seemed to grow more winning and her eyes deeper, and Jovina's "fine-cakes" lighter and more delicious. Then suddenly, almost without realizing it, he was engaged.

One Sunday evening he went to see Jovina, assuring himself, as he walked up Church street, that Jovina was the girl for him. His last call on Mary had not been very satisfactory. She had seemed less confiding, less sweet than usual, and had several times spoken sharply to him.

"She has also a temper," he said to himself. "I sink I take de cooking."

He did not find Jovina on the front door-step, where she usually received him, and, wondering a little, he opened the gate into the side yard and went around to the back porch to inquire of Mrs. Neuweiler whether her daughter had gone away. To his surprise, he found Jovina herself, in a new and most becoming pink dress, rocking vigorously back and forth in the rocking-chair.

"I sink you are fixed up pretty fine for de back porch, Chofina," he commented, gazing admiringly at her.

"Why, Benj?"

"Why, you ought to be sitting out front where de folks can all see your fine new dress."

"I am not fixed up for de folks," said Jovina.

Benjamin's mouth opened in astonishment. That coquettish remark from staid Jovina, who often harshly criticized Mary Kuhns for "making de men sink too much from demselves!" Jovina, who had yielded to an unaccountable impulse to be "flirty," blushed suddenly and becomingly.

"Shall we den go out front," she demanded with asperity.

"Well, I guess not," said Benjamin, firmly, as he sat down on the step at her feet. "I sink we will stay here — anyhow, a while. Your dress iss for sure fine!"

At this Jovina, who usually "gafe him a mousful" when he began to flatter, smiled sweetly.

"Look a little out; you might make me vain," she said.

"I guess it iss no danger, Chofina. Do you want to go dis efening in de church?"

"*Ach*, I don't know. Do you?"

"No."

"Well, den, I guess we won't go."

Benjamin gasped. Was Jovina actually making an effort to please him? Not once during the evening did she show any of her "spunk." She agreed with everything he said. Usually they had long and heated discussions about religious matters. It was just the time when the "New Baptists" were leaving the "Jonathan-Kuhns Baptists," and Jovina, who went, did not agree at all with Benjamin, who stayed. It was quite by accident that Benjamin introduced the subject this evening. He had such an exhibition of Jovina's temper the last time they discussed it that he might have known better than to try again. This evening, however, Jovina only said sweetly:

"I sink it would perhaps be better when we would talk from somesing else."

Whereupon, with all doubts driven from his mind, Benjamin proposed, and was immediately accepted.

"When shall we den get married, Chofina?" He asked.

"Oh, I sink I can be by Sursday all ready. I haf chust dis week made me dis new dress, an' I will buy me a coat an' hat."

"But, Chofina, I sought it took much longer to get ready to get married!" he exclaimed in surprise and consternation.

"It does not take so long of course as when we were going to house-keeping for ourselfs. We will, of course, lif here wis mam and pap. An' you haf dis new suit to get married in."

"Yes, b-b-but —" this mad haste took away his breath — "dis is me pretty much of a hurry. No — no — Chofina," — he saw her figure straighten in the moonlight, — "I did n't mean nosing by it! I meant — I meant — could we get a minister so soon, Chofina?"

"I sink it would be a good sing when we would go ofer to New Chersey. Den all de busybodies in Millerstown need n't know nosing about it beforehand. I heard you say once dat when you got married dat would be de way what you would do. Besides, we need ofer in New Chersey no license."

"Yes, but —"

"I will of course tell mam and pap, and you can tell Wednesday efening your mam. Den we can slip easy Sursday morning away."

So occupied was Benjamin with his own thoughts that he scarcely knew how the rest of the evening passed. Finally he bade her good night and went home.

"It iss me too much of a hurry, dat iss what it iss," he said miserably to himself. "It iss n't dat I don't want to get married, or dat I don't want Chofina; but — but dere iss Mary Kuhns."

The old puzzle rose like a specter to harass him.

"Perhaps it wass only in my mind dat Mary wass de last time ugly to me," he thought. "Perhaps she wass a little chealous from Chofina. She iss ten times so good-looking as Chofina. Chofina iss me too homely."

He forgot Jovina's pretty new dress and the flush on her cheek. He knew now, once for all, which he wanted: it was Mary. He could feel the touch of her little hand and see the coquettish gleam in her soft eyes. And poor Mary! What would she do if he should marry Jovina? Perhaps it would break her heart and she would die, and he would be to blame. Mary was such a little girl! She was not big and strong like Jovina, who was almost as tall as he. What should he do? He could not go and tell Jovina that he had been mistaken. In the first place, she might hold him to his promise, and there would be an awful scandal, which would effectually put Mary beyond his reach. On the other hand, she might angrily release him, and he did not wish to break with her entirely. That would mean that he would *have* to take Mary. Of course he wanted to marry Mary, but he did not want to be driven to it.

His round and rosy face dropped in such doleful lines when he looked in the glass in his room that it made him almost sick with pity for himself. All night Jovina, tall, dark, and inexorable, seemed to stand beside his bed.

Nor was he any less miserable on the eve of his wedding. He had seen Jovina only once. Then she was very sweet to him, and there was a soft flush on her cheek. He began to feel easier. The same afternoon, however, he passed Mary on the street, and the alluring tilt of her chin sent him back into despair. He could scarcely attend to his work in the cigar-factory. The boss frowned, and the boys chaffed him gaily.

"You act as when your mind wass away some place. Perhaps it iss ofer by Mary, or perhaps Chofina. Which one is it anyhow, Benj?"

Benjamin frowned only a trifle less darkly than John Weimer, who said, "*Esel!*" ("Donkey!") under his breath.

When Benj went home for supper on Wednesday, a big plate of crullers occupied the place of honor in the center of the table.

"Chofina Neuweiler gafe dem to me," his mother explained. "I wass once ofer dere a little while dis afternoon. My! but Chofina iss a good cook. Don't you sink so?" She looked at him inquiringly, but his mouth was full and he did not answer. "I belief perhaps she iss going somewheres off to-morrow."

"Why do you sink she is going somewheres off?" Benjamin had not yet announced the fact of his approaching marriage. That would be the first decisive step, and he hesitated to take it. Now, however, he realized that the time had come when it could no longer be put off.

"*Ach*, nosing; only her mam said to her somesing about 'when you come back, Chofina,' and I sought perhaps she wass going somewheres off."

Thereupon Benjamin announced that he and Jovina proposed to journey the next day to New Jersey to be married. His mother, who had never liked Mary Kuhns, expressed her approval; and, buoyed by this and the memory of her crullers, he went to see Jovina in a fairly cheerful frame of mind. They planned to make the journey by trolley, starting at five o'clock in the morning. He decided not to notify the men at the shop that he was not coming, but to let his mother send the boss word after he had gone. It would be a good joke on Millerstown.

As the evening wore on, and Jovina seemed to prefer long silences to conversation, his cheerfulness waned. He saw John Weimer go swiftly past in the dusk and a furious jealousy added to his soreness of heart. He did not want to marry Jovina Neuweiler; he wanted to marry Mary Kuhns. Jovina noticed his gloom, but whether or not she suspected its cause, there was a solemnity about her good night which warned him that his choice was irrevocable.

He needed neither the alarm-clock nor the sound of his mother's voice to arouse him the next morning. Indeed, he was awake long before it was time to get up, and he was not sure that he had slept at all. He ate so little breakfast that his mother was frightened.

"You will feel bad when you do not eat somesing, Benj. Come now; here is some raisin-pie."

He silently shook his head. The unaccustomed splendor of his Sunday clothes worried him, and there was something about the exceeding tightness of his high collar which reminded him of the other yoke he was about to assume. He stole through the streets to the Neuweilers' more like a thief than a prospective bridegroom, and, avoiding the boardwalk, went around to the back door upon the grass. Jovina met him at the door, the bright pink of her dress reflected in the glow of her cheeks.

"Say, Benj," she began, "you go a little ahead down to de trolley, an' I will come a little behind. Den when de folks see us dey will not know dat we are wis each oder."

Thus admonished, Benjamin sped away with a sudden lightness of heart. The evil day was postponed for a few minutes at least. When Jovina met him down on Main street, however, his despair again overwhelmed him. The next time he saw that spot he would no longer be free. No longer could he live his own life. No longer could he join the boys in the gallery of the church on Sunday evenings; he would have to sit with Jovina. No longer could he dash gaily around the Copenhagen ring at the Sunday-school picnics, winning a kiss for a forfeit from every girl whose hands he could slap. He would have to stay close by Jovina now. And, worst of all, nevermore could he join the gay group on Mary Kuhns's doorstep; nevermore could he take her walking or trolley-riding. Nevermore could his hand linger caressingly on hers as he bade her good night; nevermore would her glances at him be aught but straightforward and direct. He was back for the moment on the Kuhns's porch in the summer dusk, and Mary was laughing as she tried to get her hand away. Benjamin smiled.

"Benj!" He came back to the awful present with a start. This was not dusk; it was dawn. The girl at his side was not gentle Mary; it was tall, stern Jovina — Jovina, whom he was about to marry!

"Well?" he answered dully.

"Don't you see den de car!" she exclaimed.

He raised both arms in a wild signal to the motorman, and the car, speeding toward them like a Juggernaut, stopped with a great grinding of wheels.

"It would haf been a fine sing when we had got left!" commented Jovina as they climbed aboard.

As they passed Sarah Ann Mohr's, that good lady was just opening her front door. Benjamin ducked his head, hoping she had not seen him. Jovina, however, gaily waved her hand, and, as Benjamin looked back, he beheld Sarah Ann, her fat arms akimbo, the light of knowledge beaming in a broad smile on her cheerful face. Their engagement was announced.

As they sped past the creamery, the farm-wagons with their shining cans had begun to drive up, and again Benjamin bent his head. Jovina, however, sat all the straighter, proud in the consciousness that she wore a becoming new dress and that she was going to be married. There was little conversation between them. She called his attention to Jimmie Weygandt as he started around his wheat-field, scythe in hand, to mow the first row before the reaper; and Jimmie, who neared the fence as they turned the corner by his fields, waved his hat and shouted. Jovina's "Hello Chimmie!" was the only answer he received. Already Benj could see him seated by Mary Kuhns's side on the porch, dark in the shadow of the honeysuckles. The more his face darkened, however, the more cheerful did Jovina become. She hummed a hymn as they dashed on, she admired the goldenrod flaming into splendor in the fence-corners, and presently she slid along the bench toward Benj.

"It hardly seems true dat we are going to be married, does it now?" she asked.

"No, it don't," he said quickly. Was Jovina beginning to have doubts as to the wisdom of their proceedings? "Are you sure it iss den for de best, Chofina? Are you sure we haf not den hurried ourselves too much? Do you sink we had perhaps better go back?"

"No, indeed, Benj! I am sure," Jovina interpreted his questions as the effort of a doubting lover to assure himself of her affection.

"You will den nefer repent?"

"Nefer, Benj; nefer. I — I haf lofed you dis long time; I —" Jovina's remarks were suspended while she grabbed for her hat, which threatened to blow off in the blast created by the tremendous speed at which they dashed through the street of the next village — "I wass not fery happy for a long time till I found it wass I and not Mary Kuhns what you lofed."

Benj groaned. Was it right for a professing Christian — a Jonathan-Kuhns Baptist at that — to enter into an agreement in which the other party was the victim of a delusion? Would it not be better to break the fact to Jovina that it was not she whom he loved best, but Mary? Again, however, his old doubts assailed him.

"If I do dat, den Chofina will nefer look at me again. Suppose I should den want her! An', besides, if Chofina wants to say dat we wass going to get married, and den I would n't, eferybody will belief her; for Sarah Ann she saw us going off in de trolley. When a fellow an' a girl go off so early in de morning in de trolley, it means dat somesing iss up."

He could not understand how it was that he had happened to propose. He forgot again Mary's heavy chocolate-cake and her coldness to him. Nor did he think of Jovina in her new dress flushing softly as he complimented her.

They reached the county-seat before he was aware. There, even though it was only six o'clock, the town was thoroughly awake. The day seems to begin an hour earlier in southeastern Pennsylvania than in other places. The cars which passed as they waited for the Easton car were crowded with men going to their work down at the wire- or rolling-mills. A little later a crowd of girls and women on their way to the silk-mills and shoe-factories would fill the streets. A man who was sweeping the old-fashioned double porches of the United States House at the opposite corner threw down his broom as he helped the porter carry out the heavy satchels of departing guests of the house, who dashed wildly across the pavement and into a carriage, meanwhile calling to the driver to "Hurry up once or we miss the train!" Already the doors of an establishment at the other corner swung vigorously back and forth. Men pushed them in swiftly, then came out more slowly, wiping their lips. The car-despatcher, standing in the middle of the tangle of tracks, shouted strident Pennsylvania-German oaths at the motormen and conductors, who in turn answered him as gruffly.

When the lumbering "double-trucker" marked "Easton" swung around the corner from Hamilton street into Sixth, Benj and Jovina climbed aboard and began the second stage of their journey. There was little danger that any one would guess that they were prospective bride and groom. The frowns on Benj's brow did not lift for an instant, and, as time went on and all her efforts at conversation failed, Jovina's face also lost its cheerful expression. Benj gazed mournfully out of the window on one side of the car and Jovina on the other, he with bent shoulders, and she with head high in the air.

It was about eight o'clock when, having left the car at Easton, they crossed the Delaware bridge into Phillipsburg, New Jersey.

"I sink it iss perhaps early yet to go to de preacher," said Benj, after a long silence. "Perhaps we had better take a little walk once. De folks do not get so early up here like in Lehigh County."

"All right," assented Jovina, cheerfully. "I wonder where dese steps go." As she spoke, she pointed to a flight of steps which fell from the street-level.

"We will see once," he answered. She followed him down the steps, which lay along the side of the steep river-bank. At the foot they came upon a little railroad station. The tracks followed the windings of the river along the New Jersey side. Overhead, on another road, thundered the heavy freight-trains back to their own county-seat.

"I sink dis would be a pretty good place to rest," said Jovina as she spied the seats in the little waiting-room. "It iss noisy here, but it iss quiet, too."

She led the way thither, and they sat down. The station-agent eyed them curiously as they waited for half an hour in solemn silence. Then Benjamin arose, and Jovina, who had begun to think that Phillipsburg, even it if were slower than Lehigh County, would by this time be thoroughly awake, prepared to follow.

"You wait here a little," Benj commanded as she gathered up her pocket-book and her gloves. "I will go first out and walk up an' down a little."

"Well, I guess I go wis."

"No; you will get tired. You stay here." There was such sternness in his voice that Jovina sank back. Did he purpose to run away? She determined to change her seat to where she could watch every inch of the little platform. Just as soon as he started up the steps he would find her at his side. She yielded for the first time to her suspicions that perhaps Benj was beginning to repent, and she grew each moment more angry.

"If it wass not for one sing he might go back," she said to herself. "An' dat iss dat by dis time all Millerstown knows eferysing about it. Sarah

Ann Mohr she saw us, and besides, I told mam dat by dis time she could tell. Go back and not married, when I start out to get married! I guess not! It iss too late now for him to sneak out of it. If he only knew somesing what *I* know, he might be glad enough. But dat sing I will not tell him — not yet, anyhow. In a half-hour we will be married; den it will be time enough."

In spite of the firm purpose betokened by Jovina's tightly pressed lips and flashing eyes, she was, at the end of a half-hour, still the same Jovina Neuweiler. As Benj walked up and down the platform, he realized that the time for procrastination was past. Each moment his anguish grew more intense.

"It don't make anysing out now what happens," he thought. "I would be willing to do wisout Mary, too, and nefer get married, if only I did n't haf to marry Chofina. I don't care for cooking or nosing. Mam's cooking iss me plenty good enough."

Wild thoughts of flight sped across his brain. There, however, stern, watchful, implacable, sat Jovina. He looked nervously at his watch. It was already after nine o'clock. He expected each moment to see her at the door, beckoning him to follow her up the steps. Presently she appeared.

"Benj!" she called. "What time iss it at your watch?"

He pretended not to hear, and she called the second time in tones which admitted of no misunderstanding.

"I don't know for sure. Wait once; I look." He drew his watch slowly from his pocket.

"It iss somewheres near nine," he said weakly.

"Well?" demanded Jovina.

"Well? well?" he repeated in confusion. "How do you mean wis 'well,' Chofina?"

"I guess you know what I mean. I sink it iss a funny sing when —"

"Chofina, wait once." He interrupted frantically the rush of her speech. "I haf a plan. Wait once a minute, Chofina."

Jovina waited at least five.

"Well?" she said again.

"Why, it says here on de time-table dat a train goes to Riegelsville at nine-sirty. I used to know a preacher what wass preaching dere. Don't you — d-d-don't you —" Benj stammered madly in his excitement — "don't you sink it would be a good sing to go once down dere an' get married?"

Jovina considered the proposition for an instant. The railroad ran down the Jersey side of the river. Had it been the Pennsylvania side, she would have concluded that Benj wished to delay the ceremony until it was too late in the day to get a license. In Jersey, however, they would need no license, hence he could gain nothing by delay. She did not object to satisfying what appeared to be only a harmless whim. It was only nine o'clock, and they had the rest of the day before them.

"But, Benj," she exclaimed, "it will cost to go down to dat place. We haf spent already a good deal money."

"What do I care for money!" he said with reckless prodigality. "We haf safed on de license."

"Haf you got de tickets?"

"No; wait once. I get dem." He vanished swiftly into the station. As he waited for his change, he looked back. There stood Jovina in the doorway. Her hat cast a shadow across her face which to him appeared like a deep scowl.

"*Ach*, I'm coming!" he said hurriedly. Had it begun so soon as this, that she would watch him every minute? The cheerfulness caused by the prospect of a delay vanished instantly. He pictured Mary at his side. How differently she would have acted!

It never occurred to him to help Jovina up the steps of the car. He climbed up himself and sank despairingly into the first seat, half of which was already occupied, whereupon Jovina, who followed close at his heels, seized him by the arm.

"Are you den not right?" she demanded, and he rose and followed her to a vacant seat. Presently she called his attention to a strong odor of mint which seemed to envelop them.

"It iss a powwow doctor lifs along here," she explained. "Sarah Ann Mohr told me once from him. Lots of folks come from Beslehem an' Nazares an' lots of places in Norsampton County ofer. He gifs much medicine, an' it smells of mint."

Benjamin, however, plunged in despair, heard not a word. Nor did the conductor's loud "Riegelsville! Riegelsville!" make the least impression upon him. He did feel, however, Jovina's clutch upon his arm.

"It iss Riegelsville," she said. "Come on!"

Benjamin came. Now at last his bachelor days were ended. He made, however, another brave effort.

"I sink perhaps dat preacher has mofed away."

"It don't make nosing out when dat one has mofed away. I guess dere iss anoder."

Jovina kept her hand on his arm till, having left the station, they followed the other passengers toward the dark opening of a covered bridge.

"Wh-where are you going?" he queried.

"Can't you see de town iss ofer here? We must pay first toll, I guess. De town iss on de oder side of de bridge."

Benj paid, forgetting for once in his life to count the change. When they stepped again upon solid ground, he suddenly halted.

"Chofina!" he almost shouted, "we are again in Pennsylfania. It wass de rifer what we crossed."

"Well, what of it?"

"We can't get married in Pennsylfania wisout no license."

"Den we go back to where we come." Her voice was terrible in its sternness. Was this his little game? Benj, however, had never before been within a dozen miles of Riegelsville, and knew nothing of its topography. He regarded this as a special interposition of Providence in his behalf.

"But, Chofina, it would not bring good luck to go back to a place for a second time to get married."

"We are going to Phillipsburg to get right aways married. Dat iss what we are going to do." To Jovina the only ill luck which could possibly befall was further delay. "Come on; it iss pretty soon perhaps a train back." Again she laid her hand on his arm. "Come on. But what iss now de matter?" For Benj had suddenly stopped at the opening of the bridge.

"I — I haf — I haf lost my pocket-book."

"Well, you must 'a' dropped it here. Come on; let us look once. When did you last haf it?"

"I don't know," he almost wailed. "I paid de tickets an' de toll from some loose change what I had. I might 'a' lost it efen in Millerstown already. How will we den get home, Chofina? I haf only a few cents loose change any more."

For a few minutes they searched diligently.

"It ain't here," said Benjamin. "*Ach!* what will we do? Where are you den going, Chofina?"

Jovina had started toward the station.

"Come on!" she said.

"But I haf no money! We can't walk."

"You haf de tickets, anyhow, to Phillipsburg. We can sit in de station till de next train comes."

"But we can't walk from Phillipsburg to Millerstown, I guess."

"Benj Gaumer," she commanded, "dere iss one way, and only one, what you can get home besides walking. Dat way I will tell you when we get to de station." Thereupon Benjamin followed her.

"I haf plenty money of my own," she announced; "but I don't take no strange fellows trafeling round wis me. I would take a fellow if I wass married to him, and no oder kind; dat I can tell you, Benj Gaumer! You need n't say nosing now. When we got to Phillipsburg once it will be den time enough."

For the next hour he sat silently beside her. He slipped his hand surreptitiously into one pocket after the other, but no purse could he find. He listened greedily to the clink of silver in Jovina's pocket-book as she changed it from one hand to the other. Certainly she moved it around oftener than was necessary. There was a north-bound train in an hour, and again he left her to climb unaided to the car. Again her "Chust smell de mint, Benj!" as they passed Raubsville fell on deaf ears, and it was necessary for her to remind him forcibly that they had reached their destination.

He followed weakly behind her up the long steps, in the embarrassed helplessness of the man with empty pockets. When they reached the top she paused.

"Well?" she said grimly.

Benjamin looked up the street, then down, then he thrust his hands wildly into his pockets. The two minutes that had passed since his last investigation had not served to create a purse. Then he capitulated.

"What for a preacher, Chofina?" he asked.

"So long as dere ain't no New Baptists nowhere but in Millerstown, I don't care. But no Menisht (Mennonite) an' no Casolic (Catholic) an' no Chew! Whatefer oder preacher you can find dan dose, I don't care."

"Wh-where den will I find him?" he asked.

She cast upon him a glance of withering scorn.

"Go in dat store an' ask!" He followed the direction she indicated.

"De drug-store?"

"Yes."

The clerks looked slyly at one another as Benj entered the store after a moment's frantic struggle to push in the door which was marked "Pull."

"Where iss a preacher?" he demanded wildly.

"The second house from the corner on the next block, sir."

"Sank you." Benj started out, but came speedily back.

"He ain't for sure no Casolic?" he queried.

"No what?"

"No Casolic."

"Oh, Catholic you mean! No sir."

"Nor yet a Menisht nor a Chew?"

"A what? He is a clergyman of the Lutheran Church."

"Sank you."

"He's harder hit than most," a clerk remarked as Benj joined Jovina on the opposite corner. "Look at 'em; they're going the wrong way."

He rushed to the doorway and called loudly, whereupon Jovina stood still, while Benj moved on a few paces.

"You're going the wrong way!" he shouted. "The preacher lives up the other way."

Jovina seized Benj by the arm, and the clerk went back to the store.

"I'm afraid I've spoiled sport," he laughed. "The poor chap won't get away from her again."

When they reached the preacher's door, Jovina herself asked if he were at home and, upon being answered affirmatively, motioned Benj to precede her. The maid, whose dancing eyes gave testimony that she understood their errand, invited Jovina to walk up-stairs and lay off her hat.

"No, I won't need to lay off my hat. I can be married in a hat."

Was this another scheme of Benj's to get away? Had he mysteriously communicated with this saucy girl, and was she trying to aid him?

"Not much does she get me away!" Jovina said to herself. "I am a little too smart for dese New Chersey ones."

The maid ushered them into the preacher's study, and he rose as they entered.

"You wish to see me?" he asked smilingly. "From Pennsylvania? Ah, I understand. Yes, I can perform the ceremony immediately."

He asked them various questions. The only objection he had to his present pastorate was the fact that it lay in a town which was a veritable Gretna Green, and he was not always sure that the persons he married were truthful about their age or their residence. In this case, however, his mind was more at ease. In the first place, they were certainly both of age, and, in the second, the clothing of the groom, in which he was evidently not thoroughly at home, and the bride's gay and beruffled attire, were too conspicuous to have been donned for an elopement. As he turned from Jovina to Benjamin, however, he began to be puzzled.

"If this young woman were apparently as unwilling to be married as this young man," he said to himself, "I should feel it my duty to decline to marry them."

Benjamin's replies, however, though wanting in spirit, were correct as to the letter, and presently he and Jovina were pronounced man and wife.

As the preacher shook hands with them, Jovina slipped a dollar bill from her hand to his own.

"He lost his pocket-book," she explained.

"But — but, my friend, I can't take a fee from you!"

"*Ach!* dat don't make nosing out," she said calmly. "He will chust haf to pay it back again."

At this the preacher bowed, his chin deep in his collar. He went with them toward the door. When they reached the hall, the maid paused for a moment with her dusting, and Jovina looked at her sharply. Had she been listening? Had this saucy little thing heard Benj's gruff replies? Was she laughing at them? Jovina turned toward the preacher.

"You must excuse him because he don't seem so anxious," she explained loudly. "It iss n't as he don't want to get married; it iss because — because —" Jovina was not an habitual prevaricator, and invention was difficult — "it iss because he has new shoes an' he has it so in his feet. Good-by, *Para* (Pastor)."

Then Jovina looked haughtily at the pretty maid, — Jovina, who herself had lived out one summer at the Weygandts', where she expected to be treated as one of the family, — and waving her hand majestically, issued her commands:

"Will de serfant-girl open de door?"

Blissfully unconscious of the laughter to which master and maid yielded as she seized Benj again by the arm, she walked briskly down the street.

"I sink it would be nice when we would take de steam-cars home," she said. "We haf come by de trolley. We can walk back across de bridge to Easton."

"All right." Had she proposed an air-ship, Benj would have been equally satisfied. If she chose to waste the difference between the trolley fare, which was fifteen cents, and the railroad fare, which was fifty, well and good. She carried the pocket-book, and she had promised to get him back to Millerstown. She bought some bananas and soft pretzels, and they ate their dinner as they crossed the bridge. When they reached Easton they found that they had just missed a train and it was almost dark when they reached their own county-seat. They had scarcely spoken a word. Jovina, from whose stern eyes the sharpness had vanished, glanced occasionally at Benj with an expression curiously like wistfulness around the corners of her mouth. Benj, however, paid no heed. He mounted the train at her suggestion and rose to leave it at her word; but he had no will of his own. It simply "made nosing out" what happened now. When they reached the corner from which the Millerstown cars started, they found that again they had missed a car. Thereupon Jovina suggested that they take a walk out Hamilton street, where suddenly the faint twilight gave place to the blaze of electric lights. It was she who asked the shouting car-despatcher what time the next car departed for Millerstown, she who piloted the way across the crowded street, she who bought a bag of peanuts from the Italian at the corner. Then Benj gave the first sign that he still possessed an interest in life, for he munched them greedily. He was hungry — not, however, for peanuts or bananas or pretzels, but for boiled cabbage and pork and schnitz-pie. He realized suddenly that he wanted schnitz-pie more than he had ever wanted anything in his life. And, alas! His mother seldom baked it! It was at Jovina's alone that he had ever got enough schnitz-pie. Suddenly he drew a deep breath. He was henceforth to live at Jovina's! The black clouds which hemmed him in brightened. It was true that they were still so very gray as to be almost black; but Jovina, had she only known, had good reason to take courage. He remembered for the first time to help her into the car, and as he sat down beside her he noticed that she wore her pink dress. A loud shout from the rear suddenly drew his attention.

"Well! Well! Look once in front dere! Chust married, fellows! Hello, Benj!" It was Billy Knerr and the young Fackenthals. At their gay sally every one in the car grinned broadly, and Benj blushed like a girl. Another penalty for being married! The sense of his own misery surged over him again. Jovina was to blame for this. He looked around at her and for an instant her own glance, tormented, pitiful, pathetically unlike Jovina, held his own. That instant something new was born within him — a sense of possession. He rose to his feet and looked angrily back at his fellow-townsmen.

"You fellows had better shut once up!" he called. "It shows mighty poor manners to yell at a lady in de street-car! An', what iss more, any one what does it will settle wis me!"

So amazed were they, and so thoroughly convinced that he meant what he said, that they were instantly silent.

The streets of the county-seat and the long, ugly rows of suburban houses were soon left behind. Then they sped out into the summer darkness, where the lights were gleaming in scattered farmhouses.

"Are you cold, Chofina?" Benj asked suddenly, as the cool evening breeze blew through the car.

"N-no," she answered, startled by his solicitude. "But I am tired."

"An' I, too."

Suddenly Jovina began to tremble.

"No, it ain't dat I am cold. It iss somesing else. It iss somesing dat I must tell you, Benj. I haf known it sometime already. It — it — iss — it iss dat —"

"Well?"

"It iss dat Chohn Weimer will some one of dese days marry Mary."

"Mary? Mary who?"

"Why, Mary Kuhns."

"Chohn Weimer marry Mary Kuhns." He laid his hand heavily on her wrist. "How do you den know dis?"

"Chohn told me himself, an' it iss for sure true."

John Weimer marry Mary Kuhns! Mary Kuhns, whose steady suitor he had been for three years! Now all Millerstown would say that she had thrown him over for John. A fierce anger against her swelled within him. What right had she to treat him like this? Then at last the morning of Benjamin's content dawned.

"But — but —"

"But what, Benj?" prompted Jovina in a voice thick with suppressed tears.

"Wait once," he said, his forehead wrinkled in a frown, his grasp on her wrist growing each moment tighter. "But Chofina, it wass I what srew Mary Kuhns ofer, and not she me."

"Of course it wass," said Jovina.

"Chovina, did you haf de wedding-day so soon because of Mary's also getting married? Did you sink folks would say she srew me ofer? Did you do it den for me?"

"Of course I did," said Jovina.

His clasp this time closed on Jovina's hand. Her own, however, was suddenly drawn away.

"Chofina!" he exclaimed, "do you turn away from me?"

"No — no; it ain't dat, Benj. I haf somesing else to tell you, Benj."

"Wait once, Chofina. It iss almost time to get out. Den you can tell me."

He helped her down tenderly. Billy Knerr called after them something about a serenade they would have the next evening, but they paid no heed as they started up the dark and silent street.

"Now, Chofina, what iss den dis foolish sing what worries you?"

"It iss dis, Benj," she sobbed: "it iss your pocket-book. I picked it up on de bridge, and I haf had it all de day. *Ach*! Benj, what will you do?"

"You haf den had it all day!" he repeated dully. "Why, Chofina, if I had not lost it, it might be dat we would not haf been yet married!"

"I knew it — I knew it! I knew it all de time!" she exclaimed wildly. "Den you don't lofe me a bit! It would make nosing out to you when I wass dead!"

For the fraction of a second Benj considered. As he had said, if he had not lost his pocket-book they might not have been married. Then how Millerstown would have laughed! And now —

"Chofina," he whispered, "it iss all right. Don't you cry a minute. I am not mad ofer you, Chofinily; I am glad. Listen once. If we wass not already married, dey would all say dat she srew me ofer, and dat you wass second choice. Now we haf a good one on her!"

"But, Benj, are you sure you don't lofe her no more?"

"I nefer lofed her," declared Benjamin, sure of his mind at last; "an' now I hate her!"

THE MILLERSTOWN YELLOW JOURNAL

Originally published in the May 1906 issue of *The Atlantic Monthly*

"He is for sure not right in his head. I never heard such a dumb thing. I guess if something went wrong with him he would not want it put right aways in the paper."

Alfie Bittenbender, the Millerstown schoolteacher, looked up at his wife as she perched on the end of his desk. Then he smiled ruefully.

"If Sarah Ann's pigs die, that is news, if Sarah Ann likes it or not."

"Just you wait," Jennie went on, "till he makes many more such dumb mistakes; it won't anybody take his paper."

Alfie looked sorrowfully about him. They were in what appeared to have been a small barn, but which was now a printing office. There was a little hand press, shrouded in burlap, a tall case of type, a stove, several piles of paper, and, nailed against the wall, a large box, divided into pigeonholes. The only spot which seemed to be in use was the broad deal table, covered with papers, on some of which Madame Jennie sat enthroned.

As a small boy, Alfie had made up his mind to be an editor. Even when he was in the "small school," he had begun to gather items.

"Old Man Fackenthal is pretty sick," he would write on his slate. Or, "Julie Lorish is home with her Pop for a while from working at Zion Church." His items dealt occasionally with civic improvements. "Al Losch has fixed his crossing. It is us now pleasanter walking."

Having graduated from the Normal School, he worked for a year in a printing office, then taught the Millerstown school. Both he and Jennie Reichard, whom he married, worked and saved in order to fit out his "printing office," and talked and dreamed of the Millerstown paper which he meant to publish, and which Jennie proudly named *The Star*.

The Star, however, had never risen. Just as Alfie was ready to make his project known to his fellow townsmen, a stranger canvassed the town for subscribers and advertisers for the *Millerstown Journal*, which he proposed to publish on Thursday of each week, at two dollars a year.

"It ain't his business to come to Millerstown," Jennie sobbed. "What does he know from Millerstown folks?"

Alfie shook his head.

"He has worked already in New York on a paper. He knows everything. I sell my things."

However, he sold nothing, but covered the press carefully, and re-wrapped the bundles of paper. He read the *Journal*, which Jennie refused to touch. In point of composition, it was doubtless a good paper. Moreover, the news was presented in a manner far from provincial. The items from Zion Church did not appear in a series of disjointed sentences, but were incorporated into a letter, addressed to Elias Bittner, and signed, "Your loving nephew, J. R." Vain old Elias had no nephew, but was too much flattered to object. Once the editor printed upside down an article to which he wished to call special attention. Millerstown condoled with him for the mistake, and read the article to a man. His pages were dark with scare heads, and exclamation points, and his advertisements were couched in jaunty sentences which Alfie could never have compassed.

"Peter," one of them read, "tell John that Butz the barber wants to see him. He needs a shave." Another, which made Alfie furious, suggested that parents "ask Mr. Bittenbender whether he doesn't think the children need new dictionaries. Weimer has plenty in his store."

"This is what they call in New York 'Yellow Journalism,'" he said to Jennie. "I would be ashamed, when I was Millerstown, to make a fuss over such a paper."

There was no doubt that, for the first few months of its existence, the *Journal* was popular. Then, suddenly, Millerstown lost its enthusiasm. The editor published the fact that Sarah Ann Mohr, who prided herself on her skill in raising pigs, had lost six by cholera. The day after, several Millerstonians told him in front of the post-office what they thought of him, and Sarah Ann notified him that he need send her the *Journal* no more. Soon he offended the new Baptists by forgetting the announcement of their services, and then the Mennonites by giving them less space than the Lutherans.

Alfie watched his career eagerly.

"If he makes all the churches mad over him," he said to Jennie, as she looked down at him from her seat on top of his papers, "then he won't have anybody to take his *Journal*."

Jennie slipped down, and started toward the door.

"Just you wait once till he makes some more such dumb mistakes," she said cheerfully.

Whereupon Alfie smiled absently back, and went down to the post-office for the day's mail. When, half an hour later, he hurried home, his eyes were round with excitement.

"I tell you the *Journal* will now have plenty news," he announced.

"What is it?" asked Jennie.

"It has been some one murdered in Millerstown."

"Some one murdered in Millerstown!" Jennie clasped her hands, all covered with biscuit dough as they were. She would not have been more surprised if he had said an earthquake or a volcano. "Who is, then, murdered in Millerstown?"

"Ay, it was some fellows living in a shanty on the mountain: Dutch John, what comes always around to trim grapevines, and another, Josie Knapp, what comes always around begging. That fellow, he killed Dutch John. But they have him. Old Man Fackenthal went up the mountain for to fetch some durchwachs" (thoroughwort), "and he found him dead. Now it will be news."

"I think it is a shame for Millerstown. I don't think such a thing should go in the paper."

"Ach, but it must! He will have plenty to fill it."

Alfie did not dream, however, of the possibilities which the editor would find in the murder. His eyes grew round with horror, not at the details alone, which were really as far from harrowing as the details of a murder could be, but at the way they were exaggerated. The *Journal* said that Old Man Fackenthal had found the body at "dusky twilight," which was not true at all. Instead, it was broad afternoon. Nor did he "start with horror, and then go out to draw in deep breaths of pure air before investigating further." Old Man Fackenthal was not that kind. Nor had the murdered man's dog stood guard over the body. The murdered man had no dog.

All summer the editor made copy of the murder. He described the quarters assigned to the prisoner, his behavior, his food, his clothing. He wrote incidentally on the jail itself, its cost and design. He published biographies of the murderer and the murdered man, whose validity no one in Millerstown but Alfie seemed to suspect.

The prisoner was tried at the county seat, and sentenced to be hanged in January. The date was set for the first Thursday, and the editor began in December to prepare the minds of his readers for the event. He reviewed the trial, commented upon the demeanor of the condemned man, and gave a list of those whose privilege it would be to attend. He promised to illustrate his account of the hanging with photographs of the jail, the scaffold, and the sheriff.

Millerstown, which read each lurid paragraph more admiringly than the last, did not see the difficulty which here arose. The hanging was set for Thursday at eight o'clock; the *Journal* was printed on Wednesday, and distributed with the eleven o'clock mail on Thursday. The printing of the paper could not be postponed, because the editor planned to be married in the county seat that afternoon, and then go away for a week.

Nor did the editor seem more troubled than unconscious Millerstown. He went gayly about his business, grinning a little more broadly, perhaps, at the efforts of his assistant to talk English, and once or twice telling him that he was a "dumb Dutchman, like the rest of Millerstown."

The date of the hanging was remembered afterwards by the "great snow." When Alfie came home from school the afternoon before, there were only fugitive flakes, but before dark the ground was white. When he looked out at bedtime, he could not see the lights in the village. The snow seemed to shut him in. He fancied that he could hear it rustling softly. At dawn, Jennie called to him to look out. The familiar contours of every day were lost in one great whiteness, and under the brisk wind drifts were rapidly forming. He looked up the pike toward the schoolhouse, and the road seemed even with the fences.

"We will have to-day no school," he said at the breakfast table. "We could perhaps get out, but it will be different to get back. I will go down the street, and if it is any one coming, I will tell them they dare go home."

In his slow progress through the town, he met no one, till he reached the post-office. There, on the roughly cleared pavement, Jake Fackenthal and Billy Knerr were swinging their arms to keep warm.

"It is a bad day for the hanging," Billy said, as Alfie joined them.

"Ach, well, it is all indoors," rejoined Jake. "We can soon read about it in the paper."

"Will he have it already in the paper?" Alfie asked quickly.

"He said to somebody that he would."

"But how will he get it in the paper so quick?"

"I guess by telegraph. He is me a pretty smart fellow."

"But" — Alfie paused. He would find out for himself down at the station.

As he turned the corner, the wind nearly lifted him from his feet. It cut his face, and chilled him to the bone.

"It would not be funny when the wires are down," he said to himself. "And maybe the trains stopped. It is just now time for the hanging. He must have gone a long while ago down to the station. It is here no footprints."

The wind grew stronger each moment. When he reached the steps of the high platform, he was compelled to cling there for a moment, with the snow stinging his face. The platform had been swept clear by the wind, and he walked quickly across it to the office, where, he knew, the agent, Henny Leibensberger, would have the stove almost bursting with heat. He swung open the office door, then closed it quickly.

"But where is he?" he asked.

"Where is who?" Henny looked up from his desk.

"Ay, the editor. Will he not hear over the telegraph from the hanging?"

"Nobody will hear nothing from the hanging over this telegraph that I know of. Did he say he would?"

"Somebody said it."

"Well, it ain't so. Sit down once."

Alfie tramped up and down the room, too perturbed to accept.

"How will he, then, get the hanging in the paper?" he demanded.

"I guess he will put off the paper. Say, Alfie," — Henny sprang to his feet, — "would you care to stay here and mind the telegraph once a minute, while I go home? It won't be any trains till I get back."

Alfie consented willingly. He had learned telegraphy before he went to the Normal School, and he often relieved the agent in summer. He would not go home till eleven o'clock, then he could take the *Journal* with him. It would certainly not contain much news.

For the first hour, he had little to do. He studied the weather report, he sharpened Henny's lead pencils, then he fell to trying them one after the other, on the backs of telegraph blanks. Presently, when his scribblings were taking shape in an account of the hanging as he imagined it to be, the telegraph keys clicked with a new sound. He answered the call for Millerstown, and took the message. It read, "Number Seven stalled at Blandon." Then he fell to writing again, wondering, meanwhile, why Henny did not return. Jennie would be anxious if he did not get home in time for dinner.

The wind seemed to grow each moment stronger and more irresponsible. The track, except for a few feet, was shut off by the thick whirl of snow, on which the sun now gleamed dazzlingly. Down at the end of the platform the drifts were even with the floor.

Presently, the key called again for Millerstown. It was the operator at the county seat, who wished to exchange a few remarks about the storm.

"The wires are down up the valley," he said. "And there have been no trains for two hours."

Suddenly Alfie's eyes brightened, and he leaned down over the table as though afraid of losing one low sound. His own hand moved swiftly, and again he listened. His hand tapped the keys again. Once he smiled grimly, then his face stiffened into its eager lines. Outside, the whirl of snow drove back and forth under the bright sunshine; within, in the smothering heat, his whole being strained itself to listen to the click, click, click, which cut into the silence.

Then the rapid crepitations were no more. Alfie touched the key, he stuck it heavily. Its life had departed. It responded only with a dull, mechanical sound, as little like the animation of the moment before as death is like life. For a moment Alfie did not move.

Then — "The wires are down. I must go," he said impatiently. "Where is Henny that he does not come? But it won't be any trains; I can go anyhow."

Seizing his hat and coat, he dashed out across the platform. The wind pounced upon him as he reached the end, and whirled him off into the deepest part of the great drift. He struggled out, to find himself face to face with the station agent.

"The wires are down," he gasped "And it won't be no eleven o'clock train. And they say" —

"All right," Henny shouted back. "Much obliged."

"But they say" —

"Yes, I understand. It won't be any trains. The *Journal* has everything in it from the hanging." Henny had turned his back to the wind, and his voice came clear and distinct.

"But they say" — Alfie's words were whirled away before the agent realized they had been spoken.

"Good-by," he shouted; then the door of the office closed upon him. He watched Alfie from the window, wondering whether he had lost his mind. He stood knee-deep in the snow, his open coat flying in the wind.

"How does Henny think he could get the news?" Alfie was saying to himself. "The other folks could think it came by telegraph, but Henny knows it couldn't come by telegraph. Does he think perhaps one could ride out? It says, 'Gelt regiert die Welt, und Dummheit Berks County,'" (Gold rules the world, and stupidity Berks County), "only this time it is Millerstown what 'Dummheit rules.' Just wait till I tell them!"

Thereupon, Alfie, with his gloves still in his hand, and with flying coat-tails, started up the street. For a few yards he plunged along, then he stopped again.

"They cannot find it out!" he exclaimed aloud. Then — "But it will mean powerful work!"

A moment later, his broad shoulders darkened the little window at the post-office. He almost snatched the paper from Dave Wimmer's hand, then dashed out. A few of the pavements had been cleared, and he made rapid progress. The low gate at his own house was snowed under, and he stepped over it, almost forgetting that it was there. He sped on down the yard, without a glance at the kitchen window, where Jennie usually watched for him, and opened the barn door.

There he gathered an armful of paper and another of wood, and thrust them in to the stove, where they soon cracked merrily. Sitting down at his desk, and seizing all the blank paper he could find, he went to work. An hour later he was conscious of some discomfort. At first he could not make out what it was, then he realized that he was hungry. And where was Jennie?

He ran across the yard to the kitchen. There on the table he found his dinner and a note.

"Pop came over that I should go along to Sally. She is sick. I will come till supper home."

He did not sit down, but, taking a pie in one hand, and a plate of doughnuts in the other, went back to the barn. There, for fifteen minutes, he wrote with one hand, while he fed himself with the other. Then, gathering up the loose sheets, he went across to the type case. The fire had gone out, and the wind had forced itself in through a hundred crannies. When his hands grew so stiff that he could not work, he built up the fire, frowning, meanwhile, at the interruption.

"The ink will not be dry," he said aloud. "But I guess it will not make anything out this time. The next time I will fix them up fine. If," — he added somewhat dubiously, — "if it is any next time."

No one who had not worked steadily while the light faded could have seen to gather and fold the scattered sheets, which, damp from the press, lay all about the floor when he had finished. With shaking hands, he packed them into a half-bushel basket, and, putting it on his arm, started down the street. He planned, as he strode along, how he would announce his début as an editor.

"I would rather give them away than sell them," he thought. "But I guess it is better that I sell them. I wonder if ever before a paper was started with an extra."

He awoke suddenly to the fact that the storm had entirely ceased. The sky was still a faint gold, while the great billows of snow gleamed coldly blue in the clear light. Here and there windows were lit up, and he heard men laughing in the tavern. A ball of soft snow caught him behind the ear as he passed Oliver Kuhns's, and he called back a cheerful, "Just you wait once till I catch you!"

Before he reached the post-office, he heard the sound of many voices. Within, Old Man Fackenthal, Elias Bittner and Pit Gaumer tilted their chairs against the wall; and on the counters — relics of the days when the post-office had been a store — perched the younger generation, Billy Knerr, the two young Fackenthals, Jakily Kemerer, Jimmie Weygandt, and half a dozen others; and all the boys in the village seemed to have gathered in the space between. Dave Wimmer, the postmaster, who leaned half way out over the gate which divided his quarters from the main office, read aloud from the *Millerstown Journal*. The reading progressed slowly, for there were frequent interruptions, and demands for elucidation.

"Did n't he say no word when he was hung?" old Elias Bittner demanded, as Alfie entered.

"No, not a word," answered Wimmer solemnly. "It says, 'silent as the grave what was soon to receive him.'"

"Did n't they have no praying, or nothing?" some one queried.

"Yes," answered Dave. "Here is a grand prayer what the chaplain made. It says" —

"How does the editor know what it says?" a slightly scornful voice demanded. They turned to regard Alfie, who stood, with his basket on his arm, just within the door.

"By the telegraph, of course," old Elias answered impatiently. "How else should he know? Dave, go on with the praying."

Old Man Fackenthal let his chair slam to the floor.

"I say so, too. How does he know it?" he said. "This editor was me too much all summer for making something out of nothing. Alfie, what have you there?"

Alfie had set down his basket, and was nervously unfolding one of the damp sheets.

"I have here," — he began, his confidence suddenly deserting him, — "I have here a new paper what will tell about the hanging."

"A new paper! What for a new paper?" demanded Elias. "It can't be any paper but the *Journal*. It was to-day no train."

Old Man Fackenthal motioned him to be silent.

"You had better shut a while up, and let Alfie tell from this new paper. Now, Alfie."

Alfie's eyes burned brightly.

"It is a new paper, just to-day begun. The name shall be the *Millerstown Star*. It will tell all the news, and it will be published every week from now on, at a dollar a year. It has this time nothing in it but from the hanging."

"We all know about the hanging," said old Elias impatiently. "We" —

"You do not know about the hanging," said Alfie firmly. "Perhaps Dave will read us what it says in this paper from the hanging."

Willing hands passed it across to Dave, from whose grasp the *Millerstown Journal* had slipped unnoticed to the floor. The room was silent enough now to suit even Old Man Fackenthal. Dave adjusted his spectacles with a loud, "Well, now, we will see what all this means." His eyes grew wider as he glanced along the head-lines, then his mouth opened, and the paper shook in his hands.

"Boys!" he said faintly.

"Well, hurry yourself," some one called.

"Boys!" he ejaculated again.

"Well, what!" This time there was a chorus of exclamations. "Ain't he dead?"

"Yes, but, boys! It says here it was n't to-day no hanging. He made hisself dead with poison in the jail!"

"Bei meiner Sex, I don't believe it!" said Elias Bittner. They silenced him in a moment, and there was a loud demand for further explanation. How had Alfie heard? Who was publishing the new paper? Where had the editor of the *Journal* got his news?

"He got it somehow, and it must be true," insisted Elias.

"He made it up out of his own head," said Old Man Fackenthal. "Say, boys, what for fools does he think we are in Millerstown? Alfie, from now on I take the *Star*."

Thus was the first subscriber enrolled.

Fifteen minutes later, Alfie started out in the street, his basket empty, save for one paper which he was taking home to Jennie.

The sunset glow had vanished, and the stars were shining. Out across the Weygandt meadows, the bleeder at the furnace blazed like a beacon. Then another light, less bright, but more alluring, caught his glance. Jennie had come home. As he reached the gate, a long shaft of light from the opening door shot across the snow.

"Well, Alfie, where have you been? I was getting scared."

For answer he handed her the little sheet, damp and crumpled, blank on three sides, and sadly blurred on the fourth. It was a newspaper of one item, which began: —

"In spite of the lengthy account of the hanging of Josie Knapp, published by our esteemed contemporary, the *Millerstown Journal*, we would say that he was not this morning hung, but yesterday evening already took poison in the county jail."

THE MIRACLE

Originally published in the June 1906 issue of
Appleton's Booklover's Magazine

THE rim of the sun dropped slowly into a gap in the Western hills, lay there for an instant as though cradled in a great lap, then slid down behind the ridge. All across the wide valley the meadow larks piped softly, and here and there swallows flitted over the ponds.

Gradually a shadow spread across the meadows, the little village, and the fields, and finally up the hillside. There, where the mountain road was lost under the first trees of the woodland, a light gleamed out to challenge the last feebleness of departing day. For the space of a second there was an almost visible struggle for the mastery, then in the twilight the torches flared out, and huge shadows loomed up in the woodland.

The lights gleamed on white shapes which stood — or did they move slowly back and forth? — just outside the circle of the torches. There, where the flame shone brightest, was that the grooved surface of a slender column, vanishing upward into the darkness? Did that darkness hide a carven capital, and did there float far back into the shadows an airy roof? The torches blazed in the evening wind. Did unseen hands swing them gently to and fro?

The soft trill from the meadows deepened to a sentient note, instinct with some Arcadian burden. Was great Pan dead? Was — ah, did not the outline of the roof gleam for an instant clear against the night above it? Should one cry aloud that the folk in the valley may come trooping in wonder? Hark! there was the sound of footsteps, of many voices. Was it here, of all the world, that They, the Forgotten, deigned to receive the homage of the last of their worshipers? Or was this Tempe itself? For one blessed second one was a child again in the childhood of the world, awed, frightened, credulous, and happy.

Then — the lights flamed still higher in the gathering darkness, the white shapes swayed no more. The chestnut branches waved a caduceus, and one stared about, wide-eyed and dismayed. Then, curiously, one went forward. What folk were these who left their homes in the summer twilight to climb the mountain side? Was it a religious rite which brought them here?

Within the circle of the torches stood a rough platform. Before it on low benches were gathered several hundred persons, who sat silently and with bent heads. Had they learned the virtue of the magic communion? And how? By what strange channels had the secret of its power come down to these, the children of its enemies? How had these Germans, far from Tempe, far indeed from their own fatherland ——

"Oh, Lord, grant these our prayers!"

The spell was broken. It was no longer Tempe. Great Pan was dead.

Two centuries before their fathers had sought here a refuge from persecution, and now, divided into a score of sects, they still counted religion the chief business of their lives. These, who were part of one of the branches from the Mennonite stem, had come to hold a camp meeting on the mountain side. They had built a platform, with a mourner's bench and several hundred rough seats before it, and had pitched a score of tents, which stood out clearly now, with no suggestion of grooved columns.

Thither came many curious visitors, not only all of Millerstown, the little village in the valley below, but many others from the neighborhood.

The early experience of the Mennonites in Millerstown had been somewhat discouraging. Their pastor, young David Koehler, had established himself there during the spring of the previous year. The congregation grew so rapidly that they were soon able to build a church. Then, as winter drew near, both David and his people were troubled. They had exhausted all their resources in building the church; there was now no money to heat it or to pay the preacher's salary.

To David, tribulation centered itself in Ellie Muth's pneumonia. She was the most spiritual, the most devout of all his converts. There had been about her conversion none of the noisy rejoicing which he had been taught was one of the evidences of a true change of heart, but which sometimes almost sickened him. She had come into her spiritual heritage calmly, but with a light on her face which hallowed his religion at the same time that it wrung his heart. There was something about her virgin ecstasy which chilled him, compelling him to think of her as a saint in a niche rather than a woman.

She did not hold herself aloof. She worked in Millerstown's little factory with the other young women, she came and went with her dinner pail in her hand, her print dress covered with lint from her loom, her sunbonnet pushed back a little from her slender face. Her companions, however, seemed to feel that she was different from them. The girl who slapped her friend heavily on the back laid her hand gently on Ellen's shoulder; the boy who bade the other girls "hook on" to his arm hailed her with a gentle "Hello, Ellie," and walked with her almost silently, if he walked with her at all.

When she came to the Mennonite church, it was under strong protest from her mother. She had her own church, the Lutheran; why not stay in it? Such religious peregrinations were not respectable; it was a disgrace to leave one's church.

"And anyhow to such a church!" she had said scornfully. "Who is in that church? Old Pit Lutz, what was put out of the Baptist, and John Heinrich, what has been in every church in Millerstown already, and a lot of crazy young ones, what don't know what is good for them."

Ellen had not answered. Instead her lips set themselves more firmly.

"It will no good come of it," her mother went on. Then, unheeding the flush which reddened Ellen's face from brow to chin, "No fellow wants a girl what is running always to church, that I can tell you."

"I am not —" began Ellen, only to find herself swept into silence by the torrent of her mother's speech.

"You will get sick. That church is like a barn. You will get the ammonia of the lungs. Then what good will your religion do you if you have to die?"

Whether or not Ellen thought of the obvious retort that then her religion would help her to die, she said nothing, but the next Sunday joined the Mennonite church.

Never had Cassandra voice more prompt fulfillment than her mother's. The church was cold in October; by December it was frigid. The huge stove with its great drum and black pipes seemed to dispense a more bitter chill. The very sight of it made the Mennonites shiver. Its mica doors, through which should have glowed a cheerful light, stared blankly into the face of the congregation, who in turn, as they huddled under shawls and coats, gazed vacantly back.

On Christmas Day, David had gone through the service perfunctorily. He was conscious of some lack. Young, warm-blooded as he was, he had suffered less than any of his congregation. Now he shivered; his teeth chattered so that he could scarcely speak. There seemed to be no warmth of feeling in his congregation; the only warmth which they coveted was physical, and that he could not give them. He looked from face to face, and suddenly realized that Ellie Muth was not there. Then her face as he had seen it at the Wednesday meeting came back to him, pinched, blue, with wide eyes fixed upon his own. She had never missed a service. Could she — could she be sick?

When he went to see her the next day her mother would not admit him.

"She has it in her chest," she said grimly. "She got it at church."

Whereupon David found the door shut in his face.

Nor did she grow better through the long winter. The winter revival meeting was a success, the finances of the church were much improved by the accession of the new members, a great fire blazed cheerfully in the stove, and the neighboring preachers looked with increasing favor upon young David, who meanwhile went about his work with a sore heart. He had never seen Ellie; her mother would not let him cross the threshold. Now he could scarcely inquire how she was for fear that some one should tell him she could not live.

Even when summer came she grew no better. Old Dr. Bender shook his head and said he did not understand, and her mother's complaints grew more and more vindictive. Often they were repeated to young David, with many assurances that no one else in Millerstown thought that he was at all to blame. Each time it seemed as though some of the boyish energy had departed from his stride, some of the heartiness from his voice.

Now it was summer, and the camp meeting was open. David looked out over the congregation, realizing indifferently that Millerstown had never before known so large a religious gathering. He looked at them unmoved, however, either by their close attention to his words, or by the scene about him, so alien to all other scenes of their prosaic lives—the dim forest stretching up to the mountain top, the wind whispering curiously as though it sought to know the purpose of this strange exodus from the quiet valley, the white tents rising shadowy and dim beyond the lights, and the flaring torches sending strange shadows over the upturned faces.

A year ago the sense of his power would have thrilled him through. He knew how to change apathy to interest, complacency to terror, weariness to hysterical delight. Now he looked at his people listlessly, his thoughts away. If he had not come to Millerstown, Ellie Muth would still be well. As it was she lay sick unto death.

Some one started a hymn, and the music, a wailing minor, rose and fell with the flaming lights. It swelled now to a threnodic intensity, it softened now almost to a whisper, thrilling, awesome.

Then slowly the preacher rose. Again he looked down at them, and as they waited for him to speak, the silence grew tense, pregnant. The stillness, the darkness, the strangeness of the place of meeting, made themselves felt. They could hear the sough of the wind in the tree tops and the strange whisperings beneath. A woman began to sway slowly back and forth, her eyes closed. Next to her a young girl clasped her hands to her heart. A sigh deep as the wind itself swept across the open space.

Suddenly the preacher's eyes burned. Something clutched at his heart and tightened his throat, something which seemed to encompass him like the wind. It was an ecstasy which he could not have described, a sudden conviction that he needed only to ask for what he wanted to have it given him, a passionate realization of all the blessings which his religion promised. The congregation, watching him, needed no signal to fall upon their knees.

One by one they turned to look at him as he prayed. His voice grew deeper and louder as he gave thanks for the blessings of the past. They had had trials, but they had been sustained. They had been able to share, even though it was but in a small degree, with those who had suffered for their religion in times past. He prayed that they might be blessed now by a season of grace, and last of all, he prayed for her "who for her much serving of Thee now lies sick. May the time of her suffering be soon past, may she be restored to health, or if it be Thy will" — young David hesitated for an instant, then, obviously unable to complete the sentence he had begun, went on brokenly — "we pray that before many days she may again be one of us."

When he had ceased, the congregation rose slowly. They looked at him as he stood with open eyes looking down at them. Slowly his gaze lifted, widened, and they turned to see what it was he saw. Then, wondering, incredulous, they stared. Pale, pitifully slender in her white dress, and swaying like a narcissus in the evening wind, Ellen Muth came slowly down the grassy aisle. Her eyes were on David; she seemed to support herself on his gaze. No one moved or stirred; even the wind itself was silent. It was as though they beheld a sleepwalker to whose safety the slightest sound might be fatal. Once she put out her hand weakly, and then with a little cry dropped to her knees beside the mourner's bench.

Even then no one moved but David Koehler, who came down the rough steps with his eyes still upon her as though he had no power to look away. As he knelt beside her, a woman sobbed, and then another; then a clear soprano voice began, at first faintly, then with deepening strength, "Now thank we all our God." Some of them closed their eyes; others leaned forward to watch young David and Ellen Muth. They saw him put his hand on hers. Then he bent low to catch her whisper:

"I came — I — came ——"

"Why did you come?" he asked thickly. It had seemed to him for a second as though the miracle which had been done in answer to his prayer were enough, but now — ah, it was not her recovery alone he wanted, it was herself.

"Because I heard — she says — they say you are to blame. I did not know. And you never came. But I am going to get well. I am better. Oh —" Her voice died away weakly. Nevertheless he would not let her go.

"Did you mean that you came for my sake?"

"Y-yes."

"Do you mean that you care for me?"

She looked at him again, and he remembered how pinched and blue her face had been in the cold church. Now it was thinner, but flushed and rosy. His heart leaped.

"Do you care for me?" he said again.

"Oh, yes," she sighed. Then quietly she slid down against him, the color gone from her cheeks.

Strangely enough, no one in the congregation understood. Their God had answered their prayers and the prayers of their pastor. Their eyes, keen for religious crises, missed the emotional significance of the scene. They lifted her gently and took her home, where her mother received them, bitterly certain now that Ellen would die, and bemoaning the madness which had come upon her, and refusing to believe, what no Mennonite doubted, that Ellen would now be well.

Back at the camp meeting the congregation dispersed gradually. They tried to talk to young David, but he kept away, and moved slowly about, putting out all but one of the flaming torches. He did not want to speak or be spoken to. He was still in an ecstasy, now, however, no longer of the spirit, but of the heart. He could see against the blackness of the woods her face, her eyes, her slender, white-clad figure, the promise of a happiness unutterable.

Finally, when all was quiet, he went to his tent. The single torch blazed up, then glimmered and went out. Slowly a mysterious influence crept in from the woodland upon the trampled circle about the benches. Was it brought by the night wind or was it an emanation from the ground? There was no one there to tell, for only young David was awake and he paid no heed. A rabbit scampered with light defiance from bench to bench. Once more the walls of the tallest tent seemed to reach the chestnut branches. The night wind moved the leaves with a soft articulation.

"Io," it seemed to whisper, and again more gently, "Io, Io."

THE PERSISTENCE OF COONIE SCHNABLE

Originally published in the September 1906 issue of *Reader Magazine*

THE fields and meadows round about Millerstown were still brightened by the last glow of the sunset. Within, in the maple-shaded streets, twilight had come. It was Sunday evening, and a great volume of pious song filled the air. For once, all of the six churches were holding service at the same time. Each congregation shared the ministrations of her spiritual shepherd with a sister congregation in a neighboring town, and it was so arranged that when the "Reformeds," the "old-Lutherans," and the "Jonathan Kuhns Baptists" had services, the "new Lutherans," the "new-Baptists" and the "Evangelicals" should have none. Tonight, however, which was the time for the services of the first three, the "new-Baptists" from the next village had come over to Millerstown on the trolley to hold with their brethren a union service; the "new-Lutherans" were celebrating Children's Day and the "Evangelicals" listening to a temperance orator.

As far as one could see, old man Fackenthal and his two cronies, Elias Bittner and Pit Gaumer, were the only persons in all the village who had not availed themselves of this unusual opportunity for worship. Old man Fackenthal sat in the corner of his door-step, pipe in mouth, and Elias and Pit balanced their arm-chairs against the two maple trees at the edge of the pavement. To the beholder their attitudes seemed somewhat precarious. Elias and Pit, however, would have laughed at such a notion. Had they not balanced those chairs against those trees every summer evening for twenty years?

For a while no one spoke. Then, when the old-Lutherans' *Gloria Patri* met the Jonathan Kuhns Baptists' "Work, for the Night is Coming," just above their heads Elias said dreamily, "It seems as when de whole town wass singing. I tell you, it sounds first fine!" And Pit grunted something which might be taken for an assent.

Presently the front legs of Pit's chair struck the pavement with a crash.

"Say, I heard yesterday somesing! Dey say dat Conrad Schnable iss getting relichion. He will go pretty soon forwards in de Efangelical church an' get conwerted."

"Well, I'd like to know once where Coonie Schnable sinks he will get relichion!" retorted Elias Bittner. His voice was high, thin and querulous. One felt instinctively that he was a tall, angular, sour-visaged person, with whom life had gone hard, whereas in reality he was short and plump, with a nimbus of white hair, which made him look like a jolly old saint.

"Elias, I am for sure surprised at you," reproved old man Fackenthal. "Where does den de relichion come from?"

"I guess you know what I mean. It isn't in any Schnable to get relichion. I guess you bos remember his gran'pap?"

"No; what about his gran'pap?" old man Fackenthal asked, as though he had not both heard and told the story a hundred times. Pit groaned loudly, but Elias went on.

"Coonie's gran'pap wass fearful wild. He wass many times drunk, an' he wouldn't nefer work, an' nobody could do nosing wis him. His wife, she went home to her pap wis de children. So one time he wass drunk, an' he laid ofer night outside, an' he died. If I'd a' had my say, we would a' buried him quiet, but no, it must be a long sermon, an' eferysing to it yet. So dey couldn't decide what preacher. So at last I said: 'Well, I guess we better get old Para (Pastor) Butz. He iss a good preacher at funerals, while he says always somesing good from de corpse.' Den dey all laughed an' said nobody could say anysing good from dis one, an' I said anyhow he wouldn't say nosing bad. So we got Para Butz, an' I tell you it wass a big funeral! All Coonie's wife's relatifs wass dere, an' —"

"Well, what did de preacher say?" interrupted old man Fackenthal.

"Well, he looked for a minute down on Coonie — his name wass Conrad like dis one. I wouldn't a' named any one for such a one. I —"

"What did de preacher say?" asked old man Fackenthal again.

"Well, he looked once at Coonie, an' once at de people, an' den again at Coonie, an' den he said: 'My bredern an' sisters, what a nice quiet corpse dis one iss before us!' "

"But dis Conrad issn't wild like his gran'pap," said old man Fackenthal. Neither he nor Pit had laughed when Elias finished his story. "I don't see for why he could not get relichion."

"No," Elias acknowledged. "I don't say he iss so wild like his gran'pap. But he has yet a lot of meanness besides from his mom's side. Now, when he had in him any Kuhns blood, it would be different. Dey are always relichious. Dey haf it inside. Now wis him it would haf to come from de outside."

"I nefer yet heard anysing *bad* what he did," said Pit Gaumer.

"Ach, it ain't sings what you hear. It iss chust dat he iss underhand. Of course, he iss already a church member; he iss a Luseran, but you can be a Luseran, an' be not conwerted. You can be a good Luseran an' not go once to church in a year."

"You're chust chealous," responded old man Fackenthal, who was himself a Lutheran. "You'd like to haf him in de new-Baptist church."

"It ain't so," sputtered Elias. "We wouldn't for a minute haf him. I guess

THE PERSISTENCE OF COONIE SCHNABLE

I been telling you dis whole efening dat I don't belief dat he can get de real relichion. He iss me too soft. Once he sought for sure dat he wass going to die, an' he hadn't nosing but de wasserparabla (chicken-pox), an' it wass when he wass a grown man a'ready. He iss too soft."

"Well, 'Lias, here you wass telling us from his wild gran'pap, an' now you can only say he iss you too soft!"

"Pit Gaumer, I didn't say he wass wild *like* his gran'pap. I only said he couldn't get relichion wis such a gran'pap."

"But he don't get relichion from his gran'pap."

"Chust talk," Elias said wildly, letting his chair drop heavily to the sidewalk. "You know well enough what I mean. I mean he issn't de relichious kind. When he gets relichion it iss because he wants somesing to it yet. You chust watch once."

There was a moment's silence, while old man Fackenthal lit his pipe. The flaring match threw suddenly into high light his square chin and handsome mouth, which, since one could not see the kindly gray eyes, seemed grimly sarcastic.

"You fellows," he began, then paused until his pipe drew to his satisfaction. "You fellows are me pretty dumb dat you can not see for why Coonie Schnable goes in de Efangelical church. It iss of course on account of Linnie."

"Linnie!" exclaimed Pit and Elias together.

"Ay, of course. Iss she not a Efangelical?"

"Yes, but she has srown him already many times ofer. She won't haf him."

"Well, you chust wait an' see once if dat iss not anyhow what he iss after. She said he dasn't come any more in de house. Now he sinks dat when he iss a member of de church, she won't dast tell him dat. It would not be Christian. Don't you belief for a minute dat he sinks dat he can not get her yet!"

"I don't for a minute belief it," said Elias.

"Nor I," said Pit.

"We will see once," rejoined their host, as he put his pipe back into his mouth.

It was just ten years since Linnie Kurtz had astonished Conrad Schnable by declining his heart and hand. Their subsequent acquaintance had been marked by so long a line of refusals, all of which Millerstown knew by heart, so that it was no wonder that Pit and Elias regarded old man Fackenthal's theory as the wildest of vagaries.

Conrad was by no means to be compared with his "wild gran'pap." He never drank, nor squandered money, nor indulged in any of the other dissipations credited to his grandfather. He saved nearly all his wages, went to church, and was in every way a respectable and law-abiding citizen. Yet Conrad was not popular, neither among those of his own generation nor any other. His grandfather, for all his wildness, had never lacked for friends. Conrad had forfeited his friends by the encouragement of one little fault. He was inordinately vain, first of his appearance, his tall slender figure, his black, melancholy eyes, and his drooping mustache, which he felt was the envy of every other man in Millerstown. Next to his good looks, his greatest source of satisfaction was the conviction that any woman in Millerstown would be his for the asking. Even Linnie Kurtz's numerous rejections did not disturb him. In the end she would certainly be his.

The third just ground for vanity he would not have hesitated to express.

"I can talk English," he would have said. "I haf nosing for dis Pennsylvania Dutch English. When I talk English, den I talk it right; I do not mix it always up like some. Dere iss Chakily Kemerer, he said once, '*Die cow iss iver die* fence *gejumpt*.' Dat iss for sure not right. It should be, 'De cow chumped de fence ofer'!"

As for Linnie, she had always declared that she would never marry, which statement from the lips of so good-looking a girl had the force of a challenge. She had dark curly hair, and blue eyes, set in a round, saucy face, and she was short and plump and generally lovable. Curiously enough, she had kept her resolution, in spite of numerous and flattering opportunities to break it. She had her reward in what the women thought was perennial youth. She looked twenty, although she was already twenty-eight.

Conrad had been one of her first beaux. When she was about eighteen he had invited her to go to a Sunday-school picnic.

"I felt as when I ought to say, 'No, I sank you, Gran'pappy,'" she giggled afterward to the girls. "I sink he must be a little off."

Nothing daunted by her decided rejection of all his advances, he came each Sunday evening to the doorstep, where every one in the village was made welcome. He had little to say, but sat gazing at her with a sentimental air, which she said "made her sick." Presently, her amused tolerance changed to contempt. All Millerstown teased her.

"Why do you sit so always, an' look so dumb at me?" she remonstrated. "De folks sink you must be crasy, an' pretty soon dey will sink dat I am, too. I guess when somebody told me to stay away, I would pretty soon do it."

"*Ach*, Linnie, we could be so happy, when you had so much lofe for me as I for you!" Conrad did not forget to stroke his black mustache as he delivered himself of his tender speeches.

"Well, I haf'n't, an' dat iss de end."

THE PERSISTENCE OF COONIE SCHNABLE

"Haf'n't I enough money, Linnie? Or perhaps I am you not good-looking enough?" His hand strayed from his mustache to his white tie. He affected a somewhat clerical garb as most becoming to his style of manly beauty.

"Lofe don't go by money or good looks," she answered shortly.

"What would you do if I should die once, Linnie? Den you couldn't nefer see me any more. Den you would be sorry dat you wass always so ugly to me." There was a melancholy quaver in his voice. Linnie looked at him in scorn. This old goose, to talk about dying!

"You chust clear right away out," she commanded, her blue eyes flashing. "I don't care a snap what you do so long as you keep away. You can't act like anybody else. Eferybody talks how dumb you are. I sink you better stay entirely away."

Certainly a lover was never more harshly scorned.

Conrad may have been annoyed, though he gave no sign. His inward conviction that Linnie would be his was not shaken in the least. That was the way with girls: the more they liked a fellow the worse they treated him. Certainly Linnie must be madly in love, whether she was willing to acknowledge it or not.

When, however, a year passed, then two, then three, and Linnie grew no more gracious, he began to plan a more active campaign. She had married no one else; she must love him. He proposed again, and again she answered him by the rudest flouting. Then a brilliant scheme suggested itself to his mind. He would join her church. She was a devout Evangelical and would not think it right to treat a brother in the faith as she had treated him. If she would once let him talk to her seriously she would not be able to resist.

In pursuance of his plan, he went to the Evangelical church for about two months. Then at the winter revival meetings he went forward to the mourner's bench and was properly converted.

"I chust sought it would work! I chust sought it would work!" he said exultantly to himself after the meeting. "She came an' she held a little while my hand, which iss more as she has efer done before, an' she said, 'Conrad, I am glad you have found peace.' Now we belong to de same church, an' she must treat me nice. I bet I get her in a week!"

The week passed, however, and he did not venture to reopen his suit. There was no doubt, however, that she was much kinder than she had ever been. Conrad began to assume slightly proprietary airs. He talked glibly of "me an' Linnie," always, however, when Linnie was not present.

About this time he was much disturbed by signs of approaching age. He discovered several gray hairs, and thereafter his hair assumed an unnaturally glossy blackness. He consoled himself, however, with the fact that Linnie was twenty-eight. Certainly a man of forty, especially so good-looking a man as he, might aspire — no, he would not call it aspiration — might expect the hand of a woman almost thirty.

"She ain't ugly to me no more," he thought. "An' de oder fellows, dey don't come so much around, an' we are in de same church. I guess Linnie knows she had better get married quick, or she won't haf any more chances. She iss getting pretty old. I bet it will not be so long before she begins to get gray. De women dey get so much sooner old dan de men. I am yet twelf years older dan she, an' I don't look much older dan she. I tell you she wass frightened when I said once a couple years back, 'What if I should die!' She tried to act mad, but it wass easy seen dat she wass frightened bad. I sink to-night I will ask her. I bet she says pretty quick 'yes.'"

That evening, having finished his supper, he started upon his quest. He no longer remembered that months had passed since he had assured himself that Linnie would be his in a week.

It was Sunday evening and the church bells had rung for evening service. As he walked up the street he was conscious of the attention he attracted.

The Knerr children hailed him as he passed. A few doors above, old man Fackenthal, Elias Bittner and Pit Gaumer were smoking silently. Elias and Pit both responded cheerfully to Conrad's "good efening," but their host did not take his pipe from his mouth. Conrad was thoroughly aware that old man Fackenthal did not like him. Nor did he like Linnie's intimacy with the Fackenthals. When she changed her name to Schnable that should cease.

He was delighted to find her alone on the front step.

"Well, where are all de rest?" he asked as he sat down.

"Ollie Kuhns an' Susannah an' Mary an' Chofina an' de rest, you mean? Dey went to de camp-meeting. Chimmie Weygandt he wanted I should go wis, but I could not."

"Dat wass fery nice from you, Linnie." Conrad gazed at her tenderly. Usually she showed Jimmie Weygandt more favor than any of the rest.

"What wass fery nice from me?"

"Ay, to stay at home. You knew dat I wass coming; say you did?"

"*Ach*, yes, I knew of course dat you wass coming. Do you not always come? But I knew too dat my Mom wass sick. I wass all ready to go, an' she got it so bad in her head, so I sought I would better not go. You sink it iss going to rain, Coonie?"

Conrad paid no attention to Linnie's question, nor did he realize that she called him by the name which he bitterly hated.

"Linnie," he began, "I haf been sinking from you all de week."

"It iss not fery polite, I sink, not to answer questions. I said, 'Do you sink it will soon rain?'"

"I am not sinking from de rain, Linnie. I —"

"Oh, you are not! Well, don't you sink it would be polite to sink from it when I ask you somesing from it? I am going perhaps to town to-morrow, an' I want to know if it iss going to rain."

"No, I don't sink it will rain." This deferring to his opinion was very flattering. "For why are you going to town?"

"I am going to buy me a new dress."

"What kind of a dress, Linnie?"

"Oh, such a one like Chennie Bittenbender's, such a blue one, wis a blue hat to wear to it yet."

"Don't you sink such a dress would be nice to get married in, Linnie?" All conversational by-paths led back to the main road of Conrad's purpose.

"No, I don't like blue to be married in. I don't sink it would be nice at all. Say, look once ofer dere!"

"Where; what iss it?" he cried.

"*Ach*, it iss a little owl. It comes efery efening in Fackenthal's tree. Wait once, you can hear it holler."

The little owl, however, did not "holler," though she kept him waiting in silence until the latest comer had vanished within the doors of the Jonathan Kuhns Baptist Church across the street.

Conrad sighed with relief at the falling of dusk. It was no wonder that Linnie had kept putting him off. Who would want to accept a proposal in the bright light with old man Fackenthal and Pit Gaumer and Elias Bittner staring at them from the Fackenthal doorstep? In a few minutes, when it was a little darker, he would dare to take within his own that plump hand, and then—

Linnie wondered at his sudden silence, and was well content to lean back against the door and listen to the singing. The odor of tobacco filled the air, and now and then she could hear a burst of laughter from some doorway farther down the street. The village was like one big family on a Sunday evening. Presently two figures approached slowly. It was John Weimer and his wife, who paused for a moment to speak to old man Fackenthal, then came slowly toward them. She could see that their hands were clasped, and they were swinging them back and forth like two children. They hailed her with a cheerful "Hello, Linnie," and Conrad with a less cordial "Dat you, Coonie?"

Their attitude of open affection gave Conrad an inspiration. He could scarcely wait until they were out of hearing.

"Linnie," he exclaimed softly, "would it not be nice to walk in de efenings around like dat?"

"No, it wouldn't. I sink it would be as soft as Pussy's foot."

"*Ach*, but Linnie, I mean wis de right feller. Chust sink once for a minute how —"

"Say, Coonie, I sink you must be hungry. Come along once back in de kitchen, an' I gif you some chocolate cake."

Conrad groaned. Was ever affection so rudely repelled as this? Cake! and he was in the midst of a proposal! For a moment he held back. Then, upon second thought, he followed her to the side gate, and back along the board walk. Perhaps she was merely leading the way to the back porch. It would be much more romantic there under the vines, where it was even darker than under the maples at the front of the house, and where there was no odious tobacco smoke to remind him of the three old men whom he knew were discussing his affairs. He groped for a chair on the porch.

"Linnie," he began tenderly.

A slam of the screen door answered him.

"Why, Linnie, ain't you going to sit once down out here?"

"Ain't I what?" she exclaimed from the darkness within.

"Ain't you going to sit down once out here wis me?"

"We don't keep our cake on de back porch," she answered, as she struck another match. "You'll haf to come in here."

Conrad went.

"You sit once down," Linnie said cheerfully. "I will go once down in de cellar an' get de cake."

Instead of sitting down, as he was bidden, Conrad yielded to temptation which a looking-glass always suggested, and crossed the room to the little mirror which hung between the windows. There he smoothed his hair, and straightened his white tie. So engrossed was he that he did not hear Linnie's step until she was almost in the room. As he turned swiftly, his eye fell on several little white packages lying on the table.

"What are den dese?" he asked seeking to cover his confusion. He picked one up and the paper opened in his hand.

"You better let your hands off, Conrad. It iss some poison what I got for to put in de chicken house for de rats. You might get some, an' it would kill you sure." She took it from him as she spoke, and laid it on the little shelf by the clock. Then she cut the cake into large slices. "Come, now, help yourself. It iss fresh baked."

"But you are first a good cook, Linnie!" he exclaimed after the first big mouthful. "I don't know anybody what iss so good a cook like you."

"I am sure I am much oblighed," Linnie answered, pleased that her trick had served. She had long ago concluded that the woes of most of the men of her acquaintance could be cured by liberal doses of her chocolate cake.

Conrad was, however, not diverted from his purpose.

"Linnie," he said as he finished the second piece. "You haf made my hunger so it issn't any more. But dere iss yet a sirst wisin me."

"Well, Coonie, you must excuse me! I sink I must be getting old an' forgetful. Here you are." And Linnie placed on the table a glass of water.

"But it wass not dis what I meant," said Conrad, who nevertheless drained it dry. "It iss somesing else. It —"

"I am sorry dat de root-beer iss all gone. Mom, she made de beginning of de week some, but Chimmie Weygandt, he finished it last efening all up."

"No, Linnie, I do not mean yet root-beer. It iss yet a stronger sirst."

Linnie stopped her rapid swaying back and forth in the big rocking-chair.

"Conrad Schnable, I am den for sure surprised. *We* are temperance if you are not." Horror spoke in every tone of her voice.

Conrad sighed. It was a curious fate which had decreed that so romantic a soul as his should yearn for companionship with one so dull to all sentiment. However, that was the way that Linnie was made, and for love's sake, he would adjust his wooing to her comprehension. His exordium, however, was unfortunate.

"Linnie," he said, as he leaned his elbows on the table, placed his chin on his clasped hands, and gazed earnestly at her. "Dere iss somesing dat I must now say to you. I haf for some time sought dat you lofe me."

Linnie gasped.

"You haf, haf you! What has den gifen you such a dumb idea?"

"Well you haf been for a long time not so ugly to me like before."

"Ugly? I hope I am not ugly to no one. I am not ugly to Cheophily Hiram, but I don't lofe him."

"Yes, but if you know already a long time dat somebody lofes you, an' are not so ugly to dem like you were a while back, dat iss den a sure sign dat perhaps you haf changed your mind."

"It iss a sign dat some folks are too dumb to know dat when I say once 'no' I mean 'no.' I haf not changed my mind."

"Den you haf always lofed me, Linnie? I haf often sought dat wass de way."

"No, I nefer lofed you, an' I won't lofe you. Now!"

She looked straight into his face, all kindly desire to save him the pain of a direct refusal dispelled. As he met her eyes the romantic softness of his own gaze brightened into an angry glare.

"You must remember dat you are already pretty old," he blazed out. "An' dat you will not haf any more such a good chance. No more of de fellers will wait for you. An' dey say dat Chimmie Weygandt, too, has anoder girl. You better get married while you can."

For an instant Linnie sat as if dazed. This spiteful, insulting creature the soft sentimental Conrad! She rose and looked down at him.

"You!" she exclaimed. "You dare to sit here an' talk to me like dis! Do you sink den dat *you* are a good match? What iss den a good match, I like to know? You sink you are good-looking, but de dummy at de tailor-shop, he iss also good-looking. An' you sink I am getting old? Well, it iss twelf years yet before I will need put anysing on my hair for to make it black. Now go quickly out dat door, an' nefer, nefer come back!"

Her voice trembled. She was frightened at her own anger.

"Go on," she commanded, as Conrad did not move. "I mean now chust what I say."

"*Ach* Linnie, *ach*, little Linnie!" A sudden revulsion of feeling overwhelmed him. Had he been mad to speak of getting old? He threw himself on his knees before her. "Take me. You are not old, you are young an' good-looking. You could haf almost any one you want, Linnie, except de married ones. You will haf yet plenty chances. But take me, Linnie!"

Linnie pulled her hand away.

"I tell you once for all, go dat door out, an' nefer come back."

"Do you den for sure mean it, Linnie?"

"Yes, I mean it for sure. An' get once up off your knees. I would be for sure ashamed. It iss as when you wanted to be conwerted. Get right aways up."

Conrad obeyed. However, instead of walking toward the door, toward which her finger sternly pointed, he moved swiftly toward the table. There, before Linnie realized what he was about to do, he picked up one of the little packages, emptied the contents into his mouth, and with a great choking effort swallowed it down.

"*Gott im Himmel*," she cried, shocked almost into profanity. "Would you sink to make yourself dead, Coonie?"

"Yes, I would, an' I haf, an' it iss your fault! You haf made me dat I did it." His excited speech ended in a groan. "I feel dat it iss already killing me, an' I will die right here, where de folks will know dat you wass de one."

"Would you sink to blame it on me? Would you do such a sing as dat, Coonie Schnable? Did you swallow it all?" She picked up the empty wrapper and looked at it.

"Yes, I would blame it on you. It iss your fault. Here iss where I am going to die. Oh-h-h!" Conrad fell moaning pitifully into the rocking-chair.

"But here iss where you are not going to die!"

She laid her hand on his arm.

"Linnie," he gasped faintly. "Go for de doctor. I don't want to die so hard."

"You go for him yourself," she answered. Regardless of his pleading, regardless of the gray terror on his face, she seized him by the arm.

"Come on!"

"What will you do wis me, Linnie? Are you going to put me some-wheres an' let me die alone?"

For answer she hurried him out of the kitchen, off the porch, out the board walk and thence to the sidewalk.

"You go down to Doctor Bender," she commanded. "An' gif him dis wrapping-paper, an' tell him what you done. I guess he can cure you. But you better hurry yourself!"

Old man Fackenthal and his two guests stopped short in a discussion of the methods of the new-Baptists, as Conrad's limp figure shot suddenly out of the Kurtz gate. The early part of the evening had been devoted to a strenuous argument as to whether Conrad would at last win Linnie, Pit maintaining the affirmative, and Elias the negative, while old man Fackenthal slyly urged them on.

Now both Elias and Pit let their chairs bang to the sidewalk and sprang to meet Conrad who came weakly toward them.

"I am poisoned," he moaned. "I am poisoned an' I am for sure dying."

"For why did you take poison? Where iss den — "

"Elias, you hold once your mous till we get him to de doctor," commanded Pit Gaumer. "Take hold of him on de oder side."

Elias did as he was bid. The Jonathan Kuhns Baptists, who were just coming out of church, crowded around them with exclamations of horror, then, when neither Elias nor Pit answered, they followed them on down to the doctor's.

Old man Fackenthal, meanwhile, sat quietly in his corner of the door-step.

"I sink some one had perhaps better look once a little after Linnie," he said to himself. "It iss enough peoples to look after dat *Esel* (mule). I did not sink he had enough sense to take poison."

He started up the street toward the Kurtz house. Before he had gone many steps, the sound of swiftly-running feet made him pause.

"Uncle Chim, iss it den you?" It was Linnie herself, who, though she was not related, had called him uncle since she was a child.

"Yes," he answered. "Come once here, Linnie, an' tell me what dis *närrisch* (crazy) Coonie means wis his poison."

He went back to his corner of the step, and made room for her beside him. To his surprise, he found that she was crying.

"*Ach*, I haf had de most fearful time. I was scared nearly to deas."

"Now, Linnie, chust you take your time once. You chust cry if you haf to."

He patted her hand as he spoke.

"He said would I marry him, an' I told him for near de hundrets time 'no.' Den he said awful sings to me, an' I said somesing from his dyed hair."

"Good for you, Linnie," the old man chuckled in delight.

His mirth suddenly turned Linnie's tears to unaccountable laughter. She laughed until she could laugh no more, then she fell to sobbing. At any other time such sounds in the quiet street would have brought half Millerstown to the scene. Now every one within hearing had followed Coonie to the doctor's.

"Linnie, don't you wake your mom!" Old man Fackenthal began to be frightened. It was his first experience with hysterics. "Is she not sick?"

Linnie grew instantly more composed, though her breath still came in long gasps.

"So den, Uncle Chim, he got once down on his knees, an' he begged an' prayed like when he wass trying to get conwerted, an' I said again, 'no' and den he chumped quickly up, an' — an' — " she struggled for composure and it was several minutes before she could go on. "An' den it wass some powders on de table, some I got for to gif de rats, an' he picked one quickly up an' he swallowed it." Again she gave way to uncontrollable weeping.

Old man Fackenthal stroked her bent head.

"Nefer mind, Linnie. Bender, he has it by dis time out of him. Don't cry so hard, Linnie."

"He said I wass de blame, it wass all my fault, an' he would die dere before me, an' de folks would say I did it."

The old man's pipe broke into fragments on the pavement, and his language was too strong for the breaking of a hundred pipes.

"Linnie, if Coonie Schnable iss yet alife,

I myself wis dese two hands will smash him!"

"No, wait once. I — I —" Far down the street, there came the sound of many voices.

"De folks are coming, Linnie. You go in de house. Dey will want to know all about it."

"No, wait once." Her hands grasped his arm and drew him down. "I had some oder sings on de table, an' I looked quickly at dem, an' — an' —"

The excited voices and the tramp of feet grew nearer.

"Linnie, you go in de house."

"I sent de doctor de label wis Coonie. He will know what for poison it wass. It wass —" she laughed and cried until he feared she was losing her mind. "It wass —" Only old man Fackenthal, whose ear was close to her lips, heard the rest of the sentence.

"What!" he said. "What you say?"

"Yes, it wass. I'm now going home. Don't let de folks make such a noise. It will wake Mom."

His shoulders heaved under the stress of some strong emotion.

"All right," he gasped. "I tell dem."

She had not reached her own door before Elias Bittner's voice broke out in shrill excitement.

"You haf once missed it, Chim. *Ach*, but poor Coonie iss sick! De doctor says he will lif, but he iss for sure powerful sick. De doctor, he gafe him much medicine to make him sick. De doctor has yet de wrapper what de poison wass in. Where is den Linnie Kurtz?"

"Didn't de doctor look at de paper?" Old man Fackenthal, seated calmly there in the corner of his door-step was as cool as though suicides among his acquaintances were affairs of daily occurrence.

"No, he knew what he should gif him for rat-poison. I guess he sought it would be time for dat when he had safed once Coonie's life. He wass looking at it when we came away."

"Well, why, *um Gotteswillen*, did you den come? Perhaps you are den missing somesing!" The scorn in his voice struck his hearers unpleasantly. "I guess you sought Linnie would come hurry running to tell you all about it. Ain't it so, 'Lias?"

"Chim," Elias began gravely. "When such a fearful sing like dis one happens so close, I sink it iss a fearful sing to sit still, an' den to make fun of dose what haf saved a poor man's life."

The object of his sarcasms ignored them completely.

"Maybe when you had stayed you would 'a' found somesing else out. Maybe — what iss it den, Cheophily?" The tall, limp figure of Cheophily Hiram, the "*kleine Knecht*" (little servant) out at the Weygandt's farm, came suddenly upon them out of the dusk. He was breathless with running.

"De doctor says dat I shall tell, — de doctor says dat I shall tell eferybody dat — dat —"

To their dismay he could not go on. Cheophily was not very bright, and excitement made him lose what little wit he had. He stood looking at them helplessly.

"*Ach*," he cried softly. "I forget my mind!"

Suddenly old man Fackenthal reached up, and grasping him by the arm drew him down to a seat by his side.

"Nefer you mind, Cheophily," he said soothingly. "Nefer you mind. I will tell dem what de doctor said."

"You!" said Elias and Pit together. "You wasn't efen down dere."

"Yes, but I know about it. Linnie, she told me. De doctor said dat Cheophily should say dat it wasn't poison what Coonie took, it was cornstarch. Ain't it so, Cheophily?"

Cheophily nodded in breathless affirmation. Suddenly the old man rose to his feet.

"Now eferybody go hurry down to de doctor an' find a little more out. But don't stay here. Linnie iss not here an' her mom iss sick. Go on! Hurry yourselfs! De doctor will perhaps let you see de label from de cornstarch. Perhaps he will let you hold it each one a little in your hands. An' perhaps you can help poor Coonie home. Go on! Clear once out!" He drove them before him like a flock of excited chickens. Presently he called out a cordial "Good night, Pit, good night, Elias."

Only a confused murmur of voices answered him, a murmur which grew each moment more faint. From the trees in front of the Jonathan Kuhns Baptist church came the soft hoot of a little owl. Then quiet settled down once more. Old man Fackenthal chuckled.

"Dey are hurrying now to see Coonie an' de label an' de doctor," he said to himself. "*Ach, bei meiner Sex*, dis iss de best I haf efer heard!"

HENRY KOEHLER, MISOGYNIST

Originally published in the November 1906 issue of *The Atlantic Monthly*

"It is already eight-thirty. The school will now come to order."

The Millerstown school children of the grammar grade went noisily to their seats. Outside, the rain was turning the beaten play-ground into a lake; within there was an odor of drying shawls and steaming coats. The teacher, Henry Koehler, frowned down from the little platform. He was a tall, slender young man, with a round face, cut across with a long, somewhat sparse, but carefully-tended black mustache.

"It is first of all some announcements what shall be made," he went on, when they had settled into comparative quiet. "But Ellie Shindler shall first put her desk lid down and listen once."

A desk lid in the last row was speedily lowered. From behind it appeared a round and smiling face, and a mop of brown curls.

"First, is it any one a Geography short?"

A lifted hand followed the smile and the curls.

"Please, teacher, I can't find my Geography since yesterday."

"Well, then, come and get it, and don't leave it any more where it don't belong. It is no place for the scholars' geographies on the teacher's desk."

The girl complied with disarming speed and gentleness.

"All right, teacher," she answered sweetly, as she went back to her desk.

"And you don't need to say anything back. It is yet another announcement what shall be made. It shall be no more sewing done in school at recess. Recess is not meant for sewing."

The school turned itself as one man to look at Ellie Shindler, who was the only needlewoman among them. They admired inexpressibly the pair of pillow shams at which she worked whenever the teacher's eye was not upon her.

"We won't have this morning any opening exercises," the master went on. "The A Class made yesterday such poor marks in Arithmetic that they will now take the lesson over. A Class step out."

The A Class gathered up its Arithmetic and slate and arose. It was composed of one girl, Ellie Shindler. The school giggled.

"Where are then Ollie Kuhns and Billy Knerr?" demanded the teacher.

"Ollie, he is sick," answered Ollie's little sister. "He has it so bad in his head. Billy Knerr, he threw him yesterday with a ball. But he did n't do it purpose."

"Where is Billy Knerr?"

"Billy is by my gran'pop," vouchsafed Sarah Knerr.

"All right." The teacher's tone became savage. "Ellie Shindler can go to the board, and work Example Three, on page one hundred and one."

Ellie copied the problem carefully on the blackboard. Then she set out row after row of neat figures. The teacher watched her, frowning. For all her multiplying and dividing she did not seem to arrive at the answer.

"Ellie Shindler," he said presently, "what is the matter that you do not get sooner that example?"

"It is something that I do not understand, teacher."

"What is it?"

"Why do we here at this place — " Ellie's hand indicated one process of the problem — "why do we here at this place multiply by 3.1416?"

"Because I tell you."

"But *why* do we?" Ellie's tone was respectful but insistent.

"Why! Why!" he repeated angrily. "I am sick of this 'whying.' Why is your name Ellie? Because it *is*. Why do we multiply by 3.1416? Because it shall be multiplied by 3.1416. Because the book says it and I say it."

Ellie turned meekly to the board. At the end of the twenty minutes allotted to the opening exercises she seemed no nearer a solution.

"It won't get right, teacher," she said cheerfully.

"All right," he answered grimly. "You can stay in after school — no — " he hastily, almost fearfully corrected himself. "You can work it out at home, and copy it ten times on your slate, and you can bring it in the morning to the school. Now we will have the A Class spelling."

The A Class left the board, went to her seat, and slate and pencil in hand, went back to the front of the room.

"Return." The A Class wrote diligently. This was the one subject in the grammar school curriculum in which the present A Class never failed.

"Oblige. — Rescue. — Student. — Various. — Vinous. — Dictionary. — Testament. — Tier. — Now, A Class, read once how you spell these words." "R-e, re, t-u-r-n, turn; return," she spelled, and so down the line until she reached "t-e-a r."

"Wrong. It is ten words and one wrong. It gives ninety for a mark."

"Tear is wrong."

"But it is t-e-a-r, tear."

"Not the kind of tier what I am talking from. They have t-e-a-r in the primary school. This is t-i-e-r."

Ellie rose slowly.

"Look out that it don't give t-e-a-r in the grammar school, too," he remarked sententiously.

Ellie turned and looked at him, her lips quivering. Then she walked down the aisle, while the children smiled up at her as they would not have dared to smile at the oldest girl in school if she were in tears. The teacher caught their grimaces.

"Ellie Shindler!" he said sharply.

Ellie turned. Her lips were still quivering.

"Go to your seat."

"Yes, teacher," she answered meekly.

"The B Class spelling."

The small boys of the B Class stamped noisily out, a train of pencil boxes and books, twitched from the desks of the C Class, falling behind them. They looked half fearfully at the master, then smilingly back at Ellie Shindler. The master, however, ignored the noise and confusion. It was not the fault of the small boys that they did not behave. It was Ellie Shindler who excited them to riot. He had had no trouble with them, until, late in the fall term, Ellie had decided that she would return to school. He had not wanted her. For one thing he hated all women. His exceedingly limited conception of their usefulness had been partly inherited from his father, who had tried three wives and had found all of them wanting, and partly induced by the fact that he saw his patrimony constantly jeopardized by an increasing number of heirs, all of them girls.

"It is girls, girls, girls," he would say. "It makes me sick. I can no more have any peace. It is big girls on the front porch with beaux, and little girls on the back porch fighting. I hire them out, that is what I do, when I was Pop, or I put them in the factory."

"Why don't you get married and go off?" queried Ollie Kuhns, the elder, in whom he confided his woes.

"Get married! To a woman! Well, I guess not! Am I not already wild from these women? Shall I yet tie myself to one so I cannot get away? Shall I then fix myself, so when I want to go in the evening off, I must say, 'Dare I go?' or everywhere I go, must I have a woman along? I guess not!"

"But you would then only have one instead of — how many is it at your house?"

"It is ten, counting Mom. And I can't stand it. I go to the hotel and board."

"To the hotel! When you could live easy at home!" Ollie's economical soul was shocked almost beyond expression.

"Yes, I cannot stand any more these women."

"But it would be cheaper to get married. It is plenty nice girls."

"Who?" demanded Henry, with scorn.

"Ay, Mary Kuhns."

"She is me too stuck up."

"Well, Jovina Neuweiler."

"*She!* I guess not. She is ugly. They are not many good-looking ones."

"Well, Linnie Kurtz. Perhaps you could cut Jimmie Weygandt out with Linnie."

"He may have her. I don't want her."

Had Ollie Kuhns been more clever, he might have detected in Henry's vehement tones a certain bitterness. Once, five years before, he had paid court to Mary Kuhns, and she, of the many lovers, had declined him so soon and so firmly, that the mere mention of her name hurt him. No, he hated them all, and especially Ellie Shindler. She was seventeen years old, and the Millerstown girls seldom went to school after they were fifteen. No one knew why she continued, except herself, and she would not tell.

"She is plenty big enough to work in the factory," said her teacher. "She don't study nothing. When I was her Pop I settle her!"

Her Pop, however, did not receive pleasantly this advice. Some one reported to him Henry's remarks, and he took occasion to meet him the next day in front of the post-office.

"I pay my taxes," he said succinctly. "You get always your pay. My Ellie can go to school till she is fifty years old, and you dass n't say nothing. You learn her, that is all."

Ellie, however, would not be "learned." She took her sewing to school, and accomplished wonders behind her desk-lid during school hours, and at recess. She joined in the fun of the smaller children at his expense, she incited them to all kinds of mischief, she set them constantly a bad example, she reminded him every hour of the *ewig weibliche*, which he was sacrificing his hard-earned money to escape. Sometimes it seemed to him that it was she, and not his nine little step-sisters, who kept him in his miserable little room in the hotel, where the fare was bad, and the company worse, but where, at least, there were no women. Moreover — and all her other faults paled into insignificance before this crime — she was able to exert a curious influence over him. There were times when he felt himself staring at her curly head with such fixedness that he could not take his eyes away, even though he knew that in a minute the curly head would be lifted, and a smiling gaze meet his own. When she came up to the desk to hand him a book, she looked at him out of the corner of her eye in a way that made him send her savagely to her seat. He could endure her mischief, her defiance, but he could not endure her smiles. It was bad enough that she should be always smiling at Jim Weygandt and Al Mattern when she met them on the street. They liked it and encouraged it. But that she should dream for one instant that he could be affected. It was insulting!

To-day it seemed as though she were "verhext" (bewitched). She had brought some candy, with which she treated the children on the last row. She failed in every lesson, and seemed dead to any sense of shame.

"What two kinds picks is it?" he asked, in a vain effort to have her distinguish between the verb and the noun.

Ellie studied the wall back of the teacher's head. From window to window ran the legend. "Everybody must talk English here." Then her eyes fell to the level of his necktie.

"It is three kinds picks," she answered slowly. "It is p-i-c-k, to pick up, and p-i-c-k, to pick with, and p-i-g, one what grunts."

The teacher glared.

"I mean p-i-c-k, spelling, not pronouncing. What is now the definition of a noun and a verb?"

Ellie shook her head. Thus the eyes of Psyche might have widened at the same question.

"I don't know, teacher."

"Is it anything you do know?" he demanded. "Am I to waste all my time teaching you when you won't learn nothing?"

Ellie answered him with a slow smile.

"Go to your seat," he commanded.

He did not remember that the scholars had ever been so unruly or so "dumb" as they were that morning. It seemed as though Ellie's stupidity had set the whole school frantic with a desire to imitate her. No one knew his lessons. Little Louisa Kuhns wailed aloud when he reproved her, — which, of all demonstrations, he disliked the most.

What should he do? Ellie Shindler would not leave school, and he could have no order while she was there. He might resign and go to work in the shoe factory, but that would mean defeat for one thing, and work which he hated, for another. This morning, he could not even have the few minutes quiet at recess, for the rain continued and there was no place for the children to stay but the schoolroom. After recess things grew even worse than before. Jakie Kemerer boldly threw a wad of damp paper at the blackboard, and hit it so squarely that the teacher, standing near, felt a drop of water on his cheek. He started down the aisle, and Jakie leaped to his feet. He ran swiftly around the back of Ellie Shindler's chair, with the teacher close behind him. Then, doubling upon his tracks, he was about to pass Ellie once more. Then he could open the door, and once without he was safe. The teacher felt his heart swell with rage. Suddenly, however, he found an ally. A plump foot shot out from beneath Ellie Shindler's desk, and Jakie fell into the teacher's arms, and was led to the front of the room. The children looked on indifferently while he received the punishment meted out to such as throw paper wads. The louder Jakie's screams, the less impression they made.

"And now," the master went on angrily, "Ellie Shindler can come up and stand in the corner, while she tripped Jakie up. It shall be no tripping up in this school."

He scarcely knew what he said. His eyes had met her own in the moment of her coming to his defense, and he read there pity and the offer of aid. Moreover, he knew that his own eyes had responded gratefully. He hated her.

She came slowly, her lip trembling, now without any laughter lingering behind. Her shoulders drooped, she did not look at him, but went straight to the corner of the room. The children watched her, open-mouthed. Ellie Shindler obedient, subdued!

For half an hour there was peace. The C class knew its spelling. Jakie Kemerer settled down to his books with a celerity and willingness which he had never before exhibited after a whipping. There was not a whisper. Then suddenly the master was conscious of a stir. There was a smothered giggle from one corner of the room, an open laugh from the other. The faces of the whole school were turned toward the corner where Ellie stood. What they saw there to amuse them, he did not know. She stood meekly as before, with her hands clasped before her.

After another long half-hour he rang the bell for dismission. He had had a lunch put up for him at the hotel as he often did on stormy days. There was a scramble for coats and hats, then the boys charged noisily out the door, the girls following slowly after, until only Ellie Shindler remained.

"The school was already dismissed, Ellie Shindler," he said.

"I have my dinner by me," she answered sweetly.

The teacher spread his dinner out on his desk at the front of the room, and Ellie spread hers out on her desk at the back.

"I have here some raisin pie," she ventured tentatively, when the silence grew oppressive. "Will you then not have a piece?"

"I have also raisin pie," he answered shortly, quite as though hotel raisin pie were not to Ellie Shindler's raisin pie as water unto wine.

Presently Ellie put her lunch basket back in her desk, and took out her sewing. This was not recess. The teacher took from his desk a bundle of papers. He was desperately thirsty, but the water bucket stood in the corner nearest Ellie, and he would not go there for a drink. He heard her humming softly, and was irritably and angrily conscious of a desire to watch her. Then suddenly it occurred to him to make an appeal to her to leave. Nothing could hurt his pride so much, but he had tried everything else.

"Ellie," he began, "why do you come in the school?"

"To learn," she answered.

"Well, then, why don't you learn?"

"I do, some. But I am pretty dumb."

She smiled at him, and closed one eye while she tried to thread her needle. Failing, she drew the thread between her lips and tried again. The dimples which the process induced did not escape the teacher's eye.

"I wish you would stay away from the school."

Ellie dropped her sewing into her lap and looked at him.

"Yes, I mean it. I don't want you in the school. I can't keep school when you are here. You are a — a nuisance. You are all the time making trouble. The children will not behave, I wish — "

"But teacher, I will — "

"And I don't want no 'teachering.' I mean now what I say."

"Do you mean I should go now?"

"Yes, now, this minute."

Ellie rose slowly and folded her sewing. Then she took her books out of her desk and piled them neatly on the lid, and put the piece of raisin pie which the teacher had declined, and which she meant to save for the afternoon recess, back into the basket. She walked slowly toward the cupboard where the shawls and sunbonnets were kept, and vanished within. Then silence fell. The teacher almost held his breath. Why had he suffered so long, when all his troubles might have been so easily ended? He would strap her books together for her. But why did she not come out of the cupboard and start home? The children would soon return, and he wanted her to be gone.

"Ellie Shindler!" he said.

There was no response, and he called again, "Ellie Shindler!" Still she did not answer. The cupboard opened only into the schoolroom. She must be there. He walked slowly down the room.

"Why don't you answer?" he said. "I said you should go. Now — "

The teacher paused. Ellie stood just inside the door. Her sunbonnet hid her face, and her shawl was wrapped closely about her.

"What is then wrong that you don't go?"

Ellie's shoulders moved up and down.

"I don't want to go," she said. "I — ach, — I don't — I don't want to go!"

"Ellie — " the teacher paused again. He had flushed scarlet, and there was an uneasy expression on his face. He must not forget that he hated her, that he hated all women. All women cried. His sisters, big and little, cried when they could not have what they wanted. Nothing made him more angry than to see a woman cry, unless it was to see her get what she cried for. What did she want? Could it be —

"Ellie Shindler — " he laid his hand on her shoulder. He felt it tremble, and a strange and unaccountable emotion suddenly took possession of him. He pushed back her sunbonnet and kissed her. She drew herself gently away.

"You scold me and want me to go," she said in a choked voice. "And then you act like this. It is not right. It — "

"Wait once." He stood with his hand pressed against his forehead. Had he gone mad? If Ellie Shindler told her father that he had kissed her, the school would not be his for a day. Who would believe him if he said that she had cried and made eyes at him, that she had led him on, him who understood all their tricks so thoroughly?

"Are you going to tell?" he demanded.

"I tell! Did you think — did you think I would tell? Ach, I will go home, I will go home!"

"Wait once." His hand was on her wrist, hurting her. He could not think. He had never been so near a woman before. Something seemed to sweep him out of himself, but even in the midst of his confusion of mind, he remembered that he had been brutal to her, and that, in spite of it, she cried at going. She stood passive in his grasp and Mary Kuhns had not even let him touch her hand. "I — I —" he faltered. "Don't cry, Ellie." Her grief seemed suddenly a sacred thing. Then he drew a long breath. "I will marry you."

Ellie looked up at him. She put one tight-closed hand against her lips.

"Perhaps it is only that you shall not have me any more in the school," she said. "Perhaps it is only that you are afraid I will tell my Pop."

The teacher put his arm across her shoulders.

"I don't know what it is," he said, half angrily.

"Perhaps you did not mean it." Her voice trembled. Neither did she know why she liked him better than Jimmie Weygandt and Al Mattern and all the rest.

For answer he kissed her again. Then, suddenly, he saw that she was smiling. She looked as though she had always been smiling.

"For why are you laughing?" he said roughly. "You are forever laughing."

"I? Laughing?" Her broken, indignant voice denied the accusation to which her shameless eyes confessed.

"Yes, you. I — I — "

The disgrace of his capitulation swept over him. The word on his lips was almost "hate."

"You what?" From the circle of his loosening arm, Ellie looked up at him. Again her lip trembled.

"I love you," he finished weakly.

THE RESTORATION OF MELIE ZIEGLER

Originally published in the May 1907 issue of *Everybody's Magazine*

Peter stood in the sitting-room, which had not been opened since his wife's funeral, three weeks before. The women had left it just as Melie had always kept it, the round table exactly in the middle of the floor, the gay chairs in a row against the wall. Peter's eyes ranged higher, however, than the gay brocades, and rested on two portraits, hanging side by side. One was unmistakably himself, the other was a woman, who from the lines of care in her face might have been his mother, but who had really been his wife.

"She looks much older than I," he mused aloud.

Suddenly raising his arms, he lifted his wife's picture from the hook, and carried it up-stairs.

All Peter's married life he had suffered from lack of appreciation. His wife had never understood him. In some ways, of course, she had been a good wife. She had tilled the garden, she had scrubbed and sewed and washed and ironed and grown old before her time. It was not with her incessant labors that he found fault. It was because she could not realize that to greater souls labor with the hands is torture, because she expected him to devote his nobler talents to shoemaking or harvesting.

Now, however, at last, there was some one who understood. The day after the funeral he had received a letter, directed in a woman's hand. Opening it, he read:

> Friend Mr. Ziegler:
>
> The consolations of friendship are best withheld until the *first mad passion* of grief is assuaged. Let me remind you of the bright regions to which she is wafted on the wings of the celestials, and also that friends are left on earth.   E. J. D.

The first reading left but a vague impression upon the mind of Peter. Perhaps it was meant for some one else. Then he read it again, and slowly comprehension dawned. He was the grief-stricken soul, Melie the being borne on the wings of the celestials. But who was E. J. D.? Could it be the Reformed preacher? No, his name was Saeger. The Lutheran? His name was Mattern. There was but one other person in Millerstown who could have written such a letter — but that was impossible. He read it again. It was — it could be no other — the school-teacher. And the school-teacher's name was Eustoria J. Dodge!

Where she came from, neither he nor any one else in Millerstown knew.

She had been elected to the primary school when the board was so bitterly divided between two rival candidates that only the selection of a third was possible. Peter had seen her go past to school, and long before the departure of the prosaic Melie he had compared his wife's short roundness with this slender figure. Nothing could have astonished him more than that she should burden herself with his woes. They assumed suddenly a far greater significance in his eyes. He was bereft, widowed, and — the last did not dawn upon him for several days — since widowed, therefore eligible for further matrimonial engagement.

All Millerstown had begun to speculate meanwhile as to when and with whom he would begin to "keep company," and Millerstown gasped with surprise when one Sunday early in November he stepped proudly up the aisle of the Reformed church with the teacher by his side. Millerstown did not approve.

"They say she can't do nothing at all," said Susannah Kuhns the next day. "And Peter took Melie's picture down what used to hang on the wall."

"Not the big one!" gasped Sarah Ann Mohr, Melie's cousin, with whom the teacher boarded.

"Yes, he did," insisted Susannah.

"She'd better keep at her school-teaching," said Mrs. Billy Knerr. "Peter, he don't earn nothing."

"Now, Maria," laughed Susannah, "have you never felt love?"

"Love, your gran'pappy!" retorted Maria.

"Sarah Ann, will you let them sit always in the parlor?" asked Susannah. "I'd make them sit in the kitchen."

"Ach, no," said Sarah Ann. "It sha'n't be said that I don't treat the boarder right."

It was not the expense of keeping an extra fire that brought the worried frown to Sarah Ann's placid face. She was angry and grieved that Peter should replace Melie with this "doppas" (slouch). She thought of little else, and at the end of a week, during which Peter had visited the teacher every day, she made up her mind that for once she would disregard her dislike of meddling, in order to save Peter from making a fool of himself.

That evening, armed with a raisin pie, she entered the parlor, and in spite of Eustoria's frowns, sat down.

"It is something I want to talk about, teacher," she began. "I want to go to South Bethlehem over Christmas. Would you care to stay alone?"

"Oh, no," responded the teacher obligingly.

"But I said Peter should eat along with us. Would you mind to cook the dinner?"

"Oh, I couldn't," began Eustoria. Then she translated Peter's pie-choked speech into a murmur of pleasure. It would not do to show any hesitancy before Peter. "I — well, I — all right."

"Then it is all fixed," said Sarah Ann, as she rose.

"Well, this is fine," said Peter, when she had closed the door. Her action in leaving them alone seemed to put the seal of Millerstown's approval on his courtship. After the dinner he would ask the teacher to marry him.

~ ~ ~ ~ ~

On Christmas morning, Sarah Ann arose early. When she was ready to go, she called loudly:

"Teacher! Teacher!"

A sleepy "What?" answered her.

"You better get up. It is already six o'clock."

"All right," floated shrilly down the stairway, and Sarah Ann departed.

Nearly three hours later the teacher, sleepily rubbing her eyes, came down the stairs. The fire had burned itself out, and the room was cold. So astonished was the nearest neighbor, Susannah Kuhns, to see the smoke of a freshly kindled fire rising from Sarah Ann's kitchen at nine o'clock on Christmas morning that she sent little Oliver to find what was the trouble.

"Teacher's cookin'," he reported. "And she ain't got her bangs on. Sarah Ann is off. Teacher was putting the turkey in the stove."

"Putting her turkey in the stove with the fire just made!" exclaimed his mother. "I never heard of anything so dumb."

At eleven o'clock she sent him over again, ostensibly on an errand.

"Peter is going to eat with teacher," he said when he returned. "He has on his Sunday suit. And they ain't going to eat in the kitchen, teacher and Peter."

"Where then?" demanded his mother.

"Everything is fixed up in the sitting-room. And teacher and Peter are sitting in the parlor. Teacher has cologne at herself. It smelled fine. But it smelled awful funny in the kitchen. And Sarah Ann's kettles were cracking. I came away. I was afraid it might do me something."

Susannah looked fearfully across the fence. To her relief, she saw the teacher moving about the kitchen.

Peter had arrived at ten o'clock, according to Eustoria's invitation. To his surprise, she did not once leave the parlor to attend to the dinner. He was distressed by a curious odor when little Oliver Kuhns opened the door, and again when, shortly after eleven o'clock, the teacher went to put the dinner on the table.

At half past eleven, when Eustoria had not yet invited him to the kitchen, he considered the advisability of offering to assist her, but concluded that she would rather accomplish her labor of love alone. Finally the door opened, and he was invited to the feast. As he crossed the room he again noticed the peculiar odor.

"She must 'a' let something get dry," he said to himself. As he saw the table spread in the sitting-room he was sure of it.

"Well, this was makin' you a lot o' trouble," he said consolingly. "You could 'a' aired it."

"Aired what?" asked the teacher, motioning him to the head of the table.

"Aye, the kitchen. Didn't something get dry for you?"

"The kitchen is no place to eat," answered Eustoria emphatically.

"Oh!" responded Peter in confusion.

His embarrassment changed to wonder as he gazed at the table upon which the feast was spread. It was covered with Sarah Ann's best tablecloth, starched so stiffly that it stood out all round the table. At one end reposed the turkey, at sight of which Peter could scarce forbear an exclamation. It lay upon a bed of greens — Peter's second glance proved correct his suspicion that they were geranium leaves — and was itself almost covered by a quantity of parsley, the entire crop of Sarah Ann's parsley box, which she cultivated so carefully in the kitchen-window. There was but one dish of vegetables, and the teacher had forgotten the preserves and pickles that Sarah Ann had put out for her.

In spite of the gay decorations, the feast had to Peter's hungry eyes an air of incompleteness. The turkey did not greet his nostrils with the odor so inseparable from Christmas feasts. It lay weakly beneath its chaplet, not as if to say, "Here I am; I have feasted and grown fat that you might be merry," but as though it meant to discourage any effort at gaiety over its obsequies. Peter was conscious of a grave sinking of the heart.

Eustoria bade him say grace, and he limited it to a very few words. Then he lifted the carving-knife, tried its edge on his thumb, and rose to the occasion.

"This is the first time we have ever —" He paused in his pleasant speech as he fastened his fork in the side of the fowl, and turned it slowly over. The parsley leaves fell in a cascade down the side, and there was revealed, as though the vines had been suddenly torn from a fire-scarred hillside, a blackened surface.

"The first time we have ever —" he went bravely on, turning the bird to the other side. There was no blackness there, but a faint, pale brown. He drew his knife across it, and proceeded with his speech. "— we have ever had the chance to eat together. I — I don't think Sarah Ann keeps her knives sharp like some."

He laid the turkey down and sharpened the knife on the steel which lay beside him.

"No," said Eustoria. "She don't."

Peter drew the knife up and down with the vindictive energy of a Shylock.

"Now we try again. What part you like, teacher?"

"A little white, if you please," answered Eustoria delicately.

"And of course stuffing?"

"Stuffing? Why, no, why, n-no, I guess I wouldn't choose stuffing."

Peter laid a slice of white meat — it was well the teacher had not asked for brown — upon her plate, and picking up a spoon brushed aside the parsley around the throat of the turkey.

"Ach, of course you take stuffing," he urged. "You ——"

For an instant he hesitated. Then he thrust the spoon in farther and drew it forth, looked at it, and laid it down.

"It is here no stuffing!" he announced, as though he had said, "The world is coming to an end!"

"Well, what of it?" asked Eustoria, a sudden sharpness in her voice. "Where I come from it isn't fashionable to have stuffing."

"Oh!" said Peter. Well, Eustoria would have to learn his ways — Melie had — and that would be her pleasure.

"Well, now," he went on with commendable cheerfulness, "what have we in this dish?"

He lifted the lid. There lay two boiled potatoes — who ever heard of boiled potatoes with turkey? Moreover, the skins had not been removed.

"They are potatoes in jackets," explained Eustoria, a bright flush on her cheeks. "They are considered a great delicacy where I come from."

"Ach, yes, in jackets. But that is a good one! In jackets," laughed Peter weakly, as he passed her the plate.

The potatoes, however, for all their jackets were cold. And the turkey! Peter chewed and chewed, while Eustoria picked delicately at her dinner. Presently the door opened and little Ollie appeared, a covered dish in his hands.

"Mom says it is here some oyster pie."

Peter took it eagerly.

"But you are a good boy, Ollie!"

Eustoria declined her share of the pie. She seemed to have acquired a certain aloofness from the scene about her, and sat with folded arms, watching Peter eat. And presently, from the fullness of her heart, she spoke:

"Susannah Kuhns is a slave!"

"Why, teacher, it wasn't never no slaves in Millerstown, and it ain't no slaves anywheres now."

"There is a slave in every house in Millerstown."

"What you mean, teacher?" Peter suspended the process of eating, and gazed at his hostess, whose eyes sparkled behind her glasses.

"Any one who works like Susannah Kuhns is a slave."

"Susannah! She don't have it hard."

"Don't she? She rises before dawn. She washes, she cooks, she bakes. She is a slave."

"What else shall she do, teacher?"

"What else? Improve her mind. Let her have the same opportunity as her husband."

"But Oliver, he works all the time. He earns the money. He is a good man."

"That may be true. But how much broader his task. What opportunities!" In reality Oliver ran the engine at the cinder dump. "His wife works at the wash-tub. Her life is bounded by her kitchen. But how thankful I am that I have discovered one man worthy of the name, one man who regards the female mind as equal to his own."

"It is so," answered Peter meditatively.

Then, while Eustoria went to bring in Sarah Ann's mince pie, Peter fell to thinking. He had not understood everything she had said, but he had understood enough to make him tremble. He had never dreamed such doctrine as this. Susannah Kuhns a slave! The teacher had better not let that reach Susannah's ears!

Suddenly, as he pondered, the beautiful structure he had built up about Eustoria tottered, and Peter did not stop to think of the elements that had gone to its making; he only hastened to escape its fall.

"Teacher," he called, "I must go home. It is a important reason why I must go home. I —" He heard Eustoria's approaching footstep. There was something ominous in the sound. Without waiting to taste his pie, without even finishing his sentence, he fled.

At seven o'clock that evening Sarah Ann came home. Her tired face grew steadily brighter as she approached the house. Every window was dark. Peter was gone, and all was well. She sniffed audibly as she opened the door, then she shivered. A few minutes later, lamp in hand, she surveyed the scene.

"They ate in the sitting-room! And it is nothing put away, and she didn't wash a dish. I knew you could expect much from these English, but I didn't think it would be *so* bad. Well, poor Melie, her things won't get spoiled. This makes to me a fearful slop! I go to get Susannah to help me clear up."

Down in Peter's lonely house there was also a scene of reconstruction. He did not clearly remember how he had got away from Eustoria. He might have blamed Sarah Ann for the toughness of the turkey, he might have excused the absence of the stuffing and the presence of the potato peelings — jackets, indeed! — but the heresy to which Eustoria had given voice was beyond any madness of love to endure.

"Melie, she loved to work for me," he said to himself with something like a sob. "She would 'a' got up in the middle of the night to cook for me."

He sat for a long time before the kitchen fire, which he had built up to a cheerful blaze, and whereon he had made coffee, and heated some "bumble soup" left over from the day before. Then, stumbling awkwardly up the stairs, he opened the door into the garret. A few minutes later, Melie, in her gay gilt frame, hung once more upon the parlor wall.

THE LONG COURTING OF HENRY KUMERANT

Originally published in the September 1907 issue of
Lippincott's Monthly Magazine

Henry Kumerant paused, paint-brush in hand, his cherubic face, with its halo of handsome gray hair, wrinkled by frowns. He regarded the sign he was painting with evident dissatisfaction.

"It is something wrong at it," he said aloud. "It should go something to 'notice' yet. *Ach*, yes, it is a 't' should go to it."

A few more strokes of the brush, and the furrows on Henry's brow cleared away.

"I will nail this one up good, so it shan't anybody steal it. Wait once till I catch the young Fackenthal and Billy Knerr. I slambang them! If we had only a preacher who would give it to them once! Old Mishler gave it to them once in the church. He said this way to the young ones: 'Saturday night you are in the apple-butter match till twelve o'clock. Sundays you stand in the choir and sing, *"Nun danket alle Gott."* Lutherans you call yourselves; Indians you are.' But it don't give any more preachers like him. *Ach*, now I must go and look once how I spell this word."

He laid the wide pine board down on the floor, and, rising stiffly, limped into his little house.

"It is b-u, bu, r-e-a-u, ro, bureau," he said as he reappeared. "This English spelling is too dumb."

Sitting down, he took the sign into his lap. The bees buzzed in and around the honeysuckle above his head; a chicken, bent upon discovery, wandered unchecked into the house. Presently Henry balanced the brush carefully on the paint-can and contemplated the labor of his hands. It read:

> NOTICE
> I WILL MENT BROKEN
> BUREAU'S, SINKS, LAUNEES
> TABELS. &. SAW FILEI-
> NG AND WELBARROW
> S FOR SAIL.
> BY HENRY KUMERANT

"Now I will hurry eat some dinner," he soliloquized. "Then I will hurry make Sarah Knerr's bench done, so I can take it this evening along when I go into town. I guess all the young ones will be yelling and screeching again. They have no bringing up. I give it to them to-morrow!"

He moved about, preparing dinner. After he had been on his feet for a while, he seemed to limber up. For a few moments there was the swiftness and energy of an angry hen in his movements. Then, suddenly, he sat down and laid his head on his folded arm on the table before him. Once his shoulders heaved.

"I have no good pie," he said aloud, tremulously. "I — have — no — good — pie. Nothing tastes good any more to me. I — I ——" Then he sprang up, and the sweep of his clenched fist seemed to include the universe. "I don't care. To-morrow I settle them."

It was not alone because of physical hunger that Henry had yielded for a moment to despair. He was moved by a far more potent emotion. Fietta Weaber, who for twenty years had stayed his soul with good things, who had been his nurse when ill, his confidante in trouble—and the troubles of the cantankerous Henry were many — Fietta Weaber had played him false. One summer evening, twenty years before, Henry had sat himself down upon the wide bench before Fietta's door. At the other end sat Fietta herself, large, comfortably made, placid. Presently she had ambled into the house to bring him food, as was the gracious custom of Millerstown, and Henry, who was his own cook in the little house along the mountain road, had eaten gladly. The next day he had returned, and thereafter, for twenty years, he had spent his evenings in summer upon Fietta's bench, and in winter in a rocking-chair before her kitchen fire. During all these years marriage had dwelt only in the background of his thoughts. Of course he meant to marry Fietta — some time.

Fietta, meanwhile, if she had any matrimonial desires, did not set about their accomplishment. She made him so comfortable that he had little to gain by marrying her. She furnished his lonely table with the best of her baking and brewing. When Jennie Kramer made his shirt collars too small, Fietta, in pity, began to make his shirts. She nursed him when ill, she accommodated herself to the irregularities of his temper, she heard with sympathy his complaints against the men of his own generation who laughed at him, their sons who teased him, their grandchildren who would not obey him, and, with each successive intimacy, she put farther from his mind the thought of marriage. As for Henry, he did not notice the droop in the corners of her mouth, the sadness of her eyes. As the years went on, she grew increasingly anxious to be married. She felt constantly that her position was not dignified; sometimes, indeed, she felt it was not respectable.

Recently, the constitutional chip upon Henry's shoulder had been once more knocked to the ground. This time the *casus belli* was the arrival of a new preacher of the new Baptist church to which he belonged. The new preacher, in the first place, was young.

"I think it is a shame," Henry said to old man Fackenthal, "That they send such a long-leggy young one here to preach."

"But your other preacher was old, and you were not so very for him," reminded old man Fackenthal, who was a Lutheran. "You said he was always too old or too deaf or too dumb or something. What is wrong with this young one?"

"His voice is too loud when he preaches. It is unreligious to yell so loud. And he is too much of a dude. He eats with a coat on in summer. And he wears patent shoes."

"Patent shoes!" exclaimed old man Fackenthal. "What are patent shoes?"

"They are shiny shoes, what don't need to be blacked."

"Well, I think that is a pretty good idea," said old man Fackenthal gravely. "When I was preacher of the new Baptists I get patent shoes, too. I bet he don't have much time for shoe blacking. Well, and what else is wrong with him?"

For an instant Henry's rage held him silent.

"Maybe the new Baptists do keep the preacher busy," he sputtered finally. "But the Lutheran preacher, he was so worn out he died. And this preacher comes every Sunday late. It ain't religious."

"Well, when a preacher stops for to pull a little boy out of the creek so he shall not to be drownded, I think it is pretty dumb to scold because he is late," Old man Fackenthal's grave voice would brook no interruption. "You better tell the preacher what you think of him, and not tell the outsiders. You can't blame us when we don't think much of the new Baptists."

"I guess the new Baptists have more religion than any church in this town," rejoined Henry angrily. "I'm going home."

Instead of going home, however, Henry had gone to Fietta's, and there poured out the full measure of his wrath. He announced that he was going to tell the young preacher just what he thought of him. The preacher was young, therefore he should be advised; he was a preacher of the Gospel, therefore he should listen attentively to the word of a man older and wiser than himself. Meanwhile, Henry did not notice that for once Fietta did not hear. Her eyes were fixed sadly on the other side of the street. She was not well, she had just received news of the coming of unexpected company, and she wished to tell him about both, but the torrent of his words swept aside her own gentle speech.

"If he is late next Sunday, I settle him," Henry said at parting; then, without heeding her good-night, he strode away.

It was true that thus far in his ministry to the new Baptist church the preacher had not been once on time. One Sunday he had been called to the bedside of a dying man, another he had stopped to mend a harness for two helpless and frightened women, and the last time he had pulled one of the little Kuhns children from the creek, and had been compelled to run back and change his clothes. The Sunday morning upon which Henry had determined to remonstrate, he had made a special effort to get to church on time. Again, however, he was delayed. He was aware as he entered the church of some unusual demonstration. At other times a decorous, quiet assemblage had reproached his tardiness. Now the congregation was astir, some in the aisles, some in their seats. Across the room stood old Henry Kumerant, the flush on his face deepened to a wrathful purple, his eyes gleaming.

"Good morning," said the preacher, directly to him. "I am very sorry to be late. I assure you it was unavoidable."

"*Para* [Pastor]" — at the sound of Henry's voice the preacher paused in his swift stride up the aisle — "it is four Sundays since you came, and you have been every one late."

"I know," said the young man, with a humility which the scarlet flush on his cheeks belied; "but ——"

"It ain't a good example," Henry went on, in spite of a rising murmur among the congregation, and of the beseeching glances from Fietta's eyes. "Everybody will soon come late like in the Lutheran church. I think ——"

"Brother Kumerant," interrupted the young man, "I will do my best to be here on time, always. In case I am late again, however, will you please open the service?"

Whereupon the preacher gave out a hymn, and the service began.

Henry, however, heard not a word. An opportunity so delightful as to be dazzling opened before him. All his life he had wanted to tell Millerstown what he thought of it, collectively and individually. Here, if only the preacher would be late again, was his chance. He would make the opening exercises short, so that he might begin his remarks before the preacher should come in. Then he would not pause, no matter if the preacher should arrive. Henry could see him already, slipping into the last pew conscience-smitten and ashamed.

"It is many things here in Millerstown wrong," he said to himself. "The women, they spend too much, and talk too much, and the young ones are too sassy, and their pops have no respect. I show them."

He went over his expected triumph so often during the next few days that he ceased to remember that the preacher might be on time. For the first time in twenty years he failed to go to see Fietta. So absorbed was he in the preparation of his "speech" that for one whole day he simply forgot that she existed. It was not until the next evening that he realized his omission. And this was baking-day, and Fietta had sent him no pie!

A little alarmed, he hurried down the street. Dusk had fallen and he could see her sitting in the corner of the great bench. He would sit near her to-night, and not at the opposite end. He meant to tell her about his speech, and he did not wish the impish Kuhns children who lived next door to hear what he had to say. They would hear that in church.

He did not notice that Fietta did not turn toward him with her usual placid smile. He sat down, and, taking off his hat, fanned his hot face. The walk down the mountain road was long.

"It is warm," he said, by way of greeting.

"Yes," responded Fietta.

Then, just as he began to be conscious of a pleasant breeze, Fietta turned toward him.

"I have an engagement," she said.

He turned and stared.

"You have an engagement?" he repeated.

"Yes, I have an engagement with some one. I am not at home."

"You are not at home?" Henry's mouth dropped open. How was he to know that Elmina Fatzinger, who had worked out in Philadelphia, had said that that was the proper formula for dismissing an unwelcome visitor? He thought only that Fietta had lost her mind.

"I have other company this evening," she explained.

"You have other company?" Henry got awkwardly upon his feet as he spoke. "You mean ——"

"I mean that it is another gentleman here this evening."

"You — you — mean ——"

His eye followed Fietta's. From out the alley which led to the back yard and the kitchen door there came a man, tall, broad of shoulder, middle aged, and vigorous. In one hand he carried a pitcher, that same blue pitcher whose contents had so many times refreshed Henry, and in the other two glasses.

"Here you are, Fietta," he said in a deep, jolly voice.

Fietta looked up at him and smiled her thanks.

"But, Fietta ——" Henry paused. The stranger was pouring out a glass of lemonade for Fietta. Then he poured out one for himself. Perhaps he did not see the little man lingering in the shadow. Fietta did not turn her head, but lifted her glass to her lips. It was as if she drank to the swift departure of the unwelcome Henry, who, half running, disappeared into the darkness.

The two weeks which intervened before the next preaching service were the most miserable of Henry's life. A series of misfortunes beset him. Some one stole his sign, and it was necessary to paint a new one. Mischievous boys put a board across his chimney so that his fire would not burn. He tore his best coat, and was half-way to Fietta's before he remembered that Fietta would mend no more for him. Twice he stole along the street in the darkness to see the stranger by her side, and Pit Gaumer, who thought Fietta much too good for Henry, taunted him with her defection. He heard that the stranger was a distant cousin, and that she was going to marry him.

He could not have endured it, had it not been for the prospect of revenge upon them all.

"I tell them," he said to himself, as he went about his work. "To-morrow I tell them. I will go first for the old ones, what are always talking, and then for the young ones, what are always yelling and screeching. And Fietta — I will not say it so any one shall know, but Fietta shall feel it in her soul. For twenty years Fietta has led me on, and now — and now ——"

Unable to go on, Henry put his head down once more upon his arms. Strange as it may seem, the preacher was again late. Nor had he this time the least excuse. He had overslept, and committed thereby the last offense which early-rising Millerstown would willingly forgive. The bell of his own church, announcing that service would begin in fifteen minutes, finally awoke him. He smiled faintly as he remembered Henry Kumerant's scornful face. He had entirely forgotten that he had said that Henry should open the service. At ten minutes past the hour, he sprang up the church steps, and there paused a moment to reconnoitre. What he saw and heard within made him tiptoe a little closer to the door, and stand still, listening.

Henry had been the first member of the congregation to arrive. The sexton stared at him in surprise.

"Well, Henry, you come so early as when you were the preacher."

"You mean I come so early as when I were *not* the preacher," rejoined Henry tartly.

He established himself in his usual place in the front of the church, where, by turning slightly, he could see the congregation assemble. First came Jennie Laudenslager, with her baby. He earnestly hoped the child would cry. That would serve to introduce his remarks on children in general. He smiled as, one by one, they came — old man Fackenthal, who had come to visit — ah, he had many scores to settle with old man Fackenthal! — then Billy Knerr — he was sure that Billy had laid the board across his chimney — and Jakie Kemerer — he was sure that Jakie had stolen his sign. Ah, how sorry they would be in a few minutes, sorry for their offenses against him, sorry for the meanness of their dispositions, sorry they had ever been born! When Fietta arrived, he turned his head the other way, only to look back in an instant. She had removed her black sunbonnet, and had bowed her head in prayer. Ah, that such hypocrisy could exist in guise so pious and so sweet! Then hurriedly, he arose.

"The preacher is again late. I will now start."

"No, you won't!" interrupted Billy Knerr. "We will wait till it is time."

"It *is* time." The hands had slipped round to the hour. Henry stepped within the chancel rail and looked his neighbors in the face.

"The preacher said when he was not this Sunday on time I should open the service. We will open with a hymn — three hundred and two. 'Delay Not, Delay Not.' Two verses."

Of all the congregation, only old man Fackenthal smiled. The others looked up in surprise. "Delay Not, Delay Not," was a favorite, and they usually sang all of its seven stanzas. Henry, however, paid no heed. His eyes were fixed on the road outside, and he saw that it was bare of pedestrians. The preacher could not come before he began. Suddenly he sprang to his feet with an angry glance at the choir, who had taken advantage of his momentary aberration to strike strongly into the third stanza.

"I said two verses!" he exclaimed. "We will now have the Scripture."

He had not based his remarks upon any particular text, as none seemed sufficiently comprehensive, and, happening now to turn to the second chapter of Genesis, read that, well aware that he had omitted the prayer. Nor did he give out the hymn which usually followed the Scripture reading. Afterwards they could sing — if they felt like singing.

He stepped pompously up the pulpit stairs. Now, for once, he would have his say. His audience could neither interrupt him nor escape. All old man Fackenthal's scorn, all the laughter of the younger generation, all Fietta's perfidy, rushed upon him, firing him to eloquence. He looked down upon them sternly, menacingly, at Jennie Laudenslager and Billy Knerr, and last of all at old man Fackenthal, whose gray eyes held his own for a second. Then, before he could look away, old man Fackenthal smiled at him.

"My bretheren ——" he began, then paused. As though a wet sponge had been passed over the surface of his mind, the scathing, brilliant speech had vanished, leaving in its place only a dull terror of the faces before him. He could not remember a sentence, not a syllable, of what he meant to say. For one moment he stood, his lips parted, his cheeks paling. Then, suddenly, a gleam of light brightened his darkness.

"Dear friends," he began again. "Dear friends." And once more, after a long pause: "Dear friends. It is a important chapter, this one, in the lives of each and every one of us, in our journey from the cradle to the grave."

Various stock phrases from sermons and prayers which he had heard drifted like straws upon the sea of his bewilderment, and he clutched frantically at them, sure that he saw upon the face of old man Fackenthal a broadening grin.

"It teaches us, my friends, of the brevity of this life."

There was a puzzled expression on the faces of his hearers.

"It teaches us, my friends, that life is short — short. It teaches us that we must be prepared for that which is some day coming to each and every one of us." Henry's voice shook. He could hardly keep his teeth from chattering. "In the midst of life we are in death, my bretheren. My friends, thousands of people died last week what never died before — thousands. My bretheren and sisters, thousands will go to-night in their beds, and when they get up in the morning they will be dead, they will be corpses. My friends ——" Henry paused. What more should he say? What had he said?

"It is, my friends, as I have said: 'In the midst of life we are in death.' We must prepare." Oh, if only the earth would open and swallow him up! He saw old man Fackenthal hide his face in his hands. "As I have said, we must prepare." Once more he hesitated. Then his hands, desperately gripping the pulpit, loosened their hold and dropped to his sides. He stepped down the pulpit stairs and down the aisle, unaware that the preacher went gravely up the other aisle. Once outside, he crossed the road into the grave-yard, where, behind a sheltering *arbor vitæ*, he sat down.

It was long past noon when he started up the mountain road. He kept well under the shadow of the trees, and once at the sound of an approaching team he hid. There was no longer any pleasure in life, and, worse still, there was no longer any one to whom he could announce the fact. There was no one who cared. He realized, as he plodded desperately on, that Fietta had been the whole world to him, and now Fietta was forever beyond his reach. If he had only married her a month ago, before the coming of this cousin, who had stolen her away. In a humility new to his soul, he looked back over the twenty years of their acquaintance; he saw his own selfishness and Fietta's self-sacrifice, his indifference and Fietta's devotion.

His new sign stared him in the face. He would like to wipe out the proudly painted name. What would Henry Kumerant signify now to the passer-by but defeat, shame? He stopped for a moment to steady himself against the gate, then suddenly straightened up. A capacious figure filled his doorway.

"Fietta!" he gasped.

Fietta did not answer.

"Wh-what are you doing here?"

"I came to see how you are getting along."

"How I am getting along?" Had she come to gloat over his misery?

"Yes." Fietta sat heavily down upon the doorstep. "Because you are sick I came."

"I? Sick?"

"Yes, because you are sick, you could n't finish your speech."

"Who said I was sick?"

"I said you were sick. I said I knew you were sick beforehand. And I said ——" Fietta rose. The glow of defiance with which she had faced the new Baptist congregation came back to her cheeks. "I said it was in the Bible about people going to bed and getting up dead."

"In the Bible? Is it in the Bible?" asked Henry dully.

" 'And it came to pass that night that the angel of the Lord went out, and smote in the camp of the Assyrians an hundred fourscore and five thousand; and when they arose early in the morning they were all dead corpses,' " she quoted. "None of them remembered it. And I asked the preacher, and he said it was true. It is in the Bible. And they are all coming to see you this afternoon, because you are sick."

Henry came a little closer, walking as though in a dream. It was not yet clear to him why she had come. Where was the cousin? Why had she defended him? Could it be that, in spite of his meanness, she still —— He leaned forward and grasped her wrist. Ah, if it were only true, he would blazon it abroad. He would tell them all.

"If they all come to see me this afternoon, Fietta," he faltered, "dare I make a speech to say ——"

Fietta jerked her hand away.

"I don't care what you do," she began, then stopped, choking.

Was it for this she had burdened her soul with the lie about his sickness? For this had she defied them all, for this had she tramped the long, hot mountain road? He had no word of thanks, he thought only of his speech, and Fietta knew him well enough to guess what that speech would have been. Was it for this she had turned away the handsome cousin who had wanted to marry her? Her eyes filled with tears. "You dare make any speech you want to," she said. Then she brushed past him. "I'm going home."

"But Fietta," Henry gasped, "I cannot make a speech without you are here, Fietta. I would be afraid. I — I could n't express me. I ——" Fietta, watching him, saw the ghastly pallor of the morning return to his cheek.

"You better tell me what you are going to say," she said scornfully. "Then I can remind you if you get stalled."

"It would be only one thing to say," he faltered, bewildered by her change of tone. "It would be, 'I and Fietta are going to be married!'"

"To be married?" she repeated.

"Yes. I — I thought perhaps — you did all these things for me — perhaps your cousin — but perhaps you are not willing?"

"Willing!" sobbed Fietta. Then she looked at him with one last, fast-vanishing misgiving. "Are you, then, sure you are not really sick, Henry Kumerant?"

WHEN TOWN AND COUNTRY MEET

Originally published in the September 1907 issue of *The Atlantic Monthly*

Most of the men in Millerstown left their work and started home for dinner when they were hungry, and many of them scolded if dinner were not ready. Adam Troxell did neither, but worked steadily away in field or garden till he was summoned. Often his longing eyes gazed back over the fields to the door of the farmhouse kitchen, although he knew that the sound of his mother's horn could reach him in any part of the farm.

To-day, from his hoeing in the south field, he turned his head more often than usual, sure that the hour for dinner had passed, but not daring to investigate. Finally, he made up his mind that if the shadow of the next post had reached a certain stone by the time that he returned from the other side of the field he would wait no longer.

Before he was half-way across, however, he heard the sound of the horn, and dropping his seed-bag where he stood, he started toward the fence. When he was already astride of it he hesitated.

"She won't know if I leave it once here," he said half aloud, and jumped down on the other side. There he hesitated. "But she might ask me." Climbing back, he made for the spot where he had left the bag, carried it with him to the fence, and, concealing it carefully beneath, climbed over once more, and made his way across the meadow, around the barn, and to the house. Outside the kitchen door, he paused to plunge his face and hands into a basin of water which stood ready for him on the pump floor, then slipped out of his heavy, mud-coated shoes.

"Adam," called a mellifluous voice from within.

"Yes, Mom."

"Take off your shoes."

"Yes, Mom."

Adam smoothed his hair before the little mirror fastened to the side of the house beside the door. It gave back a reflection of his slender, stooping shoulders, narrow face, and pale eyes.

Having finished, he went into the kitchen, carefully opening and closing the screen door. The kitchen was kept almost dark so that flies might not be tempted to linger therein, although it was not yet the season for flies. Adam's eyes, dimmed by the sudden change from the light without, did not at first distinguish the figure of his mother, as she stood before the stove; then the sound of her voice helped him in his sense of direction. Mrs. Troxell was not so small that she was hard to discover. The outline of her figure, though vague, was enormous, and straight from shoulder to skirt hem.

"Just sit down once," she said.

Adam took his place at one end of a table which stood with its side against the wall. It was covered with a red cloth, and there were two plates turned upside-down, with a knife and fork crossed on each one. When his mother had heaped his plate high, she filled her own, and sat down, sighing heavily.

"What is the matter?" asked her son. "Have you got it somewheres?"

She did not answer at once, and he went on eating, not because he was not anxious to hear her reply, but because he was accustomed to have her take her time.

"Adam, I have been for some time thinking of something," she began presently. "It is that I must have help. It is so much all the time to do, and I cannot always do the things so quickly like sometimes. Till I get the cows milked in the morning, I am tired. I must get me somebody."

"You better get you a girl," answered Adam uneasily.

"But the girls, they cost so much. It won't anybody work in Millerstown for less than a dollar and a quarter."

"It is so," he acknowledged.

"And they eat so much. They eat more than they work."

"Well, I could do the milking. Then you would not have it so hard."

"But you would then have to hire a man, and it would come out the same. It is another way I am thinking from."

"What is that?"

Mrs. Troxell rose heavily, and went to the cellar for the pie. She did not answer until she was in her place opposite him.

"You might get married."

A wave of color flooded Adam's face.

"You are plenty old enough," she went on. "You are now fifteen years older than your pop and I when we were married. Then it would n't be no wages to pay, and it would be some one what would take interest. These hired girls, they don't care. And we could then keep more chickens, and put the eggs in the store, and she could help sometimes in the field, and in the garden. I am getting so stiff, I cannot work any more in the garden —"

"But, Mom —"

He might as well have tried to dam the smoothly-flowing little Lehigh with a shingle. A listener might have wondered at his seeking, the tone was so round, so smooth, like the soft bubble of the stream, intensified a hundred times.

"— like I used to. And it is plenty girls, but not so many what are good for something. I have been thinking from the girls, Adam. Not Mary Kuhns, she is too much of a *schussle* [careless person], and not Elmina Fatzinger, while she is always too much for spending money, and not Mantana Kemerer. But Linnie Kurtz, Adam. She is a good worker, and she is not so proud. I think it would be good to get Linnie."

"But, Mom, when shall this marrying be?"

"Ay, soon. It must be somebody here for the harvest, and she must be by that time used to the things. Linnie cannot have so many eggs to bake with as at home. I will learn her to be saving."

"But, Mom —"

Mrs. Troxell gathered herself together as if to rise.

"If you get done early with the planting, you can go to-night to see Linnie, Adam."

Adam rose, and went out into the sunshine, his pale eyes blinking. He sat down on the doorstep and put on his heavy shoes, then he went slowly back to his work. He could not believe that his mother was growing old, she who, in spite of her vast size, had accomplished such herculean labors. He shared her distress at the idea of paying wages. Most of the girls were not willing to do as their mistresses wanted them to do; they liked to gad about, to go to the county seat on the trolley, to have beaux, and they ate more than they were worth. He had thought vaguely of getting married before, but he had put the thought aside, because he did not suppose his mother would approve.

But Linnie Kurtz! The flush came back to his cheek. He did not want Linnie Kurtz, she was too smart. There was always a laugh in her eyes when they met his.

No, there was some one else whom he would marry. As he thought of her, a little seed of romance, tiny and neglected in the bottom of his heart, put forth a pale, green tendril. He would marry the girl whom he liked.

He finished his hoeing, then went back to the house and dressed quickly. His mother gave him his supper, then started to the barn to milk. She said nothing more about his marrying; she was accustomed to have him follow her suggestions.

It was seven o'clock, and the spring twilight had begun to fall. Adam walked swiftly into the village. When he reached the main street, the trolley car from the county seat had just come in, and he watched them change the fender, then climbed aboard.

He felt himself strangely excited, although he had scarcely thought of the girl for weeks. Her name was Florence Kramer; he had met her through his cousin, who worked with her in the silk mill, where she earned seven dollars a week. He knew that his mother would refuse to believe that, but it was true. And she was pretty and smart, and probably had money in the bank. Certainly she could not, even if she wished, spend seven dollars a week!

He had seen her only a few times, but he did not have any fear that she would refuse him. What girl would not be glad for such a home as he could offer her? Only he and his mother knew the amount of their deposits in the Millerstown bank and a bank in the county seat, kept thus divided so that prying Millerstown might not know how much they had.

His mother received his story that night with a long silence. He did not see, in the darkness of the porch, that twice she tried vainly to speak.

"C — Can she work?" she asked, at last.

"She is a fearful worker," answered Adam proudly. "She earns seven dollars a week."

"Have you asked her, already?"

"Yes, but she is not sure if she will."

Mrs. Troxell's head sank upon her breast. She made strange noises in her throat. For the first time in his life, Adam had acted without her counsel. Was this the effect the strange girl was to have upon him? Then her cold hands seized the arms of her chair.

"You bring her out here before you get married," she said, stammering a little. "I must talk to her before you get married to her. Tell her to come Sundays."

"Yes, Mom," answered Adam. "I was going Saturdays in, but I will write to her to come out."

The letter bore evidence of careful, even painful, composition. The girl, receiving it, laughed, then flushed scarlet.

"Dear Miss," it began. "I guess you are disappointed while I do not come in. My Mom says you shall come to-morrow evening out for supper."

She sat a long time after she had finished reading it, with it crushed in her hand. She had never paid any attention to this "Dutchman" until he had startled her by proposing that she marry him. The half-spoken refusal had been smothered by the consciousness of an ugly pain in her side at the end of her day's work, and of the fact that her last week's wages was all she had in the world. Marriage would mean peace and comfort for her body at least, even though Adam Troxell was as far from the man she would have chosen as any one could be. She would go out and see where he lived, and then she might accept.

Mrs. Troxell, sitting behind the vines on the porch on the Sunday afternoon, watched the girl disapprovingly as she came with Adam up the long lane which led in from the road. There were drooping feathers in her hat, and she wore gloves. She looked about her eagerly, and her face sparkled at sight of the farm-house with its broad porch. It would be pleasant there on summer evenings. The girls from the mill could come out to see her, and she could go often to town. She felt already the importance which being well married would bestow.

She could not help a sudden start when Adam's mother rose to meet her. There was something portentous in a first view of Mrs. Troxell. Her size took away one's breath.

"How do you do?" she said slowly, and her voice made the girl shiver, it was so unlike any other voice she had ever heard. "It is a nice day."

"You have a nice place here," Florence answered nervously.

"Yes," said Mrs. Troxell.

"But I should think it would be awful lonely."

Mrs. Troxell smoothed down her white apron.

"It is too much to do in the country to get lonely," she said. "It is all the time something to do."

The girl's face brightened.

"What do you do? Everything looks so quiet. I shouldn't think there would be anything to do."

For a moment Mrs. Troxell did not answer. Then she apologized for not having asked the girl to take off her hat.

"Adam shall take it in the house," she said.

When he had gone, she turned her head again toward Florence.

"What do you mean by something to do?" she asked.

"Why, there ain't no theatre here, and no people, and no places to go."

"We have no time to go places," said Mrs. Troxell, her great voice trembling. "There is too much work." Her little eyes watched the girl. "We have gardening and soap-boiling and white-washing and butchering and milking and harvesting and cleaning, and — "

"Oh!" Florence's eyes widened and she gasped a little.

"— and baking and canning and — "

At the sound of Adam's footstep, Mrs. Troxell stopped abruptly. She lifted herself heavily from the chair.

"You can take her round to look at the things, Adam," she said. "I will make supper."

"All right," said Adam in his high voice, leading the way down the steps. His mother's tone seemed to breathe satisfaction. "We will go first to the barn, and then you can go along to fetch the cows."

"But ain't you going to stay with me when I come out here?" Florence demanded. It was not that she wanted him, but that she was afraid of his mother.

"Yes, when the cows are milked. I milk Sundays. Mom has it so bad in her back."

"But don't you have a girl or a hired man?"

"Ach, no, it is too expensive to hire. But we would have to hire if I did not get married."

"Oh, are you going to get married?" she said sharply.

Adam smiled at her. He could never quite understand her metropolitan wit.

"Come now this way and see the barn."

The girl followed him slowly, lifting high her trailing skirts. She made no response as he pointed out the various improvements he had made.

"But Mom, she thought of all these things," he explained proudly. "Now, I am going for the cows. Will you go along?"

"No, I'll go back to the house." She could not imagine a more terrifying experience than close contact with cows. She hurried back across the yard, and turned the knob of the front door. It would not open. She tried it again, and shook it, her face scarlet. Had the woman locked her out? She stood hesitating for an instant, then she heard a heavy footstep. There was a great sliding of bolts and keys, and Mrs. Troxell, a gingham apron over her white one, stood before her.

"I guess I did n't hear you first off," she said. "We use always the back door."

The girl stepped inside.

"He said I should find you."

"That was right. You come along in the kitchen."

Florence looked about her curiously. The hall was narrow and dark, and the doors leading into the rooms on either side were closed. There was an odor of recently applied whitewash. Mrs. Troxell opened a door which led into a room as dark as the hall. There were faint outlines of a table with a chenille cover, and chairs set in a neat row against the wall. Suddenly she paused. Florence, in the dark, walked against her, and stepped quickly back. It seemed hardly human, the vast mass which she had touched.

"I thought I heard one," Mrs. Troxell said mysteriously, making her way to the other side of the room. She lifted the curtain, where, buzzing against the window, there was a fly. She killed it with a stroke of her hand.

"It must a' sneaked in when we came in," she said. "Or else it is from last year."

Then she opened the door into a brighter room, furnished with a rag carpet, a row of chairs set against the wall, and a table set for supper.

"You can sit here," she said. "We always eat out in the kitchen except when it is company here."

"Do you eat in the kitchen in summer when it is so hot?"

"Of course. Shall I have flies in my house?"

The expression of satisfaction had not left Mrs. Troxell's face.

The girl sat down, and watched, fascinated, Mrs. Troxell's careful exit. In a few moments the faint delicious odor of cooking stole in upon her. After a long time, she heard Adam's voice and a splashing of water at the pump. Presently he came into the kitchen and sat down beside her, whereupon she shivered and turned involuntarily away.

"Well, did you get lonely?" he asked cheerfully. "When you do yourself the milking you won't get lonely."

Florence did not answer. She was watching Mrs. Troxell's struggles with the door, her driving away of invisible flies, then her hurried entrance which left her almost breathless. This time there was a large tray in her hands.

In a few moments they sat down at the table. The meal was delicious; Florence was sure that she had never tasted anything so good. Nevertheless, she could eat but little. Mrs. Troxell's long grace, and her son's silent feeding, and Mrs. Troxell herself, frightened her. She wished herself back at the boarding-house table, with its poor coffee, and worse bread, and the good company.

Mrs. Troxell urged her to eat.

"You can't work when you don't eat," she said cheerfully, and her melodious voice seemed to fill the room. "In the country you must eat a lot so you can do country work."

Florence shook her head. She wondered whether this choke in her throat signified homesickness. And for what? What was it that made this place so terrible? Was it the silence? Was it the vast old woman?"

"What time does the next car go?" she asked, when Adam finally laid down his knife.

"Must you go already back?" asked Adam, in dismay. "I thought you should stay and go 'long in the church."

"Yes, you can just so well stay," seconded his mother.

"No, I must — I have a sick aunt. I promised to stay with her." The excuse was the sudden reckless invention of the moment.

"But I can't go 'long so early. I take always the collection in the church."

"Oh, but I can go alone." Her eyes brightened. "You need not even go to the car with me."

"Ach, yes, that he will do," insisted his mother. "Of course he will go with you to the car."

"Of course I will," said Adam. His eyes sought his mother's, and met her gaze, alert, anxious, perhaps a little pitying. He interpreted it to mean that she was as eager that the bargain should be struck at once as he.

They had scarcely left the house before he spoke.

"Well, how would you like to live here?"

"I don't like the country. It is too lonely."

"But you would n't be lonely. Mom is always here, and it is not lonely when you have work to do."

"But I don't like to work."

"You don't like to work!" He stopped in the lane and stared at her. "But you get seven dollars a week, working."

"But I only work for the money. I don't like to work."

"But you will have here a good home. It is no one in the family but I and Mom, and it is a good farm, and we have money in the bank."

She turned on him suddenly.

"Will you let me have some of the money? Will you let me hire a girl?"

"A girl," he repeated heavily. "A girl yet, with you and Mom to do the work. What would a girl do?"

Florence broke suddenly into an hysterical laugh, then she started to run.

"Don't you see the car is coming?" she cried.

When Adam got back to the house, his mother was sitting on the porch.

"She would n't marry me!" he said.

"She would n't marry you!" Mrs. Troxell's voice was non-committal.

"She wanted me to take the money from the bank, and hire a girl. Take the money from the bank!"

"What!" Now Mrs. Troxell did not need to assume surprise.

"Yes." Then his voice softened. "I guess we might 'a' made it easy for her. We might 'a' hired a girl to help. We — " he sat heavily down on the step. "I wanted her." After a long time he said again, "I wanted her."

Mrs. Troxell watched his bent head. Fear came into her eyes at this son who wanted anything she had not suggested. Then her eyes narrowed cunningly.

"The Lord does not let us have always what we want, Adam. It is some good reason why you shall not have her."

"I guess so," he answered piously, and with that, romance died. "But now we will have to hire, Mom."

"No, not yet awhile," his mother answered. "I feel good to-night. I will get a while along alone."

She sat on the porch for a long time after he had gone to bed. Occasionally she smiled and once she muttered softly,

"I settled it. I scared her. To take — " Mrs. Troxell gasped heavily — "to take the money from the bank to hire a girl!"

THE ORGAN AT ZION CHURCH

Originally published in the November 21, 1907, issue of
The Youth's Companion

The little chapel in which the meetings of Zion Evangelical congregation of Millerstown were held glowed in the morning sunshine. Its four straight walls had been freshly painted in a soft yellow, a little brighter than the tone of the oak matting on the floor. The unpainted pine benches had, after a dozen years of wear, deepened into a warm light brown, upon which the morning sunshine, streaming undimmed through white muslin shades, revealed no speck of dust. High on the walls above the line of vision hung several pictures, one of Moses with the tablets of the law on his arm, and one of the last day, the brilliant colors of which had happily faded so that only by earnest scrutiny could one decipher the design.

It was fortunate that this was so, for the pictured "Father of Lies," with his attendant imps, could not but terrorize all those who beheld him. Evidently, however, the Zionites cared little for pictures, or seldom looked upward, for the "God Bless Our Church," done in crewel, hung upside down above the door.

The room at nine o'clock on Sunday morning was absolutely still. Not a fly buzzed between the shades and the shining window-panes, not even a church mouse nibbled in the corner. Their banishment was one of the articles of Sexton Wertman's creed, and both had long since fled across the wide playground to the schoolhouse.

David allowed nothing to disturb the immaculate order of the chapel. The room as it was this morning pleased him best. It was necessary, however, that people should come in, that they should move his carefully placed benches, and disarrange the neat pile of hymn-books on the shelf behind the pulpit. Moreover, people would allow their children to eat peppermint drops and cardamom seeds, fragments of which dropped to the floor, and would be sure to attract again the mice which he had so carefully banished. Often during the services he frowned suddenly or moved uneasily as the odor of peppermint or fennel reached him.

This morning, however, as he entered the chapel, he was thinking neither of the shower which had laid the dust, which the congregation would otherwise have carried into the chapel, nor of the fact that he was to lead the meeting that morning. Zion Church had regular preaching only once a month. On the other Sundays the members took charge.

In spite of the fact that leading the meeting was the greatest pleasure of David's life, he frowned, and his blue eyes, which travelled from benches to pulpit to see that everything was in order, had no pleasure in them. He sighed as he raised the window-shades to equal distances from the window-sills. Then he filled the pitcher which stood with a glass beside it on the little pulpit.

No one had ever been known to need a drink of water while preaching, and David himself would have scorned it as a refuge of weak-throated men, but it never occurred to him not to have the pitcher there, with a china plate beneath it to prevent the moisture from marring the varnish.

Then David sighed again, his eyes on the organ, which stood beside the pulpit, the organ which was to cause the disruption in Zion Church. It stood there, glittering in its splendor of yellow varnish and bright ivory; and David, for all that he wished it many miles away, could not help stroking it caressingly. He loved all things bright and shiny and new.

Since the organization of the church, twenty years before, Aaron König had been the foresinger. It was his duty to select and start the hymns.

There was never any announcement by number or name. Aaron simply began, and the congregation dropped in one by one. On rare occasions a fearless and fervent sister got ahead of him by beginning a tune before the congregation were off their knees after prayer. After the first few lines, however, the hymn was always surrendered to Aaron, whose deep voice gave it volume and strength.

A stranger, wandering into Zion Church, would have picked out Aaron last of all the men as the owner of that voice. He was a little, slender, gray-bearded man, so timid that when it was possible he avoided meeting the eyes of his neighbors. He flushed like a girl when spoken to suddenly; he could not pray in public, although all the children in the congregation above twelve years prayed fluently.

When once started in a hymn, however, his shyness vanished. Then his black eyes gleamed, his slender figure seemed to grow large, and his big voice thundered out in never-failing volume.

The children watched him with awe and wonder as he sat on the mourners' bench directly under the pulpit, keeping time with hands and feet to the music, and often, when especially moved, swaying bodily back and forth.

It was not at these contortions, however, that they marveled, but at a certain power which he possessed of singing continuously without stopping for breath. With never a pause between the stanzas, he sang on and on, now some inspiring Reformation hymn, and again some Pennsylvania-German camp-meeting song, with English verses, perhaps, and a German chorus. The rest of the congregation omitted the first line of each stanza while they gasped for breath, but Aaron swept on with full-lunged vigor.

This he accomplished by a means which none of his brethren suspected. As the congregation sang the last line of each stanza, Aaron, with lips still moving, stopped singing. He relied on the final burst of fervor to conceal the absence of his voice and gave him time to get his breath. Then, almost before they had sung the last line, he was ready for the next.

It was small wonder that Aaron's voice had become the ruling passion of his life. It was that which made his lonely bachelor life worth living.

Now, however, the old order of things was to be changed. Led by the younger, more progressive spirits, the congregation had purchased a little organ, which was to be used for the first time to-day.

This had not been accomplished without considerable protest on the part of the older members.

"But Aaron König, what will he do?" David Wertman had demanded.

"How do you mean, 'What will Aaron König do'?" Amelia Sames had asked, sharply. Amelia had been appointed organist.

"Aye, while he has always been de foresinger."

"I guess nobody won't keep Aaron König from singing," responded Amelia. "He dare sing. Nobody won't do him nossing for singing."

"But it issn't de same wis de organ. It will be de organ now what iss de foresinger."

"Well, let him den come to de meeting an' say he doesn't like it."

Aaron, however, did not appear at the meeting at which the question was decided, although he had been notified as to the time.

"You can easy see dat Aaron doesn't care," said the jubilant Amelia.

The congregation as a whole agreed with her, and when the vote was cast there were but two noes, that of David Wertman and that of the Widow Mohr.

"Aaron will come no longer in de church," the widow said, much troubled. "An' I like de foresinging better dan de organ. If Aaron stays away, den I stay away, too."

Meanwhile Aaron König pounded shoes down in his little shop. He wished sometimes that it was the organ itself which he had under his hammer.

"It issn't relichous to haf such a music-box for to lead de singing," he said to himself. "It issn't no life in such a music-box. It iss life when de foresinger leads. An' I won't haf nossing to do in de church, in my church what I helped to make."

He had thought of going to the meeting and protesting, and had then grown pale at the mere idea. Not if he were threatened with death could he have made a speech before them all.

Then suddenly his hammer paused above David Wertman's shoe, and slowly the shoe itself slid down his leather apron to the floor. His cheeks flushed lightly above his gray beard, and he smiled. Amelia Sames should see!

The organ had been ordered immediately, but it was several weeks before it came. Now, however, it stood in its place, almost defiant in its newness.

David laid the hymn-books upon it, and then opened the Bible at the chapter he had chosen for the morning's reading. Then, as he went to lower a shade, which was a fraction of an inch higher than its fellows, he heard the heavy footstep of the first comer. It proved to be the Widow Mohr, of vast bodily dimensions and larger heart. She responded cheerfully to his *"Wie geht's?"* although panting a little from her long walk.

"It iss a fine morning," she said. "Who will lead dis morning de meeting?"

"I will," David responded. "Broder Gracely, he should lead dis morning, but he had to go off. He went to a funeral."

"So? Who iss den dead?"

"I sink it iss a cousint. It iss some one what iss already a long time sick."

The widow's eyes wandered toward the organ, and were as quickly withdrawn. She sighed heavily as she settled herself in her seat.

The congregation gathered promptly in spite of numerous temptations to linger by the way. None of them had seen the new organ, and they were all curious to know what Aaron would do. The subject had been discussed in every Evangelical household in Millerstown during the week.

Aaron walked out to church alone as usual, his hands behind his back, his nervous glance on the ground. He was surprised and embarrassed to find most of the congregation assembled before his arrival. Usually he was among the first.

He always took his seat on the "mourners' bench" under the pulpit, then fixed his eyes on the "God Bless Our Church" above the door. It was an evidence of his piety and devotion that he had never noticed the position of the motto.

It had always been his duty and privilege to open the meeting. Without turning to glance at the clock behind him, and without referring to his watch, he seemed to know instinctively when it was ten o'clock. Jim Fackenthal always insisted that the Widow Mohr, who faced the clock, and who was supposed to have a tender interest in Aaron, gave him some signal. No one, however, had ever been able to detect her in the act. Nor did Aaron's gaze ever waver from the motto before he began the opening hymn.

By the time that he had reached the second line, the widow joined in with her dulcet soprano, and by the end of the first stanza all the grown people had caught up. Then the children added their shrill soprano, and they sang on and on. There was never any omission of stanzas in the Evangelical meeting.

This morning, for the first time in twenty years, they did not wait for Aaron to begin. At three minutes of ten Amelia Sames took her seat on the organ-stool, which squeaked loudly when she nervously turned it higher instead of lower, as she had intended. At the same moment David stepped into the pulpit. He was reassured by Aaron's evident acquiescence in the will of the congregation. He did not realize that it was not quite time to begin.

"I sink," he began, smilingly, "dat we will all sing for de first time wis de organ in English, so dat all de children can choin in. Let us sing 'Work for de Night Iss Coming.'"

Amelia found the place with comparatively little trouble, and laid her hands on the shining keys. At the first note the children began to sing, and she looked appealingly at David. He held up a warning finger.

"You must wait till Amelia plays it once ofer," he corrected. "Now, Amelia, start it once again, and I will tell dem when dey shall come in."

This time all went well. They began together and sang fervently, their delight in the novelty shining in their faces. Aaron, however, remained silent, his lips twitching nervously, his eyes fixed on the motto above the door.

Then, just at ten o'clock,—whether notified by some sixth sense, or by some glance of sympathy for departed glory from the Widow Mohr,— Aaron gave voice to a protest. They had finished the first stanza, and were half-way through with the second, when suddenly his deep voice boomed out. David Wertman smiled happily to himself. The trouble was over.

Then slowly an expression of distress crept over David's face. Aaron's singing was not adding to the harmony, although he, too, sang "Work, for the Night Is Coming." Several seconds passed before David could decide where the trouble lay. Then suddenly he comprehended.

The congregation, as David had requested, sang English; Aaron sang German. They were in the midst of the second stanza; Aaron had begun with the first. They sang in the key of C; Aaron, half a tone higher.

The discord for a few moments was ear-splitting. Then gradually, but surely, it grew less. There was still lack of accord, but it was as if one weak falsetto sang against a host of true singers. The congregation had unwillingly, but none the less completely, gone over to Aaron. Amelia, with flushed cheeks, pedaled vigorously and pulled out all the stops, but it was of no avail. The organ at its greatest volume could only give forth a thin wail, ineffectual against Aaron's dominant bass.

David wisely allowed them to sing to the end of the three stanzas. Then they dropped to their knees with a sigh of relief and with tremors of anxiety as to what the leaders in the struggle would do next. The widow, who, on account of her size, never knelt for prayer, raised her head from her arm to cast a surreptitious glance at Aaron. His eyes were closed, and he was swaying back and forth, as he often did when overcome by religious fervor. It was plain to be seen that the one who yielded would not be Aaron.

It was Aaron's custom to start the hymn as soon as he heard the Amen, and before the congregation had had time to rise from their knees. It was not merely because he feared that some one would forestall him, but because he felt instinctively that the undignified scramble from their knees was appropriately hidden by the beginning of the next hymn.

Now, however, David Wertman closed his prayer without the usual long approach to the Amen, hoping to announce the next hymn, and make an appeal to Aaron to start with them.

Aaron, however, was before him. He rose from his knees with the opening words of *"Ein Feste Burg"* on his lips, and the congregation joined in. Amelia struggled vainly to find the key in which he was singing, but after striking sundry wrong chords, gave up in despair. The hymn had four long verses, and Aaron sang them all.

Then David Wertman rose.

"It iss easy seen," he began, sternly, "dat we do not understand what de organ iss for. It iss to lead de singing. Any one can gif out a hymn, English or Cherman, but de organ must lead."

Then a brilliant thought occurred to him. "Broder König, haf you a hymn what you would like to haf us sing?"

All eyes turned toward Aaron, who would not answer. His eyes were lifted toward the motto, and his lips quivered. The widow, with a desperate desire to make peace, asked for *"Ach Gott vom Himmel sieh darein,"* and Amelia struck the opening chords.

Again, however, Aaron's voice rang out in a different key, and again the congregation hesitated, made a frantic effort to sing with the organ, and one by one went over to Aaron, the children's treble swiftly following the widow's mellifluous soprano, and their elders following less willingly.

David motioned Amelia to silence, and the hymn was finished with all the Reformation spirit which it embodied. When it ended, Aaron König bent his head on his hands, and the widow rose slowly and heavily to her feet.

"Iss it any one here who wanted de organ while dey sought Broder König could not sing no more?" she asked, slowly.

No one answered.

"If it iss any one here like dat, dey can now see dat Broder König can sing better dan de organ. I sink we better let Broder König keep on wis de singing."

"But we haf spent de money for de organ," put in a careful brother. "Shall we now srow de organ away?"

"An' I am de organist. What shall I do?" demanded Amelia.

"Let us keep de organ," went on the widow, smoothly. "An' Amelia can come an' play any time in de week, but Sundays not. I make a move dat Broder König be yet our foresinger."

The motion was seconded and passed, with one dissenting vote, that of the organist.

Then Aaron lifted his head. There were tears in his eyes and he trembled.

"I sank myself," he said, in a choked voice. Had there been any one present who did not understand the German idiom of his speech, they would have understood from his eyes who it was whom he was thanking.

The organ has been pushed back to the corner of the chapel. It has not been opened, for Amelia Sames refuses angrily to touch it on week-days, since she is not allowed to play it on Sundays. To David Wertman, however, it is a source of great satisfaction. He lifts the gay calico cover, which he had his wife make for it, and dusts its dustless case carefully. It is the one thing in the room which is always in perfect order, the one thing which gratifies his passion for cleanliness.

MRS. WEIMER'S GIFT OF TONGUES

Originally published in the February 1908 issue of
Lippincott's Monthly Magazine

"Mom, the sugar is all."

Louisa Weimer, whose hands were covered with flour, raised her arm to brush the curls out of her eyes. No one could have accomplished the awkward gesture with more grace than Louisa.

Her mother gave no sign that she heard, save that the gleam in her black eyes became brighter. She continued to move about the table with a light step, and gently opened and closed the oven-door.

"Mom," said Louisa again, "shall I fetch some sugar?"

Mrs. Weimer still made no response, until Louisa, after having washed her hands, put on her sunbonnet and started toward the door.

"Where are you going, Louisa?" she asked, not in Louisa's somewhat halting English, but in Pennsylvania German.

Louisa's eyes were blue, but they could flash none the less brightly for that.

"I said I was going to the store for sugar," she answered, now also in German.

"All right," said her mother pleasantly. "Bring cinnamon, too."

The screen door closed sharply behind Louisa.

"Always Dutch," she muttered as she went down the board-walk. "This is the only place in Millerstown where it is now all the time everything Dutch."

Then, catching sight of her "company girl," Mary Kuhns, Louisa ran on to join her.

Back in the kitchen, Mrs. Weimer went on with her work. She had her daughter's habit of talking to herself. Her speech was shorter, however, and delivered in German.

"I will not talk English, not if I live to be a hundred," she said.

She knew well enough that hers was the only house in Millerstown in which English was constantly frowned upon. Nor was it because she did not understand it. One could not help understanding it. One heard little else in these degenerate days. Degenerate they were indeed. The young people no longer obeyed their parents, they were extravagant, they must always be going to the county seat on the trolley cars — Mrs. Weimer hated the sound of the gong. These things had not been when she was young. They had all come in with the speaking of English, and as for her and her house they would not speak it, nor would she acknowledge that she understood it, even though such an attitude involved not a little inconvenience.

Louisa meanwhile was exercising her English to her heart's content. Her arm lay across Mary Kuhns's shoulder, and their sunbonnets were close together.

"I tell you," Mary was saying, "if you ever want to have your picture enlarged, now is your chance, Louisa. It don't make anything out what sort of a picture you have. He can put another dress to it, or a hat, if you want a hat, or he can take a hat off. And he can make a pompadour for you."

Louisa's heart leaped. The height of her mother's ambition was to own a crayon portrait of herself to hang beside that of her departed husband on their parlor wall, and another of Louisa to hang opposite.

"But how much does it cost?" she asked, her hopes suddenly falling.

"It is a special sale. It is only ninety-eight cents."

"Ninety-eight cents!" repeated Louisa. "Is he here yet?"

"Yes, and he will go round to every house."

Louisa slipped out of Mary's grasp.

"I must go hurry and tell my Mom."

She sped on to the store to accomplish her errand, then home. This time she spoke hurriedly in German.

Mrs. Weimer was as much excited as Louisa herself. Of course they could not afford to have the pictures framed at once, but they would not mind that.

"When did Mary say he would come?"

Before Louisa could reply, there was a gentle tap at the door. Both women turned, a little startled. Who was it who had come down the board-walk so quietly?

Before them stood a young and slender man, whom they would have guessed to be the crayon-portrait agent, even without the large portfolio which he carried under his arm. There was a metropolitan air about him which impressed even Mrs. Weimer. His hat was in his hand. The Millerstown men did not go to the trouble of removing their hats when they rapped at one's door. His skin was very white, his eyes very black, his dark hair very smooth.

"Good morning," he said, in a gentle voice. "I hear you are interested in portraits. I have something here which is finer than oils."

"Yes," said Louisa, thinking regretfully of her soiled dress. "Come in and take a chair once."

"Thank you," said the young man, with a bow. "But can't we sit out here on the porch?" It was a warm morning, and the stifling air in the kitchen could be felt at the door. He held the door open, first for Mrs. Weimer, then for Louisa.

"If you will sit here, miss, and your mother here, I can show the pictures to advantage."

"What does he say, Louisa?" asked Mrs. Weimer. She always insisted that English be translated for her.

"He says you shall sit down," answered Louisa impatiently. Once more she was to be disgraced by her mother's German.

"Your mother doesn't understand English?" the agent asked politely. "But you do?"

"No, she don't, but I do. Pretty near everything is getting English. But Mom, she still talks Dutch."

The young man fanned himself with his hat, and looked at Louisa. Louisa in her close-fitting calico dress was a pleasing spectacle.

"It is a warm day," he said. "Now, I have here a very fine line of crayons, as you will see. These pictures I will show you are some of the most beautiful young ladies of the county seat. This is a young lady on Fourth Street."

He held up before them the first of his portraits. No one could have dreamed that the original came from any place smaller than the county seat. The cut of her dress, the brilliant jewel at her throat, and, most of all, the towering pompadour, proclaimed her as city bred. Louisa gave an "Oh!" of rapture, and even her mother was impressed.

"Imagine how handsome the lady will look in a fine frame. And this is a picture of her mother. It is a fine black and white effect. She is a widow."

"What does he say?" asked Mrs. Weimer.

"This is the young lady's mother."

"Would not your mother like an effect something like this?"

"I think it is grand," said Louisa. "Mom, how would you like such a picture?"

Mrs. Weimer's eyes glistened.

"Ask him how much it will cost, Louisa."

Louisa translated her mother's question.

"You cannot buy such a picture anywhere else for less than four dollars. These are special rates, ninety-eight cents is all the firm is asking. You will never have another chance like this. The firm is about to leave this section. You think you will take one?"

"He says, will you take one?" translates Louisa.

"Yes, if it is only ninety-eight cents."

Louisa translated again.

"That is our price. Your mother has a picture of herself?"

Louisa brought her mother's photograph from the album in the parlor. That she brought with her another did not escape the agent's eye.

"And now," he began, when he had put down in his note-book the directions for Mrs. Weimer's picture, "don't the young lady want one too? Excuse me, but you would make a handsome picture."

Mrs. Weimer saw Louisa blush.

"What does he say, Louisa?"

"He says, would I like such a picture?" Louisa clasped her hands. "Ach, please, please, Mom!"

"All right," consented Mrs. Weimer.

The agent held out his hand for Louisa's picture.

"Ah, this is a good one," he said, in his gentle voice. "But we must touch up these cheeks so they look a little more like what they do naturally. And what color would you like the dress to be?"

Louisa heaved a rapturous sigh which ended in the word "Pink."

The young man wrote down the directions for her picture. Then Mrs. Weimer expected him to go. He stayed on, however, asking Louisa for a drink, then, when she had given him some raspberry vinegar, lingering to show her some pictures from his portfolio. Mrs. Weimer was disturbed because Louisa was neglecting her work. She herself went back to the kitchen and finished mixing the cake which Louisa had begun. Several times she went to the door, but Louisa did not turn her head. Mrs. Weimer decided that she did not altogether trust the young man. One could never be sure about these English.

~ ~ ~ ~ ~

Millerstown talked of little else than crayon portraits during the next week. The women talked them over when they met in the store, the children whispered about them in school, until the teacher forbade all mention of the word "picture."

To Louisa the week seemed long. She had never seen any one so good-looking or with such fine manners as the agent.

For some reason, the young man did not follow the same plan in the delivery of his pictures as he had in their sale. Instead of starting at the head of Main Street and going from house to house, he went, first of all, to the Weimers'. When he came it was just eight o'clock, and Louisa and her mother were half through with the week's baking. They did not expect him till afternoon, and they were both much surprised, and Louisa much annoyed. She had dreamed all the week that he would come in the afternoon, when she was dressed to receive him.

"Good morning," he said in his gentle fashion.

"Good morning," answered Louisa.

"This is a beautiful morning," he said hurriedly. "I have brought the pictures. Will you step out and look at them?"

Louisa moved toward the door.

"Where are you going?" asked Mrs. Weimer.

"We shall go out on the porch to see our pictures."

"You tell him he shall bring them in here," commanded Mrs. Weimer. Then he would not keep Louisa from her work.

"You shall bring the pictures in here," translated Louisa unwillingly.

The young man bowed and backed out on the porch. When he returned he carried, not the light portfolio, but two heavily-framed pictures. One he leaned against the kitchen wall, the other he slowly uncovered.

"We didn't order frames, Louisa," said Mrs. Weimer.

"Well, perhaps these are not our pictures."

At first glance, indeed, the picture which he held up for their inspection seemed to belong to neither of them. It was the likeness of a young woman clad in the pinkest of pink dresses, which, however, was no pinker than her cheeks. Her eyes were blue, and her brown hair was piled into a high pompadour.

"But that is grand!" sighed Louisa. "But"—the admiration changed to bewilderment—"but—who——" Suddenly Louisa flushed a rosy red. "Is it me?"

The young man bowed.

"Who is it?" asked her mother, then saw her question answered in Louisa's face. "Is it you?"

"Of course," answered Louisa.

For an instant Mrs. Weimer said nothing. She looked from Louisa to the picture, and from the picture back to Louisa. Surely it did look a little like Louisa.

"But we cannot take the frames. Tell him that, Louisa."

"And this," said the young man, as he turned the other picture to the light—"this is your mother."

Louisa and her mother both exclaimed this time. There was no mistaking the likeness. The cabinet photograph had been exactly copied.

"Louisa, you go and get my purse," said Mrs. Weimer. The agent was already folding up the covers which he had taken from the portraits. Mrs. Weimer laid her hand on one. "Not the frames," she said in German.

The young man shook his head. The jaunty air which he had worn on the occasion of his first visit had departed. He seemed a little frightened. When Louisa returned he was standing with his hand on the latch of the door.

"Give him his money, Louisa," said Mrs. Weimer. Perhaps—but no, they would never give away such beautiful frames.

Louisa counted out the money. The young man no longer looked pleasantly at her; in fact, he did not look at her at all. Suddenly he made an incoherent remark.

"What did you say?" asked Louisa.

"The pictures are three dollars and ninety-eight cents apiece. The firm have decided they cannot sell any without the frames. This is a fine quality of gilt, warranted never to wear off."

"What did you say?" demanded Louisa again.

"The pictures are three dollars and ninety-eight cents. The firm ——"

"What does he say, Louisa?" asked her mother.

"He says the pictures are three dollars and ninety-eight cents."

"Tell him we do not want the frames. We only want the pictures."

Louisa repeated her mother's words.

"But we cannot sell the pictures alone. The firm have decided ——" The young man seemed to be taking a firmer hold on the door-latch. He had never delivered crayon portraits before, and was new to the tricks it involved. "You see, you'll have to have the frames anyhow. You might as well have them now." He spoke as though he were reciting from a book. "They are the finest gilt on the market. The firm ——"

"What does he say, Louisa?"

"He says we will have to have the frames anyhow, Mom," translated Louisa wistfully.

"I cannot afford frames. I did not order frames. You tell him to take his pictures from the frames and take his money."

"She says," repeated Louisa, "you shall take the pictures from the frames. We don't want the frames."

"But the firm ——" The young man paused and laid a hand on each of the pictures. "The firm have decided that you cannot have the pictures without the frames."

"We cannot have the pictures without the frames!" repeated Louisa. "Are you not in your right mind? We ordered the pictures for ninety-eight cents. It was nothing at all said from frames."

"I cannot help it. The firm ——"

"What does he say, Louisa?"

"He says he will not give us the pictures unless we take the frames."

Mrs. Weimer's black eyes blazed.

"What will he do with them?"

"Take them along back with him, I guess. Perhaps he will show them round like the others."

"No, he will not."

"You are sure you do not want the pictures?" put in the young man. He had opened the door, then grasped the pictures again. "Both the pictures are very fine. You will never get any better ones. They ——"

Louisa was aware that the pictures were fine.

"You are a cheat," she said suddenly.

The young man flushed from the top of his high collar to the top of his white forehead.

"I can't help it," he said angrily. "The firm ——"

"What does he say, Louisa?"

"He says he will take the pictures away. He is a cheat." Louisa could scarcely keep her voice steady.

"Good morning," said the young man. He was trying vainly to push the door open without letting go of the heavy frames. The latch had dropped, however, and he was powerless.

"What will you do with the pictures?" asked Mrs. Weimer in German.

"I do not understand. I do not speak German. I must go. Good morning." He set one of the pictures against the wall for an instant, lifted the latch, seized the picture again, and pushed the door open with his foot.

Louisa burst into tears. It seemed as though she could not let the beautiful pictures go. Nor was her disappointment less keen than her mother's. Mrs. Weimer saw the young man's shoulders move through the door, and she stepped forward.

"Not so fast, young man," she said in German.

The young man winced as he felt his arm caught as though in a vise. He started to draw it back, and Mrs. Weimer opened the door wide enough for his arm and the picture to slip back. He was in a moment again wholly within the kitchen. There he flattened himself against the wall. Before him stood Mrs. Weimer, her finger shaking in his face, from her lips pouring a torrent of incomprehensible words.

"Let me go," he said weakly.

Mrs. Weimer talked on.

"I do not understand you. Let me go. I am English. It is not my fault. The firm ——"

Mrs. Weimer caught the drift of his words. She had forgotten that he could not understand her. Her speech had all been wasted. For a moment rage held her silent; then her eyes shone.

"Louisa, you go into the front room," she commanded, in German — Mrs. Weimer did not lose her presence of mind in the greatest of excitement— "and shut the door."

Louisa obeyed, weeping.

"Now!" Mrs. Weimer surveyed the figure before her, from the wavy black hair which Louisa so admired, down to the tips of the pointed shoes. She wondered how any one could have such feet.

"You ——" She looked around to be sure Louisa had closed the door. "You are a humbug, that is what you are," she said in plain Millerstown English. "You are a fraud, you are a cheat, you ought to go to jail, that is where you ought to go. That is where you will anyhow come some day. You ought to be thrashed."

The young man put up his hand as though to ward off some physical violence.

"Let me go," he said again.

"You are a thief," said Mrs. Weimer. "It isn't such trash in all Millerstown like you English. You are a robber and a swindler. You ——"

"I will let you have them for ninety-eight cents," he said desperately. "Only let me go." His hands were busy with the fastenings which held the pictures to the frames. "I'll take them out. I can't help it. The firm ——"

"Don't talk from the firm," said Mrs. Weimer sternly. "Here is your money."

The young man received the money in a shaking hand, then lifted the heavy frames.

"G-good morning," he faltered.

"Good-by," said Mrs. Weimer meaningly. "Good-by for always." Then she opened the door into the sitting-room.

"He is gone, Louisa," she said in German. "And here are the pictures. I settled him. And, Louisa" — she thrust her hands deep into her mixing-bowl as she spoke— "now you see what it is like to be English."

THE COUNTY SEAT

Originally published in the May 1908 issue of *The Atlantic Monthly*

"I and Ollie and the children are going to—" Susannah Kuhns bent over the salad dressing which she was stirring on the stove as though it, for the moment, took all her attention. Meanwhile, she watched her guest, stout, placid Sarah Ann Mohr, from the corner of her eye. Then she brought out the rest of the sentence with a jerk,— "are going to move."

"T-to m-move!" exclaimed Sarah Ann. "When, Susannah? Where will you move? Why?"

Susannah straightened her back, so that it reached the perpendicular and passed it.

"We are going to move to Allentown. I am sick of Millerstown. Millerstown is too slow and too dumb and too Dutch."

"But you will get homesick."

"Homesick! For why should I get homesick? I have my man and my children by me. It is no one in Millerstown I care for."

"Ach, Susannah!" Sarah Ann's eyes filled with tears. She was accustomed to Susannah's tempers, but she had never seen her in such a mood as this.

Susannah poured the dressing over a bowl of crisp endive and set the empty pan in the sink with a slam.

"Oliver is sick of working at the furnace. He will go back to his carpenter trade, and in Allentown he will get two dollars a day. And my children will talk English, and when they are through with the school, they can work in the factory."

"But your things will get broken when you move."

"Pooh, that is nothing. I will just get new ones."

"But who will lead the singing in the church!"

"I don't care."

"Won't you never come back?"

"Never to live."

"But *why* do you go?" Not even a plague could have driven Sarah Ann from Millerstown. "You have here your nice house, and it is where you have always lived, and—"

"I hate it," said Susannah. Then she went to the screen door. "Dinner!" she called.

Sarah Ann rose as the two children, Oliver and Louisa, came in.

"But you won't be here for the Sunday-school picnic or the Christmas entertainment."

Little Louisa answered, her fat cheeks almost cracking with scornful laughter.

"We can go every day to a Sunday-school picnic or a Christmas entertainment in Allentown."

"Don't you sass Sarah Ann," said their mother sharply. "This afternoon you are both to help me."

For the next few days, Sarah Ann went back and forth from her own house to the Kuhnses, with tears in her eyes. Susannah gayly declined her help. She scrubbed the floors, she whitewashed, she washed and ironed and packed. Her husband helped her with the heavy things, and in the intervals of work, wandered miserably about.

"Do you want to move to Allentown, Oliver?" Sarah Ann asked him.

"Yes," answered Susannah. "He does."

Susannah sang while she worked. She had led the singing in the Evangelical Church since she was a girl, but she would sing there no more. There were great churches in the county seat, churches with stained-glass windows and crowds of people, where they would want her to sing. Then cross, unwilling Oliver would be glad they had moved.

Nearly all Millerstown came to the station to say good-by. Susannah told them again and again how glad she was to leave, and they listened to her silently. She seemed already like an alien.

"I should not be surprised if it is by and by no one at all in Millerstown," she said laughingly. "Millerstown is too slow."

The eyes of the other women met. They thought Susannah Kuhns had lost her mind. Sarah Knerr joined them just before the train pulled out.

"You forgot your soap-kettle, Susannah," she said breathlessly. "I ran all the way to tell you. It hangs yet in the back-yard."

"I am not going to take it," answered Susannah.

"How then will you boil your soap?"

"I ain't going to boil soap. I buy my soap."

"And won't you make apple-butter, and won't you butcher?" gasped someone.

Susannah did not deign to answer. She looked back as the train started. It would have been a relief to jump up and down in her seat as the children were doing. Oliver told them sternly to "shut up and sit still," but they were too excited to obey.

The crowd at the station in Allentown seemed to their unaccustomed eyes great enough for a holiday or fair week. Susannah could hardly follow Oliver, with Louisa hanging from one hand, and Ollie trying to escape from the other.

"Mom!" he shrieked every few minutes. "Look once here!"

At the big skeleton of the Powers building, Oliver stopped them.

"There is where I shall work at two dollars a day," he said.

In spite of himself there was pride and excitement in his voice.

A little farther on he stopped at the opening of a narrow street.

"It is here where we shall live."

"I see where," screamed little Ollie.

Their goods were being unloaded before the door of a tiny frame house.

"I too," echoed Louisa.

Oliver unlocked the door and let them in.

"It is not a nice house," said Louisa.

"It *is* a nice house," reproved her mother sharply. "It is while it is not yet fixed up that it don't look so fine." Then she waved back her husband, who came into the room with a roll of carpet in his arms. "Don't bring it in yet. Did you think I should put down carpet when the house is not yet cleaned?"

"But I must go Mondays to work, and Sundays it is no working, and I can only help to-day and to-morrow."

Susannah looked at him.

"Do you mean I should put down the carpets before it is everything washed up?" she asked.

"No," he answered, meekly. "But you shall wash this room first, and then I can move the things right aways in."

"Begin at the bottom to wash the house!" gasped Susannah. "And go up! I guess not. I begin at the top, like always."

She went upstairs and looked about her. She could not suppress an exclamation of horror. Then she went to the head of the stairway.

"You shall just come up once and see how dirty it is here," she called. "It will be dinner till I make the garret done."

"But the things? Shall they stand all the time out?"

"You can watch them so it don't anybody carry anything off," she replied. "I—" The rest of her sentence was lost in the sound of a stiff scrubbing-brush, pushed swiftly across rough boards.

In an hour, Ollie tiptoed softly to the bottom of the garret stairs.

"Mom," he called, in a wild whisper. "Come down, come down!"

"What is the matter?" asked Susannah in fright.

"The police have got Pop."

Susannah sprang to her feet, upsetting the pail of water. Little Ollie got nimbly out of her way as she flew.

"They'll take him to jail," he cried.

"Oliver!" called Susannah. "I am coming."

When she reached the front door she saw Oliver nervously moving the boxes. A policeman had paused in the middle of the street for a last word.

"They must be off in half an hour," he said.

Husband and wife scarcely spoke until the things were safely inside.

"This awful thing shall not come to Millerstown," said Susannah. Then she thrust a broom into Oliver's hands. "Go out and sweep a little off."

Susannah clattered back into the garret. Brisk worker as she was, it was dinner-time before she finished.

"I tell you it is clean for once," she said proudly, as they sat on the boxes, eating the lunch which Sarah Ann had put up for them. The children had begged to take theirs out on the back step, but she would not let them. "And have all the neighbors know what we are eating! I guess not."

"But at home, they know always what we have for dinner," said Louisa.

"This is home," corrected their mother sternly.

After dark, they put up two beds by the faint light which came in from the arc light outside. They had no oil for their lamps and they were afraid to light the gas. The children were already asleep on a pile of carpet, and did not wake when they were put to bed.

An hour later, Susannah lay down beside her sleeping husband. There had been one rug which she had not been able to clean before she left Millerstown, and she had taken it down into the yard and had beaten it there. She closed her eyes with a great sigh of relief. Then she sat up. What was this noise? She was conscious for the first time of the rush of trolley-cars, the roll of carriages, the tramp of feet. Somewhere in the neighborhood a band was practicing. She jumped with fright at the sound of the church clock striking eleven.

"We must get used to it," she said to herself. "It cannot be so quiet here like in Millerstown."

She was not to get used to it that night, however. She tossed and rolled, determining that she would not hear the clock strike again, then listening and waiting for it. She grasped her husband's arm in terror, when, toward morning, half a dozen men sat down on the doorstep to finish a noisy argument.

It was dawn when she fell asleep. The milk-carts and market-wagons had begun to come in from the country, and rattled noisily by, and for a while she was conscious of them in the midst of her drowsiness. Then, slowly, they faded away.

She woke to wonder uneasily where she was. The first stroke of the church clock recalled her to herself. It was five o'clock, and she must get up. No, it was six. How had she happened to sleep so long? And Oliver was asleep. She laid her hand on his shoulder. As she touched him, the clock struck again. Seven! It could not be.

"Oliver!" she called.

"Yes, yes," he answered crossly.

Then, deliberately, the clock struck eight.

She lay staring, until the stroke had died away. To sleep until eight o'clock on a day like this, when on ordinary days she got up at five!

All morning she worked feverishly, only stopping to comfort Ollie, who came in crying because some boys had struck him.

"Nobody would hit me in Millerstown," he wailed. "I don't like it here. We don't get nothing good to eat."

"You just wait once till to-morrow," his mother consoled him. "Then we go in the church and the Sunday-school, and I make a good dinner."

Susannah was growing impatient. She could not find places for her furniture. The kitchen was so narrow that the old-fashioned settle which her mother and grandmother had owned could not go there at all. Where would Oliver rest when he came home tired? And where would the children play? Besides, her fire would not burn.

She grew more and more surprised as the hours passed, that no one came in to help. When people moved in Millerstown, everybody helped. She thought with a proud catch in her throat of the morrow. Then her neighbors would be glad enough to know her. Then they would go to church, and she would be invited to sing in the choir. She hummed the first line of "Ein feste Burg," then burst into song, her high, shrill soprano dwelling on the notes as long as she could hold them. By the time that she reached the second stanza, there was a rap at the door. She answered it quickly. A little girl stood on the step.

"My mother says you shall please stop singing. She wants to sleep. She takes a nap in the afternoon."

"Takes a nap!" repeated Susannah, her astonishment for the moment holding her wrath in check. "Is she sick?"

"No, but she takes a nap. And you shan't holler."

She looked up impertinently as she went off the steps.

"'Ein feste Burg ist unser Gott,'" began Susannah as loudly as she could, before the door closed. Then she saw across the street the blue coat of the policeman, and thought better of it. They would see. Hollering, indeed!

She looked with proud satisfaction upon her family when they were ready for church the next morning. The house, too, was in fairly good order, although there were many things yet to be done. It did not occur to her to touch any of them to-day. She had never heard of any one working on Sunday. Her eyes widened with astonishment as she listened to the quick strokes of a hammer in the next house.

When the Millerstonians visited the county seat, they went invariably to St. Peter's Church. There the morning service was still held in German, there was a German prayer-meeting, and a German Bible class. Susannah would have preferred to go to an English church, but Oliver would not hear of it.

The usher showed them to seats well toward the front. The children stared round the great church. Once when a purple gleam from the rose-window fell on little Louisa's dress, she gasped with delight. Her mother had no eyes for anything but the organ and the choir. The organ seemed large enough to be a church itself. She saw with astonishment that there were only four singers in the choir. Surely they would be glad to have her.

She joined in the singing with a heartiness which made those near her turn their heads. She was pleasantly conscious of their attention.

Afterwards the preacher spoke to them in the vestibule. He hoped they would come regularly to church. They would be glad to have the children in the Sunday-school and their father and mother also.

"She will sing in the choir," said Oliver proudly. "She sang always in the choir at home."

The preacher hesitated for a second. Susannah's singing had reached even to him.

"It is very kind," he said. "But we have a quartette. We pay them."

"I don't ask any pay," said Susannah quickly.

"But you see these people are engaged for the year," explained the preacher. "Their voices are trained. They—"

"But she would be willing to sing along with them," persisted Oliver. "Wouldn't you, Susannah?"

Susannah's face had grown very red, and her black eyes snapped. She had always been quick to take offense.

"No," she said sharply. Then she seized Oliver by the arm. "Come on home." There were tears of vexation in her eyes. "He might 'a' said right-aways he didn't want me," she said.

She would not go with Oliver and the children to Sunday-school in the afternoon, but she went with them afterwards for a walk. She did not enjoy it. There was no place to go. In Millerstown they went to see either her parents or Oliver's parent, and always stayed for supper.

The children were restless and uneasy all the evening. There was no place to sit outside but the doorstep, and Susannah would not let them sit there for an instant. It was too close to the woman who said that she "hollered," and to the woman who put down her carpets on Sunday. In the morning she would take them to school, then they would have more to interest them.

Oliver started away at six o'clock. The county seat had not yet grown so English that it had forgotten its habit of early rising. Then Susannah called the children and gave them their breakfast. At eight o'clock she took them to school. Little Louisa cried as she came away. She had heard the whispered "Dutchy" from the girl in the next seat and she did not dare to pinch her as she would have pinched Sarah Knerr.

Nor did Ollie like his seat-mate any better. He hailed him, also, as "Dutchy," and when Ollie, who was braver than Louisa, kicked him, he told the teacher, and Ollie spent the rest of the morning on the platform.

His mother declined to listen to their complaints. She had spent all her patience on the stove. What would Millerstown say if it knew that she burned her pies on the bottom and that they were raw on top? She had swept the pavement three times, and still it was dusty.

Worse than all, however, had been the insult she had received from the lips of an impertinent resident of the county seat. She had discovered that with the limited storage-room in the house, they would have no place to keep one of her greatest treasures, a large feather-bed. She was trying to decide what to do with it when there came a rap at the door. The young man to whom she opened it told her that he had come to buy old clothes, old furniture, old anything.

"It is here a bed," she answered slowly. It would be hard to part with it, but it would doubtless yield the price of a new lounge for the parlor.

The young man stared at it. He had never seen a feather-bed.

"I might carry it somewhere on a vacant lot," he said. "I'll carry it away for a quarter."

For an instant Susannah could not speak. Then, —

"A vacant lot!" she repeated. "Had you never no grandmother what had such a bed? My grandmother she made it herself, out of her own feathers. What for a bed did your grandmother have, then?"

The young man put his head on one side. Whether he resented the implication cast upon his grandmother, or whether he merely desired to be sarcastic, it was hard to tell.

"How would you like to sleep on somebody else's grandmother's dirty old bed?" he asked, and was gone.

"You lie!" cried Susannah after him. It was not exactly a logical response to anything the young man had said, but Susannah did not care. It showed her wrath and defiance.

It was small wonder that she had little patience for the children's complaints.

"You will just have to get used to it," she said to little Louisa. "I cannot be always fighting."

Little Louisa burst into tears.

"I want to go back," she wailed.

"Louisa!" began her mother; then she stopped, staring at the doorway. Her husband, whose lunch-pail she had packed that morning, and whom she had not expected to see before night, stood before her. He looked pale, and sick.

"What is the matter?" she faltered. "Have you got it somewheres, Oliver?"

He sat down on the nearest chair.

"He wants I should work on such a scaffold what hangs out of the window. I fall and break my neck. I won't break my neck for nobody. He said I could go."

Susannah looked at him, helplessly.

"But if you don't work, how shall we get along?"

He shook his head but did not answer.

"What shall we do, Oliver?" she repeated.

Little Louisa looked up at her, her fat face swollen with crying.

"Mom —" she began.

"Be quiet," said her mother.

Oliver lifted his head.

"Perhaps, Susannah, if we —"

"Be quiet," said Susannah to him, also. "I am thinking."

"Listen, Mom!" Ollie began to dance up and down. "Let us go —"

"You hold your mouth, or I send you to bed," said Susannah. She stood in the middle of the little kitchen, her arms akimbo, a frown above her black eyes. No one would ever have thought that she was really in the choir-loft of the Millerstown Evangelical Church, looking down into the admiring eyes of Millerstown, which, gasping, let her take all the high notes alone.

"Louisa," she said sternly, "if you are quiet and Ollie is quiet and you Pop is quiet, we will go back."

THE OLD RÉGIME

Originally published in the October 1908 issue of *The Atlantic Monthly*

It was the opening day of the Millerstown school, already two weeks after the usual time. The Virginia creeper along the pike was scarlet, the tall corn in the Weygandt fields—tree-high, it seemed to the youngest children—rustled in the cool September wind, and above, the blue sky arched, immeasurably distant. It seemed good to be getting back to winter tasks. The fields and hills were not quite so friendly as they had been a week before.

For generations there had been a wild scramble for seats on the first day of school. The earliest comers had first choice, and the triumph of having secured a "back seat" was not entirely shattered by the later and punitive shifting which befell them.

No one but the teacher could unlock the front door. There was another way to get in, however, through the dark cellar, where at recess Oliver Kuhns played "Bosco, the Wild Man, Eats 'em Alive," as his father had done before him, then up through a trap-door to the schoolroom. Lithe, swarthy Oliver was usually first, then the two Fackenthals and Billy Knerr and Jimmie Weygandt and Coonie Schnable. Coonie might be found bartering his seat to a later comer on as good terms as he could make.

This morning, as usual, it was the rear seats which were at a premium. Ollie Kuhns flung himself into one, and the next three boys followed. Then there were no more "back seats." A wail arose. Coonie Schnable, the stingy, offered five cents and was jeered at; Jimmie Weygandt offered five cents and a new knife and was more courteously denied.

"*You* don't need a back seat," Oliver assured Jimmie. "But if Coonie sits where Teacher can see him, he gets licked like sixty."

Coonie grew pale under his summer's tan.

"He don't like my Pop, nor none of my family," he said.

"My Pop says he used to lick them till they couldn't stand," offered Ollie cheerfully. "But he learned them. My Pop would 'a' had him back this long time if the others would."

The older of the Fackenthals took from his pocket a short tin tube. Plastered on it was a ball of putty.

Little Ollie laughed. He threw himself back in his seat, his feet on the desk. It was only seven o'clock and the teacher would not be there till eight.

"You just try once a putty-blower," he warned. "You will easy see what you will get!"

Twenty years before, the children's fathers and mothers had gone to "pay school." It was before the establishment of the public-school system, and the pay-school was kept by Jonathan Appleton, of New England origin and Harvard training. Why he had come to Millerstown no one knew. It never occurred to Millerstown that he might have displayed his learning to better advantage in a larger and more cultivated town. They regarded the thirty dollars a month which he was able to earn, as a princely salary for a man who spent his summers in idleness and knew nothing about farming. Jonathan seemed to like Millerstown, — at least he stayed for twenty years, and married a Millerstown girl, little Annie Weiser, who adored him.

"You might 'a' had Weygandt," her mother mourned. "For what do you take up with a *school-teacher?*"

Little Annie only smiled rapturously. To her Jonathan was almost divine, and her marriage a beatitude. Like most perfect things, it was also short-lived. Two years after they were married, Annie died.

In another year, Jonathan lost his position. By that time the Millerstown school was free, and to the minds of many Millerstonians there was good reason for changing.

"Here is Jonas Moser," said William Knerr. "He is a Millerstown boy. He has gone for three years already to the Normal. He has all the new ways. They have there such a model school, where they learn them all kinds of teaching. The Normal gets money from the state. We pay our taxes. I think we should have some good of this tax-paying. We did n't pay nothing for Teacher's schooling. And he is pretty near a outlander."

"Boston is n't outland!" said Oliver Kuhns. "And Teacher" (Appleton was to retain the title, if not the position, till the day of his death) "Teacher is a good teacher. He learned all of us."

"He whips too much."

Oliver laughed. "I bet he whipped me more than all the rest put together, and it never did me no harm. I am for having an English teacher like him. Jonas Moser don't talk right yet, if he is a Normal. I don't want my children taught Dutch in the school."

Appleton laughed when he heard they were talking of electing Jonas Moser.

"Nonsense!" he said. "Why, Jonas Moser can't teach. His idioms are as German as when he left, his constructions abominable, his accent execrable."

"But they say he has methods," said Oliver uneasily. "They taught him in such a model school."

"Methods!" mocked Appleton. "A true teacher needs no methods."

"Yes, but—but—" Oliver stammered. Jonas Moser was leaving no stone unturned to win votes. It was as though he had learned electioneering also at the Normal. "But could n't you say you had anyhow *one* method? He has books about it. He brought them to the school-board."

"Nonsense!" said Appleton.

When he found that they had elected Moser, he was at first incredulous, then scornful. He said that he was going away. But he did not go. Perhaps he was too old or too tired to find another position. It might have been Annie's grave which kept him there.

When, at the end of the year, Jonas Moser resigned, half of Millerstown wanted Appleton back. But there was another Millerstown boy ready to graduate at the normal school, who claimed his turn and got it. He resigned at the end of a month, giving his health as an excuse. It was true that he looked white and worn. Unfortunately for the children's disciplining, he did not tell what anarchy had reigned. It might have been, however, that the school-board suspected it.

"We will now try a Normal from away," said William Knerr. "These children know those what we have had too well."

Presently Appleton's scorn was succeeded by humility. He applied for his old position and was refused. It would have been an acknowledgment of defeat to take him back. He grew excited, finally vituperative.

"Your school is a pandemonium," he shouted, his black eyes gleaming above his long, white beard. "The children are utterly undisciplined. They learn nothing. They are allowed to speak your bastard German in the schoolroom. They have no manners. You have tried seven teachers. Each one has been worse than the last."

"Well, anyhow, the children ain't beaten black and blue," said William Knerr sullenly.

"Beaten black and blue!" repeated the old man. "Oliver Kuhns, did I ever beat you black and blue?"

"No, sir," answered Oliver heartily.

"Or you, James Fackenthal?"

"No, sir." James Fackenthal was burgess and he sometimes consulted with Appleton about the interpretation of the borough ordinances.

"Or you, Caleb?"

"No, sir."

Then he whirled round upon Knerr.

"And you I never whipped half enough."

It was, to say the least, not conciliatory. The eighth "Normal" was elected.

After the ninth had come and gone, they engaged a tenth, who was to come in September. On the opening day, he did not appear. Instead came a letter. He had decided to give up teaching and go into the life-insurance business. Oliver Kuhns pointed out the fact that the letter was dated from the town whither the last teacher had gone.

"I guess he could n't recommend Millerstown," Oliver said.

"I know another one," said William Knerr. "He lives at Kutztown. I am going to-morrow to see whether I can get him."

Oliver Kuhns rose to his feet.

"I make a move that we have Teacher come back to open the school, and stay anyhow till the Normal comes," he said.

Ten minutes later, he was rapping at Appleton's door.

Appleton had been reading by candlelight and his eyes blinked dully.

"The school board wants you to come back," said Oliver tremulously. "You shall open school in the morning. We are tired of the Normals. We want you shall learn our children again."

The old man took off his spectacles with a wide sweep of his arm. Oliver seemed to see the ferrule in his hand.

"I shall be there. But I do not *learn* the children, Oliver, I *teach* them. Write it on your slate, Oliver, twenty times."

Oliver went off, grinning. The old man could joke. He had expected him to cry.

The teacher was up as early as the children the next morning. He dressed with care, looking carefully at one shirt after the other. Finally he chose one whose rents would be hidden by his coat and waistcoat. Then he donned his high hat.

All Millerstown saw him go, his coat-tails flying in the breeze, his hat lifted whenever he caught the eye of curious watcher behind house-corner or syringa-bush.

"Good-morning, Miss Kuhns!— How do you do, Miss Kurtz?— Not coming to school, Miss Neuweiler?" Such ridiculous affectation had always been his. He had called the girls "Miss" before they were out of short dresses.

The children, too, saw him coming; not Oliver and the Fackenthals or Billy Knerr, because they did not dare to leave the seats they had chosen, but the rest of the boys and all the girls.

"His coat-tails go flipperty-flop in the wind," giggled little Katy Gaumer. "We never had no teacher with a beard before."

"He looks like a Belsnickle," laughed Louisa Kuhns. "I ain't going to learn nothing from such a teacher."

Thus had they been accustomed to discuss the various "Normals."

Ollie bade Louisa sharply to be still.

"You ain't going to behave that way for this teacher," he said. Then he swung his feet down to the floor, describing a wide arc through the air. The other three boys did the same, and there ensued a wild scramble from window to seat.

"This is my seat!"

"No, my things are already on it."

"My books are in that there desk."

"It don't belong to neither of you."

"Give me my pencil-box."

"This is my slate!"

The roar of sound had not lessened when the door opened behind them. They did not hear him come in, they would probably not have heeded if they had. Then, suddenly, Coonie Schnable, quarreling with a little girl over a pencil-box, was bumped firmly into a seat, and Daniel Wenner into another. By that time, after a moment of wild rushing about, peace reigned. Each seat was occupied by a child, every voice was silent, every eye fixed upon the front of the room.

This was a new way of opening school! Usually the Normals had said gently, "Now, children, come to order." They had never begun by seizing pupils by the collar!

Teacher walked to the front of the room, and laid his hat on his desk. He was smiling pleasantly, and though he trembled a little, the light of battle was in his eye.

"Good-morning, children."

With one accord, they responded politely. None of them had been taught the manners which he had "learned" their parents, but perhaps they had inherited them.

Teacher did not allow a minute for the respectful silence to be broken.

"We will have the opening exercises. We shall sing,—

> Oh, the joys of childhood,
>   roaming through the wildwood,
>   Running o'er the meadows, happy and free."

"And remember to say *joys, j-o-y-s*, not '*choys*.' Who starts the tune?"

"We did n't sing last year because the boys always yelled so," volunteered Louisa Kuhns, anxious to be even with Oliver.

"To the corner, Louisa," said Teacher grimly. "Next time you want to speak, raise your hand."

It was a long time since a pupil had obeyed such an order as that. Nevertheless, Louisa found her way without difficulty.

"Now, who can start this tune?"

A hand went up timidly.

"I guess I can, Teacher."

"Very well, then, Katy. Ready."

Teacher stood and watched them while they sang. Then he read a chapter from the Bible. His predecessors, having respect for Holy Writ, had long since omitted that part of the opening exercises. There was not a sound till he had finished.

"Oliver Kuhns, are you in the first class?"

Ollie raised a respectful hand.

"Please, Teacher, my Pop is Oliver. I am Ollie. Yes, I am in the first class."

"In what reader are you?"

"We are nearly through the Sixth Reader."

"We will go back to the beginning. Second class, where are you?"

Katy Gaumer lifted her hand.

"We are in the middle of the Fourth."

"You also will go back to the beginning. Third class, come up to the recitation benches and take a spelling lesson."

Teacher opened the third-class spelling book at random.

"Elephant," he began. "Tiger." He laid the book down. "Why don't you write?"

The class sat as though paralyzed.

"We aren't that far," ventured Katy.

"It is the second lesson in the book," said the teacher. "Go to your seats and prepare it."

It was a sad morning for the Millerstown school. In the bottoms of their haughty hearts the children still cherished a faint desire to do well. Appleton's angry amazement at their ignorance mortified them. They felt dimly, also, that he was grieved, not, like the Normalites, because he had to teach such unruly children, but for the sake of the children themselves. There was not a sound in the room, except the impatient movement of a foot when the correct answer would not come.

After recess Katy Gaumer raised her ever-ready hand.

"Please, Teacher, I think we know our lessont."

"Lesson, Katy. You may come out." A diligent scratching responded to "elephant" and "tiger."

"Jagu—" began the teacher, then suddenly paused, his face pale. At the door stood a strange young man. Behind him came William Knerr and Oliver Kuhns. William advanced bravely into the room, Oliver remained miserably at the door. If he had only told Teacher that he was only engaged temporarily! But he had not dreamed that William Knerr would find a teacher so soon.

Appleton saw that resistance was useless. At William Knerr's first word, he passed the spelling-book politely to the young man, and walked toward the door.

"I couldn't help it, Teacher," said Oliver, as he and William Knerr went out.

Teacher turned to look back. He seemed to take the measure of the Normal with a glance of his keen black eyes.

"May I stay and visit your school?" he asked humbly.

"Certainly," said the young man jauntily. What an unprogressive school-board this must be, who would tolerate such a teacher, even as a substitute! "Do you teach Phonetic Spelling?"

"No," answered Teacher, as he sat down. "Just plain spelling."

"Oh!" said the young man. He saw also that the copy had been put on the board in a fine Spencerian hand. That would have to be corrected. His Model School taught the vertical system.

"Elephant," he began.

"We have already spelled elephant," said Katy Gaumer saucily. "And tiger."

The Normal smiled at Katy. He had determined to make the children love him.

"Jagu—" he began. But it seemed that jaguar was not to be pronounced. A ball of something soft and wet sailed past the Normal's head. He pretended not to see. Inwardly he was debating whether the moral suasion recommended by his text-book was the proper method to apply. He decided to ignore this manifestation.

"Jagu—" There was a wild clatter from the corner of the room. A pencil-box had fallen to the floor.

"Jagu—" began the Normal again.

There was another crash. The Normal saw with mingled relief and regret that the old white-bearded man had slipped out.

"Boys!" he cried nervously.

"Boys!" mocked some one in the room.

The Normal started down the aisle, realizing, not without some fright, that the time for moral suasion was past. He thought it was Oliver Kuhns who had dropped one of the pencil-boxes.

"Go home," he commanded sternly.

The children were startled into absolute silence. Hitherto, even the Normals had tried to keep their inability to control the school from the knowledge of Millerstown. This one would send them out, to publish his shame. Billy Knerr laughed.

"Go home with him," commanded the teacher.

There was a wild roar of sound. Every child was shouting, the little girls and all. Oliver and Billy sat firmly in their seats. They did not propose to be cheated of any sport.

"Boys!" began the Normal. Then he became desperate, incoherent. "If you don't go out, I'll get somebody in here who will go out."

There was another shout, and the boys sat still.

"Well, stay where you are, then," the Normal commanded. "But you must obey me."

He wished that the old man would come back. There was something about the stern glitter in his eye which made it seem impossible that he could ever have tolerated such wild uproar as this. He did not guess that the old man was still within call. If he had walked to the window, he might have seen him, sitting on a low limb of the apple tree, grimly waiting.

It is not necessary, and it would be painful, to describe the last half-hour of the morning session of the Millerstown school. Those who have plied putty-blowers and thrown paper wads and dropped pencil-boxes and given cat-calls will be able to picture the scene for themselves. Others will not credit the most accurate description. When the Normal went down the path at noon, he was consulting a time-table. Unfortunately for any plans of escape, William Knerr met him, and instead of going to the station, he went over to the hotel for his dinner.

"He is coming back," said Ollie Kuhns.

As Ollie prophesied, the Normal did come back. But he did not come alone. William Knerr was with him, and the burgess and Danny Koser and Caleb Stemmel, all members of the school board, and, all but William, bachelors, ignorant of the ways of children.

The Millerstown school was not to be thus overawed. Billy Knerr behaved well enough, for his father's eye was upon him; but a frenzy seemed to possess the others. What did Oliver Kuhns care for the burgess and Danny Koser? They were neither his mother nor his father. What did Katy Gaumer care for Caleb Stemmel? There was a chuckle from the back of the room, and a quick turning of Directors' heads. Every eye was upon a book. Perhaps, thought the Directors, they had imagined the chuckle.

The Normal announced that they would continue the lesson of the morning.

"Elephunt," he began, forgetting his normal-school training.

"It is el-e-*phant*," corrected Katy Gaumer.

"*Tiger*," said the Normal in a terrible voice. There came a howl from the back of the room. It sounded as though the beast himself had broken loose.

The Normal laid down the book.

"Learn your own children," he said hotly. "I resign."

He walked down the aisle and out the door.

The laughing children looked at one another.

"He walked in one piece away," squealed Katy Gaumer, in delightful Pennsylvania German idiom, so long unforbidden in the Millerstown school. Then Katy looked up at the Directors, who gaped at one another. Perhaps she wanted to show how quickly feminine decision can cut the knot of a masculine tangle, or perhaps, woman-like, she welcomed a firm hand after months of liberty.

"Teacher's setting in the apple-tree," she said. "I can see his coat-tails go flipperty-flop."

THE GHOST OF MATTHIAS BAUM

Originally published in the February 1909 issue of *The Century Magazine*

All Millerstown loved a courting, and considered the details of village love-affairs as common property. Few wooings yielded such abundant food for thought and conversation as those of Savilla Marstellar, who, as a young widow, rich, good to look upon, and an accomplished housewife, had many suitors. To the eyes of Millerstown its eligible men seemed to divide themselves into two classes: those who wished to marry Savilla, and those who did not.

In the first class, Al Losch and Jacob Fackenthal were most favored by Savilla. Al was a stone mason, and Jacob a carpenter. Both were tall, strong young fellows, industrious and capable, even though the older women shook their heads and said they were wild.

The second class, so at least Millerstown thought, was composed entirely of one man, Christian Oswald, whose misogynistic principles were so fully accepted that no one dreamed of connecting his name with that of any woman. He was a bachelor, said to have at least ten thousand dollars in bank, a little man, as shy as Jake Fackenthal was bold, and physically as weak as Al Losch was mighty. Millerstown would have laughed had any one suggested Christian as a suitor for the hand of Savilla. For once, however, Millerstown had made a mistake. Christian Oswald adored Savilla from the top of her curly head to the soles of her slippered feet. He had scarcely spoken to her, however. Never was love more hopeless; never passion more skillfully hidden.

Just at the moment when Al and Jake had driven all others from the field, Savilla did something so foolish that Millerstown declared that both men would "throw her over." To begin with, she had been notified that she would have to give up the house in which she lived at the end of the month.

"What will you do?" asked her friend, Sarah Ann Mohr.

"I have a place," answered Savilla, calmly.

"But where?" insisted Sarah Ann.

"Aye; out where Matthias Baum lived. I will buy that house."

"Are you then no longer right in your head?" demanded Sarah Ann, while her glasses slid unheeded down her nose. "Do you then forget that old Baum hung hisself dead, and it is ever since a schpook?"

"I don't fear me for no schpook."

"What you say?"

"I said I did n't fear me for no schpook. I never did the old man anything. He can be thankful that I give his house a good name."

She swayed back and forth defiantly in her low rocking-chair, displaying an inch or two of white stocking above a low shoe. Sarah Ann gazed at her again. Somehow or other it did not seem quite respectable for a widow to wear low shoes.

"But, Savilla, it is out there so lonely."

"I am not afraid."

"And it won't nobody go to see you."

"Pooh! What do I care! They can stay away."

"Losch he is afraid of schpooks, and Jakie Fackenthal, too, he is afraid of schpooks."

"They can stay away," repeated Savilla, defiantly.

Nor were Sarah Ann's the only protests with which Savilla had to contend. Al and Jake besought her not to go out there to live. She had to hear again and again the sinister story of the place, and as she steadily refused to be frightened, she began to realize that her friends were looking at her askance, as if she had leagued herself with the mysterious powers supposed to reign there; all of which had the effect of setting the fair widow more firmly than ever in her own way. If Al and Jake were both afraid of schpooks, she had at last a means of deciding between them. Whoever braved oftenest the terrors of that lonely path should be rewarded with her heart.

The house stood on a little cross-road about a quarter of a mile from where the pike broadened into the village street. Back of it lay the fields and meadows of the great Weygandt farm, and in front, across a narrow road, a thick grove of locust- and chestnut-trees. The first object upon which one's glance rested, however, was a hickory, which swung far up against the sky, dwarfing the locusts near it into shrubs. From its lower branches hung ropes of wild grape-vines, which clasped the young shoots of Virginia creeper on the other trees, making a dim twilight even at noonday. Years before, the house had been the home of wicked old Matthias Baum and his brood of wilder and more wicked sons. They bore so evil a reputation that they had few visitors. Once, however, when old man Weygandt needed extra hands for the harvest, he ventured to seek them there. Walking across the fields at dusk, he climbed the fence into the yard. There seemed to be no one at home, and he peered curiously about among the great vines. Then suddenly he turned and dashed madly away. There under the great hickory-tree, shrouded by the vines, and swayed gently by the evening breeze, hung a ghastly thing. It was old Matthias himself, dead only a short time.

At first it was supposed that his sons had murdered him, until a tavernkeeper in the next county testified that they had spent the day in his barroom. Besides, old Maria Kutz declared that she had met the old man that afternoon at the cross-road and that he had carried a rope.

One dusky evening a few months later, when the members of the new Baptist church were returning from prayer meeting, a wildly running figure overtook them. It was Miltie Knerr, a nervous, timid boy. He sobbed and cried as they gathered about him.

"What ails you, Miltie?" demanded his brother.

At first they could distinguish only "old Baum" in the confusion of his speech. Suddenly old Maria peered into his face.

"Miltie," she whispered, "did he carry a rope along with him?"

At that, big fellow that he was, he flung himself into his brother's arms and cried aloud.

A few weeks later Billy Knerr's horse was stopped at the cross-road by "something white." Then some of the Weygandts saw a light in the deserted house, and the ghost was born.

Such was the dwelling in which Savilla had taken up her abode. Millerstown thought she had gone mad. No one, however, was so much disturbed as Christian Oswald, who, in spite of the fact that he was a member in good standing of the Jonathan Kuhns Baptist Church, had an abiding faith in schpooks. To see Savilla expose herself to the power of one so well authenticated distressed him beyond expression.

At first Al and Jake were as regular in attendance as they had been when Savilla lived in Millerstown's main street, and Savilla, who was touched by their devotion, did not notice how much earlier they came than heretofore, nor how much sooner they departed. Jake came always on Sunday and Wednesday evenings, and Al on Tuesday and Saturday. One dark and cloudy evening in September, however, Al did not appear. Then Jake, too, missed an evening, and the rockers of Savilla's chair beat a lively tune as she waited.

As the evening wore on, she herself pleaded guilty to a little nervousness. It was the time of the autumnal equinox, and the wind shrieked about the house. Suddenly, above the storm, she was aware of a whistle, a curious, tuneless succession of shrill sounds. She stopped rocking, terrified. But how dumb! A ghost could not whistle. Her hand was on the latch almost before the visitor knocked. Had Millerstown beheld the man who stood there, it would scarcely have believed its eyes. Christian Oswald keeping company with Savilla Marstellar! Did he dream of marrying her? It was certain that no man would brave the terrors of the Baum schpook unless his intentions were serious.

"Well, Christian, come quickly in out of the wet," said his hostess with cordial welcome.

For a moment the embarrassed Christian stood still, the rain dripping from his hat and from his black beard. Then Savilla put her hand on his arm and drew him forcibly within the door. He could not have come at a more propitious time. He would help to pass a long evening, and, better than that, he would help to soothe her wounded vanity. As for Christian, he had come not only from a veritable hunger to see her, but from a desire to protect her. He knew, as all Millerstown knew, that this was Jake Fackenthal's evening. He knew also that Jake sat calmly behind the stove in Aaron König's shoemaker shop.

Christian spent the evening in paradise. At first he listened to Savilla's cheerful monologue in an agony of embarrassment. Then, as her hot coffee warmed him up, and she brought out her raisin pie, he began to talk, and Savilla herself was surprised at his conversational skill.

"You must surely come again once," she urged as he departed, and Christian, though the hour was late, and the wind blew more fiercely than ever down the dark road, and the limbs of the great hickory threatened to snatch him up from the ground, gave no thought to any ghost.

Jake Fackenthal reported early the next morning.

"But I was mad because I could n't come last evening out," he said apologetically. "But Pop he had to go off, and Mom she is n't very for staying alone."

Savilla looked him over, six feet of shamefaced cowardice. "Mom" Fackenthal afraid to stay alone! Her lips curled.

"Everybody is talking from your living out here alone," Jake broke out angrily. "It is only one thing to do."

"And what is that?" asked Savilla, coolly.

"Get married."

"Yes, I have been for some time thinking of that. Al Losch —"

"Be dast with Al Losch! I mean to me."

"I tell you what I do." For a moment Savilla meditated. "You come out here four weeks from to-day, and I give you my answer once for all."

"And Al Losch, will you give him his answer, too?"

"I will treat each one alike."

Savilla had made up her mind that she would be courted no longer.

It was true, as Jake said, that Millerstown talked. She liked both men so much indeed that their fear of the schpook offended more than her own vanity. She was ashamed of them. She would give them one more chance. Four weeks from now it would again be the dark of the moon, and they would then have an opportunity to prove that their affection for her was greater than their fear of the schpook.

During the month which followed, neither missed an evening. Fortunately, it was a month of clear, still nights. Jake bragged openly that he was going to build a house before long, and that he would not live in it alone. When this was reported to Al, he said slowly: "Just you wait and see. Just you wait till after next Thursday."

Christian heard of his reply with consternation. Next Thursday! Had Savilla promised to marry him next Thursday? That could not be, for Jake was also looking forward to Thursday! At last he hit upon the right solution. She had promised to give them their answer on Thursday. He was in despair. On the Tuesday preceding the important day, he felt as though he could live no longer without sight of Savilla. He had never dared repeat his call. After nightfall, he made his way out to the cross-road. He knew it was Al's evening with her, but he hoped that Al would be frightened by the storm. It had grown cold, and the wet leaves that drifted down from the trees touched him uncannily on the cheek. The sky was black, and there was no light save a friendly gleam from Savilla's window. Guiding himself by this, he plowed on through the deep mud. He was tempted to try a whistle. Something warned him, however, to reconnoiter before making his presence known. There, in the big chair opposite Savilla, sat Al, in his hand a great wedge of molasses cake, on his face an expression of sublime happiness. For a few minutes, Christian watched him from the sloping cellar door up which he had crept, then he turned, and picked his way dejectedly out of the yard.

Before he had gone half-way to the pike, he heard a door slam behind him, and guessed that Al was leaving early. Horrified at the thought that he might be overtaken, Christian climbed up the slippery bank, over the fence, and crouched down behind a shock of corn in the Weygandt field. He trembled as he heard Al's rapid, heavy steps. He was evidently trying to cover the ground between Savilla's and the pike as swiftly as possible. Christian heard every footfall as he splashed through the mud and water, and smiled in tremulous delight as he thought of the mire which must cover him from head to foot. Then, as Al's dim outline became for an instant visible to the jealous watcher by the corn shock, something happened.

Al seemed to be rushing to meet some creature which whirled itself through the darkness to throw itself upon him. To Christian's frightened eyes, the thing was huge,—indeed it seemed three times as large as Al Losch,—and without bodily shape. The two figures, man and monster, rose and grappled with each other. Then again the dark mass whirled about on the ground. Christian could hear the swish of the mud as the horrible something pressed Al into it. The very ground beneath him seemed to quiver with the impact. Then the mass seemed to divide itself into two parts, and Al leaped up, and with a hideous shriek sped toward the village. The other lay still for an instant, then it, too, arose. Slowly, as Christian stared, its huge proportions seemed to dwindle, its vagueness assumed corporeal limits. Schpook or no schpook, it bore a remarkable resemblance to Jake Fackenthal. Then with a mad cry, "The schpook! the schpook!" it, too, fled villageward.

It was several minutes before Christian was able to gather himself together. Then, though the mud in the field was far deeper than that in the road, and as tenacious as glue, he stole quietly away among the corn shocks.

By morning all Millerstown was alarmed. Al Losch, coming home from Savilla's, had been set upon by a creature with more than human strength, which had well-nigh killed him. If any one did not believe it, they had only to look at him. His eye was black, his nose swollen, and he walked with a limp. Half a dozen persons described the encounter to Christian between his house and the Fackenthals'. Christian, who was better able than any one else to picture it in all its horror, said not a word.

When he reached the Fackenthals' shop, he listened in vain for sound of hammer or saw. Then he opened the door, only to start back at the sound of a rough exclamation from within.

"*Harrejä!* What do you want here?" It was Jake, who sprang to his feet from a bench on which he had been reclining. Then he sank back in a vain effort to suppress a dolorous groan.

"What ails you, then?" queried Christian, tremulously.

"Nothing," responded Jake, gruffly.

Suddenly the door was flung open, and Al Losch presented himself. Truly the schpook had done its work well.

"Have you a nagel-borer?" he asked.

Jake rose and went to find the gimlet. Al looked at the two men curiously. They were probably discussing his adventure.

"I tell you it was powerful," he said pleasantly.

"Boys,"—Christian's voice sounded like a mild echo of Al's deep bass, —"when will you get married?"

The two men turned and regarded him with amazement.

"What does it then make out to you when we get married?" Al demanded.

"I have something to say about it," faltered Christian.

"You have something to say about it?" repeated Al.

"Yes, I have. What would Savilla say when she knew you was afraid of schpooks?"

Al laid his hand on his black eye.

"I guess she won't have much to say when she sees this."

"What would she say when she knew it was no schpook?"

"What?"

"That it was no schpook?"

"It was a schpook. It is n't a fellow in the world could knock me so over."

"Yes, it is." The answer came not from little Christian above whom Al towered threateningly, but from the other side of the shop, where their host had sat down upon a nail-keg. "It was all the time me. I thought it was Wednesdays already, and I was running out there and we ran together."

For several long minutes no one spoke. Then Al turned again to Christian, who, though trembling, met his eye bravely.

"What does it make out to you that it was him," he demanded savagely.

"It is that if you don't do what I say, I will tell Savilla and all the people. You must promise you will not go before Friday out there."

"But I don't promise."

"Then I tell—"

"You better, Al," counseled Jake.

For a moment Al hesitated, then a sudden movement of Christian's sent him into a spasm of terror that he might tell.

"I promise," he said sullenly.

When he had gone, Jake turned and smiled at his guest. He had no idea how Christian had discovered what he himself had guessed soon after the encounter. Nor could he imagine a reason for the little man's sudden friendliness to him, unless it were a desire to see the better man win. He remembered what Al had for the moment forgotten, that Thursday was the day upon which the widow meant to accept one of them.

"He did slambang me powerful," he said reminiscently.

"I was in Weygandt's field. And—" Christian paused until he could control his voice. No amount of moral courage can make a man forget that his enemy weighs a hundred pounds more than himself—"and I want you should promise, too."

"I! I go where I like."

"Then I tell all the folks you thought it was a schpook."

"I did n't say I thought it was a schpook."

"Yes; but you did think all the same it was one. I heard you yell. *Himmel!* but you did yell!"

"I don't care," Jake blazed out. "I'm going out there to-morrow. Savilla will give me her word that she will marry me. And you better get pretty quick out here!" He was mad with his aches and pains, and furious at this little piece of impudence who dared dictate to him.

"Then I tell her how you yelled at the schpook, and she would not have you—no, not when the minister was ready to marry you."

Jake looked at him aghast. Well, he was still bound no more than Al.

"Well, I won't go," he said desperately. "But what is it to you?"

Christian, however, did not answer. His courage consumed by this last burst of eloquence, he fled wildly out of the door, around the corner of the shop, past the pig-stable, and out through the alley gate. Stiff as he knew Jake to be, he could not risk pursuit up that smoothly scrubbed board walk.

Jake stood for a moment in angry thought.

"Why need *he* care?" he said aloud.

Then as suddenly as Al had come upon him out of the darkness the night before, there flashed across his mind a possible solution. Could Christian Oswald, that black-bearded little monkey, think he could get Savilla?

"Christian!" he yelled. "Christian!"

But only the defiant crow of a rooster from the chicken yard replied.

The next evening Christian dressed himself in his best, and started out to Savilla's. It was an evening upon which the bravest schpook would scarcely have ventured forth, clear, starlit. Across the Weygandt fields drifted the strains of the "Mocking-Bird," played by the Millerstown band. A brisk wind had dried the road, and Christian's meditations were undisturbed by any necessity for watching where he stepped. As he went along, however, he looked down at the ground. Yes, there it was, a rough depression which looked as though it might have been the scene of a wrestling-match. He gazed solemnly at it, remembering the battle of the night before; then he lifted up his voice in triumph. The German Bible class of the Jonathan Kuhns Baptist Church, to which he belonged, had devoted its attention for several Sundays to the history of Abraham.

"And the vale of Siddim was full of slimepits," he quoted slowly in German; "and the kings of Sodom and Gomorrah fled, and fell there."

With that he went his way. He was not sure of winning Savilla, though thus far he had triumphed. Ach, no! He was not surprised that she seemed a little annoyed to see him. As the minutes passed, however, and neither Al nor Jake appeared, her demeanor changed. She had not heard of Al's adventure, and her eyes grew hard and bright as he told her. So Al really imagined that he had met a schpook! Christian said nothing about Jake. Their absence sufficiently condemned them both.

"What are all the folks doing this evening?" she asked finally.

"Oh everything is like always," he answered. "The band is playing." Then a sudden inspiration came to him. That it was a bald prevarication did not trouble him at all. "It was a lot of fellows at Aaron König's—Jakie and Al and some more. They were telling schpook-stories."

Savilla's eyes blazed. That settled them! But she would have her revenge. She turned radiantly to the little man who sat in throes of love and fright upon his chair. To-morrow, when they came penitent, pleading, she would have news for them. One man at least loved her more than he feared old Baum's schpook. Then as she looked at him she thought of his good nature, his irreproachable character, and—shall we whisper it?—his reputed wealth, and revenge seemed suddenly to lose the bitterness which had bred it.

"Christian," she said softly, winningly—"Christian, would you sooner have coffee or yeast beer? And I have fresh-baked molasses cake in the cellar, and Fastnacht cakes."

Then, though Christian knew it not, his suit was won.

ELMINA'S LIVING-OUT

Originally published in the February 1909 issue of
Lippincott's Monthly Magazine

"Elmina, hurry yourself. It is five o-clock, already!"
Elmina stirred, then opened her eyes.

"All right, Mom, I'm coming."

"Remember it is baking-day, Elmina."

"Yes, yes, I'm coming, Mom."

"And, Elmina, don't let nothing burn."

Elmina made a face at her pretty reflection in the glass.

"It is plenty apples fallen from the trees for a couple apple-pies. Do you hear me, Elmina?"

"Yes, Mom, I hear you."

Elmina slipped quickly into her clothes and ran down to the kitchen. She knew as well as her mother that there were six pans of rusk, at least half a dozen pies, and a fine cake to be baked that morning. Her mother had made the fire before she started out to weed the garden beds, and the rusk was soon in the oven. Then she ran out to sweep the porches and the pavement. As she came back she heard a shrill call from the garden.

"Elmina! Elmina! Don't let nothing burn."

Her lip curled angrily as she put the potatoes and ham on to fry. Then she covered the table with a red cloth and put the breakfast dishes on it, and replaced the cakes in the oven with a fresh batch. Presently her mother came in from the garden. A stranger would scarcely have noticed the resemblance between them. Elmina was straight and slender, her mother was stout, and her bent shoulders showed plainly the weight of years of strenuous housekeeping. Elmina's skin was fresh and rosy, her mother's tanned and dark. Elmina's eyes were blue, as were her mother's, but the difference between youth and premature middle age, between high spirits and weariness, made them as unlike as though they were a different shade.

"Did you do as I told you, Elmina?" Mrs. Fatzinger slipped off her overshoes and washed her hands at the pump.

"I don't know what you told me," answered Elmina sullenly. "I baked the rusk, and swept, and cooked breakfast."

"Well, you can bake the fine cake while I work some more in the garden. Only, don't burn it."

Elmina did not respond, and the meal was finished in silence.

"Now, Elmina," began her mother as she took the last bite of a piece of pie, "you must hurry redd off the table."

Elmina, like a naughty child, seized her own plate in one hand and her mother's coffee-cup, still half full, in the other.

"Elmina!" exclaimed her mother, and Elmina set the plate down with a slam.

"Bake first the cake, then you can wash the dishes while it bakes."

"What else am I doing?" demanded Elmina.

"And when the butcher comes you can get a beef-steak for to fry. It is enough money in the purse."

When Mrs. Fatzinger reached the garden gate she turned.

"Elmina! Elmina!"

"What?"

"Don't you let him give you no tough one, and watch him once when he weighs it."

"Shall I tell him it shall come from a cow or a pig?"

Mrs. Fatzinger began her weeding.

"The girls are no longer like they were when I was young," she said to herself. "I wouldn't dast to sass my Mom."

In the kitchen Elmina plied her egg-beater with an energy which threatened to demolish both beater and bowl.

An hour later Mrs. Fatzinger came in from the garden. Her face was a dull scarlet, even under her sun-bonnet.

"Hand me once a basin water out here, Elmina," she said. "I am too dirty to come on the porch."

Elmina swiftly obeyed.

"Have you baked the pies, Elmina?"

"Yes."

"Did you burn the cake, Elmina?"

Elmina appeared suddenly in the doorway.

"Mom!" she said explosively.

Mrs. Fatzinger looked up from the wash-basin, a huge cake of homemade soap in her hands.

"I have swept the pa'ment and the porches and cooked breakfast and baked rusk and fine-cake and pies, three apple, two latwerk [apple-butter], and four cherry pies, and washed the dishes. I will yet ice the cake and make dinner and redd up the kitchen and make the beds and cook supper and wash the dishes, and to-morrow ——"

"Elmina, are you not any more right in your head, that ——"

"And to-morrow I will scrub the pa'ment and the porches and the boardwalk and make breakfast and dinner and supper and the beds and wash dishes, and whatever it is yet to do. And Sundays the same. Mondays,

I hire out."

"You hire out!" repeated her mother dully.

"I hire out."

"Where, then?"

"I haf a place. Mantana Kemerer has a place for me where she works in Phil'delphy. Mantana gets five dollars. I get three."

"Would you believe such a lie, Elmina?"

"Yes, I believe it, and I am going Mondays."

For a second the two pairs of eyes regarded each other, steadily. Then Mrs. Fatzinger began vigorously to rub her hands.

"You'd better kill the chickens once, Elmina. Don't kill no young hens."

The screen-door closed with a slam.

Mrs. Fatzinger brushed her hair before the little glass on the porch.

"It is her Pop over again," she thought. "He was once crazy to go off when he was a boy. But he had such a bossy Pop. Elmina has no bossy Pop. And she likes to work. But she will go. It won't do no good to talk."

The tears came to Mrs. Fatzinger's eyes. Presently she called across the chicken yard:

"Elmina, wipe the hatchet off good or it rusts."

The prospective journey was not mentioned between them until Sunday evening, then Mrs. Fatzinger broached the subject.

"You can take some from my aperns. You don't have many dish-washing aperns."

"I ain't going to take no dish-washing aperns."

"Why?"

"I ain't going to wash no dishes. Mantana washes the dishes."

"Elmina Fatzinger! Are you, then, going to work in a hotel?"

"No. It is only four people in the family."

"I have lived many years in this world, and I have never heard from such a place."

Mrs. Fatzinger did not sleep well that night.

"It is something wrong at places where so much money is paid," she said to herself. "But if it isn't everything all right, Elmina will come home pretty quick."

In the morning she would not let Elmina help to get breakfast.

"Suppose you should cut you with the knife or get grease at your dress. You would look fine to go in Phil'delphy!"

Breakfast over, Elmina kissed her mother good-by.

"You write right aways home, Elmina."

"Yes, mom."

Elmina started across the porch, her eyes blinded by tears. She had not even said good-by to her "company girl," Linnie Kurtz. She almost wished that she were not going.

"Elmina! Elmina!" came a loud call from behind. "Mind you do your work right. And don't you go in no se-ater, and go always in the new Baptist Church. Mind you work like I learned you."

"Yes, yes," answered Elmina impatiently.

Mrs. Fatzinger went slowly back to the kitchen. There the first plate which she touched slipped from her hands.

"Now when that was china like some, it would 'a' broke into a thousand pieces," she said to herself as she picked it up. "Ach, I don't know why Elmina had to go to Phil'delphy."

Elmina found Mantana waiting for her at the train.

"Ach, Mantana!" she cried. "What am I so glad to see you! I did n't know it was so many people in the world like I saw this morning already. And streets and houses and trolleys! It is five times bigger than Allentown!"

"Of course," said Mantana. "Come now, we must hurry."

"Is she a cross one, Mantana?"

"No, not so extra. But you must look a little out."

"Is it any children?"

"Only a little girl. It is a Mister and a Missis and Mister's Mom and the little girl yet. Now"—she conducted Elmina through a narrow alley, across a tiny yard, and into a wide kitchen—"I take you up to her."

Mantana led the way into the upper hall. At the door of her mistress's sitting-room, a soft voice bade them come in.

"Mrs. Alexander, here is the girl what I told you about from Millerstown, Elmina Fatzinger."

Mrs. Alexander looked up from her desk with a smile.

"How do you do, Elmina?" she said.

While her new mistress finished her letter, Elmina looked about the beautiful room. They had a sitting-room at home, which was too fine to use, but it was very different from this. At home there was a Brussels carpet, and a centre table, and vases of dried flowers, and a great family Bible. Here in this room the polished floor was almost bare, and the few rugs deep and soft to the foot. There were books and pictures and plants, and, most astonishing of all, sunshine. Did not these wasteful people know that sunshine faded everything? And what kind of a housekeeper could Mrs. Alexander be that she was here at eleven o'clock on wash-day morning writing letters? At that point Mrs. Alexander laid down her pen.

"Have you lived out before?" she asked.

"No, ma'am."

"Mantana says that you are a capable girl. Can you sweep?"

"Yes, ma'am. I did always the sweeping at home."

"And wait on the table?"

"Yes, ma'am." Who in the world couldn't do that?

"You may come down-stairs with me now."

Elmina followed her to the dining-room.

"Ain't they got no table-cloth?" she thought as her eyes fell on the gleaming table. "With all their grand things?"

She paid close attention to Mrs. Alexander's directions.

"Here is the linen, and here is the silver. The glass is in that cupboard and the china in the pantry. Here is the slide opening into the kitchen." She pushed back a little slide, and Elmina saw Mantana stirring something on the stove. "Now, if you need any help, ask Mantana. You will have time to dust the dining-room before you set the table."

Elmina set about her work at once. As she wiped the chairs and tables, she began to feel uneasy. Would any one pay her such high wages for such easy work? Well, if her wages were not forthcoming, she would go straight back to Millerstown. Presently she opened the door into the kitchen.

"Hello, Mantana!"

"Hello! Shall I show you once how to set the table?"

"Well, I guess not!"

"All right," said Mantana, half-offended.

Elmina shut the door and went busily to work.

"Here is nothing but tidies," she said as she opened the first drawer, which contained Mrs. Alexander's luncheon doilies. In the next she found a table-cloth, and, spreading it, laid the first plates that she could find, face downward upon it. "Now knives and forks. Whew! Silver ones. My, but they are dull! Now I hunt the napkins. I wonder if they use, every day, napkins."

She contemplated the table with great satisfaction.

"That is first fine! I guess I call Mantana to see. No, I won't. She acts as when she was mad over me."

Mantana had not enjoyed having her advice declined.

"They think it is easy to hire out in Millerstown," she thought. "Now Elmina can see."

Presently the sliding door opened.

"Is dinner ready?" Elmina demanded.

"Is your table set?"

"Yes. Slide it in."

"You tell them that lunch is ready first."

Elmina shut the slide with a bang. This was a funny place where you called folks before you put dinner on! She went out to the hall.

"Dinner!" she called. "Dinner!"

A sound near her made her turn. There in the parlor sat Mrs. Alexander, the little girl, and an old lady. Elmina smiled at them.

"I did n't know you were already here," she said.

The eyes of the two ladies met. There were some things which the new maid would have to learn.

When she reached the dining-room Mrs. Alexander paused, and her hand went out as though for support. For an instant she was shocked beyond the possibility of speech. Beside her own place, with her elbows on the table, sat Elmina.

"I put my place at this end so I could run easy out," she explained smilingly.

Mrs. Alexander's eyes took in at a glance the turned-down plates, the crossed knives and forks. Then they returned to pretty Elmina.

"I think ——" she began. "Will you send Mantana to me?"

"Ain't it right?" demanded Elmina, springing to her feet. Had she put on the best table-cloth? Or, perhaps, they did n't use napkins every day. "You shall come in," she said to Mantana. "They came and looked at the table and they act as when they were crazy."

Mantana glanced into the dining-room.

"Elmina Fatzinger!" she said.

To Elmina it seemed an hour until she returned.

"Perhaps you will not be so saucy again when I say 'Shall I show you how?' Go look once at the table before I call them."

Elmina took a furtive peep.

"Tidies!" she exclaimed. "And no table-cloth! Well, come on." Elmina started toward the table.

"She said I should wait to-day on the table."

"Well, you can. But I dare eat dinner, I guess."

Mantana paused, the bouillon cup shaking in her hand.

"Elmina, do you think we dare eat with them?"

"Aye, of course. Where else should we eat?"

"We dare n't eat with them. We eat afterwards here."

"We dare n't eat with them! Are we, then, not good enough?"

Mantana did not stop to answer, nor did she offer further conversation until lunch was over.

"We shall now eat. Then she wants to see you."

"She need n't think she can send me off. I go so away."

"She ain't going to send you off. She will show you how we do things in Phil'delphy."

"Pooh with Phil'delphy! I am not at all for Phil'delphy. Are we, then, going to eat in the kitchen?"

"Yes, we are going to eat in the kitchen," answered Mantana sharply. "Where do you eat at home? In the parlor?"

Mantana sighed as she washed the dishes.

"I might 'a' known it. The Millerstown folks are too dumb. I will now have to have an Irish one working by me again."

Elmina found Mrs. Alexander in her sitting-room. Mrs. Alexander had concluded that what she at first took for impertinence was merely ignorance. She determined to explain very carefully the reasons for the various domestic rules.

"Sit down, Elmina," she said graciously.

"I think I stand," responded Elmina.

"I was sorry that I had to go out before lunch. I thought Mantana could tell you anything you wanted to know."

"No Fatzinger had ever yet to learn anything from a Kemerer."

"But Mantana knows our ways. Now we will start afresh, and I will tell you about your work. We have breakfast at eight o'clock."

"I don't think you need ——" Elmina paused. Breakfast at eight o'clock! She would like to hear more of these remarkable arrangements.

"But first I will show you your room."

"I don't think you need to," said Elmina. "I ain't going to stay in Phil'delphy."

"But Mantana said you were so anxious to come."

"I was once. But it is here too high up."

"Too high up?"

"It is too stylish."

"Are you afraid you will have too much work?"

"Well, I guess not! You ought to see the girls in Millerstown work once, baking, and milking, and cleaning, and butchering, and making soap! And whitewashing and gardening yet! It is much harder work in Millerstown." In the vehemence of her speech Elmina forgot her dignity and sat down in a rocking-chair.

"What is it, then?"

"I don't like to eat in the kitchen. I don't mean because it is the *kitchen*. We eat always in the kitchen at home. But I think I am good enough to eat with anybody."

Mrs. Alexander concealed a smile.

"Of course you are. But then you could n't wait on the table. When your mother employs some one to help her about — about butchering, does not she expect them to do as she says?"

Elmina laughed.

"I guess not. Billy Knerr helps with the butchering. Nobody would dare tell him anything. And he sits down at the table."

"But here it is different," said Mrs. Alexander helplessly.

Elmina rose and held out her hand.

"I guess no Fatzinger ever *had* to work out. I am now going back to Millerstown. I will now say good-by. Say good-by to Gran'mom and the little girl for me. And when you ever come to Millerstown you must come to see us."

Mantana made no comment when Elmina said she was going home.

"I go along to the cars," she said.

"You need n't," responded Elmina curtly.

"Anybody what comes all the way to Phil'delphy and goes the same day home needs some one to look after them," said Mantana grimly, as she put on her hat.

She hurried Elmina along, dragging her from before trolley-cars, and bidding her "hurry yourself."

"It is easy seen that slow Millerstown is the only place for you," she said pleasantly.

"What do you think the folks will say when I tell them you are living with folks what don't let you eat with them?" asked Elmina.

"I haf four hundred and seventy-five dollars in the bank. Millerstown may say what it likes."

She bought Elmina's ticket, and had her baggage rechecked.

"He will have a fine time this evening!"

"Who?" asked Elmina.

"Mr. Alexander, when she tells him of the crazy one that was to-day here from Millerstown."

The train started, and Elmina was denied the privilege of responding.

~ ~ ~ ~ ~

Mrs. Fatzinger washed the dishes very slowly that evening.

"I don't think I go this evening out on the front steps," she said to herself. "I go straight in my bed. No, I don't." She paused. "When I don't go out, people will think something is wrong about Elmina's going away."

Linnie Kurtz joined her on the step.

"I think Elmina might 'a' told me she was going away," she said in an aggrieved tone. "I hope she comes soon back."

"Yes," said Mrs. Fatzinger. Then her lips set themselves in a firm line. She saw inquisitive old Maria Kurtz approaching.

"Good evening," said Maria. "Is it so that Elmina has gone off?"

"Why, yes."

"It is pretty sudden, this going off."

Linnie Kurtz saw Mrs. Fatzinger's lips tremble.

"Well, Maria," she said, "did n't *you* know she was going? Has something happened for once that you did n't know?" Linnie was conscious of the gratitude in Mrs. Kurtz's eyes. "And" — the color in Linnie's cheeks deepened; she seemed to look through old Maria and down the street — "and Elmina said if she did n't like it she was coming right aways home."

Mrs. Fatzinger sighed. If only Linnie's kind invention were true! If only —— Then Mrs. Fatzinger leaned forward, her face brightening to all her daughter's youthful charm.

"Well, Elmina!" she cried. "Did you come home?"

"Hello, Mom," said Elmina cheerfully.

When Maria had gone home Elmina told her story. Linnie Kurtz was there, and "Mom" Fackenthal and Mrs. Billy Knerr.

"Tidies on the table for to eat off of!" repeated Mrs. Billy.

"And no table-cloth!" said Mrs. Fatzinger.

"And Mantana wears a little cap with lace at it."

"That does lots good!" said Elmina's mother. "Give me a sun-bonnet."

"Ach, it is n't for sun. It is for style. And" — Elmina had kept the most astounding news for last — "she dare n't sit down with the folks to eat. She stands and holds a little waiter."

There was a chorus of incredulous exclamations.

"It is for sure true," asseverated Elmina.

"Well, I would n't stay at such a place. I give you right to come home," said Mrs. Fackenthal, as she rose.

"And I," said Mrs. Billy and Linnie together.

When they had gone Mrs. Fatzinger laughed uneasily.

"I guess you will sink your Mom is a poor housekeeper. My schnitz and knöpf, what I made, I fed to the chickens, and there is a grease spot on the floor like the dish-pan."

"Ach, I guess not quite so big," answered Elmina. "What am I so glad to get back to clean Millerstown! And what am I so tired of travelling round all day doing nothing!"

THE COVERED BASKET

Originally published in the July 1909 issue of *The Pennsylvania-German*

Susannah Kuhns sat upon the edge of Sarah Ann Mohr's bed, her foot swinging angrily. Beneath her stiffly starched and immaculate white apron was an equally stiff gingham apron, below that was a slightly mussed "dish-washing" apron. In her excitement she was carelessly wrinkling all three.

"Do you **want** to be murdered, Sarah Ann?"

Ponderous Sarah Ann was slowly and carefully wrapping in three towels the church-book, left to her by her father who had been a preacher. She was going on a short journey to the house of her brother in South Bethlehem, and she was about to put the church-book in its usual hiding place, her upper bureau drawer.

"I would hate to have anything happen to this book," she said, placidly. "It has all the church records for fifty years. Ellie Lichtenwalter's Mom couldn't a' got her pension if it wasn't for this book, and Fackenthal, he—"

Susannah interrupted furiously.

"I am not talking about the church-book. I am talking about Venus Stuber and his robbing. Millerstown is all alike." Last evening I said to Jim Weygandt that Venus should be put to jail, and Jim laughed and said he was a 'institution.' "No," I said, "he is not a institution, whatever the dumb thing is, he is a thief and a scalawag and a **lump**. I'll put him in jail."

Sarah Ann smiled. Ollie would not put his worst enemy to jail, even at Susannah's command. Venus Stuber did nobody any real harm. It was true that he appropriated chickens and garden produce and fruits, both large and small, but then he never tried to conceal his thefts. It was only the night before that Sarah Ann had called melodiously from her window, "You can take a few onions, Venus but don't you step on my young peas!" Tall, slouching, heavy-jawed Venus — Venus, indeed! — had waved his hand at her across the moonlit garden. He needed no such warning, he was always careful. He knew the location of every row of young peas in Millerstown. Sarah Ann tried to present this extenuating circumstance, but Susannah would not let her say a word. Upon this subject Susannah would not listen to reason.

"I don't let the children go out scarcely any more." Sarah Ann smiled again. The children were hardly ever at home, excepting for meals. "And you'd better lock your things up good, Sarah Ann. I'll watch while you're away, and if he does anything—"

Sarah Ann straightened up from her packing.

"Susannah, I will not have Venus Stuber put in the jail for taking my things. If anybody tries to put him in the jail for taking my things I will say I gave them to him." She met Susannah's blazing eyes quite steadily.

"All right, Sarah Ann Mohr. All right." Susannah was so angry she could scarcely speak. She went furiously down the steps and over to her own house, while Sarah Ann, for the first time since Susannah lived next door to her, went to the railroad station alone, and climbed into the train without Susannah's cheerful goodbye and wave of apron.

A few minutes later Susannah started across the street to the store. In her heart she knew that Venus would commit no serious crime, but having assumed a certain position, she would not depart from it. It did not improve her temper to see Venus leaning against the maple tree in front of her own door.

"Good morning, Susannah," he said, lazily. Venus was always good-natured.

"You'd better clear out." Susannah was like an irate terrier, barking at a sleepy and indifferent mastiff. "You are just looking for something to steal."

"Why, Susannah!" Venus still grinned. "I never stole nothing from you but three beets. But if you don't look out, I will."

"You just try it once! Clear out, now!"

Venus moved to the next maple tree.

"Sarah Ann don't care if I lean against her tree."

"Sarah Ann is away and I am in charge, Pack off!"

Venus went lazily.

As though she were carrying out a game with herself, Susannah stubbornly insisted, in spite of her husband's jeers, in laying a trap for Venus in the little covered alley which separated her house from Sarah Ann's.

"You are not right in your mind," said Oliver with marital frankness.

Susannah shut her lips, and went on, piling one chair upon another and a dishpan and two pails on the upper chair. She almost hoped that thieves would come. In the middle of the night when the barricade clattered down to the brick pavement, the excited voice with which she awakened Oliver was almost joyful.

"I told you so! Oliver! Venus is after Sarah Ann's things!"

Oliver flew down, willingly enough, and Susannah followed. The chair and the pans had fallen, but nothing else was disturbed.

"It was nothing but a cat," cried Oliver, angrily. "Is it not enough that I have to work all day without chasing cats at night? Piling chairs so that I shall be wakened in the night! What do you care if some of Sarah Ann's garden stuff is taken? She don't."

"I don't care if her whole house is stolen."

"For what do you care, then?"

"I don't want my children murdered in their beds."

"Pooh!" Sleepy as he was, Oliver managed a derisive laugh. "You are surely not right in your mind, Susannah."

Susannah awoke in the morning in a still worse temper. Sarah Ann with her placid "I thought Venus would n't do nothing," would be more than she could endure. She had succeeded in convincing herself now that Venus would steal from houses, just as he stole from gardens. She was positive that he had tried to get into Sarah Ann's house, if they had been a little quicker, they would have caught him.

She dressed, tied on her "dish-washing" apron and her smooth gingham apron, put the draughts on the stove, and then ran, — Susannah never walked — out to sweep the pavement. As she entered the little alley, a shadow darkened the other end. Whether it merely passed the opening of the alley, or whether it issued from the alley itself, she could not be sure. She quickened her steps. Some one might easily have been in Sarah Ann's house all night.

To Susannah's expectant eyes, the sight of Venus Stuber, sitting calmly on her own doorstep, was no surprise. Beside him stood a large basket, not open to the daylight, as Venus usually bore his spoils homeward, but covered with a lid of thin boards, tied down with cord.

Susannah's first impulse was to shriek for help. Then she remembered Oliver's unreasonable anger. If she could only get the basket into her own hands! What it contained, she could not guess. Venus lifted it as though it were heavy and it was large enough to contain a little child. She remembered fearfully the tales she had heard of Charlie Ross. But Venus had come from Sarah Ann's and there were no children there. She walked slowly across the pavement.

"What have you there, Venus!" Honey is no sweeter than Susannah's voice.

Venus grinned.

"Don't you wish you knew, Susannah?"

"Let me see once, Venus." She approached a little nearer, going as warily as though he were a chicken which she meant to sacrifice for dinner.

"What have you in your basket?" she asked again.

At that, Venus's patience suddenly failed, and with it the respect with which he treated by day those from whom he stole at night.

"Shut up," he bade her, and was gone.

For an instant Susannah stared at him, and as she stared, curiosity and alarm gave place to triumph. She had been right. Whatever Sarah Ann's loss was, she would report it first to Oliver. Then when they came to tell her, Susannah, she would laugh, and tell them to go to see Venus Stuber.

Meanwhile, not a word would she say.

It was a busy morning, and she was so occupied until dinner time that she had not a moment in which to speculate about what it was that Venus had taken. When dinner was over, and Oliver and Louisa had rushed out to play with the little Knerrs, she began to wonder what Sarah Ann owned that was so small and so heavy. Sarah Ann had neither jewels nor silver. But Sarah Ann did have,—Susannah grew weak and faint as she remembered—Sarah Ann had what was far more valuable than jewels or silver, the church-book. And it was she who had told Venus Stuber that Sarah Ann was away!

All this flashed through Susannah's mind as she stood motionless beside the dinner table. There was nothing so valuable in all Millerstown as the church record. Long since, the preacher had advised Sarah Ann to have it kept in the safe at the squire's office, and Sarah Ann, encouraged by Susannah, had refused. Its hiding place was known only to Sarah Ann and Susannah. Was it, could it have been that which Venus carried in his covered basket?

Susannah crossed the yard, took Sarah Ann's key from its hiding place between two bricks, and went into the house. As she climbed the stairs to Sarah Ann's room, her knees shook, and she stepped awkwardly upon her "dishwashing apron," which slipped off unnoticed. Then she opened Sarah Ann's upper bureau drawer and peered within. The church-book was not there!

Her first impulse was to rouse Millerstown and organize pursuit. Then, as she went slowly down the steps, a better plan occurred to her. She would go to Venus's cabin and get the book, and she would not say anything about it until Sarah Ann had been a little frightened. She had suffered. Sarah Ann might suffer also.

Without washing the dishes, without performing the post-prandial ceremony of chasing the flies from the kitchen and darkening it, she started to the mountain, carrying with her a pail, ostensibly to gather blackberries. She looked about her a little uneasily as she made her way up the overgrown wood road. The door of Venus's cabin stood open, but there was no other sign of his presence. Susannah went boldly into the little house and looked about her at the dirt and confusion. The basket stood in the middle of the floor, beside it lay the boards which had covered it. There was an untidy bed in one corner, and a stove in another. Susannah's first glance showed her that if the church-book were in the house, it was in the bed.

Unpleasant as the task was, she pulled off the dirty coverings. Then she looked in the oven, she even raked out the ashes of Venus's fire. The book was not there. If Venus had burned it, he had performed the task thoroughly. Susannah set her steps homeward, going a little more briskly than she came.

Gradually, as she went down the mountain road, cold fear beset her. If she had only told some one her suspicions! She could hear Oliver's "**Gott im Himmel!** why did n't you say something, Susannah!" Then she would answer, "But I did wake you, and you were cross," and Oliver would say, "But you did n't tell me the church-book was gone, Susannah!"

Perhaps she had overlooked some hiding place in the cabin. She stopped, meaning to return. But it was too late now. Venus might come home, and Venus might murder her. She would go back to-morrow. If only Sarah Ann had not come home!

Sarah Ann however had come. Had Susannah been at home, she might have seen her, five minutes after her arrival, rush as swiftly as her great size would allow, out of her house and across to Susannah's.

"Susannah!" she had called, pitifully. "Susannah!" Sarah Ann held no hurt remembrance of their parting, or if she did, the present fright swept it from her mind. When Susannah did not answer, she hurried to the house of the Lutheran preacher, and walked into his study unannounced.

"**Para (Pastor)**," she said, trembling. "**A-ach, Para!**"

The preacher started up in alarm, and began to pour out a glass of water for Sarah Ann.

"What is wrong, Sarah Ann? Sit down, sit down!"

Sarah Ann motioned the water aside.

"The church-book is gone!"

"The church-book is gone! Since when?" The preacher gasped.

"Since I came home, already. I was visiting my brother in South Bethlehem. He had the paralysis. I kept it in the bureau drawer. Nobody knew but Susannah. It is gone! It is gone!"

"I warned you, Sarah Ann. Have you any idea who took it?"

"Nobody in Millerstown would take it," wailed Sarah Ann. "I found a strange apron on the steps, I—" Sarah Ann's mouth suddenly dropped open. An unbelievable suspicion forced itself into her mind.

"Was it Susannah's apron?" asked the preacher, cleverly.

Sarah Ann clasped her hands.

"**Ach, Para**, don't say such a thing. Susannah can go everywhere in my house, and I don't care. What would Susannah want with it?"

"The book is very valuable, Sarah Ann," reminded the preacher. There was keen rivalry among the Millerstown churches. "Susannah is not a

Lutheran. Human nature is human nature. Now," he rose and put on his hat. "We will go to the squire."

Sarah Ann rose also, her face purple. Not all the church-books in the world could recompense her for loss of faith in Susannah.

"We will not go to the squire," she stammered. "I—I will go home and look again. I—I—Perhaps it is there. I will look again."

"If anything happens to the book, it will be partly your fault," said the preacher, stiffly. "It is a public trust."

"Yes," agreed Sarah Ann. "But I will go and look again."

When she reached her own porch, she sat down weakly in the rocking chair. She would wait for Susannah. Susannah would help her search. And, presently, Susannah came, and with head lifted proudly,—or at least so it seemed to Sarah Ann—went into her own kitchen without even glancing across the dividing fence. Sarah Ann cried. It was a terrible thing if Susannah were guilty. It was worse, if for the first time in ten neighborly years, Susannah were seriously angry.

In her own kitchen, Susannah, whose head was turned not in pride, but in deadly fear, met her husband.

"Where were you all afternoon?" he asked, a scornful eye on the uncleared table. He had been hunting her from garret to cellar.

"I—I went to—to fetch blackberries."

"Where are they, then?"

"It did n't give any." She started as she remembered her pail. She must have left it at Venus's cabin. She began to talk wildly. "I am going to make a good supper, Ollie, I am going to make flapjacks, I—" She realized with a thankful sob that Ollie had gone out.

In the morning she started again to the woods. It had rained and the paths were slippery. She had not slept and her head ached. Venus had apparently not come home. She repeated frantically her search of yesterday, and went thoroughly over the neighboring ground. There was no sign of the book, and she forgot all about her pail.

Shivering with fright, she went home. She remembered Sarah Ann's thousand neighborly kindnesses. Sarah Ann had but one fault in the world, she was too kind. And why did Sarah Ann not discover her loss? And how should she ever confess that she had allowed Venus Stuber to rob Sarah Ann of her dearest treasure?

The next day, she made another hurried visit to the woods. Her search was in vain, and, determining to go at once to Sarah Ann, she started down the road. Then, suddenly, hope flashed upon her. Perhaps Venus himself had returned the church-book. He had never been known to return anything, but he might have concluded that the book was worthless to him but sufficiently valuable to others to bring him into the long-threatened jail. That afternoon, if Sarah Ann went out, she would go over and see.

Hurrying along a little more cheerfully, she saw a crowd before her door. Had they—had they found out?

"What is wrong?" she demanded.

"Little Ollie fell from the grape arbor," some one answered. "No, no, Susannah, he ain't hurt. We thought he was and we sent for his Pop, but he only hit his nose, and—"

Susannah hurried in. The injured Ollie had already vanished toward the Knerrs, but his father was there, stern and reproachful.

"Where do you go always?" he demanded, furiously.

"For mint tea." Susannah lifted the bunch she had hastily gathered. How she hated to lie!

Oliver looked at her with horror and amazement. He knew that she was not telling the truth. Without a word, he went out of the house and across the fields toward the furnace.

Susannah walked slowly to the door behind him. Oh, what a relief it would be to call him back and tell him! But first she must see whether Venus had returned the book.

She watched that afternoon till Sarah Ann went out, then she stole across to her house. Venus might have dropped the book into the cellar window which opened on the street, she would look there first. The cellar was dark, she felt her way about, touching each spot where the book might have fallen. It was not there. Newly disheartened, she made her way back to the kitchen. There in terror, she began to cry. Sarah Ann was just coming in the door.

"Why, Susannah," she said, quite naturally, thinking that Susannah meant to make up, and had come a'borrowing.

To Susannah's ears it was an accusation.

"I tried to catch him," she cried. "It was Venus Stuber stole it. I saw him—" She was sobbing wildly.

"Why, Susannah!" Sarah Ann was too astonished to move. She was suddenly thrust into the room by the opening door. Oliver Kuhns came in, his face scarlet. Over his shoulder leered Venus Stuber, who seemed to be enjoying some huge joke. Oliver looked at them for a moment, at Susannah, weeping on her knees at the head of the cellar steps, at Sarah Ann, who stood gasping.

"What have you been doing. Susannah?" He said, roughly.

"Nothing," sobbed Susannah. "Nothing. Venus Stuber, he—"

Oliver took her by the shoulder. In his hand was the pail she had carried on her first journey to Venus's cabin.

"Venus Stuber says you've been stealing from him. He says you've been ransacking his house. He watched you three times."

"Stealing! I stealing! From Venus Stuber!" No one but Venus seemed to appreciate the humor of the situation. Venus laughed aloud. Susannah turned to Sarah Ann, who had always been her friend.

"Sarah Ann, do you believe I would steal?"

Now Sarah Ann became incoherent.

"I never told anyone but the preacher, Susannah. I never believed it. He put it into my mind. And I would n't tell the squire, even if it was the church-book. I—"

"You thought I stole the church-book," said Susannah, slowly. She was trying to make herself understand the words. Oliver turned pale. Angry at Venus's story, he had merely meant to frighten her. He had supposed it was only her desire to prove Venus a thief which had made her go to his cabin. Now they had plunged into possibilities of trouble which terrified him. Even Venus's face had lost its usual grin.

"No, I never thought so," sobbed Sarah Ann. "But you were the only one in Millerstown who knew where I kept it. And your apron was on the steps, and—"

"When did you miss the church-book?" asked Oliver, heavily.

"When I came home. I would have told you but I could n't find Susannah, and I would have given her her apron, and I would have told her everything, but she was cross over me. And when I found it, I would have told her, but—"

"Found it!" gasped Susannah. "Did you found it?"

"Why, I put it in the flour barrel, Susannah, the last thing, and then I forgot where I put it. It is here, Susannah. It is here. All the time it is here."

"Here," repeated Susannah.

It took Sarah Ann a surprisingly few seconds to go upstairs and down.

"Look once, Susannah," she cried.

But Susannah did not glance at the worn covers, she crossed the room in a bound and seized Venus Stuber by the arm. Oliver stared at her, mystification and relief alternating on his round face. Susannah shook Venus.

"What did you have in your covered basket?" she cried, furiously.

Venus looked down at her, grinning. He did not approve of such curiosity, and he had a well developed sense of humor.

"Don't you tell anybody, Susannah," he said. "If anybody asks you, you say you don't know. When I want the people to know, I leave my basket open, Susannah."

THE EXILES

Originally published in the October 1909 issue of ***Harper's Magazine***

In spite of the separation of Pennsylvania German Millerstown from the political life of the State, it brimmed in crises with political and martial feeling. When the Civil War broke out, the railroad had just been completed, and on it travelled thousands of soldiers from New York to the South. The engines stopped at the water-tank, and thither repaired the Millerstonians, large and small. Never had they seen so many persons, never had they heard such light talk of life and death, never had they felt so lifted out of themselves.

Presently the Millerstown Band enlisted bodily, and afterward half a dozen young men — a Fackenthal, a Kuhns, a Knerr, a Mohr. The only one who did not come home was Calphenus Knerr, who was of all most needed. His young wife was too ill to be told of his death and the bringing home of his body. It was not until weeks later, when she was able to take her sturdy boy into her arms, that she guessed the truth from Mary Ann Kuhns' face.

The baby was from the first too much for her. He was far too heavy for her to lift; it seemed impossible that so tiny and frail a creature as Ellie could be the mother of so rosy and splendid a boy. He looked like his father from the hour he was born, and grew each year to look more like him. Of course he was spoiled. He had example — Ellie was a good and pious soul — and precept, but enforcement with the rod was lacking. Mary Ann Kuhns offered to whip him, her arms having daily practice on mischievous young Oliver, and Ellie would not speak to her for a year. Henry Hill offered also, just after Ellie had declined to marry him, and to him Ellie never spoke but once again. Gradually her love for the boy blinded her to all else in the world — to the goodness of her lifelong friends, to her own needs; it made her forget even his father's grave. One evening, when the boy did not come home to supper, she omitted her weekly journey to the cemetery, though the flowers were already gathered and standing in the cool cellarway. Callie did not come home till eight o'clock. He had been up on the mountain with the boys. He neglected to say that they had played truant. At the end of the month he deceived his mother about his report, insisting that the teacher had forgotten to give him one. Then he forged Ellie's poor, crooked little signature to deceive the teacher. The next month he had not even the grace to try to hide his absences, and he laughed at his mother's protests. Staying out of school did not seem to Ellie a very serious offence. He knew already much more than she did, and more than his father had known.

"He is just a boy," she said to herself, not perceiving that he was in every way a little worse than other boys, more cruel, more headstrong, more lazy, just as he was more handsome. "By and by he will be a gardener like his pop, and everything will be all right."

But Callie refused to learn to be a gardener. He began to stay away overnight; then he did not come home for weeks at a time. He boasted of the places he had seen.

Ellie was now no longer deceived. Indeed, all Millerstown's prophecies of evil did not equal her anticipation. Several Millerstown girls smiled upon the boy—that was a fresh source of terror to his mother, who knew that he would keep faith with no living being. Her shoulders were already bending, expectant of new disgrace. And still she loved him, she prepared her best bed for him, she lay awake listening for his step, she gave him almost all of her widow's pension and her little income.

One evening she sat on the doorstep in the dusk, hoping that he might come home. It was early summer, the cool air was filled with the scent of honeysuckle. Her whole soul yearned for the boy. At sound of a brisk step on the rough brick pavement, her eyes strained ardently into the dusk, her heart leaped. The step came closer, she heard a voice speaking to her, she saw—*Ach Gott!* what was it she saw!

When she came to herself, she lay on the settle in the kitchen, and the boy was dashing water into her face. He wore a blue suit, buttoned to his chin, and a little visored cap.

"I thought it was your father," she cried, faintly. "Why do you wear those clothes?"

"Hush, mother," answered the boy, "the neighbors will hear you. I have enlisted in the army."

Ellie shuddered.

"No, no, no."

"Yes, I have, mom. I just came home to say good-by."

"Is there a war?" whispered Ellie.

"No; but the pay is pretty good, and a man sees the world."

"But if a war should come?" she faltered. It would be useless to forbid him to go; he would not obey her.

Terror-stricken as she was, pride strengthened her, intoxicated her. At last Callie had grown up; he was braver and better than all the boys in Millerstown; he was his father's son. During her agony of disappointment over the boy, she had begun to remember his father, who, during his life, had never failed her. She thought of him the next morning, when Callie went to church with her, Millerstown gaping with admiration and amazement. It was then that she spoke to Henry Hill.

"Callie is going to be a soldier like his father."

~ ~ ~ ~ ~

The boy did not write often to his mother. His company was sent far from his own Pennsylvania German section. Ellie thought of him daily, hourly, and prayed for him, that he might resist temptation and remember his God. He was soon invested in her mind with all the splendid qualities of his noble young father. Gratitude filled her heart; she grew stronger; she went about among her friends; she bloomed like a girl.

One evening in December she came home from prayer-meeting with Mary Kuhns, who stopped at the gate to talk.

"You are sure you are not afraid to go in alone, Ellie?" she said, finally.

"*Ach*, no!" answered Ellie. She ran lightly on the board walk, the powdery snow flying lightly from her skirts. When she reached the kitchen porch, she saw footprints leading to the door.

"Some one was here and went away again," she said to herself, as she want in. She locked and bolted the door, and closed the shutters with a cheerful slam. Then she took off her shawl and "twilight," and set Schwenkfelder cakes for the morning baking, and afterward sat down to read a chapter in her German Bible before she went to bed.

It may have been a slight sound which disturbed her after a moment. She still held the Bible open in her hands, but she was not reading. She realized suddenly that the footprints she had seen pointed only to the door. The person who had made them had not gone away; he must be in the house now. She did not think of thieves—there are no thieves in Millerstown—but of some vaguer and more portentous danger.

She heard again the slight noise, like a creaking of the cellar steps. She could not breathe. She heard the noise again. Some one was coming up the cellar steps.

When the intruder opened the door, she had not turned her head; she still stared at her German Bible. She felt a head on her lap, arms about her knees.

"Mother!" he called, faintly.

His mother looked down at him over the open Bible. She did not kiss him or put her arms round him. "What are you here for, Callie?" she asked.

"I—I couldn't stand it. It—it was too hard. I—I ran away."

The Bible dropped from Ellie's hands. "But you must go back!" she gasped. "You must serve your time out. You are—you are—a—a soldier!"

The boy looked up at her, his eyes more than ever startlingly blue in his bronzed face. They were filled with ghastly fright. Could his mother have failed him? Had he heard aright?

"I can't go back. I have been away for a month. I—I worked my way back to you."

Ellie saw that his clothes were torn, his cotton shirt was black with grime; he smelled of liquor. She drew her knees away from his clasp.

"First, you must wash," she said, "then I will talk to you."

Calphenus did not move; he continued to kneel by her side and supplicate her. "But they will court-martial me if they find me. They may be after me now. Mother, aren't you going to hide me?"

"Be still," commanded Ellie. "You must do as I tell you. Go up-stairs and wash. The shutters are closed, you can make a light. There are—there are clean clothes for you in the bureau."

The boy got heavily to his feet.

"Go right away," his mother bade him, sharply.

When he had gone up-stairs, she stealthily opened the outer door and walked in his footprints to the road, sweeping her skirts about, then she came back to the table and sat down.

When Calphenus appeared he wore his Sunday suit of long ago. It was a little tight for him; his arms hung at his sides as though he were powerless to move them. He looked at his mother with awe, and trembling as though she were a stranger. He did not even sit down until she bade him. Then his stiff tongue almost refused to move. He said he had been away from the army too long to hope for pardon. If he went back they would torture him. The regulations said that he might be punished any way but by death. He would never go back; he would rather die. Couldn't she think of anything to do? Wouldn't she even *try* to save him?

Ellie's face was hidden in her folded arms on the table which had been her mother's and her grandmother's. She lifted her head and looked round the little kitchen where she had been rocked in her cradle. The house was like an outer shell of her own soul.

"Yes," she said, heavily. "I will go away with you, and we will try to hide."

So, without farewell or backward glance, they fled.

They lived first in the county-seat of the adjoining county, where Calphenus worked in the wire-mill. They had changed their name to "Throckmorton," which Calphenus found in an old catalogue, and chose because it was most unlike any name which he had ever heard. Neither he nor his mother could pronounce it. He became "Arthur Throckmorton." They called it "Arsur Srockmorton." He taught his mother to speak English, such as it was. She destroyed her German Bible and her hymn-book, the only treasures she had brought with her from Millerstown. For a year she seemed to see the constable waiting before the door. Then, when no one had come to disturb them, she breathed more freely. Not so poor "Arthur." He was obedient to his mother; he spent his evenings in the kitchen with her; he consulted her about the clothes he bought, the pennies he spent. He never went anywhere except to his work; he had no diversions; he ate his meals silently, and went to bed early, and stole out in the cold, dark morning to his work.

One day he came home at noon, dinner pail in hand, his face white, his blue eyes almost starting from his head. "We are found out!" he gasped.

His mother looked at him with a strange expression in her black eyes. It could not possibly have been relief.

"Well?" she said, slowly.

"It was this way," he explained, trembling. "There is a young fellow, he works aside me; he said to me a while back, 'What is your name?' and I told him what it was, and I moved away to another place. And to-day he came after me, and he said to me, 'I — I don't believe it is your name,' he said to me. 'I believe you are a Dutchman.' He — he will get the police on us, mom."

"Well?" said Ellie again.

"Mom, you don't mean that you will tell on me! You don't mean that you will give me up, mom! You are not going back on me!" He began frantically to plead in the tongue of his childhood. "You won't desert me, mother?"

Ellie's inscrutable eyes darkened. "No," she answered. "We can move."

The next day their house was empty. The boy did not even go back to the wire-mill for his wages. They went to Harrisburg, and found a little house far out on the river road. It was a wretched little house with a few acres of ground.

"You can teach me to garden," said Calphenus, with a long sigh. "I can raise things and take them to market."

"Yes, well," consented his mother. They sat together on the door-step, looking out over the wide Susquehanna, shallow after a long drought. They could see, far on the other side of the river, the fiery headlights of great trains; the stars shone peacefully above them.

"It is nice here," said Calphenus; "nice and open."

His mother did not answer. She had never lived near a stream, and the sound of the water made her as lonely as had the great hum of human life in Reading. It was tiny, peaceful, silent Millerstown for which she longed.

For ten years they lived unmolested. Calphenus raised truck, learning to love his labor; he went daily to market. He was afraid of the name Throckmorton; he adopted "Vail" instead, equally absurd for a Pennsylvania German. It was painted above his stall in the market, "Arthur Vail." Once during the ten years his mother went away for two days. He was crazy with terror.

"Are you going back to Millerstown, mom?"

"No."

He dared not question her further.

"But you won't give me up, mom?"

"No."

He did not leave the house till she returned.

Slowly he began to gain confidence. One night the flame of a great fire lit the sky, and they heard the next day that the State Capitol had burned. Presently the mighty dome of a new Capitol rose above the city; he could see it building as he digged his garden. It frightened him a little. He knew that it represented a vague, indestructible something which fire could not destroy nor time change; which could neither be escaped nor resisted. Sometimes the thought of law terrified him, sometimes he laughed cunningly because he had lived so long almost beneath the shadow of that dome and was not caught.

The city crept gradually upon them. Within half a mile their road became a city street; across the river a long stretch of close-set lights marked the new railroad-yards; automobiles rushed by, each one causing Calphenus to gasp afresh with delight. He began to go about the city; he ventured once into the Capitol itself and stared up at the inside of the mighty dome; he saw the Governor's mansion flaring with lights, and women rustling up the steps, and was perfectly at ease and contented to watch so much splendor in safety and peace. There was a young girl who tended with her mother the next stall in the market; he had begun to talk to her. She was one of his own blood; when he picked her up after she had stumbled, with a solicitous "Annie, did you hurt you?" She answered, trembling, "Just a few." Then he had kissed her. He thought of her often. Why shouldn't he marry? He was safe now.

His mother had seen plainly the change in him, his growing assurance, his complacent smiling to himself. He began to look as he had looked the night that he came home in his blue suit to say good-by to her. The change did not please her. She became daily a little more silent; she spoke to him more gravely. She would not let him make any improvements in the house, or even buy her a German Bible; if he allowed himself diversion out-of-doors, he got none within. Prisoners could scarcely have lived more simply.

One day Calphenus did not return from market at his usual hour. It was six o'clock instead of two when he finally appeared. His supper was waiting for him when he had unhitched his horse and put away his crates and boxes.

"I — I couldn't come sooner," he faltered. "I — I — it was a perade. My horse, he got stubbory. I — I —"

"A perade!" repeated Ellie. "What were you doing in town?"

"I — I — I" He stood gasping.

"What ails you?" asked his mother.

"I — I have something to tell you. I saw somebody from Millerstown this morning. It was Jimmie Weygandt. I — I — he saw me; he said, 'Hello, Callie!' he yelled it out so. I was afraid. I drove a long ways round to get home and I met the perade. I — I thought he might come after me. He saw me come from the market; he might go in there and ask about me. He — he might come out here — he might — the police will find us, mother."

Ellie looked at him strangely. "Well?" she said.

Calphenus almost screamed. "Are you going to give me up?"

"No," answered his mother, wearily; "I will never give you up."

He ate almost nothing. After supper he went back to the barn to make all secure for the night. Then he stood motionless, listening to the river. For a moment its roar shut out all other sensation. He was appalled by the majesty of its sound; he was terrified by the loneliness of his own soul. He did not know where to turn. Then, dimly through the misty night he saw the dome of the Capitol rising august and beautiful. The river, the very heavens and earth, seemed to move uncertain; this other, shining in its bow of light, seemed to abide. He felt suddenly a great peace.

"Mother," he said, faintly, when he had entered the little house, "I have decided to give myself up."

His mother helped him pack a few simple things, and all night she blessed God and prayed for her son. In the morning she went into his room and helped him dress as though he were a little boy. Then he ate his breakfast, and went out to the gate.

"Calphenus," she called, faintly, "I want you to come back."

"Yes," he said. "But I will miss the train for Washington." Nevertheless, he returned obediently.

"There is something I must say to you, Calphenus." She spoke in German; there was to be no strange English between them forevermore. She stood by the table, a buff-colored paper, which she had taken from her bosom, in her hand. Her voice shook, but her eyes were steady. "Once I was away for a little while. I was in Washington. They said you couldn't have been arrested any more after two years were up. Here is a paper; you have to fill it in before the squire, and then you are free."

Calphenus took the paper from her hand and stared at it. It was a blank form; he saw the scattered words:

> "............ deserted from the army of the United States, released from liability to arrest and imprisonment, and from trial and punishment by court martial."

"When did you get this?" he asked, thickly.

"When I was away."

"It is five years."

"Yes."

"Why didn't you tell me before?"

"I couldn't," she said. The tears were running down her cheeks. It had burned like a coal in her bosom, this little paper which would have made him free, and would have taken her back to Millerstown. "I don't know why I couldn't. It wasn't time until now, Callie."

"Why didn't you tell me last night?"

"It wasn't time then yet."

Calphenus sat down by the smooth table. His mother had turned her face away and was looking out the east window of the house. She often stood there, she sat there with her work, preferring it to the wider, more lovely prospect to the west. He wondered vaguely why it was. Then his handsome face flushed. Five years ago he might have been free. Five years! How dared she keep it back?

His throat choked with rage. Then he heard again the thunder of the river, and was afraid. He tried to remember what had brought him peace; he walked to the door and looked out, and came back to his chair. He saw that his mother was watching him; she wept no more; her eyes seemed to glow like the flaming dome; he looked at her with awe; he could almost have thrown himself at her feet and begged for mercy. He feared her, his weak mother, who had punished him so cruelly, who would not tell him that he was free until he was willing to give himself up.

He stared at her curiously. How little she was, how thin, how old! For him, life waited; for her, it was past. Suddenly, with torturing clearness, he saw what her life had been. She might have been happy when she was a girl, but after her marriage grief had been her portion, and then almost twenty years of disgrace, and then these years of bitter exile. And still she could love him and punish him and pray for him! He went across the room and put his arm round her.

"Mother," he stammered. "Mother—"

For a long minute Ellie stared at him. Then she laid her head upon his breast.

"*Ach*, I have such homesick for Millerstown, Callie," she whispered. "I want to go back."

THE ETERNAL FEMININE

Originally published in the July 1910 issue of
Lippincott's Monthly Magazine

Susan Ehrhart stood at the kitchen sink, washing dishes and crying. Her tall, muscular figure shook, the tears ran, unchecked, down her face, and the little house was filled with the sound of her voice. She cried as one who knows no shame, as if she did not care if all Millerstown or all Lehigh County or all the world heard her.

"I am going right aways home to my Mom."

She listened for an instant, as if expecting a response; but none came, unless the regular tap, tap, tap, of a shoemaker's hammer somewhere in the neighborhood could be called an answer. Indeed, as she listened, it seemed to lose for a second its regularity and become animate, telegraphic, intelligible. The taps became shorter, they rose in a crescendo to a single loud stroke, then they went on evenly. It was as if they said:

"I don't care if you do."

Susan finished her dishes, dried her hands, and put on her sunbonnet and shawl. Then she opened the door and went out.

"I am going right aways home to my Mom," she announced to the quiet night.

The taps went on evenly. Susan walked across the yard to a little shop.

"I am going right aways home to my Mom."

When there was still no verbal answer, she lifted her hand and beat, not upon the door, but upon the wooden wall beside it. She heard the wild clatter of a thousand shoe-nails falling to the floor, as the boxes toppled from the shelf within, then an angry exclamation.

Without going in, she went out the road toward Zion Church. It was not long after sunset, and there was still a faint gray light in the west, against which the roadside trees stood out dimly, and by which Susan, if she had cared, might have picked her way through the mud. The cold March wind blew upon her back. As she plodded along, bowed and bent, she looked like a work-worn peasant. She might have posed for Millet. But in free, Pennsylvania German America, it was not necessary to suffer her wrongs silently. As she went she cried aloud:

"I am going right aways home to Zion Church to my Mom."

A stranger coming to Millerstown and meeting Sarah Ann Mohr or old man Fackenthal, or indeed almost any one of her citizens, would have said that the Pennsylvania Germans were kindly, hospitable folk, a little given to gossip, perhaps, but possessing in the main many more virtues than faults. Any one who met only Samuel Ehrhart, on the other hand, would be likely to say that the Pennsylvania Germans were sordid, parsimonious, and disagreeable. Samuel's character was enough to prejudice the observer against his whole race.

How he had won Susan, no one in Millerstown knew. She was not handsome, she had stooping shoulders and a long thin face, and she was six inches taller than her husband. But surely she must have had at least one better chance! And, lacking that, would it not have been better for her to stay forever in her father's house? Samuel's aunt had looked curiously at her as she stood before the stove in Samuel's kitchen, manufacturing a delicious meal out of the small rations which Samuel allowed.

"Susan," she said, the words bursting from her as if they could no longer be restrained, "Susan, what did you want with Samuel? Did you like him?"

Susan did not answer. Instead, she had looked down at Samuel as he came in from the shop. He might have been a tenderly loved child or a treasured jewel. Then she looked at his aunt as if words were powerless to express her emotion. To Susan, Samuel was then still the most wonderful person in the world.

"Like him!" her eyes seemed to say. "Who could help liking him?"

Samuel had gazed uneasily at his aunt as he came in. She rose at once.

"Never mind, Sammy. I'm not going to stay for dinner. Don't you think it!"

"*Ach*, but won't you stay once?" urged Susan. "That is ——"

Samuel's aunt saw the swift frown of disapproval, and the bride's amazement, then her prompt and tender look of obedience. This time her voice was sarcastic.

"Don't be frightened, Sammy. I'm going home."

Millerstown watched the couple for a month with wonder and amusement. Then Elias Bittner reported to old man Fackenthal that they had quarreled.

"What about?" asked old man Fackenthal.

"About insurance. Susan, she has been paying on insurance eight years already, and Samuel, he won't pay no more because he says it is nothing in the Bible from insurance, and he don't believe in making money off of dead bodies."

Old man Fackenthal laughed.

"Samuel would n't give nothing for the graveyard fence because it don't say nothing in the Bible from graveyard fences. Don't he know he will get the money after Susan is dead?"

"He says he don't trust no insurance company."

"But she will lose all the money she has already paid in."

"Well! It is n't his money."

"What did Susan do?"

"She cried and went home to her Mom. But Ellie Benner says she don't believe she said anything to her Mom, or her Mom would n't 'a' let her come back. Her Mom is spunkier than she. Ellie says Susan must just 'a' told her Mom that she came home to visit once a little."

Three times Susan had gone home. The second time it was because Samuel scolded her for inviting her former "company girl" to stay overnight.

"Do you want to land me in the poor-house, with company all the time?" asked Samuel.

The third quarrel arose when Samuel accused her of having pared the potatoes wastefully.

"I saw your potato-peelings in the bucket," he scolded. "Don't you know how to peel potatoes better than that, say!"

Each time, as Millerstown suspected, Susan had not told her mother the real reason for her coming. She cried loudly when she started; but it was three miles to Zion Church, and one may cry away the worst of griefs in that distance. By the time her journey was over, she always thought better of her rage.

Samuel was not at all disturbed. He never doubted that she would return, and in the meantime she was being fed at her father's table, and his own supplies would last longer. He thought sometimes that Susan ate a great deal, but he consoled himself by remembering that she worked a great deal also. He did not believe that this last quarrel was any worse than the others. It had begun when Susan suggested buying flower-seeds for the garden.

"Flower-seeds!" cried Samuel.

"Why yes. A few such sweet-peas and sturtians, and a few others to it yet. They only cost five cents a package."

"Five cents! Think of the flour you could buy till you have a few packages!"

Susan reluctantly yielded.

"Well, I guess I can get a few seeds from my Mom—if she kept any this year. She thought once she would buy her altogether new ones."

"I don't like flowers," declared the surly Samuel. "They take up too much room; they are only a nuisance. And think of all you could do while you are working at flowers!"

"But I must have my flowers, I must have my flowers!" Susan had a way of insisting over and over upon things when she was excited. "I cannot get along without my flowers. I must have my flowers."

Samuel looked up at her.

"You are not now any more at home," he reminded her. "You will not have any flowers."

"It won't cost nothing," pleaded Susan.

"Yes, it will. It will cost room and time. I know how it goes with flowers."

Susan burst into tears. There never was a human being who cried more easily than Susan.

"I am going home to my Mom. I am going right aways home to my Mom to Zion Church to stay."

Samuel thought of the supply of pies and cakes.

"You can go," he said.

Susan's mother was just winding the clock as she walked into the kitchen. Every one else in the house had gone to bed. Mrs. Haas was a short, enormously fat woman, who in spite of her breadth looked younger than her daughter.

"Why, Susan!" she cried. "My, but I am glad to see you! But where is your man? And what is the matter that you are crying?"

Susan's woes burst at sound of the kind voice.

"I come home to stay always," she wailed. "Please let me stay always. He is mean to me. He will not let me have flowers, he would not let me have any company girl overnight, he will not pay the insurance that Pop paid always for me, he ——"

Mrs. Haas sat heavily down in the kitchen rocking-chair.

"*Um Gotteswillen!*" she cried. "Is it true?"

"Yes it is true," sobbed Susan. "It is all true. When I came home before, it was each time something wrong. I thought I would try it again. But now I cannot try it again."

"No," said her mother firmly; "I guess you will not try it again. I guess I and your Pop can keep you. You can go now to bed, Susan, in your own bed like always, and I will bring you a little garden tea, and to-morrow we will go and fetch your things."

Samuel looked up calmly from his shoemaker's bench the next morning when Susan came in. He had not expected her back so soon.

"Well?" he grinned.

He heard Susan's answering sob, then a sharper voice. Susan's portly mother pushed her away into the shop.

"I thank the Lord I have this chance to tell you how mean you are, Samuel Ehrhart," she said. "We are here to fetch Susan's clothes. No mean, stingy man need take care of my children, that is all I have to say, and my children need n't work for such a mean, stingy man."

"B-but ——"

Mrs. Haas would not let him go on.

"I and Susan are going to get her things. You can come along to see that we don't get anything of your trash."

Samuel got awkwardly to his feet, dropping the shoes from his leather-aproned lap. He forgot that he had carefully arranged a patch, economically cut from a tiny bit of leather, and that it would be difficult to get it into position again.

"B-but ——" he began.

Mrs. Haas slammed the door and was gone. His shoe-nails fell clattering to the floor, but he did not hear. He grew suddenly pale. He knew Susan's value. He had never dreamed that it would be possible to live so cheaply as they had since her advent. She did not only her own work, but she was beginning to wash and clean for the neighbors. He had looked forward to the day when she would become as much of a wage-earner as himself. Perhaps it would have been better to let her have a few flowers. He followed Mrs. Haas over to the house.

Susan sat by the kitchen table. He saw with relief that she was still crying. Susan would be easy to manage.

"Susan ——" he began.

Susan's mother appeared at the door of the cupboard with a sauce-pan in her hand.

"Oh, you came to watch, did you? Well, this is Susan's. You can't say it is n't, for I gave it to her."

Samuel stood in the doorway, fingering his apron.

"Susan ——" he began again.

Mrs. Haas thrust the sauce-pan beneath his nose.

"It is Susan's, or is n't it Susan's?"

"Yes," he faltered; "it is Susan's."

"Well, then," said Mrs. Haas. She added it to a pile of pans and dishes on the table. "You'd better look a little over those things. Perhaps it is some of yours there." Her eyes dared him to claim any of them. "Now I am going upstairs. Come, Susan."

But Susan did not move. She was too spent with grief. Her mother patted her arm.

"Then stay right there, Susan."

Samuel's eyes brightened. He swiftly determined to say a few things to Susan. But they must be said to her alone.

"Susan," he began, "you can have ——"

Mrs. Haas's foot was on the step. She heard the whisper and looked back. She saw that the least bit of Susan's cheek was visible.

"You come with me," she commanded Samuel sternly. "I don't want it said that I took any of your things. I guess I know what I gave Susan when she got married, and I don't believe she got much since, but you come once along and see."

Samuel went with a backward glance. He grew each moment more terrified. He thought that he might promise her more than the flowers. She might keep some of the chicken money.

Mrs. Haas opened the door of the closet in Susan's room. She held up a red petticoat.

"I suppose this is Susan's?"

Samuel was too perturbed to smile.

"Perhaps Susan don't want her things taken away," he ventured timidly.

Mrs. Haas refused to see his meaning.

"I don't know why you would want any left here," she said scornfully. "You could n't wear them. You may be saving, Samuel Ehrhart, but you are not that saving. Is this Susan's?"

"Y-yes," stammered Samuel. The article in question was Susan's hat.

"And this?" It was Susan's best dress.

Samuel had edged toward the door.

"I have something to tend downstairs," he explained. "I must put the draught on for dinner."

"All right," answered Mrs. Haas promptly. "I will go along with you. Here, you can take these clothes of Susan's, and I will take the rest. You can put them on the table, with the other things, then we can pack them in the wagon."

"You might — might — st-stay for dinner."

Mrs. Haas's laughter echoed through the house. "To dinner! When you would n't have Susan's company girl overnight. I guess not!"

Samuel reluctantly picked up an armful of clothes, the familiar gray wrappers and blue skirts. They were so long that they trailed behind him down the steps, and his mother-in-law bade him sharply to gather them up.

Susan had apparently not moved. But the fire was burning brightly, and the tea-kettle was bubbling. Samuel's eyes brightened. Susan's mother also saw the steaming kettle.

"Susan, help me to carry these things to the wagon," she commanded sharply.

Susan lifted her long, tear-stained face. She was crying again like a child, without any attempt to wipe away the tears.

"*Ach*, Mom," she wailed. "I do not think I am going along with you home."

Mrs. Haas paused, confounded. She stood still, her arms round the bundle of clothes, which was as large as herself.

"Not going along with me home!"

"No, I think I will stay here, Mom."

"You 'think you will stay here, Mom'!" In her amazement she repeated her daughter's words.

"Yes," said Susan. It might have been Samuel's evident fright and repentance which moved her, it might have been the touch of the familiar tea-kettle. "I think I will stay here, Mom."

The bundle of clothes slid from Mrs. Haas's arms!

"You said he would n't let you have any flowers!"

"Yes, Mom."

"You said he scolded you for peeling the potatoes too thick!"

"Yes, Mom."

"You said he made you give up the insurance what your Pop paid, always, so you could have something when you are old!"

"Yes, Mom."

"Well, then! Are you crazy?"

Samuel came a step nearer. He still held his bundle; the wrappers and petticoats trailed again about his feet.

"You can have the flowers if you want to, Susan. And you can have a quarter — *ach*, I mean a half of the chicken money, Susan, and ——"

Mrs. Haas cut him short.

"Do you believe him, Susan? Do you believe him for a minute?"

Susan hesitated. His words sounded sweet in her ears, but she could not say that she believed them.

"Then come home," commanded her mother, stooping to pick up the clothes.

Susan hid her face in her arms.

"I can't go home, Mom. I can't help it. I know he is mean, Mom. But I can't help it! The whole trouble is — I — I — like him!"

And, with a final wail, Susan took off her sunbonnet, and sought her gingham apron, hanging upon its accustomed hook.

THE SQUIRE

Originally published in the September 1910 issue of *The Atlantic Monthly*

THE squire was a bachelor, and lived alone in his house; therefore he was able to use the parlor and dining-room for offices. The parlor contained only a pine desk, a map, hanging "at" the wall, as Millerstown would have said, and a dozen or so plain pine chairs. The law was administered with scant ceremony in Millerstown.

The squire sat now in the twilight in his "back" office, which was furnished with another pine table, two chairs, and a large old-fashioned iron safe. He was clearly of a geographical turn of mind, for table, safe, and floor were littered with railroad maps and folders. The squire was about sixty years old; he had all the grave beauty which the Gaumer men acquired. Their hair did not thin as it turned gray, their smooth-shaven faces did not wrinkle. They all looked stern, but their faces brightened readily at sight of a little child or an old friend, or with amusement over some untold thought.

The squire's face glowed. He was going — his age, his inexperience, the certain disapproval of Millerstown notwithstanding — he was going round the world! He would start in a month, and thus far he had told no one but Edwin Seem, an adventurous young Millerstonian who was to leave that night for a ranch in Kansas, and whom the squire was to visit on his own journey. For thirty years he had kept Millerstown straight; there was no possible case for which his substitute would not find a precedent. Fortunately there were no trusts to be investigated and reproved, and no vote-buyers or bribers to be imprisoned or fined. There were disputes of all kinds, dozens of them. There was one waiting for the squire now in the outer office; he shook his head solemnly at thought of it, as he gathered up his maps and thrust them back into the safe, that precious old safe which held the money for his journey. He had been thirty years gathering the money together.

The law might be administered in Millerstown without formality, but it was not administered without the eager attention of the citizens. Every one in the village was on hand when simple-minded Venus Stuber was indicted for stealing, or when the various dramatic scenes of the Miller-Weitzel feud were enacted. This evening's case, Sula Myers *vs.* Adam Myers for non-support, might be considered part of the Miller-Weitzel feud, since the two real principals, Sula's mother and Adam's mother, had been respectively Sally Miller and Maria Weitzel.

The air was sultry, and rain threatened. The clouds seemed to rest on the tops of the maple trees; it was only because the Millerstonians knew the rough brick pavements as they knew the palms of their hands that there were no serious falls in the darkness. They laughed as they hurried to the hearing; it was seldom that a dispute promised so richly. There was almost no one in the village who could not have been subpoenaed as a witness, so thorough was every one's knowledge of the case.

Already the real principals faced each other, glaring, under the blinding light of the squire's hanging lamp. It made no difference that Millerstown listened and chuckled or that the squire had taken his seat behind the pine desk.

"When it don't give any religion, it don't give any decent behaving. But God trieth the hearts of the righteous," said Mrs. Myers meaningly.

She was a large, commanding woman, who had been converted in middle life to the fervent sect of the new Mennonites, and young Adam had been brought up in that persuasion. Except for his marriage, young Adam had been thus far his mother's creature, body and soul.

Sula's mother, Mrs. Hill, was large also. She took off her sunbonnet, and folded her arms as tightly as possible across her broad bosom.

"There is sometimes too much religion," she said.

"Not in your family, Sally," rejoined Mrs. Myers, her glance including not only Mrs. Hill and Sula, but all their sympathizers, and even Caleb Stemmel, who was supposed to be neutral.

Caleb Stemmel belonged in the same generation with the squire; his interest could be only general. Caleb did not see Mrs. Myers's scornful glance; he was watching pretty Sula, who sat close by her mother's side.

Sula looked at nobody, neither at her angry mother beside her, nor at her angry mother-in-law opposite, nor even at Adam her husband, sitting close by his mother. She wore her best clothes, her pretty summer hat, the white dress in which she had been married a year before. Even her wedding handkerchief was tucked into her belt.

Sula had been strangely excited when she dressed in the bedroom of her girlhood for the hearing. There was the prospect of getting even with her mother-in-law, with whom she had lived for a year and whom she hated; there was the prospect of seeing Adam's embarrassment; there was another reason, soothing to her pride, and as yet almost unacknowledged, even to herself.

Now, however, the glow had begun to fade, and she felt uncomfortable and distressed. She heard only dimly Mrs. Myers's attack and her mother's response. Immediately Mrs. Myers told Mrs. Hill to be quiet, and Mrs. Hill replied with equal elegance.

"You will both be quiet," said the squire sternly. "The court will come to order. Now, Sula, you are the one that complains; you will tell us what you want."

Sula did not answer; she was tugging at her handkerchief. The handkerchief had been pinned fast, its loosening took time.

"It was this way," began Mrs. Myers and Mrs. Hill, together.

The squire lifted his hand. "We will wait for Sula." He looked sternly at Mrs. Hill. "No whispering, Sally!"

Sula's complaint came out with a burst of tears.

"He won't support me. For three months already I did n't have a cent."

"All this time I supported her," said her mother.

"She had a good home and would n't stay in it," said Mrs. Myers.

The squire commanded silence again.

"Sula, you were willing to live with Adam's mother when you were married. Why are n't you now?"

"She — she would n't give me no peace. She would n't let him take me for a wedding-trip, not even to the Fair." She repeated it as though it were the worst of all her grievances: "Not even a wedding-trip to the Fair would he dare to take."

Mrs. Hill burst forth again. She would have spoken if decapitation had followed.

"He gave all his money to his mom."

"He is yet under age," said Mrs. Myers.

Again Mrs. Hill burst forth: —

"She wanted that Sula should convert herself to the Mennonites."

"I wanted to save her soul," declared Mrs. Myers.

"You need n't to worry yourself about her soul," answered Mrs. Hill. "When you behave as well as Sula when you 're young, you need n't to worry yourself about other people's souls when you get old."

Mrs. Myers's youth had not been as strait-laced as her middle age; there was a depth of reminiscent innuendo in Mrs. Hill's remark. Millerstown laughed. It was one of the delights of these hearings that no allusion failed to be appreciated.

"Besides, I did give her money," Mrs. Myers hastened to say.

"Yes; five cents once in a while, and I had to ask for it every time," said Sula. "I might as well stayed at home with my mom as get married like that." Sula's eyes wandered about the room, and suddenly her face brightened. Her voice hardened as though some one had waved her an encouraging sign. "I want him to support me right. I must have four dollars a week. I can't live off my mom."

The squire turned for the first time to the defendant.

"Well, Adam, what have you to say?"

Adam had not glanced toward his wife. He sat with bent head, staring at the floor, his face crimson. He was a slender fellow, he looked even younger than his nineteen years.

"I did my best," he said miserably.

"Can't you make a home for her alone, Adam?"

"No."

"How much do you earn?"

"About seven dollars a week. Sometimes ten."

"Other people in Millerstown live on that."

"But I have nothing to start, no furniture or anything."

"Your mother will surely give you something, and Sula's mother." The squire looked commandingly at Mrs. Myers and Mrs. Hill. "It is better for young ones to begin alone."

"I have nothing to spare," said Mrs. Myers stiffly.

"I wouldn't take any of your things," blazed Sula. "I wouldn't use any of your things, or have any of your things."

"You knew how much he had when you married him," said Mrs. Myers calmly. "You needn't have run after him."

"Run after him!" cried Sula. It was the climax of sordid insult. They had been two irresponsible children mating as birds mate, with no thought for the future. It was not true that she had run after him. She burst into loud crying. "If you and your son begged me on your knees to come back, I wouldn't."

"Run after him!" echoed Sula's mother. "I had almost to take the broom to him at ten o'clock to get him to go home!"

Adam looked up quickly. For the moment he was a man. He spoke as hotly as his mother; his warmth startled even his pretty wife.

"It isn't true, she never ran after me."

He looked down again; he could not quarrel, he had heard nothing but quarreling for months. It made no difference to him what happened. A plan was slowly forming in his mind. Edwin Seem was going West; he would go too, away from his mother and wife alike.

"She can come and live in the home I can give her or she can stay away," he said sullenly, knowing that Sula would never enter his mother's house.

The squire turned to Sula once more. He had been staring at the back of the room, where Caleb Stemmel's keen, selfish face moved now into the light, now back into the shadow. On it was a strange expression, a hungry gleam of the eyes, a tightening of the lips, an eager watching of the girlish figure in the white dress. The squire knew all the gossip of Millerstown, and he knew many things which Millerstown did not know. He had known

Caleb Stemmel for fifty years. But it was incredible that Caleb Stemmel with all his wickedness should have any hand in this.

The squire bent forward.

"Sula, look at me. You are Adam's wife. You must live with him. Won't you go back?"

Sula looked about the room once more. Sula would do nothing wrong — yet. It was with Caleb Stemmel that her mother advised, it was Caleb Stemmel who came evening after evening to sit on the porch. Caleb Stemmel was a rich man even if he was old enough to be her father, and it was many months since any one else had told Sula that her hat was pretty or her dress becoming.

Now, with Caleb's eyes upon her, she said the little speech which had been taught her, the speech which set Millerstown gasping, and sent the squire leaping to his feet, furious anger on his face. Neither Millerstown nor the squire, English as they had become, was yet entirely of the world.

"I will not go back," said pretty Sula lightly. "If he wants to apply for a divorce, he can."

"Sula!" cried the squire.

He looked about once more. On the faces of Sula's mother and Caleb Stemmel was complacency, on the face of Mrs. Myers astonished approval, on the faces of the citizens of Millerstown—except the very oldest—there was amazement, but no dismay. There had never been a divorce in Millerstown; persons quarreled, sometimes they separated, sometimes they lived in the same house without speaking to each other for months and years, but they were not divorced. Was this the beginning of a new order?

If there were to be a new order, it would not come during the two months before the squire started on his long journey! He shook his fist, his eyes blazing.

"There is to be no such threatening in this court," he cried; "and no talking about divorce while I am here. Sula! Maria! Sally! Are you out of your heads?"

"There are higher courts," said Mrs. Hill.

Millerstown gasped visibly at her defiance. To its further amazement, the squire made no direct reply. Instead he went toward the door of the back office.

"Adam," he commanded, "come here."

Adam rose without a word, to obey. He had some respect for the majesty of the law.

"Sula, you come, too."

For an instant Sula held back.

"Don't you do it, Sula," said her mother.

"Sula!" said the squire; and Sula, too, rose.

"Don't you give up," commanded her mother. Then she got to her feet. "I'm going in there, too."

Again the squire did not answer. He presented instead the effectual response of a closed and locked door.

The back office was as dark as a pocket. The squire took a match from the safe, and lit the lamp. Behind them the voices of Mrs. Myers and Mrs. Hill answered each other with antiphonal regularity. Adam stood by the window; Sula advanced no farther than the door. The squire spoke sharply.

"Adam!"

Adam turned from the window.

"Sula!"

Sula looked up. She had always held the squire in awe; now, without the support of her mother's elbow and Caleb Stemmel's eyes, she was badly frightened. Moreover, it seemed to her suddenly that the thing she had said was monstrous. The squire frightened her no further. He was now gentleness itself.

"Sula," he said, "you didn't mean what you said in there, did you?"

Sula burst into tears, not of anger, but of wretchedness.

"You'd say anything, too, if you had to stand the things I did."

"Sit down, both of you," commanded the squire. "Now, Adam, what are you going to do?"

Adam hid his face in his hands. The other room had been a torture-chamber. "I don't know." Then, at the squire's next question, he lifted his head suddenly. It seemed as if the squire had read his soul.

"When is Edwin Seem going West?"

"To-night."

"How would you like to go with him?"

"He wanted me to. He could get me a place with good wages. But I couldn't save even the fare in half a year."

"Suppose"—the squire hesitated, then stopped, then went on again—"suppose I should give you the money?"

"Give me the money!"

"Yes, lend it to you?"

A red glow came into Adam's face. "I would go to-night."

"And Sula?" said the squire.

"I would—" The boy was young, too young to have learned despair from only one bitter experience. Besides, he had not seen Caleb Stemmel's eyes. "I would send for her when I could."

The squire made a rapid reckoning. He did not dare to send the boy away with less than a hundred dollars, and it would take a long while to replace it. He could not, *could not* send Sula, too, no matter how much he hated divorce, no matter how much he feared Caleb Stemmel's influence over her, no matter how much he loved Millerstown and every man, woman, and child in it. If he sent Sula, it would mean that he might never start on his own journey. He looked down at her, as she sat drooping in her chair.

"What do you say, Sula?"

Sula looked up at him. It might have been the thought of parting which terrified her, or the recollection of Caleb Stemmel.

"Oh, I would try," she said faintly; "I would try to do what is right. But they are after me all the time—and—and—" Her voice failed, and she began to cry.

The squire swung open the door of the old safe.

"You have ten minutes to catch the train," he said gruffly. "You must hurry."

Adam laid a shaking hand on the girl's shoulder. It was the first time he had been near her for weeks.

"Sula," he began wretchedly.

The squire straightened up. He had pulled out from the safe a roll of bills. With it came a mass of brightly colored pamphlets which drifted about on the floor.

"Here," he said. "I mean both of you, of course."

"I am to go, too?" cried Sula.

"Of course," said the squire, "Edwin will look after you."

"In this dress?" said Sula.

"Yes, now run."

For at least ten minutes more the eager company in the next room heard the squire's voice go on angrily. Each mother was complacently certain that he was having no effect on her child.

"He is telling her she ought to be ashamed of herself," said Mrs. Myers.

"He is telling him he is such a mother-baby," responded Mrs. Hill. "She will not go back to him while the world stands."

"The righteous shall be justified, and the wicked shall be condemned," said Mrs. Myers.

Suddenly the squire's monologue ended with a louder burst of oratory.

The silence which followed frightened Mrs. Hill.

"Let me in!" she demanded, rapping on the door.

"This court shall be public, not private," cried Mrs. Myers.

She thrust Mrs. Hill aside and knocked more loudly, at which imperative summons the squire appeared. He stood for an instant with his back to the door, the bright light shining on his handsome face. Seeing him appear alone, the two women stood still and stared.

"Where is he?" asked Mrs. Myers.

"Where is she?" demanded Mrs. Hill.

The squire's voice shook.

"There is to be no divorcing in Millerstown yet awhile," he announced.

"Where is he?" cried Mrs. Myers.

"Where is she?" shrieked Mrs. Hill.

The squire smiled. The parting blast of the train whistle, screaming as if in triumph, echoed across the little town. They had had abundance of time to get aboard.

"He is with her, where he should be," he answered Mrs. Myers, "and she is with him, where she should be," he said to Mrs. Hill, "and both are together." This time it seemed that he was addressing all of Millerstown. In reality he was looking straight at Caleb Stemmel.

"You m-m-mean that—" stammered Mrs. Myers.

"What *do* you mean?" demanded Mrs. Hill.

"I mean," — and now the squire was grinning broadly, — "I mean they are taking a wedding-trip."

THE MAN WHO WAS NICE AND COMMON

Originally published in the November 1911 issue of **Harper's Magazine**

Socrates and all his philosophic children recognize a certain "suspension" as the proper frame of mind for an inquirer. Of this Millerstown knows nothing. Millerstown's mind is made up long before the facts of a case are apparent.

Jacob Volk and the younger of the two young Fackenthals saw the stranger first from the high seat of their coal-wagon.

"Who is he?" asked Jacob.

"Where does he come from?" demanded Jim.

"What is he doing in the hotel?"

"What does he have in that satchel?"

"He is lame."

"He is thin as a switch."

"He looks dumb."

"I could blow him over with my breath." Jim pretended to strike his fat roans a mighty blow with the end of the lines. "Get up, *ihr faule Dinger* (you lazy beasts)!"

Jacob Volk prepared to climb down from the wagon.

"Let me off! I will see what he is doing in the hotel. I will see where he comes from. I will see—"

Jim Fackenthal laughed and drove on. Jacob Volk was the most inquisitive man in the universe; it was well to punish him. But Jacob, regardless of coal-dust and rheumatism, scrambled over the back of the seat into the body of the wagon and dropped to the road.

In the combination bar-room and office Jacob's low opinion of the stranger was fortified. He was even thinner than a switch, he wore glasses — ridiculous affectation of school-teachers and preachers — he walked with a slight limp, he accepted without protest the charge for room and board to which the hotel-keeper added a dollar above the usual amount. Indeed — *esel* (donkey) that he was — he seemed surprised that it should be so low. He said that he might stay all summer. Jacob flew to tell the news.

"A stranger!"

"He will stay all summer!"

"What does he look like?"

"Do you think it is anything in him?"

"What will he do in Millerstown?"

"Perhaps he will start a new church."

"Perhaps he is a insurance man."

"Perhaps he will keep summer school."

"I won't send my children to summer school; he need not think it!"

The stranger apparently expected nothing from any of them. He kept his own counsel, and divided his time between his shady corner room overlooking the village street and the little mountain back of Millerstown. The hotel-keeper's wife said also that he took medicine.

"Pooh!" commented Millerstown.

Millerstown did its best to learn his business. Sarah Ann Mohr, who lived across the street, knew when he rose, and that was shamefully late, and when he went to bed, and that made Sarah Ann lose many hours of good sleep. The post-master observed carefully the postmark of every letter he received, the address of every letter which he sent away. Most of them went to a lady by the name of Smith who lived in New York. Inasmuch as the young man's name was Smith, not much could be made out of this discovery.

The boys followed him in his walks on the mountain, but, like a famous king of France, he merely marched up and then marched down.

Ellie Wenner, who washed for him, could contribute only a single item. His clothes were mended, she said, as though he had a mother.

Presently Millerstown had recourse to plain questions. Had he a mother living? Yes, indeed! A father? No. Brothers and sisters? No. How had he heard of Millerstown? He saw the name on a time-table. Did he ever know any one from Millerstown? No. Did he like Millerstown? Very much.

But if the young man refused to divulge his own affairs, he was at least willing to listen to the affairs of others. Ellie Wenner loved to tell about her quarrels with Wenner's first wife's people, who wanted all the first wife's housekeeping things. Elias Bittner liked to tell his private woes. Pit Gaumer dealt principally with church quarrels. Jacob Volk had a quarrel with the universe. Old man Fackenthal liked to talk about Elias and Pit and Jacob, especially in their own presence. All Millerstown liked to talk all the time.

And the young man liked to listen. When he went for his laundry he sat on the bench outside the kitchen door and heard all Ellie Wenner's woes. He held on his knee the clock which the relatives of the first Mrs. Wenner had tried to steal; he was shown the faded spot on the parlor wall from which they had torn her crayon portrait.

"They came in the window when I was off," declared Ellie. "What do you think of that, say?"

"I think it was shocking." The stranger was always kind, always sympathetic; he was, as Millerstown would have said, "nice and common."

He was also excessively polite. When he fell over Elias Bittner's foot, he said, "Excuse me," and then blushed crimson when Elias responded only with a loud, rude, and suffering "Ouch!"

By-and-by he began to get on Millerstown's nerves. They were sure there was "something wrong" about him. Perhaps he was a burglar or a swindler or a safe-cracker. Then they were equally sure that he was "a little off," and to this conclusion they clung. They began to laugh at him among themselves; once or twice children yelled at him on the street. They had names for him: "Der Fratz Hans," because his fine clothes and his professed inability to speak Pennsylvania German made him seem proud and self-important; sometimes "Der Ueberg'scheit," because he was overwise; sometimes "Der Simpel," because he believed everything they told him.

Finally, from morning until night Millerstown fooled him to the top of his bent. They did not begin with any concerted conspiracy against him; no one person agreed with any other to deceive him; they simply could not help themselves. The whole joke-loving community was similarly affected.

Ellie Wenner's husband's first wife's relatives no longer crept in the window; they broke down the front door, and one of them carried a gun. Sarah Ann Mohr's pigs no longer weighed four hundred pounds; they weighed five hundred, five hundred and fifty, one even seven hundred. The single wildcat which had haunted the minds of Millerstown children for generations, and which was really an invention to keep them from straying to the mountain, grew to a nest of wildcats, then to a herd. Eventually the herd descended upon the village and carried off a child.

"We could hear them in the night always," declared Jacob Volk, with bulging eyes. "Like lions, they shook themselves and roared."

The stranger was as excited as any story-teller could wish.

" 'They gaped upon you with their mouths, as a ravening and a roaring lion,' " he quoted from the Bible.

Jacob swung his feet from the top of the hotel-porch railing to the floor with a crash.

"You have right!" he cried. "That was it, exactly."

But it was not on Ellie Wenner's wash-bench or on the hotel porch that Millerstown did its best; it was in front of old man Fackenthal's. There were three maple-trees; against each one was propped a chair; in one sat old man Fackenthal, in another Elias Bittner, in the third Pit Gaumer. Jacob Volk sat on the door-step, and in the middle of the long bench sat "The Simple." On the curb and crowded round Jacob on the step were as many Millerstonians as could be accommodated. No one sat on the bench beside the stranger; from that angle the delightful expressions on his gullible face could not have been seen. The neighboring door-steps were crowded also; the rest of the village was almost forsaken. Had it not been that the stranger was pious as well as simple-minded, the Sunday-evening services would have suffered.

There was no order of speech; no one was called upon to open the meeting; no one practiced beforehand. They behaved just as they always behaved.

"I remember—" Jacob Volk would begin.

"My pop told me—" Elias Bittner would interrupt.

"I wish you would be still." Pit Gaumer would say. "My uncle said—"

"You are all to be still," old man Fackenthal would command. "*I* want to talk."

Everybody talked, everybody invented, everybody boasted. Jacob Volk, who had bragged all his life, excelled himself; others who had never bragged now burst forth with incredible tales. There was no effort to make the stories probable or possible. Elias Bittner, caught beneath his overturned wagon when the horses ran away, had kept pace with them for two miles on his hands and knees, until, the wagon righting itself, he had leaped out, rushed to the horses' heads, and stopped their mad flight. Pit Gaumer, when a young man, had walked to "Phildelphy" and back in two days, and had killed thirty wolves on the way. Jacob Volk with his "good hickory gat" had driven off a whole army of desperadoes who had set upon him on the mountain road.

Then Millerstown grew tired of its madness. They still talked—not till the stranger departed, at the end of the summer, did their play end—but the character of the talk changed. Farce took herself off and Comedy arrived. Millerstown had not dared to laugh before for fear of undeceiving the stranger; now it shouted with glee. Tales of apple-butter matches, battalions, family quarrels, old and delicious feuds—here were stories at which one could shout and roar. The Simple did not always laugh; he sat as though enchanted. But Millerstown did not care whether he laughed or not. Millerstown was enchanted with itself.

"So they fought and they fought and they fought," said old man Fackenthal, "Johnny Wock and Mrs. Johnny Wock.

"'You shall have the half,' yelled Johnny Wock, 'and I will take the half!'

"'And you will take the biggest half!' Mrs. Johnny Wock said back at him. 'You always do.'

"'Now,' said Johnny Wock, 'rage flies into me!'

"He took the ax and the saw and the hatchet, Johnny Wock did, and he cut the things in two, the tables, the chair, the bag of flour, the sugar-kettle, even the vinegar-barrel he sawed from top to bottom."

"And then what?" asked a dozen voices.

"Oh, they made it up; they always made it up. They patched the table and shoveled up the flour."

"Oh, tell another!" cried The Simple.

Mom Fackenthal stood in the doorway. Even she was affected by this strange madness.

"You might tell them about the—"

Old man Fackenthal looked up at her and chuckled. He knew what she meant; because of her respect for preachers she had never let him tell it before; he told it now, for the first of a hundred times, his tale of "The Snorting Preacher." Afterward there was always some one who had not heard, or who pretended not to have heard, whose mighty mirth it was a joy to witness.

"A couple of years back, when Jimmie was a little boy, we had a candidate in the church, and he stayed by us overnight. He was big and fat and dumb; he was no sort of a preacher. But we had had already eleven candidates, and none suited. This one they were going to take whether or no. Mom and I, we slept in the back room, and he in the front room because there was the strongest bed, and Jimmie, he was in the trundle-bed in the back room. The doors were open into the hall, it was so fearful hot. It wasn't a breath of air, not a breath. But pretty soon there began to be a breath. The preacher snorted something powerful."

"You mean snored, pop," said Mom Fackenthal.

"I mean snorted; it was snorting. Like an elephant or a tiger he snorted. It was like it began at the church and ended a mile out the pike. I tell you, I nearly jumped out of my bed. Mom, she was awake, and the preacher, he had snorted himself awake, and Jimmie was sitting up.

"'Mom,' Jimmie yelled — 'mom! The cow is coming up the steps!'

"Then Jimmie laid down and went to sleep, and the preacher went to sleep, but mom and I, we didn't sleep, I can tell you. It was like a cornsheller, it was like a sawmill, it was like the end of the world. Three snorts he gave. And then he snorted himself awake. And Jimmie sat up in bed.

"'Mom!' he yelled out—'mom! The cow is *dying!*'"

Millerstown ached from holding back its laughter.

"And then that preacher got up, and he said little Jimmie was so and so and so and so, and—"

"Pop!" warned Mom Fackenthal.

"And he slammed the door—I ain't going to say nothing, mom—and that was the end. We didn't know if he sneaked out then, or if he kept himself from snorting and sneaked out in the morning. But he went. We didn't know if it was the snorting or the swearing that shamed him."

"That was like the time when—" began Elias Bittner.

"I guess you young folks never heard—" interrupted Pit Gaumer.

"I'm not done talking," old man Fackenthal would say.

Thus it went on, summer evening after summer evening, until, as the shadows began to fall earlier on the quiet streets, and the boys who had sat on the curb slipped into less cold seats on the bench beside the stranger, the mood of the Millerstonians changed again. They still talked, they still continued to pour out at the feet of this young man a rich burden of plot and sub-plot, a store of history and folk-lore. There were strange uses of prepositions, racy idioms, new words, coined in the slow, careful mint of their isolated, introspective minds.

Now, suddenly, Comedy followed the way of Farce, and Tragedy arrived. Evil stalked about and was punished, for Millerstown, except for a few evil-doers, is good and upright and clean; heroism was properly rewarded; religion, for Millerstown is pious, by turns inspired remorse and brought comfort.

These stories were not all true; they were pruned and polished, and each one ended exactly as it should. They were told with awe and tenderness and horror. Each man became suddenly to his neighbor what he was to himself, a primitive creature, frightened a little by the darkness, peopling the world, especially the dear, safe little mountain back of Millerstown, with evil or uncanny beings, or even with ghosts.

Jacob Volk's wildcats became suddenly real, not only to the children, but to their mothers and fathers.

There were, Jacob Volk said, a man and a woman living on the mountain with their little baby. One night the man could not get home on account of a heavy snow, and the woman and the little baby were there alone. Hitherto the wildcats had never troubled the little household; now they realized that the master was away. They were mad with hunger, full of expedient. They gathered round the cabin; again they roared and gaped. One howled upon the roof, one burst in the window, another entered at the door. There the mother sat with the baby in her arms. And suddenly she began to pray and sing, and the evil beasts slunk back. All night she sang, all the dear hymns of the fatherland, over and over again, "Nun danket Alle Gott," "Ein Feste Burg," "Oh, Haupt voll Blut und Wunden," "Allein und doch nicht ganz Allein." When, exhausted, she stopped to catch her breath, the beasts came a little nearer, and again she drove them back. Finally the dawn broke, they stole away, and her husband found her unconscious, but living and safe.

A man on the mountain — again the stage was set upon the mountain — robbed and murdered a stranger who had stopped with him, and buried his body near the house. He made the spot smooth; no one suspected him; nobody missed his poor victim; he was perfectly safe. But across that spot he could not walk without stumbling. A branch from a tree fell upon it and tripped him; a very small stone became suddenly an obstacle which no visitor could see until he had fallen over it; the long shoot of a blackberry vine made a snare. And when the man had removed the branch and the stone and the blackberry vine, he could not restrain himself from crying out, "Be careful, be careful, you will fall!"

His visitors laughed at him; they said there was nothing there; he must be crazy. And then *he opened the grave to show them that there was something there.*

"He d-dug it open!" cried Elias Bitner. "God had taken his reason."

Thus, entranced by their own invention, now minstrels casting spells, now kings and courtiers sitting at happy ease, the Millerstonians passed the long summer, until autumn came, and the stranger went away.

The stranger looked much better than when he came. He was a good deal stouter — no one could help being who led such a lazy life, who had eaten so much, and laughed so much. The Millerstown women had made fun of him at night, but by day they had sent him scores of gifts of pie and raised cake and fruit and doughnuts. He went round to say good-by to them all, at which politeness they were amused. He said that he hoped Ellie Wenner's husband's first wife's relatives would annoy her no more.

Presently doors were closed early in the evening; windows were shut to stay shut till spring; Millerstown ceased its communal life, the summer gatherings were no more. Kitchens were small; the women did not like too many men sitting round; the men met in the post-office or store. They spoke occasionally of the young man, wondering pleasantly who was playing tricks on him now. Spring came, a dull summer passed, and they heard no word of him. They tried sometimes to repeat the happy evenings round old man Fackenthal's door, but their efforts were vain. The spirit had gone out of them.

Then, one January evening, the post-master handed old man Fackenthal a letter and a package.

"A letter!" cried he, all in a flutter. "From New York? Who should write to me from New York?"

Elias Bittner hazarded a brilliant guess.

"Perhaps it is The Simple." Then he, too, was astounded.

"There is a package for you, too," said the postmaster. "And one for Pit and one for Jacob."

Not one of the old men thought of using his knife to cut the string which bound his package. Helplessly, half-frightened, they picked at the knots.

"Listen once!" cried old man Fackenthal. "What do you think of this, say?"

To an almost petrified audience he read his letter. It was, as Elias had guessed, from the stranger. It was a letter of thanks. They would see, he said, if they looked into his book, why he thanked them. He mentioned by name various Millerstonians, Ellie Wenner, Sarah Ann Mohr; he was very grateful to them all. They had restored him to health, they had given him the material for a series of stories which had been so successful in magazines that they were now being published in book form. He was sending each of his old friends a copy. He hoped some day to come to Millerstown again.

With faltering hands they turned the leaves.

"The Snorting Preacher," they read at the top of one page; "When Johnny Wock Divided Up," at the top of another; "Who Putteth Her Trust in Thee," on a third.

"Do you suppose he got *money* for them?" faltered Pit Gaumer.

"It says, 'Price, one-twenty-five,'" answered Elias. "That looks like money."

"Do you suppose—" Jacob Volk began a sentence, but did not complete it. Reading the intention of old man Fackenthal and Elias and Pit in their eyes, he followed them out.

"Just give me time once!" said Jacob Volk, speaking for them all. "If there is money in it, I can make the money! I can beat those stories. They are nothing."

Afterward they would discuss and argue and deny and refuse to believe and laugh at one another. But now was not the time for speech. Within half an hour, beside four brightly burning lamps, with four new tablets and four new pens and four new bottles of ink, four old men sat motionless, chin on hand, with puckered brows, waiting.

THE SUFFRAGE IN MILLERSTOWN

Originally published in the March 16, 1912, issue of
The Saturday Evening Post

There are few women in Millerstown who take naps or who lie down in the daytime. It is safe to say that no woman, unless she was seriously ill, ever lay down for a whole afternoon; it is absolutely certain that none but Lizzie Kerr ever spent a whole afternoon — and that in November — reclining upon an outside cellar door.

It was not a position which Lizzie chose for herself. In the first place, she had no time for this extraordinary proceeding. When one has a husband and seven children, the youngest less than a year old, and when one is the only woman on a farm where there are fourteen cows, twenty pigs and a few hundred chickens, that need constant attention, one should be busy every moment. In the second place, Lizzie found the position exceedingly uncomfortable. Lizzie was very large and she was accustomed to rest upon a feather bed — not a hard board. Besides, it is apt to be a little cool on the first Tuesday after the first Monday in November; and besides, it is neither dignified nor decent to slam a cellar door upon one's husband and then lie down upon the door.

Of all this Lizzie was thoroughly aware. Her hands were clenched; she answered the muffled voice from beneath her with a voice utterly unlike her own; at the sound of her baby screaming in his cradle in the kitchen she put her hands over her ears; at thought of her bread-sponge running over the bowl and her pies burning in the oven, she groaned. She did not cry, however, though she looked like a tender-hearted person to whom tears came easily. Occasionally she lifted herself into a half sitting posture, but almost immediately lay down again, feeling it safer to distribute her weight over as many of the flimsy boards as possible. She meant to save Alpheus from committing a great wrong, but she did not wish to crush him to death.

The baby screamed himself to sleep, and woke and screamed again; a stranger, passing in a buggy, asked whether she was ill, and, receiving her lying answer that she liked to sit on the cellar door, looked at her as though she were a lunatic; the prisoner commanded, argued, cajoled, pleaded — she grew colder and colder, stiffer and stiffer. However, for the sake of the morals of Millerstown, for the sake of her husband rushing to ruin, for the sake of her poor children threatened with destruction by the demon rum, Lizzie Kerr continued to embrace her martyrdom. Once she tried to sing Cold Water is the Children's Friend, but she did not get beyond the first line.

An hour ago she had been standing by her kitchen table working her bread, an entirely suitable and becoming occupation for the mother of seven, and Alpheus had faced her as he drew on his husking mittens. Alpheus was a little, energetic man, for whom his wife had great admiration. He was smart; his brothers looked up to him for counsel; the men at the store listened to him with respect; he read the newspapers learnedly and recounted marvelous tales of extraordinary things — of French people making a Christmas dinner on camel's meat, of women demanding the ballot and battering policemen and being battered in turn by them, of evil men blowing up bridges with dynamite. He could argue with the preacher; he could read both English and German. Until yesterday she had been proud to be his wife. She was richer than he — the farm was hers, inherited from her father; but she had been proud to marry so smart a man. Until yesterday she had been content to know no law but his will; until yesterday she had concerned herself with nothing outside her natural sphere. Now, interfering where she had no business, rushing into a situation of which she knew nothing, governed by ridiculous prejudice and feminine ignorance, she had made a fool of herself.

"I was yesterday in the store, pop," she had faltered when she could fill her lungs with enough breath to speak.

"Yes — well?" answered Alpheus. "What then?" He stared at Lizzie suddenly with some alarm; he had never seen her look like that. "Do you feel bad, mom? Do you have it somewhere?"

Lizzie leaned upon the bread-sponge which rose in great billows about her round arms. With her rosy cheeks and her bright smile, Lizzie was an attractive person — a person to whose company it was good to return after a day's work; but now Lizzie did not smile.

"They talked about the election, pop. They said that Moser was temperance, pop, and Steiner was for the taverns. I said you wouldn't vote for Steiner for the world; and then I came home — and he was sitting here and talking, pop. I ——"

Alpheus was annoyed and disgusted.

"Pooh!" he said as he started for the door.

Lizzie was before him, however. She moved with more agility than one would have expected in a person of her size. Bits of dough clung to her fingers; her face was scarlet.

"You are a church member; you have all these boys to bring up. How will you bring up these boys if there is a saloon in every house, pop? How ——?"

Alpheus was more agile than Lizzie; he dodged past her and closed the door. Then, walking briskly across the meadow to the cornfield, he laughed. Women were good for some things, of course; but they had no minds. Lizzie had no mind or she would realize that the temperance question had absolutely nothing to do with this election. Steiner might occasionally take a drink — that was none of the world's business. He was the candidate of Alpheus' party; he had great respect for Alpheus and the influence Alpheus had over his brothers and several illiterate voters; he would bring them good roads and prosperity. It was foreordained that Alpheus should vote for him. Lizzie was crazy!

Contented with himself, amused at his wife, Alpheus worked on. Presently he began to pity Lizzie. He decided that he would explain things to her that evening. He was really very fond of her.

After a long time Lizzie roused herself from the apathy in which she worked to go to the cellar for the baby's milk. The cellar was across the yard; under its slanting door was a steep flight of steps; below, in the cool dampness, stood a dozen brimming crocks of milk.

"I ought to make butter," said Lizzie as she drearily contemplated them. "I am behind with everything. Nothing will ever be right with me again. Oh, my soul!"

Then slowly Lizzie climbed the steps and heated the milk and filled the baby's bottle. Her tears dropped upon him as he lay sound asleep in his cradle. She was disgraced in the eyes of her friends; she was disappointed in the idol of her soul.

It seemed three hours — it was really but one — before Alpheus returned from the cornfield. It was not yet two o'clock and the polls did not close until six; but he said to himself that his brothers might wish to vote early or Steiner might not think him sufficiently concerned. He came whistling across the meadow. At sight of the open cellar door he turned his steps toward it.

"Mom," he called into the depths, "I am going now to town."

There was no answer; Alpheus went toward the kitchen.

"Did you know you left your cellar door open, mom?" he asked.

Lizzie was standing by the table, where he had left her. Whether the cellar was opened or closed made no difference to her.

"Pop," she began, trembling; at which Alpheus remembered.

"When I come home I will talk to you," he said indulgently. Then he patted Lizzie on the shoulder.

Lizzie began to plead.

"Ach! pop, don't vote for Steiner — please, pop!"

"Of course I will vote for Steiner!"

"When you have little children, pop? What if they come in the tavern, pop?"

"*Geh mir aweck!* — Get out!" — mocked Alpheus. "You make me laugh!"

"He takes drinks, pop. And the people in town, they said ⸺"

"I don't care what they said." Alpheus finished washing his hands at the sink. "Where is my other coat?"

"Ach! but, pop, you can talk with me a little about it, I guess. I am dumb—but I am not so dumb, pop. I ⸺"

Alpheus slid rapidly into his coat. Then he applied the brush and comb which lay on the little rack by the door. Then Alpheus could not resist a foolish but overwhelming temptation.

"I must be there early," he said importantly. "I always mark the tickets for a couple o' fellows."

"What!" cried Lizzie. Sometimes Alpheus read to her accounts of election frauds and subsequent investigations. In her confusion, it seemed that he, too, was about to commit fraud. The foundation of Lizzie's world was shaken.

"Goodby," said Alpheus cheerfully.

The baby in the cradle began to cry. Alpheus turned back to his wife.

"Shall I fetch you a little milk?" he asked as tenderly as though he spoke to the baby.

Unable to answer, Lizzie started to follow him. She meant to tell him that she had brought the milk and that the baby had the bottle; but her voice choked. She was shocked; she was hurt; she was—though she did not suspect it—furiously angry at Alpheus' superior airs. When she reached the door he had vanished down the cellar steps and she followed across the yard.

Then, suddenly a great, new, overwhelming emotion filled Lizzie Kerr's soul. Never in her life had she done a violent thing. She had disciplined setting hens; she had spanked her children; but it had been done after deliberation, it had been done with dignity. This was done without consideration, without forethought. She leaned over and lifted the slanting cellar door and closed it upon the little man within. Then, partly from pure weakness, Lizzie Kerr, mother of seven, of great size, lay down upon the door.

The first frantic sound that rose from within added the reproaches of a tender heart to Lizzie's already overwhelming emotions.

"Mom!" called Alpheus. "Mom! Somebody is shutting me in the cellar! Lock yourself in the kitchen, mom, and then lock yourself in the upstairs, mom! And holler like sixty!" His first thought was for her. It was with bursting heart that Lizzie answered.

"I am shutting you up, Alpheus. It is Lizzie. Nothing is after me. I am sitting on the door."

"What!" screamed Alpheus shrilly.

"I must talk to you about this, pop, before it goes any farther." Lizzie's voice became more clear. She did not weep—her tears seemed to be forever dry. She prayed for eloquence; she thought of the people in the Bible who had been given tongues of fire. "You see, pop, it is this way: The people say that Steiner has parties and that the people drink. It is not raspberry vinegar, pop, or yeast beer—it is real beer in bottles from the tavern, pop. They sometimes have some of this cha'pagne-water. Suppose these poor little children should get some, pop! Suppose little Lizzie should stay out late in the night, pop; and suppose little Alpheus should come home yelling and hollering, pop! Suppose ——"

The cellar door quivered.

"Get up!" ordered Alpheus. He spoke as he might have spoken to his horse or his dog. Lizzie had never heard that tone addressed to her. Her cheeks flushed, but still she spoke gently.

"Will you promise to vote for Moser, pop?"

"Get up!" commanded Alpheus again.

"Will you promise not to vote for Steiner, pop?"

"Get up!" ordered Alpheus, more furiously.

"Will you promise not to vote for anybody, pop? Will you stay here with me? Will you ——"

"Get up!" said Alpheus in a terrible tone.

For a few minutes there was silence. The door shook slightly again; but Alpheus, though strong, was short—he could get no purchase on the door. Then motion, as well as sound, ceased. Indeed, actual physical paralysis was no more numbing than the sensations that filled the breast of Alpheus. Had the barn fallen upon him and bade him lie still, he could have been no more amazed. Presently silence was succeeded by a more furious burst of anger. He would vote for whom he chose; now he was absolutely determined to vote for Steiner—nothing would keep him from it! If she had not acted the fool he might have listened to her; but he was the boss—nobody could make him do what he didn't want to do.

Poor Lizzie did not answer. Indeed, she did not hear half he said, for another sound penetrated to her ears and filled her with dismay. Presently, when he paused for breath, Alpheus heard it also.

"Your baby is crying!" he shouted. "Go to it!"

Lizzie was wringing her hands. The baby should have gone to sleep at once and slept for hours. He had a bottle and he was comfortably fixed. Had he broken the bottle and cut himself? Was something after him—the cat, perhaps? Had ——

"Your baby is starving!" said Alpheus. Shall a mother sit on a cellar door while her baby is dying!"

"He is not starving," said Lizzie. "He has his bottle; and, anyhow, he could go without a little while and not starve. He ——"

"Then something is after him," declared Alpheus. "He will die then ——"

"He will not die while he is yelling like that," said Lizzie hoarsely. Oh, if only she only had him in her arms! "That's a mad yell, pop. He is only cross. Oh, say you will not vote for Steiner!"

"I will vote for Steiner!" shouted Alpheus. He remembered suddenly Peter and George, depending upon his advice, and the incompetents expecting him to mark their tickets. He shook the door. "Let me out! Get up!"

"No!" said Lizzie. "No, pop, I cannot."

Fortunately the day was only cool and not cold; fortunately the sun shone directly upon Lizzie's bed; fortunately no one passed but the one stranger; fortunately it did not occur to Alpheus to pretend a fall down the cellar steps, or to remain silent and simulate death, or to take any other means of adding to Lizzie's agony of mind.

He told her he was cold; she advised him to get as close to the cellar door as he could and reminded him that he had a means of escape. He recalled to her her promise to obey; she put him in remembrance of her long years of obedience and suggested the Higher Power, to whom one owed a higher obedience. She quoted Bible verses at length; she reminded him of moral truths and precepts that have little to do with elections. In some strange, unconscious way, Lizzie had allied herself with those unaccountable lunatics known as reformers. Alpheus was certain now that she was crazy. He reproached her with her presumption in setting forth her opinions; and then another dam broke in the long-checked current of Lizzie's mental processes.

"The farm is mine!" said she. "I do half the work. I guess I can have some say, Alpheus."

She had not called him Alpheus for years. It was as though she chose to ignore all the relations of duty and affection that bound them together. Alpheus remembered the smashed windows of London, the dismay of London's mighty men.

"Lizzie," said he weakly, "what will my children think when they see me penned in the cellar?"

"Will you promise not to vote for Steiner?"

"No!" roared Alpheus. "Get up!"

Thus the long afternoon passed. The baby ceased crying and slept, and waked and cried again, the boards under the baby's mother grew harder, the air colder; but Lizzie still lay upon the cellar door.

At length, now, with infinite patience, Alpheus explained to her the political situation. Steiner had nothing to do with the taverns.

"Except drink in them!" said Lizzie with a new quickness of thought.

Steiner would bring them good roads.

"But he is a bad man!" said Lizzie. "It is better to have bad roads. Will you promise not to vote for Steiner?" she asked.

"No!" shouted Alpheus. "Get up!"

It was half-past four when the children came home from school. Alpheus, the oldest, was twelve; Lizzie, who was next to the baby, was five; they were the most obedient children that ever lived. Their mother had risen now to a sitting posture. Seeing her, they hurried up the lane.

"You are to go to your Aunt Sally," she said. "You can go to Aunt Sally till six o'clock."

The children stared at her and at each other; then they trotted off. Only little Alpheus looked back.

"Why do you sit on the cellar door, mom?" he called.

"Because I like it," said Lizzie.

From the earth beneath came a reproving voice.

"Ain't you ashamed, mom, to lie to children! Ain't you ashamed?"

"Will you promise not to vote for Steiner?" asked Lizzie with the same deadly monotony.

"No!" yelled Alpheus. "I won't."

After a long time the clock in the kitchen struck five. The sound reached the cellar. In an hour the polls would close.

"That was six o'clock," said Alpheus.

"It was five," corrected Lizzie.

It seemed to Lizzie, shivering without, and to Alpheus, shivering within, that hours passed before there was another sound. Then Lizzie spoke once more:

"Will you promise not to vote for Steiner?"

To her amazement Alpheus returned a prompt "Yes."

"W-what?" faltered Lizzie.

"I said 'Yes,'" repeated Alpheus. To Alpheus' shame, be it said, Alpheus did not tell the truth. An expedient had occurred to him. If he could only get to the polls in time!

For all her weight and stiffness, Lizzie almost sprang from the door. It was at once lifted and Alpheus thrust up his head. Then he bounced out.

"You dare not make a man promise something when you have him penned up!" he shouted. "It says so in the law. I am going to vote. I ——"

Alpheus paused. Up the lane came the children.

"What time is it?" Alpheus demanded furiously of his wife.

"It struck six already," she said heavily; "I thought I would give you another chance to do right, Alpheus."

"What!" began Alpheus—then paused.

Seeing the wild-looking creature before him, Alpheus was suddenly appalled. The recollection of his wrongs, of Steiner's probable rage, of his own little, unshepherded political flock, vanished from his mind; he saw instead those wild, window-smashing Londoners.

"Mom," said Alpheus, "are you going to parade like—like those others? Will you vote, mom?"

Solemnly Lizzie returned his gaze. She was stiff and sore in body and mind; she was a stranger to herself.

"I do not know yet what I will do," said she ominously.

Alpheus was distracted with fright. It would have made no difference to him now if Steiner had been plunged into the sea. He tried to take Lizzie's unwilling hand; he called to the children to "Come quick to mom!" Then he rushed into the kitchen.

"See, mom!" he cried. "Here is the baby—the little baby, mom! It cries for you, mom! See!"

Thankful for the fierce screams with which the baby resented being torn from his bed in the midst of sleep, Alpheus bore him forth and placed him in his mother's arms. Then, as the amazed and terrified children surrounded her, Lizzie returned—for the time at least—to woman's sphere. With a loudness which inspired a like demonstration from all her frightened offspring and made Alpheus declare that hereafter he would do everything she liked and nothing she did not like—with a heartiness that branded victory as a not unmixed satisfaction—poor Lizzie wept.

THEIR SENTIMENTAL JOURNEY

Originally published in the September 5, 1912, issue of
The Youth's Companion

The question burst like a blast from a cannon into the silent peace of twenty years. Sarah Ann Mohr and Aaron König, to whom it was addressed, gasped as they sat at opposite ends of the long bench before Sarah Ann's door in the quiet evening. To Sarah Ann, it was almost an accusation of crime, to Aaron it was a sudden sharpening of the twinges of conscience that had bothered him for twenty years.

Ollie Kuhns, lounging on his own bench next door, shouted out the impertinent, the outrageous inquiry.

"Sarah Ann!" he said, and waited for Sarah Ann's placid "Yes"; "Aaron!" and waited until Aaron, too, had signified that he heard. "Haven't you two been going together long enough to get married?"

Neither Sarah Ann nor Aaron answered a word. Like a fat and startled pigeon, Sarah Ann rose and vanished into the covered alley that separated the two houses; like an angry sparrow, Aaron went hopping down the street.

"*Ach!* How could anybody say such a thing!" wailed Sarah Ann.

"And now," said Aaron König, when he had shut behind him the door of his little shop, "now I will have to get married!"

"It shames me," Sarah Ann wept. "I suppose all Millerstown is talking over me."

"I would almost rather die than get married," said Aaron König.

But Aaron was no coward. For twenty years the Widow Mohr had allowed him to occupy her bench in summer and a rocking chair in her kitchen in winter. For twenty years she had fed him from her rich store. She had not only treated him to molasses-cake, cold meat, yeast beer, fine cake in the evenings; she had sent him warm crullers, fresh rusks and hot raisin pie — the caviar of his menu — in the mornings. She had supported his deep bass with her mellifluous soprano in the prayer-meetings; she held the last note of each stanza until he caught his breath and could swing into the first word of the next. She was on his side in all church disputes. She had visited him when he was sick, she had even mended his clothes. However hateful might be the state of matrimony, he could not fail Sarah Ann, now that the subject had been broached to them both. But he wished that he might clutch Ollie Kuhns by the throat and choke him black and blue.

The next evening Aaron put on his best coat. It was perfectly true that it so closely resembled his every-day coat that even the sharp-eyed

Millerstonians, greeting him from their door-steps as he passed, noticed no difference. To Aaron, who had spent the larger part of a day and night praying for strength to do his duty, it seemed like a sacrificial robe.

The air was hot and thick, and there was the almost constant reflection of distant lightning in the sky. It was the sort of atmosphere that frightened Aaron and made him nervous.

Sarah Ann had not ventured again into Ollie Kuhns' irreverent neighborhood, but sat dejectedly on her back porch. She was mortified and troubled to the bottom of her soul, a fact that Aaron did not observe in the least. He did not think of her; he thought only of himself and his own wretchedness. He did not say good evening; he sat himself down, mouse-like, on the bench beside Sarah Ann's monumental figure.

"Sarah Ann," he said, shortly, "Sarah Ann, will you marry me?"

It was evident that Sarah Ann, too, had made up her mind.

"Yes, Aaron, I will marry you," she answered, gently.

Aaron's brave voice gave no hint of the panic in his soul.

"Then let us be married to-morrow. You take the nine-o'clock train for Allentown, and I will take the nine-o'clock train for Allentown, and we will be married there."

Without another word, ignoring the roll of thunder that had suddenly become ominous, Aaron went out through the little alley and home—there to realize that he was lost.

When he had gone, Sarah Ann went into the house. She hardly realized that Aaron's behavior was strange. Her first husband, who had left her comparatively rich, after grudging her the money necessary for her clothes during his lifetime, was much more queer than Aaron König. Aaron was quiet, he was neat, he was small—she was used to his ways.

She closed the kitchen shutters; then she went into the cellar to get herself a piece of pie. She ate it there, looking about meanwhile at the bins waiting for apples from her fine trees and potatoes from her garden, at the shelf filled with baked things, at the cupboard overflowing with preserves and jellies. Then she went up-stairs. The kitchen was immaculate. Each chair stood in its place, the red table-cloth hung straight. The kitchen might have been a parlor.

She went on into the little sitting-room, as neat as the kitchen, and into the parlor, as neat as both, and then she climbed the stairs. In her room the great bed gleamed white, like the catafalque of a princess. It had a valance and a mighty knitted counterpane, and sheet-shams and a bolster, and two huge pillows and elaborate pillow-shams. On one a sleepy child bade the world good night; on the other, the same child waked with a glad good morning. The edges of the pillow-shams and the sheet-shams and the pillow- and bolster-cases were ruffled and fluted.

Sarah Ann glanced into the other bedroom, only a bit less wonderful than this; then she went into the attic, and took from its hook her best black dress, wrapped in a sheet. Back in her room, she laid it at length upon her bed, as if it were the princess herself. Then she looked down upon it.

"Ach, Elend!" (Misery!) wailed Sarah Ann. "Must I then have a man once more in my nice house?"

Worn with sleeplessness and distress, she and Aaron climbed together into the train the next morning.

Just in front of them sat a fat and voluble man who insisted upon talking to them. Neither had told any one the purpose of the journey, although now that their feet were so firmly set upon their desperate path, it would not have added to their trouble to have all Millerstown know. The fat man assumed that they were husband and wife, yet it embarrassed neither of them. They were far beyond the point of embarrassment.

"Now I don't have no wife to look after me," he said jocularly. "I am a lonely single man. But I come and go as I like. I come from Reading, and I am going to-day to Sous Beslehem. I am such a traveling man. Now if I want to stay all night I can, and if I don't want to, I don't need to, and it don't make anything out to anybody, and I don't get a scolding, see?"

Neither Sarah Ann nor Aaron made answer. Their hearts were too full. Did not each one know only too well the advantage of single blessedness? Besides, the time of their bondage was at hand. Already the church steeples of Allentown were in sight, already the brake was grinding against the wheels. The fat man called a cheerful good-by to them, but they made no response.

For an instant they stood together on the platform. Beside them a Philadelphia train puffed and snorted; they could make no plans until the noise had ceased.

"I — I think I will buy me some peppermints!" shouted Sarah Ann into Aaron's ear.

But no marital duty was to find Aaron wanting.

"I'll get them for you," he offered.

Sarah Ann shook her head. "I know the kind!" she screamed.

On arriving at the candy-stand, she stood perfectly still. Aaron's offer terrified her. It was but a forecast of his constant presence. Hitherto she had always bought her own peppermints. It was one of the joys of her life. She looked uncomprehendingly at the candy man when he asked her what she wanted. She did not know — oh, yes, in her heart she did! She wanted to burst this iron band of fright that opposed her; she wanted — it was the first murderous wish of Sarah Ann's benignant life — she wanted to throw Aaron König into the river.

Then, as if this monstrous desire bred others as new and strange, Sarah Ann was guilty of the first impulsive, unconsidered act of all her uneventful years. The Philadelphia train puffed more loudly, the conductor called "All aboard!" The steps of the first car were near at hand. Without a glance at the place where Aaron was patiently waiting for her return, without a thought of her base cruelty, Sarah Ann mounted the steps. Before she had found a seat, before she had time to catch her spent breath, the train had started. She was free!

For the first twenty-five miles she sat in a daze of excited joy. She felt as light as air, her heart beat so that she could feel it — she regretted that her life had been spent in such uninterrupted quietude. She paid for her ticket with-out a pang, she bought peppermints from the train-boy, she invested in a newspaper and threw it away without opening it. She had plenty of money. It would not be like Sarah Ann to go anywhere, even upon a wedding journey, without money. She spread her skirts comfortably over the seat, rejoicing in the wide space. Aaron was small, but even Aaron crowded her.

As she made her plans to stay in Philadelphia overnight, the thought of Millerstown's opinion troubled her. All her life she had had great respect for Millerstown's opinion. But Aaron would go home alone, and Millerstown would suspect nothing. Fortunately, Aaron was close-mouthed, and even a loquacious person hardly acknowledges that his bride has fled from him. It seemed incredible, even to Sarah Ann herself, that she could be thus coolly considering the distressing plight of one who had been her friend for so long.

She determined to go to a hotel in the city. It was true that Manda Kemerer lived in Philadelphia, and that it would be sensible and economical to stay with her. But Sarah Ann said to herself that she was not out for economy; she was taking — and the thought brought an excited and unbecoming giggle — she was taking a wedding trip, and economy on a wedding trip is a crime.

For the first half of the journey, her mood held. Then, as suddenly as Ollie Kuhns' question had shot out of the dark, and with the steady, constant fire of a machine gun, came the reproaches of a guilty conscience. It may have been that the motion of the train, of which she was suddenly uncomfortably conscious, had something to do with her repentance.

She said to herself that she claimed to be a Christian, but she had behaved like a heathen. She claimed to love her neighbor; she had treated Aaron worse than an enemy. She prided herself upon her truth; she had acted a wretched lie. As the train passed Jenkintown, she drew her skirts close about her, as if their spread had symbolized her proud heart; when the train entered the suburbs of the city, she wept. But she could not marry Aaron König, she could not!

Climbing ponderously down from the train, she started up the long platform, her heart aching. Aaron was her dearest friend, and she could never look at him again. His visits, quiet as they were, had given variety to her dull life.

He was a man of importance in the village; his attentions had gratified her vanity. He had never been anything but kind to her, and she had treated him vilely. Had it been possible for Sarah Ann to blot out the last two hours, and stand once more by Aaron's side on the Allentown platform, there is no telling to what depth of humble atonement she might have plunged.

As it was, she moved along helplessly with the crowd toward the waiting-room.

Then, suddenly, Sarah Ann gave a little cry. Just beside her and about to pass, totally oblivious to her presence, moving rapidly as if he were pursued, was the object of her tender penitence.

"Aaron König!" she cried. "Why, Aaron König!"

Seized in a firm grasp, dazed by her sudden appearance, which he failed utterly to comprehend, overwhelmed apparently by some wild grief of his own, Aaron stood still. For an instant the hurrying crowd protested against this blocking of the path; then it divided round them.

"I am sorry, I am sorry!" cried Sarah Ann. "But I couldn't think of this marrying!"

"I — I will get married if you say so," faltered Aaron. "I —"

Then, suddenly, Sarah Ann and Aaron cried out together.

"What are you doing in Philadelphia?" demanded Sarah Ann.

"Did you run away from me?" cried Aaron.

"I — I — I —" stammered Sarah Ann.

"It — it was this way," stuttered Aaron. "I — I —"

Then Sarah Ann took the bull by the horns. Trembling, yet hoping, she asked:

"Don't you want to get married, Aaron?"

Whereupon Aaron, gasping, hating himself, but realizing that the happiness of his life hung on his reply, answered briefly, "No."

"Nor I," said Sarah Ann.

Together they went into the station and sat down. For a long time neither spoke. Then Aaron lifted a tremulous voice:

"It was all Ollie Kuhns."

"Yes," agreed Sarah Ann.

For a moment neither spoke. Then Aaron murmured, "And now, Sarah

Ann, let us have a little something to eat."

The trains seemed especially arranged for runaway and repentant lovers. At one o'clock there was a train for Allentown, at five they could be in Millerstown. They ate their dinners, each paying for a share, and then each bought a ticket. They did not even utilize the remaining time in sight-seeing, they did not even walk to the windows and look down upon the busy street; they sat side by side, enjoying as of old their quiet, friendly communion.

Their state of calm continued until their journey was almost over, and in the Millerstown train they sat once more behind the fat man. He explained, with many digressions, unheard by them, why he had decided to return to Reading.

Suddenly an almost purple flush came into Sarah Ann's cheek. Her lips trembled; she seized Aaron König by the arm.

"We are almost there!" she cried, anxiously. "And what will Millerstown say that we two go away like this and come back together? What will we tell them, Aaron, *ach*, what will we tell them?"

The fat man was still talking; had he been dumb for a year, he could not have talked more constantly.

Aaron, as greatly terrified as Sarah Ann, appreciating more thoroughly than she the infinite and eternal pleasure that Millerstown would wring from such a joke as this, sank back weakly in the seat. His mind put forth vague, inquiring tentacles, as if the roar of the train or the flying fields or the steady stream of the fat man's talk could answer Sarah Ann's question.

"There was a man in the Beslehem train," the fat man was saying. "He went out on the platform and his hat blowed off, and he came back and he yelled it over the car like a fool. 'My hat blowed off!' he said. 'What do you think, my hat blowed off!'"

The fat man paused for a breath, then went on: "Now he oughtn't to have told nobody. It is dumb to let your hat blow off. If he hadn't told it to nobody, nobody would 'a' knowed it. My hat blowed off once and—"

The fat man went on past the village, past the great pipe-mill, through the lovely open country, within sight of the curving hills back of Millerstown, into Millerstown itself. He was still talking when they rose.

"That is it!" said Aaron König, almost hysterically, as they went down the aisle. "That is it! If we don't tell Millerstown, Millerstown will never know. Like the man said, Sarah Ann!"

Overjoyed to be back, excited over the hoodwinking of Millerstown, Sarah Ann and Aaron stepped from the train, lovers no more, but friends forever. And to this day, their secret has been kept.

THE CURE THAT FAILED

Originally published in the December 1912 issue of
Harper's Magazine

SITTING on the broad bench against the front wall of her house, Sarah Ann Mohr sighed heavily. The Millerstown *Star* lay unopened beside her, her eyes were dim, her round face was pale.

Presently, with another long sigh, Sarah Ann opened the paper. Usually she read with many exclamations, now an amazed "ei yi!" to herself, now a call to one of the Kuhns family who lived next door.

"A snake crawled out of the pulpit in the Zion Church, Susannah!" she would cry. "What do you think of that, say!"

Or,

"Can this be, Susannah? It says a preacher in Allentown ran off with the collection!"

On the inner pages were much more remarkable announcements. Here a German professor had succeeded in planting hair on bald heads by means of tiny gold wires; here a man attempted to commit suicide because he had grown so fat that his wife no longer loved him.

But vainly Sarah Ann tried to become interested. Even the account of the woman who put glass into her husband's pies brought from Sarah Ann only a slow shake of the head. Sarah Ann folded the paper and clasped her hands and closed her eyes. The thought of eating was not pleasant. For it was doubtful whether Sarah Ann would ever again in all her life have a full meal.

It was two weeks since the old doctor had been called in for the first time in twenty years. He had a short, sarcastic way of speaking. He looked down upon Sarah Ann as she lay on her bed.

"What did you eat, Sarah Ann?"

Sarah Ann answered with a weak "Not much."

"But *what?*" Insisted the doctor.

"*Ach*, some corn and fried tomatoes and sliced peaches and some doughnuts and a little pie. I have often eaten that much already, doctor."

"But you never were as old as you are to-day. And you take no exercise, Sarah Ann."

Upon this first visit the doctor gave only medicine, upon the second he gave advice.

"You must eat only the simplest food, and little of that."

"But I don't eat much, not what *I* call much." Sarah Ann's appetite was returning. She thought of the ripening corn in her garden. "And the pies and cakes I make myself, and the things that you make yourself, they are always all right."

Even as she spoke, Sarah Ann made up her mind to disobey. When the doctor had gone, she crept down-stairs and cooked a little lunch for herself; she made herself coffee and fried a few corn fritters. In the afternoon the doctor came again to look down upon Sarah Ann as she lay in her bed.

"You will be worse before you are better, that I can promise you," said he. "And if you do such a dumb thing again, you may die."

Now life was sweet to Sarah Ann. But though she did not wish to die, neither did she wish to live in a state of constant starvation. When she was able to rise once more, the doctor limited her to soft-boiled eggs, soup, toast, and the like. Drearily she looked down upon her garden with its nodding tassels of corn, its scarlet tomatoes, its tall vines of lima beans, its heavily laden peach-tree. This year her cantaloup and egg-plant were unusually fine, and they would go to waste with the other fruits and vegetables.

Sarah Ann preferred to sit on her back porch, but now she could sit there no longer and be tortured. Each evening, hungry and discontented, she went to the front of the house. The doctor promised her that she would become accustomed to smaller rations. In the mean time she longed for a meal of fried chicken and cucumber salad and boiled corn and sliced tomatoes, a meal fit for a grown person.

Sitting on the bench, now thinking with closed eyes of her own misery, now gazing idly down the street, Sarah Ann saw presently a strange man approaching from the direction of the station. The sight of his tall, thin figure diverted her for a moment.

"Who is he, then?" she asked herself. "Where is he going? What is he doing in Millerstown?"

Her questions were promptly answered. The tall, thin man approached nearer and stopped before her.

"Is this Mrs. Mohr?" he inquired politely.

"Yes," answered Sarah Ann.

The gentleman sat down beside her.

"My name is Simpson," he explained, as though he had heard Sarah Ann's mental questions. "I came to see if you could give me board. To-morrow evening I am going to deliver a lecture in your hall. After that I have nothing to do till next Monday. I should like to stay here till then."

Sarah Ann considered. She would recover all the faster if she had something to occupy her time. She could board the strange gentleman without any cost, and his money would help to pay the doctor's bill. She and the strange gentleman came speedily to terms.

"Yes, well," said Sarah Ann. "I guess you dare stay."

The strange gentleman was sympathetic; it was not long before Sarah Ann told him of her illness, and her hunger, and her prospect of being hungry forever.

"He says I dare never eat, never," said Sarah Ann, mournfully. "And what is it to do but to eat? I used to couldn't leave a speck of dust lay, but now I can leave a little lay sometimes, and so I could have more time for cooking. I —"

The strange gentleman turned and gazed for a moment at Sarah Ann.

"Oh, sister!" cried he. "You are foolish indeed! Not eat! Why, eat everything you want to! You have within yourself the means for your own cure. Let no doctor persuade you that you can't eat."

Sarah Ann had always had great confidence in the doctor.

"He says I have a weak heart."

"Did weakness ever grow to strength from starvation?" demanded the stranger, triumphantly. "Food, plenty of good, nourishing food is what you need, sister. To-morrow"— the stranger turned more squarely toward Sarah Ann —"to-morrow in your town hall you will hear what you shall do. I have come to bring a message to Millerstown, a message which will banish sickness and pain from this ideal community, which will —"

"You mean that I will dare to eat anything I want to?" cried Sarah Ann, excitedly.

"I mean that."

"Corn?"

"Of course."

"And cantaloup? And tomatoes?"

"To be sure," said the stranger.

Sarah Ann could have wept. Instead, she rose solemnly and went to her garden and cut her best cantaloup for the stranger. She wished that he would tell her his message now, so that she could have a little lunch before she slept, but she supposed he would wish to keep his good news to tell all the village.

Early in the morning, Sarah Ann set about preparing the stranger's breakfast. She had fine ham; she fried a generous slice and half a dozen eggs and some potatoes to go with it. She remembered having heard that in some places people eat warm bread for breakfast, and she baked a batch of biscuit. But she still confined herself to her boiled eggs and toast, tantalizing as were the odors which rose from the various skillets and pans on her stove. The stranger praised her cooking until she blushed with pleasure.

THE CURE THAT FAILED

When breakfast was over, Sarah Ann planned a dinner over which her guest went into ecstasies. At supper she fed him even more generously. He was pathetically thin; she determined that if good food and plenty of it could make him fat, he should have every chance.

Millerstown had not many diversions. Even to-day no moving-picture show has cheapened that blessed village, and at the time of Mr. Simpson's lecture on Electrotherapy, Millerstown was glad to assemble for any sort of entertainment.

Sarah Ann sat on the front row in the crowded hall. Her good spirits had returned, the prospect of being fed once more had made her well. For breakfast and dinner and supper of the next day, Sarah Ann had planned three feasts which would make yesterday's meals seem like nursery diet.

The stranger opened with a magic-lantern entertainment. He exhibited a few pictures of Niagara Falls, then he recounted the mournful story of some one named Little Christie who got up in the middle of the night to play a barrel organ for an old Mr. Treffie. At this pathetic recital Sarah Ann's tears fell.

Then the stranger stepped briskly to the front of the stage. With oratorical eloquence he declared that the day of doctors was past, that doctors were old fogies. He said that a recent marvelous discovery was to make self-healing possible in nearly all diseases. There were in the body, the stranger explained, electric currents. He reminded each one present of how he or she had as a child lighted the gas with a spark from his finger generated by swift walking about a carpeted room — an illustration which was lost on Millerstown, since Millerstown had no gas-lights. He then mentioned the terrific power of the lightning, and Sarah Ann and the other ladies present looked at one another in some alarm as though they might momentarily flash like summer clouds.

Having proved the power of the electric current and its existence in the human body, the stranger lay down upon the floor of the high platform and crossed his ankles. He then rubbed his hands rapidly together.

"The electric current is thus produced," he explained. "The crossing of the ankles prevents its escape from the body. When the hands are moved directly above the spot affected" — the stranger indicated an imaginary trouble which might have come from too free indulgence in corn and tomatoes and sliced peaches and doughnuts and pie — "when the hands are moved directly above the spot affected, the electric current, working powerfully upon that part, brings about an immediate cure.

"I have been eating three large meals a day," boasted the stranger, springing to his feet and bowing in the direction of the pleased and blushing Sarah Ann, "but I have no fears of indigestion."

Having finished, the lecturer took up the collection and the entertainment was over. Millerstown had been interested, but its citizens seldom suffered from illness of any sort and it did not feel drawn to contribute very generously. Only Sarah Ann put in as much as a quarter, and there were many more pennies than nickels.

Sarah Ann walked home as one in a dream. She believed the stranger — she had felt the electricity snap from her finger to the spigot in her kitchen in winter, and she had often been frightened by the summer storm. She walked rapidly, thinking of the cantaloup in her refrigerator. When Mr. Simpson arrived, they would feast together.

When she had almost reached her gate, the doctor called her from his porch. The doctor had not gone to the lecture.

"Better, Sarah Ann?" said he.

Kind-hearted Sarah Ann could not help a pang of sympathy for the old man whose business was to be taken from him.

"I am well," she answered.

Then Sarah Ann's pity changed to mild exultation.

"Obey my directions," commanded the doctor in his unpleasantly dictatorial way. "You'll be laid out again if you don't."

Sarah Ann smiled.

"All right," she answered, complacently.

With the greatest impatience Sarah Ann awaited the return of Mr. Simpson. She cut the fine cantaloup at once and put the halves on two plates, and, with each, two pieces of black chocolate cake.

Mr. Simpson entered the gate with his head bent and his hands clasped behind him. In the darkness Sarah Ann did not see that the expression of Mr. Simpson's countenance had changed. It may have been the ridiculously small collection which troubled him, or it may have been that he was subject to spells of melancholia. He did not seem to wish to talk; his hostess's questions about electrotherapy seemed to afflict him with great weariness, her starved condition to have become a matter of indifference.

"Do you use it every night?" asked Sarah Ann. She did not venture to try the name of this wonderful remedy.

Mr. Simpson yawned.

"I use it when I need it."

"Say you were only *afraid* that everything was not right, would you use it then?" asked Sarah Ann.

The careless "I guess so" with which Mr. Simpson answered planted the first seed of doubt in Sarah Ann's mind. She began to tremble. Suppose all her hopes were in vain!

With knit brows Sarah Ann went into her kitchen. There with great longing, but with greater fear, she put both pieces of cantaloup and all four pieces of chocolate cake on one plate and carried it out to Mr. Simpson, who ate it in grim and ungrateful silence and went up to his bed.

When he had gone Sarah Ann sat still on her porch. She could hear the old doctor laughing, and it reminded her of her sufferings; she could see Mr. Simpson's empty plate, and it reminded her of her miserable hunger.

"I could eat the crumbs," said she, wretchedly. "And to-morrow I am going to cook all these good things, and I am afraid to eat them."

Again Sarah Ann reflected. Mr. Simpson had been short; he would not answer her questions about the new cure. But (it was not until long after the old doctor had gone to bed and the street was quiet that Sarah Ann's mind worked to real purpose) it was possible still to test the cure.

For breakfast, Sarah Ann gave Mr. Simpson ham once more, since he seemed fond of it, and with it she offered him pie, cake, and doughnuts. At noon Sarah Ann gave him fried chicken, fried as only Sarah Ann in all the world could fry it. As accompaniments she served the lima beans, the tomatoes, the corn, at which she had been staring hungrily for days. For dessert Sarah Ann baked fresh peach pie. For supper Sarah Ann made chicken salad, and fried eggplant, and sliced cucumbers. For dessert Sarah Ann had ice-cream.

Of all these Mr. Simpson ate heartily and in rude silence; at them all Sarah Ann only gazed hungrily. She asked no more questions; she only looked at Mr. Simpson with curiosity.

"To-morrow," said Sarah Ann, with joy—"to-morrow I will eat."

It was eleven o'clock that night before Sarah Ann, moving slowly, was ready for her bed. Once, after Mr. Simpson had had his evening lunch of cantaloup and cake, and had gone up-stairs, Sarah Ann had opened her refrigerator door. But she closed it at once. An observer might have thought that Sarah Ann had a listening air. But all was quiet.

At twelve o'clock Sarah Ann sat up in her bed. She was conscious of having heard a sound, but she could not tell from where it came. She was about to lie down when she heard it again, a peremptory call in a man's voice. Were the Kuhnses in trouble? But Oliver Kuhns would not address her as Mrs. Mohr.

Drowsily at first, then vividly, Sarah Ann remembered Mr. Simpson. She went as rapidly as she could to her door and opened it.

Then Sarah Ann's heart stood still. Mr. Simpson was moaning.

"Ach, what ails you?" called Sarah Ann. "What is it? Where do you have it?"

"I am ill," groaned Mr. Simpson.

"From what?" asked Sarah Ann, stupidly.

"From your food!" shouted Mr. Simpson.

"From my food?" repeated Sarah Ann. Mr. Simpson spoke as though she had poisoned him. "I didn't give you nothing but a — little — a little pie and some ice-cream and some tomatoes and —" Then Sarah Ann was silent, remembering with terror that she had listened for sounds from Mr. Simpson's room. Sarah Ann began to cry and to call to Mr. Simpson.

"Why don't you cross your ankles?" she wailed. "*Ach,* why don't you rub your hands? Why —"

Sarah Ann was rudely interrupted. Mr. Simpson pounded upon the head-board to compel her to listen.

"Be still!" yelled he. "Stop your nonsense! And *fetch your doctor!*"

With faltering steps Sarah Ann crossed her room. She was too frightened to remember the great hopes which had vanished, or to realize that Mr. Simpson's voice was that of a very angry rather than a very sick man. Trembling, she lifted the window and called a wild "*Ach,* doctor, doctor, come once here quickly!" out into the quiet night.

THE SPITE FENCE

Originally published in the July 1913 issue of **Harper's Magazine**

THE great wind whirled upon Millerstown in November. The fall had been open. John Henry Leidigh did not pack his celery away in his cemented celery-pit until the 15th of the month, and then Lizzie, his wife, laughed at him because he worked late at night, by lantern-light. Lizzie stood between two of the slanting supports of the tremendous fence which divided the property of John Henry from that of his neighbor and brother, John Adam. She was a short, round, pretty woman, with flying, curly hair and a discontented mouth. She stood with her arms akimbo and her apron blowing about her. She had come to call John Henry to his supper.

"Just feel this warm air once! It isn't going to make anything down to-night! Come on, John Henry!"

John Henry's head lifted from the celery-pit. He had bright eyes and a firm mouth; not much more could be seen of him in the dim light.

"I'm busy to-morrow. I have to drive to town. You know I have to drive to town. And by to-morrow evening we will have a big storm."

Lizzie said no more. She had conquered John Henry in the one great struggle of their lives; since then, in matters which concerned them both, John Henry had had his way. Lizzie ran across the yard, out of the black shadow of the enormous fence which stretched up and up far beyond the circle of the lantern-light. She ate her supper alone, then she prepared to go to a cottage prayer-meeting. Lizzie and her husband were Lutherans. Her husband's brother and his wife on the other side of the great fence had left the Lutheran Church and had become Evangelicals. Neither of the men, however, attended service regularly.

When Lizzie had finished eating, she covered the bread and cake with a cloth and put the steak and fried potatoes in the warming-oven and pushed the coffee to the back of the stove. Then she went to the Fackenthals' to prayer-meeting.

The night was clear and starlit. The air was crisp but not cold; it had begun to seem as though winter might actually have forgotten the latitude of Millerstown.

"To-morrow will be a fine day," Lizzie said to herself. "I don't care what he says about it."

Lizzie was right. The morning dawned clear, and there was no frost. The zinnias and chrysanthemums and cosmos still bloomed abundantly, and even the nasturtiums had not been nipped. John Henry Leidigh was a gardener and truck-raiser by profession, and he had remarkable skill with all growing things.

By noon there was a light haze in the west. Lizzie took one of her husband's horses, and with Susannah Kuhns drove to the mountain for life-everlasting to add to the bouquets of dried grasses and grains with which she decorated her parlor mantelpiece; and they rode without hats or wraps. Lizzie had no children; she was free to come and go as she liked.

At supper-time she reminded John Henry that his prophecy had not come true. John Henry, who was a silent person, did not answer. He rose from the table and lit his pipe and went across to the little house where he kept his gardening tools and bulbs and flower-pots and the various instruments of his trade. In the little house was a small heating plant from which John Henry warmed his green-houses, and a desk at which he read or figured or pored over flower catalogues. He did not like to be interrupted; if any one knocked he was a long time answering, and the interloper, even if it was his wife, was made to feel that a great liberty had been taken. The enormous fence extended from the front of the lot backward for about a hundred and fifty feet, and the little house stood close to it at its farther extremity.

When John Henry opened the door to go out, the great wind came in. It lifted the corner of the tablecloth and blew it into the dish of apple-butter; it whirled a newspaper round the floor; it sent the glass of spills crashing from the chimney-shelf to the hearth.

Lizzie cried out, "Ach, John Henry!" as though John Henry were to blame. Again John Henry did not answer; he pulled the door shut with great effort and went across to his little garden-house. The sky was overcast, and there was a greenish light upon it from the lingering glow of the sunset. The elm-tree creaked as it did only in a very high wind, and the air seemed already filled with things in motion. The great storm had begun.

In springtime twenty years before, John Henry Leidigh had put his horse into the high, red-wheeled buggy which was his pride, and had driven to Spring Valley to court Lizzie Schaffer. He and his brother were orphans, and were singularly devoted to each other. The mating instinct, though it developed late, was strong, since it could separate the two men.

John Henry courted Lizzie Schaffer exactly a month; he knew his mind, and Lizzie knew hers even better. They went to housekeeping at once in the old Leidigh homestead at the north end of Main Street, and John Adam lived with them.

Lizzie was very good to John Adam. She was much set up over her good match. She had come from a quarrelsome family, and she had never been greatly sought after. She liked now to appear at church with John Henry on one side and John Adam on the other; it was almost as pleasant as it would have been to be a great belle in Spring Valley.

The next fall John Adam borrowed his brother's fine buggy and went courting also, and brought home Lizzie's sister, Anna, to his brother's house. Anna was older than Lizzie and not at all good-looking, and she resented in the Schaffer way the preferring of her younger sister to herself. The Pennsylvania Germans say, probably in allusion to some long-forgotten and certainly well-forgotten custom, that a younger sister who marries first makes her older sister "dance upon the pig-trough." Poor, homely Anna had had to endure a good deal of teasing.

In a little while John Adam's new house was finished. It was built upon the homestead land, between the homestead and the open country, and was naturally smaller and less handsome than the old house. It was probable that John Adam would never be as rich a man as John Henry. John Henry had a brighter mind, and his trade of gardening gave him more chance for enlargement than did that of John Adam, who was a carpenter.

The two brothers rejoiced that they could be so near.

"The women can see each other often," said John Adam, innocently. "Sisters must always talk together all the time."

"And I can read to you, like always," said John Henry. John Adam was slightly near-sighted; since they were children his brother had read to him.

For six months the two families lived peacefully. It seemed as though the natures of Lizzie and Anna had been changed and improved by their association with their husbands. They did their mending together, either in the dark, raftered kitchen of the old house, or in the bright, shining, much smaller kitchen of the new house. They even gave each other an occasional compliment.

"It certainly is nice to have so much room to move about, like you have, Lizzie."

Or, "You have everything so handy, Anna. And everything is so new and clean."

Once they spoke of their old life and of the quarrelsome brothers and sisters at home.

Near the little house in which John Henry kept his gardening tools John Adam built his workshop. The doors faced each other; when both men were at work, it was like being in one room. In the evenings John Henry read to John Adam as of old. Their wives began to go about; they joined church societies, and they made friends in the village. It was fortunate that the two men had each other. John Adam was not bright-eyed and firm-mouthed like his brother; he was weaker in character, and depended a great deal upon John Henry.

The summer after they were married Lizzie went to her husband with a complaint about her sister.

"She tells the people that she helps with my work. You tell him to tell her to stop it."

John Henry stared. "But she does help you. I saw her baking biscuit for you last week."

Lizzie blushed scarlet. "I hadn't the chance to learn at home like she had. But she needn't tell everybody."

"Whom did she tell?"

"Susannah. You are to tell him to tell Anna about it."

"I won't do anything of the kind!"

"You are on her side!" Lizzie burst out. She was not yet accustomed to keeping house, and she was tired. Now that her fine house and her position in Millerstown were beginning to seem less strange, her old ill temper was returning. She did not see that her husband looked at her as though he thought her mad. "She was always ugly to me. She used to whip me when I was a little girl, and she was cross because she didn't get you, because she had to wait for your brother, John Adam; that is what is the matter with her."

"Don't talk so dumb!" said John Henry.

"It is so! It is so! I am just sorry for your poor brother."

It was not long before Lizzie said laughingly to some one that she had made Anna dance on the pig-trough, and the some one repeated it to Anna. Anna went furiously to John Adam.

"You tell your brother to make her stop," wept Anna. "I hate her!"

John Adam dropped knife and fork and gaped at his wife.

"What!" he said. "You hate your sister!"

"She was always ugly to me," wept Anna. "She had always the best because she was good-looking. She was always conceity over it. She never had to work like I did. She has a wicked tongue. I am just sorry for your poor brother that he married her. You must tell him to make her stop talking."

"I won't tell him anything," said John Adam. "You must settle this between yourselves." Perspiration stood upon John Adam's forehead. The very sound of an angry word terrified him.

Within another month the two sisters had ceased to speak to each other. They had often refused to speak for months at a time at home. To feminine Millerstown, after receiving promises that her confidence should be respected, Lizzie told her opinion of Anna. To feminine Millerstown, without exacting any promises, Anna told her opinion of Lizzie. Almost with the promptness of telegraphy the various opinions were reported to the various subjects. At John Henry, Lizzie stormed; at John Adam, Anna cried. Gradually John Henry and John Adam did not call to each other so frequently as they went about their work and John Henry no longer read to John Adam every evening. Lizzie said that she could not be left alone, or Anna commanded John Adam to stay with her. The two brothers ceased to regard each other with the old placid, friendly gaze. The tie which had bound them had seemed eternal, but here was this new tie which proved utterly incompatible with the other.

"Your brother says you cheated him in the division," said Lizzie to John Henry. "Anna counted it up to Susannah."

John Henry went to John Adam.

"Your wife says I cheated you. Is it true?"

John Adam was terrified at his brother's tone and at his brother's question. He did not know whether John Henry was asking whether he had cheated him, or only whether Anna had said that he had cheated him.

"Yes," he stammered, "that is, she said—I—Ach, John Henry!"

John Henry had gone. He was too angry to argue; the division had been just—indeed, he had given John Adam the advantage wherever he could. He did not speak to John Adam for a week, nor had John Adam sufficient courage to speak to him.

Helplessly John Adam sat about the house after his work was done. Suddenly one evening Anna began to cry.

"You could anyhow plant a few trees and bushes in the yard so I would not need to see her so plain. It spites me to see her. She has everything better than I."

John Adam promised to plant the trees. "John Henry will give them to me." He rejoiced over the prospect of having an errand with his brother. "He has fine trees."

"He doesn't have the right kind," objected Anna. "His grow too slow. You ought to get young shoots from the school-house trees. They grow quick."

"But they have such an ugly smell in the spring; they—" Tall, homely Anna cried again. "I will get them! I will get them!" promised John Adam.

The next day John Adam brought the young ailanthus-trees from the school-house yard and planted them on the smooth lawn. He knew that the shoots would spring up everywhere and that they would be a source of great trouble, but he made up his mind cheerfully to weed them out. Anna's temper had been better since he promised to plant the trees.

That evening John Henry visited John Adam in his kitchen. John

Henry was furiously angry. He had expected his brother to apologize for his cruel accusation of cheating; instead John Adam had insulted him and his wife.

"You will have to take those trees out," he commanded. "They are not fit trees. They poison Lizzie when they bloom. Anna knows they poison Lizzie."

Anna's face grew white. "That is foolishness about their poisoning Lizzie. She would say soap poisoned her if she didn't want to wash the dishes."

"You are not speaking the truth," thundered John Henry. "You know they have always poisoned Lizzie." He turned to his brother. "Will you take them out?"

John Adam looked up with an air of desperation. He was confused once more; he did not know what to say. He saw clearly, however, that he must now choose between peace in his house and peace with his brother. He gasped with distress, but he made the only possible choice. He planned crazily that he would advise his brother in private to take out the young trees in the night. Aloud he said in trembling voice:

"No, I will not take them out."

John Henry stormed at him. His emotion was not all anger; it was part jealousy of the woman who had taken his brother from him.

"I will put up a fence between us. Then you won't need your miserable trees, and if you keep them the wind can't blow your pollen to us."

Slamming the door, John Henry left his brother's house.

In the morning the fence was begun; in two weeks it was finished. It was a solid board wall, almost thirty feet high, and it was braced to stand the storms of fifty years. It sheltered the house and gardens of John Henry from the north wind, and obscured only a little of his view. To John Adam it did great damage. It shut from his eyes his old home; it darkened his lawn; it cut off several hours of sunshine from the lower floor of his house. Both men had to turn their little work-shops; they stood now back to back against the towering fence.

Lizzie and Anna seemed actually benefited. Lizzie walked as one in whose behalf a righteous deed has been accomplished; Anna was able to point to a visible evidence of her sister's and her brother-in-law's wickedness. Millerstown, which enjoys guerrilla warfare, but not open slaughter, was horrified, and carried no more talk from one woman to the other.

Millerstown undertook to argue with the brothers, but to no purpose. John Henry was grimly silent; John Adam wept. They would listen neither to the squire nor to the preacher who besought them to be reconciled. Anna left the Lutheran Church and joined the Evangelical Church, and her husband went with her.

For twenty years there was peace. When strangers came, the origin of the spite fence had to be explained; at other times Millerstown almost forgot that the two brothers who now passed each other without speaking had been inseparable companions until they were nearly forty years old.

After John Henry had reached his little garden-house on the night of the great storm, he did not go in at once, but stood for a moment meditating in the doorway. Then he began to lift long boards which he took from a pile at the side of the house to the tops of his cold-frames. The cold-frames he could protect from any branches which the wind might tear from the trees and send flying about. For his greenhouses he could do nothing. It was not certain that they would be harmed, and he had grown rich enough to stand the loss of a few panes of glass without worrying.

The sound of his brother's hammer was borne to him clearly by the wind. John Adam spent a great deal of time in his shop; to it he retired much as John Henry retired to his little house. He had acquired, as the years passed, a surly manner a good deal like his brother's.

When John Henry had finished placing the boards, he went into the little house and got paper and shavings ready to light a fire in the stove. There would surely be a great fall in temperature before morning, and there were some tender plants in the greenhouses which needed heat. He would light the fire before he went to bed.

Then, as was his custom, he drew down the single shade and locked the door. There were new catalogues and a farming magazine on his desk, and beside them a plate of Baldwin apples and a bag of pretzels. John Henry was settling to a quiet, pleasant evening. If the sound of his poor brother's hammer still reached him, he was able to forget it in his reading. He opened the catalogue first, turning his head for an instant while he listened to the prodigious wind, which came to his ears in the little house at the foot of the great fence as to one in a deep pit.

The wind grew higher. Lizzie and her fellow-church-members at the Fackenthals' added a prayer for its quieting to their other petitions. John Henry in his little house began after a while to read aloud, as though thus only could he fix his mind on the words before him. John Adam's hammering had ceased, but he had not left his little shop. In the kitchen, Anna sat alone mending. She never visited her husband at his work; the spite fence had divided other hearts besides those of John Henry and John Adam.

Then, at ten o'clock, Anna, sitting in her kitchen, and Lizzie, hastening home with her friends, heard above the terrific roaring of the wind a fearful rending and tearing, and then a fearful crash. It was not one short sound and then an end; it continued, it seemed to their frightened souls, for one long moment after another. Every one who heard it — and all Millerstown heard it — screamed. Those who were in their houses were afraid to go out, yet they were equally afraid to await the descent of their own roofs about their heads. Those on the street began to run madly, seeking shelter, yet afraid of it. It was too dark to see a hand before one's face; the roar of the wind was so terrible that no one heard his neighbor's cry.

Lizzie, her arm clasped tightly in the arm of Susannah Kuhns, put out a groping hand.

"I can feel John Adam's gate." she cried, hysterically. "Only a little farther and we are at our house. I — I —" Lizzie stood still and uttered scream after scream.

"What is it?" shrieked Susannah, in her ear. "Ach, what is it?"

"The spite fence is gone." cried Lizzie. "Here; feel! It should begin at this post. It touched the front fence here. It is gone!"

"It is a good thing!" shouted back Susannah. "Ach, let us go on!"

But Lizzie would not move. She began to scream again.

"But John Henry is in his little house! He is in his little house!"

Stumbling, holding to each other, the two women made their way toward Anna's light. Into Anna herself they crashed at the gate.

"John Adam is in his workshop!" she cried. "The spite fence has fallen upon it!"

Appalled, the women clung to one another. The voices of approaching men came fitfully to their ears. Millerstown guessed at once what had happened; the men were saying aloud that it was a good thing.

"But John Henry is in his little workhouse!" cried Lizzie.

"And John Adam is in his workshop!" cried Anna.

Millerstown is quick-witted. There are two automobiles owned in the village; from these their powerful lamps were unscrewed and set up to guide the rescuers. They created a glare which made the scene as bright as day. It was apparent as soon as the light fell upon the great, twisted mass of wreckage that in John Adam's carpenter-shop could be no living thing, nothing even that retained the shape of humanity. Like chips on a pile, the fragments of the workshop lay upon one another. The great fence, which had seemed to preserve its shape for a wild gyration, had ground the building to pieces like a flail. Where the little house of John Henry had stood, the wreckage was piled high; whether there remained within it space for a living body could not be told until some of the wreckage had been lifted off. It would be a work of great delicacy. The light was so glaringly bright, the shadows were so deceptively black, a board lifted carelessly or a fresh blast from the wind might make still more complex the ruin.

There were a hundred willing hearts; there was the cool, directing head of the squire; there were the mighty shoulders of the Gaumers and the Fackenthals and the Knerrs and the Kuhnses. Some of them wept as they worked. They forgot the danger to which every living thing seemed to be exposed; they forgot their own homes; and while Lizzie and Anna and Susannah Kuhns watched in horror, they toiled like giants. Frequently they shouted, but there was no answer. As their hearts sank lower, they worked the harder. Lizzie and Anna refused to go away; they stood together dumbly watching what seemed like the opening of a grave.

Suddenly there was a lull in the wind, and at the squire's command a great section of the fence was lifted and flung away from the little house. In an instant, forgetting his constant charges against unnecessary jarring of the mass, the squire himself pushed open the door. Then the squire, standing on the threshold, gave a mighty shout. What he said no one could hear, but Millerstown crowded as close as it dared to see.

Within the little house, in the glare from the acetylene lamps, each in an arm-chair, with an empty plate and an empty bag between them, sat John Adam and John Henry. Back of them the garden tools of John Henry had been removed from the corner where they stood, and there, opening against a mass of splintered boards, was a door. It was a small door; it looked really like the entrance into a dog-kennel; but it was amply large for the passing of a man's body.

Open-mouthed, Millerstown stared. Slowly, forgetting that they were hand in hand, Lizzie and Anna moved forward. Then came a lull in the wind, and to the two men, still sitting in their chairs, the squire put a question. The wind, the danger, the delivery from suspense were forgotten, while the squire and his friends waited for the answer of John Henry and John Adam.

"How long have you been having these little meetings, boys?" asked the squire.

John Henry and John Adam looked their fellow-townsmen and their own wives for a moment in the eye. Then John Henry and John Adam together spoke up bravely.

"For about twenty years," they said.

THE "ROSE-AND-LILY" QUILT

Originally published in the October 2, 1913, issue of
The Youth's Companion

Grandmother Miller sat before the fire in her wide kitchen, with her hands clasped in her lap. The kitchen was warm, sunny, and with its plain walls, its rag carpet, and its beautifully carved mahogany dresser, even handsome. A Pennsylvania German kitchen is usually dining-room and sitting-room both. In this house there were many other rooms, but they were closed, and, since it was November, as cold as Greenland. There were other great pieces of furniture, carved like the dresser, and worth a large price from a dealer in antiques, if he had known of them, or if Grandmother Miller could have dreamed for an instant of parting with them.

Grandmother Miller was a picture of beautiful old age. She wore a black dress, and had a little black-and-white checked breakfast shawl folded about her shoulders. Upon the table and upon the chairs lay spread three new dresses, and many colored and white aprons — evidence of the loving care in which she was held. If a stranger had looked in at her through any of the four windows, — two on the side toward the pike and the church, and two on the side toward the village, — he might easily have grown sentimental about gracious and placid old age.

But Grandmother Miller was at least not placid. Her black eyes snapped, her hands clasped each other tightly, and occasionally her foot struck the floor a sharp tap.

"They have made my clothes for me!" said grandmother, angrily. She repeated it as if she were not only angry, but frightened: "They have made my clothes for me!"

She rose and paced the floor.

"I am no child! I am no baby! They want to make out that I am old enough to die! I will not have it! But" — Grandmother Miller sat down once more in her chair before the fire — "I cannot help myself!"

In her misery she began to rock back and forth.

"My own children that I brought up have respect for me," she thought. "But these others have no respect for me. They are not like their pops and moms. I say yet to-day to my children, 'Do so and so,' and they do it. But these others are different. I was kind to them always. I learned English for them. I let them cut whole pies in the cupboard. When their pops and moms were little, they did not dare to take pie except what was cut. I let them sleep here, three, four at a time. I let them fight with pillows, my good feather pillows. I let them walk over me. This is what I get. *Ach,* in a year I will be in my grave with trouble!" Grandmother Miller lifted one clenched hand into the air. "If they do not make it different, I will — I will — yes, what will I do? I am old, they walk over me. *They have made clothes for me!*"

Six months ago Grandmother Miller's subjection had begun. Hester, her namesake and her darling, pretty Hester, with whose bringing up she had concerned herself as much as Hester's father or mother, was the first aggressor. Hester had almost finished her schooling in Millerstown; after another year she and her Cousin Ellen would go away to a normal school. She came into her grandmother's kitchen one bright June morning with a basket in her hand.

"Here are doughnuts, gran'mom, and here are 'schwingfelders,' and here is bread."

Grandmother Miller looked with delight upon the viands. She had taught Hester to bake, and she had reason to be proud of her pupil. She patted Hester on the shoulder, praised the bread and cake, and planned to carry some of her own baked things to the Weimers, in whose home were five small children. Hester had on a pink calico dress with a tight waist and a full skirt, such as the girls in Millerstown wore in the seventies, and her curly hair lay damp about her forehead.

Hester had no sooner gone than her Cousin Ellen ran in. She was much darker than Hester, but she and Hester dressed alike, because their grandmother wished them to do so, and presented them constantly with pieces from the same bolt of cloth.

"I have some pie for you, gran'mom," said she, "and some fine cake."

Grandmother patted Ellen on the shoulder as she had patted Hester. Now she could carry all her baking to the Weimers.

To Grandmother Miller's astonishment, Hester and Ellen appeared the next week on baking morning, and each carried a basket.

"Here is pie and fine cake, gran'mom," explained Hester.

"And here is bread and doughnuts and schwingfelders," said Ellen.

"We changed round once," they said together.

Their grandmother looked at the two girls proudly. They wore pink sunbonnets this morning, and they were even more engaging than usual.

"They are fine," said she. "But don't bring me any more. I get all the time so many things on hand. I will bake myself to-day. But the things are fine. I have a new dress for each of you. You are good girls."

"But mom baked the bread and the doughnuts and the schwingfelders," explained Ellen.

"And my mom baked the pies and the fine cake," said Hester.

"Then why do you bring them?" I thought you wanted me to see how good you could bake."

"Ach, no!" said Hester, laughing. "It is because you are not to bake any more, ever."

"Not to bake any more!"

"You are not to have it so hard," explained Ellen. "We have it all planned."

Grandmother Miller laughed until she could hardly see. When the girls had gone, she chuckled, "The dear children!" She got out her baking-board and heated the old-fashioned oven, and decided that she would bake rhubarb pie and cherry pie. "Then I will send one to each of these girls for a present," she thought.

One morning early in July young John Adam appeared on his way to school. He and Hester were the children of Adam, Grandmother Miller's oldest son. John was short and sturdy and blue-eyed, and he went about work or play with equal vim.

He now took the broom from his grandmother's hands. "You are not to sweep the porch any more, gran'mom," he said. "I am the sweeper. And John Edwin is coming to hunt the eggs in the evening always and feed the chickens."

Grandmother Miller did not laugh. She had laughed at Hester and Ellen, but they continued their unwelcome gifts of pie and cake. She stammered out a Pennsylvania German equivalent for "Nonsense!" and made up her mind grimly that she would sweep the porch and the pavement in the morning and gather the eggs in the evening long before John Adam and John Edwin should appear.

In August, grandmother protested angrily to her son Adam.

"What ails these young ones? Why are they all the time after me?"

Adam looked down at his mother uneasily. Although he was forty years old and six feet tall, and she hardly came above his elbow, he was still a little afraid of her.

"Come to us to live, mom. You oughtn't to live here alone any more."

Grandmother laughed. Adam was her child; she had borne him, nursed him, spanked him. She knew how to deal with Adam.

"Pooh!" said she.

As August changed to September, and the days grew shorter, Grandmother Miller began gradually to be aware that she was never alone. Accustomed to visits from her grandchildren, she was slow to notice that before Ellen, who had slept with her, departed, Hester came in to do the breakfast dishes, and that Edwin's children stopped on their way from school at noon, and Henry's children on their way back to school.

When in September grandmother wondered idly whether she should have turkeys or geese for the Christmas feast, Hester told her that she was not to have the Christmas feast.

"We will have it at our house, gran'mom. You are not to have Christmas dinners any more. It is too hard work."

At that, when she had a few moments to herself, grandmother wept. She was hurt and angry, but, worse than that, she began to feel old.

"I didn't know it would ever be like this," she said to herself, bitterly. "I did not think the day would ever come when I would wish to die. But now I wish to die."

Grandmother Miller always did her winter sewing in November. At that time she made herself three warm dresses and many white and colored aprons. But in September Ellen and Hester, sewing after school hours and in the evenings, made grandmother's aprons and dresses, and a new silk sunbonnet. Ellen and Hester sewed with lightning speed; it was the one art in which they had not obeyed their grandmother's instructions. Grandmother did not like their sewing; their stitches were too long, and an occasional pucker showed where all should have been smooth.

When they presented their grandmother with her wardrobe, she was at once too polite and too confused to express the amazement and disappointment that she felt. She laid down the apron that she had begun, and looked at them stupidly.

"But how will I fill in my time?" she asked, with a mighty effort to keep her voice steady. "What will I do from morning till night?"

"You will rest," said Hester, affectionately. "You are to rest, so that you will be with us for many years."

"Your hand trembles, gran'mom," said Ellen. "Let me thread your needle."

Speechless, grandmother let Ellen take the needle from her hand. When the girls had gone, she sat for a long time, and looked at her gifts spread out on the chairs and the table.

"They have made my clothes for me!" she said again.

Then her gaze wandered. She looked down the street toward the village and up the road toward the church. Opposite the church was the cemetery; from where she sat, grandmother could see a tall monument.

Suddenly, as if some firm foundation were slipping from beneath her feet, or as if she were being dragged down by some powerful force, Grandmother Miller clutched the arms of her chair. Then she rose, and without stopping to put on her shawl, ran down the street to the village store.

"I want muslin," she said. "Muslin and cotton batting and tailor's chalk."

Still moving as if she were pursued, Grandmother Miller returned to her kitchen, climbed thence to her garret, brought down her quilting-frame, and set it up in the kitchen.

"I must have work!" she cried. "Cannot sew! Cannot thread a needle!

I will show them! I must have work!"

Overseaming neatly and beautifully, she sewed the breadths of muslin together, laid the cotton batting between them, and fastened them into the frame. Upon them, by means of an intricate pattern in which tiny rose was set close to tiny rose, and tiny lily close to tiny lily, she printed a design for her quilting. Then, although night had come, and Grandmother Miller was seventy years old and owned no spectacles, she began her work. After her thimble had clicked against her needle for about fifteen minutes, she breathed a loud "Ah!" of complete satisfaction.

"Cannot sew!" said she again. "Cannot thread a needle!" Her eyes sparkled. "Whichever leaves me the most alone, Hester or Ellen, will get this quilt."

"But, grandmother, you cannot see!" protested Ellen, when she came to spend the night.

"Perhaps she could if I threaded a lot of needles." Hester spoke a little absent-mindedly; perhaps she was already planning the great surprise for grandmother.

In the morning, after Hester and Ellen had gone, grandmother unthreaded their needles.

Every fall grandmother visited the farm that she had inherited from her father. Thither her son Adam took her in the high buggy, and for her arrival her tenants made great preparations. It was not, as a matter of fact, necessary for grandmother to make the eight-mile journey; the Dieners could easily bring in the fat goose and the red ear of corn and the panhas and the sausage that they annually presented to her. It would even be easier for them to bring in the new baby than for grandmother to go to see it.

But to grandmother's amazement, she was allowed to go this year without protest. Adam's wife and Ellen and Hester and a few other women of the family were on hand to wrap her up, and to charge Adam to keep her wrapped up; but beyond that they did not interfere.

Grandmother was unspeakably happy. The thought of her rose-and-lily quilt, growing slowly under her exquisite stitches, gave her great satisfaction; her mind had now something to rest upon when she sat before the fire or lay wakeful at night. Never was quilt so carefully made. With its beautiful close pattern, followed in fine white stitches upon the white background, it would be handsomer than any Marseilles spread. Moreover, grandmother loved to visit, to go armed, as she was now, with gifts—a gold piece for her tenant's Christmas present, a shawl for the mother, a coat and cap for the newest baby, and nuts and candy and oranges for the other children.

Having made her visit, having eaten her dinner with the Dieners, having listened to Mr. Diener's report, and having even inspected the corn-crib and the barn and the spring-house, she let herself be lifted into the buggy, and she and her son started homeward. They stopped at the store for a fresh supply of tailor's chalk to make a new section of the rose-and-lily quilt. Adam did not call for the store-keeper to come out, as Ellen or Hester would have done. He said, "There, mother, hold the lines," and went in himself.

Sitting there in the dark street, grandmother was for an instant disturbed in her contentment. Two women, hooded and shawled against the cold, came down the street, talking busily.

"Ach, she is too old!" said one, and the other answered with a hearty, "You have right!"

"They are talking about some poor soul," said grandmother to herself. "But I am not old."

To grandmother's surprise, Ellen and Hester and the others were not at hand to help her down when she got home. She was delighted. Now she would work a little upon her quilt. Adam held the horse while his mother clambered out; then he handed her the basket, and she trotted happily up the brick walk. The girls, her daughters-in-law and granddaughters, were fine girls; they would have the fire burning brightly and the lamp lighted. After supper — seventy-year-old grandmother meant to have a little of the fresh sausage! — she would stamp the new section of her quilt, and work one rose and one lily. She dreaded the moment when her dear task would be accomplished.

She opened the door of her kitchen. Then she put her basket down and supported herself with her hand against the frame of the door. The fire was burning, the lamp was lighted, on the table was spread the cloth for her supper, and on it were the precious silver spoons and the sugar-bowl and the cream-pitcher that Ellen and Hester insisted she must use — "While you live, gran'mom."

But the quilting-frame was gone, and on grandmother's armchair lay the finished quilt!

Presently, when she could gather strength enough, grandmother walked across the room, picked up the quilt, examined it, and laid it down. Then she climbed into the garret, brought the frame down once more, set it up, and into it sewed the finished quilt. It was not only quilted, it was hemmed. The girls must have worked with incredible speed. Grandmother lighted two other lamps, flung wide the closed shutters, and began to work at the quilt. But she worked with a long pin, instead of a needle. It was pathetic to see her bending close over her eager strokes.

It does not take long for news to travel in Millerstown. Within five minutes, some one coming down the road saw grandmother's brilliant light, went to find out what in the world she was doing, and then flew, saddened and horrified, to announce that grandmother had gone mad. Hester and Ellen were all ready to start to her house to spend the night; the others ran with them, and all came, panting and breathless, to grandmother's door.

"O gran'mom! gran'mom!" wailed Hester, as she flew. "Oh, dear gran' mom!"

"We should 'a' stayed every minute by her," said Ellen.

Then, with their fathers and mothers and sisters and brothers behind them, to say nothing of other uncounted Millerstonians, they burst into grandmother's kitchen, where grandmother stood by the quilting-frame with the long pin in her hand. The rush of their coming would have been enough to drive a sane person into insanity.

"Oh, what are you doing, dear gran'mom?" said Hester.

Grandmother straightened her shoulders and flung back her head.

"I am ripping," said she, in the steady tones of one who, after unendurable provocation, rejoices to give battle. "I am ripping, and I will keep on ripping till every long, crooked stitch is out of my quilt. I thank myself," — grandmother's tone was firm, her eye was bright and steady, — "I thank myself for all the trouble, but from now on I will do my own quilting."

"And" — grandmother did not know that at this moment she was adding just twenty happy, independent, useful years to the seventy that she had already enjoyed — "from now on I do my own sewing and sweeping and cooking and baking and egg-hunting and chicken-feeding. And on Christmas, one month from to-day," — grandmother's voice became excited, jubilant, laughing, and she waved her long implement for ripping in the air, — "on Christmas I will roast here in this oven, for whoever will come, a turkey and a goose!"

THE PICTURE-TAKER

Originally published in the November 1913 issue of
Lippincott's Monthly Magazine

EVERY one on Church Street had gone to bed except Ellie Edelman and Albert Kutz, and the night was dark and silent. Ellie sat in a corner of the bench in front of her mother's house, her rosy, smiling face lifted, her hand patting the bench beside her invitingly.

"Come sit down once, Albert. You don't need to go yet."

"I am not talking from sitting down," replied Albert, from between set teeth. "I am talking from the picture-taker. What do you know about him? Where does he come from? What is his name?"

Ellie laughed a gurgling laugh.

"He never asks no such questions about you, Albert. He never talks about other people when he is with me."

Albert controlled his voice with difficulty.

"Did you ever let him take your picture?"

Ellie still smiled.

"What is that to you?"

"What it is to me?" repeated Albert furiously. "It is this, that if you don't stop going with him, or if you ever let him take your picture, I won't marry you, that is what it is."

Ellie's laugh could have been heard a square away. It wakened old man Fackenthal across the street, and he smiled, sleepily; it made Annie Warner frown. Annie had no beaux.

"You won't marry me! Who wants you to marry me?" She patted the bench again. Ellie hated quarreling. "Come sit down once, Albert."

But Albert went without another word, his footsteps ringing sharply against the brick pavement. Ellie watched him go. When he had vanished in the dim light, she said, "Pooh!" and laughed. Then she strained her eyes to see down the street. Whether she expected him to return, or some one else to come, she was disappointed. She sat still a few minutes longer, a lazy, sleepy smile on her face, then a little owl above her head hooted softly, and she went into the house. A few minutes later she was asleep, rolled up like a kitten, her tousled, curly head deep in her soft pillow. And, like the cat who remembers the helpless mouse with which she has played, her expression was one of entire satisfaction with the world.

The "picture-taker," who had registered at the hotel as Arnold Smith, told Ellie that he was spending his vacation in Millerstown, and Ellie asked no questions. She did not care where he came from; the pleasure of hearing him talk, the delight of watching his pleased eyes when she answered, were enough for her. He did not dream that it was in amusement, and not in admiration, that his eyes brightened; it never occurred to her that he was laughing when she said, "Shall I move a piece ways up so that you can get this nice bush also in the picture?" She had thought that Albert Kutz was good-looking, but he was nothing to compare with this stranger. She could never marry Albert now. It was only because she could not help being happy that she was still kind to him. Soon he would have to know — that is, as soon as the stranger asked her — that she was going away. The stranger would never settle down in this stupid village, she was sure of that.

He took a dozen or more pictures of her, she went for long walks with him, he showed her how to roll his cigarette, an operation which would have scandalized even Ellie's easy-going mother. Presently he told her that he was going away. Ellie's eyes filled with tears.

"You are going away?" she repeated unhappily.

"Yes. My vacation is over. I must get back to work."

"B-but you will come back?"

The stranger pinched her rosy cheek.

"Of course. Some day."

"When do you have off again?"

"Have off? Oh, a vacation, you mean! At Christmas."

When he bade her good-night, Ellie lifted her face to his. She was almost irresistible, but the picture-taker conquered any impulse he might have had, and went down the street. He was not entirely unprincipled.

The remembrance of his presence left Ellie in such a glow that she hardly realized that night that he was going away. In the morning she cried. Then she dressed hurriedly. Perhaps if she went down to the station, she could see him once more. But she had slept too long. The train had gone.

Albert Kutz came to see her that evening. He was like a silly moth; he could not stay away. He was prepared to forgive Ellie everything at the first sign of repentance. He had seen the picture-taker depart, if Ellie had not. The picture-taker might have shivered if he could have seen the stare of hate which followed his handsome shoulders down the street.

Ellie received Albert silently. Once he thought that he saw tears in her eyes, and he ground his teeth together. He had sense enough not to ask her what was the matter. When he proposed a walk she acquiesced languidly, and they went slowly out the pike, a favorite walk with Millerstown lovers. It was there that Ellie had once almost promised to marry him.

"Are you tired?" he asked presently.

"No."

"I guess we will have to turn now round. I must go in the post-office before it shuts up."

Ellie turned like a flash.

"*Ach,* I will go along to the post-office to see if it is anything for me."

All the way down the pike she was her gay old self. She would not let him ask for her mail. He stood watching her and biting his lips. When he saw that there was no letter for her, his heart jumped. She turned listlessly away from the window.

"I said to my Mom I would come early home," she said sadly.

~ ~ ~ ~ ~

Summer changed to autumn. The leaves of the Millerstown maples turned red and yellow and dropped; there were butcherings, house-cleanings, apple-butter boilings, and all manner of preparations for winter. The weather prophet in Reading, who judged the temperature of the approaching season from a specially selected breast-bone of a goose, prophesied bitter cold, and the Millerstown housewives covered their roses well, and added quilts and comforts to the ridiculously large store they already possessed.

Ellie's spirits rose with each drop in the temperature. The day of the first frost, she went about smiling; when warm weather returned for a few days, she was listless and sad. Her busy mother, who, every one thought, had spoiled her, scolded. She knew nothing about the stranger except that for a while he had fallen a victim to Ellie's charms. Most men did. Mrs. Edelman was proud of it.

"Why don't you take Albert?" she asked. "You will never feel settled till you are married. I never did till I was married."

"I am not going to marry Albert," declared Ellie.

"Humbug!" answered Mrs. Edelman. "You'd make a nice old maid."

Ellie continued to let Albert come to see her upon condition that he would say nothing about getting married. One day Albert, whose patience was exhausted, seized her by the arm.

"Is he coming back?" he demanded.

"Yes."

"When, then?"

"Over Christmas."

The next evening he went with her to the post-office. He saw her lips quiver at sight of the empty box.

"Don't he write to you?" he demanded.

Ellie looked him calmly in the eye. She had never had a line from the stranger.

"Not with the evening mail, he don't."

Even after that Albert could not keep away.

At first Ellie had expected the pictures to come. Surely he would send them to her. He had taken so many. Then she concluded that he would bring them at Christmas-time. It never occurred to her that he would not come. If she grew pale and listless, it was only because the time seemed so long.

And now Christmas was almost at hand. Twice the fields had been covered with snow, there had been a little skating, and practising for the Christmas entertainments had begun. To Ellie, it seemed that spring was coming. She laughed and sang, and her mother teased her about Albert Kutz.

"Will it soon give a wedding?" she asked.

"Perhaps," sparkled Ellie.

Although New York was not much over a hundred miles away, it was as distant to most of the Millerstonians as London or Paris. Philadelphia, where the Kellner family had gone to live, and where Mantana Kemerer "worked out," was a much less awesome place. Many of them had been to Philadelphia. But New York! You had to cross water to get there, there were cars overhead and underfoot, and cars beside you, and huge buildings which were likely to fall on you. You had to be "dog-sharp" to come home alive, and you never came home with any money.

The villagers knew what New Yorkers were like. A year before, a New Yorker had edited a paper in Millerstown for a few months, and his metropolitan ways had not pleased Millerstown. They called his paper the "yellow" journal. He had returned to New York to be a reporter on the *Era*, and they hoped never to see or hear of him again.

It would have disturbed them beyond expression could they have known that on a certain clear December afternoon, events were so shaping themselves in the office of another New York paper as to bring trouble to Millerstown. In the great office there was the cheerful rattle of typewriters, the click of telegraph instruments, an occasional yell for a messenger boy or a shout for a copy. Above, on the next floor, thundered the printing-presses. It was a place which would have terrified the citizens of Millerstown.

In one corner of the office, at a high roll-top desk, which cut him off from the rest of the room, sat the Sunday editor, a blue-pencilled newspaper before him. It was a copy of their rival, the *Era*. The heavily pencilled lines read:

Watch To-morrow's Press for Exposé of Unprecedented Deceit. Republican's Article on Life Among the Boers a Fake.

Having for years rivalled each other in the manufacture of news and the "faking" of pictures, the *Era* and the *Republican* had for some months been exposing each other's fabrications. The *Era* had pricked the *Repub-*

lican's "Prehistoric Discovery" hoax, the *Republican* had proved that the huge mounds of snow which the *Era* had accused the Highway Department of leaving on the street were really small piles, of which enlarged photographs had been taken. The *Era* had printed General Bland's unconditional denial of the interview which the *Republican* had published. The *Republican* had shown that the pictures which the *Era* labelled "Houses of Anthracite Miners" really represented the miners' pig-sties. Then the *Republican* cheerfully awaited developments. They had come.

The Sunday editor rang a bell and summoned a reporter.

"Any fake about your Boer article?"

"No, sir."

"Where'd you get your illustrations?"

"Denworth's."

The Sunday editor handed him the paper.

"Pooh, they can't touch it," said the reporter.

"Well, you be ready to defend it."

~ ~ ~ ~ ~

It was two days before Christmas in far-away Millerstown. Mince pies were baked, turkeys killed and hung in cold cellars, Christmas trees were locked in barns, ready to be taken in and trimmed after children had gone to bed. Old man Fackenthal, who played Belsnickle and went round with a bundle of switches for naughty children, had tried on a marvellous suit of red flannel and cotton-batting. In all Millerstown, only Albert Kutz was sorrowful. He had been so foolish as to buy a ring for Ellie, knowing that she would not take it. She seemed more dear and desirable than ever, now that the color had returned to her cheeks, the light to her eyes, even though he knew it was because the stranger was coming back. He went to the Edelman house each evening, fearing that it would be his last. Mrs. Edelman obligingly went out to visit the neighbors, and left them alone. She asked Ellie why they did not sit in the parlor instead of the kitchen, and Ellie said it was warmer in the kitchen. It was really because it would be easier to dismiss Albert at the kitchen door when the stranger arrived.

And presently her straining ears were rewarded. There was a knock at the front door. Albert rose miserably.

"Good-by, Ellie," he said unsteadily.

"Good-by," answered Ellie cheerfully, no more able to keep the thrill of joy out of her voice than Albert was able to keep the quiver of pain out of his. At that moment Albert was no more to her than the cat under the table. She only wished that he would go, and go quickly.

When she opened the front door, she was so startled that she almost cried out. The man who stood there was not tall and broad-shouldered, as the picture-taker had been, but short and stout. When he lifted his hat, the blood came back to Ellie's heart. No one but the picture-taker had ever lifted his hat to Ellie. Perhaps this man was a friend, perhaps —— She did not know what to think.

The man spoke in a quick, decided voice:

"Is this where Miss Edelman lives?"

"Yes, sir."

"Is she at home?"

"Yes, sir."

"May I see her?"

"Yes, sir."

The man came in and closed the door, and Ellie led the way to the parlor. It was in immaculate order, and there was a bright fire glowing behind the mica doors of the double-burner. Ellie was too confused to do anything but stare at the young man.

"Will you please tell Miss Edelman I should like to see her?"

"Yes, sir — I mean — I am Ellie Edelman."

The young man was upon his feet at once.

"Oh, I didn't understand!"

Ellie realized that he was waiting for her to sit down. She did not see that the kitchen door had opened a tiny crack.

The young man wasted no time.

"Miss Edelman, did you ever have your picture taken?"

"Yes, sir."

"Where and when?"

"Once long ago, and once a tin-type at the fair."

"Never any other time?"

"No, sir." A wave of color came into Ellie's face. "*Ach,* yes, sir." He had surely come with news of the picture-taker.

"When?"

"Last summer."

"Here?"

"Yes, sir."

"Do you remember in what positions?"

"Positions?" repeated Ellie helplessly.

"Yes, how were you taken; standing or sitting or ——"

"Oh, why, sometimes standing and sometimes sitting and sometimes walking, and — and ——"

"Who took them?"

"A — a man."

"Did he say what he took them for?"

"Why, he said ——" Ellie began to stammer. He had said that he took them because she was so pretty. "No, he did not say why he took them."

"Did he take one in which you were leaning on the fence with a pail in your hand?"

"Yes, sir. But he said he would n't finish it up, because—because I was not fixed up like sometimes. He——" Ellie was almost crying. The young man was so stern. And the picture-taker must have showed him her picture in her old dress. The young man did not heed her tears. He was there to vindicate himself from a charge which might make him lose his position. The clerk at Denworth's denied having sold him the pictures, and he was accused of having taken them himself, or of having secured them, knowing that they were not what he represented them to be. He could not spare this young woman, if she did cry.

"What was the name of the young man who took your picture?" he asked.

Ellie began to sob. She could not say that she did not know. Neither she nor the stranger saw the door open.

"What was his name?" he repeated.

"What was whose name?" asked Albert Kutz. Then Albert found himself pushed back into the kitchen by the quick shutting of the door in his face. The stranger was pleased to see that Miss Edelman was a girl of sense and spirit. At least, she resented the eavesdropping of her family. He took a paper from his pocket.

"I am a representative of the New York *Republican*. Two weeks ago I wrote an article on 'Life among the Boers' for the Sunday edition. I got the illustrations from a photographer in New York. They were chiefly pictures of Boer girls. A reporter for the *Era* declares they are not Boer girls. He says they are Pennsylvania-German girls, and that they came from this town. Do you know this picture, Miss Edelman?"

He unfolded the paper before Ellie's frightened eyes. There was the picture of her in her old dress, the milk-pail in her hand. The picture was labelled, "Typical Boer Girl."

"It is me," gasped Ellie.

"And this?"

"It is Mary Kuhns."

"And this?"

"It is Jovina Neuweiler." Ellie suddenly stopped crying. "He said he did n't take pictures of nobody but me," she said hotly. "I don't want to have nothing to do with him and his pictures."

"No," said the young man heartily; "of course you don't. The *Republican* wants to help you punish him. Now what was his name?"

Ellie stared at him dumbly.

"You want him punished, don't you? You see, we are going to sue the Denworths for misrepresentation and fraud, and we want you for a witness."

"A witness?" repeated Ellie.

"Yes."

"In — in such a — a court?"

"Yes."

"And have all the people know he took my picture?"

"Oh, everybody will know that." The young man took another paper from his pocket. It was a Sunday *Era*. It reprinted the *Republican's* pictures of Boer girls, but they were labelled differently. "This is not a Boer girl, but Ellie Edelman, of Millerstown." The other pictures were labelled, "Other Millerstown girls." Ellie seemed to be the only one whom the former editor of the Millerstown "yellow journal" remembered by name.

Ellie stared wildly. To have to go to New York, to confess before all the world that she had let the stranger take her picture, and that she did not even know his name! And to have all New York staring at her in her old dress and apron! If she had been fixed up, it would have been different. And here she was alone with this stern young man. Her mother would not be back for an hour. Albert had gone — had she not slammed the door in his face? They might take her to prison — they might — Ellie burst into tears.

At that the stranger lost all patience.

"Do you like to be branded in the eyes of the world as a dirty, ignorant Boer girl?" he demanded.

"No," said Ellie wildly. "No, no——"

"Then what was the name of the man who took your picture?"

Ellie did not answer.

"Miss Edelman," said the stranger, "are you a Boer girl or are you not?"

"I do not know what you are talking about," cried Ellie wildly. "But I am not a Boer's girl. I — I am ——" Ah, surely Albert would not mind, even if he never spoke to her again, "I am Albert Kutz's girl."

She realized that the kitchen door had opened once more. Had Albert stayed? Had he heard? Would he with righteous anger repudiate her? Her eyes besought him piteously.

Albert fronted the stranger like a lion.

"What do you want?"

"I want to know whether Miss Edelman is a Boer girl," said the stranger impatiently. "You see, it was this way——"

But Albert opened the front door.

"She told you whose girl she was," he said. "Now clear out."

THE DEVICE OF MISS BETSEY

Originally published in the February 5, 1914, issue of
The Youth's Companion

Large, placid Sally Baer endured her troubles in silence and patience. Thin, nervous Betsey Baer endured hers with angry protest.

"'The cousints will come three months from to-day,'" Miss Sally said on the first of March, with angelic sweetness, just as she had said it on that day for many years. "Those new quilts what we made because Cousint Sadie did not like the heavy ones, they are now ready. The new sheets, they are ready. It is won*derful* how Georgy kicks out the sheets. The new tablecloths are ready, too, and I mended the old one what little Edis cut with her knife."

Miss Betsey, who was sewing carpet rags, sniffed and snorted; she pulled her thread with such viciousness that it snapped short before she had set the few stitches required for the fastening. Three times she opened her mouth, and then closing it, pressed her lips firmly together. She had already said everything that she could possibly say upon this subject to her sister. She sought now a more sympathetic listener.

"I am going to Sarah Ann," she announced. "I must borrow a new apron pattern from Sarah Ann, so I can have plenty aprons to wait on these cousints."

Carefully she wrapped her little black and white shawl about her head. It had been her mother's shawl, and, like all material things, was highly valued in the Baer household.

Miss Betsey shut the door behind her with ominous quietness. When she was herself, she was apt to slam doors; but when she was trying to control an angry temper, she shut them softly with great pains. Down the long board walk she went swiftly; her face was very red.

Into Sarah Ann's kitchen she walked without knocking. Sarah Ann, who was a fine seamstress, was making an elaborate apron; even into the hems of her gingham aprons she set the tiniest of stitches.

"Well, Betsey," she said, and went on sewing.

"October and November are nice months in the year!" announced Miss Betsey, with a fury that did not seem appropriate to the remark. "October and November I can enjoy; in October and November, I can do my work, and read my Bible, and play a little on my parlor organ, and go a little round to see the folks. But in January it begins. In January we made new quilts, because those that we had were too heavy for the cousints. In February we hemmed table napkins and tablecloths, and sewed carpet rags, because the cousints wore out our other things. Now it is soon time to begin to plant onions for the cousints to eat. Then it will be time for us to plant other things for the cousints to eat. The first of June the cousints come. A week before she writes a letter. 'Dear Cousint Sally,' she writes always. 'It is time that we are thinking of pleasant Millerstown and our dear cousints. Will arrive next Saturday if convenient.' She means if it is convenient to her. To us it is never convenient in this world. It is too much to have them. They do not get up till eight o'clock, even these children. They go to tell us how we shall talk. Georgy told me I should not say 'The butter is all.' I *will* say the butter is all! How else should I say it when it is no butter any more? They spoil our nice things, and they are sassy. I like it not!"

Sarah Ann looked at the complainer over her spectacles. "Why do you not tell these cousins to stay away, Betsey?" she suggested.

"Sally would die before she would do such a thing. It would not be Christian."

"Or to come, but not to stay so long?"

"That would not be Christian, either."

"Or to behave theirselves?"

"They cannot behave. I tried once to train these children. Their mom was off, and I shut Georgy in the upstairs and Edis in the cupboard, and Edis tore my best dress, and Georgy poured water from the pitcher on the bed. I said to Sadie, 'Look once what these children did, Sadie!' And she only laughed. She said my dress was old, and the bed would dry. Oh, I would learn them if I had them! Nobody will come to see us because Georgy and Edis make fun of the people to their faces, and Cousint Sadie makes fun behind their backs."

"It is six years since they first came," said Sarah Ann, sympathetically.

"Six! It will be ten this summer."

"Indeed, I would do something," advised Sarah Ann, vaguely.

Miss Betsey rose, clenched her hand, and brought it down on the kitchen table so hard that Sarah Ann jumped in her chair.

"I will! I do not know yet what it will be, but I will do it!"

But for the welcome of Cousin Sadie and Georgy and Edith — neither Miss Sally nor Miss Betsey could say anything but "Edis" — preparations went on. A fine garden was planted, rooms were cleaned, and in spite of the fact that Miss Sally and Miss Betsey were probably two of the best cooks in the world, cookbooks were studied. Cousin Sadie did not care for Pennsylvania German dishes, — Cousin Sadie called them Pennsylvania Dutch, — and Georgy and Edith cried when they did not have what they wished to eat. There was no doubt that Cousin Sadie and her children were very selfish persons who were anxious to save money by visiting their relatives. Miss Sally and Miss Betsey might have had their reward if they could have heard the accounts of "My cousins' country place" that the cousins carried back to New York, and could have beheld the picture that they drew of two handsome ladies on a great estate.

The spring was wet, and gardens flourished.

"It will be plenty to eat for the cousins," said Miss Sally, as, scarlet and soiled with earth, she bent over the garden beds.

"We wouldn't need to have a quarter so much garden if it weren't for them!" muttered Miss Betsey.

"The things grow well with this weather," said Miss Sally, gently.

"This weather means that we will have a dry summer like three years back, and I must sleep in the attic because the cousins must each have a room alone."

Miss Sally heard the mutterings. "It is nice that we have such a good young preacher." Thus she tried to pour oil on troubled waters.

"We cannot hear him, except once in awhile alone. And these cousins do not care for the Millerstown church."

"Cousint Sadie is a widow."

"But she has money. She could go somewhere and pay board. *Ach*, if I could just have one summer in my life once more!"

"Perhaps" — Miss Sally alluded to a hope long since grown dim — "perhaps she will this summer ask us to visit her, so we can see a city yet before we die."

Miss Betsey straightened her thin little body from its cramped position. "I do not want to visit her; I want her not to visit us. She will never ask us; if she thought we would come, it would frighten her to death!"

Soon only two months remained before Cousin Sadie and Georgy and Edith would come, soon only two weeks. Miss Sally drooped and began to grow thin; Miss Betsey's eyes grew harder and brighter. The prophetic goose bone in which Miss Betsey had great confidence, warned all to prepare for a hot summer with many heavy storms.

"And Cousint Sadie makes us all get up and get dressed," complained Miss Betsey. "I would rather stay in my bed and wait what the Lord sends."

Miss Sally and Miss Betsey rose earlier in the morning, and went to bed later in the evening.

"Here are early strawberries already. We must make a few preserves for them to eat when the fruit is scarce," said Miss Sally.

"And have none ourselves for winter!"

"We can buy a few canned things."

"And get the lead poison and die! I will cook for them, and make their beds, and wash for them, but I will not commit suicide for them!"

Miss Betsey sat for several hours composing a letter. The day she mailed it, she received from the post office Cousin Sadie's annual letter, announcing the day on which her family might be expected to arrive in Millerstown.

The day that she set was the next after Memorial Day. She would not come earlier, because Georgy wished to see a better parade than the one in Millerstown. Cousin Sadie did not mean to be insulting; she wished only to show the cousins what a man Georgy was growing to be. At thought of him Miss Betsey's heart sank.

"Last year he pulled out the roosters' tails," she cried, "and threw eggs at the cow, and put molasses on the door knobs! What will he do now? O dear! O dear!"

"We must try not to think of these things," said Miss Sally, in her patient voice.

"No, because we will soon have worse things to think of from this wicked boy."

~ ~ ~ ~ ~

Together Miss Betsey and Miss Sally sat on the porch in the twilight. They heard the evening train whistle; their neighbor, Billy Knerr, called to them that he would bring their mail from the office. Miss Sally thanked him in a faint voice. There would be no mail; Cousin Sadie's annual letter had come a week ago, and Cousin Sadie herself would come on the morrow.

Presently Miss Sally laid her hand on the arm of her sister's rocking-chair, but Miss Betsey paid no heed to the caressing gesture. If she answered it, she would cry.

The smell of the honeysuckle was sweet, that of the grape blossoms even sweeter. Children laughed and played on the dusky street. But poor Miss Betsey took no pleasure in anything. "I thought we would help Louisa Knerr with her little baby," she said. "Louisa is a nearer cousin than Sadie, and the baby is my name child."

Miss Sally made no answer.

"And there is Maria Eckert so sick she cannot move with rheumatism. I cannot even go to Zion Church to see her. And she was my company girl."

Still Miss Sally said nothing.

"We cannot even invite this young preacher to eat with us for Sunday dinners. Can you not even answer me, Sally?"

"There is somebody coming in," said her sister, as the gate slammed.

"Here is a letter from New York!" Billy Knerr cried. "Perhaps they are not coming!" In Millerstown one person's affair was every person's affair. "I wish you would give me the right to settle that boy, Sally. Shall it be a good whipping in the beginning, so he learns better, or one at the end, so it is punishment for everything he does?"

"*Ach*, Billy!" said Miss Sally. "It is not right to talk so."

Miss Sally turned the letter over and over in her hands. "What could this be, Betsey?"

But Miss Betsey made no offer to take the letter. Her eyes widened; her hands clenched; she swallowed as if to rid her throat of some obstruction.

"I do not know, Sally."

Miss Sally rose with a painful bending of stiff joints, went into the kitchen, and lighted the lamp. After she had found her spectacles she opened the letter with a kitchen knife. Then for a long time she read in silence. She must have read over and over again what was written. When Miss Betsey turned to look at her sister through the window, the tears were running down Miss Sally's cheeks. Miss Betsey sat in her chair and questioned her.

"What is it?"

"She is going to the seashore this summer, and in the winter she is going to board; she is going to give up housekeeping. What does she mean by giving up housekeeping? What —" Miss Sally was dazed.

Strength seemed suddenly given to Miss Betsey. She sprang up and faced Miss Sally beside the kitchen lamp.

"Are they not coming?" she gasped.

"No, they are not coming." Miss Sally sat down heavily. "I prayed, Betsey. I did not have much faith, Betsey, but I prayed for one free summer before I died, and my prayer is answered. O my soul!"

Miss Betsey seemed to grow in stature as she stood by the kitchen table. The color returned to her face, and her eyes flashed. She took the letter in her hand.

"You may have prayed," she said, solemnly. "But I was the instrument. It was put into my mind to write these cousints a letter. I said Cousint Saidie would be frightened. She is going away this summer, and in the winter it will not suit her, either. She is so frightened she will never come again."

Miss Sally raised her hands in horror.

"Did you tell these cousints not to visit us?"

"No," answered Miss Betsey, firmly. "But I said when they came we would go back with them for a nice long visit in New York."

A MILLERSTOWN PRODIGAL

Originally published in the February 28, 1914, issue of **The Outlook**

"Addison!"

Lying prone upon a pile of sand in the corner of the cast-house, Addison Miller lifted his head from his arms. Above him the boss towered threateningly.

"Where is that shovel with the broken handle, say?"

Addison lay down once more. On the opposite side of the cast-house the other men sprawled about also. There was nothing to do in this last half-hour before six o'clock but rest. The boss did not need the shovel; he was only mocking Addison.

"She is over by the wall," answered Addison, sullenly.

"'She!'" shouted the boss so that the other men might hear. "What 'she'?"

"Ay, the shovel," said Addison. "You said, Where is the shovel? I say, The shovel, she is there."

Addison was prepared for the yell which rose from the group across the sanded floor. They were English — Irish, Millerstown would have called them scornfully; they laughed at Addison's good Pennsylvania German.

"You just wait once!" he yelled back at them. "Some day I give it to you. Then each one will get a hit!"

Having hurled his pitiful defiance, Addison lay down once more. His body ached, his soul was burdened by the thought of his great labors. He said to himself that the work was killing him, that he might even now have some terrible disease which would make an end of him here in the little boarding-house which he hated, or which might overwhelm him as he helped to direct the stream of molten iron from the tapping-hole and plunge him to a fiery death. Even his mother, who drove him to work, would relent if she saw the danger of his task. It was true that other men survived and grew old, but Addison knew that he would never grow old. He saw himself filling an early grave in Millerstown, provided, alas! that there were anything left of him to send to Millerstown.

Presently Addison sat up and looked about him. The October twilight was rapidly fading; his fellow-workmen who jeered at him were gathering together their dinner-pails and coats. In a moment the great siren whistle would begin the wail which to Addison was like the cry of his own despair. Already the noisy voices of the incoming shift could be heard across the yard. For the next twelve hours these advancing men would take up the unholy task of relieving the groaning monster of its burden. Next week Addison would be changed to the night shift, whose boss, even more brutal than the day boss, hailed him always as "Dutchy" and who had probably already planned his death.

All Addison's motions were slow, strong and well as he looked. He blinked round him at the great cast-house with the dim shadows under the high roof, at the sanded floor laid out in patterns for the next cast, at the monstrous shaft of the furnace vanishing upward into the blackness. One familiar with cathedrals might have compared the cast-house to a great, dim church. Addison, however, was not familiar with cathedrals; the only churchly association which the scene had for him was its resemblance to a great picture which hung in the attic of the Millerstown Sunday-school, in which creatures clad in red garments and carrying strange forks and instruments of torture rushed about in just such a light as streamed from the molten iron at casting time. If his good little mother could see this place, she would be appalled.

Now Addison climbed slowly to his feet, his companions still jeering.

"Elephant!" called one. "He gets up like the elephant at the circus."

"And you like — like — " But Addison could think of no comparison sufficiently insulting.

Addison groaned aloud. He was stiff. He had never been accustomed to any work harder than helping his mother in her garden or driving the cow home from pasture. He did not know how he should get back to his boarding-house to the meal which was not fit to eat.

"My mom would have good pie for supper," he said, miserably, to himself. "She would have crullers to it yet and shoo-fly pie. She would not buy bread from the baker and cinnamon buns, she would cook things. It is like eating stones to eat such stuff. She would make me anything I wanted for supper; she would —"

Suddenly Addison straightened his shoulder and drew in a long breath of the cool air. He stood inside the gate which led out of the furnace yard contemplating, not the quiet evening, nor the dark hills, nor the faint golden light in the west, but his own joy. His heart leaped, his knees shook; like the prodigal, Addison came suddenly to himself.

"I am going home to my mom," he said aloud. "This evening yet I am going home to Millerstown to my mom."

Stirred by excitement, Addison began to walk rapidly. His motions were so sudden that he knocked the dinner-pail from the hand of a workman coming in through the gate. Then he fell over the tracks outside, and got to his feet again, laughing to himself. Any one else who had worked at the furnace for three weeks would have been familiar with the position of the track. But Addison in his misery had observed nothing.

"I am going home to my mom," said Addison to himself once more. "I am going rightaways home to my mom."

Addison's landlady was not one who gave herself up, body and soul, night and day, to work and the planning of work, as did Addison's mother and the other women in Millerstown. She had put the supper on the table, and she sat now at her mechanical piano playing comfortably. There were lace curtains at the windows and a red carpet on the floor. In Addison's eyes Millerstown possessed nothing half so magnificent.

Addison climbed the stairs to his room three steps at a time. Then he got into his best clothes, his hands shaking.

"I will leave these old things here," he said to himself. "My board is paid till to-day, she may have these for to-day's board. I am going back home to my mom."

At the supper-table he answered sharply the sallies of the men. They had made a butt of him because he was a German. They should tease him no more. He would not tell them that he was going away. He was afraid that they might stop him; that they might have been told by his mother to have a watch upon him. His mother was little, but she had a tremendous will. He could not understand such energy as hers. It frightened him. He could not work as his mother wished him to work; it was impossible. His mother had found this place for him, she expected him to keep it, but she would not want to have him killed!

"I will talk to her," planned Addison. "She said often already that I am all she has. She will want me to stay by her. I will stay in Millerstown, and when I have rested me up a while, then I will get work in Millerstown."

The fare to Millerstown took half Addison's money, but he was not disturbed. He would need no money at home; his mother would take care of him. He thought of her again as he sat in the train.

"My mom can do anything," he said.

Once he remembered uncomfortably how she had insisted upon his working. From the time that he was fourteen years old she had been after him, night and day. He could recall a hundred pleasant mornings when he had been roused from sleep, first to help her, then to go to Farmer Weygandt's to learn to farm, or to the smith's to learn to make horseshoes, or the store to learn to sell goods. He had never kept any position very long. His mother had not punished him—a hundred pounds cannot well punish a hundred and seventy. She had only urged him in season and out of season. She had not even reproached him; a certain pride restrained her from accusations of neglect.

"She can do anything!" said Addison to himself with pride. "And now I will help her."

Millerstown lay dark and quiet at the foot of its little mountain. Addison remembered as he got off at the end of the train that it was prayer-meeting evening and that his mother would not be at home. He was hungry; he wondered eagerly what she would have in her cupboard; he thought, as of a long-past horror, of the bought cinnamon buns and the baker's bread of his boarding-house.

"That woman, she rests all the time," he said to himself. "My mom does not rest."

It occurred to him as he went up the street that Millerstown would be surprised to see him back. He was conscious that his ways did not have Millerstown's approval. But his mother would explain why he had come, his mother would allow no one to speak against him.

He desired suddenly to see her at once, and he turned into the yard of the little New Baptist Church. He would not speak to her before all the people, he would look in at the window, and, having seen her, would go home and await her there.

The prayer-meeting was over, but the New Baptists had lingered to talk, as was their custom. He was still less fond of these fellow church-members of his mother's than he was of Millerstown in general. They assumed an air of proprietorship over his mother. One of them, fat Lizzie Miley, had once dared to reproach him because he did not work!

His mother was surrounded by them now; beside the huge bulk of Lizzie Miley she looked almost like a little girl. She had begun to wear the black silk sunbonnet of the older women; it was that, Addison thought, and the fact that he was so far away from her and she missed him, that made her look older and more tired. But now he would stay with her and work for her.

He did not mean to let any of them see him, but he heard Lizzie Miley mention his name in her sharp voice, and unconsciously he moved a little closer to the window.

"Is he there yet?" asked Lizzie Miley of his mother. "Is Addison there yet in his place? Or has he given this place up already?"

Addison's mother looked brightly back at Lizzie Miley.

"Yes," she said proudly, raising her voice so that all the New Baptists might hear. "He is at his place yet. When he gets a start, he will begin to send money home. He gets good pay. He—" Addison's mother glanced around at her interested audience. Never in his life up to this time had she been able to boast of him to the New Baptists.

Then suddenly the color left her cheeks and she gave a little cry. Outside the window she had seen her son, his blue eyes staring into the room. Addison was certain that she would speak to him, and say that she had been mistaken and that he had come back. Deception was not possible to her simple soul.

Instead, she turned her back upon the window and reassured the New Baptists, who were frightened by her cry.

"I am all right," she insisted. "It is nothing. A little pain took me, that was all. It took me in my side. . . . No, not in my heart, Lizzie. I —" She finished with a gasp, looking at Lizzie Miley. "He has still his place, Lizzie."

Then, with shoulders straightened, Addison's mother walked down the aisle and out of the door.

For a few minutes Addison waited. He ought not to have come upon her like that; he had frightened her — he thought of it with awe — he had frightened her into telling a lie. The other members of the New Baptist Church followed her, they would soon catch up to her. But she would get rid of them and be waiting for him, and she would feed him, and they would talk together. He had never been willing to make plans with her, but now he would plan.

In half an hour Addison opened the gate of his mother's yard and went to the kitchen door. The familiar latch waited for his hand; he smiled as he touched it. Then he felt of it curiously. To his amazement, it did not yield to his grasp. Could his mother have stopped by the way? But she had seen him; she would have gone home as quickly as possible to greet him. He remembered the tears with which she had bade him good-by; surely she would be anxious to see him now. Perhaps she could not get away from Lizzie Miley. He would sit down on the step and wait.

At the end of half an hour Addison tried the door again. The latch did not lift.

Then he began to call, frantically. Perhaps the shock of seeing him had hurt his mother. Perhaps she was lying ill. Addison pounded on the door.

"Mom!" he called. "Mom!"

Addison thought he heard a slight stir.

"Are you sick?" he called. "Open the door, mom!"

"I am not sick," said his mother, clearly, from within.

"Then open the door!" commanded Addison, in amazement. "It is Addison!"

No sound responded to his call. He shook the door again. Then he listened. Again he heard her move.

"Are you cross over me, mom?" he asked, bewildered at the silence.

His mother did not answer.

"I have come home to stay with you, mom."

Even this announcement did not serve to unlatch the door. Addison began suddenly to tremble. He remembered that he had something to explain, and explanation is not easy to a closed door.

"The work was too hard, mom. I had to carry heavy iron, mom. I was afraid I would do myself something. And I had to take a shovel to dam the iron when it flowed out. It was hotter than live coals. I was afraid it would kill me."

Still there was silence in the little kitchen.

"They laughed all the time over me," explained Addison, with less assurance.

Then suddenly Addison got down on his knees and began to talk through the little hole above the latch. It seemed to him that the world was turning turvy.

"I am hungry, mom."

He thought he heard his mother crying. He began to coax like a child.

"Let me in, mom. I will work for you, mom. You won't have anything to do all day." He could see into the room through the little opening. His mother sat by the kitchen table with her head bowed on her arms. The little kitchen spoke of hard, never-ending toil. He thought suddenly of his landlady sitting at her mechanical piano. His mother had never seen such a thing. "I will work hard for you, mom."

Still his mother did not move.

"I am your boy Addison, mom," he said, wheedlingly. He thought with a gasp of the dark shadows in the cast-house, of the early hours, of the terrible rush of molten iron. "I am going to stay by you. I am your boy Addison."

He could see his mother rise to her feet, clinging to the table. She spoke in a hollow, broken voice; she looked like an old woman. To her son she was suddenly the dearest and most desirable creature in the world.

"My son Addison has yet his place," she said, as she had said to Lizzie Miley. "He works like other men. Other men lift heavy things and tend to iron, and he does it too. He earns good wages. He is no longer a shame to me. I am getting so I cannot work so hard. My things are getting old. I will soon need new clothes to cover me. All these things my son will get for me. I—"

Then Addison's mother swayed and her voice thickened.

"My son has made me lie," she said.

"He has made it that for the first time in my life I have told a lie."

Then Addison's mother sat down and once more hid her face on the little table.

"Mom!" cried Addison, frantically; "let me in!"

"No," answered his mother, "I cannot let you in."

Again, wildly, Addison began to plead. He said to himself that she had turned against him, that she was all he had, and she had turned against him.

"I am your son," he repeated. "And I am hungry."

With his mother's answer it seemed to Addison that the world came finally to an end.

"I cannot help it," said she. "I cannot let you in."

In confusion of mind which was torture Addison looked about him. The dark shadows of the night reminded him of the dark shadows of the cast-house; he seemed to hear in the stillness echoes of all the sounds which frightened him; the groaning of the furnace, the shouts of the boss, the clang of iron against iron. Then a real sound penetrated to his ears— the whistle of the train at the next station. It was like the first breath of the siren which roused him from his heavy sleep.

He got dizzily up from his knees and straightened himself to his great height. He said to himself that he must win his mother back or he would die.

"Mom," he said, "I am going back to my work."

Then, without a moment's lingering, he started to run down the dark and shadowy street.

THE SAVING GRACE

Originally published in the June 1914 issue of *Women's Stories*

"A strong will and an unthankful heart" had Beulah Miller, and her mother could do nothing to change them. But when Beulah went to the limit of her childish daring, and saw what she had brought upon herself, she suddenly understood how fine and different her mother was. A story of unusual strength and homely human interest.

Anna Miller looked into her daughter's room, aghast. Her lips moved, but no sound came forth; her hand fumbled vaguely for some support. It was not from the untidiness of the room that she shuddered, though the room was like a vague spot in the exquisite neatness of the Pennsylvania German house; nor at the cheap pictures disfiguring the white walls; nor at the wickedly poor and tawdry dresses which lay scattered about, in such remarkable contrast to her own serviceable apparel.

It was the fact that her daughter was not there, curled up sleepily in the high bed, at six o'clock on Monday morning, which dismayed and alarmed her. She could not say that she was surprised; she had been wondering for weeks what Beulah would do next.

After a little time she began to speak aloud; she said over and over again, "Beulah! Beulah!" as though the repetition of her name might bring Beulah back.

She had often said to herself that motherhood meant heaviness of spirit and bitterness of soul. There was nothing which lured so irresistibly, nothing which paid with such ample joy, nothing which exacted in turn so swift and continuous a toll of pain. A woman thought of children from the time she could play with a doll; she married so that she might have children. For a few years the baby was hers, then it became a changeling, no longer depending upon the creature whose whole happiness lay in serving it. It grew disobedient, impertinent, a source of anxiety and sometimes of shame.

Anna Miller had married at twenty-five — a late age for Millerstown — the elderly pastor of one of the village churches, who died in a few years, leaving her with a little girl whom she called Beulah. The child was pretty, with black eyes and curly hair, and with not the least resemblance to father or mother. Her mother tried in vain to trace a likeness to some member of her own family, and was forced finally to conclude that the child "took after" some unknown relative of Mr. Miller's. As Beulah grew up, her mother thought less and less well of the person who had given her

her strong will and her unthankful heart.

It was not because she was not disciplined that she was not well behaved. She was penned into the cupboard, she was deprived of this pleasure or that, she was even whipped. She was by no means wholly bad. As a little girl, she had had short and infrequent seasons of gentleness and docility. But as she grew older she became more and more willful, she listened less and less to her mother's admonitions.

Mrs. Miller had determined long ago that her child should be a good child, that she would make any sacrifice, go to any pains to make her good. She began now to put her fears into concrete form, praying that Beulah might not be "like Albert Weidner."

Albert Weidner, during Beulah's childhood, was the village prodigal son.

"He smokes already, and he is only ten years old," Millerstown would say.

"He goes off alone to the county seat. Who can tell what he does over there?"

"He leads a high life."

As Albert grew older, Millerstown looked at him more and more askance. There was no doubt that he was both idle and evil. More than one mother prayed that her son might not be like him. But no mother save Anna Miller feared such a fate for her daughter!

When the child played with little girls, she terrified them with her roughness. The boys admired her too much, even in her selfishness and cruelty, to hurt her. As for her mother's punishments, she knew perfectly well whom they hurt! She was presently equal to disobeying merely to see her mother suffer.

Until she was fourteen her mother allowed herself to hope that she would change. Thus far she had been kept to a certain extent within bounds. Then suddenly she realized that there were no bounds. She wished now a different style of clothes from the simple dresses which her mother made her; she asked for imitations of cheap dresses in the shop windows in the county seat.

"No," said her mother, with her gentle firmness, "they are ugly and immodest."

"Then I will make my own dresses," declared Beulah.

Whereupon Beulah clothed herself, with surprising skill, in close-fitting dresses which showed every line of her rounding figure. She also spread her pretty hair over a strange skullcap which offended all her mother's notions of propriety and tidiness.

By and by she declared that she would go no more to church to listen to the interminable German sermons.

"He preaches round the world and through the middle," said Beulah to her mother. Beulah always spoke in English; she considered her mother's preference for German an evidence of ignorance.

"But it is your father's church!" protested Mrs. Miller in vain. Now another hold upon Beulah was gone.

She continued to go to Sunday school, taking pains to arrive in her cheap finery after the long prayer, and giggling steadily until the end, when she went down the pike in the face of the older people who were coming to church.

She went one summer evening with several of the Millerstown boys to walk to the next town. They expected to ride back on the nine-o'clock train, but, loitering by the way, they arrived too late, and had to walk the five miles in a storm. A reporter, spending his vacation in the neighborhood, sent an account of the journey to a city paper, illustrating it, to the scandalizing of Millerstown, with an easily won picture of pretty Beulah. The boys were punished by their parents, and had, besides, the grace to be ashamed, but Beulah looked at her picture in the Sunday *Globe* and laughed.

By this time the Millerstown mothers had begun to hope that no girl of theirs would be like Beulah Miller.

"What shall I do with you?" said Anna finally in her despair. She had followed Beulah from Sunday school, where, since her newspaper notoriety, she was more than ever stared at, and they came down the pike together, Beulah a step or two in advance.

"Why don't you stay in the church, mom?" said Beulah by way of answer.

"I can't."

"Then don't come behind as if you were following me!" commanded Beulah irritably.

Her mother looked up at her. It was not like Beulah to be out of temper; usually she took her own way in serene and cruel good nature. Her mother saw now that she was staring over at the empty porch of the hotel. Was it possible that its emptiness irritated her? Had the necessity for men's eyes grown already as strong as that? Her own poor heart stood still.

Then her heart began to throb. A man appeared on the hotel porch and stood looking at her daughter and smiling, and in Beulah's cheek flamed a deep glow, different from the bright color which came and went so constantly. The man was Albert Weidner, handsome, of ill repute, ten years older than Beulah.

It was evident that there was more than a casual acquaintance between them. Beulah's mother did not speak her horror — Beulah would only have laughed. She merely walked by her side, as she had been commanded, until they reached the little kitchen.

"Have you ever talked to Albert Weidner in all your life, Beulah?" she gasped.

"Often," answered Beulah lightly.

"I mean" — her mother hardly knew how to put her question into words — "I mean do you *know* him?"

"Of course, I know him!" Beulah laughed consciously, almost proudly.

A week later, Mrs. Miller, sitting at her bedroom window, heard the sound of voices and looked out. Beulah stood on the step, and Albert Weidner was with her. Beulah laughed, an excited, strange laugh, a laugh which was wicked to her mother.

Mrs. Miller uttered no useless reproof. She sat down beside her little table and read her chapter for the night, and Beulah saw her there as she passed to her room. She had not deprived her mother of all comfort.

But now Beulah had gone, leaving her mother and her home. A stranger would have said that this untidy room was like a trail of evil. She did not belong in this house. It was better that a person who could keep such a room in such a house should go away. Never could there be unity between them.

She had written a note to defy her mother, rather than to save her anxiety. She said that she was going on the first trolley to the county seat, there to be married to Albert Weidner. Her mother found the message after she had begun mechanically to fold the scattered clothes. Her mind worked curiously; she said that she must go after Beulah, and, at the same time, she said that now she could put this dreadful place in order.

Then she sat hopelessly down on a littered chair. She must go after her and try to bring her back. But how? She was not familiar with the county seat as Beulah was. Beulah went thither often, but never with her mother, of whose plain appearance she was ashamed. The crowds frightened Mrs. Miller, and now she would not have the least idea how to begin her search. They might not have stopped at the county seat; they might have gone elsewhere to be married. And Beulah would not come back with her; she would only laugh. That, her mother said, would kill her. But she must go.

The clothes were sorted out on the kitchen floor, ready for washing. It had been for that that she had gone to call Beulah. She was able to do the washing alone, but Beulah must learn. Now she laid the things back into the basket, and put away the breakfast she had prepared for Beulah, and changed her dress. There was ample time; she could not leave before the next trolley, which passed at seven o'clock.

No one saw her go, prim, exquisitely neat, her little bonnet tied beneath her chin. The Pennsylvania Germans of Millerstown wear no religious garb which differentiates them from other Americans; she looked like any other dear, old-fashioned little woman. She looked also as though she were stricken with mortal disease.

It was eight o'clock when she reached the county seat. She had no plan of procedure, no clue, except that she remembered that persons could not be married without licenses and that licenses were to be had at the courthouse. There she discovered, in answer to her faint, terrified inquiries, that the clerk of the orphans' court, who gave them out, had not yet opened his office. She sat down on a bench along the wall to think. They would have to get the license, and she would wait for them. She would find some way of persuading Beulah to go home; she would coax her, would promise her anything, a ring, a chain; she would do some sort of work to increase her little income so that Beulah might have more pleasures.

A reporter of the same ilk as he who had sent Beulah's picture to the Sunday paper came presently and sat down beside Mrs. Miller.

"Madam," he said smilingly, "perhaps there is something that I can do for you."

Mrs. Miller did not answer.

"Are you waiting for the clerk? Are you interested in licenses, madam? For yourself, madam? Or perhaps a son or a daughter?"

Mrs. Miller looked at him, dumb, tortured. He became more insistent.

"Perhaps it is someone under age?"

Mrs. Miller's lips moved at last.

"What do you mean by 'under age'?" she asked.

The young man explained volubly. Persons who were under twenty-one had to have the consent of their parents before they could get married. Did she not know that? At sight of the intense relief on Mrs. Miller's face, he determined all the more firmly to keep her in sight. There was a story here, a story worth having, and he meant to get it.

The morning passed; a hundred persons passed through the narrow corridor and stared. Mrs. Miller did not return their gaze; she had seen as they entered the distant doorway that they were nothing to her, and her glance lingered behind them, waiting.

At noon the clerk of the orphans' court went for his dinner, but Mrs. Miller did not stir. Neither did the reporter. The person for whom she was watching might come at any moment, and she might persuade her daughter—he decided that it was a daughter—to go away, and then the story would be forever lost to the *Daily News*.

It was not until four o'clock in the afternoon that a new and fearful possibility came into Mrs. Miller's mind.

She began now to walk the city streets. She had had nothing to eat since early morning, but she was neither faint nor hungry. She knew only that she must find her child, she *must*. Beulah was no longer the tall, handsome girl of to-day; she was a helpless, dependent baby, who, for a while, had filled her mother's heart with ecstasy. And she was lost, lost in this evil place!

Mrs. Miller went into store after store until she was finally shut out at six o'clock; she peered with terror into nickelodeons, to her mind wicked places; she went into restaurants and waited, looking about helplessly. But there was no Beulah. At eight o'clock she stood on the street corner staring wildly about. It was long after dark, but the electric light turned night into strange, uncanny day. She could hardly resist the impulse to scream out her daughter's name high above the creaking of cars, the shout of the starter, the laughter of the pleasure seekers. She wished to call out: "Oh, Beulah, come home! come home!"

At the curb near her stood an automobile, in which were two women; it was with difficulty that she restrained herself from asking them whether they had seen Beulah. They were plainly dressed, they had kind faces; perhaps they would take her round the streets, and she might find Beulah yet. She laid her hand on the machine which yesterday she would have touched about as soon as she would have touched her stove heated for baking.

"Oh," she began, "please, I——"

Then suddenly she heard a voice.

"Well, mom!"

Mrs. Miller looked up. It was only physical weakness which kept her from throwing her arms round the tall girl. Instead she looked at her wildly. Beulah wore a gigantic new hat; her clothes were even more untidy than Beulah was usually willing to have them; her hair showed its strange and unbeautiful padding. She laughed sharply.

"What are you doing here in town?" she said in German. "Let us go home."

"Where is Albert Weidner?" asked her mother slowly.

"Albert Weidner?" The girl's voice became shrill. In it were desperate disappointment, hurt pride, chagrin. "He fooled me; he didn't come."

Her mother made no motion to obey. It was relief now, wild, inexpressible relief which sealed her lips and weighed down her limbs. To Beulah it was something far more alarming. She thought that her mother was looking at her angrily, that she refused to take her home. The women in the automobile stared curiously, evidently not understanding the German speech.

Beulah did not see the strangers. The weary day, her sudden, terrible sinking of the heart when Albert Weidner did not meet her, her despairing waiting on street corners, her panic when she realized that she had spent her every penny on a hat designed to please him, and that she had no car fare to take her back to Millerstown — all weakened and affrighted her. And now her mother made no motion of forgiveness; she only gazed at her sternly.

"Mother!" cried Beulah.

Still Mrs. Miller stood motionless, clutching the automobile.

Now suddenly, in her despair, Beulah's eyes were opened. Here was the only person in the world who would shelter her and love her, in whose bosom, against which her head had never rested willingly, she could not hide that head, which she felt was forever shamed. She saw suddenly for the first time the beauty of her mother's quiet face; she comprehended the adequacy of her mother's life. Every one loved her mother, trusted her, admired her. She had called her mother ignorant, she remembered that the preacher had said that a thorough knowledge of the Bible was a good education and that her mother knew the Bible better than he.

Then, if possible, abasement was made yet deeper. The ladies in the automobile spoke to each other in English.

"What a dear little woman!" said one clearly.

"Yes," agreed the other. "And what a vulgar, ordinary girl!"

Poor Beulah put out her hands blindly. She was faint from lack of food, she could hardly stand. She expected to fall, face downward, on the pavement. But she did not fall. Instead she caught sight of a great mirror in the brightly illuminated window of the store before which they stood. She saw in it her mother's white, slender face, her little bonnet, her simple dress, she saw the ladies in the automobile, who must be rich, but who dressed as plainly as her mother, who looked like her mother. Beside them she beheld herself, conspicuous, untidy, absurd. For an instant, as her outward apparel seemed to her the unpleasant symbol of her soul, she wished that she might die; then, like a flash of light, there came to her aid and her salvation the common sense, the humor which distinguishes her race. Laughing and crying, she took her mother's hand.

"Oh, mother!" she cried. "Look at me in there! I *am* vulgar and ordinary! Oh, take me home and make me good!"

THE CHILD THAT WAS TAKEN TO RAISE

Originally published in the August 1914 issue of
Lippincott's Monthly Magazine

"Oh, my soul! oh, my soul! oh, my soul!"

Like a crazy person — Millerstown would have said "like a schpook" — poor Lizie Schaup roamed through her mistress's house, up and down the steps, from the stiff parlor out to the spotless kitchen, then down the smoothly scrubbed board-walk to the barn, then out to the gate. She knew every crack in every board in the house, she had set out with her own hands every plant in the garden, she had washed and ironed every sheet and towel, washed and dried every dish, and never from the day that she came from the poorhouse at sixteen until the present moment when she was sixty had she broken even a tumbler. She had helped to nurse "him," her mistress's husband, in his last illness, she had prepared the bodies of her mistress's children for burial, she had been at once a daughter, a sister, and a servant.

"Lizie!"

Some one was calling her sharply; her back straightened as though jerked at the end of a string, her chin set itself. She saw Sarah Knerr peering between the lilac bushes.

"Where did she go?" asked Sarah Knerr.

Poor Lizie's back grew even straighter.

"She went off."

"Is it so that she went to the station to fetch the lawyer? Is it so that she will take a child to raise? Is it so that it will be a Diller?"

Poor Lizie's head went back another inch. It was all true, alas, alas! But Sarah Knerr's curiosity need not be gratified yet. Lizie answered shrilly:

"She does not have me to tell her business to strangers."

Sarah Knerr laughed. She had been born in the next house, she had known Lizie and her mistress all her life.

"You'll get over your ugliness when the Dillers come in, Lizie Schaup."

"Since when are the Dillers coming in?"

"Well if it is n't the Dillers, it will be the Wagners or the Kolbs or the Prutzmans — it has to be one of those four that is adopted. They are her only near relatives. I guess ——"

Sarah Knerr's guesses were wasted on the air. Poor Lizie had vanished. She went into the stiff, grand parlor and sat down, rocking her body back and forth in her misery. She was a little, thin woman; sometimes, in moments of fanatic passion for cleanliness, when, scrub-brush in hand, she scoured the pavement or the outside of the house, she looked wild. Now, desperate, frightened, she might have been thought mad.

"The Dillers or the Wagners or the Kolbs or the Prutzmans," she repeated aloud. "Swully Diller is as thin as a thorn—they are always ugly when they are so thin. John Wagner is fat as a pig and dull as an ox, and he would never wipe his shoes while the world stands. The Prutzmans—they are all big-feeling, and the Kolbs, they are all mean. *Ach, Elend, Elend!* why does she do it, then?"

Seeing that one shade hung unevenly, poor Lizie rose and rolled it up and down, trying to straighten it. Finally the cord slipped from her hand, the curtain snapped to the top of the window and stayed there. Each one of the four nieces of Lizie's mistress would see it when she came in. Fat Emmeline Diller would make a "tchk" with her tongue and teeth, loud-voiced Mary Wagner would scornfully direct her husband's attention to it, tall, thin Dillie Prutzman would order poor Lizie to adjust it.

"You are not my boss *yet!*" poor Lizie would answer wildly.

Already they were coming up the street, dressed in their best, stared at by the neighbors. There were four nieces, four stupid nephews-in-law, four grandnephews, all bursting with curiosity and anxiety and fear. "Aunt Mena" was about to adopt a son to take the place of the children who had died, to be given her name, to inherit her wealth, almost the greatest in Millerstown. Emmeline Diller had put the notion into her head, first by sly hints, then by open suggestion, finally by frank coaxing. "Swully"—the boy's name was really Walter; Millerstown has barbarous nicknames—Swully was the oldest of eight children, he was smart, he ought to have an education, which she and her husband could not give him. He might even make a preacher—think how fine it would be to have a preacher in the family! She mentioned even his thinness as an argument, as though she and her husband could not feed him.

Aunt Mena had made her crazy with delight. She had agreed entirely. It was true that she had no direct heir to inherit her money. It was true that she was growing old. It was true that she had recently had a long sickness, and that she might "go off" suddenly. It would be a splendid thing to take a boy to raise.

But Emmeline's happiness was short-lived. She discovered that John Wagner and Israel Kolb and Frankie Prutzman had each been offered by his mother. She said then to Aunt Mena that it would be much better to divide her money among her four nieces. "Like the china set," she said.

A queer glitter had come into Aunt Mena's eyes.

"China sets are different," she had said. "You can't divide a house in pieces, and you can't divide a lot when the house stands in the middle. The thing is to take a child to raise."

Poor Lizie heard the creak of the gate. The nieces were at hand. She rushed wildly to the kitchen, that loved, spotless home of her happiness, and looked about. It would never be the same, never, never. The adopted son was to come there to live; whether Diller, Wagner, Prutzman, or Kolb, he would be intolerable. The house would never again be clean or quiet. Besides, they might drive her away, and she had nowhere to go. But there was no time now to think of that.

She heard their footsteps on the porch. She flung out her arms, then crazily she stooped and kissed the handle of the tea-kettle. She had grown to believe that all these things were hers.

She reached the front door in time to open it to her mistress's guests. They were all solemn, all important; since the last Weimer funeral, none of them had come to the front door. This was a great occasion. Emmeline Diller did not glance at Lizie as she stood in her blue calico dress and her white apron against the wall, Lizzie Kolb said, "Well," Dillie Prutzman smiled with haughty, twisted mouth. Swully attempted to step on Lizie's foot as he passed. John Wagner asked whether there were doughnuts to be had. She was not more to any of them than a piece of furniture. Two of the nieces had decided to keep her after they moved in—at least, as long as she could work. The other two planned to dismiss her at once.

Against each side of the parlor wall, Lizie had set three chairs, according to her mistress's directions. The Prutzmans sat to the north, the Wagners to the south, the Dillers and Kolbs to east and west. In the centre of the room stood a marble-topped table, on it were pens and paper, beside it two chairs, one for Aunt Mena, one for the lawyer who was coming from town. Aunt Mena was the most formal and exacting person in Millerstown, and she was now planning to bring riot into her house.

There was no place for poor Lizie to sit, but she did not go. She stood in the doorway, a hand on each jamb, a poor Samson in the midst of the Philistines.

The nieces paid no heed to her, their eyes were glued to the corner cupboard, where, in unbroken perfection, stood Aunt Mena's Wedgwood set. Not a piece was nicked, not one missing from the dozens of plates and cups and saucers. There were four platters, one with a deep gravy ditch, there was a great, broad-bodied tea-pot, with its attendant cream pitcher and sugar bowl, perfect in form, exquisite in their clear white and blue. The set was Aunt Mena's most valuable personal possession, it was perhaps the most valuable possession in Millerstown. It was to be divided among the four women who eyed it so hungrily, and it was to go to their children after them. Not a piece was even to be given away. Aunt Mena had great family pride—it was that which made her adoption of a son so certain. In the eyes of each niece, her own son was a god among his cousins.

"And Aunt Mena," said Mary Wagner, giving complacent expression to part of her thoughts—"Aunt Mena will see what is best. She is pretty smart yet."

Aunt Mena might still be smart, but she was no longer either young or well. The young lawyer from the county seat put a supporting hand under her elbow as they came together into the room. Poor Lizie, her eyes fixed watchfully and in terror and foreboding upon the nieces, did not hear them until the lawyer asked her to let them pass. Then she stepped back with a gasp.

Old Aunt Mena was white and bent, with bright eyes and a set mouth. She bore bravely the burden of her years and her many sorrows. She walked past poor Lizie without looking at her, and the lawyer followed her. His expression was non-committal. He looked at them all and bowed, even to the servant standing in the doorway. It is probable that he had never had such a case before. He put old Aunt Mena into her chair with an air of courteous respect which made the men in the room gape at him and the boys snicker and the women sit up a little straighter in their chairs. Then he sat down beside her.

He took no papers from his pocket, he simply sat still, waiting for Aunt Mena to begin. Emmeline Diller thought she would help out the situation; she presented to the lawyer her husband and her son. Mrs. Wagner and Mrs. Prutzman and Mrs. Kolb also introduced their husbands and sons. The men said stiffly, "Pleased to meet you," the boys squirmed in their chairs. They all began to be a little frightened.

Then Aunt Mena began to speak. Her voice, tremulous at first, strengthened as she went on.

"I was eighty years old this March," she began. "I have not so many years to live any more."

"Ach, Aunty!" murmured Mrs. Diller pityingly.

"You mustn't talk that way, Aunty," whimpered Mrs. Kolb.

Aunt Mena paid no heed.

"My man left me well off, and somebody must have all these things. There is this house and the lot and the barn and the furniture and the china set and the money in the bank. It is all in all worth about thirty thousand dollars."

The nieces were almost paralyzed.

"What!" cried Mrs. Diller.

"Ach, Aunty!" Mrs. Prutzman's delighted exclamation was almost a squeal.

"Now, this must be given to somebody. Emmeline and Lizzie and Mary and Dillie each think I should take a child to raise and give him my name, so that the name shall last a while yet. That is what I think I will do. I have picked out already the one for whom I will do this. It is all to be done right, and each one is to know before I die where she stands, so that there shall be no fighting. Everything shall be fixed. He" — she nodded toward the young lawyer — "he will see that everything is right. Emmeline, do you believe that I am yet in my right mind?"

Emmeline laughed in sudden, blessed surety.

"Of course you are Aunty!"

Then Emmeline's heart sank. One by one her cousins were similarly questioned and responded as heartily. Then Aunt Mena spoke again, this time a little more sharply:

"It was a time when you did not think so, any of you."

The nieces flushed scarlet. Six months ago Aunt Mena had been ill and they had crowded jealously to her bedside. They had thought that she was going to die, they had thought for two days that she would never rouse from the unconscious state in which she lay. And they had talked and talked and talked, watching with her at night. There was nothing that they did not say. It was before the scheme of adoption had entered the head of any of them; they had divided her property among them. Then, suddenly, they had realized that Aunt Mena's eyes were open, that she was awake. But she had heard nothing — they were sure that she had heard nothing. Only now they began to be a little frightened.

"You talked when I was sick," said Aunt Mena. "You said that a man had come while I was sick and had offered six hundred dollars for the china set. You promised together to sell it to him after I was dead. Each one was to sell her share."

"It wasn't me, it ——" began Emmeline Diller.

"I said all along ——" interrupted Mary Wagner.

"We didn't ——" thrust in Lizzie Kolb.

Aunt Mena raised a frail hand.

"You needn't say what you said or what you didn't say. I heard what you said. I saw that man afterwards. I hunted him up. It is all fixed. A museum is to have the china set. He was buying it for a museum. I am going to give it to the museum. The museum does not need to pay a cent for it. It will all be kept together.

It will have a name over it in large letters, 'Gift of Mena Weimer, Millerstown.'"

"To will it out of the family!" cried Lizzie Kolb.

"Aunt Mena!" protested Mary Wagner.

"But you promised it to us!" declared Dillie Prutzman.

Aunt Mena wasted no time in answering argument with fact. Afterwards, they would have time to discover the ridiculousness of their protests.

The women's eyes sought one another in dismay and anger. Their husbands stared helplessly at the floor, their sons continued the series of insane grimaces which they were making at one another after the manner of their kind. Swully Diller stretched his long legs in a vain effort to reach poor Lizie's foot. Lizie still stood in the doorway. She had resumed her Samson-like attitude, her eyes were upon her frail, stubborn mistress whom she loved.

Suddenly Aunt Mena turned and looked at her.

"Do you think I am in my right mind, Lizie?" she asked.

Lizie's hands loosened their clasp of the door-frame and clutched each other.

"Ach, Mena!" she cried. There are few titles in Millerstown, even between maid and mistress. "Ach, Mena! I — I guess so, Mena." Then poor Lizie hesitated. There had always been perfect openness between them. "I — I am not sure, Mena!"

The nieces shrieked out their horror and disapproval.

"You'd better clear out, Lizie Schaup," cried Emmeline.

"*You are not sure, Lizie?*" repeated Aunt Mena.

"I thought you were, Mena," wailed poor Lizie. "Indeed, I thought you were. But now I do not know. Don't have any Swully or any Israel Kolb come in till you are dead, Mena. Let them come in then, Mena, if you must, but not now. Mena ——" Lizie took a step forward, then stepped back again and seized the door-frame. "I must talk, Mena. You took me from the poorhouse and you gave me a home, but I must talk. Johnny Wagner, he will eat you out of house and home, Mena, and he will never wipe his shoes. And Israel will bring his dog, and Frankie says nothing all the time but 'Shut up' and 'Hold your mouth' and worse things, and whichever comes will bring his mom and his pop and all his folks and ——"

There were stirrings of rage, mutterings, then a chorus of interruptions. Dillie Prutzman's voice rose to a shriek:

"Lizie Schaup, you lie, you ——"

The young lawyer raised his hand.

"Mrs. Weimer asked her to speak," he said sharply. "Go on, Lizie."

Lizie did not go on because he bade her, but because she could not help herself. She would have spoken though their voices had drowned hers utterly, though they had attacked her bodily. She had never said her whole mind about them in all her life; the accumulation of speech threatened to burst her.

"They sit up front in the church!" she cried. "They bake ten kinds of fine cakes for the Sunday School picnic, and they have the preacher to sit at their table, Mena. But they went through all the bureau-drawers when you were sick, Mena, they know everything that is in your house. They looked for papers, Mena, they——"

Again the tide of feminine speech swelled furiously. The wild mob at Versailles could have been no more clamorous.

"It is a lie!"

"She is crazy!"

"It is not true!"

"I was awake when you thought I was asleep," reminded Aunt Mena grimly.

Poor Lizie put up her arm as though to shelter herself from blows. She was still brave, still defiant.

"Do not let them come in, Mena," she wailed. "Swully steps on my feet now; he will step on yours till everything is at an end."

The lawyer looked at Aunt Mena, then he laid his hand on her slender arm. It seemed merely a warning gesture. In reality, his fingers pressed the vein in her wrist. Its pulse beat dangerously.

"I'd tell them, Mrs. Weimer," he said gently. "No one will gain anything by putting it off."

Aunt Mena too felt the wild racing of her heart.

"All right," she said slowly. "Then you must go quietly home and do your talking there. Half of my money will go to the church and the orphan asylum. The china set goes as I have said. The other half of the money will come some day to you four. But as long as my child that I take is living, nobody will get anything."

"Your child!" repeated the women, still confused, still furious, but suddenly restored to hope.

"Yes," said Aunt Mena; "I have already taken a child to raise. It is all fixed. The papers are already made out, and it is fixed so nobody can bother my child." Then, cutting the air like the arrows of the returned Ulysses, a single, shrill, excited sentence smote them, nieces and nephews and grandnephews alike: "The child I have taken is Lizie Schaup."

THE EIGHT-HOUR DAY

Originally published in the October 31, 1914, issue of
The Country Gentleman

IF Oliver Kuhns had learned from experience anything of the contrary ways of women, especially of his wife, he might have ascribed to its true source the uncanny sound that waked him from sleep at midnight. Instead he lay shaking with fright, unaware that Susannah was no longer beside him. He tried to persuade himself that he had dreamed the sound; he assured himself that no one could have reached the attic without going through his room, and that, though he might have slept, Susannah would have been roused in an instant.

In a moment Oliver heard the noise again. It was too loud for the scratching of a mouse or even of a rat; it was the sound of a stealthy footstep passing back and forth over his head. Nerving himself by the thought of his wife — though Susannah had lost her mind he still loved her — and by the sight of his children in the next room dimly outlined in their trundle bed, he rose and crept to the foot of the stairway. He had not deceived himself: above was a faint light, steadily passing to and fro was the quiet step.

Setting his bare foot close to the wall so as to make the boards creak as little as possible, trembling, yet trying to be brave, Oliver Kuhns climbed the steps. Then at the top, his lighted candle dropping from his hand and rolling with a clatter to the bottom, Oliver sat heavily down upon the floor. It was not a burglar who fronted him; it was Susannah, whom he had thought safely in bed — Susannah, dressed as though it were daylight and carrying weapon-like before her the household broom.

It had been the improvident Beidles who, two weeks before, had received the first intimation of Susannah's madness. Then, upon a hot Monday morning, the six Beidle children had advanced into the Kuhns' yard, carrying as was their custom two baskets to be filled with scraps. Susannah was at her washtub; far down the long, narrow yard the two Kuhns children, Oliver and Louisa, watched her from the boughs of the apple tree.

To the amazement of the Beidles, Susannah made no motion toward filling their baskets. She lifted her soapy hands from the washtub only to wave them in wild and forbidding gestures.

"Go home!" cried Susannah, her black eyes snapping. "Don't come round here! What do you want? Go home!"

The oldest of the Beidles ventured an explanation:

"We come for scraps."

"I have no scraps."

"We come"—the voice of the oldest Beidle sank to a frightened whisper—"we come like always."

"I have nothing for you," screamed Susannah. "If I had I wouldn't walk into the house to get it. I am tired of you. Go home!"

As a snake works its way backward, so the young Beidles pushed their way out of the Kuhns' yard. Even the oldest could not remember the time when Susannah had not filled their baskets on Monday morning. But they dared say no more, they dared not even stay to listen to Susannah, talking now apparently to the empty air.

"I am tired," repeated Susannah as she thrust Oliver's grimy shirt up and down in the soapy water. "I am tired of everything. He might help me a little. I get up at five o'clock in the morning so he can have his breakfast the way he likes it. I pack his basket. I wash, I scrub, I iron, I bake, I cook, I raise pigs, I garden, I make clothes for the children and for him. I belong to the Sunday school, I mend, I flute the pillowcases, I help to clean the church, I sing in the choir. Nobody can say I am lazy."

If the loud declaration was made in anticipation of an answer it received none. Sarah Ann Mohr, Susannah's neighbor, was away; nobody heard but the children perched in the apple tree.

Suddenly Susannah's tears dripped into the washtub.

"I am tired," she wailed pitifully. "I ought to have a wash machine. My bones feel like dried sticks in me. He ought to help me."

Susannah's tears continued to drop while she finished Oliver's shirts. There was small prospect of help from Oliver. In Millerstown man's work was as clearly divided from woman's as night from day. Man earned the money and woman kept the house.

Susannah still wept while she starched the wash and hung it on the line in the hot sunshine. Then she put the tubs and the wringer away and scrubbed the porch, and because the water had run down on the boardwalk she scrubbed that too. Afterward she went to the store for sugar and baked two cherry pies and got dinner.

But of the delicious dinner Susannah ate nothing. The children had clambered down from the apple tree when she went to the store; they appeared promptly at twelve o'clock, remembering their mother's outburst and aware that they had soiled their clean clothes. But their mother said nothing; she did not seem to notice their disarray. Nor did they notice that their mother did not eat. The young Kuhnses were hungry, and when hungry devoted themselves to food.

Their father was also given to devotion to food, but today he was excited and talked as he ate.

"We had good news at the furnace," he announced. "We are to work in eight-hour shifts from now on. I guess——"

Susannah made a single sharp comment:

"We cannot get along with less wages."

Oliver beamed upon her. He was too much occupied with his own satisfaction to see her red eyes, her set mouth.

"That is the good thing. I get the same pay like always."

"Oh, you do!" commented Susannah shortly.

"One time I work from five till one, then from one till nine, then from nine till five. Then I——"

"Then you can weed the garden," said Susannah, "and you can pick cherries, and you can help wash."

Help wash! A man! Oliver laughed. It was ungracious of Susannah to respond to his announcement of good fortune with this nonsense. Weeding garden and picking cherries and washing were her work. But she would get over her ill temper; she always did. Oliver finished half a pie, washed his hands at the pump and took his way, whistling, down the yard. Susannah said to herself that she believed she hated him. She washed her dishes as she had washed the clothes—partly with tears; then she brought the clothes in from the line. Ordinarily she would have prepared to iron the sheets and towels as she cooked supper, leaving the starched wash for the morning. Today she thrust the basket with its high-heaped burden under the kitchen table, and without darkening the room or slaying the three flies which by fine strategy had made their way in in the morning she went into the dark sitting room and lay down upon her face on the floor.

There for a while Susannah cried, then she slept. And between tears and slumber a monstrous plan formed itself vaguely in Susannah's mind.

~ ~ ~ ~ ~

The next morning she rose from her bed at four o'clock instead of five and got Oliver's breakfast and packed his basket. It was warm, and it was necessary for her to call Oliver twice, facts that did not add to her good temper. Oliver, once roused, was cheerful.

"It is a little hard getting up an hour earlier," said he, "but then at one o'clock I will be home. Then I can sleep."

"Oh, you can!" muttered Susannah.

"And I will be powerful hungry," prophesied Oliver. "You might keep a little something hot from the dinner, Susannah."

"Oh, I might!" said Susannah.

Oliver departed, whistling as usual. Susannah was sure now that she hated him.

Then Susannah set to work. She killed the three flies with the vicious slap of a folded paper, she sprinkled the great basket of wash, furious with herself because she had not done it the evening before.

"It will not iron nice," she said to herself. "And Louisa's best dress is in, and my best dress and my ruffled petticoat what I must have for the Sunday-school picnic." A fresh weariness came into Susannah's eyes. She thought of the wash basket to be packed with food, of the picnic guests who always arrived uninvited at the Kuhns' table on such occasions. "I will not go to the Sunday-school picnic," declared Susannah to herself.

All the hot morning Susannah worked. She swept the pavement, she got the children's breakfast, she finished the ironing, she baked two raisin pies, she got dinner.

"I was going to make doughnuts yet," she said wearily. "I was going to start to make soap. Nothing gets done any more."

Until one o'clock Susannah kept up the fire in the hot kitchen so that the stew and the coffee might be warm for Oliver. Oliver was enthusiastic about the new hours. Having finished his dinner he stepped round the basket of ironed clothes waiting to be carried upstairs and betook himself to the hammock, unconscious of the glare that followed him. It was three o'clock when Susannah lay down on the sitting-room floor. Yesterday's nap had made her stiff, but any other bed was intolerable in the heat. In her discomfort Susannah matured her plan.

On Wednesday Susannah got Oliver his breakfast and packed his lunch pail, began to give the garret its monthly cleaning, baked two lemon pies, gave the children their dinner, kept Oliver's warm for him, went to the store, did the week's mending, got supper, washed dishes and went to bed. Her plan was complete now.

On Thursday morning Susannah, waking at four o'clock, did not rise. The sky was rosy, the unfinished garret waited, it was time for workers to be about their business. Oliver stirred presently beside her.

"Susannah!" he exclaimed. "Ain't you up yet?"

"No," answered Susannah. "I ain't."

"Well, Susannah!" teased Oliver good-naturedly. "It is ten minutes after four already."

Still Susannah did not stir. Oliver looked at her, puzzled.

"Come, Susannah."

"I am not going to get up," announced Susannah.

"Are you sick?" asked Oliver with alarm.

"No," said Susannah. "I am not sick." Susannah sat up in bed as though her remarks could not be made from a supine position. "I am well. But I am going to lie here till seven o'clock. Seven o'clock is a very good time to get up. You will find things in the cellar for your breakfast and you can pack some things in your kettle. If the children don't want to wait till eight o'clock for their breakfast they can eat some pie now. Eight o'clock is a good time for breakfast."

And then, having finished her speech, Susannah lay down.

For an instant Oliver stared at her, his mouth open, his hands clasped round the bedpost.

"Susannah!" he cried.

"You will be late and lose your job," answered Susannah.

When Oliver had gone, stumbling down the steps in his confusion, Susannah sat up again in her bed.

"At seven in the morning I begin my work," said she. "I work till two; that is seven hours. Then I work again from five till six. That is the eight-hour day for me."

Again Susannah lay down; again, suddenly, she sat upright.

"I will buy baker's bread and perhaps baker's doughnuts. I will also buy soap and I will get the children's clothes in Allentown, and I will not iron anything like stockings and underclothes, and Louisa cannot wear all the time white dresses, and I won't cook anything fancy, and I will get things in cans."

Again Susannah lay down; again Susannah popped up.

"Oliver will just have to pay for the things," said she.

If Oliver Kuhns was astonished his children were frightened and Millerstown was incredulous. The children, clamoring loudly for their breakfast, were advised to eat what they could find. Sarah Ann Mohr, seeing that Susannah's shutters remained closed, and traveling hastily and ponderously over from her house and up into Susannah's bedroom, was told Susannah's plans in detail, and waddled out to fetch Susannah's mother to her sick daughter. Susannah's mother and her sisters and her aunts, hastening to her side, were laughed at and their reproof was scorned. Still Susannah lay in her bed.

At seven o'clock, according to her schedule, Susannah rose. At eight she served breakfast, prepared in leisurely comfort, as she prepared supper when she had company in the kitchen. At half-past eight Susannah swept the pavement, singing in her high soprano voice. At nine Susannah walked slowly down to the store and ordered a washing machine, some store soap, half a dozen cans of soup, and some ready-made gingham aprons. Both going and coming Susannah stopped to talk with her neighbors. At eleven Susannah looked into her cupboard.

"I'll heat the soup," said she. "And there is pie and cake left over and hash to warm up, and that is enough for anybody. Tomorrow I will bake at one time five or six pies; they cannot have pies fresh every day; that is settled."

Susannah's children ate their dinner with murmurs which their mother hushed. For Oliver no dinner was kept warm.

"It heats the kitchen too much," she explained to Oliver. "If you want you can put the draft on, but you will have to black it again. Here is the new wash machine. I think that with a machine I will perhaps keep on with the washing."

Oliver sat down heavily. He earned good wages, and with Susannah's economical ways he had been able to save. Now he saw his hoard vanishing, himself plunged into bankruptcy.

"Who else would do it?" he asked weakly.

"*Ach*, perhaps I will hire some one," said Susannah. "Or perhaps I get me an ironing machine. I like an eight-hour day."

It is astonishing how quickly one can accustom oneself to leisure. It is astonishing also how quickly a house and its inhabitants can begin to look uncared for. The grass was not cut; the garden was not weeded; the children, who had been hitherto the most carefully washed and brushed children in Millerstown, began to look untidy; there was dust under the beds, and the cellar had a musty odor.

Susannah sat round in apparent ease of mind, the children followed their own devices, and Oliver sat round, also, but not with Susannah. When Susannah sat on the front steps or on the broad bench beside the front door Oliver sat on the kitchen porch or down at the end of the lot. Oliver was ashamed of Susannah.

And at Susannah's side there established herself comfortably one evening, as though she belonged there, the improvident mother of the Beidles. Susannah's ways were bringing her into congenial and appropriate company.

To Susannah once more came her mother and her other relatives, and once more Susannah laughed. Once more Sarah Ann slipped sidewise through the narrow gate between the two yards and gasped forth her disapproval.

"But I am getting fat," boasted Susannah. "My hands are getting like a lady's hands, my bones don't feel in me like sticks any more. I don't do anything but what I must do. My garret is half done and it lays that way. If you were smart you'd do like I do, Sarah Ann. I buy my bread, I buy the children's clothes and Oliver's shirts, I don't cook soap, I don't clean or scrub any more like I used to, I will never flute anything if I am killed for it. I put the fluting iron down the well."

Sarah Ann's hands, raised to heaven at the beginning of Susannah's remarks, dropped limply to her knees. She bent forward and fixed Susannah with her eye.

"Susannah," asked she, "do you like it?"

Susannah looked about her, at the long grass, at the littered porch, and finally up toward the garret window, against whose pane leaned a broom, forgotten for two weeks.

"Yes," declared Susannah firmly. "I like it."

Now, at midnight, in her ignominy discovery and retribution had come upon Susannah. At the sound of the approaching footsteps she had laid hand upon that same forgotten broom. At sight of Oliver her hand loosened and the broom, sliding the stairway, joined the candlestick at the bottom. It was a long time before Susannah standing, and Oliver sitting at her feet, found tongue to address each other. Susannah had nothing to say and Oliver was smitten dumb.

Then Oliver's eyes, traveling round the dimly lighted garret, saw a strange sight. All it contained, a chair or two, the boxes, the children's cradle, the chest in which the winter clothes were packed, had been pushed to one side of the room. The floor on the other side—it must be remembered that the hour was midnight—was wet; upon it stood a pail, a wet scrubbing rag, a scrubbing brush, and beside them lay a cake of soap. Open-mouthed, the dazed Oliver contemplated them. Then from his lowly position Oliver looked up at Susannah with hope in his eye.

"Is the eight-hour day over?" said he. "Will it—will it"—Oliver's voice trembled—"will it be again like always?"

With a sudden catching of her breath Susannah looked down at him.

She had expected jeers and reproaches; she was prepared to meet them with defiance. It was true that she was working tonight; she would work on that account the less tomorrow. But Oliver did not reproach her; he seemed not to see how embarrassing was her position. She realized that she still held in her own hands the terms of her capitulation.

"When you work nine hours," said she, "then I will work nine hours. When you work ten hours I will work ten hours."

"But I can't!" cried Oliver, his hopes dashed. "The shift is eight hours. You cannot understand. You——"

"I can understand," cried Susannah. "I have nothing to do with easy work like eight-hour shifts. What I mean"— Susannah looked her husband in the eye — "what I mean is washing pavements for me and——"

"What!" cried Oliver.

"And weeding the garden, and picking cherries in the afternoon and working also——"

Susannah paused to get her breath, and her husband moved a little nearer to her. He looked at Susannah first with startled curiosity, then with the amazed conviction that Susannah meant what she said. He bent his head, awaiting the naming of his last, most humble and ignominious task, aware that he entered at this moment upon a strange new service, in which he was to be first laughed at, then unwillingly followed, by every one of his fellow men of Millerstown.

"And working also," said Susannah firmly, remembering in her restored vigor her old weariness, "and working also for me on Mondays my wash machine."

THE HIGH CONSTABLE
A Millerstown Burglar Story

Originally published in the April 28, 1915, issue of *The Outlook*

It is a difficult thing to hold spite for four months even against a neighbor. When the object of one's resentment is the husband with whom one lives, the difficulties are multiplied. But this evening, when Oliver returned from hearing the report of the election, the period of Susannah's resentment would end. She would then give expression to the anger which had for four months been growing stronger in her breast. If Oliver were annihilated, it was Oliver's fault.

Susannah lay deep in her bed one night early in July, in the heavy sleep which followed naturally upon the completion of a large washing and ironing in one day. The silence of the Millerstown night is unbroken; there, if anywhere in the world, can the weary rest. Then—

"Clang!"

The sound was that of a giant gong set, not in Susannah's room nor in her house, but out of doors, as though its business were the rousing of the countryside. At once Susannah rose to a sitting position. She could see her bed, smooth and neat; she could follow the dim outlines of the room and the faint oblong of the window opening against the thick foliage of a maple tree. Oliver, her husband, was at work on the night shift at the furnace; only she and the two children, Oliver, Jr., known to Millerstown as Ollie, and Louisa, were at home. She could hear the regular breathing of the children in their beds in the next room and the gentle motion of the leaves in a pleasant breeze.

Awaiting the terrifying second clang of the great bell, Susannah put one slender foot out upon the rag carpet, then the other.

"It is the alarm!" The words formed themselves in the region of Susannah's diaphragm, but were unable, on account of tense muscles, to rise farther. "The burglars have come!"

By day Susannah washed and ironed and scrubbed and cooked and trained her children and managed her husband. Susannah, judged by Millerstown's standards, was a success. Susannah, judged by her own standards, was a failure. She was not one of those comfortable women who can fill their lives with plans for their children.

"I have trained those children," Susannah would say to Sarah Ann Mohr. "There are no children in all Millerstown who come so quick when you say come and who go so quick when you say go. I feed them good. I wash them till their bones almost come through. More I cannot do now."

"But you, Oliver—" This complaint was addressed only to Oliver himself. "You, Oliver, should be something. So long as you earn your wages and eat and sleep you are satisfied. Billy Knerr is tax collector, Jim Fackenthal is road-master, Eli Fry is High Constable; but you are nothing!"

"I want—" This said Susannah to her pillow when all plans for Oliver had failed. "I want to do something myself!"

When Susannah slept, she dreamed. If life's waking feast had given her only a half portion, sleep gave her full measure. Susannah dreamed that she rescued children from drowning, that she dashed into burning buildings, rushed across tracks before swiftly moving trains to save the imperiled. If the Presidency of the United States had been open to her sex, she would have beheld herself occupying that high office. But most clearly of all did Susannah see herself entrapping the marauders who had recently made life in Millerstown so exciting and perilous an experience.

Millerstown lies ten miles from the county seat, and here the long freight trains make their first stop to take water from the tank at the railway station. They bring with them at times, in addition to their legitimate burden, human travelers. Tramps and other undesirable citizens, warned away from the county seat, leave the train at its first stop to seek a meal or a lodging for the night, or sometimes to steal. The Millerstown store had been twice robbed, several kitchens had been forcibly entered, and even mammoth bolts on the doors of the bank had been attacked with a file. It was Ollie Kuhns and his sister Louisa who, playing with other children in the yard of the bank building, had found a flask filled with nitroglycerine. Then it was that the bank officials set upon its wall the thunderous alarm.

Now the marauders had come. Sitting upon the edge of her bed, Susannah ceased to breathe. The alarm was set to continue indefinitely, fiercely, almost unendurably. Susannah awaited, terrified, the shock of its clangor, the sound of rapid steps, perhaps the sound of gunshots.

But Susannah heard no second stroke of the bell, no running steps, no commotion of any kind. In a flash, she realized that the alarm had been tampered with, that it would ring no more. Moreover, Millerstown had not heard its single stroke. Millerstown did not move or stir.

Susannah rose, her eyes gleaming, her breath sharply drawn. Her hour of glory had dawned. She dressed herself with trembling hand; she locked her sleeping children, the restless Oliver and the excitable Louisa, into their room, and she went down the steps and out of the house. The hour was half-past three, which was not far from the time of Oliver's return. But to Susannah it was still midnight, the traditional period for the operations of the wicked.

For an instant Susannah stood on her kitchen porch, her heart throbbing. She thought that she heard a stir in the house of Sarah Ann Mohr, and then remembered Sarah Ann's oft-declared intention of covering her head with the sheet and yielding herself to prayer in circumstances such as these. Susannah wished no help. She saw Millerstown's quiet head upon its pillow; she saw its treasures, a dollar saved here, a half-dollar earned there, lying as peacefully in the bank. Susannah was a little over five feet in height and she weighed ninety pounds. But alone, unarmed, she was going forth to rescue the treasures of Millerstown.

Two courses were open; she could steal out through the tunnel-like alley between her house and Sarah Ann's to the street and thence to the bank; or — and here was a far more perilous undertaking — she could go through the gate into the yard of Sarah Ann, then climb four paling fences, running meanwhile the risk of being taken for a burglar herself, and approach the bank from the rear. Susannah chose the latter. Somehow, her skirts almost torn from their bands, Susannah accomplished ascent and descent.

The bank building is an ordinary dwelling-house, its lower floor, in which the bank is situated, reinforced by iron shutters, double doors, and many bolts. Behind it, in a little yard, stands a shed in which the supply of coal and wood is kept. This shed is empty in summer, and here the children often play.

About the shed lilac bushes form a thick hedge; in their shadow Susannah approached the bank. With a quickened heart she saw that she had not been mistaken — the rear shutter was open. Moreover, as she watched, clinging to the fence in sudden weakness, a tall man stepped out of the window upon the slanting cellar door, and, with a large tin box in his hands, approached the woodshed, passing so close to her that she detected the hateful smell of whisky upon him.

Susannah ceased again to breathe. Like a cat after a mouse, she paced after the marauder. As though it were a stage burglary and the burglar had arranged his progress to be caught, he stepped into the little shed. The ready hand of Susannah shot out, the door closed, the wooden button turned, the burglar was trapped. The button was tightly fastened with a screw; only a few days before Susannah had had to hammer it with a stone in order to release a terrified Louisa, locked into the shed by her brother.

The burglar made no sound. For a moment Susannah stood still, drawing her breath in great gasps to fill her empty lungs, and peering about to assure herself that there was no accomplice waiting in the shadow. Then, panting, elate, living as she had not lived in all her life, Susannah sped down the street to the Squire's.

But in her delay Susannah had lost precious time. It was, as has been said, almost morning. Had she not been so absorbed in her capture, she would have seen the brightening sky, have heard the swelling chorus of the birds, and have realized that at dawn the shift of the furnace would change and that Oliver and his companions would return. Poor Susannah was to enjoy her triumph but a moment.

Traveling rapidly along in the thick shade of the maples, she heard a cry and stopped to listen. There was a sound behind her, the padding of feet moving more swiftly than her own. In an instant a tall man rushed past her, in his arms a box, his head bent low. In furious pursuit, with yells of "Stop, thief! Murder! Help! Men! Everybody! Stop, thief!" rushed another man, a dinner-pail in one hand, an upraised billet of wood in the other. Past Susannah both sped without seeing her. But Susannah saw them both. The tall man was the burglar, the pursuer was Oliver Kuhns.

Now windows were raised, and citizens, roused by the shouts of Oliver, assured him wildly of their speedy assistance. The box in the stranger's hands crashed to the ground, as though he were casting all burdens aside. Half-clad men appeared in doorways, women screamed questions out of upper windows. Some, indeed, joined their husbands in the race. There were other brave women in Millerstown beside Susannah.

Susannah neither asked nor answered questions, nor did she aid in the pursuit. Susannah was wakened from her dream of glory; somehow her thunder had been stolen from her. She said to herself that she did not care if the bank were carried off bodily. She was, when the chase passed her, before her own alley gate. Unseen, she entered it and regained her yard.

There another clamor saluted her ears. Ollie and Louisa were demanding an explanation of the locked door and of their mother's silence.

"Mom!" screamed Louisa; "I want to get out."

"I *will* get out!" yelled Ollie.

Calmly ascending the stairway, Susannah bade them return to their beds. Then, as though all Millerstown were not abroad, Susannah followed their example. As high as her spirits had risen, so low they now sank. How the prisoner had escaped from his prison, how Oliver happened to be chasing him down the street, she did not know. But the outrageous explanation was imminent. Susannah's spirit had still lower depths to explore.

Oliver rushed in presently with a shout. Was she asleep? How could she sleep? The bank had been robbed! He, Oliver, had driven the burglar away.

"I was coming home," he gasped. "There was a man. He hollered to me. He heard me. I was whistling"—Oliver called it "vistling." "It was a burglar. He was in the shed. He heard me vistle and he yelled pitiful, 'Let me out!' I let him out and I grabbed for him. I—"

"You let him out!" said Susannah in an indescribable tone.

"He said he was sick. I didn't know he was a burglar. But then I saw the shutter open and I grabbed for him. But he ran faster than I. He had everything packed up. He carried the tin box, but he dropped it. Sarah Knerr, she ran out and picked it up. She got all the things."

"Sarah Knerr!" repeated Susannah in the same tone.

"Yes; and everything is in it what ought to be. Everything is safe in the bank, and they are watching with guns."

Susannah closed her eyes. When she was very angry she could not speak. She became silent for days. But after days, or perhaps weeks, her anger burst forth, strengthened by nursing.

"Then you caught this man?" she asked presently. "You have him?"

"Why, no," confessed Oliver. "He got the start of me."

"So," said Susannah; and turned to sleep.

"What is wrong?" asked Oliver in astonishment.

Susannah made no verbal answer. In her heart she said, "Wait!"

Susannah was considered, even by Sarah Ann Mohr who loved her, to be a little queer; and never had Sarah Ann so good a reason for her opinion as in the weeks following the burglary. Susannah was a great talker about village affairs, but about this great affair whose hero was her own husband Susannah would say nothing. From morning until night, as was natural, Millerstown talked. The shutter had been pried open by the tool of a professional house-breaker—Millerstown must examine both shutter and tool. Everything had been removed from the old-fashioned safe, all was packed in a bag in the shed—Millerstown must handle the bag. In the shed lay a larger, deadlier flask of nitroglycerine than that discovered by the Kuhns children; this must be gazed upon as it stood upon the shelf in the Squire's office. The burglar, thanks to his long legs, escaped entirely; it was surmised that he had put the width of the continent between himself and Millerstown's vengeance. Sarah Knerr, the wife of Billy, the tax-collector, already sufficiently honored, told at all the meetings of Millerstown women how she had gathered the scattered gold and papers in her apron.

To the thousand speculations Susannah contributed nothing. Susannah stayed at home; she did not join her friends. And within her heart resentment deepened. Oliver had cheated her of glory; that the act was wholly innocent signified nothing.

That her spirit had separated itself from him, Oliver understood. What had he done? Nothing. What was the matter? Nothing.

"Why are you, then, so cross over me?" he would say.

"I am not cross over you," Susannah would answer, her eyes glittering.

In his desire to appease and enliven Oliver frequently recounted his adventure. Presently he began to suspect that Susannah was irritated.

"Don't you like to hear of how I caught the burglar, Susannah?"

"I am tired of bolts and bars and nitroglycerine," answered Susannah. "How was that burglar locked in the shed?"

"The door blew shut, and the button just dropped," explained Oliver.

"So," said Susannah, aloud. In her soul, Susannah said again, "Wait!" Susannah was almost ready for the interview which should make of Oliver a humble man; the clearing storm was at hand. Oliver was still on the night shift at the furnace; until the evening of election day, when the shifts changed, Susannah would not have before her that clear hour or two when, secure from interruption, she could have her say. By day, after Oliver had had his sleep, she saw little of him. He went away from the house, for which she was thankful.

"I went down over the fences in the night alone." This was to be the beginning. "I locked him in that shed alone myself. He would have been caught and sent to prison. And you let him out!" The end of her remarks also had Susannah planned. Susannah had dealt with a shrinking Oliver before.

All through election day Susannah went about absently and with a flushed face. Oliver had a holiday, but he was at home only for meals. That he was excited Susannah did not see. When he had had his supper, he went, according to the custom of mankind, to hear the returns. When, at nine o'clock, he appeared, the children were still up. In her miserable brooding Susannah had loosened the hands which held the reins over that spanking pair, and Oliver and Louisa no longer went "quick" or came "quick." They misbehaved in school, they stayed out on the street in the evenings, they had to-day tied a tin can to the tail of their dog, and had put walnuts on the feet of Sarah Ann's cat. Now they sat quarreling, one on each side of the kitchen table.

Oliver's step was a little unsteady; his eyes were bright. So blinded with anger were the eyes of Susannah that she thought her sober husband had been drinking. She commanded the children sharply and sternly to go to bed.

"Go!" said Susannah.

"No," said little Louisa.

"It is not time," said Ollie. "I will not go!"

Susannah rose and moved in their direction, scissors and thimble clattering to the floor.

"Ach, let them stay!" begged Oliver, still more unsteadily.

"Go!" commanded Susannah, still more sharply.

"Billy Knerr is Burgess," announced Oliver, in apparent madness.

"Susannah's soul said no longer "Wait!" but "Go to it, Susannah!"

"Oliver," she began, in spite of the presence of the children, "in the summer-time when the burglar—"

"It is that for which I am elected," said Oliver, more unsteadily than ever.

"Elected!" repeated Susannah, in unbelieving scorn. "You!"

"I am High Constable," announced Oliver, his voice steadying in his pride. "I worked for it all summer. I thought you would like it. It was because I saved the bank."

A confusion of tongues spoke now in the ears of Susannah. Again she heard "Wait!" again she heard "Go to it!" but she heard also a gentler "Make up, Susannah!" Oliver had ambitions; Oliver had worked to please her; Oliver might in time be himself Burgess. Susannah put her hands across her face and burst into tears. When Susannah cried, peace was at hand. Oliver crossed the room and put his arm about her.

"What is wrong?" he asked, bewildered. "I did it for you. I worked hard for it."

Susannah only cried the more. She was fast becoming hysterical. Then a sound recalled her to herself. Little Ollie began to pound on the table with his knife.

"We are High Constables!" he cried. "Louisa, we are High Constables! We can do what we like to the people!"

At once Ollie found himself rudely taken in hand and moved toward the stairway door. Ollie's impertinence had served a good purpose.

"Your father is High Constable," said Susannah, once more mistress of her house, of her children, and, best of all, of herself. "Your father is High Constable over the town, and I am High Constable over you. You are nothing. Now go to bed."

When the door was shut, Susannah looked at her husband. Heroically she spoke, heroically and with consummate kindness she put out of her mind her great achievement. Life had keener pleasures to offer than revenge, and a better portion than glory.

"There was nothing the matter with me all summer but meanness," said Susannah. "Oliver, I am proud of you."

SARAH ANN'S DELIVERANCE

Originally published in the November 1915 issue of
The Cornell Women's Review

D<small>REARILY</small> Sarah Ann made ready her Saturday evening supper, sadly she shed an occasional tear upon plate or cloth. Slowly she placed the platter of potato salad in the middle of the table and flanked it with cake and pie, and jellies and preserves, and bread and cold meat. There had been a time when each detail of Sarah Ann's housekeeping was a joy to her, but such was the case no longer. The pies were good because long practice had made it impossible for Sarah Ann to make any other sort of pie, the cakes were light because her hand could not err, and not because she brought any enthusiasm to her task.

Sarah Ann was tired of everything; she hated the pattern of her dishes; she hated the clean, bright red of her table cloth; she hated, most of all, the three chairs set 'round her table.

"It used to be only one," mourned Sarah Ann. "For twenty years it was only one. Then I had no orphants and widowers 'round me. Then I could eat in peace and the folks would come in and it would be quiet and nice, and afterwards I could go to bed and rest. Now it is all the time noisy, and all the time some one is talking and laughing, and nothing is ever nice and straight."

Heavily, Sarah Ann sat down in the rocking chair on the porch. Here also were two chairs beside her own, each with a white tidy over its back, perpetual reminders of the orphan and the widower to whom she had given shelter.

"I have no peace," wailed Sarah Ann. "They will stay till the end of the world. When Millie's Pop died I took her in; I thought it would be a good thing for her to come to Millerstown, because in a strange place she could perhaps find some one and get married. It is easier for one like Millie to get married in a strange place. But now Millerstown knows Millie. And I took Peter in for the winter and he is here yet, and it is August already, and Aaron König is mad over me and won't come any more to see me, and" — Sarah Ann's round face flushed scarlet — "Peter, he keeps at me and at me, but I won't take Peter for good, and" — Sarah Ann hid her face in her hands — "if only I hadn't let these people into my house!"

Peter Ziegler, who worked in the shoe factory, and Millie Probst, who worked in the shirt factory, were late. Peter was by nature slow, and in his widowhood his habits had become worse, and Millie Probst was prone to linger at doorsteps and talk with her friends. As she waited, Sarah Ann let her thoughts travel backward to the cold November evening when she had weakly listened to Peter Ziegler's woeful plea.

Well did Sarah Ann remember how she had trembled with emotion as she had climbed to her bedroom. Like all persons who live alone, she often talked to herself, and such speech was a great relief. But now she dared not speak until she had passed the door behind which slept Millie Probst. Millie was not a person whom one wakened lightly.

"When she sleeps, she sleeps," Sarah Ann would have said to herself. "When she sleeps, she is not talking."

Slowly, Sarah Ann's ponderous figure had traveled down her hall. Peter Ziegler, who sought a home with her, was not even a blood relative; he was connected with Sarah Ann only through his wife, the diligent and departed Amelia, who had been dead for three years, a space of time which seemed ten to her husband. It was not so much for Amelia that Peter mourned—he had made various efforts to provide her successor—but for the creature comforts with which she made his life soft. Once, when he was about to select a person whom Sarah Ann thought unworthy to follow Amelia, he had been circumvented by that stout and placid lady.

Now traveling down her hall, Sarah Ann wept. Peter had looked so pale as he made his plea, his collar had seemed so much too large for him, his pink string tie so limp, that her tender heart had softened. It was characteristic of Sarah Ann that the more rapidly her heart throbbed with sympathy, the more slowly and unintelligently her mind operated. When she had closed the door of her room and speech was possible, she could scarcely shape the words for tears.

"'I eat a little bumble soup,'" quoted Sarah Ann from Peter's pathetic speech. "'First when I go home, I have to make fire, then I warm a little bumble soup left over from yesterday, and then I sit down and cry.'"

Sarah Ann crossed her room to the rocking chair beyond the bed. The edge of the bed itself was a nearer haven for her tottering steps, but Sarah Ann's imposing couch, with its high-piled chaff bag and feather bed, was not meant to be sat upon except by a giant, and that a giant who had no respect for smooth, white coverlets and sheet shams.

"I am so sorry for Peter," Sarah Ann had wept. "I guess for the winter I must take Peter in."

Regardless of starch and fluted ruffles, she hid her face against the end of the bolster.

"But I like my home," she wailed. "If I wanted a man all the time 'round, I could get married to a man I like better than Peter. But I do not want a man in my house!"

Presently Sarah Ann undressed and climbed into her bed. But she did not sleep. Before the coming of Millie Probst, her mind, ranging about her quiet dwelling, contemplating the key turned in the lock, the shutters barred, the clock wound, the cat banished to the barn, beheld everything in order; it visualized no best room bedcover raised in a large mound over a sleeping form, it beheld no best room bureau littered with a comb and brush and hymn book. Millie Probst was neat, but she was not as neat as emptiness would have been.

"Now she is in the spare room," wept Sarah Ann. "And he will go in the other room, and it will be no place in my house where everything is right. He will have to take his boots off in the downstairs, though, and I will put strips of rag carpet where he walks the most, and I can make him such a bib to wear when he eats. The men are always spilling things at themselves. He could"—Sarah Ann could plan no more for the coming of the vandal. Instead she fortified herself by repeating Peter's pathetic complaints.

"I come home at night and everything is cold. I warm me a little soup from yesterday. Ach, Sarah Ann, take me in!"

Sarah Ann blushed as she lay in her bed.

"He needn't think it will mean anything," declared she in a whisper. "I told Peter these many times I would not marry while the world stands."

In the morning, Sarah Ann, with her usual consideration for others, had approached her already established guest.

"I am thinking of taking a boarder," said she, bravely, as though she were not about to burst into tears.

"Well, now!" Millie was immediately alert. She was a large young woman; to Sarah Ann, who was herself by no means small, she seemed to fill the room, to fill at times, the whole world. She could let no simplest statement pass without comment, no wildest extravagance without polite and immediate agreement. Millie was nothing if not affable, and with this coin she paid Sarah Ann for her many favors.

"It is Peter Ziegler," explained Sarah Ann.

"No!" Millie's negative had entirely lost the significance of a negative and had become merely an exclamation. Its eagerness escaped Sarah Ann, deep in her trouble.

"His wife, Amelia, was my cousin; that is why I do it."

"Well!" cried Millie.

"He is away all day working in the shoe factory, and when he comes home at night, he—"

"Does he work in the shoe factory?" Millie knew all about the occupation of Peter Ziegler, but Millie allowed no previous information to prevent her from helping on a conversation. As steadily as others breathed, so Millie talked.

"He has no one to cook for him, and —"

"Ach!" cried Millie sympathetically.

Sarah Ann frowned, not in anger, but in confusion. Millie's interruptions often threw her off the track of her discourse.

"He wants I should let him live here this winter."

Millie threw up both her hands and opened her mouth. As a matter of fact, she had overheard the conversations between Sarah Ann and Peter.

"What do you think?" inquired Sarah Ann, politely.

"Think! *I* think! Oh, Cousin Sarah Ann" — Sarah Ann hated to be thus addressed — "It is yours to say what shall happen in this house. But, Cousin Sarah Ann" — Millie burst into a Niagara torrent of approval — "I think you are a noble woman!"

"Ach, Millie" — Sarah Ann lifted her hand as though the violence of Millie's approval might become physical.

But Millie would not be halted.

"It is grand! It is Christian!" Millie's arm made now a vain effort to encircle the waist of Sarah Ann, and Sarah Ann moved away uneasily. She did not like to be touched. There was a sudden excitement in Millie's speech and she began to pile the breakfast dishes, a task in which Sarah Ann needed no assistance. "I will help, Cousin Sarah Ann. It is a Christian act. Is it not awful how the men get by themselves along? It was a man in Long Swamp, he had everything so nice while she lived, but she died for him. Then it was terrible. He could 'a' got a woman, Cass Beidleman, to work for him, but he wouldn't, he was too tight, he —"

Sarah Ann nodded. She would have liked to tell a little about her plans for the disposal of Peter, but she could only gasp, as though she would help Millie get her breath. Still handling the dishes, Millie continued to describe the miserable condition of the Long Swamp man.

"He could 'a' come sometimes to our house to eat. I told him. But he wouldn't. And" — A flush reddened the cheeks of Millie, and she moved her head in a little toss — "and he got married then. She wasn't better than nothing, she hung the stockings on the fence post to dry, and —"

"It is this way" — Sarah Ann succeeded in raising her gentle voice above the tumult — "Peter can —"

"She only scrubbed the kitchen once in two weeks, you can hardly believe such a thing, she —"

Making an incoherent noise, Sarah Ann tried to escape from her kitchen. Never, never would she take another lodger into her house! But, turning, she met Peter Ziegler at the door and could not refuse him. Peter had wisely come early in the morning.

"I was soft," said Sarah Ann, sitting now with her head on her hand, waiting for Peter and Millie to come to supper. "That was what was the matter with me."

There was no denying the fact that for a little while Sarah Ann had been happy in her sacrifice. For a few weeks Millie's speech seemed less profuse, for a few weeks Peter forbore to make love, for a few weeks Aaron König, the little elder from Sarah Ann's church, who had come for almost every evening in twenty years to sit in Sarah Ann's kitchen or on her doorstep, remained faithful. But presently Millie's speech flowed in its old volume, presently Peter began to press his suit, and presently Aaron, terrfied by the noise and laughter, came no more.

Peter reminded Sarah Ann daily of his loneliness; he implied that a person was selfish to have as much as Sarah Ann and to refuse to share her comfort with a soul who so loved her. Peter gave, moreover, no sign of leaving. Spring changed to summer, a season when a man may be perfectly comfortable without anyone to keep up fires in his house. But Peter did not go. Cheerfully he continued to remove his boots so that Sarah Ann's stair carpet might not be worn out, cheerfully he wore at table the bib of dark oil cloth which Sarah Ann provided; cheerfully he endured all the other contrivances by which Sarah Ann protected her house and its furnishings from harm. When Aaron König ceased to come, Peter's assurance became impertinence.

"You will marry me sometime," said he. "You might as well now as later."

He even dared to remind Sarah Ann of the hand which she had taken in his affair with the school teacher.

Worse than the open proposals of Peter were the sly insinuations of Millie Probst, who, in spite of her generous offer, did not speak in a friendly tone.

"I can go always to my room in the evenings, Cousin Sarah Ann. I am never one to be in the way. When the time comes, you need only to say it, Cousin Sarah Ann."

Sarah Ann made no answer. Teasing of this variety always made her blush; applied to herself by Millie, it made her creep.

"Will they never go away?" asked Sarah Ann in despair, and her sad heart answered, "Never."

"If Millie only had a place to go!" sighed Sarah Ann, her tired head sinking down almost to the arm of the rocking chair. The August evening was warm and Sarah Ann had worked hard. "But she hasn't and she won't have. Millerstown knows her."

Then, nervously, Sarah Ann started up from her rocking chair. From the front of the house, through the little covered alley, there echoed the sound of Millie's mighty laugh. Millie laughed with an open throat and there was room within for all the winds of Aeolus. Millie had brought home a new story or a new joke about some citizen of Millerstown; from it she and Peter would wring every possible drop of amusement. She was recounting it now to Susannah Kuhns, who sat on the bench at the front of her house awaiting the return of her husband.

"Ain't that a good one?" demanded Millie of Susannah.

"I cannot stand Millie to come in here!" cried Sarah Ann. Sarah Ann turned toward the kitchen door. But the kitchen offered no refuge, for in another moment Millie would be upon her. Sometimes, in the joviality of her mood, Millie kissed Sarah Ann when she came home from her work.

"I cannot stand it!" repeated Sarah Ann. Then, with all the uncomfortable weight of her two hundred pounds, at actual risk to her life, Sarah Ann ran down the smooth boardwalk.

"If I can only get away!" she panted. "If I can only get for one meal away from these people in my house!"

Sarah Ann did not stop to think of the supper, she did not stop to wonder whether Peter and Millie would be anxious about her; she heard Millie's laugh once more and she let the garden gate swing shut behind her.

"I do not know where I will go," she said, aloud. "I cannot go anywhere in Millerstown because it is supper time and I would make trouble for the people. I will go" — Sarah Ann looked up at Millerstown's wooded hill — "I will go to the mountain. I cannot hear them there."

Sarah Ann was not accustomed to walking, except back and forth in her kitchen and her garden and over the smooth pavement to church, but she climbed the mountain road with steps which were almost brisk. She did not remember that she had eaten nothing since noon and that it was past her regular hour for supper; she did not recall the painful effect which tall trees and the soughing wind always had upon her. She turned presently into the woods and sat down upon a rock.

"It is quiet here," said Sarah Ann. Then, nervous and worn and hungry, she began to cry. "I wish I was in the graveyard," said she hysterically. "There I would have peace."

It was dusk when she rose from her hard seat on the rock. She had cried until she could cry no more. She had thought with actual regret of her husband, penurious and hard to get along with as he had been. At least he had been a silent man, and at least in his lifetime there would have been no Millie Probst and no Peter Ziegler in his house. She thought longest of all and with sad regret of Aaron König whom she had driven away.

"But it is not Christian to act like this," said Sarah Ann to herself. "It is not even grown up, it is like a little one. They will perhaps be hunting me, Millie and Peter. And if I stay longer, they will perhaps be making a fuss over me when I get back. I cannot stand a fuss made over me."

Now Sarah Ann was conscious of the tall, ghostly trunks of the trees, of the strangely colored patches of evening sky which she could see through the branches, of the rustling noises made by the wind, and of stranger, more alarming sounds of the woodland which she could not identify. Stiff and sore and almost helpless as she was from her long sitting on the cold rock, Sarah Ann started rapidly down the mountain road. Soon her rapid walk quickened, against her will, into a run. Once she had to throw her arms about a tree in order to save herself from a fall, once she went down upon her knees, and continually she cried out sharply. Faster and faster she flew down the mountain road and along the grassy lane to her dear garden gate. There she stopped, breathless, clinging to the familiar palings and trying to get her breath.

"Oh dear, I am back with them!" cried poor Sarah Ann, panting.

When her gasps and pants became more even, Sarah Ann listened for voices from her house. But there was no sound. They had gone about hunting her, they had missed their suppers, the coffee had grown cold, the lettuce leaves had withered. The duties of hostess were sacred to Sarah Ann; in keen repentance, she started up the board walk.

Then, suddenly, in the darkness by her great syringa bush she stood still, and put out a trembling hand toward the frail branches. She heard a sound. Millie was not worried by her absence, Millie had not gone to rouse the town, Millie was close at hand, laughing.

Still trembling, Sarah Ann waited for strength to endure once more the cacophony which made life miserable. In the light which streamed from the kitchen window she could see that Millie and Peter sat comfortably side by side in the rocking chairs.

But Sarah Ann could see more. Millie had put on her blue dress, and Peter his best suit.

"As if it was Sunday," said Sarah Ann to herself, "or as if — as if — as if —"

Sarah Ann took a step forward so that she might lean against the porch pillar. For Peter Ziegler, who had asked her only yesterday to be his, and Millie who had teased her constantly about Peter, were sitting hand in hand!

Sarah Ann gave a little cry. She did not stop to analyze the strange scene or to consider the duplicity which could have at the same time one lady in mind and another in hand; she did not observe the guilty look of Millie or the chagrin of Peter. (In the experience of Sarah Ann philandering had had no place.) She did not even wonder how Millie could care for Peter or how Peter could care for Millie. She thought now that Love had suddenly seized these two creatures in his mighty grasp and had thereby incidentally freed her from a burden which had become too heavy to be borne. Suppose she had not fled to the mountain and left them alone together!

With a single bound, Sarah Ann soared across the steps. Grasping Peter by one hand and Millie by the other, she cried aloud to them so that Susannah Kuhns and both her children came running up at top speed. A marriage ceremony could scarcely have committed Peter and Millie more irrevocably to each other than did Sarah Ann's shout of congratulation.

"I am surprised!" cried Sarah Ann. "Well! Well! But this is the way it should be. Oh, how many things I will have for you! You will not need to wait at all. Quilts I have! Rag carpet I have! Even furniture and dishes for a present! Ach!" — Sarah Ann's mellifluous voice shook, her English forsook her, she relapsed into Millerstown's broad and pleasant speech. "I wish you choy!"

MOTHER'S GIRLS

Originally published in the July 1917 issue of **Woman's Home Companion**

— *Daughter Nellie hired Lizzie Wenner*
— *Daughter Sarah hired Annie Bach*
— *Son Thomas hired Katy Froelich*
   But none of them stayed

GUILTILY, as the clock on the secretary down in the "winter kitchen" gave its preparatory whir, Grandmother Snyder opened her eyes. It was five o'clock. At last she could get up. For an hour she had lain sleepless, planning how she should meet the difficult situation of this day.

As Grandmother Snyder rose, dawn began. A soft light spread over the sky; she could see a dim, gray, lonely house across the fields toward Millerstown, and a moment later the clustered houses of Millerstown itself with the smoke beginning to rise from their chimneys. Presently in her own room she could distinguish the framed face of Dr. Martin Luther above the tall bureau, and the German motto "God Bless This House" opposite. Grandmother Snyder had worked the motto herself some sixty years ago.

With the window wide open, Grandmother Snyder shook the sheets violently and beat up the pillows.

Having finished in her own room, Grandmother Snyder crossed the hall to another room and there drew down the shades as though she were afraid the rising sun might fade her carpet. She gave also a smoothing stroke to the coverlet, bending over it as though she meant to study the pattern, or as though she remembered the day when she had stooped over that bed to kiss the rosy faces of her children. Afterward, briskly for a lady of seventy, she pursued her way down the stairs and through the wide room which was used in the winter for sitting-room, dining-room and kitchen, and in summer for sitting-room and dining-room alone, to the "summer kitchen" beyond. Thither the stove had been moved, there all work was done from May till October.

In the summer kitchen, Grandmother rattled the stove and pulled out the drafts. Then, before she put on the coffee or brought from the cellarway the eggs for breakfast, she read a letter lying open on the kitchen table where she had left it the night before.

Dear Mother [it read], Sarah and I are coming to Millerstown together on Wednesday. We shall arrive on the noon train and stay until the next afternoon. We shall leave all cares and babies behind us. It is a great comfort to feel that you have this good girl — you have never told us her name, by the way. Tell her that we will have something in our satchels for her. Now, Mother, be sure to let her get the meals alone, and let us have a nice time together. We —

Grandmother Snyder laid the letter down. Her clear bright eyes clouded, her hand trembled as she lifted the coffee pot, she began to talk to herself.

"In August they said I was to have a girl, and Nellie got me that Lizzie. In October, Sarah got me that Annie. In February, Thomas was here and he got me that Katy. I will not have another. It is no use to talk. I will not." After a while Grandmother Snyder tossed her head. Into her eyes came the expression to which her children had always given instant heed. "I have a girl."

It was in August that Nellie, arriving unexpectedly, had found things at Grandmother Snyder's at a pretty pass. Grandmother Snyder was not at home when she arrived; therein lay the first cause of offense. Nellie was a bustling, important little person, she had almost run up the street, so anxious was she to see her mother. It was certainly not pleasant to find her mother's house locked and no one to greet her. Worse still, when Grandmother Snyder came she was pale and tired. She had spent the night with a sick woman.

"A sick woman!" Nellie had exclaimed. "Now, Mother, what sick woman can there be in Millerstown who has no one but you to sit up with her?"

Grandmother Snyder pointed across the fields.

"They live in that house. They came only a little while ago. They are poor and both are sick. They are English people" — Grandmother Snyder used Millerstown's term for those who are not Pennsylvania Germans. "There is no one but them and the little girl. She has black eyes. Her name is Amelia. She is often here by me."

"Why don't they hire someone?" Nellie asked.

"They are poor."

"How many times have you been there, Mother?"

"A few times," answered Grandmother vaguely.

"Well, you mustn't go again, Mother. And one reason I came to-day is to get you a girl."

"A girl!" cried Grandmother Snyder with a terror-stricken expression.

"Yes," said Nellie, "a girl. We have talked it all over. You must have a girl. It is not safe for you here alone."

"Not safe alone!" repeated Grandmother Snyder. "Who would get me?"

"It is not safe," said Nellie, still more decidedly.

"She will spoil my things," objected Grandmother.

"A good girl will not spoil your things."

"I cannot afford it." This in a feebler tone.

"Why, Mother, what nonsense!"

"Who is this girl to be, then?"

"I will find her. There are plenty of girls in Millerstown."

"I would have to be all the time here to watch her," she offered as a last, feeble objection.

"Here is where you ought to be," said Nellie, grateful for an irrefutable argument.

Grandmother Snyder said no more. She inquired about all Nellie's children; she got out sundry caps and mittens which she had been at work on; she listened silently when Nellie announced upon her return from the village that she had persuaded Lizzie Wenner to come. Then Nellie with an affectionate farewell and a heart at ease took the train for home.

Grandmother Snyder received with dignity the girl whom Nellie had found. The Wenners were not good housekeepers. Grandmother Snyder's eyes opened wide with astonishment at the Wenner method of washing dishes, and of cleaning the kitchen.

For three days Grandmother Snyder stayed at home and watched her companion. The sick woman was better, she was able to be out of bed and to prepare meals for her husband and her little girl. On the fourth day, Grandmother Snyder observed upon rising that a light burned in the little house. Before she was dressed she saw a little figure making its way across the fields. But when she reached the kitchen and opened the door the little figure had turned and was making its way back.

"Wasn't there someone here?" asked Grandmother Snyder of Lizzie Wenner, suspiciously.

A conscious expression came into the face of Lizzie. It was suddenly clear to Grandmother Snyder that this new maid had been assigned other duties besides her housework.

"The little girl is not to come here," said Lizzie.

Grandmother Snyder ate her breakfast with dignity, but with some haste. Then she addressed herself to Lizzie. Grandmother Snyder knew the Wenner temper.

"You do not do your work right," said she gently. "You clean, but it is funny cleaning. You don't scour right. Just see this knife, Lizzie! It will be rusted soon through. And your oatmeal is very lumpy, and the eggs are always hard-boiled or else they are all water, and —"

"I don't have to work," answered Lizzie shortly. "I can leave if I do not suit."

"You do not suit," said Grandmother Snyder in a voice like honey.

All the pleasant October weather Grandmother was busy. It took some time to clear up after her maid, and to that task she could not at first apply herself steadily. The English people were worse, the wife had taken to her bed. Grandmother Snyder feared to stay away from them for more than a few hours at a time. Little Amelia turned to Grandmother Snyder as to a light shining in a world of darkness. For her Grandmother Snyder made clothes, for her she baked cookies in the fantastic shapes she had modeled for her own children. It was pleasant, after all these years, to feel that one was necessary once more to a little child.

In late October another of the Snyders came home unexpectedly. This time Grandmother Snyder was in her house, had been there for at least ten minutes. The kitchen was pleasant and warm, and Grandmother Snyder sat at the window knitting, as is becoming at seventy. Little Amelia's mother was better, little Amelia when she appeared after school to stay for supper was sent home by a somewhat excited Grandmother Snyder, who met her outside the door and spoke to her in a whisper. Grandmother Snyder and her daughter Sarah had a pleasant and uninterrupted visit together.

"But Nellie found you a girl!" said Sarah, amazed. "Where is she?"

"She was not neat," answered Grandmother Snyder, "I had to tell her. I told her politely, but she got very cross over me. She left. The Wenners are that way."

"To-morrow before I go, I'll get you another," promised Sarah.

"I do not want anyone," protested Grandmother Snyder.

"But you must have someone, Mother."

When Sarah had departed Annie Bach appeared. Annie was neat and tidy. For a day Grandmother Snyder despaired. She had nothing to do, the English people were still better, there was no garden to be worked in October, she had visited all the old and sick that she knew, and made dust cloths and dish cloths and iron holders for all the newly married, and caps for all the babies. But the next morning, black-eyed Amelia came early to the door.

"Oh, dear Grandmother Snyder," wailed little Amelia, as she flew into those outstretched, friendly arms, "my mother cannot speak to me."

"I will come right away," promised Grandmother Snyder. It was a good thing, after all, that Annie Bach was capable and needed no watching. But suddenly Grandmother Snyder stood still and stared. Upon the face of Annie Bach was an exact likeness of the conscious expression which had appeared upon the face of Lizzie Wenner.

"You are not to take care of those people," objected Annie.

Grandmother Snyder regarded Annie for a long minute with half-closed eyes. Then she began to fill a basket with bread and eggs and other food.

"Annie," said she gently, "There is something I must talk to you about. Last night a young man came to see you. This must not happen again, Annie. We are two women alone in this house."

"What!" cried Annie. Annie may have been good-tempered, but she knew what were the rights of a human being. "If John Miller cannot come evenings, then I will not stay."

"Well," said Grandmother Snyder gently.

Through a series of fortunate happenings, the departure of Annie remained unknown to Grandmother Snyder's family. Grandmother Snyder wrote frequent letters which gave an impression of leisure and fine-ladyhood. There were many little folks in the houses of Sarah and Nellie, and the annual Christmas journey to Millerstown was prevented by chicken pox in one house and measles in the other, three successive cases in one, four in the other. Many letters traveled from New York to Millerstown, Grandmother Snyder's Christmas box was tremendous, the letters she received almost too many to be counted. Back to New York went two fine turkeys, two great fruit cakes, and innumerable cookies.

The poor English people were by this time in sad case. Soon after the New Year the father died, it would be only a question of a few weeks when the mother would follow him. Grandmother Snyder had no time to read her letters until they had been in the house for several days.

In January came Thomas from Chicago. Thomas, his mother's darling, Millerstown's darling. Thomas found his mother preparing supper.

"I thought you had a girl, Mother," said he, when the first greetings were over. "Nellie said you had a Bach girl."

"I had, but she left me."

"She did!" said Thomas, sympathetically. "That was too bad. I tell you what, Mother, you do the cooking while I'm here, and I'll get you another girl before I go."

"All right," agreed Grandmother Snyder. Then, in search of the pie for dessert, Grandmother vanished into the cellarway. There she drew down her chin in a droll grimace. The report was spreading in Millerstown that she was difficult to get on with. Thomas would not be able to find another girl willing to come.

But Thomas brought Katy Froelich back with him, a pretty girl, to whom he had offered dear knows what outrageous retaining fee.

"Pay her well, Mother," advised he. "Here are a few bills to help out."

Grandmother Snyder took the bills. She had a place at present for all extra bills that came to her.

When Thomas had gone, Grandmother Snyder looked at the curly-haired maiden. She could see little Amelia starting across the fields.

"There is one thing I must say before your trunk comes, Katy." There was no reason why a good device should not serve more than once. "We are two women living alone. You cannot have any callers, Katy."

Katy pouted.

"I didn't say for sure I'd stay," said she crossly. "I think I won't stay."

"Well," said Grandmother resignedly.

In March came Nellie for a day, Nellie, full of protest and affection.

"Think of it, Mother, I haven't been here since August! And now I can only stay a day on account of Baby. But, Mother, where is your girl?"

"She is at a funeral," said Grandmother, which was true that day of all Millerstown. The poor English lady had died.

When Nellie's train had puffed away, Grandmother Snyder went to the house of mourning and put herself in charge.

Through late March and showery April Grandmother Snyder seemed to have again leisure and inclination for letter-writing. She even answered all questions put to her. Was her girl really a good girl? The best she had ever had. Did she have beaux coming to the house? Not a beau. Did she seem likely to stay? Forever. Was she neat? Very. Respectful? Grandmother Snyder used the Pennsylvania German word for "superlatively." "She even goes to church and prayer meeting with me," wrote Grandmother Snyder in her German script. "It reminds me of my own girls."

Tears came into the eyes of Sarah and Nellie as they read. To Grandmother Snyder's companion to church and Sunday school they sent grateful gifts, some dark red stuff for a waist, pretty white stuff for aprons, and a little pin. Relieved, Grandmother Snyder's children postponed their visits.

Now May had come. Fields were green, apple trees were in blossom, flowering shrubs in bloom. But Grandmother Snyder felt none of the happiness which the springtime usually brought her. It seemed as though she had purchased peace with a large price. Hitherto, through all her life, she had told the truth.

Discovery, also, was now at hand. Not one, but both of her daughters were coming at noon; it was natural that Grandmother Snyder's deception should lie heavy on her heart.

Having finished her breakfast, Grandmother Snyder began to prepare what seemed to be a propitiatory feast. Chickens had been killed yesterday, as soon as the letter had arrived. To the chickens were now added pies, cake, all procurable good things.

It was exactly noon when Sarah and Nellie arrived from the station, and their mother met them at the door and took them up-stairs to lay off their things. The two ladies were glad to see this bit of formality, it signified that their mother was taking her ease.

Then, at once, the two were ushered to the feast. The dinner was smoking on the table, the dessert was set forth on a smaller table at the side.

"She cooks almost like you do, Mother," said Nellie, when she had had a second helping of everything. "Could she cook like this when she came or did you have to teach her your way?"

"You have to teach them all," answered Grandmother Snyder briefly.

"Where is she?" asked Nellie.

"She is in the kitchen."

Sarah rose and opened the door.

"There is no girl here," cried Sarah. "There —" Then, "What!" cried Sarah.

At the table sat Grandmother's girl. She was little and she had black eyes and her legs were pathetically thin. She wore a dress made of pretty dark red stuff and an apron made of pretty white stuff and a little gold pin. She looked up frightened at the two fine ladies. Perhaps the sorrows of her short life had saddened her, perhaps Grandmother Snyder's nervousness had imparted itself to her. At any rate her lip trembled, her head dropped on her breast. It was she who had been Grandmother Snyder's companion to church, she who had been respectful and obedient and neat, she over whom Grandmother Snyder bent so tenderly in the great bed.

Grandmother Snyder went to her and laid her hand on her shoulder and the little thing turned her head against that hand. Into Grandmother Snyder's eyes came the expression to which her children gave instant heed.

"Now, girls," said she briskly, "you asked me whether I had a girl, and I said 'Yes.' I have a girl. You asked me whether she seemed likely to stay, and I said 'Yes.' She will stay. She is the best girl I have ever had, I have taken her to keep."

THE MUSIC LESSON

Originally published in the February 28, 1918, issue of
The Youth's Companion

SITTING by the deal table in the kitchen, with her eyes flashing and her hands moving impatiently, Susannah Kuhns awaited the return of her daughter Louisa. The basket of close-packed, sprinkled wash beneath the table proclaimed that the day was Monday; the orderliness of the kitchen signified that the hour was somewhere between the putting away of dinner and the preparing of supper. To be exact, it was half past four o'clock. At three Louisa's music teacher had come and at four had gone, at two precious dollars an hour, but Louisa had taken no lesson. Neglecting her opportunity, defying her mother, indifferent to the waste of money, Louisa had walked out of her mother's house.

Susannah, who was slender and spry and just twice as old as her seventeen-year-old daughter, struck her hand sharply on the edge of the table, then rose and walked up and down the room.

"I will tell her the meaning," Susannah declared. "Once more I will put it before her as it is. To want to be all the time cooking and baking and scrubbing and preserving and making soap when she could sing! Have I my mind any more that this can be! Shall she be educated, or shall she be forever dumb — that is it. That is what I will put to her. I — "

A train whistled down at the end of Main Street. It carried the music teacher back to that abode of learning, of musical knowledge and musical appreciation, the county seat. It was a coincidence that it should also carry young Jimmie Fackenthal, the mail clerk, who came into Millerstown each Monday at twelve o'clock and left at half past four. It was no thought of young Jimmie, however, that made Susannah pace the room in excitement. The man in the moon was as little connected with this great trouble as was Jimmie Fackenthal, friend of Louisa though he was. Louisa was not to marry; her mother did not think of her marrying. She had higher plans for Louisa than a life of drudgery and dullness.

"I will put it before her," said Susannah again, almost sobbing in her excitement. "Again I will put it before her as it is."

Now pacing the floor, now sitting on the edge of her chair, Susannah waited. Since her childhood she had longed for adventure, since her marriage her spirit had escaped only once from the monotonous duties that filled her life. Then, when for three days she and her husband, Oliver, and her two children, Ollie and Louisa, had taken up their abode in the county seat, she had learned to her dismay that her singing, the one pleasure of her dull existence, was laughable.

Thereupon, returning to Millerstown, she had ceased to sing except on rare occasions when she climbed to the garret, or locked herself into the parlor. She had even refused longer to lead the choir in church, although the congregation besought and her husband commanded.

"What is funny in Allentown is funny here," poor Susannah had explained grimly.

"It is not funny to these in Millerstown," her husband had declared sensibly; "they like it."

"It is funny to me," Susannah had said, and then her eyes had shone. "Louisa will sing when she is big. Louisa has a voice. Louisa will take lessons."

No one ever suspected the height of renunciation to which Susannah rose. To live in the success of your children is not always easy at the age of thirty-four!

At noon it had been Louisa that had cried. Then Susannah, standing by the stove stirring her endive dressing, had gone on furiously. She did not forget the dressing for an instant. When you have been an expert cook for twenty years, you are not likely even in emotional crises such as this to waste the good eggs and flour and vinegar and the morsels of bacon that give to endive dressing its distinctive (Pennsylvania German) flavor.

"Singing," declared Susannah, "is not just hollering. You — "

"I — " Louisa opened her mouth and closed it helplessly.

Louisa was a pretty girl, but she was fat, and the tears that stood on her cheeks were not becoming.

"You will be quiet," said Susannah with decision. "I have brought you up from little. I have trained you. I have saved you so that you wouldn't need to work so hard. I — "

"I like to work!" wailed Louisa. "It is to me no trouble to work. I — "

But Susannah cut her short ruthlessly.

"I kept all these years egg money for you, and the little money I got from my pop. You are to take these lessons, you are to learn, you — "

"I would rather work. I can sing already, I — "

"Louisa!" Susannah almost shrieked. "I am talking. Be still, Louisa, till I am done! You think you can sing! O my soul! I know what singing is. I thought I could sing, too; then we went off, and I heard singing. They made it different in Allentown, and they made it right. They put their singing up here." Susannah indicated the roof of her mouth. "They didn't put it down here, as if their collars were all the time choking them. They — "

"I don't want to — "

Susannah lifted the endive from the stove to the table.

"I don't care what you want. It makes nothing out if you want or if you don't want. You are to learn to sing. The lady, she comes to learn you. Two dollars I pay her to learn you, she —"

Defiance blazed suddenly in Louisa's blue eyes. There was at that instant a long whistle as the twelve-o'clock train came shrieking round the curve.

"*You* didn't take singing lessons," she said bravely. "You got married."

Susannah flushed. It was irritating to be reminded of the fact just then.

"Yes," she agreed. "I got married, that is so. It was nothing else for me to do; that is why I got married. I had no piano. I had no mom to tell me to sing. I had no nice teacher to learn me. I sang till — till that time in Allentown —" Susannah's voice sank to a broken whisper; it was not easy to speak of the great humiliation of her life. "They looked at me in the church, and the people laughed over me how I sang. I saw them! And when I sang in the house, a little girl came running, a little neighbor girl, and she said I should stop my hollering. I —"

Susannah's voice had thickened until she could not speak.

"Pop, he thinks I can sing good enough already," said Louisa sullenly.

"Pop!" repeated Susannah scornfully. "Pop! What does he know about it, tell me that!"

"He says to spend two dollars a week that way is not right, he says it is wicked, he —"

Susannah took a step toward her daughter.

"Is it your pop's money?" Her voice rose in shrill demand. "Would you rather learn to sing and get money for singing — those in Allentown in church got money — and perhaps learn others to sing, or would you rather stick here in Millerstown and scrub and bake and —"

"Yes, I would," insisted Louisa stubbornly.

"Well," said Susannah, "you're not going to. After dinner you are to practice till she comes, that is what you are to do."

"It makes me feel like a fool!" Louisa wept now with sobs and cries like a baby. "It is just opening my mouth and yelling, 'Ah, ah!' — that is what it is. It is the dumbest thing in the world. Ollie, he mocks me, and the neighbor children they make fun of me, too. They say 'Ah, ah!' at me, and —"

Tears had no effect upon Susannah. "You are to sing," said she.

"I would rather scrub the whole house every day. I would rather dig the garden and plant onions. I would rather —"

"If you are so fond of working, you can set the table," said Susannah coolly. "It is almost time that your pop comes."

Still sobbing, Louisa set the table; with angry eyes Susannah served the pot pie and poured the fragrant coffee into the cups.

When her husband arrived for his dinner, he looked at the two women and rubbed his chin and sat down at the table in silence. There was nothing to be said. Susannah knew her mind, Louisa knew hers, and Oliver, who had not the least sympathy with musical ambition, knew that a word from him would only do harm to Louisa's cause.

As she ate, Susannah's eyes began to shine. The weekly visits of the young music teacher were the joy of her life. The teacher played and sang; she talked about music; she was romance and poetry to Susannah. To her and to Louisa's spiritless imitations of her Susannah listened with rapture.

Louisa had a voice like her mother's, except that her collar seemed an inch or two tighter. But for that difficulty the young teacher promised a cure.

"She has a voice," she assured Susannah. "She uses it as incorrectly as possible, but the voice is there all the same. Did you never sing yourself?"

"*Ach*, a little," answered Susannah in great mortification and heart ache. "Just in church I sing a little."

There was nothing surreptitious in Louisa's defiance. She went upstairs and put on her best pink dress, which her mother liked her to wear for her lessons, and she tied in her hair the enormous pink bows that her mother thought ridiculous, and donned her white slippers, which were the envy of all the girls in Millerstown. Then she walked boldly out the kitchen door.

Susannah thought she knew why Louisa was setting forth.

"That is right," she said approvingly. "Get some flowers for the parlor till teacher comes."

But Louisa got no flowers; she did not turn down the board walk, which, with flower beds on either side, bisected the long yard; she went round the side of the house and out the front gate.

"Louisa!" called her mother presently; but Louisa did not answer.

"She went to Sarah Ann to get peonies for teacher," said Susannah to herself. Then she dried her hands and went upstairs to brush her hair and put on a clean dress and apron. Louisa's arraying herself for her music lesson was a tribute paid to vanity; her mother's was homage paid to art.

When Susannah came down, Louisa had not returned. The girl was not in the house, she was not in the yard, she was not visible at Sarah Ann Mohr's, next door.

Susannah called across the fence, "Did Louisa come to get flowers, say?"

"No," answered Sarah Ann from her rocking-chair. "Louisa went walking fast down the street."

It was two o'clock before it occurred to Susannah that Louisa had defied her. Even then Susannah thought that it was only in the matter of practicing. Louisa hated to practice. That she would stay away from her lesson Susannah did not dream until she heard the clock strike three and saw the teacher standing at the door. Then, with face white as her stiff apron and with trembling hands, poor Susannah let the teacher in.

Now, at half past four, trembling once more, by turns white and flushed, Susannah waited. The teacher had gone on the train that was also Jimmie Fackenthal's train. Susannah walked nervously up and down her kitchen. It was time to begin supper, but to supper Susannah gave no thought. The shock of disappointment seemed to have stunned her. She had deprived herself of luxuries, even of comforts, had made many sacrifices, had prayed that the desire of her heart might be fulfilled, and Louisa had proved unworthy, ungrateful, cruel.

Once Susannah took a long drink of water, as if her throat were burning; several times she spoke to herself, enumerating the monotonous duties from which she had meant to save her child.

"Scrubbing!" The words came out jerkily. "Soap boiling! Butchering! Washing! Rag-carpet sewing! Mending! Preserving! Canning! Fruit-juicing! O my soul!"

There was an unaccountable excitement in her manner. Once she went to look at herself in the little mirror by the door, as if to see the ravages that this grief had made upon her.

At a quarter to five o'clock Louisa, in her brave array, walked in. Her face was crimson, and her hands shook like her mother's; she looked as if she, too, were disquieted by some great emotion. Never in her life had she disobeyed her mother; she feared her too heartily for that.

For a long time Susannah stared at her. Louisa looked unlike herself with her scarlet cheeks and her quivering mouth. Her curly hair lay in ringlets on her forehead, and there was a strange, shining light in her blue eyes.

Under her mother's scrutiny, Louisa began to cry.

"I can't sing, mom," she declared. "I won't sing, mom."

"Sit down!" commanded Susannah with decision.

Louisa sat down on the edge of the kitchen rocking-chair; her mother sat on the other side of the room. Susannah spoke in a low key, as if she, too, were suddenly a different person. Louisa was frightened by her mother's gentleness, her strange voice, her trembling hands.

"It is things I must ask you, Louisa."

"I can't sing," repeated Louisa wildly. "It is no use to talk, mom."

"Once more, Louisa, for the last time in this world, why will you act this way?"

"I hate it!" declared Louisa. "It is dumb. I am not for singing. It is wasting time."

"It takes one little hour in a whole day, Louisa." Susannah's voice quivered in her excitement.

"I could do better things in that time than say 'Ah, ah,'" objected Louisa.

"What could you do?"

"I could learn to sew and bake and cook better than I can now," replied Louisa. "I don't know how to keep a house and I want to."

"What! To keep a house!" said Susannah sharply. "You needn't think about keeping a house. I will keep the house like always."

"I will not sing!" cried Louisa. "I will not sing!"

The flaming red came back to Susannah's cheeks.

"I told you how I was once shamed in Allentown," she said. "Think of it, Louisa, to take music lessons, to improve yourself, to learn! To have some one tell you the right way!" She spoke as if she described an actual experience of her own, and not one forever denied her. "To feel every Monday that you are learning! And to have the people listen to you when you sing, Louisa, think of that! Remember how I have saved for you, Louisa, remember — "

"I can't help it," answered Louisa, weeping. "I am sorry, mom, but it is too late, mom. I — "

"Too late?" echoed Susannah. "What do you mean by too late?" Suddenly Susannah's voice rose shrilly. "You talk about keeping a house! For who, then, will you keep a house?"

Louisa covered her hot face with her hands.

"For Jimmie Fackenthal. He don't want me to sing, he don't care for singing, he wants me to cook, he — I — "

"What!" cried Susannah.

Then Susannah crossed the room to Louisa's side and laid her hand on Louisa's heaving shoulder.

"For the last time," said she solemnly. "Will you cook and bake and scrub all your life, Louisa, or will you sing?"

Louise wrung her hands.

"I will cook and bake, mom" she cried hysterically. "I am sorry for you, mom. I am sorry for the wasted money, mom, I — "

For an instant Susannah stood looking down at Louisa. Her face quivered, her lips opened and closed, as if she were seeking to master herself. Then she took her daughter into her arms.

"I am happy for you, Louisa," she said. "If it is what you want, I am happy for you. But you needn't worry about the money, Louisa. Because, Louisa," — Susannah stopped a moment and gasped for breath, — "because I am already taking those lessons myself."

GRANDMOTHER'S BREAD

Originally published in the April 20, 1918, issue of *The Country Gentleman*

At twelve o'clock at night on the third Sunday in September, Sarah Ann Mohr invariably rose from her bed, dressed partially and descended into her kitchen. There in the tightly closed hot room she took from her cupboard a dough trough, a jar of homemade yeast, a can of flour, a cup of salt and a bowl of potato water. With sweeping, ample motions she put potato water, yeast, a little flour and salt together and stirred them well. Then covering the mixture with many wrappings of red tablecloth and shawl she climbed back to bed.

At five o'clock on the morning of the third Monday in September Sarah Ann rose again. Now she threw her shutters open, laid back the handsome coverings of her ample bed and dressed completely. Millerstown was by this time awake; Susannah Kuhns, her fire made and her water for washing heating in the boilers, was sweeping the pavement and singing "Beulah Land." Seeing Sarah Ann at the window, she waved her broom but did not stop her chanting.

Descending into the kitchen for the second time, Sarah Ann opened the windows and the shutters and then closed the windows tight. When she had stirred more flour into her rising and had transferred the mixture to the dough trough, she got her breakfast in a leisurely fashion. Another woman would have peered frequently in under the covering of red tablecloth. Not so Sarah Ann. Sarah Ann knew.

At nine o'clock Sarah Ann lifted the coverings from the bread trough and looked with satisfaction upon the white and swelling mass within. She rolled up her sleeves, scrubbed her arms with a thoroughness that would have pleased Pasteur himself, and bending over the dough trough as above a washtub plunged her tightly closed fists into the sponge. Even her pummelings and beatings were solemn. The third Monday in September was not, it was clear, an ordinary day.

At eleven o'clock the bread was kneaded once more and the loaves were molded into their pans. At half past eleven Sarah Ann prepared for herself a substantial but plain lunch. Though the top of the stove was reddening, though she was fond of good things, she cooked nothing, but ate only bread and jelly and cold meat. This was not the time for indulging in the pleasures of the table.

At twelve o'clock, when Sarah Ann had put the bread into the oven, she sat down to rest and to watch. Within the stove were crackings and murmurs which spoke to her delicate ear of a fire exactly right.

At one o'clock Sarah Ann opened her oven door and drew out her loaves — two square and high loaves, of a shape prescribed by custom which went back much farther than Sarah Ann could remember, and two long, cylindrical loaves, according to a modern fashion. All were perfectly baked with only those slight irregularities of shape and color which proved that the hand of the artist and not the mechanism of a machine had molded them. Sarah Ann set them on a folded cloth and covered them so that they might not cool too swiftly.

Still Sarah Ann was not through. Climbing the stairway, not without signs of irrepressible weariness, she put on a black dress and laid out a black bonnet and shawl. At three o'clock, her bread in a large basket, she went out through the little covered passageway between her house and the next and started on a journey. For ten years she had traveled in a buggy, now for nineteen she had traveled in a trolley car. Everyone knew where she was going, and everyone wished her, for her own sake and for the sake of Millerstown, well.

"At 'em again, Sarah Ann!" someone was sure to call.

Sarah Ann smiled beatifically but made no other reply. She did not like to talk on this journey; she liked to sit still, sometimes shutting her eyes, to feel the basket on her knees, to remember and to anticipate.

After a few years of terror she had grown used to the trolley car which traveled on a somewhat irregular roadbed and which was guided by a series of somewhat dull intelligences, first through a pleasant stretch of country, then through a busy village, then through a shorter stretch of pleasant country. Having come this far, Sarah Ann opened her eyes, first, because if any accident happened on the high bridge outside the county seat she wished to face calamity awake; secondly, because there were many interesting people to see. The car was now crowded with women having baskets and packages. Sarah Ann was not acquainted with the women, but she knew both them and their bundles by sight. There was the woman with the eight embroidered pillow shams, one pair with "Good night" and "Good morning" in English, one with "Good night" and "Good morning" in German, one pair with the Lord's Prayer and the Creed, and the other pair with intricate floral designs. Sarah Ann had meant year after year to speak to the bearer of this proud burden, but she had never had a good opportunity. The woman looked straight ahead, aware that she was the creator of articles of aesthetic worth. Sarah Ann sympathized with her air of aloofness; Sarah Ann, too, had a responsibility.

There was a woman with a stuffed parrot and a woman with a live parrot. The two always rode on the same car with Sarah Ann, but though they lived near together they did not seem to be on friendly terms. The live parrot talked incessantly and had all the passengers laughing. They laughed also at a fat and snarling poodle.

Some of the baskets were heavy. Sarah Ann knew them to be filled with jellies and preserves. Other baskets, she knew, contained fine cakes. She could see as distinctly as though her eyes could pierce opaque matter the cake in the basket opposite, of ten layers, decreasing in size from bottom to top, covered with white icing and thickly sprinkled with tiny pink candles. That cake was certain to take a prize, and the woman who had baked it and now carried it was aware of that certainty.

Before Sarah Ann reached her destination it was necessary to change from one car to another, and here, at a congested street corner, alertness and care were demanded. It was difficult for her to descend from a trolley car at any time, but when the descent was into a maelstrom the task was formidable. People crowded upon her, automobiles threatened her, confusion of mind hampered her. She had for many years followed closely in the wake of the woman with the stuffed parrot, a tall creature who seemed indifferent to noise, to confusion, to the laws of motion and of gravitation. More than once Sarah Ann had seen an automobile change its course to avoid her.

Safe in another car, she always sighed with relief. She would have the same perilous change to make upon the return journey, but she would not then have her precious burden.

The car came to a stop outside a large fenced inclosure and there all the passengers alighted. They went through a wide gate, each carrying carefully her basket or package. Then they separated; the woman with the live parrot walked rapidly to a distant building marked "Livestock, Fowls"; the woman with the fat poodle dragged that unwilling beast toward another distant building marked "Livestock, Dogs." Sarah Ann and the woman with the stuffed parrot and the woman with the eight pillow shams went in the same direction and entered different doors of the same huge structure marked "General." Now Sarah Ann needed no guiding. Before her were the miles of tables at which she had looked in wonder for thirty years, already laden with samples of every conceivable product of the garden, the kitchen and the sewing room. Here were rows upon rows of jellies, hundreds upon hundreds of sofa cushions, dozens of pillow shams, tier upon tier of cakes, disk after disk of pies.

The judges were usually beginning their almost interminable task when Sarah Ann set down her basket. They greeted her always in the same cheerful and complimentary fashion.

"Well, I guess the prize for bread is settled!"

For the first five years Sarah Ann had smiled, trying to demur. Latterly any protest would have been affected.

"We will see," she answered invariably in her mellifluous voice.

She set her four perfect loaves in the space left for them. One of the judges gave her a ticket and she put it carefully in her little purse. On Friday afternoon she would return and get her basket and her bread, and—at least so had it been for almost thirty years—her prize of five dollars. Upon her loaves would lie a long blue ribbon, before all the crowd of other aspirants for prizes—prizes for stuffed parrots, prizes for the largest ears of corn, prizes for curiosities like pictures made of human hair, prizes for sofa cushions, prizes for pickles, prizes for bread—she would hear "You've got it again, Mrs. Mohr!" In the newspaper would be printed "Prize for Bread, Sarah Ann Mohr, Millerstown, Pennsylvania." Life at such moments was rich indeed.

The prize had seemed hard to win nearly thirty years ago. There were then many competitors and the judges inspected bread, weighed bread and tasted bread till they wished never to see bread again. Sarah Ann's victory was a triumph indeed. But year by year the winning of the prize had grown easier. Fewer persons competed, fewer persons baked bread at all.

"What do they eat then?" asked Sarah Ann of her neighbor Susannah. "What do they put their spreads on?"

"Perhaps they are all eating baker's bread."

"Baker's bread!" repeated Sarah Ann in contempt.

Presently Sarah Ann's question was answered. Each morning the trolley delivered to Millerstown's new storekeeper a large box and each evening took it away. Sarah Ann inquired what it contained. For answer the storekeeper handed her a leaflet. From it a rosy-cheeked old lady looked up at her, not a little like Sarah Ann's own reflection. "Grandmother's Bread," read the legend beneath it. "Made in Philadelphia. Better than any homemade bread you ever tasted."

Sarah Ann's cheeks grew as red as those of the old lady.

"I do not believe you will have sale for such bread in Millerstown. The people bake themselves."

"I am going to get two cases from now on instead of one," said the storekeeper jubilantly. "Better try it."

Sarah Ann said no more. She pitied the storekeeper.

On her way home she stopped to see Maria Fackenthal. Maria was resting on the back porch and so unusual was it for her to rest that Sarah Ann feared she was ill.

Maria said there was nothing the matter with her.

"I just sat down to be thankful I did not have to bake a big batch of bread."

"Are your folks away?" asked Sarah Ann.

Then Sarah Ann flushed. She could see on the kitchen table four loaves of bread, each neatly wrapped, each bearing upon the side of its wrapper in bright red letters the label "Grandmother's Bread."

Maria followed the direction of her friend's eyes.

"No. But I'm not going to bake bread any more."

"Why, Maria!"

Maria rose. What she had to say she could say best standing.

"Never! I've reckoned that if all the pounding and back-bending I've given to bread were added up I could have lifted the whole blast furnace. I'm tired of it."

"But for health's sake, Maria!"

"This is healthy bread. Ordinary bread I wouldn't touch. But Grandmother's Bread is good. Would you eat a little if I spread you some, Sarah Ann?"

Her guest, too, had risen.

"No, thank you," said she. "I am not hungry."

Then Sarah Ann went home and set her bread solemnly. She blushed for Maria when Millerstown should discover this letting down, this degeneration.

"Sometimes I will send those poor men a loaf," she planned kindly.

But Sarah Ann was destined to greater surprises. The storekeeper had divined her opinion of his venture.

"Still more people eating Grandmother's Bread," he called. "From the end of Main Street as far as your house, everybody's eating it."

"Not the Gaumers!" gasped Sarah Ann.

"Yes, and the old Kuhnses and all the people in the frame row."

Sarah Ann backed away.

"The Kreiders don't!"

"No," answered the storekeeper. "But they will."

On her way home Sarah Ann stopped at a little brick house set back from the street. Years ago two little children, John and Mary Semmel, had been left orphaned in Millerstown and she had taken them in and kept them. The boy worked in a store in Philadelphia, the girl was married to Albert Kreider. When Sarah Ann knocked, Mary was taking her loaves from the oven.

"You see what I am doing, Aunt Sarah Ann. I well remember what you taught me."

Sarah Ann's ruffled feelings were smoothed. The children had been dear obedient children.

"You and John too," said she. "John could bake as good bread as you. It certainly spites me to think of people eating such Grandmother's Bread. What do you hear from John?"

"He is well. He sends his love to you."

"Does he still have his good place in your cousin's store?"

Mary bent suddenly to close the oven door. John had a better position, but for some reason Mary did not choose to tell Sarah Ann.

"Come and see my garden, Aunt Sarah Ann," said she.

It was this year that Sarah Ann found that in all the county she had only six competitors where there used to be sixty. The change opened her eyes to other conditions. The fair had changed, the crowds lingered no more to admire the fine hens and the beautiful pies; they watched the airplanes and the clowns and surged in a close press up and down what was to Sarah Ann the scandalous "Street of Wonders." Bent upon investigating, she went herself to see and thereafter woke at night blushing.

But Sarah Ann wished to exhibit her bread once more, to round her twenty-nine to thirty, to see once more before she died, though death seemed not yet to threaten, her name in the paper. She was moved not only by ambition, but by a desire to stand once more for correct principles, to bestow once more upon Millerstown that honor which Millerstown had ceased to appreciate. Even Susannah Kuhns, neighbor and friend though she was, fell finally before the rosy old lady who offered her wares so smilingly.

"I'm not going to get all wore out before my time," she explained. "I wish we had a laundry so I could send my wash to it. They say there are places in the city where you can buy pie."

"Buy pie!" repeated Sarah Ann.

Sarah Ann escaped narrowly a more serious blow. For a day she was unable to use her stove which was being repaired and she went to supper with Mary Kreider. She did not announce her coming, but walked in when supper was on the table. Mary looked at her husband and for some reason flushed scarlet.

"We haven't such a fine supper, Aunt Sarah Ann."

"Your homemade bread and coffee are plenty good enough. I see you bake in the new kind of pans."

Sarah Ann ate heartily. Afterward she dried the dishes for Mary. At such moments the heart opens.

"I am going again to the fair with my bread. Then it will be thirty times."

"And thirty prizes!" said Mary. Mary spoke and moved nervously and her cheeks were flushed. She had managed to destroy the wrapper of Grandmother's Bread.

"I hope John will soon come to Millerstown," said Sarah Ann. "Does he still have his good place?"

"John is doing fine," answered Mary. "He sends always his love. You must see my flowers, Aunt Sarah Ann."

Again Mary had avoided answering Sarah Ann's question about John.

At twelve o'clock at night on the third Sunday of September, Sarah Ann rose for the thirtieth time from her bed. Never in all her years of prize-winning had she begun her work on Sunday. She moved now with more than her accustomed solemnity. The occasion was more than solemn, it was funereal. When she had finished setting her sponge she did not return to bed, but sat down by the window. Her prize-winning was not easy to give up. But Sarah Ann was wise; it might be that some day her hand would fail and that even if they continued to give prizes she might lose. A dread that she might fail now overpowered her; it made her hand tremble when she kneaded her dough and shaped her loaves. This last triumph she desired greatly.

The morning was cloudy and to Sarah Ann the clouds seemed ominous of failure. But when she drew her bread from the oven her spirits rose. She had never baked more beautiful bread.

When late in the afternoon she left the fair grounds her heart was quite at rest. The same judges greeted her with the same gay assurance of success as last year; the same parrot and the same pillow shams assured her of a continuation of all things as they were. Outside the grounds as she waited for her car she watched the completion of a mammoth billboard, beside which billposters waited with their long rolls of paper and their brushes and pails. On Friday she would see what the posters were; doubtless they would be very interesting, like that of the tall, thin man who pointed so sternly at the crossroads directing the citizens of Millerstown to go to Keipers' for their clothes.

The most of Tuesday and Wednesday was spent in sleep. On Thursday the dread of failure returned. It was a small thing which Sarah Ann asked of Fate, that she, who had taken so many, should take one more prize. It was really a larger blessing than she knew. Though she did not dream it, though no one dreamed it, the fair was holding its last session. Next year exhibition rooms and grand stand, restaurants and hangar would be filled with soldiers in training, and the race track would be a parking place for ambulances. She had won the prize for bread since the beginning; it would be sad indeed if she lost the last year!

Friday was a day to dull the liveliest hopes. A heavy storm was imminent and all the morning there were dashes of rain. Sarah Ann prepared herself as best she could to accept defeat. But her large and treasured basket must be brought home and her bread disposed of. She had a tender feeling for the loaves, even though, dusty and handled as they were, they could only be given to the pigs. She could not leave them to be swept by the caretaker into dear knows what receptacle, with the reflection that these were the loaves which lost the prize!

Her spirits sank still lower on the journey to the county seat. It was raining now and the landscape was hidden. She looked longingly at the woman going to fetch her stuffed parrot, but won no answering glance. Life was as gray as the day. She remembered the traits of her husband, long dead and never lovable; she remembered departed friends; she remembered all that was sad and gloomy and miserable.

When it was time to change from one car into another, Sarah Ann in her confusion laid a hand upon the basket destined to receive the stuffed parrot. She meant not to rest the least weight upon it; she meant only to touch it and thereby save herself from destruction. But its owner detected her, glared at her and she had to find her way as best she could.

Her curiosity about the tall billboard returned as the car drew near the fair grounds. She could see the bills from afar, the brave black and red upon them as yet unhurt by the rain. She bent her forehead upon the window pane, trying to make out their design. A little dancing child or a grinning clown, or a picture of a horse race would have been at this moment helpful. But neither dancing child nor grinning clown nor lively race was to be seen. She drew back her head with a sharp "Oh, misery!" A smiling grandmother, enormous, red-cheeked, offered her a loaf of bread!

After this Sarah Ann's motions were those of one in a dream. She went through the gate and paid her fare, forgetting that as an exhibitor she was entitled to free admission. Within a smiling grandmother in the flesh, followed by a string of small boys, offered her a tiny loaf made of pasteboard. Yonder she saw another smiling grandmother and still another. It was indecent for grandmothers to be so indifferent to the rain and so numerous. If she had not had a well-nigh unconquerable spirit she would have fled. As it was she went bravely on.

Inside the great building she found a throng. Driven in by the rain, they surged back and forth, admiring this, laughing at that, ready to be attracted by any slight stir. She made her way through with difficulty. It was now four o'clock and she would be allowed to take her bread and her basket and go. She knew that the prize was not for her.

Sarah Ann was right. A poor pink ribbon lay across her loaves, the blue ribbon lay across two loaves near by. She looked at them bravely. If her loaves were perfection, these were a little more than perfection. The crust was delicate and brown, the grain fine and even and the shape of the loaf was absolutely symmetrical. A young man stood beside the table receiving the congratulations of the multitude. There was something the least bit familiar to Sarah Ann about his shoulders, but her impression was too confused and fleeting to be held. To his side approached one of the perambulating grandmothers.

"Sample all gone, sir," said the perambulating grandmother in a deep bass voice.

"Time to stop," answered the man.

The whole ignominy of her situation came over Sarah Ann in a wave. This prize-winning bread was Grandmother's Bread; this assured young man was the person who had set the grandmothers walking. Sarah Ann would fly, not even taking her basket. Especially would she fly before the judges saw her and announced her defeat.

But Sarah Ann was too late. One of the judges had seen her and now called to her "Pink ribbon, Mrs. Mohr!" meaning to be congratulatory. She nodded her head and tried still to turn and go. But the press held her and the people looked at her. In another moment she would cry.

Then insult was added to injury. The pert young man, turning swiftly at sound of her name, laid his hand on her arm.

"Aunt Sarah Ann!" said he.

Sarah Ann struggled with confusion.

"Don't you know me?"

A deeper flush came into Sarah Ann's cheeks. "Yes," said she at last. "You are" — amazement, affection and involuntary reproach struggled in her faint voice — "you are John Semmel."

John Semmel looked steadily into Sarah Ann's eyes. Sarah Ann had never looked at him like that! Then John looked down at the table and saw the pink ribbon. He remembered suddenly an item from his sister's letter. Self-confident though he was, he felt the hot tears in his eyes.

"My soul, Aunt Sarah Ann!" he cried.

Then John, still holding Sarah Ann's arm, lifted the blue ribbon from the loaves of Grandmother's Bread and laid it on Sarah Ann's. The pink ribbon he dropped.

"Same bread," said he to the judges and the crowd, in Millerstown's broad and pleasant tones. "I taught the company how to make it, and I learned it off of her."

Then Sarah Ann began to tremble. She had a keen imagination and she saw a hundred bakers baking, saw a hundred wagons traveling, a hundred trolley cars gliding and a thousand persons eating. There was laughter and handclapping about her, but that she did not hear.

"My bread!" she faltered.

"Your bread," answered John Semmel. "We feed it to a million."

The End

This first edition of *Katy Gaumer and other stories of Millerstown* by Elsie Singmaster Lewars consists of one thousand copies published in December 2008. The book was printed in the Commonwealth of Pennsylvania on acid-free, 55# Natural Vellum stock. Printing support was provided by Thomas E. Turner III of Seaber Turner Associates, 436 Coronet Drive, Blandon, Pennsylvania, who coordinated all printing and binding production details with Jostens Book Manufacturing of State College, Pennsylvania.

All of the Millerstown stories contained in this 2008 anthology are printed exactly as they were first published, without any attempt to edit Singmaster's original work. As such, they provide a unique window into the evolution of her writings throughout the early period of her development as an author.

Many of the pen and ink illustrations contained in this work are based on actual photographs and artifacts contained in the collection of the Macungie Historical Society. Some of the photographic images were originally created by Elsie Singmaster's uncle, William Mickley Weaver, during the time that Elsie and her family called the Macungie community their home.

The mission of the Macungie Historical Society as set forth in its Articles of Incorporation: *The support of an educational undertaking by promoting the discovery, collection, preservation, archive, display, interpretation, and publication of the history, historical records, culture, landmarks, artifacts, memorabilia, and data of, and relating to, the Borough of Macungie and its surrounding area.*

Macungie Historical Society
Post Office Box 355
Macungie, PA 18062
www.macungie.org

Jane Ramsey
Macungie, PA 18062
www.janeramsey.com

Copyright © 2008 by the Macungie Historical Society, Inc.
All Rights Reserved.

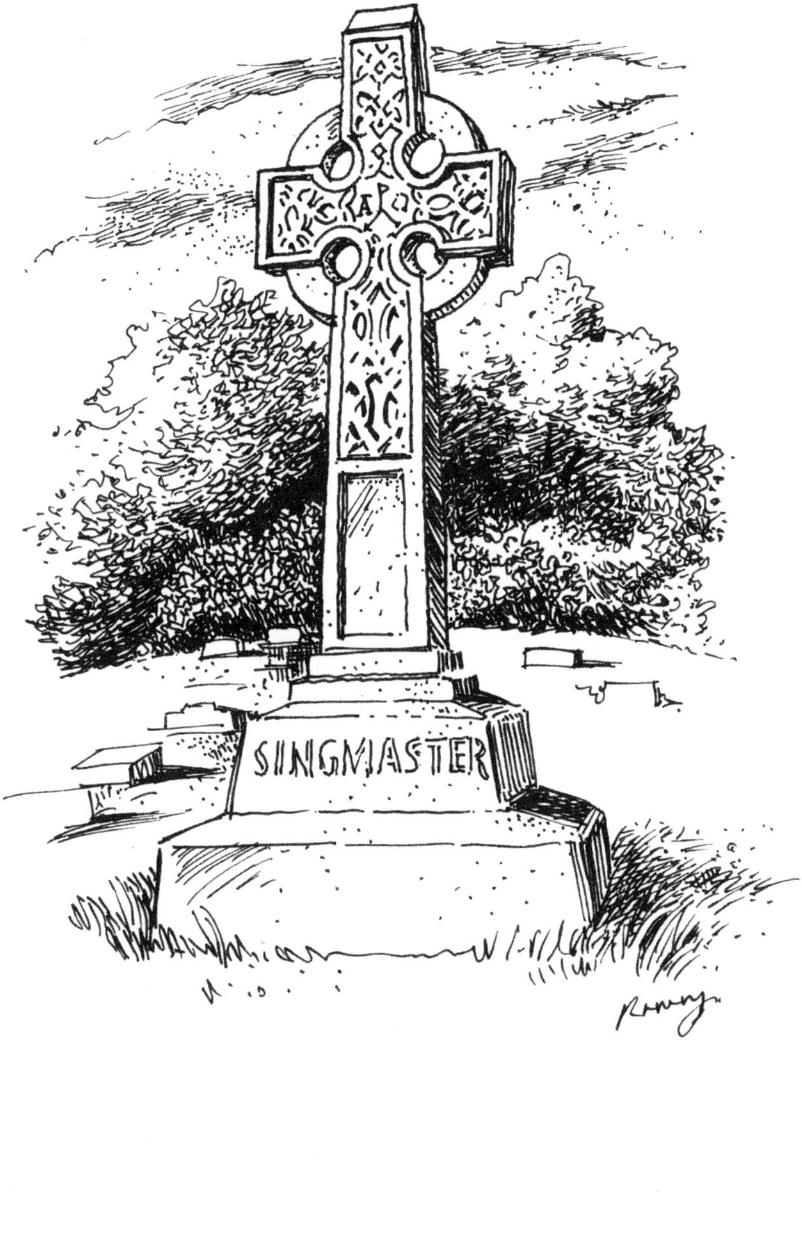
SINGMASTER

DRAWN BY T.M. FOWLER MORRISVILLE PA.

1. PUBLIC SCHOOLS.
2. SINGMASTER HALL.
3. KEYSTONE HOUSE. L.M. HOLBEN PRO.
4. KEYSTONE ROLLER MILLS. FRITCH BROS. & BOGH. PROS.
5. CRANE IRON CO. FURNACE.
6. PLOW WORKS. JAMES MILLER & SON PROS.
7. CIGAR FACTORY. NAGLE BROS.
8. CARRIAGE WORKS. J.W. GERHARD. PRO.
9. VALLEY KNITTING MILLS. R.P. MOYER & CO PRO'S.
10. EAST MACUNGIE HOTEL. HENRY SCHANKWEILER. PRO.
11. EAST PENN. R.R. STATION.

-CHURCHES.-

A. SOLOMONS REFORMED.
B. GRACE LUTHERAN CHAPEL.
C. ST. MATHEWS EV. LUTHERAN.
D. GERMAN BAPTIST.
E. EVANGELICAL.
F. BAPTIST.

Library of Congress, Map Division